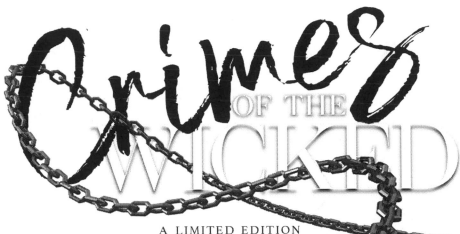

Crimes OF THE WICKED

A LIMITED EDITION
CRIMINAL MAYHEM COLLECTIVE

N.K. STACKHOUSE • A.J. MACEY • SUKI WILLIAMS
N.J. ADEL • CHIQUITA DENNIE • BEE MURRAY
DJ SHAW • MANDY MELANSON/ELLE RYAN • LASHE LACROIX
BROOKE SUMMERS • VICTORIA GALE • J.N. PACK

CONTENTS

Crimes of the Wicked: a limited edition criminal mayhem collective

Corruption and, deception mixed, with little redemption;

It's the code most of us live by and the same code we'll likely die by.

Once you enter this world, there's no going back.

Come join these 12 authors as they release mayhem on the immoral underground and the notorious criminal masterminds that reign there.

Some stories send you back into familiar territories, while others throw you into new adventures.

One thing's for sure- this won't be the last time you'll play with these demons!

From elite mafia ties to deadly cartel crews and even dangerous motorcycle clubs, there is sure to be a baddie for you in this law-breaking collection.

Authors include; N.K. Stackhouse, A.J. Macey, Suki Williams, N.J. Adel, Chiquita Dennie, Bee Murray, Mandy Melanson/ Elle Ryan, Lashe Lacroix,

J.N. Pack, Brooke Summers, Victoria Gale, DJ Shaw

THE PAWN IN PLAY

The Elite Players
Book 1 - Part 1

N.K. Stackhouse

The Pawn in Play

In this game played by Kings, they forget it's the Queen that holds all the power.

Ripley Quinn

The game of life plays dirty and let's just say I'm not on the winning side.

A dying mother. A shitty job. And a shattered vase.

Three events that change everything.

When I fall into the Elite Players'- Paxton King's- world, I do so in a very literal sense.

The darkness of their world hides Mafia wars and deadly coups, and I'm now in the middle of it all.

They offer me a ticket to a better life,

The price; be the final pawn in their grand scheme.

To play the role of a puppet and allow Paxton to control my strings.

And he knows exactly what strand to pluck to get me to play this game until the very bitter end.

Paxton King

That little green-eyed snake thinks she is the innocent in this story

But don't be fooled by her trembling lips or pitiful pleas

Ripley Quinn might be able to pretend for a while

but she is just like the rest of us, driven by a need to survive; a hunger for control

and I am determined to prove to her that she is willing to kill to get what she wants

Money is the ultimate Power Play

and right now, I hold the reins over her past...and her future.

What she doesn't know is this game won't end until the final shot rings.

And I intend for her to be the one pulling the trigger.

Author Note

The Pawn in Play, is the first book in the new Darker Mafia Standalone Series, **The Elite Players**.

Please note that this will only contain PART ONE of **The Pawn in Play** so you will be left with a CLIFFHANGER!

The Second and final part will be published after Crimes of the Wicked is finished it's run.

The Elite Players Series will each follow one couple within an interconnected group, each with a guarantee HEA after THEIR book.

The Pawn in Play will contain heavy Mafia themes with all the blood, lies, and violence that comes with playing with the Mafia.

If you don't LOVE Enemies to Lovers dynamics, M/F (1 male, 1 female) relationships, and heavy use of the word *fuck* this might not be the story for you.

CHAPTER 1

Ripley

I s it too early in the story to throat punch a cunt?

"Did you really want to be a janitor when you grew up?"

This bottle blonde bitch is seriously trying my very last nerve. Like seriously, the very last one.

"Oh yes! I used to dream about one day going around and cleaning up someone else's shit."

The sarcasm could not be any clearer unless I literally wrote it in bold sharpie on my fucking forehead. But of course, this ever so clever receptionist's ruby red lips scrunch up in disgust, believing every word that left my mouth to be the truth.

I mean it's not like she seems to be the brightest cookie in the bunch, but I had held a shred of hope that stereotypes might be wrong about this one. But it seems the typecast holds true. Go figure.

The funniest part, she probably makes more in a single week by just sitting behind that desk wrapped in skintight dresses than I make in a month.

Sometimes I want to reevaluate my life choices.

I don't bother correcting her assumption though. I really just don't give a shit what some entitled little elite thinks of me. I ignore the snide comment she mumbles under her voice and go back to dusting the empty cubicles.

Glancing at the clock on the far wall, I passively wonder why Bottle Blonde is still even here at this hour. Maybe there is some meeting or whatever she has to be around for? Lord knows she isn't actually working if the strong fresh acetone smell from her nail polish tells me anything.

Her cell phone lights up blaring some top 40 jingle. When she answers she goes about beginning very loud and very inappropriate for work conversation, with who I can only guess is her 'bestie' on the other line.

After hearing about sucking her boss' 'enormous cock' for the third time in less than five minutes I give up on trying to just blatantly ignore her. I pull out the beaten-up earbuds from my jean pocket and plugin with the hopes of drowning out the world for a little while.

It is my first solo day with this new cleaning company, and I can only hope this is not a recurring occurrence with Bottle Blonde staying late. Because that could really make this rotation a lot more troublesome than I am ready for.

As the heavy rock beat blares in my ears I reflect on the shit show that has been my day. And it isn't even over yet.

Just this morning I received that oh so awesome letter from the community college I attended last year that 'due to not registering for classes for over three semesters, I would have to reapply next fall for reconsideration,' so yeah there's that. I mean who wouldn't want to pay for another application fee just to pay a shit ton more money to get a fucking piece of paper at the end of it all?

When I graduated high school, I stupidly thought I could actually make tuition payments if I worked as many hours as I could stay standing for. It could have almost worked if that was all my paychecks were being used for. But just when everything seemed to normalize mom relapsed.

With the hospital bills piling up and her being too weak to make it to work, I quickly realized the role I had to step into. I convinced her to let me take the following semester off so I could help out until she was feeling better. I refused to make her feel bad about me dropping out to help with bills so I promised I would go back as soon as everything got back to normal.

That was almost two years ago.

At least most days mom isn't in pain, thanks to the medicine, but the bills keep building and building. I try to grab the mail and hide the late notices as much as I can hoping I can save her from the added stress.

There is no real point in complaining though, you just deal with the hand you've been dealt.

So that's where this extra job comes in. The hours fit perfectly into my 'downtimes.' I work mornings and lunch rushes at the diner around the corner from our apartment, then I have this one cleaning office building from three to nine. And then from eleven till two on weeknights and all day on weekends I have a decent bartending gig, where the tips alone usually cover rent every month. But even working around the clock like this I barely make enough for us to survive, but hey that's life, right? You have to take the good with the bad, no matter how bad the bad gets.

I give the cart I am pushing an extra shove as I open the heavy conference room door. Mindlessly going about grabbing the discarded Styrofoam white cups that litter the large dark table as *Partners in Crime* by *Set If Off* clicks on in my ears. I absently hum along with the upbeat rhythm easily busying myself with dusting the shelves that take up the back wall of the large room. I catch my reflection in the wall of windows that overlook upper Manhattan. And it's not exactly a welcoming sight.

I take in the warf of a girl staring back at me. Okay maybe 'warf' isn't the right word to describe her but I miss the more rounded curve to my hips and the brighter sheen that used to exist behind my eyes. You know when I wasn't surviving on four hours of sleep and deli to-go meals.

I take in the dull hue of the unwashed black strands that hang limply against my cheek. I can't even remember the last time I added some color to my hair or even gave it a good deep conditioning treatment. The more I stare the more my hair begins to irritate the skin it touches. Annoyed, I quickly snap the hair tie from my wrist and twist the straw-like strands into a high ponytail. I push the feel of breaking delicate strands far from my mind, but I make a pact with myself to stop into the market on my way home for some decent conditioner.

With my hair finally out of my face, I take in the paleness of my cheeks that the light dusting of freckles across my nose can't even hide.

Holy hell, I look like death. When did I start not caring about my appearance? I mean I was never high maintenance, but I at least used to make sure I didn't have stains on my clothes before leaving the house. The bleach stains that dot my black t-shirt seem to multiply the longer I stare.

A movement of human proportion in the reflection behind me has me turning fast. The world spins around me as I twist around. I instantly lose my balance on my too-small sneakers, reaching out quickly to try to steady myself with anything I can reach. I make contact with the worst possible object.

The expensive-looking lamp follows me crashing to the floor. The shattering of the heavy glass base drowns out any other sound that could be happening around me. To be honest I don't even know if I make any sound of distress. As the glass sprays out around me the world slowly comes back into focus and I finally notice the group of suit-clad men glaring down on me. And I do mean fucking glaring, like I killed and dismembered their puppy, glaring.

The one that pulls my full attention though is the one front and center. His dark perfectly styled hair is swiped away from his forehead in a way that comes with practiced precision. The deep color of his hair is in stark contrast with his crystalized sapphire eyes that crawl over my sprawled appearance with pissed indifference. The hard lines of his cheekbones and sharp edges of his jaw beg for my submission and are meant to cause as much pain as possible. Everything about this man screams 'I will fuck up your world and leave you ruined on the floor.'

But it isn't his handsome face that calls for my soul, no, it's what is swimming in that apathetic gaze. The demon that lives behind his tailored persona and sculpted suit. I know it sounds oh so cliché, being drawn to his darkness and nearly reveling in the warning bells that scream in my head. The absolute undoing and destruction he'd rain down terrify me as much as it pumps electricity straight through my fucking veins.

The way his tailored suit pulls tight in all the right places makes it obvious that every muscle is sculpted with hard work and dedication. Blood. Sweat. And death.

Wait, what the fuck?

I try to find my voice within the humiliation clouding my judgment, but his deadly baritone growl drowns out any apology I was trying to muster.

"You better have a good fucking reason for being here?"

Chapter 2

Ripley

"I ...um...cleaning?"

The words stumble out of my mouth in a rush with no conviction to them. I dart my eyes around each of the four men that have crowded in on me. I hate to admit that each one is just as gorgeous as the other. Like I seriously wish they didn't look like GQ models, maybe then I could find real words within my head.

Life just isn't fair.

I notice, while my throat is trying to recall my speaking ability, that each man has a dangerous air blurring around the edges of their personas. However, it is possible that my mind is just associating danger because of the situation I have found myself in...

Yet none of them pull me in the same way the first one does. Something about the predatory aura emanating from every pore on his body feels like crisp wine buzzing in my nerves. Because of my blatant staring, I notice the vicious change in his demeanor at my words. Darkness clouds his eyes alerting me that my less than stellar answer did not fend off the beast.

To be honest, under his inspection even I feel like they are lies. *I am supposed to be here right?*

Hell, it isn't hard to tell this bastard is a master of manipulation. Just one precise flick of his eyebrows will have you saying whatever the hell he wants you to.

I swallow the hard lump forming in my throat and pull up the 'I don't give a fuck' personality I am infamous for and let this bastard have a taste of his own medicine- or at least that's was the plan.

Instead of words coming out of my mouth I just stare with lips gapping on empty air.

Well fuck.

Okay, a backup plan. I swallow and tuck my legs under me, pushing my body off the floor being cautious of the broken glass. I make these bastards wait on my explanation without giving two fucks.

It should also be noted, not one well-dressed devil makes a move to offer a hand to a fallen damsel. Not that I wanted them too nor expected it, I just wanted that particular fuckery noted for future references.

When I am finally standing upright and on even footing with these guys, I can take in the full effect of what they are. I can't help but notice-very begrudgingly- just how much I have to crank my neck back to meet Mr. Grumpy Pants' eyes. I ignore my disheveled appearance and bleeding scraps, instead, I focus on my step into his personal space, wanting to make him step back from my advance.

I *horribly* underestimated my opponent.

The second I step at him his hand snaps out and twists into my ponytail. He tugs it back...hard.

A surprised squeak echoes around the darkroom. I slam my teeth together painfully when I realize that embossing noise was made from my own throat. If looks could kill, this bastard would be nothing more than ash right now.

He smiles.

"Can I ask you, *what the fuck* you think you are doing?"

The words grate out between my clenched teeth. The shock of the assault has tears stinging at the corners of my eyes that I beg not to fall.

"If I remember correctly, I asked you first."

An equal amount of death is pushed into his own words. The sick smirk does nothing to lessen the blow.

I want to hate him. I want to despise him. I want to fucking catapult my knee into his balls and watch him whimper.

My body has the very opposite idea.

Because while one half of my head wants to inflict pain- the other half, is mesmerized with the swirling of crystals in his eyes.

And for that very thought, I hate that half.

It's clear to see which is currently winning within this debate. But that doesn't mean I won't slash with deadly claws.

"And if I remember correctly, I told you I was here cleaning."

Fire sparks in his eyes and instantly I know I just hit a match he wasn't expecting. He wasn't expecting a fight. But he sure as hell wants one.

I don't know if that's exactly a good thing or a 'my body will be discovered in the dumpster tomorrow' kind of thing.

"Well doesn't she have a massive set of balls; I'll give her that much."

A new voice pulls my eyes from the bastard, who by the way, still has a death grip on my hair.

I turn until I am met with a set of cruel chocolate eyes and a smirk that holds the power to leave a nun drenched.

"Shut the fuck up, Jameson."

Mr. Personality cuts his voice toward the group and the man's smirk instantly falls back into his emotionless expression. Guess we know who's the leader of this little death crew.

When the silence is about to choke the last of my air, I turn my head back to the one with his hold attached to my head.

This is really fucking pissing me off.

"I have a job to do so if you wouldn't mind, could you please release my hair?" The sickenly sweet pitch of my voice has the absolute opposite effect I was going for. Instead of letting me go his grip tightens and he shoves me into the nearby conference room chair.

Seriously what the fuck?

As soon as my ass hits the plush cushion his arms cage him in, and his hands dig into the arms of the chair. I absently notice a tattoo peeking out from the top of his collar, it almost looks like the points of a crown?

The very idea of this corporate suit having such a visible tattoo strikes me as odd, but I don't have the time to analyze the situation much further.

"See here, that's the part I have fucking problem with," his eyes blaze with fury and his lips ground into a hard line, "we are very particular of who is allowed in this building. And I sure as fuck never approved *you*."

"Sorry to burst your ego, buddy, but I just got a job with Fairhope Cleaning and I was sent here to clean the floor today," I ground out my own reply.

I hate nothing more than having to explain myself to this dick. Everything about this situation is rubbing me the wrong fucking way.

"Do you need to see my badge?"

The sarcasm that bleeds into my words is accidental but its' too late to pull it back now.

"Okay fine. Let's say I believe you," his own dark sarcasm runs through each word, "what possessed you to be in here, right now?"

"Oh, for fucks sake, Pax. Quit with the bullshit riddles. Just ask the girl point-blank."

Chocolate Eyes steps up. Drilling me with a look that can only be described as death, his voice is clear with words not meant for me.

"Just ask the girl what she heard."

I am starting to think I stumbled upon something more than just your everyday meeting. And just like that, I start to realize how fucking screwed I really am.

"What the hell is going on?" I question the room in general.

My eyes scan each man in turn. The final two that have yet to speak look unamused with the antics their little leader is playing at.

Movement pulls my attention back to the towering man before me as he reaches his hand into my front breast pocket- and yep totally going to ignore the unwanted tingling that his fingers leave through my shirt. Pulling out my employee ID he scans over the information. After way too many silent seconds, his eyes collide with mine once again. The threat sparks in his gaze before it leaves his lips.

"Well, *Miss Quinn* here's what we are going to do. Because I don't much care for you or trust a fucking word that has left your mouth, consider this your last day at Fairhope. Now get the fuck out."

"Who the fuck do you think you are? Other than breaking that lamp I didn't do anything wrong."

The fire builds in my stomach and I etch for a fight.

"You don't have the power to fucking fire me."

"That's where you're wrong, Ripley Quinn."

Every word drips contempt and irony.

"I guess I haven't introduced myself."

Every single fucking syllable that leaves his mouth feds a fire about to explode.

14

The Pawn in Play

"My name is Paxton fucking King and I own your fucking ass."

* * *

I SLAM the apartment door like it physically wronged me in its previous life. Rage bubbles and boils in my stomach and I need to seriously find an outlet for this emotion before I take the entire apartment down with me when I blow. As I stomp through our small foyer, I kick off my black flats and revel in the thump that sounds as each smack against the wall.

Who the fuck does that Paxton cunt think he is? Like fucking seriously? Getting all up in my face and telling me to get lost. Yeah, that shit doesn't fly with me.

I may have been handed the shit cards in life but that sure as hell doesn't mean I'll take it up the ass lying face down. I have been called a lot of names in my short nineteen years, but a pushover, a weakling, and especially timid, have never been amongst those words.

Blame it on being raised by a strong single mom but I put up a fucking fight when prompted.

I throw open the fridge door in hopes that mom has an opened bottle of wine chilling but come up empty. Actually, the shelves are looking pretty empty if I allow myself to think about it. In my rage, I forgot to stop by the corner market to grab dinner for us.

I close the fridge door in a soft thump, all my earlier fury evaporates within the cool rush of air that follows the door. Reality sinks back in and the fight burns cold.

Fuck I just lost my job, a job we really freaking needed.

I let the quiet of the apartment overtake my cluttered mind. The soft hum of the air conditioner; the New York traffic buzzing by outside of the thin windows; the pitter-patter of dripping water in the bathroom, wait, that sounds like overflowing water, not a leaky faucet...

I spin on my heels and sprint down the hall and come to a heart-stopping halt.

"MOM..."

I hit my knees in a painful crash as I make a grab for the woman lying hazardly over the threshold of the bathroom and hall.

I take in the entire scene with horrifying clarity; the blood pooling under her head; the overflowing tub water that is soaking through her thin night-gown; the 911 operator barking orders in my ear after I dial the number with a blood-covered hand; and the tears that freely fall as the paramedics cart my mother out of the apartment.

Everything plays out like a bad movie...desperately trying to turn away from the screen but unable to force the images away from your closed eyelids.

CHAPTER 3

Paxton

"So, what was with the bastard routine?"

My cousin is seriously fucking asking to get his ass handed to him tonight, isn't he?

"Seriously J, why poke the beast?"

The ever voice of reason finally speaks up. Thankfully Bishop's warning distracts Jameson from his inspection of my reaction to that little Green-Eyed Reaper.

All it took was one look at the mix of midnight black hair, pale skin, and bright green eyes to call her bluff. Anthony truly must think we are fucking dull not to recognize his little spies. The man has a very specific type that he...likes to keep close. And *Ripley Quinn* is that type to a T all the way down to that feisty innocence that nearly got her killed.

But hey I called a spade a spade and sent her running as gentlemanly as I could.

Hey, I didn't kill her so that was a damn nice move on my part.

However, just because I let her go doesn't mean I didn't send someone tailing her to see just what she brings back to that old bastard.

"Yo, Pax, you coming back?"

Knox, the member that rounds off as our fourth calls from the open door on the far side of the conference room.

You see we have a private little *playroom* adjacent to the conference room, the only entrance is the secret door that opens from the conference room. But before you go thinking some *Fifty Shade Red Room* bullshit, it's not that kind of playroom. No, this room is for business only.

The business we only conduct after hours. A business that leads to Anthony trying to 'checkup' on us.

Just thinking of that bastard and his little stunt tonight has my blood boiling. I need to fucking hit something. In one movement I tear at my suit jacket and turn away from the midnight city lights. I toss the jacket over the chair that sits just within the small brightly lit room, stepping up to the man that sits in the center of the room tied to a chair, just the sight has a violent smirk cracking over my lips.

I let the rage course through me, and I release it on the broken man. My fist connects with his bloody jaw. The reaction is immediate and his body jerks sideways with the force. The chains wrapped around his arms and legs stop him from toppling onto the floor. The poor bastard is barely conscious, so I barely get so much as a grunt from his raw throat. The lackluster response does nothing to stifle my need for pain.

An arm lands on my shoulder as I wind up to use the guys as a punching bag.

"Dude, if you hit him again, he'll go under and we aren't done with him yet." Bishop is the only one I have ever let lay a hand on me when I'm in an 'interrogation.'

Jameson made that mistake just once before he learned. Knox made it a few more times, but after he ended up with ten stitches down his arm, he finally got the idea. Bishop, however, has made it through unharmed, from me at least.

I back off, leaving Bishop to the questioning. Since I am obviously in no state of mind for it right now.

Fuck, why does this chick have me so fucked up? I've caught Anthony's spies dozens of times before and they always throw up the same claims, so what was different with this chick. Although, they usually try a little harder to act the part. I mean this chick was blatantly staring at our reflection in the window, not even trying to pretend otherwise. Anthony must have lost his edge with finding *smart girls.*

Fuck, whatever, stop thinking about it. Wait until Jones gets back to us.

"So, Fred, ready to talk yet?"

Bishop's to the point question lacks any emotion, the act usually messes with their heads. The man cracks a swollen eye open to find Bishop crouching in front of his slouched position.

"As I have already told you, I don't work for The Elites and I don't know who the fuck called for the hit."

Hysteria is clear in the way his broken voice cracks with the effort to speak. We may have gone too far to get any real information from this guy. I step back into his eyesight, loving the next part of this conversion. It shouldn't make me this giddy, but it is oh so fun.

"Well you see here, Freddy, we already know all that."

I don't even try to hide my glee. Twisted right?

"Then why the fuck am I here? I don't have anything for you."

Ah, the begging, the pleading, the desperation...

"Because *Fred,* you see, you have information that we want."

"I don't fucking have any information!"

It's almost too easy to call his bluff with the way his body shifts on the chair. Nervous energy oozes from his sweat.

"As I keep telling you, I don't know who The Elites are and I sure as fuck don't know about a group operating inside of them that are planning a takeover...why won't you just believe me."

"Well, you worked for Cyrus King before he was murdered six years ago correct?"

Just saying his name reaffirms our plan through my head.

"What the fuck does that have to do with anything?"

I have too much fun getting them all confused before I blow their fucking minds.

"Because Cyrus King ran The Elites here in New York."

"I didn't fucking know anything. Please you have to believe me."

"Oh, I do, Freddy, but you see, we have reasons to believe you're an informant for the Violante's head."

"I don't know where you heard that I am not in the mafia,"

I let the wheels turn for a few seconds in his head. Then recognition slams into his one good eye and I know he finally knows,

"You...you're his son...you're one of them...you're an Elite..."

Pure terror steals his voice and I leap at the cue.

"Ah, there it is, some recognition. Finally."

* * *

"So now that one snake is taken care of, are we going to talk about the green-eyed one?"

Knox levels my stare with his dark gaze as he tosses back the tumbler of scotch. I nonchalantly sip my own amber liquid, buying time for my response to form.

"You sent Jones after her right?"

Jameson walks into my office dressed in nothing more than a pair of grey briefs.

"Couldn't you fucking grab a suit from your own office before strutting in here?" The growl is unintentional but I'm in a shit mood so I am sure as fuck don't need to see his dick flopping around with every step.

"Well if you hadn't made a bloody fucking mess of that bastard, I wouldn't have had to ruin my spare suit."

He strolls over to the closet and swings the door open as if he owns it.

"So I'll be using one of yours."

"Did you at least get Miles to drop him off at County Med?"

Knox turns his attention to the dressing bastard in the corner. Annoyed with the whole situation I ignore them and instead stare down to the slowing waking world. The sky is just barely turning blue with the impending morning and the sight alone through the foggy windows reminds me how long we spent with that fucker. Even after hours of "questioning" he never broke. I give Anthony credit for getting legit informants but fuck, we didn't get shit from him. My fist slams into the desk, three heads snap my way with the sound.

"How the fuck are we not getting anywhere?"

I push away from the desk and stand needing an outlet for the frustration.

"We have been at this for months and have nothing to fucking show for it."

"Obviously Anthony is smarter than we gave him credit for?"

Bishop says the words I have dreaded the most. Did I underestimate that bastard?

"If that's so, what was up with that chick earlier?"

Knox's low tone is packed with the same frustration we are all feeling.

"I know none of us want to give it a thought," Jameson calls from the closet as his buttons the last button of the crisp white shirt, "but what if she wasn't lying? What if she really was just here for work?"

"You're joking right, J? She was the very personification of Anthony's bitches?"

I can't even pretend to give the very idea a real thought.

"Hear me out, dick."

Jameson struts over to my vacant seat and sits his ass down before my desk. "Do you realize the trump card that just fell into our laps if she really wasn't attached to him."

"I'm sorry, what the fuck are you even coming up with?" Knox fires

He gulps down another shot of amber before turning his gaze my way. Seemingly thinking I can fix my own cousin's fucked up head.

Tried that.

Failed more than once.

"You fuckers don't even realize. Look, we have been dragging every one of his informants in here for months and we have nothing to show for it. What if we tried a more *delicate* approach?"

He won't let the idea die; words just keep spilling out of his mouth. However, if I can look past the fact that James' plans usually end up causing more trouble than they're worth, it might not be the worst idea I've heard him spout.

"That is if she is not, in fact, one of his whores. And that's a big fucking if, but you just might be onto something." I tell him.

A plan swirls in my head. A coup that Anthony Violante wouldn't even see coming. We have been coming at him with a force he's been able to counter, but maybe, just maybe, the only way to take down the head is to capture him by his fucking balls.

And that's when my phone lights up with the update from Jones.

CHAPTER 4

Ripley

"Here you go, Ries."

A steaming cup of tea is forced into my hands. I accept the warmth numbly. "You really need to drink something."

The worried octave of Charlie's voice breaks through the shock and I turned exhausted eyes over to my best friend. Her pastel lavender hair is piled high in a messy topknot. Even without a speck of makeup her statin grey eyes still have an effortless sparkle to them.

The constant beeping of the heart monitor by the head of the bed drags my attention back to my reality. My mom looks so frail laying there motionless on that bed. God, I hate hospitals.

"Thanks for being here, Chaz."

The scratch in my throat is the result of the hours of crying. After the ambulance drove off with my mom, I somehow had enough reason to call Charlie, who in turn flew out of her nearby apartment to pick me up. We made our way to the hospital a few minutes behind the ambulance.

By the time we parked and made our way to the front desk, they had already taken mom back. From what I understand she suffered a seizure as she was getting into the bath and that in turn made her lose conscience. Hitting her head on the tile floor in the process. She only needed a half dozen or so stitches for the gash on the back of her head, but she still hadn't regained consciousness, and no one can tell me why. The only response I can get from the doctors is vague and annoying 'it's just a waiting game now, be patient.'

Fuck patience. It's overrated anyway.

"It'll be okay, Ries, she'll be fine."

Charlie's hand reaches out to squeeze my shoulder reassuringly. I rapidly blink away the fresh tears that threaten to fall.

"Can you believe it was almost two years ago that I met you at this same hospital?"

Instead of thinking about the current situation, I indulge in the past for a little while. Thankful for her distraction.

Her light eyes drift off into memories long gone as well and a bittersweet smile graces her delicate lips,

"God, I can't believe it's been that long already. You and Miss V really helped me through those last hard months with dad."

Instead of thick tears building in her voice, I hear her strong acceptance echoing through.

When mom had that relapse that ended with me putting college on hold, I ran into Charlie, who's dad was in the hospital room a few doors down from mom. Her dad was in the last stages of lung cancer and mom's breast cancer had just relapsed.

To say we found refuge within our collective devastations would be putting it mildly. Even after mom was released, we still came by to check on Charlie, mom took to her like a second daughter. We were there for her when her dad passed a few months later and she has been there for us ever since.

Charlie's mom passed away when she was young, so her dad was all she had left until we entered the picture. Now she's the sister I never had. And it's times like this that remind me just what her presence means to me.

"Come on, girl, there's no reason to cry anymore."

Her fingers swipe at the tears I hadn't even realized were falling.

"Shit, sorry, it's just...I don't know what I'd do without you, Chaz."

I reach my arms over the chair I have tucked myself into to wrap them securely around her neck. I end up dragging her down onto the armchair with me and we both squeeze into the small chair.

We stay like that, just enjoying the comfort of another person's body heat until there is a soft knock on the opened door. We both turn simultaneously and my heart stops at the bastard standing in the threshold of my mother's hospital room.

The same man who oh so rudely fired me not more than a handful of hours ago.

Paxton fucking King.

* * *

"I'M SORRY YOU, FUC...WHAT?"

The stunned words shoot out of my mouth in a rush. After Paxton knocked, he asked, more like demanded, I step away to discuss a matter at hand. Charlie could barely contain her drooling and seemed to think it was a fucking grand idea. I hadn't even had the chance to fill her in on everything that happened before mom collapsed so the bitch probably thought the suited-up devil was some doctor there to talk about mom's treatment.

"Jesus, are you always this dense?"

He gently brings the steaming cup of coffee to his lips while his shining personality brightens up my night.

Ah, sarcasm and I are very good friends.

I brought him down to the cafeteria with the intention of questioning him about...well...everything. Starting with this little stalking spree and ending with asking for my job back. What? I'm not above making my financial needs known.

That brings me back to my earlier exclamation.

"Seriously, Paxton, what the fuck? Why would you want to pay for my mother's hospital bills?"

The words taste bitter knowing there has to be a price. Nothing in this world comes free, and nothing is ever done for just *good intentions*.

"What's in it for you?"

"Look, Miss Quinn, like I said, I have a job that I believe you'd be perfect for." The smugness just oozes from him and it is taking everything in my power not to walk away from this table right now.

Sure, it seems easy enough; do this *job* and get *paid*. But it's also easy enough to realize that when a man like Paxton King offers you a *simple* job, you better be smart enough not to fucking take it.

"I may not know you but I sure as hell know you aren't a man to get involved with," I pause giving him the chance to dispute my claims. He stays silent. "So, I'm gonna stop you right here. I don't want your 'special' job or your money."

I make a grab for my own untouched coffee and go to stand when his hand snaps out to grab onto mine. Not with the same force as he put on my hair earlier tonight but enough to stop me dead in my tracks.

"I'll give you one thing, *Ripley*, you are smarter than I originally took you for."

I go to throw in a comeback worth his insult, but he doesn't pause long enough for me to get a word in.

"But you might want to think of that sick mother of yours upstairs. She needs top-notch medical care and expensive medications and let's not even begin with your atrocious living situation. I am offering you a chance to give her everything she needs with just a little under-the-table dirty work."

This bastard did his research. That alone terrifies me enough to want to run as far from him as possible.

Oh, and let's not even touch the fact that he just admitted whatever it is he wants me to do is considered 'dirty work.' So, yeah, I have all the information I need to outright turn down this fucked up offer. I might be broke, but I'm not desperate enough to accept something with so many red fucking flags.

"Fuck you, King, I won't be your fucking whore," I spit out.

I shove out of his hold and stomp away from the table. It's a good thing that the cafeteria is empty, thanks to the late hour because his next words reach me all the way to the entrance. And the emphasis of each syllable has ice shooting through my veins.

"I'm not asking you to be my whore."

Chapter 5

Ripley

When I make it back to the room all the anger has bled from my exhausted body. I want nothing more than to crawl into bed and sleep for the next five days. However, as I watch my mother's unconscious body, the likelihood of not being able to rest for the foreseeable future settles into my soul.

Charlie is slumped over in the chair fast asleep and I just can't bring myself to wake her, so I let her rest as I go to find the doctor. I need to find out what the next step is, and how much that step is going to cost.

Hours pass slowly with little to no improvement in mom's condition and even the doctor is at a loss. Which doesn't give me a lot of hope. I did however find out what little our insurance covers for this hospital stay.

Paxton's horridly stupid offer plays over and over in my head, each time the tempting idea of financial security pulls at me just a tiny percent more sanity rushes back in. My stomach turns violently even considering it for a split second. Apparently, I need to remind myself that with a money offer like that comes, I don't know, something not good that's for sure.

I might not even know what 'it' was he was offering but it cannot be anything within the realm of legal, right?

"What's with the disgusted look, Ries?"

Charlie's sleep-heavy voice tells me she's finally awake.

"How'd you sleep?"

I push the nasty feeling in my gut as deep down as I can get it to go.

"Shitty but that wasn't the question," she pulls herself from the chair and stretches her arms high above her head, "what's on your mind, girl?"

Okay, you know what, what the hell, let's see what she thinks of this non-detailed job offer.

"Funny you should ask. You remember the suit that stopped by early this morning?"

I pause waiting for her to catch up.

"You mean that scary sexy looking god that I want to lick from head to toe?" This bitch doesn't even flinch at her words. The fact that she is very serious means I need to quickly move on from this before the conversation takes a drastic erotic turn.

"Yeah him, sure. Well get this, that guy works in the building I was cleaning yesterday, and that fucker fired me."

"Okay, but then why and how was he here?"

Her confusion is totally warranted.

"The latter I don't even know and more importantly I'm scared to ask. But the kicker is that he came to offer me a different job..."

I let the sentence drift off to see if she can even make sense of anything.

"An under the table job that would pay for mom's hospital bills and a better living situation."

"Um okay? So, what...is he like a pimp or something? Because that sounds way too good to be true and most definitely illegal."

"Yeah, that's why I turned him down without asking any more questions. I don't need blood money to survive."

"Wait, he actually kinda looked familiar. What was his name?"

"Um, Paxton King, he works at the King Tower on fourth."

As soon as the words are out of my mouth, she has her phone out and her fingers zip over the screen. I guess it wouldn't be a bad idea to learn a little bit more about this guy. Since the fucker seemed to know way too much about me.

"Paxton King. As in the notorious billionaire King family?"

The spark that ignites in her eyes worries me. Something tells me this bitch is about to come up with her own fucked up fairytale plot.

"Chaz, stop whatever it is that your fucked up little dreaming head is coming up with. I turned him down. I outright refuse to even consider whatever it is he wants from me."

I need to put my foot down hard now or next thing I know Charlie will have me bound, thrown into the car and heading towards King Tower before I can give any real struggle.

"I'm serious Charlie, I will not go along with your plans this time."

Not going to happen.

* * *

THE EARLY AFTERNOON light bounces off the mirrored windows of King Tower and I try to remember how the ever-loving fuck I ended up in the passenger seat of Charlie's Beamer in front of this building at ten-thirty in the morning.

Honestly, all I can remember is an hour and a half of bartering and auguring in my mom's room. Somewhere between the 'honestly whatever he wants can't be that bad' and the 'shouldn't you at least hear him out before you turn him down?' I lost count of my fight.

For the record though, I am just humoring her, there is no way I'm going to whore myself out for simple financial security. At least I don't *think* I will.

Anyway, here we are, and I still haven't found the courage to get out of this car. I don't even know what I am supposed to say after everything I spat at him this morning.

"Maybe he won't be here, I think we should try calling from home..."

I try one last time to get her to let me off and take me home. She doesn't bite.

"Come on, Ripley, at least hear him out. For once, just get all the facts before you throw in the towel."

"Come with me?"

"And what would you learn if I came along holding your hand? How about you keep me on the line the whole time, so I know if you need help?"

"But if this guy really is connected to the mob wouldn't they have, like, some sort of thing set up to screw up cell service?"

Oh yeah, that's something else we conveniently found out in our information search. The King family is rumored to have fucking Mafia ties. Specifically, with the infamous Violante Family that has its hands in everything from money laundering to international terrorism to black-market murder trade.

Seriously what the fuck am I even doing here?

"I think you watch way too many movies but okay, fine, maybe it wouldn't be that bad to have me come up with you?"

I finally gather up the courage to open the car door, and with Charlie close on my tail I walk into the building that is sure to be the death of me.

CHAPTER 6

Paxton

"There is a Ripley Quinn here asking for you, sir"

"Quinn? As in the girl who turned you the fuck down?"

Jameson lounges back in the chair in front of my desk. Not a single care in the world for the work that is piled in front of us. I ignore his bantering.

But what a fun turn of events. I can't say I am all that surprised with her showing up here. I saw a spark of intrigue behind her hardened exterior this morning, but I wasn't expecting her to come around so soon. I expected more of a fight. The sharp sting of disappointment that clenches my gut takes me by surprise. I brush off the feeling like nothing more than a sick need for entertainment in my life.

"Send her in, Heather."

I release the intercom button just as the door opens. The second the fluorescent lights hit her midnight hair, allowing the blues and black hues to bounce around her head, my world stops.

Which is really fucking bad.

I shake off the uneasy need building in my dick and notice the same woman she was cuddled up in the hospital room follows in behind her. Did she bring back up? Or a safety net?

Either way that's not how this is about to go.

I look over at Jameson to try to get him to get rid of the chick. Instantly realizing that won't be a problem. James is all but eating up every inch of this five-foot whatever, pastel haired bombshell. I scan over her body once more quickly to try to find the appeal. Don't get me wrong she is absolutely stunning just, not as intriguing as the raven-haired spitfire.

"Mr. King, thank you for having a minute to talk."

Her voice drips with professionalism I find hilarious. I don't dare let a smile slip through. No, if I want this to work, I need to get her on board.

And more importantly, I need to do that while keeping my dick dry.

I stand to extend my hand to capture the one she offers.

"Miss Quinn, I can't say I was expecting to hear from you again after our *chat* earlier."

"Um, yes, well," she stumbles through her words and it makes me want to tease her, "I was able to think it over clearly and I have decided it would only be right if I were to hear you out."

Again, she doesn't say what I anticipate, the uncertain outcome leaves an unsettling lump forming in my gut.

"I thank you for your reconsideration, may my colleague here give your friend a tour while we speak?"

Her eyes flash with worry and it isn't hard to see her friend is the one who talked her into this. Which is yet another reason why I want her gone. I want to see just what Ripley Quinn can do on her own.

The girls share a silent look that is packed with an entire conversation before her friend nods, reluctantly.

"Jameson, would you take Miss..."

My eyes find Ripley to fill in the rest.

"Charlie Kentrell."

The girl, Charlie, steps forward and slides her eyes up and down my cousin in a way that leaves my skin crawling. The blatant lust zipping between them is horribly uncomfortable to be around. She doesn't even pretend not to check him out and James does his own sick inspection. These two need to get a fucking room before I lose my lunch to their eye fucking.

I do have to admit though, it sure as hell looks like Ripley isn't the only one with a set of balls.

Jameson leads Miss Kentrell out of the room. And with one final worried look shot over to Ripley, her friend disappears behind the closed door.

She takes an audible breath and I let her have the first words since it looks like she is gearing up for a battle.

"Before we start, I want to make something very clear, Mr. King."

She glides up to my desk, leveling her green gaze with mine. With the sun gleaming off the unique color I can't help but compare the hue to mint chocolate ice cream. Cold and refreshing with dark specs sprinkled within the milky green. It's an odd comparison, I know, but it's the first thing that pops into my head. Memories of sneaking ice cream at midnight with my father. And with that flavor always being his preference the comparison sticks. It really is the silliest thing that brings up the nostalgia of times long gone.

"Paxton, are you even listening to me?"

Annoyance rings clear and it snaps me out of my pointless thoughts.

"What was it you wanted to clarify?"

I ignore her question, hoping she'd just move on without any more inspection of my flyaway train of thought.

"I will listen to your idiotic proposal under one condition."

Her shoulders set in a no-nonsense pose and I prepare for her ultimatum. Though I can already guess what she'll demand.

"When I turn down this job, I want to be unfired. I expect you to contact the cleaning company and allow me to resume my job here."

"That seems reasonable enough, Miss Quinn."

The funniest part is she has no idea what she could have really bargained for. She has no idea the cards she holds. Guess she's about to find out.

"Please, won't you sit."

I motioned to the chair that Jameson conveniently forgot to push back into place under the desk.

"So, what exactly is the job you are offering?"

She eases herself down, getting right down to the most important part. But she won't get those answers that easily.

"Firstly, before I tell you anything, I will need you to sign this NDA. Since what I am about to offer will never be allowed to leave this room."

I open the drawer to my right, and I pull out the contract I always have handy.

"And what happens if I decide not to take it?"

A delicately shaped eyebrow arches.

"Well, I'm sure you did your research before coming to me, right?"

I know she isn't stupid so there is no need to play into any false ideas. I will need her to understand exactly what I do, or this won't work.

"About who the internet says you are?"

The confidence in her voice sends a shot of something dangerous through my veins.

"Exactly. And what did you find out?"

I lean forward and let my elbows rest against the desk.

"That the King name has Mafia ties with the Violante family."

Oh, this is going to be fun. I love pulling the rug out from unexpecting victims.

"No, sweetheart. We don't just have ties; we are the fucking Mafia. The King and Violante are one and the same."

"So, your offer isn't exactly on the legal side of the spectrum then?"

She hides her surprise rather well.

"Something like that."

I can't help but wish for a reaction she isn't giving me.

"But you have to sign this little piece of paper before I divulge into any other details. I will let you walk right now, though."

I level my gaze with hers and allow my hard edges to show through. To show her just what she's about to get into if she decides to hear me out.

"So, what are you going to do, Little Reaper. Are you going to walk away or stay to listen to an offer that will change your life?"

Without enough thought, she bends forward and scribbles her name across the page. Sealing her fate. And tying her to me in more ways than one.

"I don't know what you know about me, but I can assure you I have no outstanding talents that could be of use to you."

Oh, modest one, you have no idea, do you?

"I am not so sure about that."

Again, her eyebrow pipes up in disbelief,

"All I would require of you, are your looks and your acting ability."

"Oh, that's all is it?"

She lets an unintentional laugh slip through her perfect lips. The light wisp of sound awakens my dick in a way that it absolutely shouldn't. I instantly drop all pretense, needing to get on with this pitch before I do something stupid.

"One year of your life then you'd walk away with one point five million and an all-expense paid medical bill and an apartment on the upper east side."

"I'm sorry, what?"

This time she can't hide the blatant surprise. Or the instant draining of color from her face.

"What's the catch?"

The words stumble from her mouth.

"Are you asking me to kill someone for you because nothing that good comes without an ultimate price?"

"See I knew you were a smart one."

I can't help the smirk that crawls over my lips.

"The catch is we would use you as an informant of sorts."

"And..."

"You would become a faux mistress of the current head of the Violante family."

"But I'm guessing only those in this room would know it would be fake?"

"You're quick."

I debate just how much to tell her at this point. The guys wanted me to keep her as much in the dark as I could, but something in me wants her to know everything.

I shut that part of thought down real fucking quick.

"You'd do what we asked with no questions and the second your job is over you go back to your little safe life and pretend nothing ever happened. And let's just say if you were to talk about anything you saw within this world... there'd be *consequences*."

"So, wait, you really do want to whore me out?"

"You would not be getting paid to fuck him, only become a mistress."

"Isn't that the same thing?"

"There might not seem like much of a difference between the two but there is. You'd be allowed to draw the line..."

My words trail off not knowing how to explain Anthony's *tendencies*.

"That isn't an answer."

She might just be too *smart* for this job.

"Get used to it. You can question all you want but that sure as fuck doesn't mean I'll give you any answers."

"I'm also assuming, if I were to get caught by this dude, you'd deny ever meeting me."

The laugh that barks out of my throat is all the answer she needs. Watching her mind work over every possibility is amusing as fuck to witness. I can honestly say I really didn't expect her to stay after I got through with the initial pitch.

Chapter 7

Ripley

Why the ever-loving hell am I still sitting in this goddamned glass office? I mean, come on, I have to have some sick twisted death wish to even be considering this deranged plot against a mafia head. And the worst part of it all, this fucker thinks he already caught his pawn.

He hasn't. At least I don't think he has.

"I didn't know I said something humorous."

The ice in my words is intended to slap the ridiculous smirk right off his gorgeous face.

Yeah right.

Without taking his eyes off of mine he hits the intercom on his desk.

"Heather, can you send for the three?"

"Anything for, Paxton," Bottle blonde purrs through the speaker.

"Heather..."

"Yes, Mr. King."

The reluctance is clear. It also isn't hard to figure out their relationship. Ugh...just the thought that the conversation I heard last night when she was bragging about 'her boss' huge cock'. It was in reference to the fucker in front of me, the thought leaves a disgusting taste in my mouth. And a horrible clenching between my thighs.

Seriously what the hell is wrong with me?

Is it just because I haven't been laid recently?

I mean I don't *get around,* but it has been a while. But not even that can be the reason for the stupidity running around my head.

While I'm fighting with my own sexual frustration, the door behind me opens to reveal the other three men I had the pleasure of meeting last night. I do notice the absence of my best friend.

Should I be worried about what the chocolate eyed devil did with her?

No one gives me the chance to ask though, for the atmosphere shifts immediately from one 'playful' banter to a professional business meeting.

36

I barely have a chance to catch my breath before I am motioned from the desk to the large table situated in front of the window overlooking Manhattan.

The view calls for my attention, but I keep my focus directly on the men around me. I keep my mouth shut waiting for Paxton or one of the other men to speak in this 'meeting.' I don't have to wait long.

"I see you've reconsidered Paxton's offer?"

The same man who had earlier commented from the other side of the room. The humor dancing in his eyes unnerves me to no end. Something about his easy light-heartedness has danger swimming in my veins. Like, his whole demeanor is nothing more in a carefully crafted facade.

I don't answer his question.

They know why I'm here so any answer would be pointless. Plus, I don't feel like playing their games today. I want cut-and dry rules and I want to quit with the runaround. something tells me getting those things isn't going to be easy. That the men before me like toying with their prey before they finally strike.

After a few beats of silence, Paxton takes control of the room simply by taking his seat at the head of the table. I can't help but fixate with the pure power that exudes from every pore of his body. It wraps around you like a living being demanding every part of your attention.

All you can do is beg for mercy and submit. It's a terrifying power.

"There is no need for idiotic questions, Jameson."

The gorgeous man, Jameson, actually has the guts to roll his eyes.

I would have laughed if the tension in the room wasn't trying to choke the life out of me.

"But yes, Miss Quinn here, has agreed to come aboard."

He merely flicks his wrist in my direction.

"No, if I remember correctly, I said I would hear you out. I haven't agreed to anything yet."

Swallowing the tremor in my voice, I straighten my back and refuse to allow them to walk all over me.

He finally turns his head, landing his eyes on mine.

"My apologies..."

There isn't an ounce of conviction in his words but at least I made my point clear.

"But she did sign the NDA, so why don't we give her a slight rundown of what we would expect."

A dangerous look enters his eyes that challenges me to run.

I stand my ground And I hold my stare. I won't allow him to see my fear. All he would do is use it to destroy me.

"I'm sure Paxton has filled you in on the surface details, but the job is quite simple. Keep Anthony Volante distracted."

A new baritone voice has me turning my head.

"That's really all you need to know."

This one, just as gorgeous and just as terrifying. Blonde hair styled similarly to the rest, but there's just a hint of a curl underneath the styling products. Another sharp jawline, hard cheekbones, and imposing physique. The thing that makes him stand out as different is the way his dark blue eyes seem to hold the power to stare directly into your soul and capture every secret you hold close.

He is intimidating as fuck.

I can't pull myself away from his mesmerizing stare. This feeling is far from the lust-filled tension that overtakes me with Paxton. No, this is more like being a rabbit frozen in a cat's line of view, thinking that with less movement it somehow has become invisible from the predator.

"Knox has sure made an impression."

Jameson's husky chuckle finally snaps me out of *Knox's* trap.

Three out of four. Only one name left.

Instead of turning back towards Paxton or Jameson, I find the last body.

This one has yet to come over to the conference table, choosing instead to find a seat on the luxurious leather couch in the center of the room.

His skin is darker than the rest, like a warm deep tan. That paired with black hair and dark almost black eyes. everything about him seems coated in a golden hue all of which makes me think he has southern European or Mediterranean ancestry.

While the other three are wearing full suits, his jacket has long been discarded. His crisp white dress shirt has the arms rolled up to his elbows leaving colorfully tattoos on display. Both forearms are adorned with gorgeous colors, I noticed Paxton's neck tattoo last night so it's likely all four have some expanse of ink. After one too many seconds staring at yet another member of the group, I shift my eyes to absently gaze around the room.

Actually, I finally take stock of the impressive office. Like CEO impressive- but there's no way, right? I mean sure Paxton King did tell me 'he owns my ass' but shit, he can't be more than twenty-three or twenty-four. His demeanor might bleed years of knowledge and demands respect but the rest of him screams of fraternities and leaving a trail of coeds-

Stop, Ries. You were inspecting the office, not the college years of some suit.

Looking past the men, wealth seeps out of every corner. From the giant dark wooden desk at one end, to the white leather couches facing each other in the center, and of course to the fully stocked bar that is set up on this end of the room. And the final piece is this long expensive wooden conference table.

I don't spend a lot of time in corporate offices, okay sure my only experience is with a cleaning crew, but even I can recognize a billion-dollar company-

Actually, pause-

"What exactly does this company do?"

All four share a look that sends a chill down my spine. It isn't dangerous, no, more like *how much does she need to know* kind of look.

I am already sick of the pick and choose game of what they are telling me. Not that I would expect them to devolve all their secret...just I hate this stupid fucked up runaround.

I hate it when colleges do it or when hospitals tell you what they think you want to hear. And I especially can't stand that shit when it comes to an 'interview'.

The longer they stay silent the more my blood heats. My fists clench to try to control my need to lash out.

"Look, I get it, you don't want to tell me shit, but you've got to give me more than just 'distract some old fucker'."

"What you don't understand is one very simple idea." Paxton somehow

39

is immediately in front of me crowding in on my space, "you don't need to know anything more than the tiny details we choose to give you. You'd be best to keep that in mind, Little Reaper"

Fuck this shit.

I stand in a rush shoving at his body to put some distance between us.

"And you'd best remember I haven't agreed to shit yet and you're not doing that great of a job trying to convince any of this is worth it."

I'm done with this bullshit. I make it to the door without anyone trying to stop me. As my hand reaches for the door Paxton's words stop me.

CHAPTER 8

Ripley

"We need you to play this part. Distract him until we can overthrow the old bastard. You'll be our finale pawn in our scheme."

"You're planning a coup against a Mafia head?"

Hysteria bleeds into my voice with the realization of what the hell I have walked into. For reasons, my brain can't comprehend, my legs turn to face the four men. My head is screaming for me to run. Walk out the door and never look back. But...I don't.

"In simple terms, yes, but you aren't a part of that."

I huff, ungracefully I might add, at Paxton's idiotic statement. *I'm not a part of that part.*

"How does that figure, Mr. King?"

Sarcasm is always my specialty.

"Because, *Miss Quinn*, all you'd be is a pretty face handing off information. you'll be long gone before we commence anything *dangerous*."

I sure as hell do not like the way he puts his own sarcastic emphasis on his words.

"Jesus, Paxton, why not tell the whole plan while you're at it?"

Jameson's voice skates with annoyance.

"She's not an idiot. A trait we knew we needed for this to work. Of course, she will have obvious questions."

The only voice I have yet to hear pulls my gaze. My eyes meet his and I see reassurance shining back at me.

"And what's your name?"

I have yet to actually ask any of their names, I have just learned them by circumstance. But this one confuses me more than any of the others. Paxton's terrifying presence sets blood racing in my veins. Jameson has sadistic humor radiating around him. And Knox just straight up has a psychopath vibe. But this one doesn't fit. He may look the most intimidating but there is a kindness in his eyes that...feels *human* while the others are monsters. And they know how to play up that fear.

"Bishop."

There is definitely just a hint of an accent but other than guesses pulled purely from his skin I can't place it.

"Great, now that you know the whole crew," Jameson is suddenly right in front of me, "tell me are you going to accept this position, or do we need to find someone else?"

I am about to make the most stupid decision of my life.

"One year, unless I get what you need earlier; one point five million; all medical expenses paid for; and an apartment, right?"

I look around Jameson's stunned expression. My eyes collide with Paxton's looking for a confirmation.

"That was the deal, was it not?"

A mix of 'what the fucks' and 'are you fucking insane' spin around the room from the others. Guess Paxton didn't enlighten his friends about our deal. Not my problem.

"When I get that in writing I'll accept."

* * *

It doesn't take more than fifteen minutes for the papers to be drawn up and signed. Five signatures stare at me as a sentiment. The physical recognition of no longer having the choice to run back. It doesn't matter that I can barely make out the letters, the scribbled ink is clear.

They own me now.

I clench my fist trying to control the shaking. The fear of what I've just done threatens to overtake me,

"Okay, so, now what. What do I need to know about him?"

I swallow the squeak in my voice hoping they'll ignore it and just give me some sort of details.

I look to Paxton for answers, he motions for Jameson to take the lead. Making sure I don't mistake the attraction that may exist between us as a comforting presence. I focus in on Jameson keeping mental notes of the important details.

"Look, you aren't trying to convince Anthony that you are from this world, but you should at least have a heads up on...things."

Not a fan of how this is starting but who knows.

"First things first, Anthony Violante is The Boss of the Violante Crime Family. They operate most of the New York City territories, as well as many outside territories but those aren't important to you. While of course, you've heard of The Five Families but make no mistake, just because The Volante's may not have the media recognition, they have a similar reputation. Anthony has a taste for blood and beautiful young women. He has a very *specific* type and you, my dear," his eyes crawl over my body and I have to physically hold back from curling in on myself to hide, "you check every box."

"Sure, whatever, but how is this little party connected to this whole thing?" I turn my head towards Paxton, "earlier you told me the King name and Violante were the same. What exactly does that mean?"

"Christ, Pax, is there anything you haven't told her?" Knox cuts in with a hard edge.

I ignore him.

"The Mafia has branches, if you will, The Elites are one of those branches. They consist of more 'under the radar' Mafia work while holding a high position in society. They can be anyone from politicians to billionaire businessmen. The particular Elite group in New York consist of the King family, as well as others you don't need to know. They are still under Anthony Violante's *rule* they just go by a less notorious name. Then within the Elites, you have a crew. This crew goes by the Elite Players."

"So, what exactly does this crew do?"

So they are these *Players,* that much I understand.

Cute name for a playmate.

"That, Little Reaper, isn't your concern."

"Personally, I think her knowing anything of this is irrelevant, but fuck what do I know?"

Jameson breaks the spell Paxton somehow captured under yet again. How is it that whenever he speaks, I forget there is anyone else in this world.

43

"Can I continue on the details that will keep you alive?"

Damn, he is a sassy motherfucker when grumpy. Jameson's attitude is crazy similar to Charlie's when pissed. Speaking of-

"What did you do with the girl I came here with?"

"Miss Kentrell?"

A spark flashes in his eyes that I don't like. Like at fucking all.

"She was left at reception with Heather to keep her company."

Now that spark burns with his sick humor knowing full well how good those two will get along.

Oh, poor Chaz.

"The only other person I believe is important for you to know is Lilianna Volante, Anthony's wife."

All humor vanishes from his features replaced with forced indifference,

"They just celebrated twenty happy years together."

How did 'pretend to be a mistress' never connect with the fact that he would of course be married. I don't have to seduce a happily married man, right? Just the thought turns my stomach.

Fuck, how did this not dawn on me before this?

"Mafia guys are notorious for having mistresses, right? I won't be the...first?"

"Fuck no, Anthony is a man whore like the rest of them. All their wives understand their ways. You don't need to worry about her. She's grown way too accustomed to his unfaithfulness to give much of a shit anymore. She barely sees him anymore. Her permanent residence is his mansion outside of Queens."

"And what about his children? I'd imagine he'd have kids?"

His eyes grow darker and the room falls into a silence that makes every heartbeat sound like a drum roll.

"They aren't important for you to know."

"What else exactly is 'important' for me to know?"

I don't bother holding in my snark. This whole experience leaves a nasty taste in my mouth and a desperate need for a shower.

"Nothing-" he gets right up in my face. The proximity makes me want to recoil but I refuse to give in to the instinct, "you already know too much, so this is the part where you stop asking questions."

"Well, fuck you too."

The need to roll my eyes is strong but I push it down needing to be mature...at least a little.

"There are rules you need to know."

Paxton's deep voice pulls in my immature thoughts.

"At the very least we don't want you to get caught but you dying would also put a real drag on this plan."

Oh, how his comforting words make all the fear evaporate into dust...

"Firstly; you'd better fucking *act* like your life depends on it. If he catches on to the role you play, he will kill you. No question about it. He is Mafia through and through. Don't forget that. Second; he's one mean bastard when he drinks. So, unless you want some black and blue to complement those pretty green eyes, never allow yourself to be alone with him when he's in that state. And lastly; don't ask questions. Ever. You pass along any information you find to me. You don't *think*. You don't *plan*. You don't *question*. If you just play the bimbo role, we might all make it out alive."

A smirk crawls across his face like he is flirting with pretty words and roses.

All I can do is nod like a moron. Jameson might not hide his contempt for me being here but Paxton...His words leave wounds on my soul and when those words are terrifying, they create scars with not a single hope to ever heal to normal.

How the hell did I become this person that is willing to put themselves in a position that could kill them? Maybe it's because I had a quiet, safe childhood? Maybe I've subconsciously craved adventure all my life? Or maybe I have some stupid notion that I want to live out some crazy action movie? Some sick, twisted fairytale? *Little Maid and the Mafia Prince...*

Fuck that.

I've spent my life trying to convince myself that the bad things only happen to those that deserve it. But the cold hard truth of life is bad shit happens no matter what the hell you do. It happens to the best of us. It happens to the worst of us. And it happens for completely random reasons.

It's all fucking random. And no matter how hard you work to make it better or how much time you sacrifice for more. You will never get above the fucking mediocrity of the hand you've been dealt in life.

Not that it means life doesn't sometimes take mercy on you, that you might get a lucky hand. A perfect hand of cards. A king-high flush right out of their shitty life.

Life's been nothing but a cruel bitch to me.

So, this whole game of chance with the Elite Players will either become the one decision that grants me a better life. Or I'm about to learn the true dark meaning of suffering.

CHAPTER 9

Ripley

The plan seemed *simple*. Like way too freaking simple, if you ask me.

I was going on a date with Jameson. Yep, you heard me right. Apparently, Anthony had a habit of stealing Jameson's girls. which is a whole lot of weird if you ask me, but remember no questions.

So here I am freezing my ass off as I wait in front of my apartment building in a slinky black dress. Or at least the 'sexiest' dress I own which isn't saying much, but with the added effect of the tumbles of black curls falling down my back and red-lined lips, it'll be able to pass to grab Anthony's attention.

A black Aston Martin pulls in front of me and it isn't until the engine purrs to a stop that I realize this is my ride. The sleek luxury sports car is gorgeous, not that I've really seen one up close. Jameson steps out on the other side of the car and my eyes nearly fall out of my head. The trickster Player really knows how to dress to impress. His six whatever body is wrapped tightly in an expensive-looking black suit that extenuates the hardness underneath. His blonde hair is styled with a little flip movement in the front that enhances the deep brown of his eyes. The whole effect is intoxicating. My only saving grace is it isn't Paxton. Seriously if that bastard was the one stepping out of the foreign sports car looking like a catalog model dripping in sex...let's just say I would have completely humiliated myself right here on the curb. I'm talking throwing panties and purring like a kitten in heat, kind of humiliating. And I kind of hate myself for the reaction these thoughts provoke in me. He's dangerous. He's a bastard like no other. And he has a dick personality. So why can't I convince my libido to be disgusted by him?

"Earth to Ripley. I'm freezing my balls off, can you please get in the car?"

The whine in Jameson's words snaps me back to the present. I find him standing with the passenger door ajar waiting for me to take my seat on the

47

plush leather. I shake the lingering thoughts of Paxton from my head and try to get my head in the game. I have a role to play so I better focus, or everything will fall apart before I even have a chance to start something.

I mutter a sorry as I slide into the warm car. I twitch my fingers in my lap afraid to touch anything in the car. I probably can't even afford to get this car detailed so I better not get even a drop of sweat on the leather seats.

Jameson slides in behind the wheel and pulls the car into traffic without a glance in my direction. He made it known more than once the other night that he was not on board with this plan.

After we finished the initial information part of the meeting the men started throwing around ideas on how to get me in front of Anthony naturally so he wouldn't pick up on me being a plant.

The over consensus was that Anthony would immediately call out Paxton if he was the one to bring me around. Something about their pasts and Paxton's preference for blondes, preferably those with lower intelligence.

Not my words mind you, it was all Knox and his crude comparisons that pointed out the obvious.

No one did correct him though, so I doubt he was far off with his comments.

After that, it was Paxton's idea to have Jameson bring me to The Queen's Lounge as his date for the evening. I was then explained that The Queen's Lounge was the Violante's under the radar social club. So basically, a Mafia hang-out and I'm about to be right in the middle of it. *Just super.*

By the time we pull up to the valet in front of the restaurant, my knees are bouncing uncontrollably. And it's not from the cold in the air. Nope, this is all nerves and I can feel the impending freak out isn't going to be pretty.

"Seriously, if you don't get your shit in order, I'm calling this whole thing off." My throat works to swallow down the nerves threatening to leak out.

"I've got this don't worry."

I try to sound legitimate but even I know I'm not convincing with the acting ability.

"Fuck this."

Jameson revs the engine to zip out from our spot, but my door is ripped open before he can make his move.

"Can I ask what you're doing?"

A familiar smooth voice has a whole new set of nerves bubbling up in my stomach.

Paxton is leaning over my door to look into the car. And the asshole looks just as good as I imagined not ten minutes ago. I was really hoping my imagination was exaggerating this attraction.

It wasn't.

Goddammit.

"Pax, this chick is freaking the fuck out. There's no way she can pull this off."

I hate to agree with him but

"Is that true, Little Reaper?"

The purr in Paxton's voice curls around me igniting my skin for all things naughty.

I nearly drown within his crystal iris. They swirl with so much promise it has me wanting to agree to anything.

It has to be the fucking suit...because I can normally keep it in my pants I swear.

My eyes bounce between the two men trying to focus on the questions being asked. I let my sick mother float into my head; our pile of debt; our tiny apartment. All the things I would have to deal with if I call this off right now.

All I have to do is seduce a rich middle-aged man, nothing more, nothing less. The only way this works is if I ignore the Mafia part, or what will happen after I hand over information. None of that concerns me. I just have to stay focused on my tiny part in their plan.

I allow my eyes too close to center myself. Breathe in. breathe out. Repeat. After three rounds of deep breaths I open my eyes and slip into my role.

"I can do it." Conviction rings clear, "I'm ready."

I swing my leg out of the car and force Paxton to step back as I exit the car.

"That's my girl."

I ignore the pride in Paxton's voice. I can't allow it in and waver my confidence.

I'll show these Players how a woman plays their game.

CHAPTER 10

Ripley

Stepping through the entrance felt like stepping into a completely different world. I wouldn't even be surprised to find Alice and Dorothy sipping tea in the corner booth while they wait for the hatter to bring them their food. I'm seriously not exaggerating. I stepped through a portal and left the frigid New York night behind me.

Gold drips from the surface in a way that screams luxury instead of gaudy decor. Ivory walls that swirl with red and gold that have a hypnotizing effect. Candlelight and smooth classical music add to the atmosphere.

I can barely wrap my head around the idea that this upscale restaurant is a mobster social club. I guess I was expecting the stereotypical deep red carpets, Italian persona, and thick cigar smoke. *What can I say, I watched a lot of movies growing up.*

But this makes me feel underdressed. I would have done anything to trade in this knee-length black velvet dress for a silk gown that made me belong.

Jameson doesn't allow me to cower in the entrance long before grabbing my hand and placing it in the crook of his elbow. An effective yet discreet way to keep the leash tight when needing control. I barely resist as he drags me further into the restaurant, much too busy being aware of every eye in this place staring directly at us. I pretend it has everything to do with Jameson being here and not the ditzy looking date on his arm for the reason for all the attention.

We make it to a table directly smack in the center of the joint before I notice Paxton disappeared. I ever so discreetly try to find him amongst the patrons as Jameson pulls my chair out, but I come up empty on my search.

"You know if you're to be convincing at this role you better start acting like you're on the top of the fucking world being here."

Jameson's lips graze over my ear in what would otherwise look like an intimate whisper of sweet nothings, if not for the crude words grating across my eardrum.

I turn in time to place my hand gently on his shoulder and I let a flirty smile grace my lips, fully slipping into this role.

"Oh Jameson, you truly know what to say to make a girl melt, don't you?"

His eyebrow ticks showing he picked up on my sarcasm. The sweet tone might convince a passerby but the annoyance under my words are clear.

It isn't hard to tell he's not my biggest fan but jokes on him, I simply don't give a single flying fuck what he thinks, what any of them think.

Well...

I shut down that little voice of protest in my head before she has a chance to call my bluff.

Jameson breaks our staring contest first but his immaturity peaks through when he shoves the chair in a second before I fully sit. Successfully knocking the backs of my knees that steals my graceful descent.

He tries to muffle his triumphant laugh, but the bastard fails miserably.

I tell myself I'm not going to stoop to his level...but my foot accidentally kicks out hard enough to slam into his shin resulting in a stifled oomph from the offender.

Completely accidental, I swear, must have been a random foot spasm, weird.

I ignore the stink eye he is glaring at me over the table in favor of studying the extensive menu before me.

My eyes nearly fall out of my head when I get a look at the listed prices. Which are not a lot mind you. This is one of the restaurants that don't put prices on their main course dishes, one of those places I don't even think water is free.

A place I have rarely visited, if ever, to be honest.

Gently laying the menu back on the table knowing full well I won't be able to convince myself to order anything I glance over to Jameson. He isn't looking at me. I follow his line of sight and land on a man sitting on the far-left side of the room.

Anthony Violante.

I don't know how I know but the fact is instantly solidified in my brain. This is the man that runs the Violante Crime Family. The man I am supposed to distract for The Players.

As if he heard my thoughts he shifts his head until his dark gaze collides with mine. My instincts scream for me to be embarrassed having been caught staring but I push down my impulse. This could be my in. A thought pops into my head and I enact the plan before I can think better of it. Tilting my head downwards I flutter my eyelids in a faux embarrassment while I slowly lift a side of my painted lips. I don't know if the effect worked but hey, I've seen something similar played out on hundreds of tv shows and movies.

After a few beats of my downcast eyes, I lift them slowly, finding Anthony still staring in my direction running a hand over his short beard.

Checkmate.

I turn back towards my 'date'. Jameson nods his head ever so discreetly as he sips his wine acknowledging the breadcrumbs I threw in front of Anthony's feet.

Food I never ordered arrives at our table and the array of aromas floating around the table makes my mouth water. Creamy pasta, crispy parmesan chicken, and what looks to be pawns drenched in sizzling olive oil.

"I took it upon myself to order for you since I expected this place intimidated your lower-class palate."

"Holy hell you're a through and through asshole."

The chuckle is unintentional, knowing full well Jameson was simply making a statement instead of trying to be a rude dick. He is just a shitty sense of tact. Can't fault the pretty little rich boy for that.

I tentatively dig into my food holding in a moan when the first savory texture hits my tongue. I lose myself in the food until Jameson clearing his throat draws my attention. Anthony's table is behind me, so I've been waiting for a cue from Jameson, which I just got.

"Well, I'm not here to charm you into a quick fuck so what would be the point of fake airs?"

His eyes stay trained over my shoulder.

"I can appreciate the honesty, but lord your personality is just as bad as Paxton's."

"Ha, yeah no, sweetheart, Paxton is in a league all his own when it comes to shitty personalities. You'd best remember that."

"That's not something you need to warn me about. Remember I experienced it firsthand."

"Again, I say, ha, you're cute if you think you are convincing yourself of that, but I've seen the way you look at each other. Under the enmity, there is a desire that should never be explored. This is a serious fucking plan and it'll all go to shit if King destroys your heart."

"I want nothing to do with him. I'm here for this job, I have no intention of exploring shit."

"I hope to stick to those words, Ripley," He shifts his eyes to expose the severity within the depths of his gaze, "now excuse yourself to the restroom then go to the bar. Make sure to catch Anthony's focus when you leave."

I bring my napkin up to dap the corners of my mouth while trying to calm my racing heart. I steady my breathing before I do just what he said. I stand from the table and swivel my head just enough to find Anthony following my every movement.

It's a weird feeling knowing you're being watched. Every move feels calculated yet stiff. I also can't remember the last time, if ever, I tried to grab the attention of a stranger for the sole purpose of seduction. I also can't help the disgusting feeling growing in my stomach knowing he's likely twice my age, if not older, and I've agreed to do...*things* with him. That is if I can even get that far.

Doubts swirl around my head as I make my way to the back of the building. I end up at a dead end. Glancing around the hall trying to come up with my next move without looking like a complete moron wandering around the upscale mobster front.

"If you're looking for the restrooms, that would be the other hall."

A deep voice behind has a chill running down my spine. I turn to find Anthony Violante has followed me into the deserted hall.

Everything inside me screams for me to run. Logically I know this is probably a good way to introduce myself but *fuck*...he followed me. Like that's really fucking terrifying, it shouldn't matter that I *'was giving him sexy*

54

eyes' or shit, you don't follow a fucking stranger until they are clearly lost and then block their fucking exit out of the hallway.

Goosebumps pop along my exposed skin as anger and sickness burns through me. It takes everything in me to keep my facial features in check as all this runs through my head knowing if this is to work, I can't lash out at him. I force a smile.

"Yes, restroom."

I make an embarrassing motion with my hands that likely looks like the flailing of a lunatic, but it is what it is.

He cracks a chuckle. Cool, hopefully, he thinks I'm kinda cute.

"I couldn't help but notice you earlier. I'm Anthony Violante."

He reaches out a hand that I try not to recoil at. Every word gets creepier and creepier. I instantly regret agreeing to this, not that I'll walk away just yet.

I know, I know, I sound insane right? Like, seriously what the fuck is wrong with this chick, crazy. Honestly, I don't have an answer to this. Up until a few days ago, I would have never guessed I was this girl. The gold-digger type, faux or not let's call a spade a spade, shall we? I am putting myself in a dangerous position just to get ahead in life while compromising most of the morals I've lived my life by until this point. Seriously, if this was any other person telling me this is where their life has come to...I'd probably have some crude choice words for them. But the thing is, this is the choice I have chosen whatever the outcome, good or bad. I have to live with myself after this, no one else does. So yeah, I'm fucking human I'm allowed to question my choices even after they are made.

His hand is still extended toward me and I'm slapped back to reality. I quickly slide my hand into his. A gentle squeeze confirms our interaction.

"Sorry about that, you caught me off guard."

A soft giggle slips from my lips slipping fully into the role of being flattered he followed me,

"I'm Ripley Grace, it's nice to meet you, Mr. Violante."

Oh yeah, the guys thought a fake last name would be safest. They said that even if he wanted to 'check up on my story' they'd have it covered. I didn't really want to know more so I didn't ask.

"Well, Miss Grace, why don't I point you in the right direction and you can thank me by joining me for a drink."

Another squeeze from his hand and a flirty smirk try to convince me to take him up in his offer.

"That sounds wonderful."

I smile through the skeevy vibes emanating from this guy.

And just like that, the ploy was set.

CHAPTER 11

Ripley

"Now tell me, what brought you here with Jameson King?"

King? So that's why they were so particular about not giving me their last names. Holy fuck are Paxton and Jameson brothers? And if so, why the hell did he not tell me?

Think Ries think. What was my story again?

"Oh, I bumped into him at Kings Tower and couldn't help myself after hearing his name."

Yuck. I take a sip of pinot. Funny how the fancier the establishment the less they care for alcohol.

And I should also mention no one has yet to ask my age...which should be weird right? I mean yeah, sure, I might look twenty-one and that I usually surprise people when I remind them, I am, in fact, not of legal American drinking age.

But then again, I doubt the Mafia really has time to worry about something stupid like that when there are things like turf wars and murders to deal with.

Or are turf wars just a gang thing? And what exactly is the difference between a gangster and mobsters?

Good questions for Google later, I guess. Since I doubt that is a pleasant dinner conversation.

"Tell me that boy didn't let you believe it was his name on that atrocity of a building."

Way to show your hand so soon. I mean yeah, I get that there is bad blood here, but I didn't expect him to try to cut down my opinion of Jameson this soon. But really should I be surprised.

Now I do know, at least think, it's Paxton's name but I can't let him in on that little fact.

"Is he not?"

I emphasize the pout for effect. Seriously I'm pulling up every idiotic attitude I've witnessed girls use that guys always seem to fall for. Even if I hate myself and every second while doing so.

"Ha, no. That boy works for his cousin. That bastard always uses his name to prey on pretty girls like you."

Double yuck but I play into his 'hero saved the damsel' game.

"That idiot!"

The anger is real but it's sure directed in the wrong direction.

"I can't believe he tried to fool me like that." I snake my hand over to his knee with my sincerity, "oh Anthony thank you so much for saving me from that mistake."

A secret smile and squeeze to his knee has him putty in my hand. Now to leave him hopefully wanting more

"Thank you so much for the drink, but if you'd excuse me, I have to go end this misconceiving date."

"Yes, yes, I can't believe how time got away from us."

He makes a show of checking his insanely expensive watch as I gather my bag to stand. I slow down my motions to give him a chance to stop me to ask me out again so we can get this plan going, but I can't seem eager or he might catch on.

"But darling Ripley I truly enjoyed this drink and I can't thank you enough for taking up an old man's offer."

"Silly man it was my pleasure. And I have always been a sucker for mature men. This is what I get for going on a date with a mere boy."

Nothing screams daddy issues like a barely legals having a thing for men twice their age.

"Maturity is something so important in a partner." *Come on Anthony, make this easy for me.* "I'd kick myself if I didn't at least ask to show a gorgeous mature woman what a real date should look like."

Swallowing my excitement for successfully getting him interested.

"A real date with a real man sounds absolutely sublime, Anthony."

I grab a blank business card from my purse and scribble my phone number across the back and hand it over to him. He takes it with a gorgeous smile that has daggers shooting into my gut.

Everything just became real, very terribly real.

* * *

THE GUYS WERE ACTUALLY IMPRESSED with how quickly I got close to Anthony.

Over the next two weeks, I go on a handful of dates with Anthony. The conversations were pleasant enough if not very surface which is to be expected. However, it disturbs me how easy this guise is to keep up. Apparently pretending to be interested in someone is way easier than I expected. What isn't surprising though is the twisting feeling in my gut that never lessens. Every secret smile and gentle touch intensifies my disgust in me.

For two weeks I keep this building relationship very public, never allowing for private intimacy. More so holding off the inevitable as long as possible knowing my time was coming sooner or later. So, when Anthony asks me to a nightcap at this penthouse after our fifth date...I accept.

* * *

THE DOOR CLOSES SOFTLY behind me as I make my way into the brightly lit apartment. Packing boxes litter almost every surface making walking a challenge.

The previous night plays over and over in my head whether I welcome it or not.

I make my way through the mess-making sure to keep the noise as low as possible not wanting to wake...*right*. I'm still alone.

I've barely even had time to visit the hospital with everything going on. which makes me feel like the world's worst daughter. Charlie was able to see her yesterday though and she assured me everything was fine, or well, the same. She woke up about a week ago but she's still so weak and can't recall anything from the night she passed out.

Neither Charlie nor my mother knows that I am 'seeing' a new man. Charlie tried to get answers out of me after that first meeting with The Players, all I told her was that I got my job back. I suspect she didn't believe me but laid the topic to rest.

They both do know I am packing up the apartment to move to a better location. I was able to dodge most of their inquiries about the hows and whys and the weight of my lies grow day by day.

"Why the sour look, Little Reaper"

That voice startles me out of spiraling thoughts.

"Why are you in my apartment, Paxton?"

I've barely seen much of him since everything started but Jameson's words have made their home in the front most section of my mind.

"I'm sure the better question should be what the fuck are you doing coming back at six in the morning?"

"I didn't know I was reporting my every movement to you?"

I move some boxes around in the kitchen to make a path to the coffee maker.

"Where Anthony is involved you damn well do."

Annoyance seeps out of every pore on his body. A body wearing sweats and a tight workout shirt. He couldn't have actually run here from wherever his home is right? I give in to the impulse to tease his grumpy attitude.

"You really shouldn't let your imagination run wild, King. I'm sure the story isn't nearly as sordid as you're making it out to be."

"You're telling me that you didn't spend the night with that bastard?"

Anger laces his words and it instantly sends rage firing through me.

"I'm sorry correct me if I'm wrong wasn't that my fucking job?"

"Fucking him was never a part of the job, Ripley."

"Seriously right now? Why the hell would you care?"

I spin to face the asshole who is leaning against my cluttered counter.

Emotions flash through his eyes too fast for me to catalog each one. Jameson's words taunt me, *a desire that should never be explored.* This attraction between us baffles me, it's like it's growing all on its own without concern for either party. I need to shut it right the fuck down.

"Look, Paxton, if you just came to yell at me for the way I am handling my part then you can leave. You shouldn't even be here."

I was actually able to push some truth into those words and I hope he decides to focus on that part...and not the tremor of indecision.

He decides the latter.

Paxton rounds the corner and I try to focus on anything other than how good he looks in relaxed clothing. Seriously, holy hot damn a man should not be allowed out the house with that much sex appeal floating around him.

I also want to note I absolutely did *not* focus on the movement in the front of his sweat- *seriously I didn't.*

Before I realize he's right in front of me making me feel small and exposed under his vexed gaze.

"You piss me the fuck off, Ripley, and I don't fucking like it."

"Paxto..."

The warning on my tongue is stolen when his hand snaps out and captures my neck. Way too much like that first time. Only this time it stirs my insides in a much more dangerous way. His eyes drill into mine for all of two of the longest seconds of my life before he drags my neck until his lips crash onto mine.

I lose everything in that first touch. And it terrifies me. But I don't pull away. I allow myself to fall deeper into the black waters. I allow myself to drown.

My hands reach out for a life raft and they land on tightly wound biceps. My fingers dig in for dear life causing a hiss to leave Paxton's throat. And it turns me on in a way I've never experienced before. It isn't gentle and it isn't sweet, but it allows me to bleed all my anger and confusion into this kiss. And he follows me emotion for emotion. My ass slams into the counter. This hand leaves my throat to twist into my hair pulling a desperate moan from my own throat and his other hand slides down my body until he reaches just under my ass. He lifts me in a single motion while deepening our connection. My ass lands on the counter aligning me perfectly to feel his erection grinding between my thighs with just thin material separating us. Desire tingles through my veins until I can barely think of anything other than satisfying this need. I slide a hand down his hard body reaching between us until his fabric-covered dick fills my hand. Holy fuck. An agonizing moan rips from Paxton as soon as I make contact with his cock.

And that's when he shoves me away in a brutal rush. One second I'm in a lustful bliss, the next, frigid reality washes over me.

I'm still trying to get my breathing under control and my mind to catch up when my front door slams shut. A picture crashes to the floor as a result and glass shatters over the foyer floor. I refuse to look at the millions of broken pieces glittering all over the hardwood as a metaphor for the current state of my heart.

CHAPTER 12

Paxton

"Paxy...?"

Red painted nails scrap against my thighs in hopes of pulling me from my thoughts. I concede to her whining.

I allow my gaze to follow the tight lines of her body. Each perfectly sculpted curve wrapped in blood-red velvet. The color does compliment the blonde strands which are twisted up into intricate spirals. A few pieces spill down her back.

But something is missing.

I mean, yeah, the visually pleasing body in front of me does awaken my dick but nothing more. All she's good for is a quick and dirty fuck. I know I sound like a grade-A bastard, but I try to stay honest in my own thoughts at least.

Yeah, Fucking, Right.

I push the images of midnight from my head and focus on the needy woman before me.

"I apologize, Heather, my mind just isn't here tonight."

I hope she doesn't push further.

Thankfully we step inside the gala hall and all the wealth and glamor dripping from every inch of the space easily steals her attention.

Everything in this place drips money. From the gold-accented frames that cover the walls. To the marks in the polished marble floor that echoes every footstep like a warning.

I scan the room absently trying to convince myself I'm not looking for her. But like a force of nature, my eyes find her almost instantly.

The same person I have been avoiding like the fucking plague for the last week. Ever since I left her wanting and alone in her apartment. The moment her perfect hand connected with my rock-hard dick it became too real...to perfect. So, I ran.

Right into the arms of a woman I knew would never make me wish for more.

Someone *safe*.

My eyes crawl over midnight hair piled high and every delicate curve is wrapped tightly in emerald silk.

I want to curse the bastard that sent her the green dress.

Which was me.

But that isn't important.

What is important is that I equally hate myself for it all the while I couldn't be happier with what I see.

It's an odd mix, wanting to slit your own throat for the torture you have created and yet still praising all that is fucking holy for the present before you.

In the end, I just couldn't help myself when I saw a dress that was the same stunning shade of green as her eyes.

But even with the morbid mix of emotions storming inside my head, my Reaper goddess steals the show with her unwarranted natural appeal.

It takes every last will in my body to pull my eyes from her. I finally find the strength when I watch Anthony's hands caress down her bareback and over her ass making his claim on my prize.

For the remainder of the evening I vow to myself to only focus sharply on the woman in front of me while not daring to seek out my Pawn.

I know it doesn't help that my shit mood is affecting not only my date but also the men at my side. But then again, when have I ever given a shit?

"Seriously Pax, what the fuck?"

Jameson's harsh words grate out in a hushed whisper while his busty date and my date swipe stories of who the fuck knows what.

"Leave it, J"

I drill my words home with a warning glare.

"Not gonna happen, brother," My warning goes unwarranted. "Tell me what the hell is eating at you when you should be nothing but overjoyed."

"Overjoyed? For fucks sake, man."

I shove at the table needing to distance myself from the fucker. The bastard follows without missing a beat.

I make it to the bar all of two steps in front of him but still by the time he catches up I've already downed my second shot. The burn is a welcomed distraction.

I feel his eyes inspect my mood more closely than I would have liked and I'm pissed at myself for allowing these emotions to even surface.

"Holy shit."

I level my gaze with him and I watch my truths reflect within his dark gaze.

Yep I'm fucked.

"Don't even start..."

I warn darkly even though I doubt he'd even care if that shit-eating grin tells me anything.

"Holy. Shit." he repeats, "you're shitting pissed she's actually doing a good job." I guess that's one way to put it.

"Fuck off," I mutter instead, grabbing two more shots before he says another word.

"So, tell me..." his arm drapes around my shoulders so he can lean in close, "is it the thought of him fucking her that has you sour or the thought she might-"

My fist aimed for his face flies before he even finishes. The only problem, he was expecting it and slides from my side quicker than my drunken limb.

He turns suddenly on his heels heading back towards our table with nothing but his laughter on the air in his wake.

For a second I debate letting the small shot glass fly across the room until it collides with his giant fucking head, but right as the glass is about to leave my fingers a swirl of green in the corner of my vision captures my attention.

My eyes follow the silk as Anthony parades her around like a fucking show pony. Each new asshole that approaches them, appraisers, her with hungry eyes making me see red. All the while Anthony stands there gleaming with the pride of a deranged master as everyone lusts after what he has cultivated.

The entire scene has bile boiling in my stomach and fire raging in my head.

Fucking alcohol isn't doing shit to control the monster begging to be released from the shackles I normally keep tightly locked down.

My control wavers and for the first time in years I debate what would happen if I let it out...

I grabbed a double shot of whiskey from the bartender before I make my way back over the table hoping to drown this jealousy in amber liquid and easy pussy.

That's when I notice a runaway in green looking to hide away from the excitement.

CHAPTER 13

Ripley

T he lights swirl around me like some sick fairytale.

No matter how many times I try to ignore the activities going on around me I can't help but notice the underaged girls being paraded around. Or the clutter of people that sit oh so still in the corner with their ragged clothes and downcast faces.

If there's ever a time that I fully realize the world I have been thrown into it's this fucking party. The exclusive gala Anthony oh so excitedly invited me to. I couldn't think of a reason to say no...until I walked into this prison tonight.

The gold draped chandeliers hide the black-market trading, covered in haunting smiles and ten-thousand-dollar suits.

For hours I keep my smile in place even as Anthony's hands slide over my body as he talks strategy with his crooked associates.

A girl can only handle so much. By my third glass of champagne, I find the courage to excuse myself from his sticky fingers.

I keep my head high as I strut through the hall, all the while completely ignoring the bastard to my right as he drapes his affections over Bottle Blonde, nope, sorry...I'm more mature than childish nicknames. Wasn't it something equaling as stereotypical, though?

Heather.

Okay, maybe I'm not all that mature after all.

But it doesn't matter what her name is because I care not what Paxton does in his free time.

He is nothing more than a means to an end.

At least as long as I keep reminding myself of that.

I made a pact with myself after he stormed out, that I wouldn't let him distract me anymore from my single task at hand.

I finally find my way to the furthest lavish restroom located on the other side of this grand building to get just a little privacy.

I push the heavy wooden door open to hide away for as long as possible.

As soon as the door slides closed, I rip off the damn heels from my feet. They hit the floor with the thump. The coolness seeping into my bare feet from the marble is instant relief. The sensation claws up my legs slowly wiping the night from my mind.

Realistically I know I still have hours left to play this part but alone and barefoot, this reminds me of who I am.

I don't belong in this world...not even pretending can convince me of it.

If anything, it just convinces me how far removed from this terrifying world I belong.

Maybe it's something you're born with. Something transferred through the blood of one evil to the next generation. Either way, Paxton and his 'Players' were born of darkness to continue a tradition of destruction.

And for some unbelievably idiotic ploy, they are planning a coup against the men that created them. They are plotting against the very hands that have fed them.

When this started, I wanted answers. I wanted to understand.

How fucking naïve.

That girl doesn't exist anymore. I now know the less I know, the better. That the only way I will be able to live with myself after this is done is if I never learn the truth.

My hands spread over the cool marble counter. Everything in this damned place is marble. Gold flecks sparkle within the counter. Gold and black swirl around in the floor. Pure white glitters off the wall. It's elegant but the magic is depleted knowing of the affairs taking place on the other side of the wooden door.

I stare at the girl shining back at me in the intricate mirror.

Not long ago all I saw was a ragged mess of someone just barely surviving. Now her skin glows well with rest. Her hair shines from proper care. Her curves have filled in due to the decadent meals.

But her eyes still hold onto the raged circumstances that her life contains.

"You know, I truly don't understand how someone with your opportunities still looks so truly devastated."

I no longer jump when that voice sneaks up on me.

Another pact I promised myself.

My eyes shift from my own reflection to his.

"Tell me why, Paxton? Why do you always seem to find me at my lowest?"

I don't bother lifting my voice above a whisper knowing the empty bathroom would easily echo my words.

"I wish I could say it was just a gift."

He pushes himself off the stall he was leaning against as he silently watched me.

"But we'd both call my bluff."

He steps up to me and I turn my body to meet him head-on.

Unfocused eyes tell me he is far from sober. However, there is not a single stumble in his step or slur to his words. Something tells me his version of drunk is just as dangerous as his sober self.

Maybe I can get some honesty out of his impaired judgment.

"So, what's the real reason, Pax?"

I barely use his nickname in the hopes of keeping our relationship as professional as possible.

"Because, Little Reaper...I can't get you out of my fucking head. I thought putting distance would set me straight. But fuck, that was a shit idea."

The pain in his voice tears at my heart. And to make matters worse our last interaction in my apartments plays through my head like some sick foreplay.

I was doing great keeping the spark of feelings buried deep inside, but then the fucker had to go and seal my fate with that angry confession of a kiss.

I haven't seen him since he bolted from my apartment. It was Jameson that gave me the dress. And it was Jameson that came for updates about my dates with Anthony. I liked it better that way. I may have made a pact with myself, but I didn't know how strong it would hold when presented with Paxton in the flesh.

I guess I had the same fucked up thought that distance would make it all go away. But the darkness simmering in his crystal gaze reawaken the spark of need in my heart.

Fuck. Considering my horribly unstable emotions and my need for a real release...I feel like being a little reckless.

My thoughts must be playing clearly across my face because I see the same resolve click into place on his features.

A tender finger reaches out to swipe at a stray strand of hair from my face. His intentions are clear, and I'll only have a moment to stop what comes next.

"That's a bad fucking idea, Pax."

My words hold no conviction and even as I say them my body slides closer to his and my head bends back never losing eye contact. Soft against hard. Blue against green. Sin against death.

"Oh, how I fucking know..."

The words are nothing more than a mutter as his lips find mine.

It doesn't start gentle. There is no timid experimenting. And the anger from last time is thankfully absent.

Hands grab at my ass and my fingers dig into tense biceps. The room around me fades away. The horrifying party slips from my mind. Nothing exists except soft lips roughly claiming mine. The only thing I know is how fucking good his hands feel as they kneed my silk cover thighs. His right-hand slips past the slit on my dress to grab at the delicate flesh of my thigh. His other glides up my back to capture my neck. Controlling me completely.

I feel his arms tense before my feet leave the ground. Like a perfectly orchestrated dance, my legs wrap tightly around his hips. The cool wall meets my heated back in a rush as he pushes into my body. The apex of my thighs land on the obvious erection straining against his tux pants. So similar to the first time but oh so different. A moan slips from between our warring mouths. With nothing more than a pull at his zipper, I could find heaven.

But the world he lives in doesn't deserve anything more than hell.

And just like that ice water rushes through my veins.

In an instant, my wanton limbs freeze with realization.

Paxton must feel the shift because he immediately pulls back, releasing my body. My legs slide from his body and unsteadily land on the floor.

I don't even know what to say or how to explain my stupidity. He might have stopped us the first time, but this was my mistake. Thankfully he doesn't give me a chance to say anything.

I feel the shift in his demeanor, sobriety, and darkness have replaced his lust and desperation.

"Nice to know you're perfecting your act. But then again, Anthony has always been good at training his girls."

His words are meant to cut deep. To draw blood until there's nothing left alive.

They succeed.

With that slice of malice, he straightens his jacket and strides from the bathroom.

Without a single backward glance.

Every interaction we have, Paxton destroys another piece of my soul.

I just don't know how much will be left after this job is over.

WHY THE HELL do I keep getting myself into these fucked up situations?

My heels slam against the marble floor with a force I can't control.

It took way too many minutes to get my emotions in check after Paxton left me alone. As I stared at the heartbroken girl in the mirror the hurt turned into fury.

This fucker won't win.

This whole job was supposed to be nothing but simple. Get close to a dangerous man then disappear.

The rules weren't that difficult to follow, Ries. So how did you get yourself so mixed up with the head Player himself?

Angry tears burn behind my eyes. With every step the silky material of this stupid dress brushes and twists around my legs like fire licking across my skin. I once thought the breezy fabric was a godsend, now I want nothing more than to shred every last fiber from my body to stop the crawling fire ant sensation from taking over my body.

I let that bastard get in my head. My fatal flaw. He's been playing a game and I stupidly fell for the act even though I knew the rules.

Get the dirty on Anthony.

Gain my freedom.

Never see that smug arrogant seductive bastard again.

The mantra echoes over and over again in my head as I round the corner. Colliding with the main man in question.

"Ripley, darling, whatever are you doing?"

Anthony's disapproving expression seeps into my bones and reminds me just what happens when I lose focus on my act.

I push down my anger and let the easy persona slide back into place as I lay my hand on his forearm. I refuse to notice the differences in his physique when my fingers run over the loose black material. And I absolutely refuse to think of how Paxton's tux cut tight in all the right places and how Anthony's...doesn't.

Nope...won't think about any of that shit.

Instead I gaze into aged brown eyes and try to appraise the attractive man in front of me.

"Forgive me, Anthony. I must have gotten more flustered than I expected when I couldn't find my way back. This place is a maze for sure."

I even add a light and feminine laugh at the end to sell the act.

"No matter," he gently waves a hand between us, "I had been meaning to have a serious conversation with you, Darling."

My ears perk up at that statement, worrying I've been unconvincing in my role.

"I do hope this is a good thing?"

I push a flirty smile across my lips and raise an eyebrow in what I hope is an 'delicate expression.'

He softly grabs my hand in his.

"Yes, don't worry. I was actually hoping to take our relationship to a more intimate level."

A warm metal object is slipped into my hand while my head reels with the possibilities he is implying.

I twist the object in my hand, a small gasp escaping my lips when I recognize the familiar shape.

A key.

Oh shit.

"Anthony?"

The confusion that bleeds into a single word is absolutely genuine.

"I know it's soon, Ripley, but I am truly serious about my intentions for us. Now, don't think you have to move in or anything, Darling, I just want you to feel at home at the penthouse as my main woman."

Logically I know this is a great thing. That I might be able to complete this job way earlier than expected but...there's this part of me that hates myself for deceiving this man. I mean, yes, I know he is 'technically' a 'bad guy' but shit, he has been nothing but a gentleman to me. Unlike the bastards that have put me in this situation.

Who are they to him anyway? What created this bad blood? And why the hell can't I get any answers for my thousands of questions?

"Ripley?"

My name on his lips draws me out of my internal war, I bring my eyes up from the key to his dark eyes.

"What do you say? Will you accept?"

Out of the corner of my eye I can see Paxton paying way too much attention to this exchange. In a moment of spite, I want to hurt him in the same way he has me. I exaggerate my smile as I throw my arms around Anthony's solid neck. I crash my lips to his instead of a verbal answer. Hands wrap around my waist and he deepens our kiss.

I refuse to acknowledge the lack of electricity in my veins as Anthony's lips run over mine. And most of all I refuse to dwell on the disappointments swimming in my stomach that wish for different circumstances and a different partner.

CHAPTER 14

Paxton

"Fucking shit, guess she has some voodoo pussy."

I down the rest of my whiskey as Jameson's comment floats around the table.

After Ripley very publicly accepted Anthony's offer to become his 'main mistress', they couldn't get out of the gala fast enough.

With him gone I found no reason to stay around. I throw Heather into a town car not giving a shit of whining complaints. Not even an easy fuck was going to fix my mood so having her around was useless. And she's fucking annoying when her mouth isn't stuffed with my cock.

The other three quickly followed my lead and got rid of their dates knowing there would be no fucking until we set the next part of the plan into motion.

So that leads us to why I'm chain-smoking Marlboros and emptying a bottle of Johnnie Walker.

"I'm seriously impressed with that chick."

Knox leans back on my leather sofa and sucks down a drag of his cigarette.

"I wasn't expecting this shit to work."

Smoke blows from between his lips.

"The thing I don't understand is why you have her thinking she needs to find information on him?"

"Because, it's fucking hilarious, B."

My words burn like the smoke leaving my lungs.

"You're gonna get her killed, Pax."

"And you're killing my buzz, Bishop. Christ."

I need to hurt something. I shove myself out of the chair. Only the light from the fireplace illuminates the apartment. I've always found mood lighting more comfortable than overhead lamps. Plus, the added darkness allows me the freedom of emotion I otherwise have to hide in the bright light.

I would have preferred going anywhere else, but we needed to be able to talk without the worry of being overheard.

But fuck, knowing this penthouse apartment is nearly identical to Anthony's...it's making concentrating really fucking difficult.

Shamrock eyes twisted in ecstasy.

I slam my fingers into my eyes desperately trying to rip the images from my imagination.

Does it make me a bad person that Bishop's accusations sound tempting? At least with her dead her hold of me would disappear, right?

Jesus, Pax, that's fucking psychotic. Truly psychopathic level of insanity.

Getting an innocent girl killed just because she twists up your balls?

Plus, that theory could also cause the opposite effect. Leaving me more obsessed than I already am. But at least with her alive, I have the option to fuck my obsession away if she was dead though-

"Fucking Paxton King, will you get your head out of your dick and pay attention?"

Fingers snap in front of my face. The king tattoo over his knuckles tempts me to rip his fingers clean off. I grab at Jameson's wrist before he has a chance to retract his hand and I shove his hand backward. Hard. An instant cry of pain cracks through his throat and his knees buckle under him. I apply more pressure to his wrist just to watch pain fill his eyes.

"Wrong fucking move, cousin."

I release my hold and add an extra shove to make him lose his balance. His ass hits the hardwood in a satisfying thump.

Silence cloaks the room. Good. They need to remember who runs this crew.

After of few more beats of silence, I scan the three faces around me

"Now, where were we?" No one answers my rhetorical questions

"Oh, that's right. Now that she's obtained her position as his mistress, we can now enact the next part. Sacrificing the pawn."

Sacrifice her I will.

75

The end of part 1 of The Pawn in Play

I hoped you enjoyed (even though cliffhangers are killers) this first look into my new Dark Elite Mafia Standalone series, The Elite Players.

Preorder The Pawn in Play
www.nkstackhouse.com/ElitePlayers

About N.K. Stackhouse

I have been stumbling through this crazy author world since 2017 and seriously at this point, I'm just trying to stay alive.

I am just your typical twenty-something trying to keep myself from going insane each and every day.

When I am not immersing myself within made-up worlds and combating the voices in my head, I am either; spending time with the genius Hubby, trying to keep my three devious demon cats from destroying the world, or reading my life away one page at a time.

I recently just traded in the beach for the mountains and moved halfway across the country. So far, I am *LOVING* the low Colorado humidity and can't say I miss the Florida heat.

Get to know more about N.K. by:
Website: *www.nkstackhouse.com*

TROUBLEMAKER

Rumors (The Cat's Crew book 1) Sneak

A.J. Macey

Troublemakers

(The Cat's Crew Book 1 Sneak)

Damsel in distress? Not anymore.

Hey b*tches, my name's Kiera. You might know me as The Cat, infamous cat burglar/thief.

No? Well, let me give you a little insight into my life over the last year and a half.

I was going about, doing my own thing when my entire life got flipped upside down. Alongside my little assassin, we were able to help The Aces MC with a little problem with a rival MC. Easy peasy, right? Wrong. Somehow though, I found myself falling for the club's president, his suspicious enforcer, and the VP... who just so happens to also be my asshole stepbrother. The Alloy Kings MC didn't stand a chance but they weren't alone. Backed by my bastard father and his mob of minions, we had a hell of a fight. Sound like fun to you? Ha, yeah, I didn't think so. But in the end, we came out mostly unscathed.

Six months later, I finally decided that was enough laying low. But I find myself surrounded by rumors, and I can't let them lie when there's so much to lose now. Can we figure out whose watching us before it's too late, or will we end up getting blindsided?

But I'm not the thief who became famous at 15 years old and survived the mob's hell in my past just to lay down and get surprised in my own damned house. Again.

Those f*ckers won't know what hit them.

I'm The Cat, and soon enough, they'll learn that this is just the beginning.

Author Note

Sneak Peek of Rumors
(The Cat's Crew book 1)

The Cat's Crew Series is a WhyChoose/Reverse Harem trilogy featuring MMFMM meaning the female main character doesn't have to choose between her love interests. Please note, some scenes may contain M/M contact.

This book contains references involving PTSD, sexual assault recollections, abuse, and other themes that some readers may find triggering.

CHAPTER 1

July 3rd
Friday Evening

Kiera

Six months. Six months since I'd taken such a big job, having laid low after everything went down with Frankie and the Solace mob. Normally, being cramped in the house would be stifling, my body itching to take on the next big step in my plan. This time had been different. Now that the Frankie shit was done, I was content to relax, focusing on refining my skills with smaller jobs. I couldn't lie though; it felt good, nearly exhilarating in fact, to be taking on such a large job again, like coming home after a long trip or buying a new gun. Taking a deep breath, I let my muscles relax where I had perched for the last several hours.

The sun had set about an hour ago, its bright rays shifting from pink to orange and red before finally falling below the horizon. Now that it had set, the night air was refreshing, no longer trapping the stifling heat of the sun beating down across the Vegas skyline. Everything ached from remaining still, but not in a bad way. The burn and throb was a welcome relief after being cooped up in the house for so long. Glancing at my watch, I clocked less than a minute until my opening. I readied myself, rolling my shoulders and unclenching my fists to stretch out my fingers.

Shuffling down the side of the building, the toes of my boots shifted carefully along the edge of the stone face. It didn't take long to get to the correct window, and I was having a good luck kind of night. The ledge was structurally sound enough that nothing crumbled beneath me as I crouched down and started to force it open from the outside.

"How's it going, Kittycat?" Chase asked after a few moments of me working. He had stayed relatively quiet once the sun had set in the last half hour, allowing me to focus on looking out for anything suspicious.

"Almost in," I murmured, "cameras looped and sensors down?"

"Yep, everything's ready to go, nothing odd on the scanner for the building either. I'll let you know if there's anything that pops up."

"All right, going in."

With that, the glass opened and I slipped through the slim gap. As soon as I was safely in the building, I unhooked my harness from the safety straps and pulleys. The office I had entered was large, and the scent of paper and wood polish filled the space, though there was nothing personal in the area except a single plant. *What a sad office space to work at day in and out*, I thought with a shake of my head. Pulling the chair out from the desk, I dug out the clean USB from my jacket pocket.

"Okay, Kittycat," Chase started, rattling off the log in credentials once the screen was booted up. "Files we want are going to be labeled FC-2020B1-5."

Following his instructions, I narrowed down the files and started copying them to the USB I'd shoved into the tower. As those finished, I decided to search more of the computer, poking around for anything of use or interest.

Hey, I'm nosy, okay? It's the best part of being a thief.

Other than the payouts, obviously.

There wasn't anything immediately eye catching, so I decided to drag and drop the bulk of the files and wait. I had ten minutes until the next security round went through, meaning I could take as much as the USB could download in that time.

"Oh shit." My body was immediately on edge, a wash of adrenaline flowing over me at Chase's curse. "Guards just got off the elevator, looks like they're doing their rounds early."

"Dammit," I hissed, "why do they always mess with my carefully laid plans? Do I have time to get out?"

"T-minus thirty seconds," Chase relayed, his tone hard and unyielding. It took a lot to rattle Skill Shot, and a few guards changing their routine was definitely not enough.

Fucking hell, I growled, jumping up. I darted to the window, standing on the windowsill and retracting the rope I had used to reach the window out of view. As soon as it was high enough to not be seen from inside the building, I closed the window before running back to the desk and shutting the screen off. Dropping to the ground, I crawled under the desk and pulled the office chair back in like how I'd found it.

"Three seconds."

I practically held my breath as the door opened. Everything felt electrified, my skin tingling as each moment passed, my body ready for any and all possible outcomes. A beam of the guard's flashlight swept through, landing on the chair and bookshelf behind the desk and across the bank of windows, before eventually retreating. When the door finally latched again, I sighed, the noise wobbly with relief.

Too fucking close. Note to self, definitely get a bit more practice in, can't be gettin' rusty now.

"You have about five minutes before they hit the next floor, and if they do the office above you, they'll see the pulley rope," Chase explained, the clicking of keys filling the background of the comms.

Sighing, I shifted back and forth, giving my adrenaline somewhere to go while the last few megabytes of data transferred. As soon as it was done, I got the USB disconnected and stashed safely in its spot.

"Three minutes, Kittycat."

"I'm going, I'm going," I muttered, dropping my card on the desk.

Opening the window from inside was much faster than from out on the ledge, though grabbing hold of the rope was more difficult than I had anticipated. *Fuck it*, I decided, climbing out onto the ledge without being secured.

"Kittycat, why do I see you free climbing the side of the building without your harness?" Chase asked hesitantly.

"Because I couldn't grab the rope in time," I breathed, focusing on not falling the almost twenty-five floors to the cement below.

"Get your ass secured to that rope. Right now, Dove," Ciar bit out, his deep and gravelly voice replacing Chase's upbeat one.

"I'm getting there, bossy," I huffed, reaching up to grab hold of the rope.

"If you don't, there's going to be hell to pay when you get back," Ciar continued. I rolled my eyes, the devious side of me wanting to push him, to see just how far was too far for my killer to handle. It was too risky, but the desire was hard to squash. So instead of making it obvious when I hooked myself back up to the pulley, I did it as discreetly as possible and hoped he wouldn't know.

"Dove." My nickname on his lips was nearly cruel with how cold and low it was growled. A shiver worked its way down my spine at the sound, but I stayed focused.

Safety first, fucking later.

"Calm down, Ciar," I taunted as I reached the roof. "I was strapped in, see?" I shook the connecting pieces, the metal jingling together.

"You are so getting that sexy ass smacked to hell and back for that fucking shit," he bit out. "Brat."

"Wow, look at that, you and Stone agreeing on something for the first time in over a year," I said in mock amazement, getting way too much enjoyment from riling him up. Unhooking the pulley from the roof, I strapped into the zipline I had attached to the crane that was conveniently working on the building next door.

"Aww, you scared him off, Kittycat," Chase tsked after I reached the crane. "You almost back? The asshole's getting antsy. Never once in our entire shared life did he ever give a shit about anything other than being a pain in my ass, but then you waltzed your pretty ass into our lives, and boom! Kittycat tamed cold-hearted Ciar. I'm quite impressed." A spark of pride grew at the warmth and surprise littering Chase's words. It was very rare that anyone—including me—could shock him.

And let's just say, it's one of my many guilty pleasures.

"Yes. Coming down now," I relayed as I secured the zipline to my side. Chuckling, I countered his prodding. "Oh, and I didn't tame anyone, nor did I waltz into your life. You came barreling into *my* house, my little assassin, so that's all on you two."

"Nah, it was all you. Ciar's weak spot," Chase teased, laughing to himself. "He's yelling at me now." Rolling my eyes at their back and forth, I absently brushed my hand over the USB to ensure it was still there. The small lump that it formed in my jacket helped calm me further.

I knew I hadn't misplaced it, but remember, one could never be too careful. Especially a thief.

Go on, write that down.

88

With the reassurance that I hadn't somehow lost the USB, I started down the crane, noting the adrenaline of having been almost caught was finally starting to ease. When I got to the SUV where he was waiting, I was greeted with a hard glare and a finger tap against one sleeve that told me one thing. Ciar was in the driver's seat. Instead of saying anything, I smiled and leaned over the center console.

Pressing my lips to his, I kissed him, chuckling at the deep growl that made him sound more wild animal or beast than man. He didn't kiss back, his lips thinned into a harsh scowl, but before I could pull away, he gripped the back of my head in a firm grasp.

"Don't you ever scare me like that again," he hissed, his lips brushing mine with each word. The sting from the way his fingers tangled into my hair hurt in the most delicious way now that the heist was over and my adrenaline had faded. A moan filled the car, my pussy starting to ache as he tightened his grip.

"God, those sounds," he groaned, no longer chastising me as he captured my lips in a passionate kiss. Our tongues brushed and tangled, sharp nips littering our fervid makeout session, but it was over too soon.

"We need to start getting home, Kittycat," Chase murmured, burying his nose into the crook of my neck and inhaling. "Otherwise, we'll never leave this damned place, and I'd rather take my time with you."

I pouted, but I knew he was right, so I gave in without an argument. We weren't in the clear until we were out of Vegas and back at the house, and it was a long eight-hour drive. Settling back into my seat, I buckled up and let Chase start driving. It only took a few turns before I was drifting off, my eyes closing fully before we even got on the interstate.

Who said The Cat doesn't love cat naps?

＊ ＊ ＊

"Kittycat." Chase's calloused fingers brushed over my cheek, waking me from the deep, dreamless sleep I had been in. "We're home."

"Mm, 'kay," I mumbled, my words garbled as I stretched in my seat.

"You head inside and get some sleep. I'll finish the data transfer to the client."

"I'll put the USB in the security room but hurry, you know I can't sleep without my pussycat," Chase teased, giving me a wink before taking the device I dug out and climbing out of the SUV. Rolling my eyes, I stretched once more and got out, albeit much slower than Chase who practically darted into the house.

The breeze was soft, rustling the few flowers planted in the yard. It was calming, my eyes falling shut again before I took a deep breath of the fresh air. Something shifted around me, and I wasn't sure what it was, but I was immediately on edge. My eyes popped open. Scanning the area near me, I tried to identify what was setting off my internal alarm bells. Either the rustling had grown stronger than it should have been, or it was the sense that there were eyes on me. If the past had taught me anything—especially the last couple of years—it was to *always* trust your instincts.

There's no way in hell I'm getting bested in my own damned house.
Again.

After several passes over the perimeter of the yard and house, I didn't see anything suspicious in the darkened landscape. Not wanting to walk around with no backup to assist in case shit hit the fan, I turned and headed into the house, beelining straight for the security room.

The rest of the house was silent, my men sleeping soundly, I was sure, so I shut the security door behind me and started to investigate. Currently, there was nothing odd or out of place on the cameras, or if there had been something—*or someone*—it wasn't there now.

I quickly rewound the videos for the last hour. "We really need full night vision cameras," I muttered to myself. "The ones I have clearly aren't cutting it."

There was nothing unusual after reviewing the footage several times. The only thing out of place had been a hint of a shadow shifting on a couple of the monitors, but I couldn't make out its source. *Well, when in doubt, do it the old-fashioned way.*

Shoving the rolling chair I was seated in back from the counter, I stashed the USB in the safe and locked it. The sun had just started to peek out over the horizon as I stepped out of the house, giving me enough light to scour the perimeter of our property. I had made it almost all the way around when I found something.

A set of footprints.

Or at least a portion of one.

"Bastards," I ground out, kneeling to inspect it. "First, Jace came waltzing around my home whenever he damn well pleased, and now this fucking jerk-off thinks they can spy on us."

Forcing my irritation back, I focused on the details of the impression in the dirt. *All right, logical process of elimination first.* It could have been one of my guys, but it was too small to be theirs. Humming in thought, I stood and put my foot next to it. Almost the same size, meaning whoever had been watching was a woman or a man with abnormally tiny feet. Unfortunately, that was all I could identify. The ridges were too muddled to make out a sole pattern and the dirt where the other footprint was didn't provide anything since it was disturbed. Scanning a few more times, I found nothing else nearby.

"Ugh. I'm going to find out who you are!" I called out. "So, if you have something to say to me, you should probably do it now." Nothing sounded after I shouted nonsense to the yard, not that I had expected it to, and I headed back to the house to put in a new order for additional security measures.

Because whoever they are, I'll find them soon enough.

Chapter 2

July 4th
Saturday Morning

Kiera

"Kittycat," a husky voice whispered. A wash of breath hit my shoulder and neck as rough stubble brushed over my exposed skin. "Time to get up."

"Ugh," I grumbled, "do I have to?" By the time I flopped into bed, it had been almost seven in the morning with a plan to be up by ten, so I would be running on less than three hours of sleep for the day.

"Well, I'm pretty sure Abby will drive all the way over here and drag you out of bed if you don't get to the compound," Chase reminded playfully, his fingers dipping under the blanket to tease the curve of my ass.

"That's not the fastest way to get me out of bed, my little assassin," I told him, growing horny as he continued to gently tease my skin.

"I wasn't trying to get you out of bed; I was trying to get you to wake up," he challenged. Chuckling at his clarification, I rolled over, seamlessly straddling his trim hips. "See? Worked perfectly."

"You're such a troublemaker," I murmured, folding over his bare chest to kiss him.

"You love it, and I can't say I'm mad at seeing you on top of me, Kittycat." His lips brushed over mine as he talked, calloused hands cupping my exposed tits and tweaking the pebbled peaks until my hips bucked and a whimpered moan escaped.

"Quite the scene to walk in on."

Glancing over my shoulder with a smirk, I found Brooks leaning against the master bedroom doorframe, arms crossed over his barrel chest and a matching grin on his handsome face. The combination only made my pussy pulse more.

"You could always come join us," I tried to convince him, but he only laughed.

"And risk Abby coming over and whipping all our asses before I have a chance to do exactly what I want to you because you're late? Not exactly the most exciting thought, Baby. She's called approximately seven times already." Groaning, I ungracefully flopped off Chase, popping up onto my feet and walking into the closet.

"Well, since neither of you are willing to fuck me into oblivion this morning, I expect some fun after the party. Got it?" I called out as I dressed quickly.

"You know I'll never turn down an offer like that, Baby," Brooks countered.

"Last I checked, you just did," I sassed, turning to cock a brow at him from across the room. I didn't get much farther than half a step because Chase scooped me up and tossed me over his shoulder. "Chase!" I yelped in surprise.

"He may turn down your sweet pussy, Kittycat, but I certainly won't."

Chase didn't say anything more, throwing me back onto the bed I had just vacated and yanking the shorts I had just slipped on down my legs before chucking them over his shoulder. There was no hesitation, no softness or gentleness as he parted my thighs and kneeled. With a hard suck on my clit, a moan left me, my back arching off the bed as Chase worked.

Expert swirls of his tongue worked me up quickly, then a scrape of his teeth against my sensitive skin had me shivering. Goosebumps pebbled across my body as I clawed at the sheets. *Fuck.* I nearly cried out when he roughly pushed two fingers into my slick core.

My blood roared in my ears, my heart galloping as stars flared in front of my eyes. With each pump of his fingers and circle of his tongue, I convulsed with the intensity of the quickly approaching orgasm. Chase didn't slow until I came apart, my fingers tangling into his dirty blond hair to hold him between my thighs.

"Holy hell," I breathed after another few long moments, shaking from the aftershocks of my release.

"I will always take up an offer like that, Kittycat," Chase told me with a sinful grin, crawling up until he could capture my mouth. His lips and tongue were coated in my arousal, the sweet yet salty taste of it only making me want more, but he pulled away before I could deepen our kiss. Much to my disappointment.

"Don't give me that little lip. Boss is right; Abby will drive her ass over here if you're any later than you are. Besides, seems he enjoyed himself even if he didn't do any work," Chase teased, looking over to where Brooks had been. Pushing my head into the bed, I glanced at the door, seeing Brooks slowing a pumping hand over his thick cock.

"Hey, I said *I* wasn't going to risk Abby's wrath, but I certainly wasn't going to just walk away from a display like that," Brooks countered. Shaking my head at his response, I shoved Chase off me with one final kiss.

Ugh, they may be right. Not that I'll ever tell the bastards that.

"All right, all right, I'm going," I huffed, yanking my denim shorts back on and pulling the cut-up shirt-turned-tank over my head. "Garrett and Stone already there?"

"They were getting supplies for the party with Blast and a few others, so they might not be at the compound yet. Depends on how long it took them to get everything," Brooks explained, tucking his hardened cock back into his jeans.

Cocking a brow, I glanced at him with a silent question written all over my face.

"I'm not coming until it's in that tight pussy of yours, Baby," he told me, possessively grabbing my ass when I walked by.

"Hm, then maybe I'll tease you some more. I do love watching you squirm," I challenged with a wink.

"That's if I don't toss your sexy ass over my shoulder like Chase did."

"Mhm, I'm sure," I murmured to myself as I headed down the stairs, excited to get my men home tonight.

Fucktastic group sex after blowing a bunch of shit up?
Perfect way to spend the holiday weekend.

* * *

"You're late," Abby sassed when I pulled into the clubhouse's parking lot.

"Not my fault this time," I argued with a bright smile.

"Like I believe that," she countered, her head shake accompanied by a small smile that gave away her amusement.

"Hey, Chase is very... persuasive." A laugh threatened to escape, Abby's scrunched up grimace making it difficult to keep it contained.

"I suppose that's fair. Nate definitely loves to be *persuasive* in the morning," she said with a cocked brow. Now it was my turn to grimace, immediately thinking about my two oldest friends fucking, which wasn't a pleasant picture.

"Eww," I whined. "Now that's ingrained in my mind. Thanks a lot, bitch."

"You're welcome," she smarted. "That's what you get for being late. Now, let's get to work. We have to decorate and get all the shit settled before the party. Nate's already getting the area out back ready with water and fire precautions, and the others should be back with the actual goods soon. You're in for some fun! There's no party like an Aces' party."

"I've seen a few of them before, remember?" I smirked. "I believe I yanked that blonde bimbo bitch off of Garrett's lap during one of them."

"Oh, bitch, those weekend things are nothing compared to what tonight will be. You're a girl who loves explosives, so I'm sure you'll enjoy yourself. While we wait for that, let's go help Cheryl. I'm sure that poor woman has more booze bottles to unload than she can handle."

"Eh, I'm sure she's got it." I shrugged. "She's a tough broad, and I'm about ninety-nine percent sure she just lives in some parallel dimension behind that counter."

"Maybe I do." Cheryl's smoky voice filtered through the bar as we crossed over the threshold into the dimly lit space. "It's quite lavish in my bar portal, but I still only have two arms for all of these."

When my eyes finally adjusted, my jaw dropped when I saw what was practically a wall of boxes lining one side of the bar. Cheryl and Abby both laughed at my reaction, but I was too busy walking over and opening the closest one.

Yup, full to the brim with bottles. Holy fuck balls, that's a lot of booze.

95

"Better hope there are some designated drivers tonight," I muttered, "or a medic for alcohol poisoning."

"Eh, the boys practically live in the bottom of a bottle," Cheryl told me, pulling out bottles from her box and setting them on the bar top. "They'll be good, and if not, there are a couple DDs. Some of the Old Ladies don't drink, so they tend to take it on themselves to make sure everyone safely gets where they're supposed to be."

"That's a positive at least, though no alcohol? Sounds horrible," I exclaimed with a shudder. *There's no way in hell I could deal with this leather-wearing boy band sober constantly.* Shoving the random trail of thoughts away, I looked back at the boxes.

"So, what do you want me to do?" I asked, walking over and once again ignoring the stickiness of the floor on the bottom of my boots.

"You'll unload, hand them to Abby, and she'll put them on the bar. When the wall and storage room is full here, we'll leave the boxes on the wall for when shit starts to run out."

"Also going to mix several giant batches of punch to put out in the park area for where the party's going to be, so several of these boxes will be for that," Abby outlined. Nodding, I stepped up to the box Cheryl had been emptying and got to work.

An hour and what seemed like several hundred bottles of liquor later, the boxes were unpacked, everything in its proper place. Though I might have hijacked one of them mid-way through to drink. When I had started rummaging around behind the bar for a glass, Cheryl reminded me—vehemently—that she was the bartender and would pour for me. As I sipped, the door to the bar opened, Garrett and Stone walking in with Rider.

"Hey, Kiera," Rider greeted with a wave, a bright and cheery smile lighting up his face. "How's it going here?"

"Good, got all the alcohol situated."

"Sure you didn't just drink it all?" Garrett joked, his emerald green eyes landing on the open bottle between Abby and me.

"Fuck off," I sassed, taking a drink of my glass with a raised brow.

"Eh, I think I'd rather fuck you, Kitten," he whispered when he reached me, his lips caressing the curve of my ear.

"Ew," Abby whined. "I don't need to hear that. You guys get the stuff?"

"Yeah, it's out back with Nate," Stone replied, hitching a thumb toward the door. "We were coming to get a drink before getting things set up."

"I came in for some soda because there is no way in hell I'm drinking and lighting off a bunch of shit," Rider countered, taking the can Cheryl held out.

"Aww, pussy," Abby teased. "Where's your sense of adventure?"

"I like my hands attached to my body and my head hole-free because if I fuck up something or someone on this compound with those explosives, Boss will have my head. Once things are set off and look like they're winding down, then I will... if the compound hasn't drunk all of it."

"Probably a good idea. I'll save you a bottle," Cheryl told him, plucking a bottle from the shelf and scribbling on the label with a permanent marker. "There, just for you."

"Thanks." Rider beamed. "All right, back to work for me. If any of you want to help Tank and me, feel free."

"Yeah, give me a few and I'll be out," Garrett said.

"Me too! I want to see all the pretties," I piped in. Rider laughed, but I didn't take offense. It probably wasn't every day that a grown ass woman like myself talked about fireworks like an excited kid.

"After we make the punch, bitch," Abby commanded.

"Don't tell me what to do." I did the mature thing and stuck my tongue out at her. "But since you asked *oh so nicely*, I'll help you."

"I'll choose to ignore that sarcasm." Abby snickered. "It'll be easy, just empty the specified number of bottles into those containers on the wheeled cart."

She was right—of course—that it was easy, and before I knew it, we were done. Stone and Garrett were hanging around, waiting for me to finish, the former walking over after a few moments to stand next to me.

"Good morning, Jerkface," I sing-songed when I looked up at him. An amused grin curled his lips, but when his gaze fell on my face, I could see a hint of something wrong. My head tilted, eyes narrowed in a silent question, but he didn't tell me what was bothering him.

"Morning, Brat," he said softly, leaning down to kiss me, but even the redirection didn't stop the question from swirling in my mind. *I guess I'll have to ask him about it later,* I realized when Brooks and Chase walked in. Seeing them all reminded me that I still had to give them the news about the footprints before we went out to where Nate and Rider were.

"I'm going to take this out to Nate and check on everything." Abby held up a couple of sodas clutched in her hands. She knew me well and being an officer's Old Lady had given her a strong ability to read the room. Somehow, she'd seen on my face that I needed to talk to my guys.

Her head dipped down in an acknowledging nod as she pushed out into the summer heat. "See you guys out there in a bit."

"In a bit?" Garrett asked, his brows furrowing.

"Come on," I said, tilting my head toward the office. Smiles fell as they stood up straight, all of them picking up on my grim tone when they realized I had something to tell them. Following behind me, we filed down the hall and into the cramped office. As soon as the door was closed, everyone took their usual spot in the space, including me hopping up onto the desk.

"If you tell me some ridiculous shit like Frankie or Lorenzo came back from the dead or that you're pregnant, I may scream," Garrett swore. His attempt at a joke was poor, but I couldn't help but smile.

"I will never fucking be pregnant, so don't worry about that. And I'm pretty sure neither of those fuckheads could return from the dead even if they tried. No, I wanted to bring this up now that we're away from the house."

"Oh, lord," Brooks muttered defeatedly, his hand coming to rub his eyes. "All right, what is it?"

"When we got home, I felt someone watching me," I explained. "There was nothing on video, but I found a footprint near the southwest corner of the house. Whoever it was had feet about my size, so I'm guessing a woman or smaller man, but there was nothing else to give me any idea who it was."

"Okay, so we need to be even more cautious," Brooks concluded. "I'm going to assume you've already got security handled?"

"You're damn right," I smarted with a bright smile, pleased he knew me well enough. "Shit's getting installed tomorrow. I just wanted to give you four a heads up that we have someone sniffing around."

"Any idea who it could be?" Stone questioned quietly. I shook my head, shrugging a shoulder slightly. "All right, we'll keep an eye out. Anything else we should do?"

"Enjoy tonight. I have all security well-armed, so if anyone tries to get in or get too close to the house, we'll know."

"You heard the lady," Chase exclaimed. "Sneak tomorrow, explosives today."

"You seem very unfazed having just found out the house is being watched, especially for someone who was kidnapped and whose home has previously been blown up," Garrett told Chase as we filtered out of the office.

"Eh, comes with the territory of being us." Chase clearly didn't seem to give it much of his attention. Not that I could blame him because he was right—there would always be someone out there wanting to use or kill us.

"Time for pretties!" I shouted when we reached the bar, my steps shifting to skipping as I hopped across the room.

"You would be the one who would call explosives and fireworks 'pretties' and act like a kid in a candy story," Garrett stated dryly, but when I glanced back at him, his ruggedly handsome face held a soft smile that told me he was unsurprised.

And no doubt loved it... especially if the massive rock on my finger was any indication.

"Well, duh, it's exciting. You can't tell me that you aren't looking forward to the party."

"Yeah, yeah," he muttered under his breath.

That's what I thought.

* * *

SEVERAL HOURS LATER, the party was in full swing, though the exploding part was still another half hour away as we waited for night to descend. Laughter, talk, and the sounds of happy children filled the air, the crackle and pop of ground fireworks being lit accompanying the joy of the compound's park. I was pleasantly buzzed as I weaved around patch holders and Old Ladies, doing my best to try and be social, but I found myself staying close to my guys, Abby and Nate, or Rider.

"Hey, Jerkface," I greeted with a chuckle when I reached where Stone was in the crowd of partygoers. Curling an arm around his wide shoulders, I sank into his lap. Now that we were somewhat alone, or at least not being bothered by others, I peppered him with what had been on my mind. "Why so quiet?"

"I'm always quiet, Brat," he challenged with a tired grin. There was an odd note in his voice that caught my attention and only added to my suspicions. I tilted my head in question as he wrapped me up in an embrace.

"You all right?" I asked finally, realizing dancing around the topic wasn't going to cut it.

"Yeah, just been a long day." I knew there was more to it, but I didn't push, knowing if I did it would only piss him off and make him clam up more. It took only a moment before I realized it was Fourth of July and Stone had lost fellow soldiers during deployment.

"Are the explosives and fireworks going to be a problem?" I murmured, hitching a thumb over to where Rider was doing final checks on the other side of the fence. Stone's smile grew, his head shaking.

"Nah, I'll be good. This isn't my first Fourth of July party here, and I can handle some loud noises. It's just some memories of being deployed is all. I appreciate the thoughtfulness though." He paused for a moment, a gravelly laugh shaking his chest before he started talking once more. "Except I can tell you're getting itchy by the way you're shifting in my lap, so I'll stop."

"Shut up," I huffed, halting the movements that I hadn't realized I was even doing. "See if I'll ask if anything is wrong again."

"Of course you will. You're too much of a nosy brat to not," he countered with a grin, his ebony eyes sparkling as he looked up at me. The light within his warm gaze told me he wasn't upset that I'd asked, but he definitely wasn't willing to talk about it right now.

"You havin' fun?" he redirected when I gave him a half-assed glare. The jerk got way too much pleasure from riling me up.

"Yeah, I'm looking forward to the fireworks," I told him, "but that's another few minutes away at least. Then when that's over, the fun things start." His gaze heated, his hold around me tensing as I wiggled my ass over his cock.

"That they do, Brat," he murmured, kissing me softly. After a few moments of our lips being locked, Abby called my name, waving me over. "Go on," Stone directed with a pat on my ass as I slipped off his lap.

I flashed him one final look, trying to convey that I was here for him, and when he gave me a soft smile, I knew he understood. I wanted to push him, worried that if I didn't he would lock it all up, but since I wasn't the most sociable either when it came to my past, I let the conversation drop. *We're there for each other, and that's what matters*, I reminded myself when I turned.

"We'll be here to watch the fireworks when you're done," Brooks called out as I started to walk away, the president taking a seat next to his enforcer. "Warden and Chase will be here too whenever they're done grabbing drinks."

"Aye, aye," I touted sassily, giving a little salute and wink before turning back and walking to Abby, my mind still focused on Stone.

Our relationship was different than it had been when we started, neither of us wanting to stab each other. *Usually anyway.* It wasn't something I'd ever expected when I first walked into the Aces' bar... *or carried into it, I guess*... but it wasn't something I would ever change. I had my men, my best bitch and her husband, Elliot, Rider, and revenge against the mob that had terrorized more than just me.

What more could you ask for?

"Jesus, you walk so slow," Abby huffed, snapping me out of my internal monologuing. Shaking my head, I laughed when she brought up her phone for a photo. After a few more minutes of chatting, she was pulled away by another Old Lady, leaving me to my own devices. Before returning to my guys, I hopped in line to refill my cup with the punch we had made, scanning the park area as I waited for the spout to be free.

It was odd, realizing there was a tingling and fuzzy warmth that filled me as I looked around. It wasn't just seeing everyone together since we'd had a couple compound parties before now, but a sense of home filled me this time. I belonged among the other members and families despite the fact that

I stuck out. I was a criminal, a thief who'd earned a name for herself without the help of anyone else, and the one thing I'd wanted above all else was complete.

So... now what?

Hell no to a fucking baby. I shuddered when I saw a little toddler running around with wild eyes and sugary hands.

Obviously I'll continue to steal because why the hell not?

"Kittycat!" Chase called out, his hand waving over his head as I finished filling my cup. "Hurry that sexy ass up."

Damn troublemaker, I huffed, but I was thankful he'd interrupted when he did. *Woman the fuck up, Cat, it's a party! Enjoy yourself,* I commanded, and when I was settled in with the guys and the show started, all previous thoughts faded away in a roar of explosions and bright sparkling fireworks.

Who says blowing shit up can't be cathartic?

That's right, no one.

CHAPTER 3

July 4th
Saturday Night

Brookes

The party was winding down, families heading back home with tired children passed out in their arms, while single members and prospects were breaking off with a hang-around in tow. The other officers, Rider, Abby, Kiera, and I hung around, picking up quickly, and before I knew it, the park area was cleaned. Abby and Kiera were joking about something across the lawn, Kiera's husky laughter making me smile.

She really is the most amazing woman I've ever met. Everything felt perfect; I had my club, my officers, and now Kiera giving me the family I'd always wanted but never thought I'd have. But when Abby started walking away with Nate, I saw a hint of a frown on Kiera's tan face. Seeing the down-turned curl only brought up the one negative thing that had been permeating my thoughts in the recent weeks—was my baby happy?

I knew she was happy with us. Kiera wasn't exactly quiet when it came to things that were on her mind. For me, the club had been my purpose in life since the day I was born. It's what I knew I wanted, and getting her was just the cherry on top. But Kiera... she'd just been doing her thing with her eye on the prize her entire life.

She'd taken to relaxing near the pool or training down in the basement over the last few months. Everything was going well. Kiera was pretty much always in a good mood, but when she was preparing for her most recent job, it was like a switch had been flipped. The fire in her gaze ignited, and she seemed almost hungry for the thrill, so with that in mind, I started to think of what she could do to keep that drive going.

With Frankie taken care of, her life's vendetta was complete, and she didn't have anything to fight against anymore. But fighting was built into her DNA, and I wasn't sure being with us and part of club business was going to be enough. I knew there would always be jobs for her to take, and there would always be threats that we'd deal with as criminals... Maybe she could be in charge of security here at the compound, ensuring that everything was up to date and that one mistake or mishap wouldn't lead to a major security breach. *Hm, doubt she'd want to do that*, I thought, my lips thinning as I rubbed my beard absently. Kiera was as much of an Ace as the rest of us, and I wanted her to be able to *feel* like it, not just know it.

"Come on, Boss, let's take our girl home." The nudge of Chase's elbow in my side pulled me from my thoughts. "Don't forget that promise you gave her this morning."

"Like I could forget. I'm pretty sure I've been rock hard almost all day," I admitted, following him back toward our waiting designated driver. The closer we got, the more I tucked my previous train of thought away for further contemplation. Slipping into the car, I got into the middle row of seats, Chase and Stone behind Garrett and me.

"Hey there, *Boss*," Kiera murmured, her tone thick with heat. Straddling my lap, she focused wholly on me, not caring that we were in the back of a crash SUV. Her arms rested on my shoulders, fingers tangling in my hair. "I'm glad to see you're excited about tonight." At the end of her statement, she ground her pussy over my cock, the rough movement nearly torturous after thinking about her getting ravished this morning.

"Damn fucking right I am," I growled, grabbing hold of her ass in a way that left no questions about who she belonged to, at least in part. "You've been out there for hours flaunting this sexy ass of yours in these cut-off shorts. I've been imagining sinking into that honey sweet pussy of yours all day."

Her lips crashed into mine, devouring me as I rocked my hips up. Releasing her briefly, I slipped my fingers up under the denim to cup the curve of her ass. She tasted like punch and chocolate from the party, only making me want more as I slipped my tongue around hers. I didn't care that the others were there watching. Kiera wanted my attention, and I'd be damned if I wouldn't give it to her.

"Almost to the house, Boss," Garrett told me, his voice rough, and when I looked over at him, I found a bulge straining against the front of his jeans.

Kiera seemed to notice it too, a sultry chuckle filling the car as she rolled her hips over me once more before crawling to Garrett.

God, tonight's going to be fun.

Kiera

"Hey there, Kitten," Garrett murmured gruffly, scooping me into his arms as he expertly maneuvered us out of the SUV. Wrapping my legs around his trim waist, I let him carry me to the house, the others trailing behind.

"Mm," I whimpered as he claimed my mouth, pushing me up against the wall as soon as he got into the front entryway. The others were there, and I could feel their eyes on me, but in that moment, all I could focus on was Garrett.

"You feel so good wrapped in my arms, Kitten," he whispered, his kisses trailing down my jaw and neck. The sting of his nipping hurt, but it quickly melted into a pleasurable burn as he lapped at my skin. "Why don't we take this somewhere we can all have some fun?"

"I have the perfect idea," Chase piped in. I heard a rustling, but I had no idea who or what it was. My eyes rolled back and closed, soaking up everything Garrett was giving me.

"What the..." I exclaimed when a soft, silky material was placed over my eyes, Garrett pulling me away from the wall and against his body.

"Shh, it's all right, Baby," Brooks soothed, his voice thick with desire. All of my other senses sharpened when the blindfold was secured over my eyes, the intensity of them making my skin pebble as a shiver worked its way through me.

"What are we doing?" I questioned when I felt Garrett start moving. Based on where he was turning, I would hazard a guess that we were going to the dining room or kitchen.

"A little fun twist," Chase explained, his giddy and excitable tone giving nothing away since that was his perpetual state of being.

Troublemakers, the entire lot of them.

"I'm going to set you down, Kitten. Don't roll one way or the other or you'll fall," Garrett warned. I smirked, knowing that even when I was feeling like I was going to combust, I couldn't help but be a smart ass.

"Don't you know cats always land on their feet?" I countered. A laugh radiated through me at the sound of his groaning, a large part of me loving when I riled them up.

"That was horrible," Stone told me, but I didn't have to see his expression to know he was giving me a minute grin. I beamed as I was set down on a hard, cold surface. Running my hand over my makeshift bed, I felt the ridges of the wood grain against my fingertips.

"The table?" I asked, tilting my head in an attempt to hear anything going on around me. They may have taken one sense away from me, but that didn't mean I was helpless. "Oooh, am I going to be dessert?" A gush of desire shot through me at the thought, my already slick pussy flooding when I heard the refrigerator door open.

"In a sense," Brooks replied. "But what fun would it be if we just did that?"

"Uh, a lot of fun?" I drew out like it was obvious. *Which it should have been, because come on, what woman wouldn't want to be ravished by her sexy men?*

Or women.

I don't discriminate, people.

"True, but we wanted to have a little *extra* fun." Chase took over, his voice much closer than before. His warm breath flared over my cheek and neck as he shifted closer, his lips barely brushing my sensitive skin with each word. I wanted more, his lips and hands all over me, but he was content to tease as he chuckled. "I take it that sounds like fun, Kittycat?"

"Yes." My response sounded breathy and thin with need even to my own ears, so I knew it hid nothing from them. My heart started to pound when he finally pressed a kiss to my pulse. No one told me what we were doing or what the plan for this extra fun entailed; all I felt was lips and wandering hands. It was difficult to tell exactly who was who, so I let myself go, surrendering to them.

Slowly, they peeled off my shirt and bra, leaving me almost bare for them. Knowing their gazes were trailing over me had my nipples pebbling and my body buzzing with anticipation. I very rarely gave control away, needing to be ready and aware at any given point, but right now, with them? I knew I was safe, so I waited for them to put whatever plan they had in mind into action.

"So..." I murmured after they moved away from me. "What are we doing? Because if I don't have some kind of body part between my thighs in the next thirty seconds, I just might go up in flames."

"Patience, Baby," Brooks said with a snicker. "We want to have a little contest."

"Hm, color me intrigued," I murmured, humming in thought as I tried to figure out exactly what the stakes might be.

"We're each going to get our time with you, possibly in multiples, and we want you to guess who is who," Chase stated.

"What do I get if I'm right?" I questioned, wanting it more with each moment we spoke.

"You get to lay out by the pool as you love to do," Garrett explained.

"Mhm, keep going," I prompted, curiosity growing.

"And whoever you guess correctly will get to be your cabana boy," Brooks added. "Feed you grapes or get you drinks, do whatever it is that you'd want us to do."

"Only if you do it naked," I negotiated. "I want to enjoy the view while I'm relaxing."

"Deal," Chase accepted immediately, the others following suit with soft laughter.

"And if I lose?"

Not that I intend to, mind you, but you can never be too prepared.

"You have to have a sexy photo shoot on the guy's bike. Or on my Audi," Chase tacked on to the end.

"Going to make me into a calendar?" I teased. A pair of fingers tweaked my nipple; the unexpected sharp sting shot straight through me, ripping a moan from my throat. "All right, deal," I agreed breathlessly. "Now someone please fucking come over here because I feel like I'm going to—" I didn't even get the rest of my statement out before one of them captured my lips.

The kiss was rough and possessive as whoever it was tangled their fingers into my hair and held me steady against them. I tried to focus on what I felt, noting a wash of stubble on his chin as I cupped his face, but when there was another pinch to my already sensitive nipples, I found myself nearly drowning in desire.

A second pair of hands worked my shorts off. The warmth of whoever peeled the cut-off denim down my legs radiated between my thighs as they stepped back between them. Whoever was kissing me returned once I was naked, the other pair of hands now roving over my chest and curves.

"More," I whimpered against his lips as I rocked against his cock. The hardened bulge was still confined behind a pair of rough jeans making it impossible to tell if it was pierced or not.

Hm, this may be more difficult than I originally anticipated, I noted when I realized I was surrounded with the scent of grease and spent fireworks. The concoction covered the normal scents I associated with each of my men, taking away a second sense.

But I was always up for a challenge, and I planned on winning most if not all of these. I just needed a bit more time, so instead, I took the lead. Shifting my hands down, I brushed over his chest, noting he wore a plain t-shirt. I continued my exploration, fighting against the urge to let go and enjoy the tantalizing nibbling on my neck and shoulder. Before I could find any identifying features, both of them pulled away, leaving me aching. I ground my teeth, unwilling to give them the satisfaction of pleading. *They'll be back. That's the whole point of this game. Besides, they'd never give up the chance to tease me.*

And I was right. A pair of hands roughly pried my thighs apart only moments before I felt the head of a cock pressing into my entrance. There was no hesitating, no build up to him pushing into me in short rocks, but I was wet enough that there was no resistance.

"Fuck," I moaned, my lip tucked between my teeth and my head pressed back against the hard table at the sudden stretch. Everything ached, my body taut with need as I clawed at the wood. He didn't slow, nor was he gentle, and each pounding thrust sent me deeper into the lustful fog clouding my mind. I knew we were in the middle of a fun competition, but I couldn't find it in me to care. All there was in that moment was my man rocking into me and my hyperaware senses.

Every nerve felt electrified, the nearly painful sensation making me arch off the table and into my man's heated chest. Wanting—needing—to feel his hands or lips on me, I slid my hands up his arms before cupping his jaw. I tugged, pulling him to fold over me. He obliged, capturing my lips in a searing kiss without slowing.

My release was nearing, my lower belly tingling as it approached, but instead of letting myself fall into it at full speed, I focused on the man bringing me to the edge. His hair was longer as I tangled my fingers into it, silky soft and good for grabbing hold of, and that was when I knew who it was.

Brooks.

With that smug revelation, I nipped at his bottom lip, sucking it into my mouth, and let myself go. Crying out, I shuddered, stars bursting in front of my eyes in an array of bright colors, but Brooks didn't stop. His pace slowed, but only for a moment, and a second pair of hands grabbed hold of my wrists and pried me away from Brooks's torso.

Whoever had joined held me steadfast against the table with my wrists pinned above my arms, leaving me exposed for my men's gazes. *Ugh, what I'd give to see their heated stares on me, their hands working their hard cocks as they watch impatiently.* The imagined thought filled my mind as clearly as if I could truly see it, and it made my skin flush with a wave of goosebumps.

"More," I whispered when Brooks brought me to the edge, but instead of finishing me a second time, he pulled out. A few seconds later, I felt the sticky spurts of his cum coating my thigh and hip. "You're an asshole, Brooks," I groaned, wiggling in an attempt to bring some relief.

"Damn," he murmured with a laugh, "thought I had you. Though I can't say I'm too disappointed at getting to strut around you naked."

"I'm looking forward to it," I smarted with a bright smile. "Who knows, maybe you'll actually finish me then." There was no quip in return, only a heated mouth fusing to my pussy and sucking at my clit sharply. His tongue swirled and lapped at my slick entrance, reigniting the orgasm that I'd been denied only moments ago. After a few more nips and circles, I came hard, grabbing hold of Brooks's head and tugging his hair hard as he continued to lick me through my release.

"There, Baby, all finished," Brooks countered with a husky whisper, shifting until he could kiss me. His lips were coated in my arousal, my own flavor against my tongue as he swirled it around mine.

"Mmm, good," I murmured, wiggling my arms when Brooks stepped away. "Now, who's up here?" Moving my hands, I brushed against strong forearms, nothing that could tell me who was holding me.

Someone new slipped in between my legs, a soft towel wiping the cold cum from my skin. They were gentle and soft in their movements, their free hand trailing slowly over my other thigh. The change of pace threw me off. None of my men would ever be considered gentle when we rolled around in the sheets.

Or wherever else we're deciding to fuck.

The hands on my wrist released, the calloused palms sliding down my arms to cup my tits. Whoever was above me folded over, nibbling my neck and earlobe. *Why must all my men have scruff and beards?* I thought with a slight whine, trying to figure out which two men were showering me with kisses, nips, and seductive licks.

Unlike Brooks who'd slipped in roughly, the man lined up, slowly sliding into me with one smooth motion. The feeling was different than before but no less amazing. I had no idea which guy was which, but the only one who would try and be soft was Chase, mainly because he loved when I took the lead.

I held back on spouting my answer prematurely, letting myself get lost in the heady, almost dizzying bursts of pleasure that came with each stroke. The rhythm was steady, and while the thrusts were slower, his grip on my hips was possessive. Moaning at a pair of rough fingers rolling my peaked nipples, I was quickly inching toward the edge of release. *Hm, Stone?* I wondered. *He would be the one to tease before actually fucking me.* Before I could figure it out for sure, they reached between my thighs, rubbing circles over my clit.

Lightning shot through me at the touch. My back arched off the table as the slowly encroaching orgasm slammed down. My man fucked me through my release, keeping a similar pace before slipping out. Smashing my lips together, I waited to see what was next. The one who was above me also pulled away from me, the lack of touching leaving me whimpering and wanting.

All of a sudden, I was yanked from the table. My heart leapt into my throat, and strong hands flipped me, forcing me to bend over what seemed like a chair as soon as my feet touched the floor. Bracing one hand on the seat cushion, I reached out with my other. *All right, I'm turned sideways over one of the chairs,* I deduced when I felt the upholstered back to my right. *Now what are they planning?*

I didn't have to wait long to find out since the same rough grip grabbed hold of my ass. Angling my hips, he ran his tongue over me, the heat against my sensitive pussy making me shudder. As he continued to ravish me with his sinful mouth, a hand gripped my jaw tightly and angled me up. A possessive kiss captured me, adding to the fire flowing through me. Then a sharp nip to my bottom lip made me moan, but when I tried to return the favor, the man held me in place, his mouth pulling away before being replaced with his cock. When the silken head pushed against the seam of my lips, I opened, noting that there were no rungs of a Jacob's ladder.

There was only one of my men who held my jaw that way, the one who happened to love me sucking his cock.

Stone.

Oh, I'm so going to win against him. My cocky thought was cut short when two fingers circled my entrance slightly before slamming home. As Stone rocked into my mouth, the man behind me continued to plunge into my slick core, his pace fast and intense. I had no clue who it was until I felt teeth graze over my ass cheek. The sharp bite stung, but the pain melted into a wave of tingles that had me quivering for more, and he seemed to know exactly what I wanted.

Leaving a trail of aching bites across my skin, his fingers sank into me at the same pace that Stone's cock rocked into my mouth. The painful grip on my hip mixed with the cruelness in his motions, telling me that behind me was Ciar, the coldest of my men both in and out of bed.

When his mouth returned to the tight ring of muscles, the momentum that had built between them reached its peak. It only took a moment until my orgasm slammed down on me, and I shattered. Stone wasn't far behind, my crying moans sending him over the edge. Fingers tangled in my hair as he came, the ropes of his release shooting into the back of my throat. Pulling off of him, I swallowed quickly before taking several deep inhales, riding through the aftershocks.

"So, care to guess who was who?" I heard Brooks ask. "You already got me correct, but I didn't hear any other sassy comments."

"I was quite preoccupied," I smarted, standing and ripping off my blindfold. The room was bright, blinding me briefly before I could continue. "Gentle was Chase partnered with Stone, biter was Ciar, and the blow job was Stone..." I trailed off when I realized there was one missing in there. Glancing around for Garrett, my eyes narrowed when I saw him leaning against the wall fully clothed. "You sat this one out?" He flashed me a sexy smirk, striding forward until he stood only a hair's breadth away.

"You know I could never sit out a round of having that sweet pussy, Kitten," he murmured, ending his statement with a bite. My jaw dropped at the hint he'd given me.

I really had thought the biting was Ciar, but apparently these little bastards are good at pretending to not be themselves.

"Mmm, speechless," Garrett taunted, "that certainly doesn't happen very often."

"Fuck off," I huffed, shoving him back a step. Garrett chuckled but didn't push the issue. "How did I do with everyone else?"

"You got Stone right for the blow job," Brooks told me, and I brightened, winking at Stone. The enforcer didn't say anything, but his lip quirked up. Surprisingly like Brooks, he didn't seem perturbed that he'd lost. Two won, one lost, I realized, but I knew as soon as my assassin started to smile that I had fucked up again.

Damn it.

Note to self, fuck my men more so I can identify who is who in my sleep.

At least that'll certainly be an enjoyable task.

"Gentle, my Dove, was me," Ciar hissed, prowling up behind me. Feeling his breath wash over my shoulder blades made my skin pebble and the hairs on the back of my neck stand on end. He was the predator, and I was the prey, even if he had been able to show some semblance of 'soft.' "And it was Garrett who held you to the table, not Stone."

"Two right, two wrong," I countered with a shrug, "could have been worse. What about Chase?" Glancing over my shoulder, I watched Ciar's intense gaze transform into Chase's exuberant smile.

"I found myself quite enjoying the show," he murmured, leaning forward until his lips trailed lightly over my shoulder. "Besides, Garrett and I haven't had a chance to have you yet tonight. Why not let Brooks and Stone enjoy the show?"

"Technically, Garrett did, at least in some capacity," I challenged, reaching up to tangle my fingers in Chase's hair and angling my head to give him better access to my neck.

That was all it took, and Garrett stripped out of his cut and shirt, nearly ripping his belt off his jeans before leaving those with the rest of the heap. I held my breath in anticipation as he stalked forward, even more turned on by what was about to happen as Brooks reclined in his seat like a king and Stone followed suit. Both choosing to watch and work their already hardening cocks in leisurely paces.

Chase stepped back, untangling my fingers from his hair, and Garrett swept me up when he walked away. Scrambling to hold on, I wrapped my arms around his tattooed shoulders as he wound my legs around his trim hips.

"I may have gotten a taste, Kitten," he whispered, his hands digging roughly into my ass where he held me steady. "But you damn well know me better than to think I'd settle for just that," he ground out, kissing me every few words, the gruff and possessive notes music to my ears.

Shifting me slightly, he lined up, letting gravity help me sink onto him. My pussy was sensitive and sore after my several rounds before, and the barbells of his piercing had me shivering in anticipation. Chase's warm, muscled body returned as Garrett held me still. As Chase peppered kisses along my shoulder blade, I felt the cold slippery liquid of the lube circle the ring of muscles.

"You ready, Kittycat?" Chase questioned, his words barely audible against my heavy breathing and racing heart.

"Fuck yes, I am."

Garrett distracted me with his swirling tongue, spreading me for Chase to work one then two and finally three fingers. When he felt I was stretched enough, the head of his cock replaced his fingers. I relaxed, inch by inch sinking deeper into my lustful fog.

"Fuck," I moaned as they started to rock. When one pushed in, the other pulled out. My little assassin and my asshole stepbrother who always knew exactly what I wanted created the perfect rhythm between them. I loved all of my men, but Garrett and Chase, the two I'd been "with" the longest, had seen me through many ups and downs. They knew me almost as well as they knew themselves.

And now?

I fully intend to revel in what they're willing to give me.

My moans filled the kitchen echoing off the hard surfaces as they started to move faster. I was wound tight, but my body was hovering above that blissful pool. I wanted more, to savor my time between them as I had with Stone and Brooks. Letting my eyes fall closed, I held tight to Garrett's muscled body and leaned back into Chase's chest. Both were coated in a slight sheen of sweat, their hands and mouths roving over me.

"You feel so good, Kittycat," Chase murmured, nipping at my ear lobe. The sting nudged me closer to release, my nails digging into Garrett's back as my body tensed. He took the hint, fucking me faster until he and Chase were rocking into me at the same time.

Their names were whispered on my lips as I drowned between them. I was being pulled under yet floating on cloud nine. The contrast was intoxicating, and finally, when Garrett sucked at the crook of my neck, I exploded. My vision darkened for a moment at the intensity of my release, a cry ripping from me as I heard Garrett groan. His pace faltered as he came with me, Chase's breathing growing harsher as he continued to bounce me on his cock.

"Kiera," he moaned, thrusting one final time before I felt him come deep within me. Panting and sweating, I slumped between them, both of them laughing at my antics.

"I think someone's going to have to carry me to the shower," I admitted, carefully putting my feet on the cold hardwood when Garrett set me down.

"Mmm," Brooks hummed as he got up. "I'm happy to oblige... if I get to join, that is."

"Boss, you've already had her once," Stone challenged with a smirk. "I think it's my turn."

"The two of you could always share," I offered, cocking a brow at Stone. "That is if you're up for that 'sex sharing thing,' Stone." Based on his molten onyx eyes and assured steps as he neared me?

That's a hell yes.

CHAPTER 4

July 6th
Monday Afternoon

Kiera

"You boys have fun," I teased, shifting on my bike's seat. Garrett, Nate, and Stone all shook their heads as they walked into the Aces' bar. Brooks gave me a panty-melting smirk, capturing my jaw between his rough fingers.

"You be good, Baby," he murmured against my lips, with just enough pressure to make my core spark.

Damn tease.

"But being bad is much more fun," I told him. A soft chuckle reached me, but before I could give him another sassy remark, Brooks smashed his mouth against mine. Sucking his lower lip between my teeth, I nipped sharply before laving away any remaining sting.

"If you keep up with that, Church will never happen," he bit out huskily. A smug smile tugged on my lips, knowing that's exactly what I had been trying to do. "And you say we're the troublemakers."

"You are," I countered, sitting up fully when he released my jaw. "I'm just picking up bad habits from the lot of you."

"Psh, yeah fucking right. You're the original troublemaker, Baby," Brooks said with a shake of his head. Stepping away from my side, he gave me a wink before turning to head into the bar for his leather-wearing boy band meeting.

"You and Abby better not burn down my compound!" he hollered as I started to pull away. Flipping him off over my shoulder, I laughed, knowing I would never do such a thing.

At least not to something I actually like.

The wind whipped around me bringing a bit of relief to the hot and dry Nevada summer weather as I rode through the streets to Abby and Nate's house. Thankfully, it wasn't far, so I would soon be out of the heat and in the sweet embrace of air conditioning. Pulling up to the house, I nearly melted into a puddle from lack of a breeze. I turned my bike off and practically ran into the house, not bothering to knock.

"Oh, thank fuck," I groaned, slumping back against the door. "Refreshing air conditioning." Glancing over, I found Cheryl perched on the couch with a beer in hand and remote in the other. I gave a half-assed wave, my hand flopping back down to my side.

"I thought cats were supposed to like the sun?" Cheryl asked with a brow raise.

"Sun, yes, outrageously hot weather? No," I groaned, pushing off from the door and walking over. "Where's the hostess?"

"In the kitchen!" Abby called out. "Almost done with dinner!"

"Need a refill?" I asked Cheryl, pointing at her bottle.

"Nah, I'm still nursing this one. I may be the bartender, but I don't tend to drink much," she explained. I wasn't surprised she didn't drink much; she probably had her fill of peeling more than one drunk patch holder, hangaround, and prospect off the sticky grimy floor of the bar to last her a lifetime.

"All right, all done. Who's ready for some food?" Abby hollered out with a whoop at the end as she pulled the pan out of the oven and placed it on the potholder. Shaking my head at her antics, I made my way to the table with Cheryl right behind me.

"Looks good, Abby," Cheryl commented, scooping up some of the lasagna. "Glad the officers had Church so I could come today."

"I'm assuming since they hold it in the bar it's locked and closed off during meetings?" I asked, taking the spatula from her.

"Yeah, I love working the bar, and since there's usually at least a few in every night, I don't typically get many nights off. Not that I mind," she explained.

"Well feel free to come on by whenever." Abby waved her fork in my direction. "This antisocial bitch here could use some more friends."

"Excuse you," I huffed. "I have plenty of friends." Abby's eyes narrowed skeptically. "I have the guys, Nate and you, and Rider. Can't forget Elliot."

"Elliot isn't here unless he's hitting up Rider, and the guys don't count. You need friends, and we saw how talking to the other Old Ladies went."

"Okay, those three twats don't even count as Old Ladies," Cheryl corrected.

"Thank you!" I exclaimed triumphantly. "I never actually heard what happened to them. Are they still banned? I didn't see them at the party the other night."

"For the time being, yeah. I'm sure Boss will have a hearing with their husbands soon. So they may be back in the next couple of months," Cheryl relayed.

"Regardless, you need some friends, and look! It's already working." Abby moved her arms, motioning them in a way very reminiscent of Vanna White. My face scrunched at her tone, not enjoying being the center of conversation even if I had to—silently—admit she was right.

"Enough about me." I waved my hands animatedly. "What about you, Miss Attitude? Anything new? Possibly about that thing we talked about around Christmas time?" Waggling my eyebrows, I not so subtly brought up the one thing I'd wanted to pester her about.

The baby scare.

"Ugh," she grumbled, her cockiness falling away as she muttered under her breath. "I talked to Nate about it, yes."

"'Bout what?" Cheryl asked curiously. I didn't say anything, knowing as much as I loved to poke and prod my best bitch, I wouldn't discuss the details of something so private. Abby could outline what happened if or when she wanted.

"We had a pregnancy scare around Christmas time, and *this* nosy one brought up whether we wanted to actually try for a little tot," Abby explained, throwing a hand in my direction as I ate.

"You two would make good parents," Cheryl stated without judgement. I flashed another triumphant grin, but I couldn't say much since I had just stuffed a large bite of lasagna in my mouth.

"Well... we're considering it, but it hasn't been something we've actively tried to do. Nate's definitely not opposed like I thought he may have been."

My smile softened, losing the bit of snark it had a moment ago, enjoying seeing the two pink patches growing on Abby's pale cheeks.

"Does that mean Kiera will have to throw you a baby shower if you get pregnant?" Cheryl asked, turning her teasing to me. My lips pursed, but I knew I would do it no matter how much I would hate it.

But only for my best bitch.

"I didn't hear a no," Abby observed, "so that's definitely a yes."

"I suppose... Icoulddothat," I hedged, slurring my words together in a rush of mumbles at the end. Both women beamed, thankfully letting the rest of that conversation slide... unfortunately into a different topic I didn't want to talk about.

"So, how're you and the guys? Any family plans for you five... six?" Abby asked, stumbling over remembering that Ciar was a part of this weird family we'd created. I snorted. She knew very well how I felt about children.

"No babies," I immediately asserted. "Other than that, not much... I think wedding planning? Wow, that was never something I ever expected to say."

"I have a feeling you've probably been saying that a lot recently. After everything with Frankie and the mob," Abby continued. "How're you feeling about all of that now that it's over?"

I sat there in silence for a long moment, my eyes tracking my fork as it edged the last few pieces of meat around my plate. Neither of them pushed me to answer, no teasing or prodding as I mulled over what I felt and what I wanted to admit. On one hand, talking about it at all was difficult, let alone with Cheryl, but on the other hand, I felt this strange sense of ease despite having someone there besides my bestie. Taking a deep breath, I started admitting one thing I hadn't really told anyone.

"Uh, out of sorts." My words were barely audible, but I could tell they were both listening by their attentive gazes and slowing movements. "I mean, I feel fucking fantastic, the bastard's finally fucking dead and his empire and all of his minions were burned to hell where they all belong. I had thought I wouldn't make it through everything. I went into this knowing I would more than likely take my father to the grave along with myself. Only I wasn't alone," I murmured with a shrug, "so here I am."

"Are you happy?" Abby asked.

"Yes, despite feeling unsettled. I'm hoping getting back into the groove of bigger jobs will help. All of these easy as pie gigs have bored me. Okay, for real, how the fuck is that even a phrase? Baking pie is a pain in the ass," I deflected, too uncomfortable to continue. Master thief, yes. Award-winning actress, definitely not. Even without knowing me well, Cheryl detected my discomfort as easily as Abby, and they let us move on without any pressure.

Thank fuck, otherwise I may have erupted into a giant wave of hives.

Chase

Whistling to myself, I stepped out of my car and strode over to the bar's door. I didn't even try to open it, knowing Brooks and the others locked it during their meetings to keep outsiders away.

Me, though? A flimsy little lock isn't going to do anything.

I crouched down, pulling out the lockpick set Kittycat had gifted me for my birthday. It only took a few wiggles of the metal instruments to hit the correct combinations of pins to unlock. Turning the picks, I yanked the door open.

"Hello, boys!" I nearly cheered as I strode into the room, enjoying the gaping stare from Stone. Brooks only rubbed his eyes as he always did when he didn't have much to say about a situation that was stressing him out, while Nate chuckled and Garrett shook his head. None of the officers seemed at all surprised I would invite myself into their meeting. Good. "Quite the party I'm joining."

"Chase," Brooks started, glaring at me, but his hardass persona didn't faze me—or Ciar, who nearly growled at the reprimanding tone. "You know you can't be here."

"And?" I challenged, grabbing a chair and dragging it to their circle. "When has that ever stopped me? What affects my Kittycat or my family affects me, and you know we won't be kept in the dark."

"Ugh," Garrett groaned, pinching the bridge of his nose, but he didn't argue. Stone was as stoic and hard as always.

Get it? Hard... Stone?

Ha, I'm hilarious.

"I think short of shooting him," Nate started, "there's no way to get him to go away. No offense or anything." The last portion of his statement was directed at me.

"None taken. Not that any of you bastards could probably hit me, but it's a valid point. So," I exclaimed, crossing my legs, "what're we talking about?"

"Well, the first thing should definitely be about whether or not you're going to try and patch in here at the club," Stone grumbled, "but knowing you, you'll probably just dance around the topic for an unknown amount of time."

"Normally yes, but seeing as how you three are also marrying Kittycat, I figured it would be the best option. I mean, seriously, could you imagine? Orphan turned fighter turned assassin turned biker? Hell of a resumé if you ask me," I spouted. "What do I have to do for that?"

"You're serious?" Garrett asked, shocked. Brooks's eyes narrowed on me, trying to figure out if I truly meant what I said.

"Do I usually say something that I don't mean, Gar?" I challenged. "But we can talk about that after this. I don't think me figuring out how to do all the steps and shit is really Church-worthy."

"All right," Brooks murmured hesitantly, "we were just talking about upcoming shipments and ensuring all our shit was in order, but I think we got that all figured out."

"They thriving?"

"They're steady, thankfully. We didn't want to bring too much attention to the club after everything that went down with the Solace mob. It was a huge and risky move, so we dispersed less at each drop and did a different drop schedule than normal. Now that it's been a while though, we've increased back toward regular movements. Aiming to pick up a bit more now with having pretty much sole reign of the area."

"Good, good," I murmured. "All right, now that I'm caught up, please continue."

"Well, that was the good news," Nate said grimly. "Stone and I have been keeping an eye on the target you told us to, Boss."

"And?" Brooks prompted when Nate hesitated. My interest was piqued at their conversation, my mind whirling with ideas of who this mystery target could be.

"*You think they'd just fucking say it,*" Ciar hissed in annoyance.

"*Yeah, well, they're a bit secretive. They'll give it up in a bit, so calm your balls,*" I told him.

"*They're your balls too, asshat,*" he countered venomously.

"*Yes, they are, and as you can see, they're very clearly calm, so chill the hell out,*" I huffed.

"She's gone off the grid," Nate finally revealed. As soon as he said *she,* we both knew who he was talking about.

Agent Emily Venry.

"And Kiera said the house was possibly being watched by a female," I added.

"Meaning Venry's gone AWOL from her job... and her new target is probably us or at the very least Kiera," Stone bit out, his body taut with edginess as he summarized the cold hard truth.

"If we could make it six months without any issues, that'd be fucking swell," Garrett groaned, folding over to brace his forearms on his knees, the bridge of his nose pinched between his thumb and forefinger once more.

"Well, technically we're already over six months, Gar," I pointed out, unable to help myself. Garrett threw me a glare, his green gaze hardened and spitting fire.

"I certainly don't want us to be a target, and Kiera's one of my closest friends, so I don't want anything to happen to her either. I guess the question is, what are we going to do about it?" Nate asked, looking between the four of us.

Therein lies the rub.

CHAPTER 5

July 9th
Thursday Afternoon

Kiera

U *gh*, I grumbled, staring at the full wall of papers, photographs, string, and notes. As I looked over what had been almost my entire life, the one thing that had fueled me—revenge against my father and all of his shitty men—stared back. I should have felt satisfied that I'd done it, but instead, that sense of disconnect filled me once more. *What do I do now?*

As I pondered that, I stepped forward and took down the first photo from the wall. It was of my father and Lorenzo standing in the entrance of the lavish house of horrors I had burned down months ago. They were talking about something I hadn't been able to hear, but I remembered their scowls and rigid body movements as if it were yesterday.

Tucking the photo into the box I had placed next to me, I forced away the thoughts that had started to swirl in my mind. It was slow going, dropping each pin into the container and placing the photograph or note into the box, but after a little while, I slipped into a trance from the repetitive motions. I had just finished the first quarter of the board when I heard the door at the top of the stairs open.

"Hey, Kittycat," Chase greeted as he descended the steps happily. The brown faux-suede of his jacket swung around his muscled torso with each skip, his holsters underneath briefly becoming visible with each movement. "How's it going?"

"Eh." I shrugged. "It's going. Pretty boring, but I know you're probably wondering how I'm doing mentally, and I can happily report I'm fine."

"Aww, you don't need to get that sassy tone with me, Kittycat. Can you blame me for wanting to check on you? Last time you went unchecked during a PTSD flashback, you were lost in your own head for a whole day," he reminded me with a head tilt. "Besides, I didn't just come down here for that."

"Then what did you come down for?" I questioned, turning back to the board without further comment about my PTSD. *If I pretend it isn't there, it goes away. That's how that works, right? Yeah, yeah, don't turn those judgy eyes on me, people. I'll deal with all of that shit at some point.*

In the future and not right now.

Hey, did you really *expect anything else?*

"A couple things. First, since it just popped into my head, are you planning on going through Frankie's files soon?"

"I know I should, but I think I want to get this done first," I explained, pulling several pieces off the wall. "I'll keep the box out in case there's anything I might need, but that part of my life is behind me, so I don't feel too rushed, you know? I plan on going through all his shit and narrowing down any potential targets that could try and take over in his absence, but I don't foresee that happening any time soon with us having control of the casino."

"Did you want me to help with his files?"

"Chase," I stated simply, looking at my little assassin over my shoulder. His gray eyes were focused on me, his shameless grin telling me he didn't give a shit that he was starting to make me itchy with all the cutesy caring shit. "I'm okay."

"I didn't say you weren't; you just assumed it," he joked, the curl to his lips shifting from shameless to cocky. "We all know what they say about assuming."

"Fuck off, assassin. What else are you here for other than to pester me?" Even though I was growing itchy at his persistent probing, I couldn't stop the laugh that bubbled out of me. Chase, more so than my other men, was the one who knew when and where to push me regardless of what I said or did. Always had and probably always would, not that I truly minded it.

Not that I'd tell the smug dipshit that. Ciar and him would never let me live that down.

"Wanted to see if you wanted to train with me. You know, get all hot and bothered and worked up," he proposed, his silver gaze becoming a pool of molten metal as he talked.

Fighting with two of my most well-matched men?

Fuck yes.

Ciar

Kiera's eyes sparked, her body moving almost immediately around the table and over to the practice mats. Chase's giddiness was nearly contagious, but I still stayed back and watched. My time for fighting would come, and I would wait until then, knowing it wouldn't be long.

"So, anything in particular you want to use?" she asked. As she gestured to the wall of practice weapons, we slipped off our jacket, weapons, and boots before stepping onto the mat.

"Nope, I figured some good old sparring would be good enough."

Before Dove could respond, Chase was moving. One hand went to grab her shirt, while the other struck out toward her stomach, both moves she countered with expert precision. I watched with rapt attention from the recesses of our shared mind, tracking and countering her movements as if I were the one fighting. If or when Chase pulled his control back, I needed to be able to seamlessly slip into what we were doing. If we didn't... well, that was a good way to get your ass handed to you. Years in the dirty, vicious ring had taught us that. Kicking out, Kiera tried to take out our leg, but we were ready. We moved in, closing down the option for her to use her arms or legs. Wrapping her up, we grabbed hold and wrestled her flailing limbs.

"Give it up, Kittycat," Chase taunted in a whisper, "we got you."

"Ha, like hell," she protested, her breathing shifting to sharp pants as she fought. No matter what she did, she wasn't able to loosen the hold until she went completely limp. The grasp lessened just enough for her to hit the ground running—literally. "Told you, my little assassin."

"Maybe I was going easy on you?"

Dove's brow cocked, her playful stance transforming to hard and ready. This next round wouldn't be nearly as fun or soft, but we were prepared. When Chase moved this time, Kiera kept ahead of every move. Each strike, block, and glance of her fiery gaze had my blood pumping and my cock hardening. Chase gave me a nudge against the separation in our mind, a warning that he'd be pulling back, so I readied myself.

The transition was seamless, Chase's manic smile falling into my cold grin. Kiera's lip quirked up in a mirroring expression, but what she did next took me by surprise. Falling to the ground, she did a somersault across the mat. I reached out, but instead of grabbing hold of her like I had attempted, a flash of steel appeared in the corner of my gaze.

"My dove's a little cheater," I hissed, a cruel smile curling my lips as she shrugged, the blade cutting into my skin where she held the knife to my throat. Not that I truly cared about her cheating, she needed to be ready for anything at all times, and a sense of pride swirled knowing she was willing to do what it took to win. The more we stared at each other, the more my cock started to strain against the confines of my pants at the ferocity in her gaze. The pinprick of pain against my throat only made my blood heat faster.

"Life's not fair and neither am I," she spouted after a moment of eyeing one another. We were at a stalemate. I could move and risk being cut. She was balanced precariously in her stance, so it wouldn't take much to knock her off balance. Neither of us had a totally clean win.

One of these days, I'll best her in our sparring.

Kiera

A ding sounded in the silence, mixing with our harsh breathing, the noise catching both mine and Ciar's attention. With the noise, our previous tension had dissipated. Reaching up, I popped my back and stretched the sore muscles that were slowly tightening from our workout. I swiped my forearm across my brow, wiping away the sweat that had started to drip into my eyes as I walked over to the computer.

"What is it, Dove?" Ciar asked, his words mumbled as he quickly secured his holsters across his torso. "New job?"

"Looks like it," I muttered, flopping into the office chair and clicking on the message. "Looks like an information gig..." I trailed off when I read the rest of the details.

"On? I don't like it when you pause, Dove," Ciar murmured, his harsh voice gradually coming closer as he walked over. As soon as he reached where I was seated, he folded over me to look at the screen, his hand braced on the desk. My brow cocked at his hard-set jaw and narrowed eyes.

"Quite protective lately, aren't we?" I prodded, rubbing my thumb over his jaw as I maneuvered him to look at me. Ever since we'd started to go after Frankie in earnest, Ciar had slowly started appearing more frequently. Which at the time wasn't too odd since we were going up against my bastard father and his crew, but since then, Chase and Ciar's rotation was continuing to grow more frequent. "Any particular reason why?"

"Well, you were kidnapped on multiple occasions by your stalker, captured by your father, and nearly killed more times than I really want to count," he rattled off, his gray gaze sharpening with each word. My brow only rose higher at his possessive tone, part of me surprised by his appearances and protective streak, while the other portion was happy to know he actually cared about me as much as I did for him.

Not that you'd see me complaining about their switching, I love my cold-hearted killer just as much as my little assassin.

"I think it's safe to say you're a magnet for trouble, and I'm not going to let anything happen to you."

"Aww," I cooed, pinching his cheek obnoxiously. "I love when you're all possessive, Ciar."

"Good. Now, what are you going to do about this job?" he redirected, grabbing hold of my hand and kissing my knuckles. "You going to take it?"

"It's not like it would be hard. We have all the information already," I told him, looking back at the computer. No, the job wouldn't be hard, but there was a small warning bell going off in my mind when I read the words on the screen.

Information on what happened to the Solace mob and Frankie 'Smokes' Casterelli.

"Hold, Chase is being impatient," Ciar huffed in irritation, his cold demeanor melting to Chase's happy-go-lucky vibe.

Chuckling, I shook my head at their back and forth banter, finding it more than a little charming even though I knew if it continued, it would grow to the point they'd be at each other's throats. *That's not something I want to deal with.*

"On one hand," Chase started, "it would be a good way to establish hold here in Reno. Putting out the word that there's a group good enough to take down the Casterelli mob would deter most from trying to come in and take over. On the other hand..."

"It'll possibly put a target on us. They'll think we're this new big and bad crew coming in, and it becomes an unspoken challenge. I also have some suspicions that it could be something else. Or I guess someone else," I murmured.

"Who? I mean, obviously we have lots of enemies, but the main ones are taken out," Chase countered, looking down at me in confusion.

"This job came in from the east coast. Specifically, near D.C.," I explained, pointing at the note attached to the message. I had splurged a shit ton of money to have that coded into my system, a steady outgoing payment to my long-term hacker business partner ByteMe, and in times like this I was thankful.

"Know who's in D.C.? Or *should* be?" I stated, remembering what they had revealed from their little boy meeting at the club the other day.

"Agent Venry," Chase muttered, picking up on what I was hinting at. "The one who's basically gone dark."

"She said she'd be back, and I think six months is a decent enough time to hope a target forgets about you."

"Ugh," Chase groaned. "Guess she found out that the files we'd sent anonymously were a bit... light on the details." Standing up, he didn't let go of my hand, but the one that had braced him against the desk moved to run through his messy hair. "So... is this really a job, or is it a set-up?"

"That's what I intend to find out, my little assassin. If ByteMe can't figure out where it's coming from, then I won't take it. It'll take a little while though." Worry flared to life as I looked at the message one more time.

I'd be damned if I didn't find out *exactly* who wanted to know about what had happened to my bastard father.

"I'll message your hacker, figure out what needs to be done to find out where this is coming in. You, Kittycat, go relax. I know you've been down here working your pretty little ass off all damned day with your photos." Chase's cheerful tone was laced with a hint of steel, telling me if I didn't do as he said, he would no doubt toss me over his shoulder and forcibly pry me away from the computer.

"All right, Mr. Sassy," I told him. "I'm going to go shower because I'm sweaty and gross. You stay out of trouble."

"Now you're sounding like Brooks, Kittycat," Chase teased.

Scrunching my nose, I made an unintelligible noise. Chase seemed to find my discomfort funny, his laughter following me up the stairs. The rest of the house was fairly empty, the others handling some MC business with Nate at the compound, so I wasn't surprised by the quiet.

When I reached the room, I quickly stripped out of my sweaty clothes and tossed them into the hamper on my way to the bathroom. Cranking the shower handle to the red, I waited for the water to heat. Thankfully, it didn't take long, still giving me enough time to comb out the knots that had been created during mine, Chase's, and Ciar's training session.

As I brushed through the tangles, I eyed my long bob-length hair. I had chopped it to my shoulders one day in Europe after a particularly rough night filled with booze and lots of tears. *I mean... isn't it tradition to color or cut your hair after a breakup?* But even after six months of being back and now engaged, I had chosen to keep my hair short. It was easier to maintain, though some days I missed being able to braid it and toss it over my shoulder or tuck it into my jacket during jobs.

As for the rest of me, I noted, setting the brush down on the counter, I was the same. Tanner than when I had returned, thanks to the desert sun, with a few more tattoos in the small sections of skin I had un-marked. *Hm, maybe I should get another tattoo on the other side of my neck,* I wondered to myself as I stepped into the shower.

"Kiera," Stone's deep voice called out as soon as I was under the streams of water, my thoughts now forgotten when his face appeared in the crack of the door. "Do you have any plans after this?"

"Nope," I replied, lathering up my hair with my berry scented shampoo. "Why?"

"Good. Meet me down out front when you're done and dressed," he commanded, leaving before I could ask him again.

Rude. Rolling my eyes, I went through my shower routine quickly, my curiosity piqued.

One of these days, I'll figure him out, but today is clearly not that day.

Stone

"Meeting out front, huh? What're you two going to do?" Chase's voice came out of nowhere, the assassin stepping into the kitchen silently.

"Nothing, just wanting to spend some time with Kiera since the three of you tend to hog her," I challenged, glaring at him over my shoulder.

"Four, technically," he corrected, tapping the side of his head. I didn't dignify him with an answer as I pulled my leather jacket on. "So, where are you two headed?"

"You aren't going to let this go, are you?" I huffed.

"When do I ever let things go, Stone?" His smile was cocky as I glared, and I ended up sighing, knowing he would stand there and pester me until I finally told him what I had planned.

"Just going to go for a ride, that's all," I told him, adjusting my jacket until it sat properly. He hummed skeptically, and I could feel his eyes on me as I grabbed my keys and sunglasses.

"Does this have to do with your mood the last few days?" Chase's question was quiet, no judgement coloring his words.

"Why would it?" I tried to counter, but when I glanced over, I knew he could see right through my stoic mask.

"Stone, you can pretend all you want, but you're not the only one in this family that's dealt with some shit," he started. This time it wasn't his normal effervescent tone, but having learned the difference between Chase's voice and Ciar's, I knew I was still talking to the former. "I used to be a fighter, you know. Trained hard, knowing if I didn't, it could be a matter of life and death... or at the very least a fucking ass whooping."

I didn't say anything as he talked, figuring if I interrupted, he would probably clam up, and I didn't want him to. Try as I might to keep my curiosity on a leash, I couldn't lie to myself and say I wasn't intrigued about how Chase—and Ciar—became Skill Shot.

"Even in the ring, there was a sense of bond between the fighters under the same front man. You'd think in shit like that it'd be every man for himself, that any of the boss' other fighters were an enemy, but it wasn't. Well, usually, mind you. But if we did better, even though it was individually, the ringmaster made more, and it was easier for all of us. It became this odd and fucked up bond. Hell, I'm still friends with a couple of the other fighters, one who's making some big waves all on his own..." He rattled on, trailing off before waving his hands animatedly. "Anyway, what I mean by all this nonsense is you're not alone in feeling out of place... like your life got ripped from where you were headed and chucked into the deep abyss of 'what the fuck is this.'"

I stood speechless. Somehow, he had pegged everything I had been feeling the last few days. Over the last six months together I had felt disconnected from Chase and Ciar. I had never connected. We'd talked, lived, and just genuinely existed together, but that was all because of Kiera. She was our central point, yet here he was, seemingly able to see right through me.

Damn, he's way more observant than I give him credit for.

"Uh, yeah..." I paused, stumbling over what to say. "It's definitely been something that's been on my mind lately. It happens every year on the Fourth, not much I can do about it. I have the club and Kiera. I have a life that makes me happy, and it's way better than the one I had when I was in the military."

Chase didn't say anything, nodding with a knowing smile. There was no more pushing on specifics, only a metaphorical olive branch between us, and even though he was still odd, a practical stranger, something had broken down between us. A wall or barrier, whatever it was, I wasn't sure, but in that moment we felt like an 'us' instead of an 'Aces versus them.'

Yes, probably should have dealt with that before getting engaged to the sexy brat and all the men that came with it, but I am now, all right?

"Well, I guess I'll be that stereotypical asshole," Chase exclaimed, grabbing a beer from the fridge as he talked. "If you need me, I'm here." He shuddered, his lips twisting into a frown. "Didn't expect offering help like that to feel so... odd. Guess that's how Kiera feels about the whole 'normal.'"

"I'll keep it in mind, but don't expect a sharing circle anytime soon, Chase," I told him, chuckling at his discomfort. At least it wasn't just me.

"Have fun on your ride. I know she'll enjoy it." With that, he popped the top on his beer and started toward the living room before switching on one of his usual cooking shows. Taking a deep breath, I headed for the garage to pull my bike out, only one thought swirling in my head.

I hope she does.

Kiera

Darting down the stairs, I kept my eyes peeled for Stone, curiosity brimming at his cryptic request. When I reached the main level I didn't see him, so I headed to the front door, following his instructions.

For the first time ever, yes.

Shocking, isn't it?

Yanking open one of the two heavy front doors, I came face to face with Stone on his bike. My brow cocked, head tilting as I tried to figure out exactly what we were doing. When he noticed I wasn't getting on the bike, he patted the seat, but even then I didn't get on it, wanting to know what the jerkface had planned.

"Jesus, Kiera, we're just going to go for a ride. Get on the damned bike, Brat," he bit out, his voice raised to be heard over the idle of the Harley. Struggling to keep the grin that twitched my lips contained, I strode closer and swung my leg over the back of his bike and got settled.

"Don't lie, you know you love me and my stubborn ass," I countered before he could start driving, enjoying teasing him. He gave me a half glare over his shoulder, but when I expected him to turn forward and go, he looped an arm around my shoulders and pulled me in tight for a kiss, his fingers curling into my hair to hold me against him.

"Damn right, I do. Otherwise, there wouldn't be a rock on that finger of yours," he murmured, his lips brushing against mine with each word. "Now, are you done being a brat?"

"Mhm," I mumbled, my thoughts a jumbled mess from his kiss and sexy smile.

"Good." With that, he turned around and started forward.

Wrapping my arms around his waist, I held on to him, leaning into his muscled back. His jacket was soft and warm, the soothing smell of leather filling my nose as he pulled out of the drive and onto the road.

I didn't know where we were going or if he even had any place in mind, but I let myself relax and enjoy the wind in my hair. This was truly the first time Stone and I had gone out just the two of us, typically choosing to do stuff with the guys or stay at the house. So riding through the desert with him was different, but I definitely found myself loving it. As much as I was enjoying it, there was a sliver of me questioning, why now? That was when it hit me.

Stone might not really *talk* about what he was dealing with, choosing to show and not tell that he wanted some semblance of connection. A sense of bond between us that didn't require much talking, and to be honest, I had to admit I felt the same most days. I hugged him tighter, placing a soft kiss on his back, and tried to help him realize that I understood and that I was here.

After a little while driving through the desert, we neared a large rock formation. Stone pulled off the road and put the kickstand down. When he gestured for me to hop off, I kept my curiosity to myself, excited to see what he had in store.

Shutting the bike off, Stone followed suit before starting toward the rocks. The formation was flat on top, but the surrounding portions were angled enough for us to walk up. I tried so hard to keep my mouth closed, but when we got to the edge of the red rock, I couldn't help myself.

"You're not going to shove me off the side of this, are you?" I teased, flashing Stone a smartass grin.

"Ha," he deadpanned, sinking to the ground. "No. Now, come here, Brat." Stone patted the ground next to him.

"What are we doing?" I asked, finally growing too curious to stay quiet.

"Watching the sunset. The others get you all to themselves way more often than I do," he explained. "So I finally just decided I'd take you instead so Chase, Brooks, and Garrett couldn't butt in."

"Aww, is Grave a bit jealous?" I cooed, leaning into his muscled torso and pressing a kiss to his stubbled cheek.

"Shut up," he grumbled. "Besides... after the Fourth of July party I was feeling a bit... off still. More so than normal so I wanted to go for a ride and clear my head."

"And you wanted to share that with me?" I murmured; no taunts or teasing colored my question this time. My surprise grew when he nodded, shocked that Stone had actually admitted it. "Thank you, Jerkface."

With my nickname for him, Stone burst out laughing, wrapping an arm around my shoulder and kissing me fiercely. After that, neither of us talked, our attention shifting to the sun that had started to set. One thought permeated my mind louder than any other as I watched the shifting colors in the sky.

Regardless of whatever life wants to throw at us, we'll have each other... and in a world of snakes and wolves in sheep's clothing? That's better than any weapon.

Chapter 6

July 13th
Tuesday Midday

Kiera

My eyes were crossing after four straight days of scanning and cataloging information from Frankie's files. I was supposed to hear back from ByteMe in the next day or two about where the job had come from, so I figured I should start sorting just in case. *Only issue with that? Holy hell in a handbasket, there are a lot of files to go through.* The ache in my hand grew as I scribbled yet another name down to my ever-growing list of things to check out and investigate. Several of them I recognized, while others were new. I jotted a small asterisk near the new ones, and anyone who would be top priority on my 'dig around in their business until I've determined if they're good' list got a star.

"Why are you on there..." I trailed off when I found a *very* familiar name. "What the fuck is the Deputy Director of the FBI's name doing on one of your files, Frankie?"

Why I asked a dead man rotting in hell that question, I had no idea, but logic told me that it was either a person he had put a target on or someone in his pocket. Either way, the Deputy Director got two stars and moved to the top of my list to look into before I continued on. It wasn't until another ten minutes later that I stumbled across something else interesting my internal logic didn't have an answer for. A single encrypted file buried amongst a bunch of random notes and photographs, the name at the end of the line making my eyes narrow.

Michael Landon to investigate. Possible connection to Catherine Costa.

What does my mother have to do with this? I thought. *She's been long gone for almost two decades. What could she possibly have had that would be of any use to Frankie?*

A little hint of worry settled into my stomach at the file's title, but the encryptions on it would require skills I didn't possess. So I sat there and stewed about the fact that it was taunting me and I couldn't access it. *Fucking shit,* I realized after another few moments of glaring at the screen in my bout of irrational irritation, *I need a fucking break.*

Tossing the notepad and pen onto the desk in a discarded heap, I shoved away from the computer and started toward the stairs. *A relaxing afternoon away from my bastard father's files should do me good.* Jogging up the stairs to the main level and then up to the master bedroom, I stripped and changed quickly into a bikini, and before much longer, I was stepping out to the sunny poolside.

The cement was hot against the soles of my feet, but the sun beating down on me was a welcome relief as I lay out on the lounge chair. A few moments later, I heard the roaring and rev of the bike engines pulling into the drive, and my lip couldn't help but curl.

My boys are back.

Garrett

The rumble of my bike was a comfort, the buzz ceasing as soon as I pulled up into the drive and then the garage. It felt good to be home and in the last year, the house Chase had built had become that, more so than the compound. Stone, Brooks, and I hopped off our bikes and headed inside, the others heading to their rooms for a long nap, but as I walked across the kitchen, I found something more enticing than a shower.

My kitten laying out in the skimpiest of bathing suits.

I waved the other two off, moving toward the back door instead. It was stifling hot out back now that the breeze wasn't blowing over my face like it had been on my bike, but I shoved that discomfort aside.

"Kitten," I murmured, bending over as soon as I reached her, grabbing her jaw and capturing her lips.

"Hey." Her voice was quiet and thick as she looked up at me from under her lashes. "Glad to see you home in one piece."

"Good." The more I looked at her in her deep emerald bikini, the more my blood started to pound.

"How are you not dying right now in your ride gear?" she questioned, her face scrunching up adorably as she glanced at my jeans, cut, and long-sleeved shirt.

"I am," I explained simply.

"So... why aren't you changing?"

At my smirk, her mossy eyes narrowed suspiciously. Stepping back, I shucked my cut off my torso and quickly untied my boots, readying myself for what I was about to do. Kiera had propped up on her elbows to watch me, hesitation blatantly painted in her expression. But she didn't kick or give me a sassy response when I strode over, at least not until I scooped her up onto my shoulder.

"Garrett!" she screamed. "Put me down! Why do people keep doing this to me!?" I didn't say anything as I walked.

Straight into the pool.

The water crashing over us was refreshing, the opposite of Kiera's loud screaming as we went under. As soon as we were submerged, I tugged her off my shoulder, guiding her to wrap her muscled legs around me. Breaking through the surface of the water, I whipped my head back, forcing my hair out of my eyes so I could look at Kiera's fiery glare.

"You are a fucking asshole," she bit out, but she didn't release me, her luscious curves pressing into me in delicious torture.

I had missed her, and I wanted her. If I have anything to say about it, I'll get her sweet pussy right here, right now.

Grinning, I grabbed hold of her ass in a firm grip, rocking my hips against her. The angry frown melted away in a soft moan, only making the need pulsing through me ignite. My quickly hardening cock pressed into her core, and I knew if—when—I slipped my fingers under her suit, it would be slick from her arousal.

Kiera's fingers tangled in my hair, holding tight to the wet tresses as I continued to work her up. Closing the distance between us, she captured me in a string of passionate kisses. The sun beating down on us was hot in a wonderful contrast to the cool pool that splashed around us as we devoured each other.

Slipping my hand from where I held her ass to between her thighs, I traced the edge of her bikini. Her moans deepened the more I teased, each pass of my fingers slipping closer to her core. It took everything within me not to shove my jeans down and rip her bottoms off, but I held back, wanting to enjoy her in my arms.

I'll have her soon enough.

Kiera

Even in the chilly water of the pool I felt as if I was about to burn from the inside out. Garrett's scruff was rough against my cheek and jaw as he trailed kisses to nibble on my earlobe, his fingers finally reaching my aching pussy. Until he paused, and I felt a smirk appear on his lips when I whimpered.

"Please," I whined quietly, wiggling my hips in a silent urge to keep going. A soft chuckle filled my ear, but Garrett obliged, and when he slipped a finger into me, my eyes rolled back.

A ripple of pleasure worked its way through me, goosebumps spreading across my skin as I shivered. His pace was leisurely, unhurried as he rocked another finger into me and sent me higher. Sharp nips and soft sucking trailed over my skin, adding to the fire that continued to blaze through me.

"That's it, Kitten," Garrett murmured, his husky tone shooting another wave of desire through me, taking me closer to the edge. As he continued to pump his fingers, quickening his pace, the calloused pad of his thumb circled over my clit. "Come for me."

At his simple command, my body responded. Shattering in his arms, I fell into the bliss of release but before I could come down fully, Garrett started to strip out of his jeans and boxers. When he chucked them out of the pool, I let go of his broad shoulders and started floating away from him. A smirk curled my lips at his resulting glare.

"If you want me, then you have to come get me," I taunted, swimming gracefully toward the deep end of the pool. I swam backward slowly, putting enough effort into the movement that I could make him chase me a little, while still keeping my eyes locked on him. Amidst the splashes of the water around me, a deep growl sounded, Garrett's emerald eyes blazing at the challenge. Yanking off his shirt, he threw it to join the other pieces of clothing off the side of the pool and started swimming toward me.

There was no real fight from me, choosing to float as he came closer, but his sparkling gaze told me that I was about to get fucked exactly how I wanted. Circling his arms around my waist, Garrett pulled me back down until my legs were wrapped around his trim hips once more. As he neared the edge of the pool, his nimble fingers quickly untied the strings holding the pieces of my bikini together. Before they could sink to the bottom, I snatched them up and threw them onto Garrett's clothes.

"Mmm, much better," he murmured, hands roving over my thighs and ass. A gasp left me as he pressed me against the rough stucco of the pool and thrust into me until he was bottomed out in my quivering pussy, giving no warning or time to let me adjust.

"Sweet fucking hell," I moaned. The bars of his Jacob's ladder piercing added an extra level of pleasure to each rock of his hips. Clutching tightly to his chest, I let Garrett take control.

My orgasm built slowly this time, the tingles winding their way through my lower back to my core. Each breath became a pant, a whimper, or moan every time he slammed home. I felt as if I was floating yet somehow drowning among the tantalizing desire that flooded me.

His hand shifted, one still holding me in place as he plunged in a hard, forceful rhythm while the other teased the curve of my ass. His rough fingertips circled the tight ring of muscles, my lip tucking between my teeth as I waited in excitement for him to keep going. After a few more massaging swirls, one tip slipped in. The ruthless pace of his fucking was a delicious contrast to the gentleness of his fingers.

As soon as one finger was worked in, the building tingles became almost too much to handle, and I exploded. Stars burst in front of my eyes, my body

139

shuddering in his arms. I had no clue what fell from my lips. In that moment, there was only Garrett and the feeling of his continued thrusts.

"Fuck," I cried when another burst of fire erupted, the impending orgasm approaching with lightning speed. Now, his fingers moved fast and rough as he fucked me. He was close, his body trembling against me, and when he came, he roared, the gruff sound mixing with my fervent cries. Both of us rode through wave after wave of release, clutching each other as if our lives depended on it.

"Perfect coming home present," Garrett teased, his lips brushing against the flushed skin of my neck. He started toward the edge of the pool, staying buried within me as he did so.

"Mmm, I would have to agree," I said with a contented sigh, reveling in the water as it washed over us. When we reached the edge of the pool, Garrett gave me a final kiss and slipped out so we could climb out of the pool.

Satiated and sore, I quickly dressed and laid out on my original lounge chair as Garrett slipped on his soaking wet boxers. Grabbing the edge of a lounge chair nearby, he slid it across the hot cement until it was right next to mine. He laid down, grabbing hold of my hand in the process. We didn't talk for a while, enjoying the heat and rays of the sun as it dried the water that coated our skin, Garrett's thumb brushing my wrist rhythmically as time passed.

"I forgive you for dropping me in the pool," I told him finally, knowing I hadn't truly been angry to begin with.

"Yeah, I know," he smarted with a smirk. "You can't truly stay mad at me, and when you do, it turns into sex." I huffed, my lips thinning at his prodding. "Am I wrong?"

"...No," I muttered, sulking in my lounge chair at being called out. "Though you can't say you don't love it, asshole."

"I didn't say that. In fact, I *absolutely* love it. And you." With that, he leaned over, tugging me closer until he could press his lips to mine. It was a chaste, gentle kiss compared to our passionate ones from only a little while earlier, but no less enticing.

"Yeah, yeah, I love you too," I sassed with a grin, making him laugh. As he lay back and I got situated again, he lifted my left hand, his eyes looking over the ring they had given me. I could see the pure happiness in his emerald irises, and warmth blossomed in my chest.

"So, what do you want to do for your wedding, Kitten? I'm going to go with not the white dress, tuxedo, typical gig," he asked, looking at me.

"Says who? Maybe I want to feel like a fairytale princess for a day," I countered, but I couldn't make it through the whole sentence without a laugh erupting. "Ugh, no. I can see the appeal of that, but I don't think I'd be comfortable flouncing around in a big ballgown or anything. Honestly... I don't know. I never thought I'd ever make it this far." The words were quiet, barely audible even in the near silence of the backyard. It wasn't something I talked about very often, but now that my father was dead and I had a family of my own as well as a future to look forward to... I had no idea what to do with it.

What do normal people do?

Ew, shudder, not normal. Pretend I didn't ask that, people.

"Well, we can figure it out together. If you want something quick as hell with only the compound, Elliot, and any other random criminals I know you associate with, we can do that. If you want just us, we'll make it happen. Kitten, this is about what you want. You're our girl, and that's all that matters to us," he explained.

I felt fuzzy and warm, though slightly itchy, hearing such sweet words from my asshole stepbrother, but I knew there was a sliver of me buried very deep that loved it. *Very deep, keywords there.* So, we lay there quietly as I flitted through different ideas.

The thing that came to mind? This was the desert, so whatever anyone wore needed to breathe, and I let my mind dream up a few dress ideas. Shorter would be nice but having a flowy portion that went to the ground would also be fun, especially if it was a bit more see-through to showcase my tattoos and the short hem of the main dress. *A dress, you might ask? Yes, because if it's my wedding day, you best believe I want to get fucked in and out of my dress, and you can't do that with a jumpsuit, now can you?* Then again, a long skirt wasn't the most practical, so it would have to be removable. Especially in the case if anything dangerous decided to happen, because with us being us? It was always a tossup. The guys we could figure out together, but of course the bikes and compound would be involved. Whatever we decided on, I knew it'd be great.

A ding sounded, my phone buzzing in a few staccato bursts on the table. Snatching it up, I unlocked it and scanned the text quickly.

E: Upcoming bid, very hush hush. Obsidian Auction House. Something a bit more... explosive is coming.

At first, I wasn't sure what to make of it since black market auctions were Obsidian's specialty. Hell, they were the crew that I stole from on the job that made me famous, but after reading the text a few times, my internal warning bells started to ring. Elliot wouldn't tell me about an auction unless it was something big. Opening my mouth to relay what had come in, I was cut off by Brooks practically running out to the back patio.

"There's someone here for you, Kiera," he stated. With the use of my real name instead of 'baby,' I knew it was serious, the lead weight in my stomach growing as I sat up and fully looked him over.

"Who is it?" I questioned, getting up from my spot and tossing a discarded sarong over my swimsuit. Garrett followed, all the softness he had shown nowhere to be found as he looked to his president. Brooks's icy gaze was worried, his jaw tensing rhythmically as he watched me step forward.

Whoever it was, it wasn't going to be good.

"Agent Venry," he told me, "and she says she needs your help."

Fuck.

The End... For Now

* * *

Begin Kiera's story in The Aces series.

Troublemaker

Continue Kiera's second trilogy in The Cat's Crew series coming early 2021.

* * *

Information on books, upcoming releases, and A.J.'s newsletter can be found here
www.authorajmacy.com

About A.J. Macey

A.J. Macey has a B.S. in Criminology and Criminal Justice, and previous coursework in Forensic Science, Behavioral Psychology, and Cybersecurity. Before becoming an author, A.J. worked as a Correctional Officer in a jail where she met her husband. She has a daughter and two cats named Thor and Loki, an addiction to coffee and swearing. Sucks at adulting and talking to people, so she'll frequently be lost in a book or running away with her imagination.

Read More from A.J. Macey

www.authorajmacey.com

Get to know more about N.K. by:

Website: *www.nkstackhouse.com*

BEAUTY OF LUST

Lies and Loves Prequel

Suki Williams

Author Note

Beauty of Lust is a prequel short story in the Lies and Loves Trilogy. Please note this prequel is a gay romance, but Lies and Loves is a Reverse Harem series. This 20k short story is just a snippet of Wulfric and Robin and is a HFN story.

Beauty of Lust is a mafia romance, which means it contains guns, torture, and violence. If you don't like MM/gay romance, implied sharing, and light BDSM then this isn't the story for you.

CHAPTER 1

Robin

"Are you here alone?" a deep voice whispered in my ear as the cold beer slid down my throat. I took my time before glancing to the side to face the speaker who settled himself onto the stool beside me at the bar. The air was smoky from his cigarette, but I caught a glimpse of amber eyes watching me with a hooded look. He wasn't someone who could be described as classically handsome, but he was arresting and intense, which kept your attention.

"I am." I lifted an eyebrow at him in question.

I could see the spark in his eyes as his lips twitched with a barely repressed smile. "Good. I'd hate to have to fight anyone off for this seat."

"Mighty bold of you to think I even want you here," I pointed out, intrigued by his forwardness. Waiting for his response I drank more of my Murphy's Irish Stout.

The man took a drag of his cigarette before putting it out in the ashtray beside him. Leaning toward me, I could smell the tobacco and the faint scent of liquor on his breath, but his eyes were clear and heated as he smirked at me.

"Since you took the time to check me out before answering my question, I think it's safe to say you don't mind me here."

"You don't even know me." I licked my lips, not bothering to pull away from him invading my space. I had a hard time acting like I didn't know who this man was, but damn I loved being the center of his attention.

"We could change that." He settled back in his seat and I took in the lean body I could make out under his button-up shirt and black slacks. The clothes were simple but of high quality, even I could tell that.

I mulled over his invitation and thought of the black jeans and band shirt I was wearing, a stark contrast to his tailored look. "Why me? There are plenty of other people here that seem more... your type."

He tilted his head at that and seemed to think that over. "You don't even know my type. But I happen to know for a fact—" Before he could continue speaking his phone rang. The sharp teasing expression faded from his face as he looked at the screen. "I need to take this. If you're still here in this seat waiting for me when I get back inside, I'm taking it that you're interested."

I didn't manage to say anything before he was out of his seat and sauntering through the door. Not sure what to think, I gulped down the rest of my beer. I turned to flag down the bartender for another drink only to find him in front of me with a serious expression.

"What are you doing?" His voice was harsh as he stared me down.

"I'm drinking." I put my empty bottle down in front of him. "Or I was. Can I have another?"

"Do you—"

"Yes, in fact, I do need that second beer, Anthony. Thank you."

"He's a Ricci—"

A dismissive wave of my hand cut his warning short, and I ignored the scathing glare he sent my way in response. *It's so funny he thinks that would scare me off.*

"It's your funeral, Robin."

I took the second bottle he handed me before he stalked to the other end of the bar. Just as I turned in my seat I found Wulfric walking back in. He beelined straight for me and I held up my new drink. He focused on the beer bottle before his eyes flicked to mine as he came to stand next to me.

"Did you get that to avoid leaving with me?"

"Not everything is about you, Alfonsi. It's been a long fucking day."

He considered me before slowly sitting in his seat again. "You know who I am."

I took a deliberate sip. "I do. Just like you know who I am."

Waiting to see if he would contradict the statement, I watched him. Each of us weighed the other before Wulfric gave me a wicked smile.

"Does this mean you aren't leaving with me?"

"Will I be alive tomorrow if I do?" My dick twitched as Wulfric leaned forward enough to almost brush his lips against my ear.

"I can keep you on the edge for quite a while, Robin. But a whole day is a bit much to ask for." I barely bit back a groan at the promise in those words, shifting in my seat slightly trying to adjust myself. Of course, he didn't miss the movement. "I think you like that idea. Of course, if we need to try to kill each other first, for appearances' sake, I'm always up for a challenge."

He nipped my ear sharply before rising and heading outside. No jacket for the cool fall air, just the heat of the next cigarette I saw him pulling out before the door swung closed. Tossing back the rest of my drink I threw cash onto the bartop and turned to follow, but before I could get far Anthony was back.

"Robin—"

I swung around to face him with a stony look that instantly had him shutting up. "It would be inconvenient if tonight's video footage was still here in the morning."

"I-I'll take care of it."

"I know," I told him coldly. "Keep the change."

Chapter 2

Wulfric

Putting out my cigarette on the bottom of my shoe, I didn't bother to look up as the door to the bar opened and brought with it a rush of warm air. Black shoes came to a stop at the corner of my vision making me smile.

"Are we throwing around a few punches? If so, I'd like to request not my face; I do have an important dinner to attend tomorrow."

A huff of laughter met my statement before a fist hit me squarely on the jaw. My head jerked around at the force of it and I thumbed the blood on my split lip. Looking up to meet his dark brown gaze I gave him a sinister smile. "So it's going to be like that."

Not waiting for him to reply I swung right back, fist barreling into his stomach. I enjoyed the whoosh of air that knocked out of him for a moment, but then the fight started in earnest. Fists flew through the air, each swing met with a sickening crunch and cursing. We continued until we came to a standstill, both of us trying to catch our breath as we took the measure of the other in the darkened alley our fight had moved us into.

"I can't believe you punched me in the face." I rubbed my already swelling jaw.

"Of course I did." He gave me a wheezing laugh, holding his ribs as he did so. "If you would just fully—"

"We've talked about this," I reminded him softly. "It's not the right time yet."

"You work for the O'Callaghans, Wulfric. People are going to find out. Especially given what you do for us."

I looked up at the man across from me. Short dark hair and serious eyes stared at me, waiting for a reaction to my statement. His black jeans fit him tightly and the Grateful Dead shirt seemed almost out of place if you didn't know him.

Robin Healy was a man full of contradictions. Working for the Irish

154

mafia, yet probably one of the most caring people I'd ever met. He could sing any song when it came on the radio, even if he hated it, but didn't like concerts. The biggest thing that piqued my interest though, he was probably one of the deadliest people I'd ever met, but rarely did he let that part of himself out to play. *More fun for me then.*

But when I didn't have a response right away, Robin straightened up slowly and started toward the road. I didn't let him get far. Striding over I grabbed his shoulder and spun him around to face me as I backed him up against the brick wall. He watched me defiantly as I pushed my body against his, fingers gripping his hair and pulling his face up.

"You push and push, Robin," I snarled, before biting down hard on his exposed throat. His body jerked but I tightened my hand in his hair to keep him from trying to push me off. Releasing his throat I softly licked the spot where I had left my mark, and chuckled at his barely stifled groan at the touch of my tongue.

"If I didn't push you we wouldn't even be here right now." His voice was soft, but the words brought me to a halt. Putting a small space between us I searched his face, I started to open my mouth but he gave a slight shake of his head. "Not here."

"Not here," I agreed slowly, as I loosened my hold on his hair and stepped back. "But later. There's something I need to take care of before I get home. I'll see you there?"

I waited until he gave the barest of nods in confirmation before turning and starting to walk out to the street.

"Wulfric!" I looked back at his deep voice calling out to me. His face was oh so carefully composed. "Be careful."

I lifted a hand in acknowledgment and farewell. Then joined the throngs of people lost in their thoughts as they moved along to their destinations. It was going to be an interesting meeting with these bruises, but the memory of Robin's body against mine had me grinning, then wincing since the movement pulled at my split lip. Tonight was going to be fun it seemed.

CHAPTER 3

Robin

The apartment was silent as I walked into the waiting darkness. *Too quiet.* Acting as if nothing was out of the ordinary, I threw my keys onto the kitchen counter and walked through the living room to settle onto my armchair, facing the dark shape sitting on my sofa. I steepled my fingers in front of my face as I considered them, but when they didn't move, I decided to break the silence.

"I admire the gall you have to break into my home, but I don't take kindly to trespassers, so why don't we just get this over with? I've had a long day and I would love to just relax."

A dark chuckle was their answer before a click and light filled the room. I blinked to find a man I'd never seen before considering me with an almost shocked expression. He had short brown hair that was buzzed and looked pretty clean cut with his cheap suit and tie as he stared at me wide-eyed.

"You look surprised to see me, though you're the one who broke into *my* apartment." I tilted my head slightly when he still didn't say anything. "Do you maybe have the wrong apartment?"

He shook his head jerkily, before taking a shaky breath. "No, no. This is the right apartment. I followed him here."

"You followed who here? You need to start making a lot more sense before I start asking my questions more aggressively. Who are you and what are you doing here?"

The man swallowed loudly before he seemed to steel himself. "Wulfric. I followed Wulfric here."

"That doesn't answer my questions," I told him as I removed my gun from my holster and aimed it at him. "I suggest you hurry up and get to them."

"I'm Henrik. Wulfric's brother."

The news made me go completely still, I wasn't even sure if I remembered how to breathe for a few beats until I slowly lowered the gun.

156

"That doesn't tell me what you're doing in my apartment."

"He stays here. With you," he spat out like it was an accusation. "Like I said, I followed him after our last family dinner. He was distant all evening." I wasn't sure what to say to that since this was the first time I'd heard anything about a brother or even family dinners. "You need to stay away from Wulfric. He doesn't need to get mixed up with your kind."

"My kind?" I laughed roughly. "Oh sweetheart, if you only knew. He is going to be back in a few hours. I would recommend not being here when that happens."

"Why would he lower himself to fuck an Irish?" the man sneered.

Before my brain could catch up to my actions, I was on top of him on the sofa, my hand wrapped around his throat. I watched distantly as he sputtered, fingers scrambling to pry my grip away from his neck.

"I'll say this only once, so listen to me. If you think I care about his Italian last name or that he cares about my Irish one, then you don't know the first thing about either of us, brother or not. I can tell you like to start things, just like your brother, but rest assured I am *very* good at ending them."

"Wulfric will hate you if you kill me," he managed to get out.

"I don't think you know your brother as well as you think you do," I told him with a small smile.

"You don't even know him! He's from—"

"What is going on here?" Wulfric's bland voice cut through his brother's tirade.

I looked up to find him standing in the doorway of my apartment. I slowly let go of his brother's throat and stood to walk around to meet Wulfric. His dark eyes focused on me approaching and I gave a soft smile as I brushed a kiss along his lips.

"Your brother came for a visit." My words made him freeze against me and I pulled away to find his gaze focused behind me toward the man on my couch. "I'll leave you two to catch up."

Wulfric shifted his gaze back to me and gave me a small nod, but his bruised face was empty of emotion. I brushed my hand against his and gave him a brief smile before turning to head to my bedroom.

"It was good to meet you, Henrick." I paused at the entrance of my hallway to look over my shoulder at him. "No offense, but I hope we don't meet again."

Silence was my only answer as I calmly walked into my bedroom and shut the door behind me. I didn't hear any raised voices after the door snicked shut, though I didn't hear any gunshots either. Small favors I guess.

* * *

Wulfric

"You're such a pain in the ass, Wulfric." Henrick's voice broke the silence between us as soon as Robin was in his bedroom.

"As are you, Henrick." I walked carefully toward him, ignoring the twinge from my bruised ribs with every step. "Is there a particular reason you've stopped by?"

"I can't just come by to see my brother when I'm in town for business?" Henrick watched me closely as I sat on the couch beside him. I took in his disheveled hair and the redness of his neck, and I felt a dark smile touch my lips knowing that Robin had done that to him.

There was little love lost between us, brothers or not. Henrick hadn't been happy that I had gone freelance instead of working with the Ricci's. No matter how much our parents tried to make him an enforcer with the Ricci's, Henrick was much better as a numbers man. Though, I guess they can't complain, since last I heard he had become a trusted bookkeeper for the Family for their unscrupulous and legal dealings. The contrast wasn't lost on me as I looked him over in Robin's apartment. He was sitting there in casual clothes looking put together, as I sat there with bruises forming all over from my earlier fight with Robin.

"What's wrong? You wouldn't have come here to just drop by." Henrick gulped and flicked his eyes toward where Robin had disappeared and I let out a tired sigh. "If you're worried he is going to overhear, he's in the shower. It's been a long day. So I'll ask again, what's going on?"

His fingers tapped rhythmically on his knee, a nervous tick before he took a deep breath and focused his full attention on me. "I was sent to check on you since I was in Seattle." Before I could respond he held up a hand and gave me an unusually serious look. "I did think this was your apartment, not his. So for that I will apologize. Every time I've watched you, this is where you come."

"Well, this is where we usually sleep or do other things." I laughed briefly at the amusement that sparked in his eyes at my statement. "So I assume there is a threat also being delivered? Might as well get it over with so we can move this along."

Henrick leaned back and rubbed a hand along his throat. "I believe their exact words were 'We've heard about his Irish boy; does he think that's going to last?'"

"Says the Italian and German who got together. Well then, make sure my response is clear to them." My face hardened, and I pulled out the gun from my back and set it carefully beside me. "Blood or not, if anything happens to him, I'll hunt you all down."

Henrick's eyes didn't stray from mine, ignoring the gun I had revealed. "I hope he's worth it, Wulfric. You'll never be accepted back into the fold now." Henrick stood, and as he was walking out the door he stopped right in front of me. "I'd be very careful if I were you, Wulfric. It would really be a shame to have to deal with their crazy on my own."

A slight nod is all I gave him in answer and I waited until I heard the sound of the door closing, indicating he had left before letting my guard down all the way. Taking a deep breath and rubbing my face, I let my shoulders droop. Exhaustion ate at me as I slumped back on the couch trying to sort my thoughts. Seeing Robin choking Henrick when I walked in and then my brother's words made it obvious that my balancing act was tenuous at best. I was trying to keep my official connection with the O'Callaghans under wraps and it was taking its toll. The Segreto's had to trust the enemy in their midst.

"I take it he's gone?" Robin's deep voice interrupted my musings. I looked up and all stressful thoughts fled at the sight. Just out of the shower, he had a towel wrapped loosely around his hips, though that delicious V of his teased just along the line of the fabric. Water weighed down his dark brown hair making strands fall into his face, and I licked my lips in appreciation.

"Get over here." My voice was rough, even to my own ears.

His smile was wide as he stayed exactly where he was. "I love that look on your face."

"You're not moving."

He leaned back against the wall, a small smirk playing on his face as he held my gaze in challenge. A small twitch of his hands had his towel dropping to the floor and pooling around his feet. "Don't we need to talk about your brother showing up out of the blue?"

I growled and stood. "We can talk about him later. I'd much prefer it if you didn't discuss my brother when you're standing naked in front of me." I strode over toward him, caging him against the wall.

"Your brother isn't really my type, Wulfric. No need to be jealous," he teased lightly.

In retaliation, I pressed my body against his, loving the feel of his hard body even through my clothing. Leaning forward I trailed kisses along his neck, enjoying the groan he let out at the touch.

"You keep mentioning him," I breathed hotly against him.

"I guess you need to try harder to distract me." Robin's voice was thick.

"I've got just the thing for you then," I murmured darkly. I ghosted my lips against his before slanting them in a possessive kiss. Robin matched my pace as he slid his broad hands around my waist, gripping me tightly. Lightly, I bit into his bottom lip as his hands moved to start unfastening my pants. I let him unbutton the pants and unzip me before grabbing his hands and pinning them above his head.

Robin just shook his head at me. "Touchy, but not touchable. One day someone is going to bring you to your knees."

"Are you warning me you're going to try?" I narrowed my eyes, increasing the pressure on his wrists and slamming my lips briefly on his. "Keep your hands there."

He obeyed my warning as I let him go to quickly rip off my shirt and shove my pants down so they were out of the way.

"Wulfric," he whispered, eyes heated as he got his fill of me standing naked in front of him.

I licked my lips, but instead of kissing him like he seemed to expect I slowly lowered to my knees bringing myself face to face with his dick, precum shining on the head and making my mouth water. It wasn't often I sucked him off, but I loved the taste of him and all the delicious sounds he made for me when I did. I looked up to find his head thrown back, straining not to rush me, and it gave me an idea.

"What if we made this more interesting?" I whispered just shy of where he was aching for me.

"What—" He swallowed hard. "What do you mean?"

"Do you trust me?" I licked the underside of his cock, smiling at the whimper he couldn't hold back.

"Yes." Robin's voice was thick as molasses when he got the word out. "I trust you. What were you thinking?"

Not bothering to answer with words, I stood up and offered a hand to him. I pulled him over to the armchair in the living room and motioned for him to sit. Robin watched me for a moment before slowly sitting down. Satisfied he would be there when I got back, I walked into his bedroom and went to his closet. After a little searching I found exactly what I was looking for, A moment later I brought the surprise back to the living room I held up the ties I had found and I gave a dark chuckle as his dick twitched at the sight of them, clearly liking my idea.

He simply watched me as I proceeded to tie first one wrist to the chair, then the other. I glanced up at him in question as I held up three more ties. A soft smile was the only answer I needed before restraining his ankles to the chair and then blindfolding him.

"I think I could get used to you like this," I murmured as I sat back to admire my handywork.

Robin grinned. "I'll remember you said that the next time you try to talk me into a gag."

A bark of laughter escaped me before I gave him a brief, hard kiss. "I wouldn't be able to listen to you beg if I gagged you, Darling. And beg you will before I'm done with you."

CHAPTER 4

Robin

I couldn't see anything with the makeshift blindfold over my eyes. None of the ties were tight enough that I couldn't break free of them if I wanted, which I knew he did on purpose for me. I waited, trying to anticipate what he was going to do in the sudden hushed silence of the room.

Warm heat surrounded my dick and I tried to thrust into his mouth, but Wulfric's strong hands gripped my hips firmly, preventing the movement that would make him increase his speed. His tongue swirled around the tip, and I let out a frustrated growl as I realized he would be setting a slow, meticulous pace with his teasing. Rough hands squeezed tighter, keeping my body from trying to move as he took me deeper. The warm heat of his throat drew a moan from my lips, and I whimpered as he deepthroated me, the muscles contracting around my cock before he languidly pulled off me. I tugged at my restraints, though not enough to ruin the game, and he let out a rough laugh before he started teasing me in earnest.

Each swirl of his tongue and light scrape of his teeth dragged another desperate sound from me. Each nerve in my body became hyper-aware of Wulfric's movements as he played me like his favorite instrument. Every lick, touch, and grazing of his teeth building up an orgasm he kept just out of reach. It could have been minutes or hours later, Wulfric finally moved one of his hands to cup my balls, which pushed me over the edge he so skillfully made me dance along.

"I'm going to come." At my words, the heat was gone. *That fucking son of a bitch!* I growled at the absence of him. "What the fuck?!"

A rough chuckle met my outburst, but he didn't touch me and as I calmed down, the climax fading out of reach. "Are you going to beg for me already, Darling?"

"Fuck you," I spat out, realizing the full intention of his game.

A wet tongue licked a path from my balls to the tip of my dick. "This is going to be fun."

I groaned at the dark promise in his rough voice as he continued the most excruciating, hottest foreplay I'd ever had in my life. He used everything; mouth, hands, and teeth to bring me to that sweet, desperate edge and deny me release. Over and over again. I didn't know how long he teased and denied me, but eventually I was blinking behind the tie as sweat dripped into my eyes making them sting. As he brought me to yet another edge, I gave in.

"Wulfric, please." My voice was strained, making him pause.

"Please what?" His tone was deep and just as strained as my own.

"I want to come. Let me finish." I tried to take in a deep breath, but it stuttered as Wulfric sucked the head of my dick in his mouth hard for a few seconds, letting it pop out crudely before blowing air across it.

"That's not how you beg for me, Darling. You must not want to really come yet." Wulfric moved away from me and my heart skipped a beat. There's no way he would leave me like this... wait, of course he would.

"Wulfric," I snarled. But suddenly there was light as he yanked the tie off my eyes letting me see him, and I licked my lips at the disheveled sight of him standing in front of me. He was sweaty too, a flush of arousal colored his face and chest, and I could see the hard evidence of his desire standing out from his body.

"You see something you like?" He smirked down at me. "Just give in, Robin. I can give you exactly what you need, just give in to me."

I looked up at him, and the darkness always present in his gaze was stronger today, not even the sex making it fade into the background. Seeing him struggling, seeing that fight in the face of someone I love, broke down the walls of my restraint, my pride. Not breaking eye contact, I gave him exactly what he wanted, no *needed*, from me.

"Wulfric, please. Please, let me come."

He searched my heated gaze, considering me. "Do you want me to suck you off, Robin? You want me to suck you off or do you want me to pound into your ass?" The images of both filled my mind as I let out a whimper I couldn't hold back. Then he leaned closer, his lips brushing my ear as he whispered something completely unexpected to me. "You know what, I think I have a better idea than either of those options and you aren't really in a position to fight me on it."

I shot him a glare that had him laughing, before he turned around to get a condom and lube packet from his pants. Before I could figure out what he was doing he had ripped the foil open with his teeth. My body jumped as he rolled it on my dick and then added lube.

"What are you—"

My words were lost as he claimed my lips in a hard kiss, the taste of myself making it hotter. Straddling me, he reached back and started to lower himself on my dick. When I belatedly realized what he was doing I tried to break the kiss. *He never bottoms. Ever. Not once since we had started seeing each other.* Wulfric deepened the kiss, refusing to let me voice my questions as he worked my dick inside of him. The ease with which he lowered himself made me realize that while he was teasing me, he had been preparing himself for this. *Fuck, if only I could have seen that for myself.*

Once he had taken all of me, Wulfric broke the kiss and rested his forehead against mine. I licked my lips, relishing the taste of him on my tongue, and he watched me with those golden brown eyes, so serious and heated. I saw the unspoken order not to ask why, not now.

"Wulfric, if you don't fucking move I'll kill you when you untie me," I threatened, as he continued to sit there, not moving.

His eyes flashed before there was a sharp tug tilting my head back, and teeth bit into my neck, just this side of too much, before he started to finally move. The sting of his bite contrasted the way he rode me slowly. Holding me between pleasure and pain with no way to move, to fuck into him, it was driving me crazy. The edging earlier was nothing compared to this, trapped between heaven and hell. I loved every second of it.

Wulfric released his hold on my neck to brace his hands on my shoulders; a brief look was his only warning before he began to ride me hard. Skin slapping against skin and the musk of sex filled the room. My entire world narrowed to feeling him ride me at an ever increasing pace, him owning every part of my body, as all I could do was watch him.

His hair fell into his face, gaze intent on mine, not letting me break his stare. It didn't take long before my climax hit, built up by his earlier teasing and now pushed over by his bruising pace. I couldn't hold back my frustrated grunt that although I could finally come, I was unable to pound into him as my body wanted to. When I slumped into the chair he slowly lifted himself off my softening dick. I blinked up at him as he took the condom off me, tying it off and tossing it aside as he untied my limbs, rubbing them softly.

"You didn't finish," I said when my brain had finally started to fully function.

Wulfric didn't look up at that, but his hands rubbing my wrist froze before continuing their ministrations. "That wasn't the point."

I turned my hand over and gripped his tightly to make his nervous movements stop. "What was the point? You never bottom."

He didn't say anything, instead urging me to stand up then tugged me behind him into my bedroom. Wulfric was still hard, but he ignored it. Instead, he settled onto the bed and pulled me down with him. Turning to face him, I searched his expression, but I didn't see any discomfort or hint at what he was thinking. In fact, the only thing I saw clearly was exhaustion, but I wasn't going to let it go that easy.

"You're not going to let me sleep until I answer, are you?" His lips twitched slightly as he squeezed me closer to him.

"No, I'm not." I put a hand on his face to keep him from turning away from me.

Uncertainty filled his eyes, though when he blinked it was gone. A fleeting moment I would have missed if I hadn't been looking at him closely. I was about to say something when he stopped me with a look.

"My brother."

"Yes," I replied dryly. "We met. He was... delightful."

"He came to deliver a warning. It could ruin all the plans I've set up for this hit." Wulfric's eyes were dark.

"You could always ask for help." At his look I let out a huff of annoyance. "Yes, I know you usually work alone. But it looks like, for this, you could use the assistance. So... switch up your plans and have this work to your advantage."

Wulfric honed in on me at my words, weighing the idea before humming softly. "Let me think on it. That could work."

"And actually let me in on your plan this time," I told him with mild annoyance. "As much fun as the fight foreplay was earlier, I'd like to know the plan before it was actually happening."

"If you didn't like it so much I would consider it." I heard the laughter in his voice and in retaliation for his teasing, I reached down and gripped his still hard dick.

"You aren't the only one who can tease you know." I pumped him softly.

"Robin—"

"Too bad I'm exhausted from all your teasing earlier. Maybe in the morning when I've had some actual sleep to recover." I let him go and closed my eyes.

"You bastard," he muttered and I let out a tired laugh. Snuggling into him I slid a leg over him and he let out a groan. "You're keeping that promise in the morning."

"Deal," I agreed sleepily, and smiled when he wrapped an arm around me.

"Wulfric?" My sleep slurred voice broke the silence and he just hummed in answer. "Your ass better still be here when I wake up."

A laugh then a soft brush of lips against my forehead. "Promise."

CHAPTER 5

Wulfric

I expected to wake up to the loud ringing of an alarm, but this was so much better. I groaned at the feel of Robin's hot tongue as it swirled around the head of my dick while he pumped me with a hand. I opened my eyes and tore the covers off me so I could see Robin's heated gaze as he took me deeper into his mouth. Not able to hold in the moan at the sight, I threw my head back.

"Fuck," I grunted. Robin hummed with me in his throat making me shudder at the feeling before he pulled off of me. "Best way to wake up."

"You kept your promise to stay. I had to reward you for it." His voice was rough. I opened my eyes and found him over me with an indecipherable look in his eyes as he stared down at me. "You usually don't stay."

I licked my lips, but I couldn't think of anything to say in response to his loaded statement. He gave me a soft smile, as if he could read my thoughts and leaned down to kiss me gently.

When he went to pull away, I pulled him down and then rolled so he was under me. He watched as I leaned over and grabbed a condom and lube from his bedside table. In a hurry, I opened the foil and rolled it on my dick as Robin grabbed the lube and tossed it to the side. His smirk let me know he'd already prepped himself while I slept. *Fucking menace.*

I gave him a look as he pulled me closer with his legs. I slammed into him with one hard thrust that had him groaning.

"I don't plan on going anywhere," I told him softly as I stayed still in him, letting him adjust to my sudden invasion. That made him look at me with an unsure expression that had my heart clenching at his doubt.

Trying to reassure him without words, I leaned in and kissed him. Robin responded slowly at first, but I matched my fucking to the speed of our mouths devouring one another. Slow, long strokes into him. Making love wasn't something I had ever done, but I imagined this was what it would be like. Savoring every reaction of his as I slowly built our climaxes up. I didn't break the kiss as we both came or while we both calmed. I kept kissing him until our heart rates evened out and then I finally broke away. Reaching down I took the condom off and tied it, letting it fall to the floor.

Robin didn't say anything, but I felt the bed shift before he lay half on top of me. He ran a hand along my chest and I smiled tiredly at the touch.

"I hope you aren't too tired after that." Robin's voice was soft. "You have a plan to tell me about."

I didn't move or look at him as I responded, "Simple plans are always the easiest. We're going on a date."

"A date?" Robin sounded confused.

"At Pulse, the dance club downtown. They usually have private parties in the back. I should be able to convince someone to let us join."

Robin lifted his head and I could feel his gaze as he stared at me, but I didn't bother to open my eyes. "Private parties?"

"Yes." My lips twitched slightly as I tried to hold my smile in.

"Have you been to any?"

I opened my eyes at that. "I have been a few times, actually. I do believe if we go tonight they have a swingers party in the back, which means you need a woman to attend. But I think we can convince them to make an exception since we won't be staying long." He quirked an eyebrow at me, but I just shook my head as I sat us both up. "We should get going. You have work to do and I've got some contacts to reach out to in order to finish setting up tonight's fun. Make sure Jason is there tonight."

"Are you going to share any more of your plan with me?" Robin's voice was dry as he narrowed his eyes in annoyance.

"I'd prefer to surprise you." I shifted and held his gaze. "Your real reaction will help things."

He kept his eyes trained on mine for a moment before he let out an exasperated sigh. "Did you even sleep for more than a few hours last night?"

My lips twitched at his irritation. "A few, but I made some calls to set things up. I got enough."

"Sleep is important, Wulfric. You're human."

"Are you trying to tell me I should take more care of myself?" I asked, amused as he rolled his eyes at me.

"I try to tell you that all the time but it's like talking to a fucking brick wall," he grumbled, but I ignored it and gave him a wide grin and wink instead.

I could stay here all day, but if I don't get moving I won't be able to get anything done. Pity because I can't think of anything I want more than to spend my time tangled up with Robin in these sheets. Fuck! I need to get my shit together and focus.

Robin sat still on the bed as I finally pushed myself up to standing, stretching before I grabbed the used condom from the floor to throw it in the trash. Padding toward the bathroom I turned when I didn't hear Robin move to join me. He wasn't sitting up anymore, instead, he was sprawled on the bed, the sheets barely covering the lower half of his body. An enticement that it took all my self control to turn away from.

"I guess you're not up for round two," Robin called out as I stepped out of the room.

I shook my head even though he couldn't see me. "I didn't say that, but you don't seem too interested if you're not joining me." By the time I got the shower started Robin was standing behind me, a smile pressed into my shoulder as he wrapped his arms around my waist. As soon as steam filled the small room I pulled him with me into the standing shower.

We didn't waste time going slow, but hurried through washing each other. Before I knew what was happening, Robin claimed my lips in a punishing kiss that soon led to a quickie that didn't last nearly as long as we thought it would. A brief kiss to his temple followed, and I enjoyed the smile he gave me in return.

CHAPTER 6

Robin

Memories of last night and this morning with Wulfric filled my mind, as I made my way into the Family house. The home had more people than usual walking around, but I ignored them and made my way to O'Callaghan's office. Two enforcers stood outside and at my approach they both lifted a hand in greeting.

"Hey, Josh. Hey, Benjamin. What's going on?" They looked at each other and took a quick glance around before filling me in.

"Someone is spreading rumors about Wulfric Alfonsi working for us." Josh scoffed. "Who the hell comes up with this shit?"

"Who knows." Benjamin shook his head.

"Is he busy?" I gestured at the closed door. "I'm supposed to be meeting with him."

"Someone unexpectedly stopped in, which is why all this chaos is going on. He should be ready soon though since he knows you're coming."

I nodded at Josh's answer and turned to walk down the hallway, figuring I would come back in a few minutes. Before I could make it more than a handful of steps, I heard the door to the office open. Loud voices spilled out of the room indicating an argument had broken out. I turned around, curious to see who had dropped by out of the blue, only to see Conrad, Grady, and Liam being thrown out of the office by an irritated Sylvia.

"You boys need to get out of here while your father is trying to run his business. No need for your shenanigans right now while other Families are visiting." She gave them one last glare before shutting the door closed behind her.

The Ricci's? As in Wulfric's family? Or the mafia Family his family worked for? Fuck. Well, I guess that answers the question of where those rumors came from, though I had a gut feeling that Wulfric himself also had a hand in all of this during another one of his all-nighters. The man was going to burn himself out one day.

Watching with interest, I saw Grady glare at the door as Liam and Conrad glanced first at each other, then back to Grady. Grady was clearly thinking about storming back into the room but seemed to decide against that and began to walk away down the hall.

"Boys." Josh and Ben looked grateful at my words, though Grady didn't seem as thankful to see me.

"Robin," Grady greeted me with a nod. At only twenty-one, he was so serious and already full of ideas that were vastly different than his father's. Liam eyed his younger brother with a concerned expression, and I sighed internally. It will be interesting to see what happens when Liam takes over the Family and Grady has to follow. Taking orders is not his strong suit.

"Grady." I nodded at the others. "Is there a problem?"

He didn't answer and Liam nudged him with an elbow. "No, we were just leaving. Need to get some school work done."

I watched closely as Grady managed to bite back a retort and followed his brother. It was ironic how different they were; Liam with long blond hair and a lean swimmer's body, whereas Grady was broader with red hair. Conrad stayed for a moment longer, like he wanted to say something, but instead gave a small wave before following after his uncles. Conrad was lean like Liam, but with darker blond hair and way more attitude, there was no mistaking him for anyone else. Yes, the all-American family where nephews and uncles were the same age or only a few years apart. Definitely made for interesting family dinners.

As soon as the boys were around the corner, the office door opened again and I looked beside me to see Josh and Ben moving far away from the opening as a man and a teenage girl walked out of the room. The man had meticulously styled black hair and a stone cold face that matched his icy eyes, moving with a purpose as he stalked out of the office. The girl couldn't have been older than fifteen at the most, but her long brown hair hung down to her shoulders hiding her face as she turned to follow, who I assumed to be her father, out of the house.

"Robin, come in," Dillon O'Callaghan called out to me.

Before I could move I felt a gaze settle on me. Looking up, I caught the girl who had been about to leave glancing over her shoulder to look at me.

Curiosity sparked in her brown eyes as she looked me over, before a small smile pulled at her lips. I nodded to her, and her smile filled her face before she rounded the corner going completely out of view.

"Robin?"

My attention snapped back to the office where Sylvia and Dillon were waiting for me. I walked into the office and carefully closed the door behind me. Anthony Ricci was sprawled out in one of the office chairs, wearing an expensive, simple suit in navy blue that didn't do anything to hide the dangerous glint in his cold green eyes. Beside him, sitting with ramrod straight posture, was Henrick, Wulfric's brother, who didn't show a flicker of recognition as I sat in the free chair.

"Glad you could join us," Sylvia said with a smile. "Coffee?"

"I'm good, thank you though," I told her, my gaze flicking back and forth between the men in the room. "This is an unexpected visit. What's going on?"

At my question, Anthony and Dillon shared a look before the Ricci Don sighed. "There are rumors going around about Wulfric Alfonsi. Rumors that need to be cleared up."

I steepled my fingers in front of me as I put on a curious expression. "Rumors? What kind of rumors? Isn't he one of your contractors?"

"Yes," Ricci drawled, his eyes focused on me intently. "He is. It would be something he would be smart to remember. No matter how good... other opportunities may look."

Something in his tone made my blood heat; I guess Henrick did hint at this last night. Not letting myself react outwardly, I just shot him a bland smile.

"Very true." I gave a serious nod. "But I don't see why that means you're here, talking to us. Unless there is something you wanted me here to tell me?" At my question I turned to look at Dillon with a questioning tilt of my head.

He stared back at me with a blank expression, though I could see the spark of humor hidden there. We held each other's gaze, silently communicating, until Ricci cleared his throat loudly, making us swing our attention to him.

"Your message has been delivered." O'Callaghan's voice was so cold I'm surprised frost didn't coat the walls. "Thank you for stopping by. Slyvia here can show you out."

"I'm—"

"Done." O'Callaghan finished for him firmly, turning a stern look at Ricci that had the other man snapping his mouth shut.

"Yes, well," Ricci huffed, standing up practically bristling with irritation. "I will remember your hospitality the next time you stop by Chicago."

"Until next time."

Sylvia followed Ricci out of the office, Henrick right behind like a silent shadow. We remained quiet for a few moments lost in our own thoughts.

"Interesting he would show up now," Dillon said thoughtfully, breaking the silence. "Wulfric was supposed to remain in the shadows until later. Why is he letting rumors fly?"

I hummed in thought. "I think he mentioned someone catching on and he was changing his plans. I believe I'm helping him finish things tonight. Don't worry, there won't be any evidence left when we are done."

"Make sure that there isn't. We can't have anything getting back to us. It's going to be enough of an issue when Wulfric officially doesn't go back to the Riccis."

"It does seem they are going to be upset," I agreed softly before sending a wide smile to him. "Mind if I'm here when they find out?"

O'Callaghan didn't hold back his laughter at my cheeky response. "I'll remember you asked."

"Is there anything else you wanted to see me for today?"

"No." He shook his head. As I stood to leave, he called my name, making me glance over my shoulder in question. "Grady and the boys. I want you to take them under your wing. It's time Grady actually knows how this business is run. He is getting too many foolish ideas about how to run things."

Remembering Grady's face when he, Liam, and Conrad were thrown out of here not long ago, I slowly nodded in agreement.

"I can do that."

"I knew I could depend on you. Now, don't forget to tell your boyfriend to get his shit together tonight. Last thing I need is for everything to fall apart after dismissing Ricci."

I didn't respond to the boyfriend comment and just gave a nod in acknowledgment before exiting the office. After a brief goodbye with Benjamin and Josh, I made my way out of the house and into my car.

Not wanting to linger, I pulled out and drove over to the autobody shop I had just bought. The building was busy being renovated, but I did a walk-through to check on the progress. I talked with the contractor briefly to make sure we were on schedule for the new opening.

"There is one thing I still need your decision on, Mr. Healy. Do you have a name picked yet? My sign guy is ready when you are to get started." The contractor's deep voice rumbled as he looked down at his checklist.

"Alexander's," I answered after a slight pause.

"Works for me, sir. I'll make sure he gets started in the next day or two and get you his contact information."

"Thank you." I gave him a slap on the back in thanks. "You're doing a great job. I'll be back next week."

"Thank you, Mr. Healy. See you then," he responded, before turning around to yell at one of his workers. Something about not needing to bring those materials in yet, though I didn't stay to listen. Instead, I made my way back to my car, set on getting back to the apartment. Hopefully, Wulfric wouldn't be long before I met him. I wanted to know what the hell he had planned for tonight, besides the vague idea of a party. Knowing Wulfric, that could go so many different ways.

I was in the kitchen readying lasagna for dinner when Wulfric waltzed in without knocking. I knew it was him by his measured pace as he approached me, then he wrapped his arms around my waist as he rested his chin on my shoulder.

"That smells good." He brushed a kiss against my throat.

Not willing to be distracted from my earlier thoughts, I just hummed in agreement before responding, "I hope you have a plan for all these rumors that have come out, Wulfric. I spent a good bit of my morning hearing all about it."

"I do," he answered evenly. But I continued like I didn't hear his answer.

"Because I spent time this morning in a meeting with the Ricci Don and your brother when I went to see O'Callaghan." Wulfric went still behind me at those words but I wasn't done. "There was someone else there, with a daughter in tow for the meeting."

"What did he look like?" Wulfric was like a statue around me. I tried to turn to face him, but he didn't release his iron hold on me.

"Dark styled hair, cold face, icy eyes. I didn't really pay attention since Grady and the boys had just been thrown out," I replied curiously. "Do you know who it is?"

"I have a few ideas, none of them are good." His voice was thoughtful and he finally let me turn to look him in the eye. The golden flecks were warm when I met his gaze. "But my plan is going to work. Rumors included."

"Are you telling me the entire plan?" My eyebrow quirked as I watched his eyes crinkle in amusement.

"I'll fill you in as we go."

"So that's a no," I waved a hand in irritation. "So what is this 'date' going to include? I usually just stick to the clean up afterward. " My brow furrowed in confusion, not following whatever plan he had brewing.

"I think you can handle going to a club for a night," he retorted softly as he let go of me, still avoiding my questions. "Besides, this club is more up our alley in some ways."

I let out a chuckle while I put the dish in the oven, because I had forgotten about the swinger party happening at the Pulse tonight. I walked over to the sink and as I washed my hands I remembered Wulfric saying he had been to a few of these parties before, and wondered what else they did at these things. He had more... eclectic tastes when it came to sex than most.

Shaking my head, I shifted my thoughts to more pertinent things as I turned off the faucet and grabbed a nearby towel to dry my hands. "The Ricci Don and your brother were there to talk about you." When he remained quiet I turned around to find him watching me intently. "They were especially insistent that you remember where you come from regardless of 'other opportunities' that come your way."

Wulfric let loose a laugh at that and I watched, almost concerned, as he seemed to be losing it. The tears on his cheeks as he tried to get himself under control made me roll my eyes. Letting him laugh it up, I made my way past him at the kitchen island to the fridge and grabbed two beers. Popping the top off both glass bottles, I walked over to one of the bar stools facing Wulfric as he got himself slowly under control. I slid one of the beers over to him while I took a sip from mine.

"You calm now?"

He wiped his eyes one last time before grabbing his beer. "Yes, yes. It's hilarious they came to visit."

"Hilarious isn't the word I was expecting you to use," I responded dryly.

"I became a contract killer because of Ricci. There are many reasons behind that." Wulfric waved his hand dismissing the details. "But it's hilarious he is concerned that I'd be moving onto a new Family. Believe it or not, I left on good terms with Anthony."

"Jealous or mad that you'd be joining a Family that isn't the one you come from? Because that comment was directed at me, not Dillon." I watched him closely as I drank more of my cold beer.

Wulfric still smiled, but I could almost feel the air chill as his eyes iced over. "I'll have to remember that the next time I talk to them. It will make for an interesting conversation."

"I don't need you protecting me, Wulfric. I can take care of myself."

He didn't respond to my statement, just looked at me with those empty eyes that should have scared me more than excited me. But that's something I wasn't going to look at too closely yet.

"What are you thinking right now?" Wulfric's voice was soft.

"I'm thinking that you can be a scary son of a bitch," I answered honestly with a smile. "And that I can't wait to see you try to fit in at whatever club you're taking me to tonight."

A wicked grin filled his face. "Bastard."

"Undoubtedly," I agreed.

CHAPTER 7

Wulfric

The loud music was blasting from the speakers and my lips curled in distaste at the sounds pumping into the club. People were everywhere drinking and dancing, while all I wanted to do was get who we were looking for and get out. If we hadn't been here for business, maybe I wouldn't have minded the atmosphere as much, but each person who walked by could be a potential associate of the Segreto. *Oh well, time to focus on the job at hand.*

Making my way through the mass of people, I arrived at the bar and waited for the bartender to notice me so I could put in my order. Everyone was talking loudly to each other and I rubbed my fingertips together wishing I could smoke to take away some of the tension rising inside.

"Well lookie here, I haven't seen you around here before." A high pitched voice filled my ear that belonged to a curvy body that pressed against my side. I flinched away as she tried to run a tongue along the edge of my ear. *Disgusting.*

I didn't even bother to turn toward the offending woman who had plastered herself against me. "Not interested."

"You haven't even seen what I'm offering," she whispered with a grating pitch. She was trying to be seductive, but from the sound of her voice, she wouldn't know how to do that if it fucked her in the ass.

The bartender came before I could turn to address the woman again and asked what I wanted to drink. "Scotch, neat or on the rocks, I don't care at this point. And a bottle of Guinness." Not waiting for a total, I handed him a hundred and leaned closer, dislodging the woman long enough for me to yell over the music, "Keep the change if you get her the fuck away from me. Right now."

"You got it, sir." The bartender nodded while pocketing the bill. He looked behind me and gestured to someone. That someone was a bouncer who managed to make his way through the crowd of dancing people quickly,

177

and grabbed the woman's arm with an exasperated expression. She must do this all the time for that to be his look.

"Amy, are you bothering the customers again? I'm going to have to take you back to Oscar." The man's voice was irritated, then he caught sight of me and I enjoyed watching as the blood drained from his face with recognition as his hand shifted to his waist.

"Wulfric— What are you doing here?" His close proximity made it easy to make out his shock as he stammered his question.

I gave him a bored look. "I'm here working, gathering information from the O'Callaghans. I'm going to need... a more private space eventually. Let Oscar know so I can go in the back when I'm ready."

"I'll see—"

I cut him off with a small smile as I grabbed the drinks placed in front of me. "See that you do." The man froze at my words, though I could tell he wanted to say more. "Run along now and I'll remember your cooperation the next time I talk to Segreto."

The man bobbed his head in a hurry and dragged the woman, Amy, behind him as he backed away from me and into the mess of people. "I'll let you know where you can take him soon."

"I look forward to it," I told him softly as I smirked at his stumbling steps.

I watched them both until they became lost in the crowd, before slowly turning and scanning the throng for Robin. Catching sight of him in the back, I made my way toward the table he had managed to grab on the other side of all the spazzing people that I assumed were trying to dance. The loud bumping music throbbing in the air made me clench my teeth at each pump of bass. Roaming hands that touched me as I walked by set my nerves on the edge, but I finally made it out of the larger group of dancers on the club floor.

As I approached, Robin was busy looking at something on his phone and I took the opportunity to run my gaze over him. He usually wore suits, but since we were at a club he had dressed down in fitted dark jeans paired with a simple white button-up, the sleeves rolled over his elbows showcasing his forearms and the top two buttons undone. Sliding into the bench across from Robin I placed his beer on the table in front of him and he glanced up at me with a smile as he put down his phone.

"You look so uncomfortable right now." His dark brown eyes danced with amusement as he took me in.

I gave a huff of annoyance as I sat back and sipped my drink, giving a half-smile at the taste of Johnnie Walker hitting my tongue. "Clubs like this aren't my thing."

"No, you don't say." Robin's voice was dry as he drank some of his beer. "Any idea how we are going to find Jason in all this?"

I ran a hand through my hair as I gave him a wide grin. "We should be able to get back there soon."

"Get where? What did you do?"

"What makes you think I did anything? I just got our drinks." He leveled a look at me as he set his beer on the table. I couldn't hold back my laughter at his expression and his lips twitched at the sound. "I was getting hit on by a woman who wanted to plaster herself to me while I was waiting to order. I paid the bartender to get her away from me and the bouncer that grabbed her is an associate of Segreto. I told him I was here to question you... it shouldn't be too long before he comes to take us to a party room of our own."

Robin just stared at me for a moment before he shook his head. "So touchy, Wulfric."

"I figured you would have more commentary about me questioning you," I told him seriously and watched as he just sipped his drink.

"You could try, but I wouldn't go quietly."

"You're never quiet, Robin. I like that about you." I smirked as he choked on his beer at my words.

"You're an asshole." He struggled to get out while he fought to stop coughing. "Why don't you go find that woman who was hitting on you. She can deal with your shit tonight."

"Would you really rather I let her be all over me, attempting to flirt? I'm sure I could find her again. Though to be honest, I'd rather it be someone else. Her voice alone was annoying as fuck." I took another sip of my scotch and set the glass down on the table waiting for his response.

"If I had a problem with it I would have said so with any of the others you've taken to bed." Robin's eyes heated. "Let's see, there was Diana."

"A wonderful woman we both enjoyed, as I recall." I motioned for him to join me on my side of the table so we could talk without having to raise our voices over the noise around us, which he did slowly with my eyes tracking his every movement.

"After her was Carrie."

"Hmmm... she was unique and took a special interest in you." I slid a hand along his thigh, enjoying the darkening of his eyes at my touch.

"Dylan from last month really liked you," Robin managed to get out as I pulled him closer into me, angling my body so his back was against my front.

"He didn't really fit my... tastes, though the boy did try," I breathed against his neck as I placed a tauntingly soft kiss against his warm skin. He shivered at the touch and seemed to lose his train of thought for a few moments. "No others you want to mention?"

I felt him swallow hard before continuing, "Steve."

"Hmmm..." I trailed a hand down his side stopping just short of his dick, lingering on his inner thigh. "I think he was one of your favorites, though I did enjoy the show. Shouldn't I be the one jealous that you're listing off the ones that mostly enjoyed you?"

Robin titled his head back to look at me, eyes heavy with desire. "You're a sadist. I'm not. It's easier to find people that want to play with me."

I released a dark chuckle as I gave in to the desire he showed me and cupped him through the thick fabric of his jeans. "That's true. But you let me play with you."

"That's because you don't bottom," he snarked back, though there was no real bite to his words given the moan he couldn't hold back. "Except last night."

I tightened my grip on his dick and even through the denim it was enough to make him hiss. "Darling, that was an exception, which you already know. Though I have to say, the idea of you at my mercy as I ride you however long I want to... that does hold its own kind of appeal, doesn't it?" He let out a faint whimper. "And if you didn't like my attention then you would have walked away a long time ago." Letting go of my vise-like grip on him I licked a trail on his neck, enjoying the salt of his sweat as it hit my tongue.

"I hate you." Robin tried to turn to face me, but I moved my hand to his chin to keep him facing forward.

"No you don't and you know it." I laid a soft trail of kisses along his neck until I reached his ear. "Pity for you, really."

"Am I interrupting?" A hesitant voice broke through the heat of the moment, though I didn't bother to look up as I responded.

"I will give you one guess and if it's wrong I'll shoot you."

Robin's answering laugh was gravelly, but he didn't move to break my hold as we both looked up at the nervous man by our table. He appeared to be about Robin's age, around twenty-seven. His blond hair was neatly styled and he watched us with shocked, wide blue eyes. Boy would be in for a surprise if he knew everything that was going on in this club.

"I was told to come escort you to our VIP area. If you would both like to follow me." He cleared his throat roughly before turning around to give us privacy.

I chuckled against Robin's skin. "He must just be a worker here. But we can pick this up again later."

"I'm holding you to that."

I released my grip on him and watched with a knowing smirk as he adjusted himself slightly, or at least he tried to, through the thick fabric of his jeans before standing up. I threw back the rest of my liquor, enjoying the burn as it hit my throat. Carefully putting the glass on the table, I stood and gave the man a bland smile.

"Lead the way."

Amused, I watched as he stuck closer to Robin while walking toward the back, and I made sure to stay back a pace. *No need to upset anyone since my plan is working, for the moment at least.* Weaving through the crowd we finally made it to a curtained off area where two security people searched us before motioning for us to continue as blondie promptly turned around and scurried away.

"The requested room is ready for your use," the bouncer addressed me as he held out a key.

"Perfect. I already know the way." I gave him a dark look and didn't miss the shiver that he couldn't suppress.

"What are we going to do back here exactly?" Robin whispered to me as we entered a darkened hallway. Our footsteps echoed in the startling quiet corridor, the music of the club fading the farther back we walked.

"First we are going to look at this room." I held up the key I had gotten. "When we grab Segreto we're going to bring him here."

"You're going to question him here? In the same club we are taking him from?" Robin asked incredulously as I stopped in front of a normal looking metal door.

As I unlocked it, I glanced over at my shoulder at him. "That reaction is why they won't look here until he's long dead."

He shook his head at me as I chuckled and pushed open the door. Walking inside I took in the full extent of the room. A few chairs randomly placed and a black tool chest in the corner were the only things that decorated the bland, off-white cinderblock room. The concrete floor had a drain in the center.

"Rather more lackluster than I thought it would be," I observed. Robin strode over to the chest and opened it. A distasteful expression filled his face and it piqued my curiosity. I joined him and peered inside to see what his reaction was caused by, and took in the blood-caked hammers, knives, and other tools in the top drawer.

"They don't even bother to clean any of these? And these just look dull as fuck." Robin shook his head. "Segretos are just getting lazy."

"Shame really," I tsked. "Guess we will have to make do with what they have here. Though there is something poetic about him being tortured with his own shitty tools, so when he screams we can just tell him if they had taken better care of their stuff it wouldn't be as painful."

Since there wasn't anything else to look at I grabbed Robin's arm and guided him from the room, pocketing the key as the door shut behind us.

"Now onto the sex party." Robin rolled his eyes at my sarcastic enthusiasm.

"Yes, the one you said you've been to before." Something in his tone made me pause, but I couldn't put my finger on what it was exactly.

"Jealousy isn't really your style." I ran a hand down his back. "What exactly about that bothers you?"

He didn't get a chance to answer me before we arrived at a set of stairs. I nudged him to go up and he did, though I stayed close to him. The door at the top didn't have any bouncers, which made Robin pause. Not letting him linger, I reached around him and opened the door, soft music and the faint glow of mood lighting spilling out.

"They won't bite, Darling. But I will." I leaned close and added. "We can talk about what is annoying you after."

Not bothering to look back at me, Robin flipped me the bird and walked carefully through the opening. I followed him and quickly shut the door, turning just in time to find Robin frozen at the sight before us.

"Not what you were expecting?" I kept my voice soft as I came to stand next to him.

"Shouldn't they be in separate rooms or something? An orgy out in the open isn't quite what I expected when you said a swinger party." Robin sounded a bit shocked.

"They seem to have actually done up the space since the last time I was here," I commented dryly, looking around to take in the full open room.

Slapping flesh, moans, and the scent of sex, permeated the air as I turned to take in the throng of people in the middle of sex. Men and women were all mixed in. Most were men and women paired together across the room, though I did see a few trios together. The thick carpet underneath our feet covered most of the room, and people were spread out on the random couches that were arranged throughout the space. A few tables were placed conveniently close with condom packets and lube on top of them for easy accessibility.

"Do we just yell fire to interrupt them?" Robin murmured.

I couldn't hold back my bark of laughter at the idea and shook my head as a nearby couple turned to see us standing there. "Would be a shame to interrupt everyone during their good time. Do you see Jason?"

I searched the room, though I kept an eye on the approaching woman who had spotted us.

"Hello! You must be new here. You need to bring your wives here to participate—"

I cut her off, not really caring to listen to her spiel of etiquette for a swingers meet up. "We don't have wives or girlfriends."

"Oh, oh!" She blushed a bit as she glanced between Robin and me. "I'm sorry, I didn't realize. Well, we really only let in couples with women since they initiate—"

"We were let in by Oscar." I gave her a wink and wrapped an arm around Robin's waist to pull him close to me. "So don't worry we're vouched for. We're just here to watch."

Her eyes widened a bit at the name drop, but interest flared to life at the mention of watching. "In that case," she gave us a large smile and turned to gesture to a dark set of couches I hadn't seen before, situated in the shadows of the room, "go ahead and set yourselves up there. I hope you enjoy your show."

"I'm sure we will," Robin murmured as I directed him to the dark couch. I pulled him down to sit next to me, but even as he let me do that he remained stiff for a moment before settling into my side. The people having sex were sprawled out in front of us, like we were at a live porno, though many would be classified as amateur from the looks of things. *Not my kind of scene*, was my only thought as I kept one eye out for our target.

"Do you see him?" I asked Robin softly, and I felt him shake his head in answer. I turned to find his eyes scanning the crowd, a detached expression on his face. Placing a hand on his chin, I turned him to face me. "Darling, if we are here to watch, that expression isn't going to work."

Robin tilted his head, dislodging my grip, before giving me a guilty twist of his lips. "Sorry, I have a lot on my mind."

I kissed him lightly on the lips before asking, "Anything you want to share with me?"

Robin didn't respond to my kiss, but he held my stare as he gave the small shake of his head. "Not the time or place. Do you see him?"

I paused at his redirection and searched his face, but he kept his thoughts to himself, scanning the room and avoiding my gaze. Not being able to figure out what he was thinking threw me off and left me on unsure footing. As if he could sense my feelings Robin finally turned to look at me, and, while his expression didn't soften, he did lean forward to press his forehead against mine.

"Work."

I wasn't sure if that was an answer, or him chastising me to focus, but I kept my arm around his shoulders as we looked around the room. I rubbed my hand on his shoulder, not wanting to push since he was right, we needed to concentrate to get this done. Robin laid his cheek against my hand for a moment before lifting his face again. I loved that he understood what I wanted to say even if I didn't have the words to express.

"There." Robin's voice broke through my thoughts. "He is on the floor now with a redhead, rutting her like a pig. I don't think he will last long if he keeps at it like that." I suppressed my laughter at Robin's succinct description of their sex, but just barely. "Do you have a plan on getting him out of here?"

"We could follow him out? Especially if he isn't going to last much longer," I mused. "If I pulled my gun in here it would cause a ruckus."

"Just a small one." Robin's voice was thick with amusement. "Following him could work, but we wouldn't have much time to grab him between here and the club. Plus, we just got here, wouldn't the greeting committee come ask what's wrong?"

"Not if we made it seem like we were so turned on by what we were watching that we leave to have sex," I offered, and Robin shuddered. "Not a fan of that idea? You were earlier."

"Yes but that was from your teasing. Watching some of these people..." Robin turned to face me with a lip curled in distaste. "Watching has never been a big thing for me."

"You like watching me."

"Yes, I do," Robin agreed. "But I'm attracted to you. Most of these people I don't even want to see with clothes on."

"So judgemental," I tsked. "I do see your point though. Ah, it seems you were right. The show seems to be over."

I watched as Jason rolled off of the poor woman who had been under him, though I had to give her credit, she kept a straight face as she sat up to lean over him again. Even at a distance, I could see her trying to look interested in another round. But he shook his head in irritation and pushed her away, standing and grabbing clothes off the floor instead of taking her up on her offer for round two. A flash of irritation crossed her face and I guessed, given how quick he was, she didn't get anywhere near to finishing.

"Should I leave before he does?"

I shook my head and looked at Robin. "I'll go first and get him into the room I showed you earlier. If anyone asks, I went to the bathroom; follow me three minutes after I leave. They'll just assume we went to go fuck and were being discreet."

Robin let out a rough laugh. "Well, they aren't exactly wrong. Three minutes."

What did that comment mean? Not having time to address it right now, I just gave him a look as I stood and began casually walking to the entrance. I could feel the fleeting glances from some of the people in the room, but I didn't feel Robin's attention on me. *Good, he needs to focus and so do I.*

Opening the door, I quickly made my way down the stairs and pulled a cigarette out of the pack from my pocket. A loud creaking alerted me to a door opening, followed by hurried footsteps, and suddenly Jason came into the hallway. At the sight of me, he came to a sudden stop.

"You're not supposed to smoke in here," his nasally voice informed me with a tone of superiority.

"I don't see any signs." I flicked the lighter and the flame danced to life.

At the sight of the flame his face reddened. "Just because you are in with Leo Segreto doesn't mean you can do whatever you want. You're just a dirty mixed Italian who is trying to fit in with the big leagues."

I released the button, letting the flame die. "Perhaps, but maybe you're just jealous I'm the one close to him and not the other way around. After all, we both know he trusts me."

"He trusts me!" he blustered. His hand reached for the gun I could see was strapped to his side, but as my eyes followed his movement he stopped just short.

I smirked at his ire. "If that's true, why am I here?" At my words, he froze in place and I enjoyed watching as his face paled, realizing that we were alone in the back of the club. "The walls are soundproof to not disturb the club patrons with the more... questionable activities the Family likes to conduct here. How many of the women up there were workers?"

"That's not—"

I leveled an icy look at him that cut him off. "We can do this the easy way or the hard way, which one do you want? I already know my preference." He backed up a step or two before spinning on his heel and started to run down the hallway. "The hard way it is."

I tucked my cigarette and lighter back into the pack, then into my shirt pocket. *So annoying when you get interrupted and aren't able to enjoy a smoke before a kill... though enjoying one afterward does sound amazing too.*

Grinning from the adrenaline at the prospect of the hunt, I stalked my way down the hall. I didn't bother to hurry, knowing that there was no handle on this side of the metal door. He skidded to a stop at said door and started knocking frantically, but the bouncer never answered. The closer I got, the faster his banging became until I was on top of him, grabbing his wrist to prevent him from making any more racket.

"No. No. There isn't any reason for you to question me." He started babbling as I began to drag him down the hall by his arm. He tried to pull back, but I just grabbed his other arm to get him under control. *I hope Robin gets here soon. It would be much easier to do this with two people.*

"Well, since I'm just a dirty mixed Italian then you shouldn't have much to worry about," I threw his words back at him, and his eyes widened. I could see in his gaze he was trying to calculate how he could escape, trying for one last attempt at freedom. "Don't."

He didn't heed my warning, instead he slammed his head back into mine. Pain shot into my face as his skull connected with my nose, and the crunching of cartilage at the impact had me grimacing. *Son of a fucking bitch!* Blood gushed over my lip, the throbbing causing my focus to waver enough that he slipped out of my grip. A clicking sound had me looking over to find Jason aiming a gun at me.

"You aren't so powerful now." The dim light of the hallway made his dark brown hair look dull as he kept the weapon trained on me. "Beg."

I gave a sharp laugh, coughing on the blood that had started trickling down my throat at the movement. "I've never begged a day in my life. You aren't going to be the one to change that." *Where the hell is Robin?* It had to have been three minutes already, but I didn't dare glance down the hall in case he was coming soon.

"Too bad for you." It was the only thing I heard before the echoes of a gunshot filled the hallway. At first, I thought he had missed, but when I looked down I noticed blood blossoming on my shirt over the left side of my stomach. Coldness seeped into me as blood began to run down my leg to the ground. *The adrenaline from the chase, and probably shock, are blocking the pain from hitting me just yet it seems.* I looked up to find him staring at me in surprise like he couldn't believe he had done it.

"You shouldn't, shouldn't have missed," I managed to ground out before footsteps rang down the hallway. At the sound, Jason turned to find Robin standing there wearing an exasperated expression. His face slowly filled with shock then cold anger as he took in the state of me as I slowly lowered myself to the floor. I carefully pressed my hand to the wound trying to slow the bleeding.

"Healy," Jason looked back and forth between myself and Robin as he came closer, "this is no concern of yours."

"I would have to disagree." The cold tone of Robin's voice had the man in front of me trembling. "But then again, I think it's time we clarified a few things." He pulled a gun and quickly fired it at Jason.

Distantly I wondered where Robin had been hiding the gun as I watched the Segreto stumble back and fall to the floor. A broken scream filled the air as he reached forward to grab his shot knee. Good shot to not kill him, but incapacitate him effectively. Realizing my thoughts were becoming clinically distant, I looked to find Robin lowering his gun, dark eyes focused on the downed man who was now sobbing.

Before my thoughts could begin to focus on him, Robin walked up and kicked the gun away and kneeled beside me. His calloused hands were gentle as he pulled my hand away from my side. He didn't say anything but the look on his face was enough to tell me it was worse than I thought it was.

"Robin." My voice was soft.

"I was trying to leave but the woman, Miranda, wouldn't let me walk out without hitting on me. She didn't want to take no for an answer or I would have been here sooner," he explained, his tone gruff.

"Robin," I repeated as firmly as I could. "You need to get him into the room and question him."

"You're shot!" Robin argued and I nodded.

"Yes, I'm aware," I replied dryly. "I'll get myself a ways down the street before I call for an ambulance. No need to have cops show up and raid the place. Finish this up for me. I'll be fine."

"You don't know that! You were fucking shot in the side, it could be a gut wound. You're usually much more careful than this," Robin complained.

Not bothering to comment, I couldn't stop a pained grunt from escaping as I forced myself to stand. "Let me have your shirt. I'll throw it on and ball mine over the wound to hide it as long as I can." When Robin just stared at me I waved a hand. "If you could hurry that would be best. I'm not bleeding any slower over here."

He shot me a look of pure annoyance and stood as he ripped his shirt off. I didn't get to enjoy the view before he reached forward to snag my smokes and the room key, helping me take my shirt off. I couldn't hold back the groan as I slipped the shirt off my arms. He balled up the cotton and pressed it against my side before putting his on me. The entire time he muttered about me being a fucking idiot for getting hurt in the first place.

"I'll be fine." I stopped his fussing hands. His eyes flicked up to meet my gaze and before he could retort with anything, I gave him a bland smile. "It's not the first or the last time I've been shot. It hurts like a bitch, but it feels like it didn't hit any organs."

"I hate you," Robin muttered before pressing his forehead against mine, eyes closed. I closed mine at the touch of his skin against mine and smiled.

"Not anywhere near as much as you wished you did." I pulled away and took a step back, starting down the hallway slowly. "Don't go easy on him, Robin. I can't wait to hear about it."

Chapter 8

Robin

I watched until I saw Wulfric stumble along the hallway to some exit I presumed only he knew about. Turning my attention to Jason revealed he hadn't managed to move and with a grimace I grabbed hold of his arms to haul him into the concrete room Wulfric had shown me earlier. Segreto let out a groan and a small scream of pain as I jostled his leg with each step I took. *Serves him right.*

Unceremoniously, I dropped him onto the ground and walked over to the toolbox I had looked at previously. Ignoring the dirty tools I searched until I found the zip ties I had seen before. With four in hand, I strode over to where Jason was attempting to army crawl away and lifted him onto one of the metal chairs, quickly tying his arms down. As I restrained his injured leg he let out a loud wail, but it cut off quickly as he passed out from the pain.

Stepping back I grabbed another chair and settled onto it, resigned to waiting until he woke up and I could start asking questions. Flashes of Wulfric standing there bleeding, falling down to the dirty ground, and his irritatingly calm reassurances that he was going to be fine as I worried over him all crossed my mind. How that man could go from sweet and sexy to closed off and distant in seconds I wasn't sure, but it drove me insane.

When Segreto didn't come around after a few minutes, I stood and looked him over to find him out cold, but at least he had a steady pulse. This was going to be an annoyingly long wait. I huffed in frustration before I eyed the toolbox and then zeroed in on the small utility sink tucked into the corner. *Guess I'll clean some tools so they're ready when he wakes up.*

"I don't have any answers for you, freak!" the man in the metal chair screamed out, spittle flying with his words as if he needed me to know how angry he was at his current situation. His indignation was overpowered by the fear shown in the tremor of his voice and the paleness of his face.

"Freak?" I mused aloud. "That is quite an accusation since we found you in the middle of an orgy party earlier tonight."

The restrained man sneered at me in disgust. "I was with a woman. I've heard rumors of you and that trash. Though, since you're Irish, I guess you like dealing with gutter scum."

His words made me see red, but I kept my voice empty as I merely hummed in response. "So you have an issue with gay men? Interesting. I think I could have some fun with you after all." Sitting back in the chair opposite him, I enjoyed the uneasy look he gave me at my words. I waited a beat to see if he would freak out, but when he remained silent I tacked on, "Unless you tell me what I want to know, of course."

"I'm not telling you anything!" Jason insisted, and I gave a dark laugh in response.

"I did hope you would say that." The buzzing of my phone interrupted me. Casually I answered it when I saw Grady's name on the screen.

"Hello, kid. I'm a little busy at the moment." My tone was casual.

"Robin—"

"Help! Whoever you are—" I rolled my eyes and casually kicked Jason's shattered knee, his plea for help cut off by a garbled scream. The annoying sound made it so Grady couldn't answer me for a moment.

"Sorry about that. I think he got the message." I glared at the injured man, but he was too busy focusing on steadying his breath to say anything in response.

"I just wanted to let you know that I picked up Wulfric," Grady's even voice told me, and I closed my eyes, trying to calm myself before I responded.

"You aren't an ambulance." Each word was measured, and I could feel Grady pause on the other end of the phone. There was some talking and rustling in the background before Wulfric's deep voice came over the line.

"The Family doctor will be able to patch me up just fine. He already has the antibiotics and everything ready to go when I get there." I could tell he was trying to soothe my nerves, but his even tone just annoyed me more.

Why can't he act like it's a big deal or that he could have just died? No. He has to be all macho and act like nothing is fucking wrong.

"You're a fucking idiot. I'll talk to you after you're patched up and I deal with Segreto," I answered briskly.

"Darling—"

Click.

"Trouble in paradise?" Jason taunted. I looked at him and whatever he saw there made him whimper.

"If there is, aren't you so glad you're here to occupy me? I have a few ideas on how to start but how about thumb screws? I brought my own just for this." My delighted smile made Jason try to shrink back into the chair, but too bad for him, this was barely the beginning.

Screaming and pleading filled the air as I put the screws on each thumb, tightening them when he seemed to steady himself against the new levels of pain. I watched, completely detached as he writhed in the chair.

"I'll talk! I'll talk," Jason begged. "Please just stop, please stop." His last words caught on a sob.

"Then talk," I told him softly.

"We've expanded into trafficking and the Förstner aren't happy about that. But we have a loose deal with them so we are working together." He took a few deep breaths. "But Angelo wants more. He is starting to trade with the Campbells for guns."

I didn't blink at this latest tidbit of information, that would cause a lot of problems for us if that panned out. Not wanting to let him know that this was news to me, I just hummed absently.

"Interesting. Anything else?"

"There is... there is a new contract killer in the Förstner family. Katie something. Not sure anything else, but the rumors we've heard... She is already skilled enough to make our Don nervous. They want an official alliance with her as part of it."

"Seems a bit old school to me," I replied dryly. "But it could work. Is that all you have to tell me? Rumors of a new killer, that's not new. There are new killers all the time when you are in the mafia. And some attempt to work with families on the other side of the country? That's not enough to buy your freedom."

"Wait, wait! There is one more thing," Jason pleaded with me, and I froze just before starting to push myself up to standing.

"Yes?"

He licked his lips as his eyes sought mine. "Angelo Segreto and the Don of the Ricci Family. They were in talks to try to take over the O'Callaghan Family. I don't know the specifics, but something about a double agent or ghost something..." Jason shook his head, trembling as he frantically kept trying to think of more things to tell me.

I didn't respond to him as I stood and walked away. Approaching the recently cleaned tools, I ignored all the easily accessible ones and instead chose to dig for a hammer. I tossed it back and forth before sauntering back toward where Jason was sweating and trembling. Casually sitting in the seat I had vacated, I leaned back while keeping the hammer switching from one hand to the other.

"Thank you for your cooperation—"

"I helped you! I told you everything you needed to know!" Jason frantically flicked his gaze between the hammer and my face.

"Yes, yes you did. But you also shot Wulfric, and I take exception to people who hurt those I consider mine. Maybe you should have let him be the one to do this and not me," I told him with all seriousness. "Now you're going to watch as I break you into enough pieces they'll never be able to put you back together again."

Instinctively Jason clenched his eyes shut and I took advantage of his actions to give him a surprise. I firmly gripped the hammer and slammed it down on his right hand. The thud, scream, and cracking of bones that resulted were like music to my ears, and I watched, detached, as he continued to wail. *Wulfric really might have an idea when it comes to using gags.*

"I've had a hard day, Jason. It would be best if you just listened to me and it, well, it won't make things any easier for you. But you're making your death that much harder on yourself." I tilted my head as he forced his eyes open to meet my gaze, while snot ran down his face from the crying he couldn't quite keep under control.

"Fuck you." He tried to sound forceful, but the whimper at the end ruined the effect he was going for.

"If you don't watch, I'll cut off your eyelids to make sure you don't miss a thing." My voice sounded coldly bored, even to my own ears, but I did enjoy the way he snapped his eyes open to stare at me in shock. "There is a reason Wulfric is the killer, Segreto. He would just kill you once he has the information. I'm going to play with you until I get bored."

I didn't give him a chance to respond before bringing the hammer down on his good knee then his left forearm. Gleaming white bone shards cut through the skin like a macabre shipwreck, bloody water spilled around it as the shard ripped its way through the skin. As he screamed, I reached forward. *I had almost forgotten the thumb screws and it looks like I have damaged one. Oh well, I'll get rid of it elsewhere. I don't need it linked to Jason here.*

Then I really started working him over using all the tools they had there. I channeled my rage at Wulfric being hurt, and the uncertainty I felt when it came to my relationship with him, into each swing and slice of Jason's body. My stress about his noncommittal attitude was directed into every sneering comment I taunted Jason with, until there was only a lump of bloody meat left behind. Breathing heavily, I realized he was dead and from the looks of it, he had been for quite a while.

"Well Wulfric always said, 'It's always interesting to see what people are hiding under their skins,'" I muttered as I threw down the hammer, just now realizing I was covered in blood and the room was a mess. Reaching a bloody hand into my pocket, I pulled out my phone to check the time and realized I had been here for hours and the club would be closing at any minute. As I was about to put the device back in my jeans and figure out how to clean up, the phone rang.

"Wulfric?" I answered briskly.

A slight pause. "Do you need help?" Wulfric's even tone pulled me somewhat out of my detachment, but not fully.

"I just need to clean up and then deal with Jason. I'll only be a few more hours." Walking toward the sink, I turned the water on so I could do a quick clean up, enough to get me out of the club without too many questions. "Hopefully the blood won't stand out too much and cause problems when I try to leave."

"When you get back, come to my place?"

"Did you end up at the hospital after all? Did you need me to bring you something?" I asked as I soaped up my hands and started rinsing, scrubbing under my fingernails closely.

"I'm not at the hospital." I opened my mouth to berate him, but he cut me off before I even finished taking my breath. "Before you say it, the shot was clean through. Nothing vital was hit. I'm sore, but I'll be fine. Stay with me tonight?"

"I'll come by after I clean up a bit," I answered after a moment. "We wouldn't want them to find our guy too soon."

Wulfric's cold chuckle filtered through the phone and I smiled at the sound, familiar and oddly comforting.

"I'll see you soon then."

Click.

I slipped my phone back in my pocket and I cleaned myself up as best I could in the sink. I didn't bother trying to clean up the body, though I did take the time to wipe the tools clean of any obvious fingerprints. Now that it was all done and I had channeled my thoughts into Jason, I just wanted to get home. I froze as I suddenly realized, *home is Wulfric, a man who's never once said he loves me or is with me in public. What kind of person does that make me?*

CHAPTER 9

Wulfric

Getting shot wasn't really how I expected the evening to go, I thought ruefully as I carefully sat back on my sofa, book in hand. Robin should be back soon, the club closed almost an hour ago. I glanced toward the door, lost in thought, just as a soft knock sounded. I let a small smile fill my face at the familiar two taps, then three that Robin always knocked with when he came by.

"Come in," I called out.

The door slowly opened, like he couldn't believe the door was unlocked, and Robin walked in. *No way was I getting up after being shot, but I had my gun nearby if someone else had shown up.* His concerned and faintly cold expression warmed a bit when he saw me sitting and waiting for him. His wet hair made the dark brown look almost black, I noted absently, as he came over to join me on the sofa. Sitting carefully so as not to jostle me he settled beside me.

"How bad is the bullet wound actually?" His bland voice made me smile.

"What did you do to the Italian that made you shower before you got here?" I replied dryly. He turned slightly to meet my gaze and I searched his eyes; seeing the answer I gave a small 'ah' in response.

"What does that mean?"

I closed the book and set it beside me, knowing I wasn't going to be able to read it like I had originally planned. No time like the present to ask the hard questions it seemed.

"What was bothering you earlier tonight? You were fine in the bar then once we got to the sex party you turned almost..." I searched for the right word, but Robin didn't let me find it before releasing a derisive snort.

"You really have no idea do you?" he sneered as he jumped up and started pacing. My eyes followed his barely controlled movements as he paced back and forth in my living room. Each pass brought him from my

196

bursting bookshelf, to the stocked bar cart on the other side of the living room, then back again.

"How could I know if you don't tell me? I'm not a mind reader, Darling," I answered calmly after he had done a few circuits. Robin threw his hands up in seeming frustration as he stopped and spun to face me. "You did mention work—"

"I meant we needed to focus on work at that moment," Robin bit out.

"Okay." I leaned forward, ignoring the pain the movement caused me, and focused solely on the man in front of me. "Well, we aren't working right now. So talk to me."

"Why should I talk to you, if you don't talk to me?" Robin's quiet voice seemed to echo in the apartment. His entire demeanor froze, his body braced for what, I wasn't quite sure. I tilted my head, studying him unsure of what to say exactly. *What does he want to hear? What am I supposed to say?*

"If you want to be with someone who is going to be able to tell you the truth all the time, then I would suggest finding someone not in the same line of work. The things I've kept from you are things that I do for work. For the O'Callaghans and outside of them."

"As an O'Callaghan I deserve to know—" Robin started, but I cut him off coldly.

"Then take that up with O'Callaghan, that's his choice. Not mine." Robin's eyes flashed dangerously at that response, but I kept going before he could snap back at me. "You would say the same thing if you were in my shoes."

"I just killed a man! A Segreto who said they've cut a deal with the Förstner and started trafficking people. You knew I'd find out about that." His finger shook when he pointed at me accusingly.

"The world doesn't revolve around you." I cursed as I slowly stood and turned my back on him. "I'm sorry I was too busy being fucking shot to worry about the details of who we were questioning. And for your fucking information," I glanced over my shoulder at him, "I had no idea that's what they were getting into. I kill people, Robin. I don't bother selling them."

His only answer was quick footsteps across the room and a hard hand on my shoulder to spin me around to face him. Robin's face was taut with pain,

pain he was directing at me, and I knew that that was something I could help him with.

"You were mad before you started working Jason over." I searched his gaze. "What is it you're really mad about? It can't only be me not sharing things with you, name one other thing. One! That I haven't told you." When Robin didn't respond I shook his hand from my shoulder and turned away again. "Why don't you come back when you've figured it out?"

I heard him move and turned to face him at the last moment, hand up to catch his throat in a tight grip. "I'm not perfect, Robin. But if you want a fight to work through your anger and your adrenaline, I can do that. I can meet you blow for blow or fuck it out of you. Pick."

His body shuddered in my hold, but his eyes were still defiant. I gave him a slight shake when he didn't answer. "Pick. Now."

"You want to know what the real problem is? Really?" he spat at me. "I love you, you fucking idiot, and the only thing you give a shit about is *work*." I froze, unsure I'd heard him right. But he didn't give me any time to process. He just kept slamming me with words, stunning me. "You were shot tonight and I didn't give a damn about the job. I cared about *you*! How am I supposed to do my job, huh? As for before, with the sex party... I'm the first man you've been with, Wulfric. Actually been with. What's going to happen to me, to us, when you decide you're bored and you just walk away?"

Robin

WULFRIC WAS SO STILL after I finished my rant that I wasn't even sure he was breathing. When he blinked, still staring at me shell-shocked, I pulled slowly out of his grip on my throat.

"I should go," I said quietly after swallowing hard. "I'll see you tomorrow." I walked past him and almost made it to the door before he called out my name.

"Robin." His voice was soft, almost choked as he managed to say my name. I didn't turn around, but I did pause and wait for what he had to say.

"Whatever this is with you, what we have together, it's not just some random thing for me."

I turned to face him only to find him still facing the other way as if he was literally frozen from my earlier revelation. Something about tonight and the stress of shit from the earlier meeting hit my nerves just right. His distance and cold focus weren't new, but even I was shocked when I threw out his history with women into this. I rubbed my face when he didn't say anything else, both of us at a loss of what to do next.

"I shouldn't have thrown it in your face that you haven't dated men before me." Tiredness bled into every word. "It's been a long ass day, why don't we just talk about this tomorrow?"

"Because you practically demanded we do it now." Wulfric turned to face me at that. "You wanted this conversation, so let's have it. It's true I haven't been with men besides for sex, but you knew that. We've been together for almost a year and no one knows we are, because they *can't* know about it. That was also something you knew when we started this."

His voice never raised as he kept talking, if anything, it seemed to get quieter which made the sting of each statement worse.

"I know that, I do. But that doesn't magically change how I feel." I shook my head. "And I know you don't love me. I don't even want to go there because I don't think I can."

"Robin—"

"No." I held up a hand that halted his words, but it didn't stop him from walking up to me. A rough hand grabbed mine, moving it out of the way as he leaned in and caught my mouth in a soft kiss. One soft kiss, followed by a second, and I couldn't keep myself from responding to the third. I pulled him against me, taking control and pouring everything I had into the kiss as it turned harder.

Wulfric pulled away first, his breath trembled between us. "There are things you don't know—"

I pressed a finger on his lips. "There are plenty of things you don't know about me either, Wulfric. We all have pasts and I shouldn't have thrown yours at you. Emotions can be a bitch." A rough laugh escaped Wulfric at that, "I'm more interested in your future than your past."

He became so still under my finger I wasn't even sure I felt him breathe for a minute. Eventually, he moved my finger from where it rested against his lips.

"My future?" Realizing I might have said too much, I shifted, but his grip on my hand prevented me from putting distance between us. "Do you plan on being in my future, Robin?" Wulfric pushed.

"I did say I love you, but I guess that depends on you," I managed to get out. Unsure exactly how he was going to respond to everything that was slipping out tonight, sweat began to form on my skin. *Murder highs are not the time for emotional confessions, something to remember for next time.*

When he just kept staring at me I started to fidget. My fingertips rubbed together in an absentminded gesture I had picked up from him. He grabbed hold of my hand, stopping the motion.

"Wulfric—"

"I'm not always the best at words." His voice was so low I wouldn't have been able to hear it if I wasn't standing right beside him. "Actions I can do. You don't know everything, Robin, not even a hint at some things that you probably should. Give me time to figure this out."

Taking a page from his book I studied him. I took in the dark brown hair falling into his face, the anxiety that flickered within the specks of gold in his brown eyes. His muscles were tense as he watched me look him over. Placing my hand on his chest, I could feel his heart thundering as he pulled me slowly against him. With a dim awareness, I realized that the beating of my heart matched the speed of his. Gazing at the man in front of me, I knew that I wasn't going anywhere, but I wondered just what it would take before he pulled away the few small pieces of himself that he was sharing with me. I had a feeling that it would break me when he leaves me, though I was helpless to stop myself from going forward with my eyes wide open.

I wasn't sure what Wulfric saw in my face, but whatever was there made his features soften into something almost like wonder. Before he could react, I let my body settle fully against him. I smirked slightly at the slight hitch of breath from putting pressure on his side, but when he didn't push me away I knew he didn't mind the slight pain.

"We should try to get some sleep. My phone already has an alarm set," I told him softly.

His hand stroked my back. "You're right."

But neither of us moved to go to his bedroom, as if we were nervous that the moment ending would shatter everything. I knew I was apprehensive about him letting me in piece by piece, and telling me random things of his past wasn't enough. He would have to trust me. Really trust me for this to last, and I wasn't sure if that was something he could give me. My heart hurt at the thought, but if this thing between us ended, I knew he would be the best mistake I ever made.

I started to move away, but threaded my fingers through his to pull him through his apartment and down the hallway to his bedroom. Not bothering to turn on the light, I easily maneuvered us around the room I knew as well as my own. Past the lone bookshelf he had along the far wall between a window and the entrance to the hallway, each shelf full to the brim with books, and around the bench he'd placed at the end of his bed. Once I stopped at his side I pushed him gently onto the bed and rewarded him with a soft kiss on the lips before turning to leave.

"I'll be right back." I threw over my shoulder as I stepped out of the bedroom. Quickly, I moved down the hall, locked the front door, and turned off the lights. Grabbing the book off the couch where he had put it down earlier, I swiftly walked back into the bedroom.

Wulfric was sitting up in bed watching me closely as I re-entered the room. I held out the book as I turned on his bedside light.

"Here." When he didn't take it I glanced over at him and he was staring at me with such an odd look on his face that I sat down beside him. "What's wrong?"

He took it and turned it over in his hands a few times. The book was in German so I wasn't sure of the title, but it looked well-loved with cracks all over the spine and an old receipt was tucked in between the pages as a bookmark.

"Nothing, I just—" He licked his lips, wetting them in preparation to speak as he seemed to gather his thoughts. "Thank you."

"Of course." I smiled at him before walking around to the other side of the bed. Stripping quickly out of my shirt and pants, I slid under the sheets and lay on my side to watch Wulfric who was studying me. "What?"

"Why are you all the way over there?" He went to gesture at the space between us but stopped short as the movement pulled at his wound.

"That right there would be why," I replied dryly, smiling slightly in amusement as he shot me a glare. "You need to let your body heal."

"That doesn't mean you need to be all the way over there. My left side is hurt, not my right. So get over here." Wulfric's voice was gruff as he patted the space right beside him softly. I considered him for a moment before making my way over to his side, and when Wulfric raised his right arm I laid my head on his chest, careful to not get near his bandages.

Long fingers gently played with my hair and I smiled at the touch. As I closed my eyes, breathing in the faint smell of scotch and smoke that I always associated with him, I could hear the soft hush of pages turning, and I smiled. It wasn't long before I felt sleep pulling at me and I knew that, at least for now, I'd found home. I just hoped I didn't regret it.

EPILOGUE

Wulfric

I straightened my jacket one last time while looking myself over in the mirror. *How could I possibly be more nervous to have this meeting than any of the other times I've been over for a meeting?* A light knock sounded on the bathroom door before it opened, revealing Robin standing on the other side. In a suit himself, he looked beautiful and deadly; it suited him perfectly.

"Are you ready to go?" he asked, while his gaze lingered on my left side. I couldn't hide the slight twinge that still lingered whenever I moved too quickly and Robin caught it every time. Though this time, unlike the others, he didn't mention it before flicking his gaze up to meet mine.

"Yes." I nodded at him. "Let's go."

Since I was already armed I didn't stop to get anything as I followed Robin through my apartment and out the front door. Once I clicked the lock in place we turned and walked toward the elevator and I pressed the down button. While we waited for it to reach my floor Robin glanced at me enough times that I looked over with a raised eyebrow.

"Something you want to say to me?" He didn't get a chance to answer as the elevator chose that moment to ding, signaling its arrival. When the doors opened one person stepped out, but I didn't get a good look at their face before Robin stepped inside and I quickly followed.

As the doors closed I turned toward him again. "You didn't answer my question."

"It's nothing." Robin shook his head and I let out a sigh of frustration.

I'd been healing from being shot for the past two weeks and while I was far from completely healed, I didn't want to put off this meeting any longer. These past two weeks seemed more than a bit surreal since Robin stayed with me every night. It was probably the most time we'd had together the entire year we'd been dating and I was shocked that I didn't mind. Every night I spent with him I just wanted more, and I'd never experienced that with anyone else before.

He didn't mind my dark humor or sharp comments that sometimes slipped out. In fact, Robin gave as good as he got. The only complaint I had was the no sex that had happened in these two long fucking weeks. Maybe it was time to show him how healed I really was and own every inch of his body tonight. Or, I narrowed my eyes on him as he pulled out his phone, maybe there was no time like the present.

The ding of the elevator interrupted my thoughts and Robin didn't glance my way as he walked off toward his car in the parking garage. His nondescript black sedan was tucked in the back corner and as we approached, I picked up my step to catch up with him. Robin gave me an odd look as I stepped up beside him and he opened his mouth like he was going to ask me something. I didn't give him the chance.

I gripped his upper arm and forced him to stop beside me before kissing him. At the feel of his hardened body against mine, I let out a groan of appreciation and his answering moan had my dick hardening. I walked him backward until his body hit the side of his car, reveling in the feel of his hands over my body. He was automatically avoiding my still sore side, instead, threading a hand through my hair and the other gripping my right hip tightly.

Sinking my teeth into his bottom lip, I laughed darkly into our kiss as he jerked against me at the pain. I slowed the kiss down slowly and broke away from his lips to trail kisses along his jawline.

"What—" Robin shuddered. "What was that for?"

I smiled against his cheek. "I wanted to. Isn't that reason enough?" He tried to pull away to look at me, but I held him close preventing any space between us.

"But your—"

"If you say my side, Robin Healy, I swear to god I will beat your fucking ass," I told him softly, and I felt his cheek pull up in a smile as he let out a chuckle.

"You are supposed to be taking it easy," he chided me.

"I have been." My voice was husky as I countered. "Now, I'm tired of being careful. I want you."

"You have me." Robin moved away slightly to look me in the eye. I searched his dark gaze at that and was still awed to find amusement, fond irritation, and love there as he looked at me. I had no idea what I did to deserve the man in front of me, but I hoped I could keep him with me for a least a little while longer. Family life had already taught me that nothing was guaranteed.

"I do," I answered softly, leaning forward to brush my lips against his gently. "We should go. Being late won't look good for my first official Family dinner." I stepped back from him and he smirked slightly before starting toward the driver side of the vehicle.

Before long we were on our way through the city going toward the O'Callaghan Family home and I rested a hand on Robin's knee. Automatically he put one of his on top of mine, squeezing it slightly before placing it back on the wheel. I didn't focus on my surroundings, instead, I kept my gaze trained on the man beside me. At the smile playing on his lips, I knew he could feel my attention but had no complaints about being the center of it.

As he parked in front of the house, Robin quickly turned off the car. He moved to unlock the door and get out when I tightened my grip on his knee to stop him.

"What is it?" He shot me a questioning gaze.

With a hand threaded through his hair I pulled his face close to mine and claimed his lips in a hard, quick kiss. Pulling away I took in his puffy, nearly bruised lips and the heat in his eyes.

"I told you I'm not good with words, but I want you to know... I'm happy here with you. Right now. I can't imagine being somewhere else."

A soft smile answered my declaration and he kissed me softly. "I love you too. Now, are you ready to officially be part of the O'Callaghan Family? Once you go in, there's no going back."

"Come hell or highwater, Robin. You're stuck with me."

If only I had known how true that statement would end up being. Hell or highwater indeed.

About Suki Williams

I live wherever life currently takes me and my family across the USA. I've always loved reading and writing, but after discovering reverse harem, I decided to actually give writing a shot.

I love reading whenever I get a chance, daydreaming new book ideas, and talking loudly about inappropriate things in public places. I have a love affair with chocolate that not even my hubby will try to get in between.

I've currently published Beauty of Corruption, Lies and Loves ,book one and Nexus, Forgotten Prison Book 1. I also write gay romance under Suki Gale and have released two books with a fellow author, J.J. Riley, in our Echo Bay series.

Facebook Page: https://www.facebook.com/authorsukiwilliams/
Reader Group: https://www.facebook.com/groups/SukiHouse
Instagram: https://www.instagram.com/authorsukiwrites/
Twitter: https://twitter.com/AuthorSuki
Bookbub: https://www.bookbub.com/profile/suki-williams
Website: https://authorsukiwilliams.wixsite.com/authorsukiwrites

Suki Gale
Reader Group: https://www.facebook.com/groups/JJRileySukiGale/

THE CRUEL ITALIAN

N.J. Adel

SYNOPSIS

THE CRUEL ITALIAN
She was born to be mine

After a fight twelve years ago, a little girl gave me a box of bandages and told me I shouldn't smoke because it was yucky. I couldn't take my mind off her ever since.

I wait for her to be a woman so I can make her mine, but she's scared to date the Mafia prince soon to be king.

I don't care. No one is gonna touch her but me. Bianca Zanetti was born to be mine. Whether she likes it or not.

Author Note

The Cruel Italian is an MF dark Mafia romance.

Trigger warnings: obsession, kidnapping, some bdsm.

All sex is consensual.

Please be prepared for a cliffhanger. *The Cruel Italian* is the prequel of *The Italian Marriage*. It's available for preorder and will be released August 28th.

Bianca

TWELVE YEARS AGO

His right hand was on the handlebar of his motorcycle, the knuckles scraped raw, and large chunks of skin were missing.

He was studying his injury and so was I behind the diner window. There was a lot of blood, but I wasn't scared. I was only eight, and his maimed hand was just another boo-boo. A cool one if the hand was broken.

An excited smile stretched my lips. It must have revealed the gap in my upper jaw from my missing front teeth. That was when he lifted his sunglasses and saw me.

I didn't look away, and my smile grew bigger. He was sweaty and grimy; he must have been in one hell of a fight. For some reason it made him look even more gorgeous.

After a few seconds of staring back at me, he, too, smiled. Heat burned my face, and I giggled. Then he took the last of his cigarettes and tossed the crumpled packet to the ground.

Eww.

Laughing no more, I walked out of the diner straight toward him. Then I reached into my backpack and pulled out a box of bandages. "Here."

He cocked a brow, grinning from ear to ear as he took the box. My hand felt really tiny compared to his. Then he blew out the smoke away from my face and thanked me.

"Smoking is yucky. It makes you sick," I said with a crazy lisp my missing teeth created.

His chest shook with laughter under his leather jacket. "I'm sorry, Miss." He threw the cigarette on the ground and stepped on it with his boot.

"Eww. You shouldn't litter either." I picked up the packet he'd so carelessly tossed down, walked toward the garbage can, and threw it there. "Can't believe I thought you were cool."

Another cackle of his burst behind me, and I realized I said that out loud. I turned around, my ponytail whipping, my face blazing with embarrassment. He turned off his Harley and put the kickstand down. Then he took the flattened cigarette off the ground and came to me.

"What's your name, kiddo?" He flicked the cigarette into the can, a hint of a tattoo appearing when his sleeve retracted.

"I...I don't talk to strangers."

A cocky smirk curved his mouth. "You were just talking to me."

I shrugged. "You needed help."

"I did." He smiled at the box of bandages. "How can I repay you, little missy? Do you live nearby? I can give you a lift."

I tilted my chin up to look him in the eye. He was a tall boy. How old was he? High school or college? "How stupid do you think I am? I don't talk or ride with strangers."

"Your mamma taught you good, si?"

I pursed my lips as a black car pulled up next to his bike. "You're Italian?"

"Si si. My name is Cosimo." He bent over, and the smell of sweat, cigarettes and blood filled my nose. He was so close he could snatch me up and runaway on his bike or shove me in that car with the window rolling down. I should have stepped back. I should have run. But all I did was take a mental snapshot of his eyes. They were the color of honey, so bright against his tanned skin. So haunting I thought he could have been a vampire—if he hadn't had a perfect tan—or a werewolf. So...beautiful. "Now, I'm not a stranger. Would you tell me your name?"

"Bianca! Get inside!" Mr. Alfarez, the diner owner yelled.

My head jerked back. He was furious, shooting death glares at the boy. When I didn't move, Mr. Alfarez grabbed my arm and dragged me inside the diner himself. He kept scolding me all the way inside, threatening to tell Mom, never taking his glare off the boy's face.

I was angry. I did nothing wrong. I wouldn't have told a stranger my name or ridden with them. If anybody did something wrong here, it was Mr. Alfarez when he yelled my name. How stupid!

I didn't know then, the yucky, gorgeous boy, who pinned me with his stare and didn't seem to pay attention to scary Mr. Alfarez, was Cosimo Lanza.

The son of Giovanni Lanza, the big boss of the Italian Mafia.

CHAPTER 1

Bianca

E very predator needed a camouflage. His was a suit and an intense, panty-melting gaze in honey eyes.

My pulse hiked in my chest as we both pushed doors at the same time. I was pushing the kitchen door to work my section, and Cosimo was pushing the diner front door.

I lowered my head, my hand frozen on the wood for a second, and then I turned and hid in the corner next to the walk-in cooler.

Did he see me? My eyes squeezed shut. *Please don't make him see me.*

"Your Don Corleone is here." Mona's squeak and elbow nudge in my ribs popped my eyes wide open, my heart beating outside my chest.

"Shhhh. Why are you yelling?"

She scrunched her nose. "I'm not. What are you doing here?"

"Hiding," I whispered. "Did he see me? Does he know I'm working this shift?"

"He wouldn't be here if he didn't know you were. He's not alone by the way. The other Corleone is here, too. What do you say I go give him a glimpse of the girls?" She pointed at her big boobs that earned her double my tips. "These babies never fail. Maybe they'll take us on a double date."

"A double date with the Kray twins? Really?"

She chuckled. "Girl, they look nothing like the Kray twins."

She was right. With their thick dark hair, deep eyes, perfect tans and custom-made Armani suits to fit their incredible bodies, Cosimo and Enzio Lanza looked like sin and redemption all at once.

"I don't know how Mama Lanza tells them apart. Do you think they have matching dicks, too?" She chuckled again.

I slapped her arm, my jaw hanging low.

Her thin brow shot up. "What? Aren't you a little bit curious?"

I rubbed my forehead, shutting my eyes. Cosimo's dick was the last thing

219

I wanted to think about. "No. I don't need that image or that question in my head."

Even though they were identical, for me, Enzio looked completely different from his brother. I could tell them apart any day any time. Cosimo had this effect on me no one else had, and I'd met a fair share of men. Here in Alfarez and during my one year in college before I'd dropped out. I might have been twenty, but I'd seen a lot. One look into Cosimo's eyes, and it was as if he literally put me in a trance to steal my heartbeat.

More reasons to stay away—and never get curious about any part of his perfect body—while I could still run for my life.

I stared at the gorgeous blonde I wished I'd had any of her assets, my eyes doing all the talking.

"You for real? I was kidding." She swallowed, her humor suddenly gone. "No way I'm going there. Cosimo comes here for you. He'll kill me. He's sitting in your section. At the same table he's been sitting at for years."

Two years and ten months, but who's counting?

"C'mon, Mona. Just do me this solid, please. Tell him I took off early or something. I'll cover for you all day once he's gone."

"No can do."

The kitchen door burst open and Romero stormed toward us. "What the hell? You two are babbling here while people are waiting for their coffee? Get your asses out now."

Romero Alfarez was the definition of a douche. Nothing like his dad. The old man was tough but nice. The only father figure I'd ever had. This douche? He was no brother of mine. "I need to hit the ladies' room. Girl problems." I slithered to the back as he looked at me in disgust. "Mona, can you please take care of my section for a minute?"

"I fucking hate you," she mouthed, her stare murderous.

I gave her a sheepish smile and disappeared, praying I hadn't just killed my best friend.

CHAPTER 2

Cosimo

"Of all North Beach restaurants you choose this cheap shit diner for lunch?" Enzio crinkled his nose as if he'd smelled a fart when he slid in the booth.

I took off my sunglasses, fixed my tie and slid across from him. "I like the coffee here."

He snorted. "You mean your dick likes the ass that serves the coffee here."

If Enzio hadn't been my twin, I'd have smashed his smart mouth just for mentioning her ass.

He tilted a little and glanced over his shoulder. "You sure we're in the right section? It's not the little dolcessa that's coming our way."

I spread my hands flat on the scarred table top in a way of keeping control of them. My twin or not, one more pet name or word about Bianca or her body, and I'd rearrange his face.

My gaze shifted toward the busty waitress approaching us. Maddie was it? Samantha? I never bothered to remember her name. It wouldn't matter because I was going to kill her for daring to come to my table.

The carafe shook in her hand as she poured the coffee, cheap lipstick covering her quivering smile. "Welcome back. Can I get you anything?"

"Where's Bianca?"

Without straightening her back, keeping her tits in both Enzio's face and mine, she said, "She's not in today. I'm covering for her."

I hated liars as much as I hated the coffee and the food and the owner of this dump. There was only one reason I'd been coming here for the past three years, and she was hiding somewhere while sending that bitch to lie for her.

Instead of soaking the waitress's face in the fucking coffee and watching her skin melt for lying to me, I leaned forward with a smile. "What's your name, bella?"

Her eyes widened in disbelief, her shaking slowing down. "Mona."

I let my glance roam her body and linger on her tits, giving her the wrong impression, easing her tension. "Tell me, Mona. Is Bianca just hiding or is she watching, too?"

Her fat nipples hardened into the rough fabric of her blue waitress dress, out of fear not arousal—or maybe both—her body a stiff lump again. "I...I told you—"

My fist wrapped around her wrist, and she gasped. "Don't you dare lie to me again...Mona. Be honest and play along, and you have my word I'll let you go without a scratch."

Tears sparkled in her pleading eyes. "I...I...don't know if she's watching."

I darted a gaze at the closed kitchen door, taking a deep breath. My patience was running out. I could barge in, yank Bianca out, lock her up in my house and never let her see the sun again.

I could break her, take her and ruin her in every way I wished. But I wouldn't. Not yet. This game we played I enjoyed so much I let it continue for years. I wanted those fiery eyes I'd seen twelve years ago to break for me, not because of me. I wanted that fearless heart of hers to beat for me, not to wilt in my prison.

How much longer could I wait? My need for her, her beautiful face, her scent, her voice, her body, was consuming me, eating away at my every rational thought. How much longer before the monster I was took over and claimed what he desired without a shred of care?

I was no saint. Inevitably, I'd break. Very soon.

"Sit on my lap," I ordered.

"What?" the waitress squeaked.

Enzio chuckled, rolling his eyes at me. "Do as you're told, dolcessa."

Her hesitation bored me. I grabbed her wrist, my free arm around her ass, making her obey. When she settled on my legs, I ran a finger along her jaw and down to her chest. Then I leaned into her ear. "You'll tell Bianca I was flirting with you, and I was hard as a rock when you sat on my lap."

Her clumpy mascara smeared under her eyes. "But...you're..."

Flaccid as fuck. This blonde in all her glorious tits and firm ass was not my type. Mine was a little brunette with hazel eyes named Bianca Zanetti. "You had no trouble lying to me. I'm sure you'll have no trouble lying to her."

She nodded, swallowing.

"You'll also tell her that I'm coming tomorrow for more of your sweet ass." I squeezed her toned flesh, enjoying her flinching. "And if you're a good girl, I said you might get lucky and be my date for the night. Don't forget to squeal when you do, show her how excited you really are."

A frightened laugh gurgled in her throat. "Yes, Cosimo. Anything you want."

I gave her one last stare, drawing another invisible line along her bobbing throat, and then I let her go.

Faltering, she got off me, yet she managed to throw Enzio a smile and a better view of her bust before she left.

"She has a thing for you," I said, almost jealous. I wished Bianca would have made half of her friend's efforts to get my attention.

"Ugh. Since your contessa isn't coming, can we go have some decent food now before the meet?"

CHAPTER 3

Cosimo

In the back seat of the Mercedes, I stared through the window at Alfarez Diner. Bianca was *there*, talking to the blonde bitch.

"We're going to be late," Enzio grumbled.

"I'm Cosimo Lanza. They will wait," I said, irritated, mad at myself, not him. Years of craving and not taking had worsened my temper.

The stubborn pixie with eyes forged in fire and a smile that made me believe God was real didn't know how much restraint and control I'd forced upon myself to let her play her denying game this long.

"I don't understand what we're still doing here. You've worked the blonde. Hands down, she'll play your stupid jealousy card."

I watched longer as the two girls talked, waiting for any sign or gesture from Bianca. A yell, a tear, a glare, anything at all. "I want to know if it's working."

"You'll know tomorrow when you go back there. Let her simmer, *Don Cosimo*." He stressed the last words and snorted. "I can't believe you'll go through all that trouble in the first place for some pussy."

"She has a fucking name," I snapped, my head jerking toward him, equally furious that he kept talking shit about Bianca and reminding me I was the fucking Mafia boss. I shouldn't have made a girl jealous to get her attention. I should have made her beg on her knees to be with me.

His hands lifted in surrender. "Piano. Che cazzo?"

I breathed out and returned my stare to the window. To the only girl that dared say no to me, yet her skin flashed with heat every time her gaze dropped to my mouth. To the woman that would always be mine, even if she didn't know or accept it.

"Cosimo...are you... Oddio." He sighed.

Rage surged through me again. "I'm not in love with her if that's what you're saying." A man like me had to have a dead heart. Love made you soft. Soft made you weak. Weak got you killed.

"I didn't say it, and fuck I think it's worse than that. You're obsessed with Bianca Zanetti. She clouds your mind, makes you do very stupid things."

"Basta!" I hadn't done anything stupid. Not yet.

Stupid was wiping out Alfarez and his family, upsetting mine and ruining the business we had with them for twenty years, only so she'd no longer be under their protection. Stupid was kidnapping her, using her for my pleasure, forcing her to do my bidding anywhere my heart swayed.

Stupid was shoving her into my life, knowing it would only put a target on her back.

Maybe that was why I never went through with it. Why I tortured myself in her game without trying to win.

No one could understand what I felt for Bianca, not even my half soul. Yes, Bianca Zanetti was my unhealthy obsession. But that was just one part of it.

The little girl that didn't have an ounce of fear when she walked straight to a tattooed boy on a bike who had just got out of a fight, giving him bandages and telling him to stop smoking because it'd make him sick. The woman that would make Don Cosimo behave like a stupid teen trying to get her jealous.

The heart I wanted to own and protect.

The body I wanted to devour and cradle.

My gaze traced her face. I wished I'd been Da Vinci or Angelo. I'd sketch her face everywhere I went. Try to capture the flames in her eyes when she looked at me from under her long, thick lashes. But my hands only knew how to draw with blood.

Enzio swore under his breath. "Fine. You want her this much, be smart about it."

"What?"

"Why don't you uncover the old beast and take her for a spin? She liked your Harley."

"She also liked NutJobs." I used to buy them for her and sneak them in her backpacks and lockers without her knowing. "But she was a little girl back then."

"She still is. Aren't they all? No matter how old they are, they will always be little girls. Don't be fooled with that strong, independent woman fuckery. You pamper her when she's good. You put her over your knee when she's bad."

I tore my gaze away from the window and dragged my hand through my hair. The idea didn't seem like a total waste of time.

But no. I'd rather she hurt for me like I'd been hurting for her. I was too proud to tailor myself for her liking. If anything, she should be the one doing it, like she should grow her hair back for starters. I loved her ponytail, and I'd like to grab on it when I made her scream my name. "I will put her over my knee if she doesn't show up tomorrow."

"I bet she'll keep misbehaving just so you can do that again and again." He laughed. "But if she does show up?"

I pictured her blazing eyes as she'd push the blonde away and walk to my table. She wouldn't say a word, but I'd hear her mind loud and clear. She'd contemplate spilling hot coffee on my slacks, and I might just let her if she went for it.

It'd mean she couldn't bear the idea of my getting hard for someone else. It'd mean she wanted me as much as I wanted her. It'd mean, soon, she was going to be in my arms, all for me.

For that, I'd gladly burn.

CHAPTER 4

Bianca

"He's *really* big," Mona whispered, chuckling under her breath.

Blood pounded in my temples as I glowered down and fiddled with my apron. "You...felt him...up?"

"No." She giggled. "But I could feel it when I—"

"Yeah! I get it!" My pitch raised a whole octave.

She cocked a brow. "C'mon, B. What choice did I have? It's not like I hit on your Don. That was all him. Besides, you sent me there. You didn't even want to see him. Why are you so upset?"

That backstabbing, impossible forbidden fantasy boyfriend stealing bitch. My head whipped up. "I'm not upset. Who said I'm upset? And he isn't my fucking Don. He isn't my *anything*. Enjoy your little time with the mob and...his big dick." *Up your ass. I hope he fucks it bloody.*

My hands clenched into fists as I spun and started for the bathroom, fucking tears burning my eyes. I punched the door open a little too hard. Then I locked myself in a stall, tears aching to be free.

Why the hell was I crying? Why would I care about who Cosimo did or didn't date or fuck? Why was my blood boiling when I found out he was hard for my best friend?

It was high school all over again. My first—only—boyfriend, Andy Michelson, and Amanda Stanley. He was the swim team champ, blond, tall with swimmer arms and always smelled nice. My first kiss. We fooled around a lot. Made it to second base, but nothing more. He even asked me to Prom, but he broke up with me before it. The douche ghosted me without explanation and started dating the cheerleader bitch. Amanda was blonde and pretty with big tits like Mona.

That's it. I'm mad at Mona, not the perfect, cruel, yucky, Italian asshole. If it were any other filthy slut, I wouldn't want to rip both their throats out like I feel now.

I cursed at myself. At the outright lie.

227

I wasn't angry because it was my best friend he wanted to fuck—it did make it worse, but it wasn't the real reason.

It didn't matter if it was Mona or anyone else. I was feeling as if someone had punched a hole in my chest and filled it with hellfire because I was...jealous.

There I said it.

The idea of Cosimo touching someone else hurt. Burned. Corroded my heart like acid.

Even if I'd never confess it. To him or anyone else.

No matter how much I loved...how much I loved his gaze on me that made me excited and nervous and a little bit scared. How much I loved the way he'd kept his desire for me in check but every once in a while his eyes flicked with dark need I stupidly ached to fill.

No matter how many times I'd pictured undoing his tie and the buttons of his shirt, and then gliding my hands up his chest while his lips crushed mine. How many times I'd imagined the feeling of his beard between my thighs and the feeling of his...

No matter what, I would never be with Cosimo. Could never be.

The boy on the bike I'd failed to take off my mind for twelve years was Mafia King. Raised by Alfarez, I knew exactly what getting involved with a member of the Lanza family, let alone the boss, meant without any room for speculation or doubt.

Blood.

On my hands, even if I wouldn't pull any triggers. On my soul, even if I would never be a part of any operation. On my dead body, even if I'd have done nothing to earn the animosity.

Anything related to Cosimo Lanza and his family meant blood. Period.

I didn't want to live in fear and darkness for the rest of my life. I'd seen enough of those to last a lifetime.

Sometimes I wished he would have just kidnapped me. That way I'd have had no choice. He'd have forced me to be with him, and I'd have fought against it. Of course, I wouldn't have won. Who was I to stand against him? I was only an orphaned, dropout waitress that had zero future or power.

Right?

Not that it mattered anymore. Cosimo no longer wanted me. I pushed him away hard enough that he'd lost interest. Now, he wanted Mona, the blonde with the big boobs and willing curves.

Tears gathered in the corner of mouth as my lips parted for a deep moan.

It was better this way. With Cosimo off my back, the spell he'd put me under would break. I'd finally have a chance at finding someone else. Someone good that I could dream of a healthy future with. It wasn't as if Cosimo was going to keep me forever if he had me. He'd have tossed me away once he was finished like he'd done with his smokes.

Mona didn't seem to mind. Her squeals were enough proof. They'd be better off together.

I ran angry palms under my eyes and wiped my face. Then I unlocked the stall and splashed the crying away. I didn't bother with retouching my makeup. Looking at myself in the mirror now was going to make me cry again.

Tucking a short strand of hair behind my ear, I hurried back to the counter. Then I glued my gaze to the coffee machine, avoiding all eye contact, convincing myself I'd made the right decision.

I am going to bury my feelings down until they're dead. I am going to forget about the Mafia Boss and put my stupid fantasies behind me forever.

"Goodbye, yucky boy," I whispered, and then I busied my hands wiping things down and tidying up instead of shooting someone.

Chapter 5

Bianca

M ona and I got home from work at around eleven. We shared a tiny
apartment on Fillmore Street, not too far from the diner. I hadn't
said a word all the way as she drove us home in her old Civic, but the second
she locked the door, I had to say something.

"You can't have him here."

"Huh?" Her nose wrinkled as she kicked off her shoes.

My brows shot up so high it hurt. "Cosimo. You can't have him here."
Listening to them pounding each other from my room wasn't going to be
safe. For either of them. I wouldn't be held responsible for what I might or
might not do.

"Pffft. Like he would come here. Have you looked around this place
lately? You and me barely have room to breathe."

She was right. He'd probably take her to any of his hotels or maybe even
his apartment. She'd get to dress up for him and see the inside of his home,
where he sat, where he ate, his bedroom...

I took a deep breath so I wouldn't cry again. "Okay. Just..." I turned my
gaze to the light night rain starting behind the small windows. It was June,
but San Francisco weather was never predictable. Apparently, neither were
the men in this city. "Just be careful."

A humorless chuckle escaped her. "I'll do my best." She ambled straight
to her room. "Good night."

No, it wasn't and wouldn't get any better. It was going to be sleepless,
too. I spied the cheap red wine bottle in the kitchen and grabbed a glass. The
bottle and I were going to have a long date tonight.

As I poured myself the second glass, leaning against the kitchen counter
and staring out into the rain, Cosimo's picture invaded my head.

He was a man who wouldn't take an interest in a girl like me. A gazil-
lionaire with endless power and an expensive education, who took what he

wanted whenever he wanted. Nothing in this world was out of reach for society elite like him.

Why would he be interested in a girl thirteen years younger than he was? A poor waitress who lived in a shoebox? The daughter of two junkies, one I'd barely seen and the other got very sick I had to drop out of school to take care of, only so she could die and leave me totally alone?

But he did.

From the day we first met, when I had a long ponytail and a lisp and a using mother I had to parent since I could remember, when I dared scolding him for being such a bad boy, Cosimo never took his eyes off me.

It was as if he was watching me, waiting for me to grow up. For him.

Sometimes I thought the reason behind his waiting was to make me think he liked me only to have his revenge for what I did that day.

Other times, like when NutJobs mysteriously appeared in my locker or lunchbox—I knew they were from him as I caught him once watching me buy them from the store—I thought he truly liked and cared for me. It was the nicest thing anyone but Alfarez had ever done for me. Creepy, like his lurking outside my school or the grocery store where I shopped, never saying a word, but nice.

He wasn't just watching me until I became legal. He was watching out for me.

People got guardian angels to watch out for them, and mine was the devil in disguise.

Except that he was never mine. It was all in my head. No one was there for me. Not even the devil.

I left a note for Mona to go to work alone, and I was going to split my shift. We worked lunch and dinner together, but tomorrow I'd do breakfast and then go back in for dinner after she was gone. I wasn't going to sit and watch while they dry humped in front of me.

If I could afford it, I would take the whole day off. Alfarez used to cut me slack when Mom was sick or when I had classes, but Romero wouldn't if I were dying. I had to go to work. I had debts to pay, most of which weren't mine, courtesy of my dear parents.

It was raining heavily when I reached the diner for my second shift around nine, Cosimo's car nowhere to be seen. Great.

Part of me secretly wished I'd have bumped into him. There was a big chance I'd never see him again, and it'd have been nice if I could have said goodbye in person. Had I known yesterday was the last time I was going to see him, I would have at least said a few words.

If I hadn't hid in the bathroom yesterday, it wouldn't have been the last time I'd seen him.

With a sigh and an internal swear, I stepped inside. Mona was still there, though, working her section like normal. I took off my hoodie, barely looking at her as she placed the carafe in the coffee machine. "Shouldn't you be getting dolled up by now?"

A relieved smile painted her face. "He didn't show up."

My brows hooked. "How so? And why are you so happy he didn't?"

"I...I...am not happy. But what can I do about it?" She laughed nervously. "A guy like him does what he wants without explaining. Besides, standing a girl up isn't the worst of his crimes."

"Can't argue with that." I put on my apron, the little dance my heart was doing was inappropriate. Despite how much I hated he was taking Mona out, standing her up was a dick move. Even for an asshole like him.

Did he really change his mind? Cosimo didn't do that. Something wasn't right.

My mind tried to comfort me, convincing me Cosimo felt *guilty* about breaking my heart by dating my best friend. My brain even dared imagine this whole thing was a charade to punish me for hiding or to make me jealous.

I laughed at myself for thinking so highly of him or what we had. A man like Cosimo didn't feel guilt or go through all that trouble for one girl. He must have found something better to do. Someone better. After all, we were just trash diner girls to him.

A surge of anger washed over me. I took a look around. The diner was still busy. Good. Work was the best distraction, even the shittiest kind like working for Romero.

As I marched to my section, the bell over the front door jingled, and the tall, dark, and gorgeous Mafioso walked in.

Dressed in one of his dashing suits, his hair slicked back, his glowing eyes holding me captive, he looked like one of those models on dark romance novels girls drooled over for hours.

He didn't come closer or go sit down at his regular table. He just stared at me as I stood frozen in the middle of the diner with a nagging urge to throw myself in his arms.

I took a step toward him, and that was when he turned his head and sauntered into Mona's section.

My lips trembled with a gasp. Had Cosimo just ignored me like I'd never existed? Was he really here for Mona? To take her out on a date? Did he totally forget about me? About our unspoken...

Mona sailed past with the coffee carafe in one hand and a mug in the other, interrupting my pitiful thoughts.

Out of breath, my heart in a million pieces, I watched as she approached him and gestured at a booth in her section. He nodded and took a seat. She said something, and he whispered in her ear.

Fire blazed in my chest as she glanced at me over her shoulder and grinned. *The fuck?*

She rocked back on her heels and headed toward the counter, her jaw slack, her nipples hard.

Of their own accord, my feet moved to cut her in. My mind had forgotten about my earlier decision and forsaken all logic. I didn't want to see them together for a reason; I knew I couldn't help myself. "What was he saying to you?"

"Nothing much. He was telling me to get ready. But his voice alone made my ovaries explode." She blew out a breath and fanned herself. "Wish me luck."

I hoped she choked on his dick and bit him hard in the process. Glaring at her, I yanked the coffee pot out of her hand and switched my direction to her section.

She grabbed my arm. "What are you doing?"

I shrugged her off me. "What I should have done two years and ten months ago."

CHAPTER 6

Cosimo

My back was to her side, but I'd recognize her footstep anywhere. She was coming toward me, and I couldn't help the smile curving my mouth.

When Bianca stood by my table, I pretended to be ignoring her. She cleared her throat. "More coffee?"

My eyes lifted to her face. There it was. The fire in her eyes I'd predicted and long missed. She looked even more stunning, cocking a brow, jealousy and rage sparkling in her stare. "So nice of you to fill in for your friend while she gets ready for her date."

She looked as if she was about to murder me. "Taking her somewhere nice?"

"Certo. My date for tonight is a very special girl. I'd like her to have anything she wants. I'll take her wherever she wants to go. Tonight, her wish is my command." I smirked, savoring the flames eating her up. "And if it goes well, her wish will always be my command, every night and every day to come."

The pot twitched in her grip as her lips curled in a silent snarl. Was she going for it? Would she burn me for what I'd done? *Do you have it inside you, little missy?*

Her nostrils flared as she slammed the pot on the table, sending it on the floor in pieces. The customers stopped dining, and their stares fell on the spilled coffee and shattered glass. I didn't lift my gaze off her, though. She smashed the pot instead of hurting me with it—so she wouldn't hurt me with it. My beautiful obsession, like me, had her own demons that once they whispered it was hard not to listen.

Except, unlike me, she looked for ways to silence them.

"Fuck you." Her voice cracked.

My smirk turned into a smile. "Do you know what happened to the last person who dared say that to me?"

234

"I'm not scared of you."

"You should be."

"Maybe, but I'm not."

She tried to storm away. My hand caught her arm, stopping her in her tracks. "Where do you think you're going?"

"To clean this fucking mess and get your *special girl*," she grated, yanking her arm from my grip unsuccessfully.

"I don't like it when you play dumb, or did you really think I was going out with the blonde?"

Her big eyes narrowed into tight slits, but the sparks never faded. Then she shook her head. "I can't believe this shit. What are you? Thirteen?"

"You make me feel that way sometimes."

"You know what? Fuck you again, Cosimo."

"Stop swearing, little missy."

"Or what? You'll spank me?"

"If I have to."

Her gaze darted around. People were still staring, and her face turned from blazing red to a bashful crimson. "You can't just—"

"Everybody out!"

She gaped at me, and then at the customers leaving.

"If shyness is your problem, here. Your friends in the kitchen won't dare come out either. We have the place for ourselves now."

"You can't just do that," she scoffed. "Not everything is under your command, Cosimo Lanza."

"Yes, I can. I just did. And yes, everything and *everyone* is under my command."

She took a deep, angry breath, her chest rising with it. "Well, not me." She nodded at her arm. "Let go."

Her defiance along with her tits rising and falling made my cock twitch. I grabbed her closer and let her sweet smell fill my nostrils. Then I leaned in and held her with my gaze. "Never."

She held her breath for a second or two, and then she blinked. "What do you want from me, Cosimo?"

"Go out with me tonight."

235

The way she looked at me now reminded me of the first time she laid eyes on me. The honest infatuation that didn't hide behind games. The innocent glee of an eight-year-old girl. Then she smirked and cocked a brow. "Never."

CHAPTER 7

Bianca

I mpulsive, reckless and stupid. That was me in a nutshell.

I said fuck you to the Mafia Boss, twice, and then told him no when he asked me out. Again.

The first time he did, I was seventeen. It was as if he could no longer wait, even if I hadn't been legal yet. It wasn't like Cosimo played by the rules. To him, I was old enough.

But Alfarez managed to curb Cosimo then, and my age was an acceptable excuse.

The day I turned eighteen, I celebrated with my college friends at a nice restaurant in Berkley. When they left, Cosimo was right outside and asked me out again.

I asked him to give me some time to think, and he generously gave me till the weekend. He said he'd be waiting for me at the diner to get my response. He knew that during my time in Berkley I still came here and worked for Alfarez on weekends to make some extra cash and help my mother.

The anticipation I saw in his eyes that Sunday...

I wanted Cosimo so much. I still did. Knowing that he wanted me too was mind blowing, dangerously clouding my judgment. I wanted to give in and just be with him. Fuck, with that look in his eyes, I was ready to strip naked and beg him to take me on the spot. But I wanted a life, away from all the pain I'd seen in this city, and I thought back then I could get it.

Hopeful. Add that to the impulsive, reckless and stupid? *Believe me, I know.*

He wasn't pleased, but with Alfarez backing me up, Cosimo said he'd let me have my education. The whole college experience. Then he'd ask me out again.

No need to say that boys were not a part of the experience. That was his only condition, and by condition, I meant threat. Cosimo threatened—

promised—he would chop the dick of any boy who thought about *taking what was his.*

I didn't like it, but I agreed. Between classes, my barista job in Berkley and the diner here, and taking care of my mother, I didn't have time to date.

And honestly, no boy measured up to the one man I should never have. The only man I wanted to have.

When I dropped out, I had no more excuses left. I'd been stalling for a year, and every time I saw him, every time he showed me how much he still desired me, my resistance diminished.

That was why I hid yesterday. I could no longer look him in the eye and convince him I didn't want to be with him. I could no longer convince myself I shouldn't be with him.

Even now, when I was gripping at my rage, shielding myself from his mesmerizing eyes and scent and touch that ripped every shred of sanity in my head, telling him he could never have me, my heart was hammering in my chest, screaming at me, begging me to surrender.

No. Not after what he did, how he used my friend against me.

Finally, I freed myself from his grasp and spun away from him. Or so I thought.

The next second I felt his hand squeezing the back of my neck, pulling me to him and turning me around. He was on his feet now, his head bent to mine, our mouths an inch apart.

I gasped as his eyes glued to my lips, his breaths hot as his mouth parted. My pulse throbbed in my temples, and my legs wobbled even before he forced a kiss on me. I stared at him, secretly waiting for our lips to touch, for his fire to consume me.

"I promised myself I wouldn't force you into anything," he whispered in a husky voice, his expression somber. "I don't know how long I can keep that promise."

He licked his lips. Such a simple gesture but so sexy I moaned. "You will go out with me tonight. It's not a request or a negotiation."

Goosebumps prickled my skin, and I needed a moment to catch my breath. "What if I say no?"

His hand tightened around the back of my neck as he bit his lip, sending a throb between my legs. "You'll learn the hard way what you refuse to understand."

I swallowed. "What's that?"

"You were born to be mine." He dragged his gaze up to meet my eyes. "I take what's mine even if I have to paint the world red to make it happen."

I wanted to swallow again, but my mouth was too dry. My pussy, however... Who got horny when they were being threatened like that? The wetness gathering between my thighs assured me I wasn't just impulsive, reckless and stupid. I was plain fucked up. "What's that supposed to mean?" I managed.

"In this world, there is what I want or nothing at all." He ran his thumb along my cheekbone and then across my lower lip, inducing a shudder all over me. "I can just throw you over my shoulder and shove you in a chair at one of my restaurants." His thumb made the same move across my upper lip. "Or skip dinner entirely and just tie you to my bed."

Oh my God. Oh my GOD. OH MY GOD!

"But I won't. I like my girls willing." He mused. "In fact, I like them begging. And you, my sweet Bianca, will beg me to take you out."

"Never." *Shut up!*

A hint of smile crossed his mouth and he bit his lip again. What the hell? It was as if he was masturbating me with words and facial expressions. One more gesture, one more breath, and I'd just come. "Oh you will, because if you don't get on your knees right now and beg me to have dinner with you, I'll put a hole in your blonde friend's pretty head right in front of you, *tesoro mio*."

CHAPTER 8

Cosimo

My cock pressed against the zipper of my pants painfully. The way she shivered was messing with my self-control. The softness of her lips and her sweet scent stirred a deep primal desire inside me. An urge to claim her without mercy. A beast aching to mark her.

I could just take her right now, cover her mouth with mine, tear off her ugly waitress dress and sink deep in her wetness, claiming her pussy.

But if I did it, I'd never know her taste when she truly wanted a man. The feeling of her lips when she ached for a kiss. The beating of her heart when it beat with desire, not fear and pain.

"Are you crazy?" Bianca gasped.

Crazy for you. I didn't want Bianca to be mine. I needed her to be mine. I didn't have an ounce of patience left. "It's just me, little missy. It looks like I've gone way too easy on you you've forgotten who I am. What I am."

"Cosimo...you can't—"

"Blondie!" I pulled out my gun. "Get your ass in here!"

"Mona! Mona, no!" Her eyes shone with tears. "Cosimo...put the gun down...please."

"Please what, bellisima?"

Her lips trembled, and her throat bobbed with a swallow. "Please take me out," she barely whispered.

"I can't hear you, little missy."

She closed her eyes, water tainting the corners. "Please take me out tonight, Cosimo."

"Get on your knees, look me in the eye and say it."

Her eyes opened wide. "You're such an asshole."

Even now, that fire wouldn't die. *Bianca, Bianca, what are you doing to me?* "You haven't seen how much of an asshole I am yet. You're lucky I'm only telling you to *beg* when you're on your knees." I winked.

She swore under her breath, and, slowly, her knees touched the floor. I

240

let go of her neck and cupped her chin. Her gaze, a mixture of tears and wrath, tore at me and played with my heart. It hurt me to hurt her, but it had to be done.

She must have seen me as this heartless monster that felt nothing except the whims of his cock and thirst for blood. No guilt, no shame, no mercy, no love.

It was true. I had no room for these pathetic emotions that stopped men from being kings. But when it came to Bianca Zanetti...

"Say it," I ordered.

She gritted her teeth. "Would you please take me out on a date tonight?"

I bent and smiled, feeling her lips with my thumb again, imagining how they would feel against mine. "My pleasure."

CHAPTER 9

Cosimo

She sat as far as possible in the backseat of the Mercedes, no words coming out of her mouth, only troubled breaths.

My eyes trailed on her face, every feature I adored, even the frown that wrinkled her forehead. "Smile," I demanded, but my intention was to tease her.

Her head whipped to my side. "You blackmailed me into a date with you. Smile is the last thing I'm gonna do tonight."

I fucking loved the way she snapped. "What's the first?"

She shook her head, rolling her eyes. Then she stared back at the window. "Walk into your goddamn restaurant and snag a knife."

I stifled a chuckle. "Would you look at me when you do whatever you're planning to do with that knife?"

"You mean when I stab you to death? Yes."

I scooted closer. She flinched in response, and her head jerked toward me again. "Good," I said.

"Good that I'll kill you?"

I tucked her hair behind her ear, her eyes dinner plate wide. "If that's what it takes to make you look at me."

"I...I... Don't...touch me." Her chest heaved. "I don't care who you threaten to kill this time, but if you think for one second that I'm gonna—"

"You're not some tramp I'll fuck on the first date. You're a princess, and you'll be treated as such."

Her lips parted, trembling. "I hate you."

Ouch. I knew she didn't mean it, still it felt like a punch in the gut. "Is that what I get for being a gentleman?"

"I hate that you can be so *gentlemanly* one moment, but on the next you spit on all manners and humanity, stomping over them, like you did with your filthy cigarettes."

I cocked a brow. "You still remember that day?"

242

THE CRUEL ITALIAN

"How can I forget?"

Her response was fast. I wondered if it was a good thing or a bad thing. "Because the day you met me is the worst day of your life?" I teased again, hoping she wouldn't.

She swallowed, her lashes casting a shadow on her cheeks. "I've had worse."

A warm feeling coated my heart. "I haven't smoked a cigarette in twelve years, little missy."

She fiddled with her fingernails, and then folded her arms over her chest and hid her face—her smile—in the window. "I know."

A grin triumphed over me.

When we arrived at the restaurant, it was empty of customers as I ordered yesterday. Since the little game with the blonde, I'd been planning my first real date with Bianca. The whole restaurant for ourselves. Candles, her favorite music, and food made especially to delight her palates.

But first things first. "Go to my booth upstairs."

"Why?" she asked, alarmed.

"You can't have a date in a waitress uniform. There's a nice dress and matching shoes your size waiting for you upstairs. Makeup, too, not that you need any."

Surprise stretched her face. "You knew all along I was gonna let you take me out."

"I'm a man who gets what he wants." I bent my head to her ear. "And it's *you* who begged *me*, remember?"

"Here's that asshole again." she sauntered away, heading upstairs, her hips swaying beautifully. It was like she was asking for my spanking.

Our table was set. Lilies and red roses, her favorite flowers, adorned it on top of the checkered white and red tablecloth. Massimo, the best chef in all my restaurants, appeared, carrying a bottle of wine and two glasses.

I watched the hefty, old man uncork the bottle and pour a small measure into a glass. In Italian, he asked me to sample it. I swirled the wine, sniffed, sipped, and rolled it over my tongue. Then I nodded at him. "The best from our winery. I'd recognize a Lanza Vineyard anywhere."

"I keep the fine imports for special occasions, like today." He winked, wheezing as he shifted on his feet. "But the finest, I'll only serve on your wedding."

I laughed with him as he filled my glass. "Have some yourself, Massimo."

"Grazie, Cosimo. Should I pour for the lady now?"

"The lady shouldn't be drinking." She was twenty.

He snorted and shuffled away. "I hope you'll let her drink on the wedding night."

That shrewd old fuck. "What makes you think I'm marrying this one?" *This fast before she even turned twenty-one?*

A cackle ripped from his throat. "Oh, Cosimo. I raised you with Giovanni and Marta since your dick was the size of a knuckle. You're going to put a ring on your lady's finger before the month is over."

I lifted my glass and held it out as he vanished inside the kitchen in a silent toast. I took a sip, and before I swallowed it, Bianca was coming down the stairs.

I almost spit my drink, big twitch in my pants, my heart racing like a fucking boy. The dress, light green that brought out the brown in her eyes and suited the tone of her skin, hugged her little body, tight around the breasts and hips, showing her curves in the sexiest way ever.

I was certain my eyes were popping, shining with my desire for the most beautiful girl I'd ever seen. Fuck this shit. I shouldn't show my weakness for her like this.

I just couldn't help it.

She ambled toward me, fidgeting, her hands smoothing the fabric on her thighs, and then covering her chest. "It's too revealing."

I swallowed the wine stuck in my throat. "It's perfect."

Pink blush rose to her cheeks as I took her hand in mine. She was so fucking innocent it was driving my cock nuts. It took all my strength not to fuck that innocence, let it coat my cock instead of painting her face, right here right now.

I helped her to her seat. From where I stood, I could see the perfect seams of her tits, and the urge to feel them in my hands, see if her nipples were hard for me, was never stronger.

Get a fucking grip.

As I sat, her eyes traveled around the restaurant corners and lingered on the bodyguards standing. I was so used to their existence I forgot they were there. "These are the same guys that wait outside Alfarez when you visit. You never go out alone, do you?"

"When you're King, you need protection. Especially when I'm with a girl that wants to stab me."

She rolled her eyes, biting her lip on a smile.

"Are they making you uncomfortable?" I asked.

"Yes, *King*."

I ignored the sarcasm. "You shouldn't. They're here for your protection, too."

"Am I in danger?"

"Never when you're with me." I reached out for her hand, but she withdrew both her arms and placed them on her thighs.

"And when I'm not?"

I leaned forward, twining my fingers and clasping my hands on the table. I saw what she was doing, but her worry was pointless. "I've always protected you, Bianca, whether I'm in the same room with you or not. Your safety is not in question here."

She took a deep breath and helped herself to some bread. "Do you fuck in front of them, too?"

A smirk tugged my mouth. "Sometimes."

She grunted, munching on the bread.

Swallowing a laugh, I took another sip from my glass. "I thought we're not having sex."

"We're not!"

"I'm just saying that if you change your mind, I can tell them to go."

"I'm not changing my mind, Cosimo."

I managed to take her hand in mine before she retracted it again. She yanked, but my grip caged it in. Then I lifted it to my mouth and kissed her palm. "When you're ready, no one will be there but me. I can't let anybody but me see you naked."

Her blush deepened, driving me insane. I stared at her beauty for what seemed to be an eternity, her hand in mine, our eyes locked.

Exactly how I imagined it would feel.

Beautiful.

Heartwarming.

Dangerous.

CHAPTER 10

Bianca

Dazed and shaking under his stare, I felt hypnotized. He was so beautiful. His face, his body in the elegant suit, his words...his touch. Those were his weapons, not the gun tucked to his side.

I agreed to come here to save Mona. *Only* to save Mona. Except that with every second, I was losing perspective along with my sanity. As he gazed at me with his honey eyes, I almost forgot my best friend's name, and that he was about to kill her. I forgot he'd blackmailed me into this date, and my weak, pathetic heart was enjoying every moment I spent with Cosimo Lanza.

He kept staring, and I kept trembling until I found the courage to speak. "What?" I whispered.

"Grow your hair back."

I blinked. That was not what I expected. "I'm not pretty enough for you?"

His eyes tightened, and muscle ticked in his jaw. "I said I don't like it when you say dumb things," he said it as a warning. "You know you're so pretty I almost killed for you. And as much as I don't like that you wear your hair short, it looks good on you." His intense gaze softened. "Everything looks good on you. If you were fucking bald, you'd still be the most beautiful girl in the world."

My heart back flipped. I had to break our gaze and touch to breathe again. "So you miss the ponytail?"

He claimed my hand again, his glance reprimanding as if saying, *don't take your hand off mine without permission.* "Yes."

"I'm not a little girl anymore, Cosimo."

"I can see that." His lips parted slightly as he raked me up and down. "Clearly."

I averted my gaze, heat coming in waves, everyfuckingwhere. The awkward silence blistered, and only the chef with the huge belly saved us when he brought our food.

Cosimo had dismissed the waiters and made the chef himself serve us. Was it for safety reasons? Or was it because he didn't want the waiters, who were most likely hot, young Italians, to look at me? Knowing the controlling, jealous, possessive Don, I'd say it was the latter.

"Buonasera, Signorina." The chef placed two platters on the table and a few small dishes, and for a second I was mad Cosimo had ordered for me. I didn't even get to choose what to eat. Then the incredible smell numbed my anger. The platters looked so delicious I salivated heavily.

"I made Massimo make sample platters of all your favorite food." Cosimo printed a soft kiss on the back of my hand before he set it free. "He's the best chef in town. I know you'll love it."

The chef smiled at me and left. Then Cosimo started filling my plate.

I snorted. "Is that how it's going to be?"

"What?"

"You're choosing what I wear, what I eat, and putting food in my plate like I don't know how to use utensils. What's next? You'll feed me like a baby?"

He waved a fork full of mouthwatering lasagna I was dying to taste. "Yes. Open up."

I was about to do as I was told but stopped myself just in time. He had that ridiculous effect on me that made me wanna do everything he said, which made me wanna defy him all the time, if that made any sense. "No. I'm perfectly capable of feeding myself."

"I know you are. Doesn't mean there's anything wrong with your date feeding you. Open up, principessa."

I shook my head.

"Now who's being a naughty baby?"

"Oh my God. Don't talk to me like—"

He slipped the fork into my mouth and pulled it out slowly. "That wasn't so hard, si?"

I was about to protest but the rich taste of soft lasagna numbed my senses like a sedative. I moaned.

A wicked gleam sparkled in his eyes. "If you really didn't change your mind, you shouldn't make sounds like these in front of me."

My muscles tensed, and I stopped chewing. He dropped his gaze, as if looking at me now was too much, and started to eat.

"I'm sorry," I said, my mouth full, my nipples hard. Watching him restraining himself, seeing *my* effect on him, knowing he was trying to behave for my sake, set me on fire.

Distracting myself from the wetness gathering between my legs, I chewed. Reflexively, I moaned again. Fuck me.

He dropped his fork. "I'm serious."

What was I supposed to do? My body was taking command over my mind, forcing me to do things I'd regret.

Fuck you Mafia Boss. Fuck your hot Italian accent and mouthwatering food and chiseled tanned skin and sex god bodies and beautiful curly hair...

"What are you thinking about?" he interrupted.

How did he know I was thinking about anything? "How much I hate Italians," I mumbled, savoring the magnificent taste, keeping it as much as I could in my mouth, careful not to make any more sounds.

He stared at me like I was crazy. "Hate to break it to you, but *you're* Italian."

"Half." I finally swallowed. "My Italian parent didn't stick around long enough to make me appreciate anything about the heritage."

"And your mother did?"

It sounded more of a scoff than a question. I didn't blame him. Both my parents were shitty. My dad was an abusive junkie who put my mom's first needle in her arm himself. She let him. Why a mother of a two-year-old girl let anyone do that to her was beyond me.

He bailed when I was five and left us to pick up the pieces. Rumor had it, he ODed in a crack house years ago. I didn't bother to verify.

My Mexican mom tried to get clean a few times with the help of Alfarez, but after the epic failures every single time, she gave up. In my opinion, she wasn't really trying. She loved that shit in her body more than anything. Alfarez was tired of saving her, too, so he took me in instead.

When Mom lost function of her limbs, I couldn't afford house care. I was drowning in medical bills and student loans, even with Alfarez chipping in. I gave up my education to take care of her. She was the only family I had, and she, too, left.

"Bianca, where did you go?" Cosimo yanked me out of my thoughts.

I sighed, grabbing a spoon, eying the tiny casserole on my platter. "A bad place."

"I shouldn't have mentioned her. I'm sorry for your loss."

"It's been months." I stuffed my mouth so I wouldn't cry. I didn't like to show my tears. "Her death was inevitable."

He held my hand and squeezed it gently. "Have you thought about how you're going back to school?"

"Yes. It's simple. I'm not."

His fingers brushed over the back of my hand. "If money is the problem—"

"Don't even think about it."

"Why not? My money is as good as Alfarez's. Your precious *papi* is not a saint or didn't you know he was a cartel mule?"

"I'm not an idiot, of course I knew. But that was a long time ago. He had the courage to walk out and build a clean life for himself." I stabbed my fork in something on my plate. "I accept help from Alfarez because he's like a father to me. Unlike you, he's not trying to buy me. I'm not for sale, Cosimo."

He withdrew his hand and leaned back in his chair. The way he pinned me with a razor sharp look made me self-conscious.

My gaze dipped to my plate as I groped for anything to say. "What's your beef with Alfarez anyway?"

He didn't speak right away, so I had to look up. He sat forward in his chair, folding his arms on the tabletop. "I don't have beef with Carlos. Both his family and mine have always had a profitable relationship, and a mutual understanding not to meddle in each other's business. We facilitate and protect each other's work. My father loved him, and before he died he insisted I, too, respect our agreement."

"I don't understand. Alfarez doesn't work—"

"When he left the cartel, he needed protection. He came to Giovanni and made a deal with him. Because my father loved the guy, Carlos gets his diner and a promise no one touches him or his family in exchange for a modest tax along with turning a blind eye when he has to."

"Turn a blind eye?"

"We use his diner and storage for family business sometimes. His men, too."

I swallowed, letting all this new info register in my head. "I guess when you're in, you're never really out."

"The only way out is in a coffin, principessa."

Chapter 11

Bianca

"Why aren't you eating? Do you want me to feed you again?" Cosimo smirked.

I shook my head. "I lost my appetite."

"Said no one in an Italian restaurant ever." He put down his fork and knife. "I know how to fix this. Dolce."

He snapped his fingers, and the chef appeared. He cleared the plates and mumbled something in Italian that didn't sound like a good thing. I must have offended him by not finishing my plate.

"The food was so delicious, Chef. I'm sorry I couldn't finish it all," I said.

"That's because you're so small," he said in a heavy Italian accent. "You have to come here every day. I feed you proper food. No one likes a bony—"

"Dolce, Massimo. Adesso," Cosimo interrupted, a menacing glare on his face.

"Mi dispiace. Subito." The chef wheezed as he walked back into the kitchen.

I didn't speak much Italian, but I knew enough to understand the chef was apologizing and would bring the dessert right away.

The way he silenced a man old enough to be his father, a man he obviously loved and trusted, set a lump in my throat. The truth from which Cosimo had been trying to blind me would always dance in my face. He was a terrifying, powerful dangerous man. If you obeyed him, you were safe. If you crossed him, you were not, regardless of how much he liked you.

A question that I'd been trying to suppress all night—all my life—nagged at me. I couldn't shut it up anymore. "Cosimo...what happens after tonight?"

A shadow of a smile crossed his face. "What do you mean?"

"You know what I mean. What happens after the date finishes?"

"I'll drive you home, unless you wanna come to mine."

"Cosimo, please. I'm serious. What happens between us?"

"It's simple. We'll have other dates."

"This wasn't the deal. You asked for a date *tonight*, and I did as you asked. I kept my end and went out with you."

"So I wouldn't shoot your friend?" he scoffed.

I scowled. "Yes."

"You sure about that?"

"Of course. It's the only reason why I'm here," I lied. To him. To myself. "I gave you what you wanted. Now you need to stop."

"You want me to stop?" His voice dropped an octave, clawing at something wild deep down my core.

"Yes." The lie trembled on my tongue. "Please."

Suddenly, he was on his feet, and then sitting next to me. I curled back in response. Cold sweat trickled down the back of my neck. "What are you doing?"

He gave me one of his intense stares that penetrated my bones. Then his fingers plunged in the back of my hair and pulled my head closer to him. I gasped. The heat radiating from his body made me feel as if I'd walked into a furnace. His breath, a combination of warmth and wine fanned my face. His eyes were glued to my lips the same way they did at the diner.

My lips parted against my will, and my eyes fluttered close. My body was desperate for his kiss, for all of him, even though I'd just told him to leave me be. When he was this close, it was impossible to think about anything but the painful pebbling of my nipples and the throbbing ache between my thighs.

I felt his fingers run down my back and around my waist. I hissed, and hissed harder when his fingertips glided up the line between my breasts.

Then his cheek touched mine, his beard rough in the most perfect way on my skin. "You're a terrible liar," he whispered.

Yes.

"Don't pretend you're only here because you have to. You can tell that to yourself all you want so you can sleep better at night. It doesn't change the truth."

"What truth?" I panted, my skin tingling hard.

"You want me as much as I want you." His breath slid from my ear down to my neck. "You like me as much as I like you."

253

I nodded. I fucking nodded. I didn't care if he called my bluff. I didn't care if he'd rip my clothes off and take me in front of his guards. I didn't care if he'd kill me after he took what he wanted from me. As long as I got to feel him on me, inside me, even once, I'd die a happy woman.

I just wanted him.

It was wrong, depraved and pathetic, but I did. I wanted Cosimo Lanza more than anything.

CHAPTER 12

Cosimo

Every fiber of her body was inviting. The goosebumps all over her skin. The parting of her lips. The swipe of her tongue. The hardening of her little nipples. The arch of her spine in response to *my* touch.

If I pressed my mouth to hers, would she resist? If I slid my hand between her legs, would she be as wet as I presumed she'd be?

I knew the answer to both questions without having to check. Bianca was ready for me. For my body, at least.

As much as my body was ready for her, too, my mind and heart wanted more. If I kissed her now, let her breath seep into mine, let her softness burn my lips and her tongue twirl with mine, I wouldn't be able to stop.

It would ruin everything.

Giving her the wrong impression was the last thing I wanted to do. I wasn't exaggerating when I told her she'd be treated like a princess. That was how I saw her, and, one day, she could be a queen.

How could I stop myself from taking what was always mine, though? When she was surrendering in my arms, ready for the taking like this?

Pull back. Get your ass to your side of the table.

My feet wouldn't budge. My hands refused to let go. My mouth was moving closer, ready to unleash hell.

"Dolce is ready." Massimo's wheezing and shuffling brought me to a halt. "Oh. Scusi."

Bianca opened her eyes with a gasp. I rolled mine toward Massimo, not knowing whether to kill him or thank him.

I dragged my hands off her and nodded my chin at Massimo. He cleared his throat, set down the dessert as fast as he could and left.

"Oh my God. Are these NutJobs?" She licked her lip.

I itched to have her in my arms again, but I clenched my hands into fists and scooted a little further from her. "Homemade. I told Massimo to replicate the recipe as much as he could. I know how much you love them."

"Just like you know my favorite flowers and put them on the table, my favorite food and had it made for me, my size and the perfect color for my complexion—"

"I know every detail about you and everything you love. I want to give you everything, Bianca. You deserve it."

Her eyes flickered. "Everything?"

"Everything. With me, you can have anything you want," I vowed.

"I want my freedom from you, Cosimo."

Her words felt like a cold blade slicing my guts. I was offering her the world, and all she wanted was to leave. Her defiance had tested me and my limited patience in ways that infuriated and enticed me at the same time. But not now. She was only making me angry. "Anything except that."

Her brow shot up. "I'll take the NutJobs then." She gave me a small smile and grabbed a spoon. Then she dropped it and grabbed a fork. "Never eaten one of those in a soufflé cup. Should I use a spoon or a fork?"

"Actually," I removed the fork from her hand, "neither. I changed my mind. You're not eating that."

"What? Why?"

"You're going to moan again, and I've exhausted my limit of self-control for one night." I wrapped my fingers around hers. "Dance with me."

"But I wanna try—"

"Dance."

She frowned. "Is it *not a request or a negotiation?*"

"If it makes you sleep better at night." I winked.

CHAPTER 13

Bianca

How could he read me so well, so easily?

My stupid body showed him my desire for him was roiling. But how could he know exactly what I was struggling with in my mind?

He was forcing me to do things, making them look like orders I couldn't disobey, only because he knew I wanted them so much, but I wouldn't bring myself to do them on my own. In my mind, anything related to Cosimo was...wrong. So wrong I craved him so badly.

I needed him to *make me* do it. He wasn't forcing me. He was making things easier for me.

My sweet devil. The violent soul. The cruel disaster about to swallow me whole.

I melted in his moves as he led me into his dance. My body was small against his. Even in the pumps he bought me, I stood a foot shorter. He swayed gently and then brought me back into his arms. So elegant, so agile. So fucking sexy.

His hands grew conservative, only touching my arms and back. He made sure our lower bodies never met, and I couldn't stop wondering if he was hard. If I was making him hard. I stole a few glances, but in the dim lights on the dance floor, my efforts were futile.

I liked to believe I was. He wasn't letting me closer because of it. He did say he was out of willpower.

So was I.

When he spun me back, I slammed into him on purpose. Palms on his rock hard chest, stomach on his pelvis. My heart skipped a beat. The size of the bulge in his pants rendered me speechless.

He scolded me with his eyes, a groan stuck in his throat. "You're naughty."

I was. Obviously.

"It's what you're making me become." I pressed myself harder onto him, my chin lifted, gaze on his lips.

He exhaled slowly, like he was fighting the urge to kiss me raw.

Read my mind, Cosimo, like you always do. I might have said I wouldn't have sex with you tonight, but I was ready for our first kiss. Thirsty for it. Needing it so badly.

I tilted my head back, reached up and touched his face. Then I tangled my fingers in the back of his thick, beautiful hair. "Gonna make me beg for it, too?"

"I would. But if you go down on your knees, I'll make you do something else you won't like. Not now anyway."

My trembling jaw fell low, and my body burned. The idea of sucking him... Seeing his cock alone would drive me out of my goddamn mind.

He fisted my hair, and ground his pelvis against me, so I'd feel him, his need for me, even more. "You don't know how long I've wanted to kiss you."

"I think I do. You don't have to wait anymore. Please."

His eyes sparkled with a feral hunger. Then he lowered his head and crushed his lips onto mine.

He didn't start slow or brush my lips softly. He was too hungry to be gentle. His passion was cruel like he was. Powerful. Invasive. A force of nature. He pressed years and years of suppressed desire onto my lips, bruising them, owning them. It was as though he was ruining me for anyone else I might kiss after, because nothing would ever compare to his kiss.

I moaned without a shred of care about what might happen because of it. My whole life was reduced to me and Cosimo kissing, losing ourselves to each other, all my concerns along with my resistance cowering to the back of my head.

Our tongues swirled as he devoured me, literally taking my breath away. Only when I gasped, starving for air, did he pull back.

My head was spinning, and if it weren't for his arm and fist holding me, I'd have collapsed. "This isn't fair."

"What's not fair?" he whispered in his husky voice, his lips swollen.

It was hard to focus or put more words together when he spoke and looked like this. I took a deep breath to gather any residue of sensibility left in me, tears pricking my eyes. "All this. What you're doing to me. This night. All this care. The *kiss*. You're dazzling me, blinding me. And it's working. It's not fair."

He brushed his thumb under my eye before a tear fell. "What are you so afraid of? I'd never hurt you or let anyone lay a finger on you."

"I know, and that's the worst part. I'm not afraid of you, Cosimo. I should be, but I'm not, and that's what scares me."

"You're scared you might be tempted by the life you hate so much."

"Yes." The tears fell despite me and him. "Because I know I'll hate myself for it. I don't want to hate myself or lead a life I despise. My father was a junkie and worked for gangsters. My mom fell for him and look what happened to her. Alfarez worked for the cartel. He loved his wife so much, but he couldn't save her."

"You know about Alfarez's wife?"

"Of course. She ODed on the shit he smuggled, and that's when he quit. Why do you think he took us in? My mother reminded him of his wife and he thought he could save her instead. He couldn't. Again."

He wiped his fingers under my eyes again, and his tenderness at the moment was too much. "I understand your concerns and how you feel, but the people you're talking about are small fish, incapable of protecting themselves, let alone their families."

"It doesn't matter. What matters is that when you play in a nest of vipers, you'll get bitten."

His jaws clenched. "Tesoro mio, let's talk about this later, shall we? I hate to see you so upset. I want you to enjoy the night."

I rolled my eyes, shaking my head. "Cosimo?"

"Si, little missy."

"Why me?"

A faint smile stretched his lips. "I already told you. You were born to be mine."

"What does that mean?"

He pulled me closer, both his hands on the back of my neck now, his eyes dark. "It means for twelve years I haven't spent a day without thinking about you, without having to see you, without being frustrated you were that young. I'm a lot of things but pedophile isn't one."

"You asked me out when I was seventeen."

"So? Seventeen doesn't make you a child anymore. I wanted to ask you out earlier."

My lashes fluttered. "Earlier than seventeen?"

"People date and have sex in high school. Mamma got married when she was sixteen."

His logic wasn't completely off the hinge. Underage sex was okay, but as long as there were no *adults* involved. At least, it was the law, which was irrelevant to Cosimo. The mother thing must have made him think it was acceptable. Alfarez once told me that Giovanni was twenty years older than Marta. "And why didn't you?"

"You hadn't started dating then. I didn't want to spook you. At seventeen, you did."

I did start dating Andy then. "Wait a second." I mused. Then I glared at him. "Did you have anything to do with Andy breaking up with me?"

"Certo."

"Oh my God. And you confess that easily?"

"You...let him touch you. Many times." Anger flicked in his eyes. "The fucker asked you to Prom, confessed that he loved you. You were going to sleep with him that night. I wasn't waiting for almost ten years so that a punk in high school puts his disgusting dick in what's mine." He pulled me harder into him and cupped my pussy. I gasped so loudly, my whole body tensed up. "Your pussy is mine."

I quivered. "Cosimo...you said you wouldn't force me...and you'd treat me—"

"*My* principessa." He took off his hand, but after a squeeze that left me soaking. "Don't ever forget that. If I'm not the one fucking you, your legs will remain closed your whole life." He lifted his palm to his nose and inhaled. His eyes rolled back. "Cazzo."

Yes. Fuck. I was so wet the thin fabric of my dress was probably stained, and he could smell my pussy now.

Why was I so wet when he confessed he was toying with me my whole life, scaring my boyfriend away without caring it broke my heart so I'd remain a virgin for him? Why was I throbbing with heat when he was laying his hand on my pussy without invitation? Why was I so fucked up?

His jealousy and possessiveness set me on fire and caged me in sweet surrender. Had I given in to him already? Accepted my destiny as his obsession? Forsaken my future and become a slave to the need he planted in me so deep?

He dropped his other hand that was on my neck and stepped back.

"Cosimo..."

"Give me a minute." His eyes remained closed, his lips pressed. His expression as he was savoring my smell and struggling because of it shattered my sanity.

How could I resist anymore?

There was only one question left to ask that would seal my fate tonight.

CHAPTER 14

Bianca

A long breath escaped him as he opened his eyes. "You wanted to say something?"

"I have a question," I said.

"Last one for tonight, little missy."

"Okay," I mumbled. "When you became...you know...was it by choice?"

"When I became what?" he teased. He knew exactly what I meant, and he knew I didn't wanna say it. Not out loud. Not when I was here, losing all control.

"When you became *Don Corleone*."

He chuckled. "You can't even say it, principessa, can you?"

I sighed. "Would you please answer the question?"

"When Giovanni died, someone had to replace him. I was his son."

"Why not Enzio? I mean you're twins. You're not like older or anything."

"The family chose me."

"Because you're better at it? Being the leader?"

He collected me in his arms and resumed our dance. "I suppose so."

I twirled when he prompted, my mind racing with thoughts. I hadn't gotten my answer yet, but he seemed to have had enough of my inquiries.

"You have more questions on the subject. I don't like it when you're not fully with me, so ask them," he said.

Taking a deep breath, summoning my courage, I gazed into his eyes. "If you've got a chance to get out, would you do it?"

He came to a halt, his eyes dark. The silence falling between us was louder than the music. Deafening.

When it was obvious he wasn't going to answer, I took a step forward and set my palm on his cheek. "Let me rephrase. Would you ever love someone enough to step down?"

"I love my family, Bianca. More than anything. I can't do that to them."

"I understand how important your job is to your family. All I'm saying is that you teach someone else how to do it, someone you trust, so you can... retire early." I forced a smile on my lips, hoping it'd ease the tension.

The darkness in his stare grew. "They chose me, not someone else. This is my destiny. This is who I am. People would kill to have my place. I'm not gonna give it up. Only a fool does that."

My throat closed with a huge lump, so I just nodded. My last chance to finding a way around this mess I was knee deep in was gone. I thought maybe, just maybe, he was forced to accept his position or he had a hint of a moral compass that might make him see how horrible his job was.

I thought maybe he had a heart capable of love that might turn things around. But like he said, the only way out was in a coffin.

Hopeful, impulsive, reckless and stupid.

Cosimo would never love anyone or anything more than his power. I was just an obsession to him. Nothing more nothing less.

That gave me the answer I needed, and I knew now what I had to do.

Stepping back, I lifted my dress a little and went on my knees.

His gaze wandered around. "What the fuck are you doing? Get up."

"I'm tired of our dance, Cosimo. I know what you want, and I'm giving it to you."

He gritted his teeth as he glared down at me. "You don't know anything. Get up."

"You have to have me. To fuck me. You can't let me go unless you take me. I get it. I want that to. I've always wanted to be with you, but what I want more is my freedom, and you said I could have anything but." My gaze begged him. "Can't we *both* win here? Please."

"And this is what you want? To have me just once and then go on your way?"

"It's the only viable option I could come up with that doesn't involve losing myself forever. So let's just get it over with. Take what you want. I'll beg you if it pleases you. It won't be forced. I promise you I will enjoy it so much." I nodded emphatically. "Please, Cosimo. It's the only way to end this."

"End this?" he seethed.

"Yes," I cried.

"Get. Up. Bianca. I won't say it again."

I shook my head, refusing to give up, even though it'd have been so easy. I just couldn't. My hands trembled as I reached for his belt to unbuckle it and—

The next thing I knew, pain seeped into my head, and the feeling of a fist pulling my hair. Then I was yanked to my feet, my widening eyes facing his dark ones, his free hand raised beside my temple, palm ready to smack.

My heart sank to my knees as I mentally prepared myself for a slap on my face and a reason to hate Cosimo forever. The shadow of his palm crossed my eyes, and I squeezed them shut.

Then...nothing.

There was no blow. Only simmering breaths.

I opened my eyes to see his clenched fist in the air, and a look on his face I'd never forget. The look of a heartless monster that had discovered he had a heart, and that heart was shattered.

"I've imagined the moment I'd finally hear it from you, how much you wanted me to touch you, so many times. Hoped for it. Dreamt about it. Not once had I thought my reaction would be, instead of making love to you long and hard, wanting to rip you apart."

"Cosimo—"

He let go of my hair. "Get out."

My heart hammered in my chest. A cold wave of shock hit me. "What?"

"I said I'd never hurt you. If you don't leave now, I don't trust what I'd do."

"But I—"

"Get out!" His voice thundered through my bones. "Congrats. You got what you wanted. You're fucking free."

CHAPTER 15

Cosimo

I gave her my back as she headed for the door. The beast inside me, the urge to grab her, lock her up somewhere and never let her out, rumbled menacingly. Her heels echoed behind me, her footsteps slow. Then she stopped.

I yelled at her again, and she scurried away this time.

My ass plopped down in a chair, and my eyes hovered on the door. What was I waiting for? For her to come back and tell me none of it was true? To tell me she was teasing me? To say it was all another act in our game?

The game is over, Capo die Capi. Not even you can win her heart.

She hated what I was so much she'd offer her virgin body, not for love, not for riches, but in exchange for her freedom from the prison of the monster obsessed with her.

Damn you, Bianca Zanetti. What do you know about imprisonment? What do you know about being a captive?

If either of us was a prisoner here, it was me.

Twelve years of denying myself what I desired, waiting, dreaming, searching for an alternative in vain. Twelve years of captivity to a little girl. Watching out for her. Taming myself for her. Revolving my day and my mind and my heart around her.

All that for what? So she could come here and say she couldn't bare me? So she could make me for the first time ever hate what I was?

A loud growl burst out of my throat as I flipped the table, smashing everything on it.

"Cosimo," Massimo wheezed. "Madre di Dio, you're bleeding."

I glanced at the blood trickling down my hand. Someone grabbed a napkin, Massimo or one of the guards, and tied my wound. I didn't feel any pain, only fury.

My phone rang. I fished it out of my pocket and answered. "Si, Enzio."

"How's it going with your contessa? Still working your magic on your first date?" He laughed.

"No."

Enzio fell silent for a moment. "That bad?"

I stared at my blood staining the napkin and waved my dismissal to the men. "Where are you?"

"Close. Want me to come over?"

"Ti aspetto."

CHAPTER 16

Bianca

*I*sn't that what you wanted? Why the fuck are you crying now?

The cold night air filled my heaving lungs as I wiped my face, my mind wouldn't stop running in circles. How could he let me leave like this? A woman to walk in a dress like that so late at night wasn't safe. Didn't he know it was dangerous out there? I didn't have anything on me. No money, no phone. I didn't even have a coat.

I should return and...demand my clothes back...and a fucking ride...in his car where we could forget about this shit and make out...

Fuck me. I was a hopeless case with zero dignity.

You're an asshole, Cosimo fucking Lanza. How could you let me go that easily?

I had no right to be upset. I asked for it, and he granted me my wish. If he was anything, he wasn't an asshole. He wanted to have sex with me but wouldn't without my consent. He wanted to beat the crap out of me but wouldn't because he...cared about me. He wanted to make me his woman but wouldn't because my stupid good side couldn't accept it and asked to be free.

He did everything I asked. He let me go. Forever.

Instead of feeling thankful, relieved, liberated, I was a pile of hot mess and heartache.

What would I do with myself now? Cosimo was part of me whether I liked it or not. Who was I kidding? For the past three years, Cosimo was my life. He was always there. He defined me. Anywhere I went, everybody knew me as the girl reserved for the Don.

Silly me, I allowed myself to think I did the same to him. I let myself dream our story was like a twisted fairytale that would end with a happily ever after despite everything. I let myself believe when the time came, he'd give up his throne for me. He'd never let me go.

All this time, Cosimo was my life, but I was never important enough to be in his.

Now that he ditched me, who would I become?

Why wouldn't he fight for me? Why wouldn't he try to keep me a little longer? Why wouldn't he be the asshole he'd always been and lie to make me stay?

He didn't even say goodbye.

My eyes burned with fresh tears, and my stomach clenched in pain.

I chanced a glanced over my shoulder, wishing he would have been there, chasing after me, regretting letting me go, or even looking after me from afar. Anything.

My gaze fell on nothing but darkness. Distant footsteps grew audible. Reaching the end of the sidewalk, I saw someone in a suit walking toward me.

"Cosimo?" A flicker of hope warmed me up for a second before I realized the face approaching was of a stranger.

Panic froze my insides. I crossed the street, running. The air ripped through my hair, and my lungs ached with coldness and fear.

Cutting down a side street, I could still hear his footfalls behind me. I took off my pumps and ran as fast as I could in the dark. Then I hit a dead end.

Fuck. I listened for the footsteps, but they were fading away. Thank God. I pressed my back to a wall and allowed myself a moment to catch my breath. When I tiptoed out of this alley, someone grabbed me from behind.

The snatch was so violent I lost my balance. As I staggered back, I crashed into a solid form—a man.

I screamed my lungs out, but an arm clamped around my throat. Something cold and sharp jabbed into the hollow of my neck. "Scream again and I'll cut out your throat."

CHAPTER 17

Cosimo

Enzio fixed his suit jacket as we walked out of the restaurant and lit a cigarette. "What are you gonna do now?"

I eyed the trail of smoke, waiting for the car. "I'll go home, but first, light me one of those."

He blew out, smiling. Then he rolled his eyes as he dragged another cigarette and lit it with his. "Si, si. That will show her."

"Spare me your crap. I've had enough for one night." I snatched the cigarette and sucked a breath. The taste of tobacco and smell of smoke brought so many memories. Old times when I was young and cared about nothing.

When I was free. Of Bianca. Of my duty.

Also, it reminded me of the day I first met her. My hand was bloody, and a cigarette dangled on my mouth. Except she was not there to give me bandages or tell me to take care of my health.

"You know what else you could do to show her? Pussy. Lots of it. It cures the worst cases of a broken heart."

"My heart is not broken," I stressed. "I've never been in love. With her or anyone else."

"Certo. She's just some virgin pussy you wanted to fuck. She gets on her knees to blow you, begging you to fuck said virgin pussy, and you kick her out to prove it."

Blood pounded in my skull. "Fuck you."

"Is she fair game now that you *set her free*? I look like you. She'll be hot for me. I'd love to let her tight innocence coat my—"

My fist punched his jaw so hard he swung off balance and blood flew off his mouth.

"Cazzo! You punch your fucking brother for your bitch?"

"She's not a bitch. I don't care if you're my brother or the fucking Pope.

269

Nobody touches Bianca or speaks about her pussy and lives to have anything coat his fuckin' cock."

He spat and smirked. "But you're not in love with her?"

I swore, looking at the night sky. Then I took a drag from the cigarette.

"C'mon. Let's have a foursome like the old days. Bitches still dig twin shit. It's way better than soiling your clean lungs with this filth."

"You sound like a bad commercial. Since when do you call cigarettes filth? You *love* to smoke."

"I don't. It's a nasty habit I can't quit. I wish I was mind blown by a hot virgin to give it up just for her, but that's your territory, Casanova."

"Careful what you wish for, cazzo." The car arrived. "It ain't pretty."

"Amen to that. So what do you say?" He waved his phone. "Get that foursome?"

I stomped on the cigarette and climbed into the car. "I have something better."

"Better than a foursome? I doubt it."

"Wanna bet?"

He ducked his head, and his eyes narrowed at me. "What are you up to, Cosimo?"

What I should have done years ago. "Hop in if you wanna see."

He spat again, wiping more blood off, and joined me. "Where we goin'?"

I didn't say a word until the car stopped a few blocks from the restaurant, in a viewing range of a dead-end back alley.

Enzio leaned forward and followed my gaze. "Merda. What the fuck did you do?"

I watched as my men cornered Bianca in the dark.

He blew out a long breath, wiping both hands over his face. "You ordered that. You're kidnapping Bianca."

"Si."

A chorus of swears flew out of his mouth. "Why?"

"She can't live with herself if she *chooses* to be with me. Like that, she'll have no choice."

"That's fucked up, Cosimo. Abducting women? We don't do that shit.

And have you forgotten she's under Alfarez's protection? You're pissing over decades of family pacts."

I didn't care. I'd kill the whole family of her Mexican Godfather if I had to. It'd all be her fault. If she hadn't refused me, none of that would have happened.

One of my men was trying to put a black bag over her head, but she elbowed him, ducked and twisted. Then she hurled one shoe at the second man coming at her, and stabbed the heel of the other shoe in the thigh of the first.

"Oh fuck. She's fighting back, Cosimo."

No, principessa. You're outnumbered and unarmed. Be smart about it. Just do as they say. As much as it pissed me off she would put herself in danger like that, it made me hard.

She sprinted and almost made it to the street before more men caught her. One of them grabbed her by the hair and slammed her back and head against the cement.

"Motherfucking idiots!" I snapped. "I'll kill them. I told them to only scare her off and just take her."

"Your girl might be a pixie, but she's a feisty pixie who isn't afraid of bad guys. Don't you know that about her? What made you think she'd go without a fight?" Enzio asked. "The men are hurting her, Cosimo. She'll hate you for it. Call it off."

I clenched my fists and jaws so hard they could shatter. Between ruining the plan and watching her, the wind knocked out of her like that, I couldn't think straight. I ran a hand through my hair, banging the seat with the other. "Too late now. She'll know it's me, and she'll hate me anyway. I might as well take her."

Enzio threw his hands in the air. "You're out of your fucking mind."

I grabbed his suit. "Dovresti badare a che cazzo dici! Don't forget your place."

"I'm your underboss. It's my job to tell you when you've gone off hinge." He shoved me off him. "No one is worth pissing off the family for. Now live up to your fucking name and do something before you fuck up everything."

CHAPTER 18

Bianca

My head pounded from the hit. Then one of them punched me and another followed with a kick. My eye began to swell, and my rib screamed in pain.

"We got ourselves a fucking fighter."

I looked up into the face of the man bending over me. He had dark eyes, a crooked nose and tattoos covering his neck. I registered the faces of the other two as well. If I survived this, I'd make sure these fuckers wouldn't.

A painful cough ripped out of my chest, the taste of blood disgusting in my mouth. The man's arm reached for me, and I gathered what was left of my strength to bite him.

He swore in Italian and smacked my face so hard my head whipped to the side. "You shouldn't have done that. Look what you've made us do."

"Why isn't she passing out? The little cunt is strong," one of them said in Italian, but I understood. "Knock her out already. We need to go."

The one I bit reached for his gun I could now see tucked to his side. Then he lifted the gun, aiming to hit my head with it.

My eyes closed, my whole body clenched as I waited for the blow that would knock me out.

It didn't come.

Instead, dull thuds filled my ears along with a series of grunts and groans. Then more swearing in Italian. Something big hit the wall and fell close to me with a sickening sound of bones crunching. A piercing cry of agony. More thuds, a heavy groan, and then quietness fell.

I breathed in pain, squinting into the shadows. A blur of a man in a suit standing over me made me squint harder. He stared at me with no expression and knelt down next to me.

His eyes blazed with fury. His face shadowed in the dark, but I'd recognize him anywhere, even with a swollen eye and a mind almost lulled into unconsciousness.

He looked beautiful and terrifying, an avenging dark angel to my rescue. He scooped me up in his arms. "I'm sorry. They will pay."

"Cosimo..." I said—tried. I faded into deep blackness, Cosimo's face keeping me company.

CHAPTER 19

Bianca

A needle stung in the back of my hand. Fuzziness clamored my head. I had no idea where I was and why my mouth was too dry. Sunlight streamed through the windows, and birds chirped annoyingly.

Pain poked at the edges of my awareness, faint, nothing grave. A beeping sound came into play, and I looked around to see it was a hospital machine. I was in a hospital bed, a white and blue gown covering me. The stinging needle was that of an IV.

My eyes shifted to the other side, and Cosimo was in a chair next to my cot, gazing at me. He held my hand, without a word, his face made of stone.

"You're still here," I slurred.

He grabbed a cup from the nightstand beside the chair and fed me ice chips. "You must be thirsty."

The coolness sliding over my lips and throat soothed me, and my head and vision cleared bit by bit. I noticed the bandage on his hand. "You hurt your hand in the fight?"

The slightest tension tightened the corners of his mouth. He fed me more ice chips and then fixed the pillow behind me so I could rest against it.

"Did you follow me last night, even after what happened at the restaurant?"

His chest rose with a long inhale as he returned to hold my hand.

His silence irritated me. "Do you know the men who attacked me? They're Italians."

He swallowed, his eyes darker. "I know."

"They were in suits. They didn't bother to hide their faces. Who are they? A rival clan sending a message?"

More fucking silence.

"If that's a yes, they never said anything. They didn't seem to want to hurt me either. All they wanted was for me to go with them. The beating only started when I fought back and only aimed to knock me out—"

"It doesn't matter anymore."

"Cosimo, you gotta give me something here."

He looked down at me, his eyes dark, unreadable. "I bastardi... The bastards who did this to you, I have them all. They will be dead by tonight."

I blinked lazily at him, my lack of fear or anxiety at the moment astounding. I should be dreading what he said, appalled by it, urge him not to do such a terrible thing. And above all, I should be afraid of *him*.

If any of what I was feeling now was real, not drug induced, it was relief and joy that he was here, taking care of me, and that I got to see him again.

My ovaries had taken control of my brain. If he looked like a troll, I'd be screaming for the police.

"Do I have a say in this?" I asked.

"No."

"They were following orders, Cosimo. They're not the real bad guys."

"They hurt you...because of me." His pensive gaze trailed on me as he brushed my forehead with the back of his hand. "I failed to protect you. I should've never let you leave."

"But you did."

"It's what you wanted."

"Still, you kicked me out in the middle of the night. You didn't tell your men to give me a ride or call a cab. You didn't think about giving me a coat. It was so unlike you. Unless..." I trailed off. I didn't want to believe what my mind was leading me to believe.

"Bianca, I—"

"You saved me."

He trailed his fingertips down my temple and over the unbruised areas around my cheekbone, pausing to caress my jaw with his thumb. "No, I didn't."

I enjoyed the feeling of his touch more than I should have. "Yes, you did. That's what I like to believe. That's *all* I need to know."

CHAPTER 20

Cosimo

S he knew. She fucking knew.

But...

"Why are you looking at me like that?" she asked. "I know I must look hideous, but it's rude—"

"You baffle me, Bianca Zanetti."

Her angry look faded into a more anxious one. "What are you talking about?"

"I read people very easily, especially you. I've been watching you since you were a kid. I know your every move, every thought, every need, every desire before you even do." I shook my head. "Today, I can't for the love of me read anything about you."

"Don't be silly. I'm an open book. Always have been."

"What's going on in that pretty head of yours?"

She pursed her swollen, split lips, looking cute nonetheless. "Nothing much. I'm just glad I'm alive. Thanks to you."

I closed my eyes for a moment at the lie, at the feelings it provoked in me. The emotions I'd been taught to smother until I forgot they existed. "Bianca—"

"It changes things." She stared at me, willing me to understand. "Between us, I mean."

I sighed with a nod. "It does."

There was a knock on the door, followed by Enzio popping his head in. "Scusi, a word?"

I kissed the back of her hand. "I'll be right back."

When I went out, Enzio said a few things about how he took care of the police report, and that Alfarez and Bianca's friend were waiting to be allowed a visit.

"Let them in," I said.

He squeezed my shoulder. "You okay? Did it work?"

276

"I think so. She thinks I saved her, and that changes things between us."

"Perfetto!"

I shrugged, no clue how things would play out. "I guess."

"No guess. It's perfect. You got your little contessa back." He patted me and started away.

"Hey, Enzio," I said, and he turned, his expression quizzical. "Grazie."

"Prego. You owe me one. Don't go fuck it up again, Casanova." He walked out to the waiting area.

I went back inside her room. "Alfarez and your friend are here to visit. I told them to come in."

She nodded. "What should I tell them? And what should I tell the police?"

"We took care of the police and the hospital."

"Of course you did." She chuckled. "What do I tell Alfarez?"

"The truth." I waited a second, reading through her expression and coming out empty. "A *rival clan* ordered a hit on you to get back at me."

She nodded again. "The truth."

Alfarez barged in, his dark hair slicked back, the corners of his eyes and mouth wrinkled. He mumbled in Spanish, hurrying to Bianca's side. Then he looked at me, his expression a combination of fury and gratitude.

Enzio entered with Bianca's roommate. The blonde squeaked with annoying girly stuff and baby sounds. I waited it and Alfarez's inquisitions out until they hit the chat that mattered.

"When are they discharging you, mija? I'll set a room ready for you at my place," Alfarez said. "We'll take good care of you."

"It's okay, Papi. I'll take care of her," the blonde volunteered.

"I'll feel safer if you're with me, Bianca," he insisted.

Bianca gave her thanks, and the other two continued their fight over who was gonna take care of my girl. Too much noise to tolerate. Time to end this shit. "She's staying with me."

The room shrank in silence, all eyes on me.

"I am?" Bianca asked, surprised.

"No way in hell," Alfarez protested.

277

"Basta cosi! It's not a request or a negotiation." Only Bianca smiled at my words. I glanced at her. "Your things are already in my apartment."

"What? When?" She looked at her friend. "How?"

A dummy look on her face, the blonde raised her hands. "I didn't know anything about that, I swear."

"It doesn't matter. Bring them to my place, Don Cosimo, por favor." Alfarez frowned.

I didn't bother repeating my command. She *was* staying with me. I just gave him a menacing glare, Enzio joining the stare-off.

Bianca cleared her throat. "I think it's better if I did stay with Cosimo. I...I mean the attackers have beef with the Lanzas, apparently. Cosimo will know better how to take care of that. I prefer to stay with him until it's sorted out."

Alfarez broke our stare and switched his toward her. "That's plain stupid. It's because they have beef with the Lanzas, you should stay as far from them as possible."

"But Cosimo saved me." Her eyes flickered between me and Enzio. "I'll feel safer with the Lanzas. Besides, they have extra measures of security we don't have."

Enzio winked at Alfarez. "You heard her."

Alfarez shook his head at Bianca, but she gave him a small smile and a begging look.

He gritted his teeth. "Well, can we visit?"

The guy thought I'd be holding her captive. I couldn't blame him. It wasn't a stretch from the truth. I was going to do exactly that last night, but now things were a bit different. Or were they?

"Anytime, Papi Carlos. You're always welcome at the Lanzas," Enzio said.

With that, Alfarez was sedated. A few minutes later, they all left me alone with Bianca.

"Is it true?" she asked, her tiny hand in mine.

"What?"

"I'm allowed visitors?"

I chuckled. It seemed to be *I* was the open book to this little girl. "You're not my prisoner. I only want to protect you. Take care of you. Until you recover, at least."

"And after that?"

This was by far the hardest question I had to answer. Once she was in my house, in my bed, would I ever be able to let her out? "Leave the future in the future, little missy."

CHAPTER 21

Bianca

The first thing I noticed about Cosimo's penthouse was how big and open it was. The hall alone was bigger than my apartment. The whole city twinkled in the incredible view. I could only imagine how he felt standing out there on the terrace or even sitting on the couch facing the floor-to-ceiling walls, watching the city from the top. Owning it. A king like he said. Instantly, my feet froze in the doorway. I felt so small, so out my league.

Cosimo bent and put my arm around his shoulder, and his arm under my hips, and then he picking me up, cradling me like a baby.

"What are you doing?" I gasped.

"Carrying you to bed. You're too tired to walk."

"But—"

"You don't get to argue in here." He started down the hall, dim lights illuminating the way on automatic, dancing with the bright city lights, the security guards following us. "My house, my rules."

I wasn't too tired to walk or argue, but I was enjoying myself in his arms too much to object. My palm pressed to his firm chest, and I curled closer, savoring his warmth and smell. "Can I get a tour of the house first? Choose a room?"

"I'll give you a tour in the morning."

"And the room? Don't I get to choose?"

"Stop the dummy talk." We entered a room, and the guards closed the door behind us. "As long as you're in my place, you're sleeping in my bed."

A shiver ran down my spine, and my pulse raced. More lights flicked on, and another shiver hit me. My mind couldn't grasp how I should behave now that I was in Cosimo's bedroom.

My body... Fuck.

All my aches were reduced to the one between my thighs, as if I wasn't almost beaten to death two days ago.

The room was huge and spacious like the hall, dressed in black, gray and red as well. A marvelous fireplace at one end and a *huge* bed at the other. "What the... How many people do you sleep with at a time?" My voice rose with a sudden burst of jealousy.

He flashed a teasing smile. "As many as I want."

My jaws clenched. "Put me down."

"In a second."

"Cosimo, I'm not gonna—"

"Quiet."

My eyes widened at the command. I shot him a glare, and he stood near the edge of the bed, taking in my angry expression. Then his tongue darted out and licked his lips.

I blinked, my emotions a jumbled mess. My rage vanished for a second, replaced by a dire need to kiss him. Then the rage slammed back tenfold. How could I feel this way when he'd just blurted out he he'd have as many girls as he wanted?

His smile stretched wider as he settled me down on the red duvet on the bed. I wondered if he'd still be smiling if I was the one having more than one man in my bed.

"I should have my own room. Your bed might fit all the sweet ladies you're planning to have but won't fit the boys *I'm* planning to have, too. It'll get too crowded."

The smile disappeared. His eyes went dark. His *whole face* went dark. Suddenly, his big body was over mine, a rumble in his chest. He pinned my wrists over my head and flexed his hips into mine.

My pulse skittered as I squirmed. His body was so strong and heavy on top of me I barely moved. I opened my mouth to protest, to ask him to stop, but nothing came out. I was furious yet turned on so much I couldn't bring myself to say no.

He pressed harder, and I could feel it. His throbbing bulge against my pussy. "Have you forgotten what I promised you a couple of years ago? If any fucker does as much as look at you, I'll chop his dick off and feed it to him."

He sealed his warning with a kiss. He took my mouth in his with animalistic hunger, an angry lion gnashing at his prey.

My body bubbled with arousal and conflicted emotions that even my own skin felt so tight I could explode. "Women can get jealous and possessive, too. If you want me to be only yours, you'll have to be only mine," I chanced.

He stared at me, smoldering. Then he kissed me again. "Deal."

I swallowed, giddy. "Deal?"

"Yes."

"Okay."

"Okay."

Fuck me. What the hell just happened? Cosimo and I...had become a thing. An exclusive thing. *Fuck me.* "I..." The taste of his lips on mine, the way he held me immobile and the growing erection, dry fucking me, scrambled my brain. I could barely breathe, let alone speak. "I...I'd like to take a shower before I sleep please."

He didn't move, a dangerous gleam in is stare.

As much as I wanted to touch him, I was not ready mentally or physically. Suddenly, how sore my body was, especially when his weight was crushing me, came to my awareness. "I'm in no shape to... I don't want my first time to be—"

"I wasn't planning on. I'm many things, but a man who uses an injured girl isn't one of them." He glanced at my mouth. Then he clenched his jaw. "If you keep misbehaving, though, I'll have to teach you a lesson."

Letting go of my wrists, he got off me. I should have felt relieved, but all I was doing was mourning the loss of his weight on me. He retreated to a couch and chairs clustered into a sitting area near one of the windows, and made himself a drink from the adjacent bar.

I allowed some air in my chest and rose. "Where's the bathroom? And my clothes?"

"The bathroom is on the right. The door to the dressing room is behind you."

A dressing room. Of course. I cleared my throat as I found my way to the door. I turned the knob, but it was locked. My eyes fell on the electronic pad on the wall. Seriously? "Can I have the code?" I snorted.

"Just hit the shower. I'll pick something for you and join you in a second."

Blood froze in my veins. Who said anything about showering together? With small steps, I headed back to the middle of the room where I could see him. He was sipping his drink, his free hand in his pocket, his face to the window.

"I'ma shower alone." There was no way I'd let him see me naked for the first time when I was bruised like this.

He glanced at me over his shoulder, cocking a brow. My tone must have irritated him. It was a statement, and I wasn't asking permission or willing to back down. "What if you need help?"

"With what?"

He smirked. "Anything."

My cheeks burned, but my pussy didn't shy. It double pulsed. "I won't need any help."

He set his drink aside and took off his suit jacket before he ambled toward me. His palms brushed softly over my face. "Don't be too stubborn. You're hurt. Let me take care of you."

"I don't want you to see me like this," I confessed against my will, whispering, melting with his abrupt sweetness.

"You think I care about a few scratches here and there? You'll always be gorgeous in my eyes, little missy."

"Thank you. But please." I lifted my gaze toward him. "For me."

He held my gaze for a long moment, his expression unreadable. "Giulia!"

I flinched at the yell. "Who the hell is that?"

"The maid. She's at your disposal during your stay. Don't hesitate to ask her for help even for the tiniest thing. If you don't, I'll have to come in myself."

I smiled. "Okay."

"I'm still picking your clothes," he said as the door opened and a stunning girl in a French Maid costume walked in.

"*That* is Giulia, the maid?" Fuck.

He kissed my temple. "Yes, and yes."

"I only asked one question."

"The second is in your head. You wanna know if I fucked her. I did. Many times."

Before my rage bubbled up, he kissed my other temple. "But I plan to honor our deal for as long as we both shall live. You can trust me. On this, at least."

My heart skipped a beat. "For as long as we both shall live?"

He ignored me and told her something in Italian. She nodded in obedience. Then he sighed at me. "I'll go find myself another shower."

CHAPTER 22

Bianca

I stopped short when I walked out of the bathroom, all the relaxation the double Jacuzzi in the shower provided my battered body gone.

Cosimo was on the bed, waiting, staring, in nothing but a towel covering his lower body. My heartbeat in my throat, I clung to my towel and wrapped it tighter around me.

When Giulia excused herself and the door closed, leaving me in the room alone with Cosimo, I shuddered. "Why aren't you dressed?"

He ran a hand through his wet hair, looking so hot I wanted to cry. And drool. "What makes you think I wear anything when I sleep?"

Oh my God. Oh my God. OH MY GOD! "Even if that's true," I breathed, "you're gonna have to put something on while I'm here."

He stood. "I don't have to do anything I don't want."

I stared at his tall form and tattooed, sculpted muscles for a moment before I stumbled back a step. "Me neither."

He kept coming my way, and I continued to step back until I hit a wall. He caged me in with his palms pressed on the wall on either side of my head.

My pulse rocketed painfully. "What are you gonna do? I told you I'm not ready." But if he keeps staring at me like this, looking like this, smelling like this, I wouldn't give a shit if I was ready or not.

"If anyone is in danger here, it's me." He nuzzled his nose against the side of my neck and inhaled. Then he moaned. "I should be the one scared of you, not the other way around."

Every inch of my skin broke out in gooseflesh, my nipples hard. I rubbed my thighs together in a feeble attempt to stop my pussy from clenching. "What does that mean?"

He didn't answer. His big, warm palms slid down, curled around my hips and squeezed. His nose moved to the crook of my neck for another

285

inhale, and then as he squatted down, he smelled between my breasts and my stomach.

The last stop was between my legs.

He inhaled audibly over the towel. Many times. I trembled and throbbed with every intake, unsure what I was supposed to feel. He looked like an animal, sniffing for his mate. It was weird and debauched and...so sexy.

My hand dug in his hair, and, shamelessly, I pulled his head closer.

"Easy," he groaned.

I couldn't obey. I pressed him to me harder. "You make me want to say hell with everything."

His mouth set a hungry kiss over the cotton as he inhaled sharply. "You're not helping."

"Neither are you," I moaned.

"Oddio, you really are dangerous," he murmured, taking my hand out of his hair, and rose to his feet. His eyes were hooded with arousal, his hair messed up and wet, his upper body naked and perfect, and his erection...oh dear God.

My ovaries just exploded. I had to close my eyes and force my spreading legs shut. "We should just go to sleep. With a lot of clothes on."

He sucked in an angry breath and exhaled it next to my ear, causing my heart to hammer. "The *second* you're healed, I'll fuck you *so hard* you'll forget your own name."

I was clenching so hard if he did as much as breathe, I'd come.

He leaned back, cursed, and marched to the dressing room. "Your clothes are on the bed. Get dressed."

CHAPTER 23

Cosimo

For ten days, we did everything together. Ate, talked, went out, slept and woke up together. To say I loved every moment was an understatement. The longer I had her close, listened to her voice, watched her every gesture, carved her scent in my memory, savored her warmth as she nestled in my arms when she was fast asleep, the harder I fell.

Bianca was light and innocence when all I had was darkness and sin. She made me feel everything I shouldn't, and I was letting her. I knew I'd pay for this later, but I just couldn't bring myself to stop.

"I love to see you smile, fratello, but this is getting ridiculous," Enzio said behind his newspaper.

I didn't realize it at first, but when he mentioned it, I caught myself smiling, daydreaming about my little princess. I crossed my legs and frowned, glancing over my shoulder toward my bedroom direction. The doctor had been taking too long to finish his examination routine.

"At least, tell me she has a magic pussy," Enzio teased, still hiding behind his paper.

I left my seat and snatched the fucking thing. Then I scrambled it and tossed it away.

He waved a hand. "Hey, I was reading that."

"I told you to never speak of her pussy again."

He looked me up and down. "Cazzo," he snorted. "Ten days, sleeping in the same bed, and she's still a virgin?"

"She's injured!"

He folded his arms across his chest. "Are her *lady bits* injured?"

My jaws ticked as I plopped down in the sofa next to him. Bianca's pussy was fine. The injuries on the rest of her body weren't the reason she hadn't let me sleep with her yet, either. It wasn't her body that wasn't ready. It was her mind that still resisted the idea of me.

If she were any other girl, I wouldn't have waited. I'd have taken what I desired until I was full without a second thought or regret, never giving it a shred of my attention.

Bianca was different as everything I had with her.

It'd been killing me, having to go this slow with the girl I wanted the most, but I fucking *cared* about her more than I cared about my cock.

"You're so fucking in love," Enzio scoffed.

I was going to jump into a defensive argument, but I found myself wondering in a different direction. Was falling in love such a terrible thing I had to deny it so aggressively every time it was mentioned?

A warm feeling wrapped around me so strange it freaked me out. I mentally slapped myself and shook my head as if shaking the feeling out.

This can't be happening. Don't even think about going there.

I gave Enzio a mocking, humorless sneer. "Fuck you." And fuck that foreign emotion sneaking up on me, slithering around me like a fucking serpent.

The doctor came out and told me Bianca's health was great. He cleared her to work and...have sex.

"That's great news." Bianca would have no excuse, and I'd ease that sexual tension that was messing with my head. "Thank you, doctor."

I told Enzio to see him out and take care of today's meetings for me. Then I went to my room.

Bianca's big eyes widened when she saw me. She was standing in the middle of the room, her hands on her hips, as if she had no clue what she was doing here or what to do with herself.

"I think we should go out," she said, scratching the back of her head. "Shopping. I'd like to go shopping."

I chuckled. I'd already bought her a thousand new things, put them in her side of the dressing room and gave her the pin code. She never touched them. "Later in the evening. I'll take you myself."

"But I wanna go now."

"I said later." I closed the distance between us and cupped her chin. "I've tried to be patient for years. To give you space. That's not like me. I'm done. The doctor said you're all well now. You can't run from me anymore."

Her chin and lips trembled. Words wouldn't come out of her mouth. I grabbed her waist and pulled her closer. She swallowed. "I don't want to. I'm just...nervous. I'm afraid you've built me up in your head to an ideal I can't live up to. I don't want to disappoint you."

I dropped my hand to her bare arm, feeling the cold goosebumps on her skin. Her innocence fueled my desire like pouring alcohol on fire. "You could never disappoint me, principessa. Everything you need to know you'll learn from me." I kissed her. "Only me."

She kissed me back, leaning into me, burning up in a split-second. "You said you were gonna...do it so hard... but I need you to promise me you'll go slow the first time."

As she stumbled through her words, so vulnerable and shy, she was even sexier. My erection ached against my zipper. "I'll go real slow with you, little missy. I promise."

"Thanks. Should I wear something...you know...sexy...for you?"

"I don't want to see you in anything right now. I want to see *you*, Bianca," I said with urgency I hoped it reached her. She had no idea how much I wanted her. How many times I'd pictured her naked, how warm and wet her pussy would be, how tight she'd be squeezing my dick when I took her virginity, how I'd savor every inch that I gained inside her.

Kissing her neck, I pushed the straps of her dress down her shoulders. I wanted to rip the fucking thing off, but I just promised her I'd be gentle. I let the fabric slide down her arms, exposing half of her tits. Then I watched with pleasure as she shivered when it fell to her waist.

Her nipples were pointed out, and I wanted to taste her, suck on her tender skin, make her sore, mark her hard. Instead, I squeezed her tits gently, the feel of them in my hands incredible.

Her eyes fluttered closed as she licked her lips, moaning. "They're so small," she whispered.

"They're perfect." I added more pressure, cock twitching crazily. Then I put one of her nipples in my mouth and suckled with frantic need. There was so much gentle I could be when she was half-naked in my arms. "You're perfect."

The violent beat of her heart worried me for a second. I looked up to make sure she was okay. Her eyes were open now, glazed and fiery. Her lips parted with gasping breaths. I pinched her nipple and watched her reaction. She didn't object. Then as I pushed her dress down her hips, I bit the tender flesh of her tit, marking her mine.

She moaned loudly. "Cosimo, please."

I released her from my mouth and took a step back to watch her body. She stood in only her panties, the dress pooled around her feet. I was so wound up I'd hurt her if I touched her now. "Take off your panties."

Fear flashed over her face, but something else ignited underneath. Something more primal. "You do it."

"I'll tear them off and won't keep my promise."

Her fingers shook, almost unsure as they dip into the sides of her panties. She must be fighting with herself. Arguing about what she wanted and what she thought was right.

She shook her head as if she couldn't believe what she was about to do. Shame took over her expression as she shoved them down.

Her body was perfection. That look on her face needed to go, though.

"I can't let you feel this way. I can't let you question this. We are made for each other, Bianca."

"I was born to be yours," she murmured.

"Yes. We're two sides of one dark soul. And you're here, naked in front of me, ready for me to claim you, because you know deep down, I'm not the monster you're making me out to be."

She took a step toward me and started unbuttoning my shirt. "I know exactly what kind of monster you are, Cosimo." She pulled the end of the fabric out of my pants in jerky, unconfident moves, but I loved that she wanted me naked, too. Then she stretched on her toes to reach my shoulders and shrug the shirt off me. "But I saw something in your eyes at the hospital. Something new, different. Hopeful."

"What did you see?"

Her fingers hesitated as she reached for my belt, as if all the courage she had was used to get me out of my shirt. I unbuckled it for her. There was no backing down. I was going to make her mine now. "What did you see?"

Her hands hovered around the zipper of my pants, and she met my gaze. "Something human."

Before I responded, she lowered her eyes and finished pushing my pants and underwear down. A little gasp escaped her as she saw the erection I was sporting for her. When she trembled and stumbled back, I had to do something before she freaked out on me.

I kicked my pants and shoes off and grabbed her waist. As I carried her up, she kicked and screamed, but I tightened my grasp, threw her on the bed and pinned her down with my weight. "What do you think you're doing, little missy?"

"That," she nodded at my dick, "will hurt. Have you seen the size of me and the size of...you?"

I bit my lip on a laugh. "It'll fit."

She shook her head vigorously.

"I won't hurt you. No matter what. I want to make you feel good. Do you want that? Do you want me to touch you?"

Her teeth sank into her bottom lip.

"You have to say it," I said hoarsely, running a finger under the swell of her tit. "Say you wanna be mine. Say you want me to own you." The back of my hand slid down the dip of her waist, and she hissed. "Is that what you want?"

"Yes, but not with that." Her voice was so soft I almost didn't hear her.

I grunted. "Fine." I bit her earlobe and kiss under it. "But when I'm done touching you with my hands, you'll be begging for my cock."

I breathed her in with a hungry kiss. My lips moved across her jaw, down her throat and reached her throbbing pulse. Her hands found my back, and tiny nails sank into my flesh. I played with one tit before switching to the other until she was panting.

My balls ached as I trailed down her abdomen and ran my finger over the top of her pussy. My name shuddered on her lips, and I couldn't wait to see the same reaction when it was my cock inside her.

I dipped my hand lower. "Spread your legs."

When she did, my thumb found her clit. I couldn't risk plunging into her wetness. Once I felt that, I knew I couldn't hold back. I moved in slow circles first, easing the tension, waiting for her to relax. As she gave a few approving moans, I fluttered my finger against her clit and watched. Something wild took over her face, and the fire I loved so much smoldered in her eyes.

"How does that feel, little missy?"

She tugged her bottom lip into her mouth. I was tempted to bite it like she did, but I focused entirely on her pleasure. "It feels...so good," she panted.

"See what my touch does to you? You were made for me, Bianca."

"Ye-s-s."

"Fuck, I want to be inside of you so bad." Pre-cum leaked from my cock. "But I want to watch you come apart all over my hand first." I upped the pace. "And my mouth."

She mumbled some incoherent words, and I teased her opening carefully, maintaining the pressure on her clit. "Fuck, you're soaking wet and not even my finger is inside you." I had to stop.

"Oh no, why did you stop? Please don't stop," she pleaded.

"Say that you need me."

"I need you. I need you so much. Please."

With a groan, I slid down and rested her ankles on my shoulders. Exhaling all the air in my lungs, I took in her little, pretty pussy. "I have to, at least, taste you, or I'd go bonkers." I dove in and slurped her glistening juices. Then I fucked her with my tongue, my thumb gaining back its rhythm on her clit.

She tasted so fucking good. I was desperate for a release, desperate to fill her with my fucking cock. But I needed to know first what it felt like to have her fall apart for me. To watch her crumble in my hands and taste her when she did.

Her pussy clenched, and her whole body tensed up. "I'm..." She didn't finish as her back arched, her fingers pulled at my hair, her screams filled the room, and gushes of her orgasm filled my mouth.

I looked at the fucking face she made as she came, and I almost shattered with her like a fucking teen watching a girl come for the first time.

Heat ripped across my skin. My heart thundered in my chest. I had to be inside her. Now.

I glided back up and devoured her lips, and then I aligned my cock with her opening. Fuck. Even though I drank her up, she was still so wet I could just slip in without effort. "You want more, don't you, little missy?"

Sweat covering her forehead, her eyes lazy, she nodded. "Yes, please."

"Do you want my cock now?"

"Do I have to say it?"

"Yes. Or I'll tease you till you break and beg for it." If I didn't break first.

"Oh my God, Cosimo." Her face turned from pink to crimson. "We... we'll need condoms."

"Not gonna happen. The first thing you'll feel inside your pussy is me, not some fucking rubber."

"But...it's gonna be messy."

"I'm counting on it."

Panic flashed in her eyes. "Can you, at least, pull out?"

I didn't want to. The idea of coming inside her made my balls swell harder. "Only if you want me to."

"Yes. Please!"

I nodded, the tip of my swollen cock pushing inside her. Then I held her gaze. "If anything hurts, you have to tell me. I'll stop right away."

Her breath snagged. "Okay."

I kissed her one more time before I thrust a little deeper, the whole tip inside her now. She moaned a gasp. Very slowly, I sank into her tightness. "Touch me."

She felt my chest and went down to my abs, tracing my tattoos. Then her hands moved to my waist and back to my hips. "You're so beautiful."

"*You're* so beautiful." I pushed again, groaning. "And so fucking tight."

She moaned, but then she blinked. "Is that a bad thing?"

"No." My eyes rolled back as I went full in. "It's a very good thing."

Her cry was so loud it worried me. "You okay?" I asked.

"Yes. Yes. It's just..."

"What?"

"I'm so stretched."

"You'll get used to it." I pushed my hips back and thrust in again slowly, thick fluids covering my shaft. "This is my pussy." I did it again, enjoying the little noises she was making with each thrust. "It will obey me."

When I was sure she could take my whole length, I started to move. Her eyes wide, her mouth, too, she dragged her nails across my chest as she screamed, leaving red marks.

"Easy, kitten," I said, the burn from the scratches only heightening my pleasure. I moved her hands to my ass. "Take it out here."

More thick warmth coated my cock as I slammed harder, taking my claim. Bianca's virgin pussy. My pussy forever.

I filled her good, and she squirmed beautifully with my strokes. She squeezed my ass as I pushed deeper, as much as her pussy allowed for the first time, until she was falling apart in my arms, her sweet pussy throbbing and clenching around my cock.

I couldn't hold back anymore. Pressure erupted from my aching balls, and every muscle in my body tightened. Just when I was about to blow a fat load, I pulled out, sticky virginity blood covering me. Then sticky ropes of cum spurted from my cock and landed against Bianca's stomach, marking her mine.

CHAPTER 24

Cosimo

As she requested, I took her shopping myself. I spent endless hours in the waiting areas with my guards as she tried a gazillion outfits and asked me if her ass looked big in them and if one of the dresses was better in lilac than in lavender.

She was so tiny to even worry about the size of her perfect ass, and the two colors that puzzled her so much were identical, but I didn't care. Patiently, I answered all her questions, and when she was done, I made my guards carry the bags while *I* guarded her on the streets of San Francisco.

All that with a genuine, silly grin on my face the whole time.

Anything for my little missy.

I linked my arm with hers. "Where else would you like to shop, principessa?"

She giggled. "I think that's it for tonight."

"Good. 'Cause I can't wait to see again that face you make when you come."

A deep blush colored her cheeks as she glanced at the guards and back at me. "Cosimo."

"I love it when you blush like this. It drives me crazy. But there's nothing to be shy about."

She cleared her throat, a little frown on her face. "Speaking of... Was it... what you expected?"

Was she asking me if I enjoyed myself? What we had was the best moment of my life, and I was Cosimo Lanza. I'd seen and had everything. "No."

She froze, and we all stopped to a halt with her. She barely looked at me, but I couldn't miss the deep grimace on her face.

I tilted her chin with my finger to make her look at me. When she did, I leaned in. "It was way better."

295

Her tiny fists punched my arms and stomach. "Fuck you."

I laughed instead of telling her to stop. We were in public, and my guards were watching my girl swearing at me and attempting to punch me. "Any time, little missy."

She continued her hilarious fist throwing, and I held her thighs and carried her over my shoulder. She yelped. "Cosimo, put me down!"

I spanked her, and she yelped again. "When you behave."

"Oh my God. Just put me down."

"Say please."

"Fuck this shit. Please."

"Excuse me?"

"I said please, Almighty Cosimo, would you put me down, kind sir?"

Laughing loudly, I cradled her in my arms and slid her body down gently. I held her arms tight and gave her a kiss that made us both giddy.

"We'll need condoms." She was pressed to me and could feel my instant hardness.

I kissed her again, the memory of my bare cock inside her vivid. "No, we won't. We're both clean, and I gave you my word. I won't be with anyone else."

"It's not just about that." She glanced at the guards and lowered her voice when she looked back at me. "I haven't been sexually active till today. I'm not on any birth control."

My balls swelled, and my cock got even harder. Why was that turning me on so much? "So?" I asked, baffled at myself.

"So I can get pregnant. Pulling out isn't exactly the best prophylactic," she whispered, explaining like I was an idiot.

Maybe I was. Because I was picturing her pregnant with my baby. "You'll be so fucking hot pregnant."

"Cosimo, can you be serious? This isn't the time to joke."

I locked my gaze with hers, making sure she understood I wasn't joking.

All the blood rushed out of her face. "Oh my God. You are serious. You're crazy."

I squeezed her arms. "I know you're afraid, but there's nothing to be afraid of."

"There's everything to be afraid of." Her voice was low and dark. She jerked out of my arms. "Get the condoms or what happened today will never happen again."

This was the first time I saw Bianca scared. Truly scared.

CHAPTER 25

Cosimo

S
he didn't say a word all the way home and once we got there, she locked herself in the bathroom.

I leaned against the door frame. "Bianca, can we just talk?"

"Go fuck yourself, Don Cosimo."

There was so much I could take. I pinched the bridge of my nose. "You know I can break the fucking door, right? So why don't you just come out?"

"Why would I make things easier for you? Go ahead. Do what you do best. Destroy things."

A surge of anger hit me. I stalked to the bedroom door and let the guards in. Then I nodded at the bathroom.

They smashed the door, and I entered. She was curled by the bathtub, a pinch to her mouth. "Come out now," I ordered.

She grabbed some toiletries and started throwing them at me one by one.

"Seriously?" I dodged the little bottles and reached her in two strides. Then I grabbed her out.

"Ow! You're hurting me!" she yelled.

I threw her on the bed and dismissed the boys. Wiping a hand over my mouth, I stared at her. "Now talk."

She yelled again, but I couldn't tolerate any more of this shit. "None of that," I warned. "You're childish behavior is no longer cute."

"I'm not a child. I'm obviously the responsible adult here. If there's anyone being childish, it's you. Happy to play with your new fucktoy however you like, and you don't give a shit about the consequences."

"You're not my fucktoy."

She shrugged and continued as if she didn't hear me. "I mean, why would you? If I got pregnant, you'd force me into an abortion or you'd take the baby and kick me out. I'd never see her or you again..."

I raised a hand and shushed her. "Che cazzo?" Was that how she really saw me?

298

"I'm not an idiot, Cosimo. I know—"

"Yes, you are. If you think that I waited twelve years only to play with you for a little while and toss you away when I was done, then you *are* definitely an idiot."

Her throat bobbed, and her eyes shone with tears. "Even if that's not your intention with me—"

"It is not," I hissed.

She looked away in defeat. "Your family will never accept me, Cosimo. I'm barely Italian and have no family or assets of my own. You think you can just introduce me to Marta one day and have her blessing? She won't take me in her arms. For all I know, she'll have me killed before I set foot in her house."

I'd be dead before anyone laid a hand on Bianca. I took a deep breath and sat next to her. "How many times do I have to tell you that you're safe with me? I'd never let anything bad happen to you. All your fears are for nothing."

She shook her head. "We both know I'll never be a Lanza." Her hand, cold, fell on top of mine. "So, please, let's just keep...whatever this is between us simple. With no complications we'll both regret."

"Whatever this is between us? Complications we'll regret?" Something stirred in me. The beast that I tried so hard to tame around her. But she woke him up with a roar.

"Cosimo—"

"I don't wanna hear another fucking word." I shot to my feet and slammed the door behind me.

Chapter 26

Bianca

Cosimo didn't touch me after that day. We still slept in the same room, but he made sure he was gone in the morning before I woke up and got to bed late after I'd gone to sleep.

Still, I felt him next to me in the middle of the night, his breath, his warmth I'd become addicted to. Even his erection that drove me insane and he pretended to neglect.

He made sure I was well-fed, but he barely shared any meals with me, and when he did, he didn't say a word.

Sometimes, he'd come home from God only knew where, doing what, in the late afternoon or early evening. He'd stay with me in front of the fireplace in utter silence. Then he'd head out and never return before my bedtime.

I caught him watching me often. Sometimes pensive, most of the time dark. No matter how dark, his gaze always burned with longing and reprimand.

The silent treatment was killing me, and the dull pattern we fell into got on my nerves. After a week, I was dying. Desperate. For his attention. For his touch.

He'd opened Pandora's box when he took my virginity. Such an asshole. How could he open that new dimension for me and then leave me there all hungry and alone?

Didn't he know that when you never had sex, you didn't know what you were missing, but when you did, it was like an insatiable beast inside you that needed to be fed or it'd eat you alive?

I could just apologize, try to be sexy, seduce him or whatever, but I wouldn't. I just couldn't do what he was asking me to do. I was stupid enough to put my own life and heart in the hands of a dangerous man like Cosimo, but there was still a shred of sanity left in me that wouldn't let me ruin another innocent life.

300

Regardless of how desperate and horny and sad I was. It didn't matter that I felt like I was fucking dying in here.

I cried myself to sleep as I came to terms that my days here were coming to an end. A man like him would never back down or compromise. His mind was set on something, and I couldn't change it for him.

My mind was set, too. Tomorrow when I woke up, I'd pack my things along with my broken heart and go.

Chapter 27

Bianca

I heard Cosimo get dressed, but I pretended to be asleep. I only stole one last glance at him as he opened the door and left.

Tears dropped on the already wet pillow as I dragged myself out of the bed. I washed my face and started packing. I only took my old things and left the new clothes. I had nowhere and no one to wear them for anyway.

Before I cried again, I darted to the nightstand to get my phone to call Mona and tell her I was coming back home.

Standing there, a cream envelope on Cosimo's pillow caught my attention. Who would leave him a note here? As I grabbed it carefully, I saw it had my name on it.

There was a blunt note on Cosimo's restaurant card inside. *Be there at eight. Wear the red dress.*

An order more than an invitation. But what was the occasion? Some celebration he needed to have some arm candy for?

I stared at the card for a while, and then at my almost ready-to-go bags. If I didn't go, he might get his men to bring me to him by force or even worse, wouldn't let me leave at all. He might have lost interest in me, but I knew better. He wouldn't allow me to leave if he still wanted me here for any other reason.

Obviously, he did. For one more night, at least.

At 7:45 his guards came to collect me. I rode with them to the restaurant, and once I was in there, they shut the doors and waited outside.

What the hell was going on?

The place was empty like it was on our first date. No party, no celebration, no shit. Was Cosimo even here?

I called for him, and then for the chef. Nothing answered me but the walls. Why did he tell me to be here when no one was? Why did the guards stand outside?

I ran to the door and tried to open it, but it was locked. What the fuck?

"Trying to leave me again?"

A gasp ripped from my chest as I twisted. Cosimo was leaning against the kitchen entrance in a black dress shirt and pants, his hands in his pockets.

"I called for you. When you didn't answer, I thought..." I blinked. "Why is the door locked?"

He straightened and took a few steps toward me. "Why were your bags packed?"

My pulse hammered. "Is that why you brought me here?"

"Answer me!"

I flinched, stepping back, but he was an inch apart from me now, his hand around my throat. "Where the fuck did you think you were going?"

"Home," I choked.

His stare darkened. Then he pushed me until my back hit a wall, and he was pressed to my front. "Your only home is with me."

My eyes teared up from the choking. "You said I'd stay with you till I was better. The doctor cleared me a week ago. At the hospital you said I could go whenever I wanted after I was better."

"I never said that."

He said leave the future in the future. It seemed that, now that we were in the future, he wouldn't allow me the freedom.

I didn't want him to.

"I thought you didn't want me anymore. You don't speak to me. You don't touch me..."

His free hand hiked my dress up and slipped between my thighs. Then he pushed the lace of my panties to the side and plunged a finger inside me. I choked a moan, surprised at how wet I already was.

His lip curled under his tooth, his eyes burning honey. "Is this what you want? Is this what gets you to stay?"

When I didn't answer, he crushed his lips onto mine, pushing two fingers inside me now. My head pounded, my chest heaved for breath, and my pussy clenched hard around his fingers.

"Say it. Say you want my touch. Say you want only me to touch you." He squeezed my neck harder. "Say it!"

"I want you to touch me," I slurred. "So much. No one else. Only you."

He let go of my neck, and I sucked in a deep, loud breath, only so he could rip off my panties. Then he spun me so that my back was to him now and returned to choke me.

The chime of his belt unbuckling rang in my ear followed by the sound of his pants unzipping. Then I felt his breath on the back of my neck, and the tip of his cock at my entrance.

But he didn't move. "How bad do you want my cock?"

"So bad," I panted, my mind numb. "Please."

He grabbed my pussy. "Whose pussy is that?"

"Yours, Cosimo. Only yours," I cried, meaning every word. I wished things had been different, but that was the truth I couldn't deny. I was his, and I loved it. I didn't want anyone else. I belonged with him. Born to be his, just like he always said. "I'm all yours."

With that, he thrust into me. He fucked me so hard I could no longer think or see or breathe. All that was there was the pleasure and the pain he was pouring into every cell of mine.

After I screamed his name, he pulled out of me and turned me. Then he shoved his cock into my mouth and shot his thick cum down my throat.

His eyes flashed with a look I couldn't understand. "Go clean yourself up and meet me in the kitchen."

CHAPTER 28

Bianca

Cosimo was cooking.

The man who had just fucked me against a wall and shoved his cock down my throat while choking me was standing in the kitchen of his own restaurant, a gun tucked in the back of his pants, making gnocchi from scratch.

"Come," he said.

I ambled toward him, but he—impatiently—grabbed my arm and squeezed me in the tight space between his body and the counter. He pressed his front to my back, forcing me to brace my palms on the floury counter for support. "Is it always gonna be this rough?" I asked.

He rolled tiny pieces of dough with his finger. "Are you always gonna try to leave me?"

"You might not believe me, but I don't want to leave you."

He inhaled deeply and took my finger, dipped it in flour and made me roll the gnocchi with him. It was strange and intimate at the same time.

"So you brought me here, all dressed up, to punish me?" I asked, my skin tingling as his breath caressed me.

"No." He kept moving my finger, the feeling of my little hand inside his soothing, comforting, safe, even though I perfectly knew what he was capable of doing with his hands. "That I could have done at home."

My nipples hardened as if I ached for him to punish me again. "Then why? I don't think it's the cooking class either."

"You're right. I brought you here for another date."

I glanced at him over my shoulder. "You're cooking for me?"

"That was the plan. I make you nice food, have a pleasant talk and then..."

"Then you fuck me."

"That, too. But I had to change the order of things." he rested his fore-

305

head on mine. "Because you've been a very bad girl...and you look so sexy in that dress I couldn't help myself."

I smiled, a warm, happy feeling folding me. "I'm sorry for a being a bad girl."

"Are you?"

"If every time I misbehave that will be my punishment, then no, not really."

He spanked me, and my stomach tightened. "If you ever think about leaving me again..."

"I told you I don't want to leave. Not even the first time I was here. When I did leave that night, I felt so angry, so empty. I'm that stupid." A flood of emotions threatened to spill from my eyes. "I came to your house knowing I might never leave, knowing I might lose everything, even my own life, but my stupid heart..." I sighed. "I'd rather die than not be with you. I'm in love with you, Cosimo."

"I'm in love with you, too."

Dazed, I just gazed at him. He said it so naturally without hesitation, as if he knew it all along, believed it, accepted it, felt it beyond any doubt. For so long.

"Surprised that I love you? I have a heart, too, principessa. And you fucking stole it with a box of bandages." He put his hand in his pocket and showed me the twelve-year-old, blue box.

"You kept it," I breathed, swirling.

"For when I missed you so much."

"Cosimo..." I trembled.

"Open it."

I did, and my heart skipped a beat. I stared inside the box, forgetting to breathe, and then I gasped for air, tears betraying me.

"The family you're so afraid of will stop being so scary when you're one of it," he said.

The bling of the diamond on the ring in the box dazzled me. Crippled my thoughts and my tongue.

He held my hand and put the ring on my finger. "Marta is a huge influencer in my family, but don't forget who runs it. If I want you to be a Lanza, you will be a Lanza."

For as long as we both shall live. I knew now what he meant. Cosimo had been in love with me all this time. He wanted to marry me all this time.

My head was spinning. I pressed my temple, shaking my head in awe at the ring, my heart throbbing violently. Cosimo, the man I gladly gave myself to, the man who owned me with his heart before his power, was proposing to me.

If I said yes, huge part of me was screaming yes already, pushing a grin on my face, I'd be the wife of the Mafia boss. I'd be a part of the Lanzas.

That also meant I'd carry Cosimo's children. The Mafia boss's children. The ones who would grow up to take his place.

Suddenly, I felt so cold, the grin vanished, and the heart that was beating frantically with happiness changed its rhythm to a frightening dance.

"But it turns out *being a Lanza* is what you're really afraid of," Cosimo said.

I closed my eyes, wouldn't dare look at him now, afraid if I saw any sign of hurt or blame or sadness in his gaze, I'd surrender without a fight. "I'm in no place to judge you or your family. I mean, look at my parents. Even the man who raised me when they couldn't used to be a gangster." I shrugged. "And since the day at the hospital when I agreed to go live with you, maybe even before that, I accepted you and what you do. Because I truly love you, Cosimo, and despite everything, I found out you were more important to me than anything else."

A sudden burst of courage took over me, and I peered up at him. His eyes were steady on me, barely showing any emotion. "I want to say yes, Cosimo, so fucking much."

"But?"

"I don't want my children to live in fear."

"Neither you nor them will ever have to live in fear. I will protect them like I will protect you. The whole family will," he vowed.

"As long as you're alive?"

"Yes."

307

"What happens if you're not?" My voice cracked. "What happens if you die, Cosimo?" Tears dropped heavily down my face. "You belong to one of the most vicious mafias in the world. There's greed, betrayal, feuds, blood. This is your world, and you surround yourself with guards and carry guns at all times because you know it's not safe to be a Lanza. So what happens if you no longer there to protect us? Have you ever thought about that? Because I have, and it gives me nightmares." I clutched my stomach in pain, shuddering.

"Hey." Cosimo held me tight in his embrace. "Easy. Easy, amore."

"You and I are two ends of a dark soul like you said, and I accepted my fate, even willed and welcomed it. I'm ready for the risk, but how could I want to bring a child into that world? And how could you be so sure you can protect them?"

"My brother and I are living examples that the Lanzas are well protected. Bianca, Giovanni died peacefully in his bed. Enzio and I lived our lives like everyone else. We had everything, and we're still kicking for over thirty years."

"But how many times have you come close to death? How many men have you killed so you could still be alive for over thirty years?"

His jaws clenched, and then he sighed. "What do you want me to do to make you feel safe?"

I locked my blurring gaze with his. "Please, Cosimo. Please, just step down and give your chair to Enzio. That's all I'm asking."

He shook his head and pushed me out of his embrace. "You're asking for the impossible."

My heart sank to my knees. Every time we were at a crossroad like that, when I felt I was about to lose him, my heart shattered into a million pieces all over again. Every time, I put all logic aside and risked everything just so I wouldn't lose him.

Would I do it this time, too?

Could I?

"You know I could *make* you marry me, but I don't want to force something this big on you. I want you to marry me because you love me as much as I love you, so I'm still waiting to hear your answer," he said. "Will you marry me, Bianca?"

I stared at the ring and at the blazing war in his eyes, my heart split, two sides fighting, and an answer on the tip of my frozen tongue.

To be continued...
Can't wait to know what happens between Bianca and Cosimo and Enzio Lanza?
Get your copy of The Italian Marriage now

* * *

Newsletter
http://njadelbooks.com/newsletter

About N.J. Adel

N. J. Adel, the author of The Italians, All the Teacher's Pets, Her Royal Harem and I Hate You then I Love You series, is a cross genre author. From chocolate to books and book boyfriends, she likes it DARK and SPICY. Bikers, mobs, rock stars, dirty Hollywood heartthrobs, smexy guards and men who serve. She loves it all.

She is a loather of cats and thinks they are Satan's pets. She used to teach English by day and write fun smut by night with her German Shepherd, Leo. Now, she only writes the fun smut.

Read More from N.J. Adel and Follow everywhere

JOAQUIN FUERTES

Struck In Love Spinoff
Fuertes Cartel Book 1

Chiquita Dennie

Author Note

*Please note the following story is only the first part of book 1 of my new book series, **Fuertes Cartel Book 1**.

Each story will have a HEA but as this is only part 1 of **Joaquin Fuertes (Struck In Love Spinoff Fuertes Cartel Book e1)**

please be prepared for a cliffhanger. The rest of the story will be released once this boxset is unpublished.

Joaquin Fuertes (Struck In Love Spinoff Fuertes Cartel Book 1) is an M/F (one male, one female) dark contemporary Mafia-ish romance that deals with intense violence and illicit themes. I would advise skipping this story if you don't like the word fuck; guys that use ANY means to get what they want; or have a problem with badass chicks that don't mind putting people in their place and doing whatever they need to in order to survive.

Joaquin Fuertes (Fuertes Cartel Book 1)

Sofia is a world-famous actress and singer on Broadway. Being on the stage has been a lifelong dream. Living in New York, her life is a non-stop roller coaster of parties, magazine shoots and more. Once her friendship with Sabrina Washington became public, any and everything was put on notice.

Joaquin is a quiet deadly force. He's known in the illegal business as Ghost. Someone that shows up only when the client needs to disappear. The second he bumps into Sofia after a meeting at the restaurant, her beauty causes his heart to beat faster. He reminds himself to not fall in love only continue working in the shadows to keep his clients' businesses out of the spotlight.

Will these two opposites see the storm that is brewing staring right there in front of them? Or can one split second of losing your breath cause you to lose control and cause destruction when that foundation is broken?

PREVIOUSLY....STRUCK IN LOVE 4

As the son of Joaquin Fuertes, the longest-running Mayor in Portugal, and founding father of the Fuentes Cartel, he had groomed me to run the family business with an iron fist. They knew me as the Ghost because I'm good at making problems disappear. The young lady sitting across from me in a chair gave me a forced nod of agreement, which told me I had failed to persuade her to do as I requested. A deep frown crossed my face. This bitch was looking to destroy not only the De Luca Cartel but ours as well here in Italy. Queen was known as a hard-ass, and Antonio had made it clear not to cross him again, or her entire bloodline would be extinct. I stepped out of my chair as she sat with tape wrapped around her mouth, keeping the screams at bay, blood dripping down her body from numerous injuries.

She had a chance to leave when Antonio confronted her back at the meeting. Afterward, she continued with her plan, and Antonio agreed for me to put an end to her plans. Both the De Luca and Fuentes' Cartel had an agreement that as long as we made money together, we wouldn't interfere with each other's territory. I'm not an abuser, unlike other men in the Cartel. I had my ways of getting what I need out of my enemies. Raising my sleeves on my crisp white shirt, stepping forward as my enforcer, Gabriella continued the ritual of cutting off one finger at a time when she didn't comply and answered my questions. I didn't need to have a gun on me like my counterparts. I've lived in Italy for the past two years, and recently an opportunity came up for me to visit America, more specifically the Big Apple, for a business exchange that would extend the Fuertes Cartel territory in the illegal underground dealings.

"Take the tape off, Gabriella."

"Joaquin, you don't want to do this. We can forge a new deal, and I can get you all the territory you need plus guns. Your father isn't the only one with ties in America." Queen said weakly, trying to convince me to betray my father. Not wanting to hear any more of her lies, I winked, and Gabriella smiled, knowing this was the signal to end her life. As she prepared to have fun, I gathered my jacket off the chair and walked out of the back of Antonio's; the restaurant was a front for the De Luca Cartel, even though it was the top celebrity spot for politicians. Everyone knew what happened here. As Queen's screams finally died down. I walked up the stairs and opened the door. I bumped into a soft body, and before we both fell, I gripped her by the waist.

"Ohh...Excuse me."

A light sweet smell invaded my nostrils. Our eyes connected, and my grasp grew tighter.

"Hello, you can let me go now ," she said with a chuckle as we both leaned against the wall away from the restaurant.

"Joaquin, the car is here, and Gabriella texted you. What's going on here?" Monica pointed between the mystery goddess and me. I somehow could not make myself let go of my thoughts of her. I was only trying to prevent her from falling, but my eyes never left hers. Something about them kept me hypnotized.

"Mira a donde vas hermosa?"

"Huh?" she asked as I grinned at the perplexed look across her face, dropping my hands from around her waist. Monica followed behind me and passed my phone over as Gabriella texted the package was cleaned up.

Gabriella: The package is secure.

Me: Inform De Luca and let him know we should have dinner plans while he's here.

Gabriella: Any other guests?

I looked back over my shoulder as the woman I just knocked into headed toward a seat that a man pulled out for her. A strange suspicion came over me, and I couldn't explain it as she peered up and caught my eye. Turning away, I opened the car door and got inside, ignoring whatever odd feeling came over me from being in her presence.

"Joaquin, are you listening to me?" Monica asked, sitting beside me in the limousine, rubbing a hand over my thigh.

"Not right now, Monica," I said, moving her hand off my thigh and focusing on texting Gabriella back.

Me: My father.

Chapter 1

Sophia

Three Months Later

I'd finished my tenth performance of my Broadway show, *Regret, My Love*. Sitting down at my vanity mirror, I turned the radio down low as Nina Simone played in the background. I needed a shower and bed from being on my feet for over four days with two shows daily back to back. I removed my makeup, tightening my robe over my sweatsuit. A knock on my door interrupted me, and my assistant walked inside without waiting for a response to come.

"Your stalker just left ." Cassidy closed the door, walking inside with a bouquet of red roses and placing them down on the vanity mirror. I pulled one stem out and took a sniff. It smelled fresh, sweet, and clean. Nothing like the man that I had come to know as Joaquin Fuertes. A dangerous, angry, menacing, but deadly Cartel Boss I met a few months ago. It was in all the journals about the Fuentes family. In New York, they were untouchable as from the stories I saw people went missing because of them. They seemed to have multiple businesses here and their connections reached up to the top of the food chain from police to governors, from the cops to governors, to politicians in Washington. The rumors say they came together with the DeLuca Cartel, which is run by club owner Antonio DeLuca, who's married to Sabrina Washington.

"Did he do anything to you?" Her head moved to wagging back and forth. Opening up another Revlon makeup remover and wiping the foundation and lipstick off my lips, I glanced up through the mirror and saw her shake her head no.

"No, he does what he always does when you have a performance. Come up here, sit in the back, watch you, bring you flowers and then leave. Should

I contact the police to have him removed from the property?" Cassidy replied.

I should probably be afraid of him. As the daughter of a southern father and mother, Latoya and Leroy Chambers, they were a regular hardworking family, and their three children are everything to them. I was born and raised in Mississippi with two brothers, me being the youngest. I was five-seven in height, twenty-seven years old, single and working on my career as an actress and singer. I had an oval face and long nose, which my manager wanted me to get fixed. My lips were full with a small gap in between, and I had a copper skin tone, with dimples in both cheeks. I was told repeatedly that I'd never make it in this business; five years later I'm the lead actress on a Broadway show. Ten movies and one TV show, with one album release, which still blows my mind coming from the south to live in New York and make a living doing what I loved. Things were opening up for me and having a distraction like this would be stupid.

"Has he threatened you, Cassidy?"

She sighed, running a hand down her face, turning toward me, walking closer to read the card. "Beautiful performance by a beautiful woman. I don't know, Sofia, the man never speaks to anyone, but he has a box seat to watch you perform. You've never gone out with him or had sex. But he sends you flowers for every show ," Cassidy said.

"I know it seems strange, but we met one day by accident. I ran into him when I was coming out of the restaurant the day I had a meeting with the producer for the show."

I had immediately noticed the man who was tall with broad, muscled shoulders. I notice men don't like to consider themselves beautiful. There was nothing too special about me and it made me curious as to what he wanted from me. We had never held a single conversation ever since I bumped into that muscular broad chest of his, that day. I tried one time to send the flowers back and ended up with more in my room the next day.

"What did you think about my performance tonight ?" I asked.

"Don't change the subject, Sofia, I expect you like the chase from the baby boy."

"I don't have time for that, right now. I have the play, my family and a movie coming up, dating is the last thing on my mind," I told her while removing my robe. I grabbed my jacket and flowers to leave Cassidy to follow behind. "I'll call you tomorrow once I find out back from Jordan about the audition ," I also added.

Opening the door, and walking outside through the back alley, I saw a long sleek black limousine sitting and running with the door wide. The driver said to me, "Ma'am, he's waiting for you."

"I'm not getting in your car," I respond.

"The boss doesn't take no for an answer, please get in. He's had a long day, all he wants to do is take you home." The driver took my flowers, and I looked around, there was no one behind me.

"What are you doing here?" I asked.

He says nothing; he just sits near the window, turns his head to stare at me, and stare at my mouth. He then licked his lips and turned back, looking out of the window. "You can get into the car, beautiful, I won't bite. I'm safe." He holds his hand out for me to take while staring into my face. I place my hands in my lap as I hesitate to take the next step and he extends a hand out and I grasp it, then look out the window. The driver goes around to get into the driver's side; he pushes the partition up to give us privacy, and I sit near the door crossing my legs, wondering if this is the worst mistake ever.

"Thank you for the flowers," I comment. He nodded in response.

"You're welcome ," he answered.

"Are you always this quiet? You're a big-time mobster from what the paper says so I figured you have some backup ." It was very quiet in the limo as we drove home, so I kept rambling.

"I live in Manhattan. I live near Waterline Square. My assistant feels you're crazy, and I'm crazy for indulging you; sending these flowers, she thinks you're probably a stalker."

"And what do you understand?" he asked.

"I guess she's right." He smiled at me as the car pulled up in front of my apartment building. I moved to open the door, and he grasped my hand. I turned to look at him.

"Joaquin Fuertes."

"I recognize your name from the papers."

"Have dinner with me ," he commanded.

"My story is simple, and one dinner can't change everything."

"Does that scare you, Sofia?" he questioned.

"It depends, are you planning on hurting me?" He held my hand as I stepped out of the car, then watched as they turned off into traffic. I stood on the sidewalk, watching the limo leave with him inside while thinking about the Tonight Show and the audience applause, knowing he was there watching me in the private booths. I turned to walk inside and saw Mr. Simon, who worked as one of the doormen for the past ten years.

"Wonderful evening, Sofia. How was your performance?" Jerry questioned.

"It was sold-out, Jerry; remind me to get tickets for you and your wife." He held up his hands in a thank you motion. Living in a condo had its advantages, staying at the penthouse level while I'm here until I wrap up the show in six months. I had a private gym and pool. My laundry gets picked up once a week, and I have a chef that prepares my breakfast, lunch and dinner when I'm home. Although on nights like tonight, I know I'll find some gourmet meal waiting for me. I rode the elevator up to my twenty-fifth-floor penthouse before stepping off. I opened the door, hung my coat up then checked my mail that my housekeeper left.

Passing to the kitchen, I saw food wrapped on the counter. Tonight, I'll open a bottle of wine, shower, and sleep the next day away. I had a full schedule coming up the following week and being distracted by a man that appeared to want me, who is dangerous on top of that, eswas the last thing I needed in my life right now, especially since I suspected he'd be the type to want to control my every move.

Chapter 2

Sofia

J oaquin...Ughh..this is-his large, strong hands gripped my neck while his
fingers gave me pleasure beyond my imagination. His whispering of
how good my pussy tasted, the groans and moans mixed between us
caused me to shudder while gripping the sheets, and our juices trailed down
onto the sheets. He surprised me with a trip to Spain. We had his entire villa
to ourselves. He gripped my thigh, squeezing gently as I called out his name.

"Sofia! Sofia! are you listening?" Edward asked, snapping me out of my
daydream.

"I'm sorry, Edward, what did you say?" The following morning, I had
the day off from the show, but back-to-back meetings for a potential movie,
album discussions with the label now that I'm established from my first
album, and I was lining up a tour potential along with a new film. Edward
arranged for a car to pick me up. And now we're sitting at the same restaurant then I crashed into Joaquin a few months back. There's a part of me that
wonders if he still comes by.

"If you would ever focus, you'd realize I said we have four meetings with
producers that want to work with you ," Edward replied.

"Sorry I haven't been sleeping lately."

He reached over and caressed my cheek, and I moved out of his hold,
before looking around and making sure no one saw us. Edward Anderson
has been my manager for the last seven years of my career. The first three, I
was struggling with the working actress playing small rolls until my big break
in the comedy, *Riley Home*.

"Cassidy, did you set up the recording with Deras Jones?"

"I did and scheduled you to do a few social media interviews with influ-
encers. It could be beneficial to show your face online a little more."

"I don't know, that ends up being more time than it's worth. I have to
study my lines. And getting distracted by weirdos on the internet is too
draining."

327

"Cassidy has a point Sofia, this could be good for us, especially with your music coming out soon."

"Let me think it over for a few days."

"I have a photo shoot set for you, so make sure you don't hang out with your boyfriend all night ," Cassidy called off from the laptop computer.

"He's a distraction. Get rid of him ," Edward demanded.

* * *

Joaquin

"Joaquin, are you listening to me?" Monica screamed, while she accompanied me out of my office building. She showed up without calling and wanted to talk. I never returned her calls two months ago after I bumped into who I now recognize as Sofia Chambers. Something about her was mesmerizing and calmed me down. Those brief moments played in my mind repeatedly until I had my people investigate and locate her information when they left Antonio's that day. She didn't acknowledge my question about dinner, but over time she'll open up to being my friend and then my lover.

"Monica, go home."

Gabriella pulled up in the black SUV that we did business in that called for a fast exit. Tightening my black gloves, I kissed Monica on the forehead and told her I'd be in touch with her later. She stepped in front of me, blocking me from leaving.

"What is this?" I questioned, anger making my tone harsher than normal.

"No, you are not leaving without me. I don't see what I did wrong, but please forgive me ," Monica whined, running her hand up to my chest, standing on her toes to plant a kiss on my lips. I turned my head, and it landed on my cheek.

"We're work acquaintances, Monica, nothing more."

"Do you have all your work acquaintances sucking your dick?" she snapped harshly.

"Do you think embarrassing yourself in public would get me to agree to speak with you privately?"

"I-"

"No, I've never thrown you the impression we had anything other than friendship. Go home, and I will call you. Never come up here again without calling me first."

"But you never answer my calls Joaquin, and you know Gael hates me." She leaned her head into my chest, and I gently leaned her head up, wiping the tears off her cheek.

"Go home. I have a business to handle."

Monica agreed, smiling weakly and stepping out of my way, and I headed in the car's direction before getting inside, and Gabriella drove off.

"She will be a problem, boss ," Gabriella implied, typing in the warehouse's address where the guns were located. Gael got a call late last night that they stole a shipment of our weapons, and they suspected it was the Russians. I had my suspicions; it was a local gang poking around our business. Antonio could negotiate a three-way sale of guns from Germany without going through the Russians, and we'd split everything down the middle. Now to have a shipment come up missing not even twenty-four hours later, I had my concerns. It was only two in the afternoon, so traffic was heavy, and everybody was out. The warehouse was near the loading dock. Antonio shuffled things around after his situation with Queen months back and destroyed the old warehouse that was closer to the city. This was further out by the Hudson River.

"Monica is needy and weak. Her entire existence is based on my approval, and I've never given her that impression. She doesn't even know my parents' names or where I live," I answered in my native Portuguese.

"If she becomes a problem."

"Then I'll take care making sure you understand that being in my life won't be her result." I grunted, lifting my gun out of my holster and removing the safety and cocking it back. Gabriella pulled into the entrance to the warehouse. Gael, Hugo, and a few more men were standing by. I walked out of the car and slammed it shut.

"Any visitors?" I interrogated.

Gael rubbed the back of his neck, sounding nervous.

"Speak," I urged.

"There are women inside working, we can't go inside. I think it was a false call," Gael responded.

Turning and wandering into the front door, I opened the gate to see a room full of women sewing, all ages and races. The low hum of merengue played in the background. Searching around, it looked like a sweatshop as the racks of jumpsuits were labeled Fashion Den. Grating my teeth, I shot my revolver in the air and everyone screamed and scrambled to run off. I pointed at Hugo to block the front door. Scanning around the room, I looked everyone in the eye to see if they'd give away who was in charge.

"Excuse me for my interruption. Who is in charge here?" I demanded, marching down the aisle.

No one spoke and I pointed to Gael to help. He's more of a negotiator. He came over and got out some money, and one woman stepped up and took it in exchange for giving us information.

"The supervisor stepped out, he said that he would get back in an hour after dropping off a package," the young lady explained; she didn't look over the age of twenty, and was dressed in worn jeans and a dingy blue vest with Fashion Den spiraled across her chest.

"How long have you worked here?" I sought.

"One year, sir."

"Any other rooms in this place? A basement or office?"

She nodded and pointed to the exit sign. I waved for Gael to follow me and for Hugo and Gabriella to stay upfront.

I jogged over to the door and pushed it open. It was a dark hallway that led to another door. There was rat shit on the ground, and empty food containers. It looked more like the trash area than a business office and I wrinkled my nose at the noxious odors that surrounded us. Gael and I drew our guns and opened the door on the count of three. Crates, small and big, sat open. I walked over and checked one and noticed serial numbers on the inside of the container. Gael checked another box, and we continued for the next five minutes, coming up empty-handed. We left out of the room and ran back to the front entrance. Hugo was standing at the window and cocked his shotgun.

"We have company, about three cars and eight men that I could see," Hugo whispered.

"Take the women to the back and find an exit," I shouted at the young lady who was in charge. She pushed them to follow behind her right as Hugo busted a hole in the window and started shooting. I moved to the other side of the window and peeked out as gunfire was returned.

Pop! Pop! Pop!

"It has to be Vitale's men." Gael yelled.

"Go through the back and come up on the side. I'll hold them off, and you get a clean shot. Gabriella go with him," I yelled as I motioned to the two of them before running a hand down my face, sweat staining my shirt.

Narrowing my eye, I aimed the handgun toward his ankle and pulled. He screamed in pain, falling, and the other men tried to help him, which opened a doorway for Gael and Gabriella to get off a few more rounds until Hugo and I walked outside to clear the area. I kicked the gun away from the only one that was left alive. Stooping down, I smacked him in the face, getting him to focus.

"Aye, focus!" I snapped my finger.

"Fuck you, Joaquin!" he shouted in pain. I took the tip of my gun and pushed it into his wound as he cried out.

"Who sent you, and where are my guns?" I sneered, cocking my gun in his direction.

"I know nothing."

Gabriella grinned, thirsty to kill.

"Then you're of no use to me," I responded, shooting him in between the eyes, and walking off toward my car to leave.

Chapter 3

Joaquin

Two Days Later.

I was born in Spain and raised in Portugal, as the son of Mayor Joaquin Fuertes and Italian mother, Alba Fuertes. They're still married to this day, even as he's retired from politics. When you join the Cartel, you never retire, and his hands advise me when needed. Mother wasn't happy about her oldest son getting involved in the lifestyle and while being groomed with two grandfathers in the underworld. Tiago Fuertes, on my Dad's side, was an underboss to his brother that started the Fuertes Cartel, and my mother's father, Piero Giordano, was his accountant. Growing up, I watched my dad work both sides of the law. He was able to walk into dinners with politicians and governors, then at the drop of a hat cut a man's throat that betrayed him. They set life for me before I was born. My younger sister, Alessandra, who is now twenty-two, wished to follow me to America, and I refused to allow her to do so.

I promised my mother that I'd never put her in a position, that she'd have to lose any of her children. I was the one behind Queen's death, and time was ticking because someone out there was waiting and planning to bring an end to my door. At twenty-nine, I should be out dating, living life, traveling around the world, preparing for a future with a wife and children. Here I was standing in my office thinking about her. The minute our eyes connected, my heart felt inclined to protect her and protect her near me. It didn't matter if she was with someone at the restaurant that night. If I ahadn't had business to attend to she would have been with me for the rest of the night. That's the side of me that pushes the other part away in order to have a moment of happiness. Ghost is the one I go around as all day and night. The amount of death and destruction, bloodshed, and ripping families apart has forced my soul to harden, and I refuse to push the darkness into Sofia. Could I have protested? No. My family would have made sure that they immediately changed my decision. Even when I came to America to get an education, it was under strict protection. Not only am I the Don of the most prominent underworld mafia family, but I also have my investment company I've built from the ground up with my right-hand man, Gael Velez. We've been childhood friends since we were five years old in boarding school. The Velez and Fuertes families ran all over Spain and parts of Italy that we gained through our collaboration with Antonio De Luca and his clan.

"He's right here. I'll tell him ," Gael responded, hanging up the phone. I was peering out of the window of my office on the tenth floor while he dealt with a phone call. Instead of having to share the space, we bought the entire building. This way, we don't have anyone around who shouldn't be there.

The Alba Industries is a venture firm with more than two hundred clients with our money tied into everything from sports teams, entertainment, and local mom and pop shops that we help refinance while taking a small percentage as payment.

"What is the problem?" I slid my palms in my pocket.

"That was Carlo updating us from his contacts in Italy. They've found out that Queen was involved in something with Antonio, and now that's she's dead, they think he was assisted by us because the last sightings had you photographed with him and Bruno."

Scratching my neck, I squinched my nose, looking at the guy harassing the young woman sitting at the bus stop. Working on Madison Avenue, people think because it's in part with business people that things are clean. The shit I've seen from here to Italy would blow your mind. *Filho da puta*, which meant son of a bitch in Portuguese, because the guy yanked the woman by her jacket while getting in her face and no one stopped him.

Grabbing my gun out of my desk, I strode out of my office, avoiding the elevator and my assistant and Gael calling my name.

"Joaquin! Joaquin!" Gael yelled, chasing after me. He knew my temper and how I felt about abuse. My mom taught me about men treating women with respect and love. When I became of age and capable to fight, she took control of her life and wanted to do things outside of the mafia family. I said I would never love someone that much to the point of controlling their happiness. Alba Goridano was a strong woman that only wanted to be a teacher. Once she fell in love, her dreams slowly faded, and she became a stay at home mom and wife. The same was now happening with Alessandra, and gshe has to fight to have some freedom.

I stormed down the stairs, pushing the entrance of the door open. At ten in the morning, I could see a small crowd of people standing at the corner waiting for the light to change so they could cross. A typical day on Madison Avenue as folks tended to their lives. I narrowed my eyes at the guy and acknowledged he wasn't as big as I originally thought when I saw him out of my window. Placing my pistol behind my back, I walked toward him.

She tried to push him away. "Please let me go!" she cried.

"Shut up, bitch!" he growled.

Stepping behind him, I tapped his shoulder; he didn't remove his grip on her and turned his head toward me. I punched him with my right fist, and he fell out on the ground. The young woman started screaming, and I strolled back to my office.

"Joaquin, you can't do shit like that and bring the heat to us." Gael texted on his phone as I opened the door to return to the office. A black car pulled up and Gabriella stepped out with Hugo. She nodded at Gael and me.

"He's not dead," I stated.

"That's not the point," he argued.

"Brother, you need to calm down; you looked stressed. Tonight, we do bevande ," I insisted.

Lately, we've worked a great deal of overtime. With the business. I had him not only as my underboss and right hand, he also served as the VP of Alba Industries. His family has ties to the gun sales, and we've brokered deals with even our worst enemies by Velez mafia. Gael was a year older than me at thirty-two and more rational and patient. I'm called Ghost for a reason. I like to get in and out without being noticed.

"You need to call her." Gael followed me back into my office and shoved his hands in his pockets.

"Call who?" I questioned, taking a seat at my desk.

"The American actress and singer. Sofia Chambers. You know the one you're consumed with and keep stalking."

I glared at his comment, and he held his hands up in apology.

"I'm not obsessed, she's a talented actress and I've attended a few of her shows."

"Stop following and ask her out. Maybe she can help you release some tension."

"I will forget you're my brother and expect to never hear you mention her name again and releasing anything in the same breath," I said through gritted teeth.

"We have a meeting tonight to discuss the Queen situation, and then a new shipment is coming in from Italy," he advised, effectively changing the subject.

Chapter 4

Joaquin

The best way for the family to go unnoticed is by staying a productive member of society and working to keep our money clean. Laundering it through some local business is what my father wants me to do, and I've been fighting him on it for the last few months. The situation of killing Queen was resurfacing. We paid off some police officers to keep things out of the paper. A week ago, it popped up on all the social media about a high ranking mafioso being killed in America.

"Where's your assistant? The last girl you fired because you slept with her, and she got attached ," Gael said, looking out into the lobby of my office.

"That's the problem with women, and they get too attached. Monica's constantly calling me like we're a couple. She's known for the last year that she's just sex for me." I shrugged, leaning back in my chair, raising my hands behind my neck.

"Have you talked to Alessandra?"

"No, why?"

"She texted and requested if I'd convinced you to let her visit."

"No."

"Joaquin."

"She's not coming, and she can stop asking and going behind my back to everyone except her brother. She's too young for this city ," I said, standing, picking up my black trench coat off my hanger, and heading out.

"Alessandra is twenty-two. A grown woman that you and your father seem to refuse to let grow up." I stopped walking and turned to him, narrowing my eyes.

"Are you sleeping with my sister?"

"Joaquin, you know me better than that. Alessandra is like a little sister to me, and she wants to be taken seriously and not smothered by her family."

"I'll talk to her, and I propose you stop talking to her ," I suggested as we walked to my limo parked out back. Leonardo was my longtime driver and bodyguard when I needed him to cover my back.

* * *

"Boss, Gabriella said I need to take the trash out ," Leonardo advised, leaving the passenger side door and walking back around to the driver's side. I had hundreds of men that depended on me, and unfortunately, I didn't trust any of them in this business.

"Thank you, Leonardo, take us to Ryde. I need to speak with Carlo and Antonio." He nodded and stuck the key in the ignition and pulled off into traffic. While living here in New York, you become hyper-focused on the next thing you have to do, and the fast pace ends up making you crash and burn if you don't take every little moment and enjoy the people you love or things. Gael was more sensible about things than I was, because the second someone crossed me, I killed them. I learned from the best, and Grandfather Tiago was no pushover. He and my father took me to my first kill at twelve, and I didn't understand at first when we walked into the basement, and a man was naked, lying on the floor. Tiago explained that he stole from the family and needed to be punished. They handed me a gun and I held it up, pointing it at the man as he writhed crawling and crying to be free. I smiled and pretended like I would shoot him, and he peed on himself. I was taught to always put the Fuertes family first. My mother knew what was happening; she cried all night about me being taken to be initiated into the lifestyle. My father promised her I wouldn't have to do anything except observe, but that was a lie. I passed the gun back to my father and asked why I was giving it back. I said it was too loud, and the feel of a knife to someone's throat, while you're staring intently into their eyes as they take their last breath, was what brought me joy. Am I a serial killer? Yes. Do I go around killing random people? No. Am I heartless and cold-blooded? Absolutely, and I wouldn't change a thing about me. That's what gets you through life, not caring, not letting anyone get too close.

"We're here, boss," Leonardo shouted and got out of the car to assist us. I waved him off that we'd be fine as Gael and I got out of the limo.

"Will be awhile here, make sure Miss Chambers gets my delivery and send my regrets about not being there." He agreed with a thumbs up, and I shut the door weaving through the afternoon lunch crowd outside of Antonio's.

"So you don't believe in love or dating, and yet you send flowers to a woman you don't want any relationship with?" Gael started patting his side to make sure his gun was ready. We have a working relationship with Antonio and Carlo, but swe don't even trust our allies.

"I'm not interested; like I said I think she's a great actress."

"I heard you asked her out to dinner the other night."

We saw Carlo sitting in his usual booth, eating and laughing with the bartender. She was tall and lean, with big breasts and a small butt. The uniforms they wore had the girls in black dresses and men in black slacks and dress shirts. The smell of fresh garlic sauce and Italian meatballs drenched in marinara caused my stomach to rumble. Last year I was here, and I'd met Sofia.

"Carlo, we've heard the rumors about your wife, Janice. I suggest you try not to enjoy yourself too much with your staff."

"Alana is a friend, and Janice knows I would never cheat on her ," Carlo replied, gesturing for us to take a seat.

I smirked, taking a seat opposite him in the booth. Alana sauntered over with a glass of wine and menus for Gael and I. Taking it out of her hand, Gael smiled and winked at her as she giggled and walked away.

"No ," Carlo replied.

"No, what?" Gael asked innocently.

"Stay away from her ," Carlo informed him.

Gael chuckled and winked at Carlo.

"So tell me what you've heard from your contacts in Italy ," I demanded, changing the subject.

He sighed, driving a hand down his face, before he leaned forward, clasping his hands together.

"We can look at this a few different ways. She came after us first and tried to take down our family, we had no choice but to retaliate. Antonio is onboard with whatever you need to do, but the Vitale wants blood as a replacement for killing her. Basically, Queen went off on her own with trying to make moves that went above her paygrade."

"Should we prepare for a retaliation?"

Alana strolled back over with the second plate of fetticuni pasta for the table this time. I wasn't in the mood for food. I needed to be clear on what Carlo was telling me to be prepared for before I carried out some calls to Italy and Portugal. My parents split their time between Portugal and Italy, and Alessandra was in Italy last time, I learned.

"Antonio explained that Vitale is making moves with the Russian mob, and we've already had a strained relationship with them over the past few years after they tried to kill him. Ghost, I know you like to kill in silence, but they're coming with big guns compared to your knives. De' Luca's family is finally content and happy; I cannot pull our children and wives back into any drama. Move in silence and move fast."

"Cut off the head, and the rest will fall," I mumbled to myself. Gael scooped some pasta into his plate, take a bite of the famous dish that Antonio's sales,

"What are you thinking?" Gael questioned.

"Traveling to Italy may need to come sooner than expected. Ensuring the family is protected is my only concern and stopping this before it gets out of hand and they strike us in New York. I'll contact my sister tonight and see if our parents stayed in town or not. Mother likely has. I pushed my father to travel more with her, thinking it would slow him down from sticking his nose in Cartel business. The man is sixty-five years old, he'll never stop pulling strings.

"Uncle Joaquin is dangerous when your mother isn't around to keep him preoccupied and focused on her. As his junior, your personality is the same, brother. You're silent and deadly."

"Leave my father out of this and tell me more about the Vitale and Russian partnership," I demanded. Right as Carlo spoke, I picked up a familiar laugh that caught my attention.

I took in the sight of Sofia and the same guy she was here with last time, laughing together. He held her around the waist, running a hand up and down her back. I felt a twinge of jealously. This was the second time we have seen her out with him in public. Maybe that's why she turned me down; because they have a relationship together.

The hostess walked them through the front section of the restaurant and down to the side and sat them at a table near to us with her back to us. Our booth was more toward the corner enclave, but I still had a perfect view of her sweet smile. He caressed her cheek, and I grabbed the fork in my hand, ready to push it into his eye. "Do you know why this is all happening? I mean, the real reason behind the hate between Vitale, Fuentes, and De Luca,." Carlo questioned.

"Didn't it originally start with Joaquin's grandfather, Tiago, killing someone that stole from them a few years ago?" Gael asked.

"Joaquin, you want to explain?" Carlo suggested.

"It wasn't Tiago that killed someone; it was me."

"Wait, you!"

Rehashing my first kill over twenty years ago always stirred up bad memories, not from the killing, but the aftermath. Like Carlo said, this war was long standing because that man that I killed was Queen's Uncle, Federico's twin brother. I had Gabriella investigate deeper and if it came to light that it was me, this war would be personal. Perio Vitale was working with my grandfather and father and tried to cut them out of a deal that would have made them millionaires. Over the years, a truce was called if we paid them a set amount, and when I refused to continue the payment of fifty million to be transferred to them, and then Queen dying, it must have all come full circle and we'll be back to destroying each other.

Loud laughing brought me out of my daze, looking at the cause of the giggles I stood ready to put an end to Sofia's lunch. Gael reached out to stop me. "Joaquin, no. We're in public, and she's well known. Let them be."

He knew my temper and what I'm capable of doing.

"Am I missing something?" Carlo asked.

"I'm just going to say hello. I won't hurt him, yet ," I informed.

Chapter 5

Joaquin

"Anytime you say I won't hurt anyone it's code for call Gabriella to clean up the mess ," Gael joked as I was removing his hand from my jacket. I grinned, and observed Sofia remove her hand from her little boyfriend's grasp. Marching over to the table, I slid my hands in my pocket so I wouldn't get the urge to kill him in two seconds. Clearing my throat, I stated, "Sofia, I see you were able to get out to have lunch. I hope you haven't filled out too much and have left room for me."

"What are you doing here?" Sofia questioned.

"Come talk to me, your boyfriend won't mind. Right?" I requested, furrowing my brows, just waiting for him to say the wrong thing.

"Uhhh, no. That's fine. The food hasn't come out, anyway."

"Grazia." I thanked him in Italian. Having two different languages after having an Italian mother and a father from Portugal came with the privilege of me getting to travel the world and speaking multiple languages was something our mother instilled in us.

Sofia stood up, and I let her walk in front of me toward the back. I nodded to Carlo that I was going toward the office at the end of the restaurant. Either he or Antonio would work out of there when they came here.

Opening the door, it didn't look like anyone had been in here today; it was spotless.

"Have a seat."

"I'd rather stand, and why did you choose to talk with me ?"

"I want to have dinner with you."

She sighed, rolling her eyes, and I grinned at her annoyance. Antonio told me the story of how he pursued his Sabrina, and she always pushed him away.

"I can't."

"That's not good enough."

"I know who you are and your family. I don't consider this is to be a great idea. Sorry, but I'm not trying to get involved with a mob family."

I chuckled at her statement and stepped closer, filling the gap between us. "I'm a legit businessman, Sofia Chambers, actress and singer."

"I don't think that's true, and besides, you don't seem like the one-woman type of guy. Am I missing something, or did you not arrive with your girlfriend from the last time we bumped into each other?"

"She's not my girlfriend."

"At least you'rehonest and admit the woman that showed up with you."

"Monica is of no importance. I'm talking to you, wanting to spend a few minutes of your time getting to know you a little better, is that so sinful ?"

"It is if it ends up with me having a bullet to my head because of your mobster friends."

"You don't think I would protect you? Sofia, I'm a simple man and my family has dealings in that world, I won't lie. But I'm a businessman ," I lied, and she seemed to believe me.

"What type of business do you have?" she quizzed.

Explaining myself to anybody was a death wish any other day. Seeing the determination in her eyes to push me away only caused me to want to press forward.

Chapter 6

Sophia

It felt like a standoff in the room—me on one side and him on the other. Neither one budging to give in, and I couldn't help but admire what he was wearing and how sexy he looked in his black trench coat and dark grey suit. Usually, I saw him at night time when he came to the show, and the one time I rode with him in the limo. His beard and mustache is nicely trimmed and his black hair is slicked back. Tall, at least over six feet, and well-manicured sideburns made him look distinguished. His eyes were the color of black coal and when you stared into them, it made you feel as though he was looking into your soul.

"I run an investment firm called Alba Industries, named after my mother."

"Still can't go out with you, my life is public, and being seen with you in it would bring unwanted attention toward my career."

"Is that your boyfriend out there?"

"dWho? Edward? I'm single, and I plan on keeping it that way for a while. He's my manager. Now, if you'll excuse me, I have to go finish a business meeting ," I explained, leaving out of the office. H grasped my wrist and turned me around, pushing me up against the door.

"What are? You-"

"Mmm... have dinner with me," he moaned, gripping my waist, pressing his entire body against mine.

"I...I..shouldn't," I stuttered, losing all sense as my legs automatically opened wider for him. Feeling his erection against my stomach, it pulled me back into the realization of what I was doing and where I was at. Shoving him again, I announced, "No, this isn't right. I need to leave and forget this ever happened." I opened the office door, heading back up front to Edward and my lunch.

* * *

EDWARD JUMPED up as I approached him and lifted my chin. "What are you doing?" I asked. I'm annoyed with all his touching and reaching for my hand today, making it seem like we're a couple.

"You looked flush, and I was checking to see if he hurt you. Did he?"

"Did he what?"

"Do anything to you?"

"Uhhh..."

"Sofia, bellissima, I'll call you tomorrow for our date," he stated behind me, walking back off to join his friends in the booth that I just noticed was close by. At least now I know how he saw me enter with Edward. I knew bellissma meant beautiful in Italian. I'd learned a few distinct words when I worked in Italy on a movie shoot a few years back.

"Sofia, what happened back there?" Edward pointed to where we came from. I picked up my purse to exit and glanced over my shoulder at Joaquin, and he smugly winked at me as I stared. Edward followed behind and met me at my car, opening the door to my Tesla. He wanted us to drive together, and I said no because I wasn't going back to the studio when I had a studio session tonight.

"Tell me what he wanted to talk to you about. Isn't he the guy from the news that's a gangster or something? Sofia, stay away from him and his friends. Nothing good can come from this little date." Edward closed my car door and leaned through the window. Turning the key in the ignition, I rubbed my temples hoping my headache wouldn't turn into a migraine.

"My dating life isn't your concern, Edward, you manage my career, and that's all, we have no personal relationship, and we've discussed this plenty of times."

"Fine. Get involved with New York's most wanted, at least call me when you finish looking over the contracts for the album." I waved goodbye and was pulling out into traffic when he walked out of the restaurant with another guy. Talking, they headed to his Mercedes limo that sat in front of my car and got inside. He didn't notice me because the only time he's ever seen me was inside of the theater. I rarely drove my car unless I had a meeting to attend.

Shaking off today's events, I left and drove to the music studio Edward rented for me to do a recording session for my next album. I was arriving forty minutes late in uptown. I left my key with the valet and stepped inside as the music blasted through the walls. Edward set up a meeting with a writer and producer that was hot right now in New York and LA, he's a little younger than me, but talented and works with all the major artists. Deras Jones was the person to call when you wanted a hit ballad or a hot one hundred song on charts. Tapping on the door, I heard him shout to come inside, and I slowly opened the door to see he was sitting at the booth, mixing some beats.

"Deras Jones? Hi, I'm Sofia Chambers, nice to meet you." I extended a hand, and he shook it, gesturing for me to sit. I did so, sitting my purse down on the mixer board.

"The Sofia Chambers, wow! I'm honored to be in your presence. You're a stunning woman, sorry if that makes you uncomfortable, I mean. I apologize. Damn."

I chuckled at his nervousness., I was the one that was star-struck when on a movie set with a major actor and to have someone feel the same way about me outside of my usual fanbase was flattering. He's an industry person who understands the way the business works.

"No worries, I'm flattered and huge fan of yours. I loved that song, Sinful Touch, that Kimberly Maxine sang. Outdid yourself there, sir."

"Thank you. Did Edward tell you what was happening today?"

I shook my head, no.

"Okay, no problem. Well, I wrote a few songs already, since I met with him and he gave me your vision of what you wanted to do with this album. All we'll do today is read through them and cut the list down."

"May I look?"

"Sure."

He passed the folder to me and I noticed it was labeled with my name. Impressed, I opened the envelope and turned one, two, and five, ten pages of musical lyrics written.

"There are over fifty songs in here."

"I know."

"When did you meet with Edward?"

"Two weeks ago," he answered, taking out another folder that had nothing written on it, and he grabbed a pen and passed me one.

"Wow! I didn't think you'd have this much done for me in two weeks."

"I eat, breathe, and sleep music. Sofia, between the two of us we can cover up with a few hits."

"I believe you," I replied and picked up my purse, removing my vibrating phone to see a message from an unknown number.

Unknown: 917-4320575# save this number.

Me: Who is this?

Unknown: Your date for tomorrow night

I frowned at the comment. Then a light bulb went off, and I remember my earlier interaction with Joaquin. He must be sitting there with a hard glare on his face waiting for me to answer. He didn't seem like a patient man at all. And from my past relationships, the men I've been with have all been fickle with being consistent. The moment I invest an interest, he'll pull back and ghost.

Unknown: Still there?

Me: Thank you for the offer, but I have to decline our date.

Unknown: Save this number.

Me: Did you not see my earlier response?

Unknown: #$

He sent a winking emoji, ignoring what I said earlier. I didn't have time for stroking a man's ego. My career, family, and friends were more important. Closing out of the chat, I turned my phone on silent and washed it back in my bag.

"Boyfriend problems?" Derian inquired, offering me a bottle of water. I thanked him and screwed the lid off the top, taking a sip. On my off days, I tried to focus on my singing and recording most often. I'd have a small tour planned for the summer. Edward is an egomaniac like every other industry manager, but he's loyal and works hard for my career and believes in me. We needed to get past his little crush so we could continue to work together. The last man I was with was about a year ago. I wasn't practicing celibacy or anything, far from it. I loved sex. The problem was finding a guy that could understand I'm not looking to become what they want me to be. I need

346

someone that supports my goals and sees the real me. The blogs can say I'm a diva or whatever. The biggest reason I've stayed so long in the industry is by being sure of myself and demanding my worth.

"No, why do you say that?"

"The little wrinkle in your nose when that text came through, you looked pissed off about something. I hate to be on the receiving of you being mad ," he joked.

"I'm free as a bird. Not interested in dating life. Besides, I'm not into the same things as I was before in my early twenties. I can't hang in the clubs and be asleep by ten if I'm not on set anymore ," I answered, laughing at my comment.

"Whoever you spend that time with, he's a lucky man."

The entire room went silent as he stared into my eyes, then stood up and went to the recording booth. He gestured for me to follow him, and I stood, grabbing my pen and notepad heading into the booth to record a few verses. Over the next three hours, we recorded about twenty songs repeatedly until I felt right with each concept. We ordered food and laughed, talked about our childhood and beginnings in the industry. Deras was a cool, laid back type of guy. Not too flashy or in your face about all the money he had or flaunting it like a massive star. We worked well together, but I'd do nothing more than friendship with him. One thing you never do is mix business with pleasure. You just end up on the first paper of a gossip magazine saying you've gotten married, had a baby, and divorced within a week. Arriving home, I noticed Jerry still standing at the door, and he tipped his hat to me, then opened the door for me to pass through.

"Late recording, Sofia?"

"Yep. I have to get this album ready for my fans. Been over four years since I've released music, I hope that they'll still remember me." I laughed and walked off to my private elevator then rode up to my penthouse.

Plopping my bag down, I kicked off my shoes and checked the clock on my wall. Just turned one in the morning and I felt beat up from the long day I had. Removing my clothes, bra, and panties, I walked to my bathroom and dropped my clothes in my hamper for my housekeeper to pick up in the morning. I had one more performance then I was done with my Broadway show, and I moved on to filming full time. Juggling both and trying to make music was taking a toll on my body. I stretched in front of the mirror, then picked up my toothbrush and paste. I was thinking of remodeling my place and renting it out and moving into a house. Mom always talked about creating roots and having stability and foundation. Glancing around my bathroom, it was the modern-day style with a clean, off-white color, more eggshell. I had my goddess tub installed with the gold trim at the bottom. A walk-in shower with four different heads installed for the front and back. My personal vanity mirror with my name up above. Stepping in the shower, the heat sprayed against my back, and I let my hair get wet this time to cleanse the day away. I began thinking about Joaquin and the kiss. Even considering a date with a family that has been in the news for years would be the end of my career. I couldn't risk being seen in public with him. Imagine what he could do to me based on that kiss in private. Twenty minutes later, I stepped out of the shower and dried off with my towel that hung against the wall on the shelf rack. Drying my hair wasn't an enormous deal tonight, and I could open it up and throw my bonnet on top to keep it down and not frizzy up. Sliding the covers back, I pulled my phone out of my purse and plugged it into the wall charger and turned it off from being on silent. I noticed a barrage of text messages and emails pop up. Mostly from friends, family, and a few from Edward about filming starting soon. The next one that piqued my interest was the one from the earlier number that I now knew was Joaquin.

Joaquin: You have a good recording session?

He's following me. I thought to myself.

Me: Are you stalking me?

Joaquin: Have a good night, Sofia, and see you tomorrow after your show.

I bit my bottom lip and grinned at his response. I shook off any weird vibes because if he wanted to do anything to me; he had the chance a few weeks back when he drove me home or the setting off in the VIP booths and watching me perform. He had many opportunities to ask me out. As a well-known actress, if I went missing, people would talk and notice, I had to shake him out of my mind and get focused. Pulling the covers up, I laid down and closed my eyes, drifting off into a deep sleep.

Chapter 7

Joaquin

Sleeping alone wasn't easy these days when you had the entire world on your shoulders. Running a business that dealt in the public eye and masked my underworld dealings caused many sleepless nights. I was in my car, heading to a meeting with the Chinese mafia (Lin-Sae). The underboss was meeting me at neutral territory at Antonio's restaurant, a place where most deals were struck. Gael was driving, as I had let Leonardo have the day off to be with his family. Gabriella was driving behind us with Hugo and a few more men. She was the only woman on my team that was a better shooter than me. Even though Gael was my right-hand man, I called on Gabriella to handle the cleanup as the enforcer. We met when she tried to steal from my family's store back in Portugal, and my father wanted to make an example out of her and murder her in the middle of the street. I pleaded with my mother, and she convinced him to give her a job at fifteen, and we've been friends ever since.

"Antonio will be there today ," Gael said out loud, stopping at the light. The cars honked at each other; bikers rushed through the streets, cutting off pedestrians. A typical Friday in New York. The smell of street vendors and barters on every corner yelling to get a sell. I smirked—my kind of town.

"He told me. Gabriella has more weapons stashed inside if we need anything."

"Today shouldn't be anything but getting answers about the Russians and their dealings with Vitale ," Gael told me.

"I appreciate how you stay optimistic, my friend. I go nowhere without my knife beside me."

"Have you spoken to your actress?"

Shaking my head no, I replied, "I texted her last night to say goodnight."

"Did she take you up on your offer to go on a date?" He finally parked, and we stepped out, and he handed the keys off to the valet. Gabriella and Hugo followed behind me, and I waved for my other men to stay in the front and back on post. I hadn't killed anyone since Queen, and I was itching for someone to step out of line.

"Her show is tonight. I plan on taking her out afterward ," I said, walking through the door, nodding a thank you to the doorman. The hostess pointed to the back room that the men were sitting at waiting on us. I observed the place was closed today. Antonio came over and extended his hand.

"Joaquin, really think about what you're doing before she gets hurt."

"Why would she get hurt? I'm not asking her to marry me, one date, simple and possibly a friendship. We're both adults, and my lifestyle will never cross into her world."

"My wife is angry with you ," Antonio stated as he pointed at me.

Gael and I looked at each other then back at him.

"What did I do?"

"I'm not home with her and the kids ," he replied.

"Admit you're happy to be out of the house and not around four kids constantly screaming your name. I hear you're thinking of a fifth baby?" I questioned. He smirked, rubbing his chin in thought.

"If it were up to me, I'd have ten kids by now, but Sabrina's the boss at home, and she's put that on hold. Anyway, let us meet with our guests."

We trailed behind him, and he opened the door to the private room in the back. Three men standing and two sitting at a table looked over at us. I nodded in respect, they did the same, and everyone took a seat at the table.

"Mr. Fuertes, how are you?" Lin-Sae asked. He was the underboss to his brother and brought his enforcer, Jin, and his bodyguards with him. In the past, we've handled business together without any problems, and I expected the same today if they answered my questions truthfully.

"Lin, you know why we requested your presence today?" I asked, unbuttoning my jacket showing my gun on the side. Knives are my favorite killing tool, but in certain situations, when I needed to be quick and deadly with one person, I brought along my backup. The nine Glock that I used for special occasions.

"My counsel brought to my attention you have some Russians upset with you behind the killing of Queen Vitale. Joaquin, I've known you, and your family a long time; this brings me disturbance ," Lin-Sae answered.

He'd been the underboss for the last fifteen years and had aged rather quickly, the grey streaks in his hair and beard, the wrinkles in his forehead and around his eyes. For someone that was only forty, he looked sixty.

"Your counsel has misinformed you. I had nothing to do with Queen's death. Antonio can vouch for me ," I lied, not wanting to play my hand too fast.

"Lin, cut the bullshit. We know the Vitales are working with Russians to start a war and bring it here on our turf. I recommend you convey how wrong that would be for everyone's safety ," Antonio informed, leaning back in his chair and nodding for his security to bring something to the table.

"What is this?" Lin-Sae questioned.

"I took the liberty of getting insurance in case this meeting didn't go in our favor. These are documents that show Sae Mafia selling drugs to the undercover FBI. Now we don't work with the police, but I can't say it wouldn't unanimously get out to some of our friends in the Cartel if they knew you were giving the product to the very people trying to stop their business ," Antonio announced, before he opened the briefcase and pulled out a manila folder then spread pictures of the Sae Cartel talking with the FBI and handing off bags of money and drugs.

Lin-Sae slammed his hand down on the table, cursing us out in Italian.

"Sae Cartel does not work with the police. These are fake ," he spat, pulling his gun out, pointing at Antonio.

Neither of us flinched as our enforcer and bodyguards drew their guns right back at him. Gael stepped up, gesturing for calmness, for everyone to put their guns down. "Gentlemen, we're on the same side. Put your guns away, and let's talk about this."

"Gael, you told me he'd be reasonable," Lin-Sae stated, and I glared at Gael for overstepping and thinking someone could control me.

"Lin, everybody in this room knows I can't be controlled. You want to know if it's true about Queen?"

He nodded his head in answer.

"She's dead, and I enjoyed every minute of torturing her when she came after this family. The Bosses all know families are off limits, and she stepped out of bounds with no authority, and I took care of the matter."

"Then you will pay for killing the daughter of Federico Vitale ," Lin said, waving for his men to put their guns away. He stood and walked out, stopped at the door and looked over his shoulder back at us.

"Family for family ," he said, walking out of the room.

Antonio jumped up, ready to shoot.

"No, we need to think and regroup ," I responded, cracking my knuckles and neck.

"They're working together, any other time he'd be neutral, and you see how quick he was accusing you about the murder ," Antonio murmured.

"Carlo told us things were bringing in Italy behind her death. The only way to secure protection is to keep them out of New York."

"The Russians won't be quick to come here unless they have to, but Vitales will hop on a plane fast. If they get the Sae Cartel to help, then a war is bound to happen ," Gael informed us.

"Should we have someone following them?" Gabriella spoke, checking the chamber on her gun. I nodded for her to take the men and leave.

"The Warehouse is empty tonight, and we can gather everyone up. Bruno is visiting from Italy with Liz; we can call him to help ," Antonio suggested.

"This is my problem; I can't get you involved. It will be fine."

"Joaquin." Gael started to speak, and I held my hand up for him to stop.

"I'm not worried about them. Gael will be in touch once we've spoken with my contacts in Italy. My father is retired, but he knows a few men higher up that can get information on what Vitale is thinking about doing."

"Try not to get blown up or shot at my friend." Antonio stated, patting me on the back, as he walked us out of the private room toward the front entrance.

Gael and I laughed at his response and shook hands with him, leaving out of the restaurant. Heading toward the car, I opened the passenger side door, and he went around to the driver's side. Turning the key in the ignition, we pulled off with two black bulletproof SUV's tailing us for protection.

"Where am I dropping you off?"

"To the theater on Forty-fifth and Broadway."

"I forgot you had a date."

"Two people are having dinner and getting to know each other."

"Is that what you do with Monica?"

"Monica knows her purpose in my life."

"Last I checked, Monica was stomping into your office looking for you, after not calling her a week after you got back into town from Italy. Joaquin, she's the only woman you've kept for the last five years for fun. How do you think she'll take it when you date this Sofia actress?" Gael queried.

"I can handle Monica."

* * *

FORTY MINUTES LATER, Gael arrived at the back of the theater. A crowd of photographers started taking pictures and yelling our names. I checked my watch and noticed she was near time for ending her final show and had Leonardo come with flowers. He was near the entrance, and I walked up to him to grab them with Gael behind me.

"She's inside, boss, and I hear they sold the show out. They reserved your seat as usual."

"Thank you. Gael, leave the keys with me and rides back with Leonardo ," I requested.

"Joaquin, you shouldn't be out here in the open alone. At least call Gabriella or have Hugo follow you tonight ," Gael said, shielding me from the cameras as we headed through the back entrance.

"I'll be fine. Keep me updated on what you find out and set up a flight to Italy ," I reminded him as I walked toward the dressing rooms and finding her door. I knocked and waited for an answer.

"Come in!" I heard and opened the door.

The girl I always saw her with was packing up her things.

"It's you!" Cassidy said.

"Excuse me."

"Her stalker boyfriend ," she insisted on calling me.

I chuckled and placed the flowers down on the side table. Peering around the room, I saw all the posted pictures of her performances in various newspapers and magazines, saying the show was superb and continuously sold out.

"Hello, I'm Joaquin ," I introduced myself, reaching out to shake her hand. She shook it and crossed her arms over her chest, tapping her index finger to her chin.

"I'm Sofia's assistant. My name's Cassidy, and she told me all about you."

"All good things, I hope."

"Mostly about you being the quiet, brooding type of guy. Except you've being dropping flowers off to her every time she's performed on stage. Why is that?" she questioned.

"I'm a fan."

Before she could delve more in-depth into questioning, the door swung open, and Sofia came inside with Edward behind her. Gabriella researched him and found out he's some big-time manager and producer. A little shorter than me with a thin build, probably a jogger. He's been her manager for the past seven years and lives off in Long Island. He had a girlfriend he occasionally sees from time to time and his parents were still alive.

"What are you doing here, Joaquin?" she questioned nervously, and I pointed toward the flowers.

"This room is off-limits to fans, and we need you to leave ," Edward said, opening the door and waving for me to leave.

Chapter 8

Sophia

The entire time my stomach turned into knots watching the two of them glare at each other. I knew Edward was no match for Joaquin, and I'd hoped he'd keep his mouth shut and not cause a fight. Tonight was a huge success, and I sold out my show, and the cast was getting ready to go out to a wrap party and celebrate. When he texted me last night, I didn't think he would really comment on the dinner. I cut the tension before Edward said anything to cause Joaquin to hurt him.

"Uhm. I have plans tonight. I didn't believe you were serious about dinner."

"What are these plans? Maybe I can come along," he replied in his strong accent, staring at me and licking his lips. Clearing my throat, I walked over and grabbed my bag to change.

"I have to change, and then we have a party to attend for my show. Sorry, maybe another time," I suggested.

"I like parties, maybe I can call my friends to meet us there." He pulled his phone out of his pocket, and my eyes rose in fear.

"Wait!" I shouted, trying to think of a way to get out of this without causing an even bigger issue.

"Sofia, you can't be serious," Edward fussed, gripping my arm, turning me toward him.

"Take your hands off of her," Joaquin demanded with a low growl. Edward probably didn't think Joaquin would do anything in front of me, but his posture was giving off mysterious vibes. Yanking out of his hold, I stepped in front of Joaquin to calm him down. His eye twitched, and his fists clenched at his sides.

"Where did you park?" I queried to get him to leave; I cupped his chin, forcing him to look me in the eye and away from Edward. It was like he transformed into a killer gearing up for his prey.

"My car is out back. I can take you to this party," he answered, sliding his hands on the lower half of my back. Cassidy smiled, and I rolled my eyes. She'd always been attracted to the bad boy types, and anytime someone put Edward in his place, she loved to see it.

"Okay, we can go. Edward, I'll see you at the party. Cassidy, are you coming?" I questioned, grabbing my purse and shawl. She was dropping off all my gifts and flowers, as well as clothes from my dressing room later tonight so I only needed my keys and wallet for the evening. I'd already changed into my black bodycon dress, adding light makeup and a few pieces of jewelry.

Everyone followed out behind me, and Joaquin reached for my hand and escorted me over to his car. It differed from the limo I rode in the first time, and he seemed more typical in an SUV compared to being chauffeured around by Leonardo. Opening the door for me, he helped me slide in and winked once the door closed. The second Edward mumbled something under his breath, Joaquin glared, ready to go off. Coming around to the driver's side, he hopped inside before putting his seatbelt on and turning the ignition.

"Here's the address of the party." I pulled out my phone, locating my email with the address. He drove off toward a club called Ryde. I've never gone there before, and he seemed to know exactly where it was located.

"Why do you hate Edward?" I investigated.

"He's not worthy of my time or yours, and he wants to sleep with you."

"And you don't ," I challenged snarkily, crossing my arms over my chest, leaning back into the seat against the window.

I must have hit a nerve as he glared over at me.

"I want to be your friend."

"Tell me something about you, Joaquin?" I questioned, changing the subject to lighten the mood.

"What would you like to know, sweetheart?"

"Let me see your name, age, parents dead or alive. Siblings, the usual."

"Like a date ," he responded and grinned.

"Ughh, you're an ass."

"I'll tell you everything about me if you have dinner with me right now."

He turned down near Ryde, a local night club.

"What about the party?"

Shrugging his shoulders, he stated, "Come with me right now for dinner and drinks, and I'll answer your questions."

"That's it? Dinner and drinks only?"

"Yes ," he replied, stopping in front of Ryde nightclub. Not turning the car off, we peered into each other's eyes, neither one willing to open the door and leave. Internally I was cursing myself out for falling for this man that I had no business being with right now. The photographers started clamoring and noticing us in the car and began filming. I shield my eyes and nodded to go. "Okay, fine I'll have dinner with you, just hurry and go before it becomes a madhouse."

Signaling to get in the left turn lane, Joaquin pulled off right as a mob of fans and photographers captured us together.

Chapter 9

Joaquin

I didn't want to do a regular restaurant, so I had dinner arranged at my apartment. I've lived in the Flatiron district for the past two years. No other woman has come here and usually when I meet with Monica, it's either at a hotel or I stop by her place. Ever since I pushed her away at my office, she hasn't called to see me. Parking in my parking space, I turned off the car and leaned over, cupping her chin and capturing her lips in a tender kiss.

"Where are we?" she muttered through the kiss.

"My place," I replied, and her eyes grew wide in shock.

Opening the door, I got out, walking around to her side and helping her step out. Right as we headed toward my door, Hugo and Gabriella pulled up and got out.

I nodded, and they returned the gesture, following behind us into the building.

"Are they having dinner with us?" she asked.

"No, I have need to talk to them quickly. You can take my key and head up to the penthouse. I'm right behind you."

"Joaquin."

"I promise a minute."

Sofia sighed and took the private key and left toward the elevator. I watched until she got on and the doors closed.

"What did you find you out?" I questioned Gabriella.

"Sir, Lin-Sae drove off to the meatpacking district and then the loading dock where most of the shipment of cars come into the city. He could have been throwing us off, but I doubt it."

I ran a hand down my face.

"Keep an eye on him and let me know what happens. I don't trust him, and if we need to remove him from power, we only have one chance. The bosses are meeting in two months to sign off on expanding into a new bureau. Last-minute interruptions will not be tolerated. Do I make myself clear?"

Hugo and Gabriella nodded in answer and walked off. I didn't need overnight security, the same way my parents have in Italy and Portugal. They have trained snipers on roofs and posted twenty-four hours a day. A few minutes later, I was unlocking the door to my penthouse and stepped inside to find Sofia standing on the balcony. I shut the front door and removed my jacket, unbuttoning my cufflinks. Stepping out to the balcony, I stared at her, leaning against the door. She turned facing me and had a sly smile lifted at the corner of her mouth.

"I'm here at your place, which you didn't tell me we'd be going to for dinner. So you owe me."

"What would you like to know?" I asked, heading towards her.

"We can start with your background. I mean, I can imagine you've done a background check on me and probably know my blood type," she joked.

"I'm Joaquin Fuertes; nice to meet you, Sofia Chambers."

"Nice to meet you, Joaquin."

"You're right, I did do a background check on you, mostly the basic information; your name, age, and your birthplace. More interested in hearing it from your beautiful lips." I said, running a finger across her bottom lip.

"Where are you from?"

"My father is Portuguese, and my mother is Italian. They've been married for over forty years. I was born in Portugal and split my time between both places because my father was the mayor."

"Any sisters or brothers?"

"I have a younger sister, Alessandra, that's twenty-two, and I'm thirty-one."

"Are you one of those big brothers that won't let his sister date?" she teased, walking out of my hold and entering back inside. Sofia plopped down on the couch, crossing her legs, exposing her left thigh.

"I am, and I don't want to talk about her. Tell me something about you," I initiated, walking over to pick up the two champagne glasses on the table. I had dinner already set up with candles, and I wanted to move at her own pace. Passing her a drink, she thanked me.

I sat down next to her extending my arm around her shoulders on the couch.

"You know I'm from the south, and I moved here to pursue my career. At twenty-nine, I'm in the prime of my career with multiple films, tv and Broadway shows on my resume. So if you're looking for a wife or girlfriend, I can't be that, and I won't put my dreams on hold."

"I'm looking for friendship, nothing more."

"We can be friends."

"Close friends?" I placed my glass down. Running a hand alongside her cheek, she smiled, taking another sip.

"What do you want with me, Joaquin, and be honest?"

"Are you hungry?"

"I am, but not for food ," she answered, surprising me.

She initiated the kiss, leaning into at the same time putting her glass on the table. Sofia attempted to straddle my legs, and I restrained her by the wrists.

"Sweetheart, what are you doing?"

"Putting our cards on the table. We've been at this for months with the cat and mouse games, we're both grown adults that are interested in only friendship with benefits and nothing more. You can tell your little girlfriend she can have you back by tomorrow. The last time I've had sex was a year ago, so this right here will break the streak and satisfy my appetite."

"So, you're using me ," I commented.

"We use each other."

"What if one of us wants more down the line?"

"It can't happen."

"But what if it does?"

Sofia sighed, removing her wrists out of my hold. "Joaquin, men are a dime a dozen, even if I wanted more I wouldn't be able to commit because my career is ever-evolving. I travel almost every other month for acting, plus my music career. I can't give any man a long-term answer. I was only fulfilling our sexual desires. I need to get home, I'm filming the next day, and need to sleep. Can you call for a cab?"

She stood up, ready to leave, and I reached for her hand before pulling her into my chest.

"Stay, it's late, and you've been drinking with no food. Tomorrow I'll take you home personally."

"I can't do that."

"Why not? You would be here anyway if we'd slept together."

"Normally a one-night stand doesn't sleep overnight ," she joked.

"I wasn't planning on sleeping at all."

She hiked her eyebrow. "Fine, and the food is probably cold by now. Answer me this. How many women have you brought here before?".

We headed over to the dining room table, and I slid the chair out for her, and she thanked me.

"None. You're the first one ," I answered truthfully.

"A part of me, thinks you're lying."

"Why would I lie? It doesn't gain me anything in your favor, sweetheart. Do I have women friends? Yes, I take them to a hotel. Never my home."

"What if I never agreed to come to dinner? All of this food would have gone to waste."

Shrugging my shoulders, I placed the napkin on my lap and picked up my fork, removing the top lids off her dishes.

"Eventually we would have had dinner. I see our paths would have crossed one day."

"As a mob boss, do you kill people personally?" she asked out of the blue.

"Would that cause you to not want to talk to me If I did?"

"I don't know. A part of me is saying run for the hills, and the other part is curious about those deep black pearl eyes looking back at me, making me feel like you have a lot of secrets to tell."

"Do you know what I see when I look into your eyes?"

"What?'

"Loneliness. Someone that has everything they've ever wanted except someone to share it with. You're afraid to get close because you think they'll leave you unless you have them in some capacity at arm's length. Dangling them on a string to want to be in your presence, but not too close that they'll see the little girl that's still dealing with the loss of her father."

"Mob boss, Business owner, and therapist. Do I have that right?"

"You're only right if what I said is truthful. Does the reason for your celibacy have anything to do with keeping me on a short leash because you'd instead prefer not to get close and get your heart broken?"

The stare off continued for three minutes straight. The tension was thick as her eyes narrowed in slits. I leaned back in my chair, waiting to see her response. Was she a flight or fight type?

Chapter 10

Sophia

"Mmmm...Yes, Joaquin." I gripped his hair in my hands. We never got a chance to eat dinner. He told me I was his meal. The reason why my dress was thrown on the floor with my heels, as I was arching my back, and gripping the back of his head. He was still clothed and running his tongue up my inner thigh. Logic faded a long time ago when I agreed to get in the car and let him take me to the party. There was something so explosive about our interactions. A deep gravitational pull where either one of us needed to be in the other's presence. Am I a fool? Probably. But neither of us could change the turn of events with me in his bed as he skimmed his fingers over my wet sex. I kept my legs apart, giving him room as he used both index fingers to open my slit and swipe his tongue across.

"Ohhh.."

The scent of my arousal drove me mad. I need him to be inside me. He grabbed my hips, keeping me from locking his head between my thighs.

"Shit!" I cried out as his tongue explored my backdoor.

No man had ever taken it there with me licking my asshole. This would be new territory for me.

"I love your taste, sweetheart."

"Ughhh...Please don't stop."

He released my left thigh and claimed my breast, squeezing gently as his tongue speared my canal. I cried out, digging my nails into the covers on the bed.

"Don't worry; I won't ."

Joaquin licked me in long, sure strokes as though it was his dick. In and out, slow, then fast.

My hips pumped up from below, meeting his rhythm. As he held my left breast, I squeezed and tweaked my right one. The sight of him, exploring my body after all of these months, was bringing tears to my eyes. No one had ever focused all of their energy on pleasing me fully without wanting anything in return.

"I'm cummmming!!"

I gasped right as he pressed against my spot that had me leaking on his sheets. I was exhausted and ready for bed.

...

Two hours later, I woke up alone in bed, under the covers in a white t-shirt. Admiring his bedroom, I saw it was neat, nothing was out of place. Almost as if he didn't have any clothes. The room was large, with a tv hanging on the wall. His closet was open with all of his pants and shoes tidy. I got out of bed and walked over to the mantle with the fireplace underneath, and it held pictures of a couple with two kids, a girl, and a boy. I assumed it was him and his family. They looked happy while posing in front of a house. I saw more photos on the wall of him in Italy and Portugal, posing with other men wearing suits. His father was prominent in the middle with a Portuguese flag. Checking his drawers, I saw all of his shirts were folded neatly, socks and pants.

"Find anything interesting ?" he asked, startling me. I turned, and looked at him wearing only pajama pants and no shirt. A large tattoo across his chest spelled out Fuertes, along with an arm tattoo of the Italian flag.

"Sorry, I didn't mean to snoop ," I told him.

He walked further inside, closing the door.

"I have nothing to hide, sweetheart ," he replied, taking a seat on the bed.

"Did I pass out?" I inquired, sitting on the edge of the bed.

Joaquin chuckled, staring at me, running his tongue across his lips. He leaned over and kissed me on the lips.

"You did."

"That's never happened before."

"You're welcome."

"Ugh, you're an asshole."

"And you're beautiful with a fiery tongue that needs to be disciplined properly."

"Let me guess, you'd be the one to dole out the punishment ," I commented.

He smirked.

"Are you hungry?" he questioned.

"No, I need to get dressed and go home, though."

"It's late, Sofia, stay here. I promise I'll take you home in the morning. You shouldn't be out this late."

"What time is it?" I looked around the room for a clock. He lifted his wrist and showed me it was midnight.

"Tell me about your tattoos?" His boldly handsome face smiled warmly down at me as I tucked myself under the covers. Joaquin pointed toward the tattoo on his arm.

"I take pride in where I come from. My heritage is important to me, both Italy and Portugal. This tattoo on my chest is my family crest. All the men in our family have them."

"Tell me about the woman that I saw you with the first time in Antonio's. She seems overly jealous of anyone being in your presence that's the opposite sex."

"Monica-"

"Monica, nice name. She's cute."

Joaquin chuckled at my response.

"Monica is a friend; I've known her for the past five years."

"Wow! I need to go."

"What does that mean? Sofia, stop, talk to me." I attempted to get out of the bed and leave. He'd been dating her off and on for five years and never proposed.

"She's your girlfriend, Joaquin. I'm not a cheater and refuse to be friends with anyone that would allow that to happen!" I spat.

"Shushh..calm down, sweetheart. Monica understands that I am not interested in her for a relationship. We have an arrangement that is beneficial to us both. I don't cheat, and I would never put you in a position of being a cheater."

"I don't know. I think we took this too far."

"Get some sleep, I'll be in the guest room, and I set the alarm to wake you at seven. I'll take you home after we have breakfast in the morning, and I don't want to hear any more about Monica. Get her out of your head.

Besides, I've had a taste of your pussy, and I refuse to give it up to the next man ," he informed me, gripping my chin before he leaned over to peck my lips and forehead. He walked out of the bedroom and left me alone with my thoughts of the past few hours. Have I invited more trouble in my world? The pleasure with the pain isn't something I'm built for, I thought to myself, drifting off to sleep.

Chapter 11

Sophia

Aweek later, I still hadn't spoken with Joaquin since that night at his place after he dropped me off at home. I blocked his number and worked overtime with getting my tracks laid down with Deras and started filming my latest movie in Atlanta temporarily. Being out in Atlanta was a nice distraction without having anything or anyone reminding me that I entertained a cartel kingpin. I can hear my parents now yelling and cursing at me that I'm crazy for even giving someone like that the time of day. Right now, I was running lines with my co-star in my hotel room. Edward was on the phone, taking phone calls and managing my schedule with Cassidy.

"Dante, what do you think about this line?" I asked, highlighting in my script, sitting next to him on the couch. We had today off and decided to run through our lines and rehearse. Cassidy was managing my schedule and social media and returning emails. We're here for a month and then back to New York to continue filming. Something more dramatic with a romantic undertone. Atlanta is the place to be for film production and networking, almost rivaling Los Angeles.

"Tomorrow we'll need to have the director rehearse with us a few times, that's a big scene ," he responded. I nodded in agreement.

"Sounds good. Cassidy, how is everything with my schedule? Deras texted me earlier about coming to his showcase when I get back into town ," I investigated, replying to his text.

"Right now, you're free; you only have two off days when you get back and then two photoshoots, a magazine interview and back to filming and recording ," Cassidy informed me.

"Get an appointment for a spa day in the hotel. I need to get these kinks removed in my back ," I requested.

"Okay, uhmm, Sofia, have you seen the latest gossip?" Cassidy probed, passing me the laptop computer with my name and photo on the front page with a shot of Joaquin holding his hands up to block the shot. It was taken when we were in the car heading to dinner.

"OMG!" I jumped up off the couch, pacing back and forth.

"Let me call you back ," Edward said, walking toward me and looking over my shoulder at the article.

"Sofia, WTF! I told you to leave that thug alone ," Edward fussed.

"I really don't need an 'I told you so' from you. How about be my manager and help fix the issue?"

"Fix it, your name's plastered on every news gossip sight with you named as the next Donna of Fuertes Cartel. Do you understand how this can set your career back, shit my career?" Edward murmured.

Dante comforted me with a hug when all of a sudden loud banging came from the front door.

"Did you order room service?" I asked, walking off to answer.

Edward and Cassidy shook their heads no. Opening the door, the last person I ever expected to see was standing in the middle of two big burly men and one woman. All were wearing black suits and ties. I suspected the handguns, but the trench coats easily probably covered them from being detected.

"Who's at the door?" Edward yelled.

I hurriedly slammed the door behind me.

"What are you doing here?" I whispered harshly.

His bodyguards moved aside, and he stepped forward, closing the space between us; the hard glare and bushy eyebrows stared into my eyes, willing me to say the wrong thing.

"Can I come inside?" he asked.

"No."

"Why is that? Are you entertaining someone? Having a party? I like parties, invite my men and me inside ," Joaquin queried.

"I'm busy."

"I'll ask you again, invite me inside, or I'll force my way in, and you won't like my way, sweetheart ," Joaquin insisted, winking at his bodyguard; he called Gabriella. A smile crept on her face, and she pulled a gun from behind her back.

"Put that away, are you insane, we're in a hotel room. You can't go forcing your way into people's private rooms. I'm busy like I said."

He gripped my waist, pulled me in close, bent down and whispered in my ear, "I missed you, sweetheart." He gently moved me behind him and opened my room door. I tried to stop him, and his bodyguards grasped my arm, stopping me. He glared at his men, motioning to let me go.

"I want to meet your guests. I remember you, Cassidy, correct? The assistant," Joaquin stated. He moved into the room, taking my hand, introducing himself to Cassidy. As a sick love puppy, she was giddy when he kissed her hand.

"Who is he?" Joaquin pointed at Dante, and I attempted to respond, but Dante cut me off.

"Hi, I'm Dante, her co-star."

"Hello, Dante, her former co-star."

My mouth dropped open in shock.

"You can't do that ," I snapped, yanking my hand out of his hold.

"I can, and I did. Grab your things, we're leaving."

"Joaquin. I don't know what goes on in your world, but this control and trying to force my client to become your alibi won't stand. Sofia is not your mistress, girlfriend, or any of that bullshit that happens in your country," Edward shouted.

Joaquin peered from Dante to Edward, sliding his hands in his pockets.

"Edward, let me talk to him," I said.

"Sofia, grab your things, please. I am only going to ask you this once. We have a lot to talk about."

"Sofia, I'll see you tomorrow, hopefully on set." Dante tried to hug me, and Joaquin's men moved in closer. I can't believe he came all the way here acting an ass.

"Cassidy, can you and Edward go downstairs and reserve a table for dinner? I need to talk with Mr. Fuertes for a moment."

"Sure," Cassidy said, meekly.

Edward refused to budge until our eyes connected and I silently asked to leave. Joaquin wouldn't hurt me. I was more worried about him getting hurt.

Chapter 12

Joaquin

Her people stepped out, and I motioned for my men to leave us alone. She looked beautiful, dressed down like this in a large t-shirt and leggings, displaying her curves. Sofia walked up to me after the door closed and she slapped me across the face. I smirked, rubbing the sting away. When I reached out to caress her cheek, she smacked my hand away.

"Sweetheart."

"I'm not your sweetheart, and who do you think you are coming up here demanding I leave with you."

"Why did you run?" I shouted angrily.

"What?"

"The second I dropped you off, you disappeared. Huh! What did I do?"

"I don't have time to babysit your feelings. My career could be over because of you,"

she snapped, picking up the open laptop and shoving it into my face.

"I don't read gossip or entertain it, sweetheart. They'll have something new to talk about by tomorrow. We need to talk." Putting the computer back down on the couch, I followed her to the window, standing behind her as she looked out into the park.

"Talk then," she stated.

I ran a hand down my face, stepping back away from her; I removed my coat, suit jacket, and gun. I eased my hand across her shoulder and toward her neck, applying a little pressure.

"I'm done playing these games, sweetheart." I moved my left hand under her shirt, gripping her left breast, I brushed a gentle kiss across her lips once, twice, smoothing her lips with demand. No woman had ever caused an ache or need that I had to be in their presence until I met Sofia Chambers.

"Mmmm...Joaquin ," she moaned.

"No talking," I muttered in between kisses, lifting her up by her ass and carrying her to the bedroom.

I turned the knob and plopped her on the bed, removing my shirt and pants, she tossed her shirt on the floor and eased out of the leggings. Capturing her mouth once more, I was shocked at her eagerness. Whirling her around, I nudged her to bend over and spread her legs. Grabbing my wallet out of my pocket, I removed three condoms, tossing them on the bed. I reached around, and her nipples firmed instantly under my touch.

"Ahhh!"

"Bellissima." My favorite word to call her beautiful in Italian. She writhed, tossing her head back. I grasped her chin, crushing her lips to mine, challenging her to not want what was building between us.

Smacking her left, then right butt cheek, I bent down to kiss the sting away. Licking my thumb, I spread her ass cheeks and ran a finger over her sweet sex, to her asshole.

"Ughhh...shit!"

I tasted her with a slow lick; I inserted a finger and curled over her hard bud.

"Baby!"

"Louder!" I shouted, smacking her ass again. She quivered in anticipation. The moist flesh between her thighs glistened.

"Mine."

Deeping my tongue lashing, I slid a hand into my pants, squeezing my dick, praying I didn't go too fast. She was so soft and smelled the same as the first time we met.

"Oh, God."

Removing my pants, they fell to the floor, and I sheathed myself, gliding into her pussy. There's no way in hell I'll ever let her go now.

"Fuck!" I yelled, rocking in and out slowly.

She almost fell over, screaming, "Ahhh!"

Kissing up her back, we soon found a matching rhythm.

"Sofia...Mmmm." I leaned into the mattress, covering her back, grabbing both breasts as I picked up the pace. Cursing and grunting in her ear, whispering how beautiful she was the first time I met her and saw her show. Thanking her for giving herself to me. Flipping her over with me still inside, one hand slid down her taut stomach to the swell of her hips. I bent down, showering kisses around her lips before thrusting my tongue inside for her sweet taste. Sofia cupped my face briefly before pulling me into a tight embrace. We continued to explore each other for the next two hours using up all the condoms.

Chapter 13

Joaquin

A month later.

S ofia was in the car with me as we drove over to the hotel to visit my parents. They were in town with my sister for a few days. Gael was meeting me there with Gabriella and Hugo as extra protection for them. They didn't want to stay with me at my place, so we compromised with the hotel that was only a few minutes away. Sofia was nervous and changed her clothes at least three times because she was worried about what they would think of her outfits. I didn't care what she wore. The only opinion that mattered was mine.

"Are you sure your parents are okay with me coming? I hate to be the surprise girlfriend, and she's black."

I chuckled at her comment. We never really talked about how people would perceive our relationship beyond our occupations. A few times, she had to beg me not to put a bullet in a photographer's head for following us.

"You'll be fine, sweetheart."

"Has any woman of yours ever met them?" she questioned. I groaned because I know the second I tell her that Monica met them she's going to explode. Even though it was by accident. Once, I talked to them on Face-Time, and she interrupted me in my office, and they asked who she was. It ended quickly before it even began.

"Monica met them once."

"Of course, she did."

"Sofia ," I grunted, squeezing her hand.

She tried to move closer to the window and out of my hold.

"I like this jealousy."

"Don't flatter yourself."

"It was by accident, she burst into my office, and they asked who she was. Please, sweetheart, not today."

"The big bad mob boss can't take the heat from his girlfriend."

"Don't flatter yourself ," I repeated her statement.

"Tell me why you came for me in Atlanta a month ago. What caused you to take a leap from just wanting to be friends to us being a couple."

Flashback

One month ago.

I pounded my fist into his face over and over. He groaned, trying to cover his face. He set up the guns being stolen and then tried to get us killed. Lin-Sae was a snake, and I was ready to bury him.

"Joaquin, that's enough!" Gael yelled, trying to push me off of him. I kicked him in the stomach.

"Pussy ," I said, spitting on him. Antonio and Carlo stood to the side with their guns drawn.

"Where are the guns, Lin?" Antonio inquired, bending down to hear him speak. Blood was all over his face and clothes. We picked him up in the early morning on his way to the city. We managed to box him in since he only took two bodyguards with him when traveling.

"Fuck you ," Lin-Sae grunted, holding his stomach.

Walking over to the table, I grabbed my jacket to take my knife out.

"Joaquin, hold up, you can't kill him. He's a cartel leader ," Gael pleaded.

Grinning, I bent down to the ground, taking the knife and placing it in the middle of his forehead.

"See you in hell," I whispered in his ear, stabbing him in the heart.

"Fuck!" Gael shouted. As my best friend, he knew I couldn't be controlled, and with Sofia running off and not taking my calls after the other night in my apartment, I haven't been able to focus. Everything pissed me off.

"A war will start because of this, and we're still dealing with Vitale and the Russians behind Queen ," Antonio stated.

"He's right, Joaquin; I understand your hurt is behind your girlfriend leaving ," Carlo said, pulling his phone out of his pocket and calling for the cleanup crew.

"That has nothing to do with me killing him."

"It has everything to do with you not keeping your cool and jumping off and killing people without really think it over. I had you kill Queen because you're methodic, clean and think things through. I've been where you are. Carlo can tell you about when Sabrina and I butted heads early on. Then she was kidnapped, and all I wanted to do wais kill anything that ever harmed her ," Antonio reminded us of his relationship conflicts.

"Queen Vitale was a gift to you. This one was fun. Call me when you locate the guns," I replied, grabbing my coat and walking out with my men following behind.

Present.

"I needed you ," I said.

Chapter 14

Sophia

Joaquin stopped in front of the Hilton Hotel, stepping out and passing the keys to the valet. He came around to open my door and help me out. I wore wide black pants and a wrap top that wore like a suit jacket. All of his men came and opened the door for us to walk through. I nodded thank you. I thought we were headed to their rooms, but he pulled me into the restaurant and pointed at the older couple and the young woman sitting at a table with six tall men standing around them.

"Father, Mother, good to see you. Alessandra, don't you look beautiful."

Joaquin's sister and mother jumped up in excitement and hugged him around the neck; he switched between them both for a hug. I glanced over to his father, and he stared at me with a harsh glare. Clearing my throat, I extended my hand to introduce myself.

"Hello, I'm Sofia; nice to meet you, Alessandra, Mr. and Mrs. Fuertes." His mother gave me a hug, and his father sat without acknowledging me.

"Joaquin, get up, and hug your son," Alba said. I smiled, standing behind as he continued talking with his sister and mother.

"Son, nice to see you again; we need to talk ," Joaquin, Sr., demanded.

"We will later," Joaquin said.

"You're so cute, Sofia, I'm a huge fan of yours. I can't wait for the second album ," Alessandra said excitedly, hugging me.

"Thanks."

Joaquin stepped off with his father, and I hung back talking with his mom and sister.

"How did you meet my son, Sofia?" Alba questioned.

"He stalked me ," I joked

They both laughed and asked if I wanted anything to eat.

"I'm fine, thank you, but we actually bumped into each other a few months back, and then he appeared one day with flowers at my show, and we've been in each other's lives since."

"Joaquin is like his father. They're sincere and forward with what they want. I get the hesitation, honey. I was the same way when his father asked me out over forty years ago when he saw me standing in a window in a boutique trying on perfumes ," Alba recalled.

"Yeah, I've learned that about him."

"Sofia, tell my brother I would be okay living here. He thinks I'm too young to move here. I could live with him and go to school ," Alessandra begged, grasping my hand. She looked like the girl version of Joaquin, except with long black hair. She had a small dainty nose, plush pink lips with a thin build, like a model.

"How old are you?"

"Twenty-two."

"He can't tell you what to do; you're an adult."

"Not in this family ," Alessandra moaned in frustration.

"Alessandra, stop pouting. We will discuss this later ," Alba commanded.

Joaquin and his father came back over and sat down. He kissed my cheek and held my hand under the table.

Chapter 15

Joaquin

I could tell my father was not happy with my choice in Sofia. Dating someone that's extremely high profile brought a lot of unwanted attention the family didn't need. She thought it was because of her race. I knew better. My father hated drawing attention, and if we're involved, the public will want to know more about me and dig into my background and family. Sofia was quiet, partially because I kept her up all night having sex.

"Miss Chambers, my son tells me you're an actress and a singer ," my dad questioned.

The waitress came over to pour Sofia and me a glass of water. I wasn't hungry, so I passed her a menu.

"Yes, sir, I'm currently filming a movie and recording my second album ," Sofia answered.

"How long do you plan on doing this?" he asked.

"Uhm.. Well, I've been in the business for over ten years, so hopefully for another ten or fifteen."

"Do you ever want to get married and have kids?"

"Drop it ," I insisted. He was getting too personal and making her uncomfortable.

"She's your girlfriend, correct?"

"She is."

"Then she can answer my questions."

"Joaquin is happy, that's all that matters. Please, honey, let's change the subject ," my mother says, kissing his cheek.

He does but only because my mother requested he do so, but later on, he'll bring it up to me in private.

"Joaquin, tell Papa to let me move here. I want to go to fashion school, and I can stay on campus ," Alessandra pleaded.

"You're too young," I said.

"She's twenty-two. I moved out when I was seventeen to pursue my dreams. You can't smother her forever," Sofia stated calmly toward me. My father squinted his eyes, offended that anyone would chime into his relationship with his daughter. Our family is very traditional, even to the point of arranged marriages. Mother and I convinced him to not push that on her because Alessandra can be headstrong at times. Her love of fashion and photography is what she wants to study in America.

"This isn't the time right now, Alessandra. I'm busy and can't watch you while I'm working."

"That's not fair! I'm twenty-two. Sofia can help me find a place to stay, right?" Alessandra whined.

"Silence!" Father shouted. The entire room went quiet, other guests gasped in shock. Gael walked up to the table and kissed my mother and Alessandra on the cheek. He then gave my father a handshake before taking a seat next to Alessandra. He tucked a piece of her behind her ear, and she blushed like a high school girl with her boyfriend. My gaze cut between them; if he's interested in my little sister, it's something he will need to forget about before it ever becomes a thought.

"Gael, you're looking well, my dear," Alba said.

"Yes, ma'am, eating healthy and following behind your bigheaded son." Gael whipped his head around to face me.

SOFIA SHIFTED BACK in her seat; I lifted her hand to lay a kiss. Hugo and Gabriella stood around us along with my father's men.

"You seem tired, are you ready to go?"

"I don't want to put you out with your family. I can take a cab and meet you back at your place later. I need to meet with Cassidy and Edward about Deras's upcoming performance. "

"I can take you." I started to stand up, and she tugged at my coat jacket to sit back down.

"Stay here with them; your mother hasn't seen you in two years. I promise I'll call when I get done." Sofia assured kissing me on the cheek.

"Take Gabriella or Hugo with you. I'd feel better when I'm not around; you have protection."

Sofia smoothed down her shirt. "What do I need protection for? There something I need to know about?"

"Take someone with you for my peace of mind."

"Okay," Sofia commented, pointing to Hugo.

Hugo nodded and walked behind Sofia as she left out of the restaurant.

"Alba, take Alessandra up to the bar and look at the desserts. I want something sweet, and would prefer you personally pick it out for me." Father patted her hand, and she stood up, grabbing her purse. Alessandra did the same. He watched as they looked over the wall case of the cakes and pies.

"Joaquin, I'm getting phone calls that Lin-Sae is no longer with us. Tell me how this happened?" Father asked.

"He stole from us, and I sent a message."

"The type of message that has me getting phone calls all the way in Portugal from the President that talks about how you've created a new dynamic that will have the family in the newspaper for the wrong reasons. They say it's a drug deal with Fuertes Cartel ," Father muttered angrily, shoving the empty plate away.

The waiter appeared with their food and we both got quiet.

"The calamari and stir-fried rice ," the server announced.

"Thank you ," he said.

"We have two strawberry salads with oil and vinegar ," the server informed, placing the dishes on the tables and walking away.

"Antonio spoke with Bruno this morning since he travels back and forth between Italy and New York. He stated a council wants you to come out there and speak with them about the killing ," Gael explained. Alessandra walked back over and sat down.

"What are we talking about" Alessandra questioned.

"Nothing of importance ," I said. Easing my phone out of my pocket, I sent a text message to Sofia.

Me: Dinner tonight, my place?

Sofia: Not tonight, I'm hanging with some friends.

Me: Where?

Sofia: Dera's performance.

Me: Keep me updated.

Lunch continued without a hitch, and my sister talked about her favorite actors and seeing Sofia's movies. Mother gushed about her garden and getting Father to eat healthier. The day was going to be long because I ended up going shopping and talking for the rest of the day.

Chapter 16

Sophia

Two months later.

E dward and I were inside of my dressing room as I prepped for my
scenes with Dante, I was starting to regret signing on to this project,
knowing once Joaquin finds out we have a love scene he's going to go ballis-
tic. He's on occasion flirted after we hung out in Atlanta, but I prayed he
kept his thoughts to himself, unlike Edward professing his undying love. He
was always telling me to leave Joaquin because I was too good for him, and
he's a better man for me. I tried establishing a professional relationship. Now
he's looking to destroy that.

"Sofia, this guy is dangerous. You know how I feel about you."

Tonya's eyes rose up in surprise. I was wearing a robe, with a lingerie set
for the next scene; today was only this scene that was the big compilation of
our characters coming together. The soundstage on the studio lot was
booming with film and tv shoots all around. My nerves were still a little off-
balanced after meeting his father in the restaurant. Over the past month, the
arguments between us came back to my insecurity of him trying to make it
seem as though I was crazy for feeling the way I did. Seeing up close and
personal the lifestyle is something I didn't need to see firsthand.

"Edward, now is not the time. I have a scene in a few minutes ," I
remarked, pushing him off.

"Funny, you've brushed me off all these years, and yet the second this
mafia motherfucker threw the door, you dropped to your knees!" Edward
snapped, and before I could react, the door swung open, and Joaquin walked
inside with his men behind him.

"What the fuck did you say to her?" Joaquin questioned, popping his
knuckles.

I started to speak, and he held his hand up, cutting me off.

"No, let him speak ," Joaquin said, standing in front of Edward as he cleared his throat before speaking.

"You aren't allowed on the studio lot without permission ," Edward told him, trying to throw his weight around.

Joaquin smirked, winking at me before punching Edward in the face with a right hook.

"Joaquin!" I yelled, bending down to help Edward up.

"Leave him ," Joaquin demanded.

"He's hurt, and I could have handled him."

Joaquin scowled at me, adjusting his tie.

"As your boyfriend, I take it upon myself to handle things for you. It's my job, sweetheart. What are you filming today?" Joaquin tugged on my robe.

I was shifting on my left foot, placing my hand on my hips.

"I'm working, and you need to apologize to Edward and leave. I'll contact you later."

"Baby, I'll do a lot of things for you; apologizing to him is not one of them." His bodyguards laughed, and I broke eye contact with him to glare at them.

"Get out and take them with you now."

"The director stated we could watch you perform. I haven't seen you on stage since your Broadway show. I'm your biggest fan, sweetheart." He threaded a hand through my hair. I smacked it away.

"Joaquin, you can't see the filming today. It's a closed set, and I don't care what the director said. Mhmmm...wait." He gripped my hips, pulling me in close, covering my mouth and shoving his tongue inside.

SOMEONE CLEARED THEIR THROAT.

"Joaquin, she's right. We should go and meet with your contractor for your house ," Gabriella said, winking at me to distract him. I mouthed thank you, and he pulled away.

"You're buying a house?"

"I am, will you decorate it for me?"

"Depends."

"What does it depend on, Sofia?"

"Alessandra and I have kept in touch, and she wants to move here. Thinking if you talk with your father, then he would agree with letting her come here. Maybe I could decorate and do other things." I fluttered my eyes, trying to seduce him.

Joaquin grinned and gestured for his team to leave out and take Edward with them.

The trailer door closed, and he pushed me up against the wall, both his hands on the wall closing me in, loosening my robe running a hand down my chest. His chest rose and fell.

"Would this make you happy, having my sister here?"

"It would make her happy."

"What would make you happy?"

"You leaving and letting me work."

He chuckled at my statement. I drew in a shallow breath as he lightly bit my shoulder, easing his hand down my thigh, lifting my leg up, wrapping it around his thigh.

"Joaquin we can't, I have to be on set, baby."

"Give me five minutes."

I chortled; he damn well he wouldn't be only five minutes.

"Five minutes will turn into an hour with you."

"Then give me what I want, and I'll grant my sister her wish," he said, unbuckling his pants, pulling his dick out and rubbing it against my slit— sliding inside.

"Yesss...Fuck."

Grabbing my other leg, he picked me up, holding me against the wall. I wrapped my arms around his neck as he was pounding inside of me.

"Ughh,..shit."

"Right there, Joaquin!"

"You like this, sweetheart. Let me hear from you."

Someone started banging on the door, calling me to set. Sweat clung to my brow, and I tossed my head back as he walked us over to the couch. He laid on his back, and I lifted up, riding the tip of the dick.

"Ughhh...You feel so good, Sofia," he groaned, squeezing my ass.

"Is this all yours, baby?" I teased, reaching behind my back inside his pants, massaging his balls. I needed him to come fast so I could clean up and get back to work.

"Aghhhh!!!" He gripped my knees, pumping from below, as we both came at the same time. I fell on his chest out of breath, and he dozed off to sleep. I smirked slowly, crawling off of him and rushing to the bathroom to clean up. A few minutes later, he was still sleeping on the couch, and I left him there to go start filming. Stepping out of the trailer, his men stood at attention.

"He's taking a nap. You may want to wake him up in an hour or two," I said.

Chapter 17

Joaquin

T he next day we finally found out that the Russians had help from Lin-Sae to steal our guns. I got word from the council about having a sit-down meeting to go over the details of how we could rectify the situation for all parties. I was in a war with myself to end things or continue down a destructive path. Antonio talked about slowing down when he got married and finding a woman that understood him. Sofia was that person for me, and if we got to that level and decided to get married, I know she'd want me to leave this lifestyle. Tightening my bulletproof vest, I was in the car with Gael, Hugo, and Gabriella as three more cars followed behind. A source said the Nigerian gang in the Bronx was meeting with some Russians for some crates of guns.

"Are you sure about this, Joaquin? The money can be replaced ," Gael exclaimed.

"It's not about the money anymore, it's about principle and the disrespect of stealing from this family."

"I know better than anyone about disrespect toward the family, but you've killed two high profile leaders of rival families without any consequences. Now going into a possible shootout would put a bigger target on our back," Gael explained, his face twitching in irritation.

I ran a hand down my face; a sigh escaped my lips.

"I did what needed to be done. Am I not Ghost? People call me because they are not willing to make hard decisions, and I am."

"Si, I understand, brother, but you're putting a bigger target on the wrong people's back."

"What are you talking about?" I demanded to know as the car pulled up to an abandoned building. Our contact said the men would be inside and to go through the back.

"I received photos of Sofia, and this came from Italy, and your father doesn't like you together."

"My father doesn't tell me who I can date."

"Is she going to be your Donna?"

"Focus on today," I answered, getting out of the car, checking to make sure my guns were locked and loaded. We had on fake FBI vests and hats to get in and out without any questions.

I motioned for Gabriella to follow me as Gael took Hugo to the left side, and we went on the right. The other men stayed in front in case someone tried to get out or come in and see what was going on.

The sun was shining in the afternoon with a small window of time to get this over with before kids were let out of school and decided to play outside. I met Gael's eyes and pointed on the count of three we go in quietly. He nodded in agreement with a dark shadow marred over his face.

Tilting my head over to look through the back screen door, it was open with no one in the kitchen. I placed my hand to my lips for everyone to be quiet as we walked inside so as not to be detected. Holding my gun and knife in my hand, I edged in further, not seeing any people around. Staring at the stairs, I heard talking, and we followed the voices, stopping at the door' it was slightly ajar.

The Russians had three men, and the Nigerians had two; the crates were open as they inspected them. I tapped Gael on the shoulder without talking, showing five fingers, and he acknowledged, pulling out a second gun. Taking the lead, I closed my eyes, thinking of Sofia, and smiled. Opening them back up, I wore a devious smirk because I was out for blood.

Pop! Pop! Pop!

Right as I held my gun up to shoot, we heard shots outside, and it alerted the men, so I started blasting in the room, and one got a chance off hitting me in the arm. Running inside, I punched the one guy that held the automatic rifle, and he stumbled. Slicing his throat and shooting as many people as I could. I never noticed the adjoining door that connected to the bathroom, I miscalculated, and someone peering out pointed a gun in my direction. One bullet hit me in the leg and I shot back, hitting him between the eyes.

"Aghhh!!"

"Joaquin, hold on!" Gael shouted.

Gabriella, she would cover us so she could pick me up and take me outside. As the firing stopped, all of the Nigerians and Russians were dead. Gael picked me up, helping me walk as Hugo started packing up the guns. Gabriella was still in front of us, keeping an eye as we ran to our cars. The bodies laid out on the ground were more Nigerians.

"Russian, Vitale, Chinese, and now Nigerian mafia are going to be looking for your head," Gael informed me.

"I'll be ready."

Chapter 18

Joaquin

Antonio walked inside of the basement of his restaurant. He didn't look happy to see me. I removed the vest, as the in-house doctor tore my shirt open to look at the bullet wound.

"Joaquin, you need to be in a hospital, I can only patch you up ," the doctor said

"What happened?" Antonio asked, sitting on the edge of the conference table.

Carlo sat his gun on top of the table, keeping the safety on. I furrowed my brow.

"I had a disagreement with some people ," I played off.

"How many people?" Carlo questioned.

"Russians, Nigerians," I answered.

"You realize that you will end up having a bigger issue now. Did you get things cleaned up before anyone saw you out there?" Antonio pressed.

Waving them off, I tried to push through the pain. It wasn't life-threatening, but it hurt, and I'd probably be sore for a while.

"You have anything for the pain?" I questioned.

"Yes, and you need to take a few days off ," the doctor suggested.

I was shaking my head, no.

"I have too much work to get done, and I'm flying to Italy soon, and my sister is moving here," I said.

Gael's jaw dropped on my comment. "When did your father agree to this."

"A few weeks ago. She's going to be staying with me, and that was the biggest condition to him agreeing to let her come out here."

"Can we get back to the problem that could potentially destroy all of our lives. If the Russians team up with Chinese, Vitales, and Nigerians, we won't be able to fight them," Carlo fussed.

"Pay the Nigerians off, and the Chinese won't do anything if we have something bigger that they want. At the end of the day, killing Joaquin off is more of a treat for the Russians and Vitale's people," Antonio stated.

"What do they want more than my head on a platter for killing their leader?"

"Territory which you will happily give up to end this feud with them," Antonio commanded, starring into my eyes.

"They can have New Jersey."

"Jersey is your lowest profitable location; they'll want more than that ," Carlo insisted.

"What if we give them Jersey, Brooklyn, and Atlanta?" I questioned.

"What! You can't give them all of Atlanta. That's your second-biggest market Joaquin," Gael shouted.

"You're right I can't keep bringing on more problems, and I need to smooth a few relationships over before we get to Italy. Let them have Atlanta and we'll regroup," I told them.

His emotions flitted across his face. As my best friend, he was the only one that could tell me when I was wrong and cause me to question my motives. Ever since I came to America and killed Queen, things have gone downward except for Sofia.

"Sofia," I mumbled to myself.

"Where is Sofia?" I asked Hugo. As her bodyguard, unless he was with me on a mission, I assigned a man on her to keep her safe.

"At a photoshoot ," Hugo answered.

"Call her."

He took his phone out of his pocket and dialed her number. Her voicemail picked up. He then tried her assistant, and no one answered. Snatching my phone out of my pocket, I dialed her number and still no answer. The doctor finished cleaning up the wound, and I leaned up off the table, standing upright. I slid another shirt on then my jacket, preparing to go find her.

Chapter 19

Sophia

I was on a photoshoot with Edward when Cassidy came inside, followed by a huge gift box.

The shoot was supposed to be about four hours, and it looked as if we'd already hit over eight hours and it was not looking like it was going to end any time soon. Cassidy placed the gift box down on the table. She picked up the card and passed it to me as I stood getting my makeup retouched, along with my hair. This was a shoot for Destiny magazine spread as the hottest star this year. I had deals across my desk for multiple movies, tv guest appearances, and even starting my own makeup line if I wanted to venture in that direction. My first love was acting and singing; having a big responsibility on my plate I know would be a challenge, starting a new business and partnership with a company would send me into traveling a lot more, testing and not just adding my name onto something just to have a product out and my fans end up disappointed.

"Seems your boyfriend sent you a little surprise, read the card, Sofia," Cassidy said. My brow arched because he figured I was out of town, the last time I talked with him earlier today.

"We aren't ever far apart, Love Joaquin," I said, reading the card out loud.

"Sounds romantic." Cassidy swooned, removing the ribbon and the wrap around the box. It was the size of a square flat box that looked like it held a book. Something Joaquin knew I loved doing was reading on my down time.

Right as Cassidy was about to lift the top, Joaquin and some of his men busted inside with guns drawn.

"Don't open that!" Joaquin screamed, running toward me, pulling me behind him.

"What are you doing? Joaquin, I'm working, and you are embarrassing me," I hissed, pushing his hands off me.

"I let a lot of things go, but this bullshit is ridiculous, Sofia tell your gangster boyfriend to leave, or I'm calling the cops," Edward stated, pulling his phone out of his pocket.

Joaquin glared at Edward and gestured for Gael with his right hand to grab Edward's phone. They scuffled for a second, and Gael gripped Edward by the neck.

"Joaquin, stop him now. Gael, stop it!" I yelled, trying to move around Joaquin to help Edward.

"Hugo, take him outside and wait for me. Cassidy, steps back from the table," Joaquin commanded.

"Why, what's wrong?" I questioned.

"Where did this package come from?" Joaquin asked.

"I don't know. I thought you sent it over to me. Cassidy brought it in from the delivery guy." He balled his fists up at his side. I swallowed a lump in my throat. Did we do something wrong?

Cassidy was scared shitless; she hadn't been around Jaoquin for long periods of time when he was dealing with any mafia business. If he got her caught up in any type of violence, I would never forgive myself.

"Boss, look at this," Hugo insisted, holding the top of the lid. I leaned in over Joaquin's shoulder, and the box contained a clock running down on top of dead flowers, possibly a bomb inside with another note that said, "We can get her at any time."

"OMG, I have to go, where are my keys. Cassidy, call the police!" I cried out, trying to pull away from Joaquin's tight hold.

"Sofia, baby. I promise nothing is going to happen to you. They were sending a message and wanted my attention and knew how to go about doing so."

"I can't do this with you; I need to leave now."

"I'll take you," Joaquin suggested, entwining our hands, and I jerked back in fear for the first time of what this could have been. My friends could have lost their lives because of me.

* * *

"No! Edward can take me. We need to call the police, OMG! Somebody tried to kill me." I fell to the floor and Joaquin tried to pick me up and I shoved him away, holding my hand up for him to give me space.

"Sofia, please, it's me, baby. I'm not going to hurt you." He slowly approached me, and I slapped him across the face, hitting his chest and cursing him out as he tried to calm me down.

"Stay away from me. This has gone too far; I don't care what you're involved in but to bring this to my door is unforgivable."

"Silencio! You knew who I was, Sofia, you're mine and nothing is going to happen to you. Understand?" The line of his mouth tightened a fraction more, the dark eyebrows slanted in a frown.

Shaking my head, I couldn't pretend this was going to be a fairytale whirlwind romance anymore. I was blind to think he was untouchable when at the top, but that's the spot everyone is gunning for, so his entire life is about watching his back and making moves to protect his family. Removing myself from this situation was my only chance at getting things back on track. Already the newspapers and gossip blogs had my name mixed in with drug dealers and killers. I was foolish, and my pride wouldn't let me see the love I had for him was overshadowing my life. Grabbing my purse and keys, Cassidy followed behind me toward the door carrying her jacket and purse. Right as we got to the door, Joaquin's men blocked the front entrance, cutting us off from leaving.

"Let me through," I demanded; even though he towered over me and could probably snap my neck in a split second, I would make sure to go out with a fight.

"He moves at my orders."

"Then tell him to step aside so I can leave, or I'll call the police."

"Like that? You won't let me fix this, mi amor?" I knew that translated to my love. I learned a few words while dating him for the past few months.

"I need to think and make sure my people get home safely. Release Edward and let him go. I will talk with you once I'm able to clear my head."

"That's not enough; I need to make sure you're safe; let Leonardo take you home and put some security outside your building. I promise to not contact you for a few days."

"Fine, but I'll call you when I'm ready." He did not like my response, but nodded in agreement and kissed my forehead. I flinched at his touch and backed up, waving to his security to allow me to walk away.

* * *

Joaquin

I was still dealing with a gunshot wound from earlier today, and having Sofia stand in fear was breaking me down. Sticking my hands in my pockets, I eyed the room, wondering how they found out about this place, and that she'd be here at this time. Gael came strolling inside once Leonardo and Hugo pulled off with Sofia and Cassidy.

"Edward was sent home with a warning. Hugo will stay and monitor her place, that Cassidy woman is staying with her tonight."

"Fuck," I shouted, tossing everything off the table. Rubbing my temple, I needed to regroup, and figure out if this was a warning from the Russian deal or coming from one of Antonio's crew. Too much shit happening all at once to deal with and lose the woman I love.

"She needs time, Joaquin. I usually stay out of your affairs, but this fucked up her image of you. The most important thing a woman wants is security and, brother, you failed to protect her. In time she will come around." Gael slapped me on the back and headed to the photographer to pay him off. My phone vibrated in my pocket. I pulled it out and saw it was a message from an unknown number.

UNKNOWN: That was a warning.
      Me: mI'm the wrong person to fuck with; who is this?
      Unknown: We'll meet in due time.

Walking out of the studio, Gabriella was waiting in the driver's side, and I hopped inside as she pulled into traffic. It wasn't too late, and so it wouldn't take us to long to get to the loft. I let the window down to get fresh air. "What's the plan ?" Gabriella asked as she stopped at the light.

"I need you to look into Edward and follow Sofia. I don't want anyone thinking they can touch a single strand of hair on her head and think I would not skin them to the bone and watch as their entire family is shot in front of them and tossed in the trash like I believe they are," I snapped.

Chapter 20

Sophia

Four months later.

Security walked me to my car after the media had a field day with the bomb scare. The movie was put on hold until things smoothed out in the media. I haven't really shown my face in public after the photographer sold his story to a tabloid about the situation at his shoot. Talking about Joaquin busting into his building, yelling and screaming to leave. Saying that he was almost killed by my boyfriend, and he'd never work with me again. Giving photos and interviews of bruises he had on his body saying Joaquin's men tried to torture him so he would keep his mouth shut. My entire life was under a microscope, but the music was still helping to keep my mind at ease. Joaquin and I haven't spoken in over four months, my heart and mind are conflicted. He tried calling and texting as soon as things went down, but Edward finally convinced me to take a break from him when the movie was shut down, and all of the news outlets wanted to only talk about my love life. Social media didn't help because some fans started accounts with our photos of us together and saying I should take him back.

Tonight, I was headed to The Blue Bell, a local nightclub for singers, and Deras was performing, and he wanted me to sit and relax. I was going to try and take my mind off things. Cassidy was in the car with me. Edward flew to Los Angeles to try and find some work for me. The cab stopped in front of The Blue Bell, and we stepped out. I put on a baby blue jumpsuit that zipped up and left a little bit in the cleavage area. My hair needed a change, so I cut it into a shoulder-length bob. Turning my phone off, we walked in together. The bouncer knew that we were coming and showed us to a reserved VIP section.

She pressed a hand to her mouth to stifle her giggles. "What's so funny?" I questioned.

"Nothing, Sofia."

"No, tell me, Cassidy."

"I had a serious moment of thinking that your life is more like a movie than the actual movie you were filming." Cassidy laughed.

The whole world was moving in slow motion. I felt like I was walking in a dream world, a nightmare. Some people saw him as a corrupt businessman, a mobster. He showed me the softer side of him, and maybe in the future, we could be friends again. For right now, I needed to focus on me.

"Hey, you came," Deras said, approaching us.

"We did, and I can't wait to hear your set. Deras, this is Cassidy, my assistant."

"Hi, nice to meet you, Deras. I'm a huge fan ," Cassidy stated.

"Nice to meet you, Cassidy. Do you guys need anything? Please let the waitress know if you need anything. Everything is on me."

"We're fine. Go so we can get to twerking in our seat," I joked.

"You got it," Deras said, heading to the stage.

Cassidy took a sip of the wine and swayed her hips. The section had champagne, wine, fruit, and cheese trays. I placed my purse on the couch and clapped my hands as Deras started talking.

"Ladies and gentlemen, I want to thank you all for coming tonight and hanging with my people and me. I'm going to start it off and sing a few songs, and then the rest of the evening, you'll be joined by a few friends of mine. Is that all right with you?" Deras asked.

"Yesss!!" The crowd cheered.

Cassidy jumped up and down, clapping.

"SLOW DOWN WITH THE DRINKS, ma'am. I'm not babysitting you," I told her.

"I'm fine, you need to take a few shots and get some dick," Cassidy commented, the corners of her mouth curled upwards into a smile.

"I can't stand you."

"You know you love me, friend." Cassidy wiggled her hips from front to back joking of missionary sex.

"Let me get drunk, so I can ignore you," I announced.

"That's my girl!" Cassidy cheered.

"Mhmmhuh."

The music started, and Deras smiled at me and started to sing a sweet melody.

When I see your smile, it lights up my day

When I hear your laugh, it brings calm to my heart

When I talk to you, baby, you are all need

Everything comes back to you

Back to you

Back to you

Back to you

He never took his eyes off me as he sang. He thanked the crowd and plopped down in my seat, and Cassidy stared at me. I didn't know how to feel about this new revelation.

If he was interested in me, I had no clue. Whenever I was around him at the studio, he never made it known that he was concerned.

"Wow, you have all the luck!" Cassidy said, joining me on the couch.

"Cassidy ," I groaned, sitting back on the couch, closing my eyes and covering my face.

"Sofia, if Joaquin finds out-" I cut her off before she even finished putting that thought in the air.

"Sofia," Deras called out for me. Opening my eyes, I sat up and scooted over for him to have a seat.

"I'm going to go to the bar and get another bottle of Moscato," Cassidy explained, holding the bottle up.

"I know this comes as a surprise," Deras stated.

"A big surprise."

He reached out and grabbed my hand, entwining our fingers.

"Am I interrupting something?" Joaquin questioned.

"What are you doing here?" I moved away from Deras to put space between us.

Chapter 21

Joaquin

Sofia didn't know that she was being watched even over the past four months. She should have known from the last time that I would never allow anything to happen to her. The break was needed because I had business to take care of; making sure that my enemies didn't see she was as important in my life helped to calm things down. The family wasn't in the clear, but I bought some time before going out to Italy in the new few weeks.

I stalked, over glaring at her little boyfriend that professed his love up on stage. I had Gael check him out when I saw them going in and out of the studio a few nights. The owner of the studio didn't mind a few extra dollars in his pocket when I asked to get information on Deras Jones. A famous writer and producer, but he still performed in local clubs. Sofia didn't know the spell she put on men because her personality not only matched her beauty, but she was genuine and caring with her friends and family.

"Joaquin, how did you know I was here?" Sofia queried.

"Do you know him?" Deras asked.

"The question is who are you? And why are you holding her hand?"

"Joaquin, that's enough. I'll call you tomorrow."

"I don't think so."

"Listen, man, she doesn't want to talk to you. You're the mobster ex-boyfriend, right?" Deras pointed his finger in my face.

"Put your finger down," I commanded balling my fists up.

Sofia jumped up, standing in between us, pushing me back.

"I'm out with my friends; we can talk tomorrow when you've cooled down."

"Come home with me now."

"Sofia, you can stay with me; you don't need to listen to him," Deras advised.

"What!" I reached over Sofia and grasped his neck. Sofia screamed as Gael and Hugo attempted to pull me away.

"Joaquin, please let him go. I'll leave with you, I promise."

"Let...me...go...," Deras stuttered out.

Cassidy came back over during all the commotion, and tried to pull Sofia away. I cursed him out in Italian and then Portuguese for inference on him, trying to act tough in front of Sofia.

"I mean it, Joaquin, let him go, or I'll never speak to you again." Sofia shoved me back. I stumbled, and Gael caught me before I fell.

"Are you all right, Deras?" Sofia asked, checking his neck.

"Grab her," I demanded and walked out as Gael gestured for Hugo to pick Sofia up and grab her purse.

"NO!!Put me down! Joaquin! You can't do this ," Sofia screamed. Cassidy followed behind as we walked out to my limo, and Hugo put her down on her feet. Leonardo was standing at the driver's side door.

"Get inside," I gritted through clenched teeth, peering into her eyes.

"Joaquin," Gael called my name, and I threw a hand up for him to hush.

"I'm not leaving with you."

"Yes you are, willingly or forcibly. But you're coming home with me tonight and we're going to talk," I explained.

"Gael, please tell him to leave me alone and lose my number." Sofia tried to walk off, and I blocked her exit. She smacked me across the face, and I didn't move; she raised her hand again to slap me and I grabbed it, kissing her palm, then her lips.

"I'm sorry, sweetheart; please come home with me so we can discuss some things. We've drawn a crowd, and I don't want to stay out here arguing and cause more photographers to show." I said, caressing her cheek.

She looked over at Cassidy for assurance.

"We can drop you off, Cassidy," I reassured.

"I'm fine; my Uber will be here soon," Cassidy informed us.

Shaking my head no, I snapped my finger for Hugo to take her home in the other car.

"Hugo will drive you home, you've been drinking, and I wouldn't feel right leaving you alone with a stranger. Hugo has protected Sofia with his life, and he'll do the same for you," I said.

"Are you sure?" Cassidy replied.

"Positive and Sofia will call you tomorrow," I stated. Hugo took the keys from Gabriella and walked off with Cassidy. Sofia sighed and finally got in the car, and I slid inside next to her. She sat closer to the door, far away from me. I was left staring out into the night sky.

Leonardo pulled off as Gael followed, trailing us to my new home in New Jersey. With Alessandra moving here, I thought it was best to leave out of the city with more privacy with security twenty-four hours.

"Where do you live now?" Sofia queried.

"New Jersey. Alessandra is moving here, and I wanted her away from the city."

"So you can keep her under lock and key ," Sofia mumbled under her breath.

Chapter 22

Joaquin

The drive was long, but we finally arrived. She looked in awe as the spiral gate opened, and Leonardo drove up the winding road. I lived on eight acres of rolling lawn. It was a brick and slate colonial manor with a main reception room, each with the finest woods and marble floors. There were eleven spacious bedroom suites throughout the house on two levels with a separate guest house that had its own entrance off the side. I hoped to make this our home as a union one day. She had no clue how much she controlled me. The past few months without her left me broken. The engagement ring still sits in my pocket.

"Thank you for coming."

"Did I have a choice?" she muttered, rolling her eyes, closing the door, and stepping aside. Her hips had spread, and she'd gain a few extra pounds on her ass. I couldn't wait to be inside her again; she was teasing me. I hadn't even thought of another woman since meeting Sofia almost eight months ago.

I opened the door and stood off to the side, and I gestured for her to come into the kitchen.

"You want anything to drink?"

"No, so get to talking."

Groaning, in frustration, I calmed down, not letting her attitude get me out of character and give her an excuse to leave. Grabbing a bottle of water out of the fridge, I took a sip and leaned against the counter, peering into her eyes. She looked away, and I stepped around the island that kept us separated and turned her around in the chair and stepped in between her legs.

I bent down and kissed her lips. She allowed me that moment of passion.

"Did I ever tell you that I'm grateful to you for coming into my life?"

She drew in a sharp breath. "You have a funny way of showing that side of yourself, Joaquin, when I constantly have to defend you to my friends, family, and the public."

"Never apologize, I'll never act like someone I'm not. This around you is me, my life. Can you understand it? As the son, brother, and friend, born into this lifestyle, I had no choice."

"What I understand is that you've been on a destructive path during these past four months with killing people, closing down businesses. I'm surprised your little girlfriends aren't complaining about you pulling me out of the club tonight."

"What girlfriends? You're the only one for me."

"I want a simple boyfriend, not a crazy kingpin called Ghost!" she screamed, shoving me away and jumping up, storming toward the front door.

"Who told you about that?"

"It's all over the blogs about you being a killer for the mafia. I knew you probably sold drugs, and I could try to distance myself, but killing people, Joaquin. I don't know if I can be with you."

"Do you love me, Sofia?" I asked.

"What kind of question is that, Joaquin?"

"Answer me."

"No!"

I chuckled, not believing her at all.

"What's so funny?"

"If you didn't love me, Sofia, you would have never gotten in the car with me from the beginning."

"I didn't have a choice, if you remember. Hugo would have hounded me until I came with you."

"Not tonight."

"Then, when?"

"The first time you walked out of the building and I drove you home—sweetheart, you're in my heart and mind. Every second of every day, I think of you. All of my thoughts are about making sure you're okay, and no harm comes to you before I even think of myself."

"That's not love, Joaquin."

"It's my love."

I pulled the ring out and got on my knee. She was speechless.

"Can you see yourself loving a crazy, mafia, obsessed, and extremely in love with you, man?" I questioned.

"Yes," she whispered.

I slid the ring on her finger and pulled her into a kiss.

"No more killing, crazy kingpin. I need the sweet Joaquin more than the other one. Promise me you'll work on being mindful of not overreacting at certain situations when I'm with someone else," Sofia suggested.

"I promise."

Chapter 23

Sophia

Joaquin was sleeping on his stomach in my bed. The sheet showcased his thick broad shoulders. The night we had reconnected played again in my mind, and I was fully ready to commit as his Donna and take his engagement ring. I slid the sheet off completely, and he didn't stir in his sleep. I removed my robe, climbing to the edge of the bed, tightening my hair in a bun on top of my head. I ran my hands up his legs slowly. Positing my legs on both sides of his body, I kissed behind his left and right ear; he finally mumbled under his breath and turned around facing me with his eyes still closed. I smiled, knowing he was about to get a big wakeup morning. Getting the chance to visit Spain with him after the movie shoot was done later this year, I couldn't wait to explore Spain with him.

I moved down, picking up his dick; it hardened at my touch. I sucked the tip into my mouth, placing kisses on the sensitive head. Joaquin shifted his left leg wider giving me more room, grasping my hair. I moaned, sliding him further down my throat. His smell was still fresh from the shower we took together before bed last night after our fourth round of sex. Every time we made love felt like the very first time. My soul was shifted, mind ignited, spirt rejuvenated with his touch. He was a bad guy; my parents taught me to stay away from that type of man, yet I agreed to be his wife. Was I making a mistake? Possibly. But the limits that he was willing to go to make me happy did bring a smile to my face. As I massaged his balls, I slid my tongue across, taking them individually into my mouth, breathing through my nose and fondling his pubic hair. Removing his balls, I spit on each one, pushed my breasts up against them, rubbing against the base of his dick.

"Fuckkkk! Stop before I come."

"Not yet."

I kept stroking him up and down between my breasts, taking the tip of his penis down my throat, squeezing between my pillows as he moaned out.

Joaquin jerked in my hands, spilling his seed, a small drizzle spilling down my cheek.

"Shit! Get up here," he groaned, reaching for my shoulders to pull me up to ride him.

"This is my show, Mr. Fuertes," I replied as I licked across his balls.

Once I got to spend more time with Sabrina and the girls; I learned how she coped with being in this lifestyle. Anticipation for more launched through my body, I paced our time together because neither one of us had to be anywhere today.

"Sofia, don't play with me, get up here now," Joaquin demanded, gripping his dick and stroking himself. I crawled up his body, slapping his hand away and straddling his lap, planting my hands around his neck, pressing gently.

"This is mine, and you can't touch until I allow you to." He slipped his arm around my waist, grabbed the back of my head, leaned up, and captured my lips. The cruel ravishment of his mouth was punishing and angry.

"Never deny me." His slow drugging kisses had teased me so much, I was ready to take him into my mouth again.

"Take me."

I was burying my hands into his thick hair, pushing his head back. His black brows winged down. I lifted up, placing his dick at my opening; the searing contact of our bodies moved through us and a low groan left his lips. I grabbed a handful of the sheets as I rode him slow and steady. I felt his heart pound underneath my fingertips. His gaze turned soft as we made love for the rest of the morning.

* * *

JOAQUIN HAD a few errands to run, and I decided to invite Sabrina and Janice over to hang out while he was out before I start running my lines for the movie I just signed on to film.

Hearing a knock at the door, I headed to place the plate of snacks and wine down on the table. Changing into a pair of leggings and Joaquin's shirt, I felt more comfortable around the house without all the makeup. Hopefully, they wouldn't think I'm superficial like other actors that have to stay on point at all times.

"Sabrina, Janice, welcome, please come inside."

Sabrina hugged me, then Janice and walked into the living room.

"Your home is beautiful, Sofia ," Sabrina said, picking up a bottle of water.

"Thank you."

"For real, how many bedrooms are in here? I can see Carlo and me fucking in every room," Janice joked.

"Janice don't you start," Sabrina insisted.

"It has eleven bedrooms and eight bathrooms, plus a guesthouse."

"Where's your boo?" Janice questioned.

"He's probably out with your husband cooking up some problems that we'll hear about on the news."

"Yeah I heard about your man. Honey, you need to make sure you have insurance on him when you get married because of the way he's running around you'll need something to cover the expenses in this place ," Janice said, gesturing around the room.

"Janice, please don't start, and that's rude," Sabrina spat.

"It's fine; I get it now. You two have been in this world for years, and I'm still fairly new to being in love with someone like him."

"You can say it out loud, Sofia; your boyfriend is a mafia boss. A leader, the boss of all bosses, sweetie, and you need to understand that's never going to change. The only advice we can give you is to own and embrace your status as his woman and be his peace, never question or doubt him in front of his men. Let the women know you own that dick and let him know that you run the family in the household, and he runs the people in the streets. The moment you lay down those rules, your life will be much easier," Janice exclaimed.

Joaquin filled me in on his friends' wives and the stories of how they met at Ryde nightclub almost ten years ago. They were way more forthcoming than I thought they would be, and I needed someone to keep things real with me.

"I agree with Janice, maybe I would have said it a little nicer. I've been through everything with Antonio and tried to end things many times. I still remember him sending his bodyguard over to me with a gift, and I turned him down. You can't win my heart with gifts, and Antonio thought his charm would do the trick. Let's not get me started on when he thought I was sleeping with Spencer. That man is so jealous and possessive," Sabrina said shaking her head.

"Joaquin's the same way."

"So why did you take his ring?" Janice questioned.

"I love him above all of his flaws," I responded.

For the rest of the afternoon, we drank and talked, they showed me photos of their kids, and we made plans to do this often.

Chapter 24

Sophia

A week later.

I stepped off the elevator walking toward the front door as Jerry stood at the door laughing with other residents as they left out. "Miss Chambers, how are you doing? I know that the bomb scare was rough."

"I'm fine, Jerry, thanks for asking, the police are still investigating, they even added around the clock security when I leave here or go to the studio, but I declined."

"That decline wouldn't have anything to do with Mr. Fuertes?" he quipped.

"Something like that. I'm moving in with him soon; I'll see you tomorrow, heading out for the evening."

"Be safe." He waved goodbye and I waved and smiled back at him as Leonardo held the door of the stretch limo open. It was a beautiful Saturday night and couples were out walking. I check my watch. It just turned eight o'clock. Joaquin called earlier. He had a surprise for me and said to get dressed up.

I was wearing a black dress rouched on one shoulder with a split on the side . "How are you?" With me starting a new movie tomorrow I decided to keep my hair pinned back with stud diamond earrings as well as a diamond bracelet.

"Doing good, Sofia. Mr. Fuertes is calling on the car phone." I slid inside picking up the phone hearing his deep, dark raspy voice.

"What is the surprise, Joaquin?" I questioned biting my bottom lip, crossing my legs.

"I have Leonardo driving you to my yacht. I am taking you on a trip." I sighed not sure about taking this trip. With me starting a new movie tomorrow and recording my album this wasn't the best time to leave. "Joaquin."

"Don't disappoint me, Sofia. We need this, just the two of us alone, I've already told Antonio I was taking some time off, so we have two weeks together traveling by sea." These past few months Joaquin and I have grown closer even though the work he does put him at risk but, our bond has never wavered. Even when his ex-plaything, Monica, didn't understand the connection we have. The door closed a few minutes later and Leonardo got in on the driver's side and headed into traffic.

"Appreciate the thought, baby, but what about my movie, and album? My manager wants me to do a tour."

"You've been through a lot, Sofia, and it's partially my fault. Can't you push the movie back for when you get back in town, and I'll talk with your manager about postponing the tour ?" he asked. The car arrived at the dock fifteen minutes later. I smiled tilting my head against the window looking out at the stars, I noticed another limo pull up and park. A tall man wearing a business suit, trench coat and gloves got out and I noticed he had a harsh scowl on his face. He had a medium build, short black hair, bushy eyebrows, and thin lips. Made me wonder who he was married to.

"I told you already, Joaquin, you don't run my life."

"I'm not trying to run your life, I'm trying to love you ," he responded groaning in frustration. I turned toward shouting out the window and saw multiple cars arrive.

"I love you too, what's the name of your boat?" I watched Leonardo get out of the car and shake hands with a man I'd never seen before. They exchanged words, and he passed Leonardo a black bag.

" It's called Sophia. I had all your favorite foods ordered and clothes picked up, so you don't have to worry about anything."

Leonardo turned, headed toward the car, and opened the passenger seat. I grabbed my purse as he opened the door, then yanked the phone out of my hand. "Leonardo, what are you doing!" I shouted.

"Bitch, let's go, she's all yours."

I screamed at Leonardo, trying to get out of his hold on my arm. I tried yelling for Joaquin to help me. Leonardo placed his hand over my mouth as I kicked and screamed to get out of his arms. I could hear Joaquin yelling through the phone. "Sofia! Sofia! Leonardo, I swear to God if you hurt her, your entire bloodline will be extinguished."

"Bitch, you bit me ," Leonardo yelled, before he slapped me across the face. I fell on the ground in shock and pain as he ripped the back of my dress trying to pull me back.

"No let me go! Please... Please, I won't tell ," I begged as he handed me off to the other guy.

I should've known something was wrong when the smell of rotten eggs was in the air but my tears spilled down my face as the guy holding me shook his head in disgust.

"Please let me go."

He grinned, licking his lips, not caring. Leonardo walked off, heading back to the limo, while we went in the opposite direction toward the loading dock. He dragged me up the steps pushing me through the door, and I fell to the floor. I looked around until the smell of a cigar caused me to look up.

Into the eyes of the last person I expected to see. He sat there in a white suit with his legs crossed, puffing on his cigar. I'd seen him before in the newspapers. I'd never forgotten that scar over his right eye.

"Hello, Mrs. Chambers ," he said in his Portuguese accent. He was grinning down at me.

"You can't do this."

"I can, and I will. Now remove your clothes, including the jewelry." The ship started to move, and I jumped up trying to run out. I banged on the door until I finally noticed men with guns.

Tears poured down my cheeks. I finally saw men with guns standing at every corner of the ship.

"You can play nice, or I can get ugly, it's your choice Sofia ," he suggested, puffing on his cigar, standing up, and walking toward me as I continued calling for help.

To be continued.......Joaquin and Sofia with Bated Breath Part 2 coming in 2021.

* * *

This is the end of part 1 of 'Joaquin and Sofia with Bated Breath'
Follow the format here for your final chapter or epilogue. When the story is done, put "The End" centered. Then add a scene break, and then your "pitch" for sell through. We're provided an example of a sell through pitch. You can either use a "Continue the Series" line or you can use a one-line blurb.

The End

* * *

This is the end of part 1 of Joaquinn Fuertes (Struck In Love Spinoff Fuertes Cartel Book 1), the rest of the story will be available after Crimes of the Wicked is unpublished.

www.chiquitadennie.com

* * *

Newsletter
(https://landing.mailerlite.com/webforms/landing/r7j2s6)

About Chiquita Dennie

Chiquita Dennie is an author of Contemporary, Romantic Suspense,
Women's Fiction,
and Erotic Romance.

She lives in Los Angeles, CA. Originally from TN and before she started
writing contemporary romance, she worked in the entertainment industry
on notable TV shows including the Dr. Phil show, Tyra Banks show,
American Idol, and Deal or No Deal. But her favorite job is the one she's
now doing full time – writing romance.

A Best-Selling Author and Award-winning Filmmaker, her first short film,
"Invisible," released in Summer 2017 and screened in multiple festivals and
won for Best Short Film. She also hosts a podcast that showcases the latest in
Beauty, Business, and Community called "Moscato and Tea." Her debut
release of Antonio and Sabrina Struck In Love has opened a new avenue of
writing that she loves.

If you want to know when the next book will come out, please visit my
website at
http://www.chiquitadennie.com, where you can sign up to receive an email
for my next release.

OBSESSION

OBSESSION

Bee Murray

The Pawn in Play

The Players are plotting Destruction

And I just became their final Pawn

I've been dragged into a game I have no intention to play.

And the first rule I learned was don't mess with the King's Pawn

Ripley Quinn

Learning the world is nothing more than just a deadly facade covered in light and glitter,

is a hard fucking lesson to swallow.

I used to think in simplicity,

that hard work actually paid off and

I could save myself with determination alone.

That was until I stumbled into Paxton fucking King.

The Elite Players are a name feared by those

that dwell within the darkest parts of this world,

and he is their leader.

Now they are plotting against the hand that feeds them

and I have been dragged into their ruse whether I like it or not.

Paxton has me by the strings and knows exactly what strand

to pluck to get me to play along until the very bitter end.

Paxton King

That little green-eyed snake thinks she the innocent in this story

But don't be fooled by her trembling lips or pitiful pleas

Ripley Quinn might be able to pretend for awhile

but she is just like the rest of us, driven by a need to survive; a hunger for control

and I am determined to prove to her that she is willing to kill to get what she wants

Money is the ultimate Power Play

and right now, I hold the reins over her past...and her future.

What she doesn't know is this game won't end until the final gunshot rings.

And I intend for her to be the one pulling the trigger.

Author Note

Author Note

    Thanks so much for picking up *Crimes of the Wicked: A Limited Edition Criminal Mayhem Collection!*

I am so excited to introduce you to my upcoming dark contemporary/mafia romance duet *Dark Desires & Wicked Crimes.* This series has two planned full-length books plus the prequel *Obsession.* Let me preface this now: we're gonna go on a journey together. It's going to be dark and twisted. At times, it's going to be violent. It's absolutely sexually explicit and profane.There is triggering content in this series and it's very different from what I normally write. There are cliffhangers and you might hate me at a few different parts but I ask you to hang in there -- this story is complicated but it's also pretty freaking amazing. I hope you enjoy it!

Without further ado, please enjoy part one of *Obsession!*

<3 Bee

Dominic
10 years ago

"Since when do we make a special trip to kidnap some piece of ass for Frederick fucking Confi? How is he suddenly so important that he can't even acquire his own pussy? And you want me to deliver it to him, too? This entire job is bullshit."

My father raises his hand and takes a long drag on his cigar, stopping me mid-rant. From the look on his face, I know it's high time I either shut the fuck up or get the fuck out. I'm also hyper aware that being the son of the boss has its advantages. If anyone else spoke to him that way, they'd be in a world of pain, or wishing they were dead. Hell, if my brother was still alive, he would have already smashed a fist into my insolent mouth. Luca was the one who was supposed to take over for my father, not me. Second sons are the spares, he was the heir. It was never supposed to be me. But Luca met the business end of a knife in a shitty club in Moscow and left me here to take his place in this shitshow.

It's hard to carry on the family business if you're dead.

I'm all the old man has left, unless he somehow manages to knock up his latest trophy wife.

He knows it and I know it.

We both hate each other for it.

"Dominic, you forget yourself. You do as ordered and you do not question." My father's voice is pure steel and I get the urge to push him even further. Arturo, his ever-present right-hand man, gives me a tight lipped smile and shakes his head. I step back, rolling my weight back onto my heels in defiance. I may be the son of Tavian De Marchi but Arturo is the one who served as a father figure to Luca and I more often than not. I toe the line with my father for Arturo's sake, not my own.

I don't know how much longer I can get away with that.

"What can you tell me about the target, *father?*" I grind out, my fingers

421

itching with the need to wipe that smug expression off his face. I can feel the fight building in my muscles.

"I can tell you, *boy*, that she's a high value target and retrieving her for Mr. Confi is seen as a favor to the family. She's the daughter of Senator Andres Christophe. It would seem that the Senator made a deal with Confi for election assistance. When he failed to deliver on his repayment schedule, Confi elected to take the girl as payment on the debt and leave a small scene for his former clients to remember him by. You will deliver as we promised or you will suffer the same consequences as any other insuborindate fuck in this organization. Do you understand?" Blotches of red color his cheeks and spittle flies out of his mouth as he half-raises out of the chair to shout at me.

My face is stone cold and I nod, not trusting myself to respond verbally. This isn't just kidnapping some piece of ass for a ransom. If Frederick Confi was taking her as payment for a debt, the poor bitch was going to wish she were dead for a long, long time before that mercy was granted to her.

Arturo holds out a thin manila envelope and I take it, pivoting on my heel and stalking out of the room.

"Dominic," My father's tone holds a warning and I can't stop the cocky grin that crosses my face as I turn to face him from the doorway. He's standing now, pouring a glass of his precious Scotch. *Your time is coming, old man. Make my day and make it today.* "This is your last chance to prove to me you are a part of this family and not just a feral dog that needs to be put down. Surely you can manage a task as simple as *go fetch* without fucking it up?"

Hatred runs hot through my veins and my facsimile of a smile turns into a bitter snarl.

I spy an autographed baseball on the shelf next to me. Without even breaking my stride, I grab it and throw it as hard as I can at the gilded mirror hanging over the fireplace. It shatters into pieces and the room is silent for a heartbeat before all of my father's guards burst into the room with their guns drawn, looking for the source of the noise.

The baseball rolls to a stop close to my foot and I reach down to pick it up and put it back on the shelf.

"Looks like I can fetch just fine."

Without another word I push my way past the guards and back out of the office. Judging from the explosion of profanity and yelling, I half expect to be dragged back by my hair to face him but no one stops me as I stride through the corridor and out to the garage.

Throwing the manila envelope into the passenger seat, I pop off a quick text before I slide behind the wheel of my Maserati and peel out of the driveway.

Dealing with my father always results in one thing: the need to do violence. The darkness I carry in me spirals to the top and I let it take control for now, speeding down the highway as I make my way to the one place in this entire goddamn world that is my own. With any luck, my father will have sent me one of his goons after me, presumably to teach me a lesson. My father may be untouchable as the boss of the De Marchi family, but his men are not. I push my foot down on the accelerator harder, the thrill and anticipation of a fight making me weave recklessly through traffic.

* * *

Colt's head snaps backward as my fist crashes into his face and he staggers back to the ropes. A warm spray of blood bursts forth after the satisfying crunch of a broken nose. His eyes are streaming, the blood gushing from his nose and dripping down on his pristine white sneakers. He lunges at me but his anger and pain makes him sloppy. I dodge him easily, driving my fist into his gut and enjoying the whoosh of air that escapes his lungs as he doubles over in agony. A knee to the face and the scream of pain when I crush his already broken nose makes me break out in a feral grin. All it takes is a brutal elbow to the back of his neck and he's down, gasping for air on the mat.

Stepping back, I survey him with mild distaste. He's a huddled mess on the floor and I only got five punches in. Like a child whose toy has been taken away, I sigh in disappointment. Another fight over before it could begin. Another one of my father's men sent to teach me a lesson only to fail miserably. Killing Colt would be momentarily satisfying but it would likely bring holy hell down on my head.

I aim a final kick at the prone man's kidneys before stalking out of the ring. If you ask my father, he will tell you I'm out of control and on a path that will only end in death. To him, I am a liability. A feral dog that he tolerates because blood is blood and that's what we do. His introspection falls just short of the realization that he made me who I am today. The blood lust that courses through my veins, the rage and darkness that simmers under the surface? It matches his. He tolerates me because he knows that I, perhaps even more than my exalted late brother, have the necessary skills to get my hands dirty.

For 25 years I have been shaped and molded, my anger cultivated and my skills sharpened. For one purpose and one purpose only: hunt and destroy. Luca was the political one. He ruled over backroom dealings and Boardrooms alike. He was savvy and charming with a brilliantly twisted mind for the business.

Compared to him, I'm nothing but fists and bullets. I fuck shit up and leave a trail of blood in my wake. But it's what I'm good at.

They cultivated this darkness and taught me to let it take over.

Joke's on them if they don't like the results.

I walk away from the ring and motion to Davis to go check on Colt. He grimaces as he steps over the blood pooling around Colt's prone body and reaches out to take his pulse.

"Jesus Christ, Dominic -- he's barely alive." Davis' exasperation puts a satisfied smile on my face.

"Ah, yes, but he *is* alive. Get him out of my fucking sight. We have a job to do."

I flip him the bird and keep walking towards the private office area I keep at the gym. I don't need to look behind me to know that Davis already has his phone out and is texting for our private medic to come rescue Colt.

"He should have fought harder. He hits like a drunk sorority girl," I call back, reaching for the bourbon I keep in my desk drawer and taking a swig directly from the bottle, "Make sure you mention that in your *report.*"

Davis snorts a laugh, "He's one of your father's best men."

I flex my fingers and note the ache in my hands as I grip the bottle. If one of my father's 'best men' can be taken out in five hits, maybe we have bigger problems. I lift my eyes and notice Davis is watching me from the shadows again. With an eyebrow raised, I give him a sardonic grin and take another swig of the bourbon and motion to the manila envelope on the desk.

"Our next target is in there."

For a man built like a mountain, Davis moves like a cat and he slinks out of the shadows to tear open the envelope and pull out the dossier.

His eyebrows rise as he looks at the glossy picture of a beautiful, blonde woman on top of the stack of papers. She's smiling wide and I can see the logo of an animal shelter on her dog's jaunty bandanna. Goodness radiates out from her.

I slam the bourbon bottle back on the table in disgust.

"Who is she?" he asks finally, studying the picture thoughtfully.

"Debt collection. Her Daddy didn't pay so she's Frederick Confi's newest pet."

Davis swore and tossed the picture down on the table. He grabbed the bourbon bottle to take a swig of it himself.

"It would seem that she is the only daughter of one Senator Christophe. The esteemed Senator went looking for some extra campaign... assistance. He chose to go to Frederick Confi for that. The Senator is behind on his agreement and Frederick has asked us to intervene and collect his debt."

A flash of rage shines in Davis' eyes and he looks down at the photo. He has no problem putting a bullet in any man for virtually any reason, but he's a protective sonofabitch when it comes to women.

I rub my eyes, suddenly tired.

As much as I enjoy fucking shit up, kidnapping women is not high on the list of things I enjoy, either.

And kidnapping a woman only to turn her over to Frederick Confi? That's an entirely different kind of game. Confi was well known for his peculiarities and his brutal tastes. He craves the innocent ones for his... projects. I don't know a goddamn thing about this girl, but giving her to that sadistic asshole will not only destroy her. She will pray for death and a shot to the head would be much kinder than the future that awaits her.

"Her father used her as collateral? What the fuck, man?" Davis mutters.

She doesn't deserve the fate she has waiting for her. No one deserves that except maybe her shitstain excuse for a father who sentenced her to it.

425

My fingers itch to have the Senator in my ring. To slowly break him down with my fists until he is nothing more than a huddled mess on my floor, pissing himself from fear. I want him to beg for the mercy his daughter will not be granted. The mercy that allows for a quick death; a death with dignity.

"When do we go get her?" I finally ask, my voice rough with anger. Davis looks at me questioningly but shrugs and pulls out the folder behind the picture to study the instructions.

"Tomorrow night. She's attending a private fundraiser. Frederick has requested that she be delivered to his ranch facility near Reno."

I nod grimly. The need to hurt something, to feel it break apart in my hands is almost overwhelming as the rage courses through me again. I look over to see that our private medic team has already removed Colt and I feel even more anger that I can't finish him off. I need to beat the shit out of someone and I need to do it now.

"Enjoy your last night of freedom, Miss Christophe," I mutter before grabbing my jacket and stalking out the door and into the brisk night air.

CHAPTER 1
OBSESSION BEGINS

Sabine
10 years ago

"Try not to be a disappointment, Sabine," my mother's parting words echo in my head as I grab my fourth glass of champagne and chug it down. I hoped that the buzz would numb the paralyzing social anxiety I get in large groups of people, but it hasn't happened yet. The room is packed with people all vying to be the center of attention and yet I am trapped here, wanting more than anything in the world to hide and blend in.

But I can't.

Day in and day out, my picture is plastered in the media alongside my parents.

"America's Perfect Family" they call us.

According to the last Sunday Times, we are on track to being the next great political dynasty.

My father is a third generation Senator, the scion of two of New England's oldest monied families. My mother is a former TV-star turned media mogul. She has made her fortune telling poorer women how to 'work harder' to achieve their goals and selling her inspirational words at a premium to all who can afford it.

And me? I'm quite literally their poster child. I'm the blonde-haired, blue-eyed piece of arm candy that they stage and position like a doll to make them seem relatable to the common people.

I can't remember a time in my life where I wasn't followed by cameras or coached on how to sit, stand, eat, or walk in a way that caught the perfect light. When I had to have braces in the fourth grade, my mother turned the entire experience into a made-for-tv documentary about the need for expanded dental insurance coverage.

Every single moment of my life has been documented, edited, and passed out as media content to assist my parents with their careers. From my first bra to my first period and the embarrassing first kiss. And, because I was a minor? I couldn't do a goddamn thing to stop them.

That ends now. I turned 18 last week and turned the tables on them.

My parents and I have an agreement. If I play the part of a dutiful daughter for the campaign trail, they'll allow me to switch my college registration from pre-law at a prestigious ivy league school to a small art college upstate. They even promised to leave me alone the second the semester starts.

No more events.

No more press.

No more photos.

Just a normal life as a normal college freshman in a dorm. It's the kind of freedom I've spent years dreaming about.

I have three weeks left of this hell and then I can get on with my own fucking life.

But until then, I have to survive with the sharks. I grab another flute of champagne from the passing waiter to fortify myself.

The bubbles tickle my nose and make me want to sneeze but I still chug it down. My parents paid good money for this champagne and they paid good money for me to be here. It would be a shame to waste either of those purchases. The dark blue dress my mother insisted that I wear is supposed to look demure and classic; a reminder to the men in the room that I am a woman, but yet also innocent.

The feeling of being watched is stronger now and I resist the urge to whirl around to search for the person who has fixated on me. My mother doesn't notice. She's too busy trying to make a deal. She's always making a deal.

My father may be the Senator, but it's my mother who is the genius that knows how to win an election. She's everything you could want in a political operative: charming, brilliant, ruthless, conventionally attractive, and most of all: rich. People have underestimated my mother for her entire life. They often come to regret that. Georgia Christophe, despite her "good old fashioned family values" look, should never be underestimated. There's blood on those perfectly manicured hands. Now that I'm of an age to be useful to her, I am not unconvinced that the next blood on her hands won't be mine.

"Sabine! Where have you been hiding, my dear? You're going to give an old man a heart attack with legs like those!"

A cold shiver makes it's way down my spine as I slowly turn to the unwelcome presence interrupting my quiet reverie. Frederick Confi in the flesh.

Frederick is, for lack of a better term, a friend of the family.

In reality, he's my father's main campaign financier.

My parents always encouraged me to think of him as the rich uncle who likes to spoil his adopted niece and, consequently, fund political campaigns with seemingly never ending streams of cash.

I have always thought of him as creepy.

When he started pinching my ass at events 2 years ago, I told my mother and she flew off the handle at me and accused me of making up accusations to get out of doing my duty to the family. That's when I started to realize that, in my mother's eyes, my value was directly related to what she can get out of me.

Rumors surround Frederick Confi like spiderwebs and it doesn't take an overactive imagination to see that he is deeply connected to criminal elements that range from the Russian *Bratva* to the Colombian cartels but none of it has ever been substantiated.

Three more weeks and you never have to see the slimy motherfucker again, Sabine. Pull it together.

"Good evening, Mr. Confi, I trust you are well?" I paste the most neutral smile I can manage onto my face and angle my body slightly away from him.

"Well, I'll tell you what, sweetheart. I wasn't having *nearly* as much fun until I saw you. Come dance with your Uncle Frederick—we have so much to catch up on!"

He reaches for my wrist and I have to stifle a gag. The last thing I want is to be pulled out into the middle of a crowd of people only to be trapped next to *him.*

"Oh, I am not much of a dancer, Mr. Confi. Thank you though." My smile is brittle and the feel of his sweaty hand on my wrist is making my skin crawl.

"Come on now, sugar, how many times do I have to tell you, you can call me Uncle Frederick!" He tugs harder on my wrist and I stumble. My hand flies out in front of me to brace myself and lands on his shoulder.

He leers at me, his eyes dropping to my cleavage. Taking advantage of my being off-balance, he pulls me into his arms and slides a hand down my back to rest on my ass.

I freeze. This is bold, even for him. Glancing around, I am both relieved and horrified that no one is paying us the slightest bit of attention.

"Fine, one dance. But keep your hands up higher, *Uncle Frederick*," I say through gritted teeth. I reach behind myself to grab his wrist and move it back up to my waist.

He laughs as if my demands are amusing, and then takes my hand and pulls me out onto the dance floor. I catch sight of my mother who notices my dance partner. She raises her glass to me in approval and my heart sinks. I stifle the outrage that threatens to spill out, wishing against all wishes that I had drunk something stronger than champagne. Something that would allow me to check out.

His fleshy hands are damp with sweat and he presses my body flush against him. Bile rises in my throat and my muscles feel frozen and tight.

"Come on now, sugar. You just need to relax! You just do what your mama said and let dear Uncle Frederick take you for a spin on the dance floor, ok?" His breath is hot against my ear and I can smell whiskey, sour on his breath. His hand inches down from my waist and hovers right above my ass.

I hate him. I hate him and every single asshole in this room who would do the same if given half a chance. I see my father in the corner, but he's busy glad-handing the Who's-Who of the city's business elite. No help would be coming from that quarter.

Frederick takes advantage of my distraction and disgust to pull me closer. His hips bump into mine as he grinds against me. The look of satisfaction on his face when I struggle to free myself makes my blood run ice cold.

He enjoys my defiance and the way he looks at me makes me feel like he has been expecting this. And worse? He wants it.

"Did you know I have the power to give your father the election tomorrow, my pet?" He whispers as his hand strokes down my arm, "All I would have to do is endorse him and my people will ensure he is elected."

My blood runs cold again and I feel him spread his hands wide across my hips. He presses me into him, grinding the semi he has been sporting since we started dancing into me and making my throat tighten.

I try to pull away but he holds onto me still and I start to panic.

"May I cut in?" A smooth, slightly accented voice sounds over my left shoulder and I find myself being twirled out of Frederick's arms and into the arms of someone younger, hotter, and infinitely preferable to the handsy old lech.

My new partner expertly maneuvers us away from Frederick and we end up at the opposite side of the dance floor. Once we are free, he drops the pretense of dancing and grabs two glasses of champagne from a passing waiter and hands one of them to me.

I sip it gratefully, unsure of the best way to thank a ridiculously hot stranger for saving me.

"Um, so, thank you," I start awkwardly, "I really appreciate the save. That guy is a... problem. But he's a friend of my parents so he can pretty much get away with murder and they won't bat an eyelash."

His dark eyes widen a little bit in amusement and he sips his champagne.

"Your parents are good friends with Frederick Confi? I was unaware he had any friends, only contacts." The accent in his voice is hard to place, it sounded Eastern European or maybe Italian, but I can't be sure.

"Where are you from?" I blurt out, the buzz from all the alcohol making me slightly less inhibited than I would normally be.

He smiles at that and I swear my entire world narrows to only his face. He is mysterious and hot when he is dancing and chatting, but when he smiles? He is devastatingly handsome.

"I'm from New York. But my family is from Sicily."

I gulp the rest of my champagne, choking slightly when the bubbles irritate my throat. I look everywhere but at him and that's when I spy my escape. Two empty chairs have been moved into the shadows near the catering entrance. *Perfect.*

Impulsively, I grab his hand and pull him after me, the two of us weaving through the crowd until I arrive at my blessed destination.

"A beautiful woman dragging me off to dark corners of a ballroom. Are you going to seduce me?" he teases.

I snort with laughter.

"I sincerely doubt I would be successful if I were to try as I don't know the faintest thing about seducing strange men in dark corners. I just like to sit in the dark."

"Well, then, perhaps we should find some place even darker?"

The buzz from all the champagne is starting to really hit me now and I feel a strange, floaty sense of freedom. It's nerve-wracking, but also enjoyable. I feel...impulsive.

Chapter 2
STOLEN MOMENTS

Sabine.

"Where did you have in mind?" I giggle as he pulls me along, looking carefully around to see that we aren't being watched before he pulls me behind a curtain and out of sight.

The door next to the kitchen is propped open and I can feel the cool breeze flowing in from outside. A faint hint of cigarette smoke floats out from the alleyway beyond.

When we burst out of the door, my giggles startled the small group of servers and catering staff that had huddled in a corner to smoke. They look up at us guiltily but I have no intention of ratting them out. I'm on an impulsive adventure. Who knows? Maybe I'll even light one up!

"Are you hiding from the infamous Mr. Confi?" my stranger asks, a note of concern in his voice that I find exceedingly flattering.

"Frederick? No. He's an asshole and he gets handsy, but I am more than 90% confident that he wouldn't try anything more scandalous than feeling me up on the dance floor. Especailly since we're in public."

He nods slowly and then pulls out a pack of cigarettes from his vest pocket and offers me one.

I don't smoke. I never have. But now seems as good a time as any. *All the rebellion, all the time.*

He raises his eyebrow at me when I take one and I hold it up to him to light it. "These things will kill you, you know."

I glance over at him and roll my eyes. "Thank you for the update. Just light the damn thing."

"You shouldn't have to endure such indignities just because the man is a friend of your parents. Surely they would intervene if they knew?" He flicks his lighter, and I lean forward slightly and watch the flame ignite the end of the cigarette.

Indignities. That word covers a multitude of sins. I take a long drag of the cigarette, hoping I'm giving off a femme fatale vibe of indifference.

It fails. Miserably.

I am choking as the acrid smoke fills my lungs and I fling the cigarette to the ground. Doubled-over I wheeze and cough until my eyes water. Several chuckles fill the air around me and warm hands grab my shoulders, holding me steady as I try and cough out all the offending smoke.

"Care to try again, *principesa*?" I can't see him in the shadows but I can tell he is smiling at me. I bare my teeth in his general direction and take in a huge gasp of air.

"No, thank you," I mutter weakly, thankful for the darkness that is hiding my flush of embarrassment.

There's something off about this stranger of mine.

He sticks to the shadows and when he is partially visible, it feels like he is purposefully trying to project a dangerous sort of vibe. Unlike the political flunkies, jet setters, and nouveau riche that surround my parents, it's difficult to identify exactly where in the whole shitshow Mr. Tall, Dark, and Mysterious fits in.

He fits the stereotype of literally half the men in here. Tall, dark haired, handsome, decent suit. Rather than the penguin suit most men chose, he is wearing all black with a black tie and a gunmetal grey shirt. He is young. There is no way he is more than a few years older than me. The way he moves his hands, as if he is flexing them constantly, let's me know that he's not as comfortable as he wants to let on. His knuckles are split and bruised as if he was in a bare knuckle boxing match the night before.

He reminds me of a criminal in a James Bond movie. The idea amuses me so much that I decide to cast him as that in my imagination from here on out. *Mafia maybe? He says he's Sicilian. Probably an enforcer. Maybe training to be a bodyguard.*

"What makes you think my parents don't know?" I ask him curiously, rubbing my bare arms to keep from shivering.

A warm jacket is draped over my shoulders and against my better judgement I snuggle into it. It smells like smoke and something citrusy and I pull it around myself like armor.

"You're telling me that your parents are aware that their... *Associate*... Is taking liberties with their daughter and they do nothing?" He sounds so incredulous that I almost tear up. It's been a long time since anyone was outraged on my behalf.

"Well, it's not like they *openly* condone it. They just choose to view it as a necessary evil. My duty is to help my parents portray the image of 'America's Perfect Family' in whatever way I can so that my father can stay a Senator for as long as possible. People like my mother and Mr. Confi work behind the scenes to fund the election campaign and keep my father in office. If feeling me up on a dance floor and making lewd remarks in private keeps Mr. Confi happy, I imagine my mother would consider it a worthwhile cost for what she gets. No one cares what I think. My role is to shut up and smile."

My words come out flippantly but there's a deep ache in my soul as I hear them out loud. I don't want it to be true; but I know that it is. I am important to my mother as a tool, not as a daughter.

I know better than to share family business with a stranger. But there's something about him that makes me want to tell him, to ask for his help. For once, I want someone to rescue me, but I know it's an impossible wish. This isn't a fairy tale, and I'm not a captive princess waiting for a knight in shining armor.

"Have you ever wished you could escape your duties?" I ask him finally, leaning back against the pallets and pulling his blazer around me tighter. "I wish I could every day. My mother tells me there is nothing greater than the duty I have to our family goals—to my father's goals, but this time they're asking too much."

He let out a sharp, wry laugh and took a long drag on his cigarette.

"Duty to family. I understand that more than most people. And yes, I would escape it if I could."

A desperate giggle escapes my lips and he turns to look at me, his eyebrow raised. "I'm sorry," I whisper, trying to hold back the hysterical giggle that threatens to overwhelm me.

I stare at the ground, the pit of my stomach churning with anxiety. For

435

all I know he could actually be a criminal or worse—a journalist. I shouldn't be out here.

I stand up and remove his blazer, "Thanks for letting me borrow this.. And for the rescue. And the smoke."

I try to brush past him, but his hand snakes out and grasps my wrist, stopping me short. My heart rate accelerates and I pause, wavering on the fence for what I want to do and what I should do. The truth is, I want to stay. I want to stay hidden in this strange little corner with this incredibly hot man for the rest of the evening. I feel safe here.

"I know you are thinking about how I make you nervous and how much you dislike events like these. As you should. You are a beautiful rose surrounded by thorns. You deserve to be protected from the dangerous elements all around you."

I stare at him for a full minute before bursting out in raucous laughter.

"Oh, Jesus. That's so good. Thank you. Thank you for that. You're like a Bond villain come to life. I love it. Fuck, I needed that moment." My eyes are actually watering in unexpected mirth.

He looks at me with a thoughtful expression on his face.

"You know," I tell him conspiratorially as I calm down, "I know things too."

Grinning that megawatt smile, he leans in, "Then tell me *principesa!* Tell me what you know!"

"I know that you, my dark-eyed and mysterious new friend, may actually be part of the dangerous crowd that hangs around these events. But you aren't the Big Man you want to be, are you?" I ask shrewdly, "No, you're stuck much like I am and fate has yet to allow you to make your move."

When the lighter flares as he lights another cigarette, his dark eyes pierce through me. He is tall and broad-shouldered. Everything about him screams power. As he stands next to me, I notice he wears a heavy golden ring on his pinky finger.

"And what, *gattina,* will be your move? If it is, as you say, a game and we are merely players?" His deep voice causes me to break out in goosebumps and I carefully lean away from him.

After a long moment, I answer, "I will find a way to just be Sabine. Not

America's Perfect Daughter, not a political princess or whatever else they come up with. I'll create a life that is just mine and leave all this behind."

He blinks and looks at me with those deep, soulful eyes that I want to get lost in. "Shall I have your mother killed for you? A terrible accident, perhaps?"

The seriousness of his question makes my chest fill with laughter again.

"You could try, but alas, you would be killed immediately after, so the loss would be twofold, wouldn't it?" Before he could bluster out his outrage at my assessment, I lean in:

"My friend, you may in fact be an up-and-comer in this world. You have the hunger for it, I can tell. But I have lived and breathed this for my whole life. My mother is protected by very powerful men. Men that outrank you on every level. You wouldn't even get close before they took you down."

"What if I were to tell you that I will one day rule it all? These men you speak of. They will answer to me and me alone." His voice is cold but the intention is there. I believe him.

"Then I would say come find me when you do, we can rule this bullshit together. I am getting out as soon as I can. The only one that will drag me back is the king."

He catches my eye and his gaze makes my heart skip a beat.

"I'm not the king yet, *principesa*, but perhaps tonight you'll settle for a mere prince?"

I don't know what to say. It's like the atmosphere has suddenly changed dramatically and my brain has fizzled along with it. When he looks at me, I am no longer chilled by the cool night air but blazing hot. Buzzed on champagne and drunk on his presence, it's like I'm living out a twisted fairy tale. When he offers his hand to me, I take it.

"Dance with me?"

His dark eyebrows arch with mischief but the expression on his face is pure sin.

I glance around the alley. The catering staff have all returned to their stations. We're entirely alone. There's a tension between us that makes me nervous and excited at the same time.

I nod shyly and he pulls me to him, this time holding me close against him. His body is radiating a raw, primal sort of strength and it calls to me.

This is a stolen moment.

Realistically, I only have minutes left before my mother will send someone out to look for me and if she sees me like this? There will be hell to pay.

Whatever consequences rain down on me will be worth it. I love the feeling of his hands on me as we sway together. When he reaches up and pushes a stray tendril of hair away from my cheek, I melt. He's gentle with me and I get the feeling gentleness is not his default. He's like a dark angel lurking in the shadows with an air of protective danger. I should stay away but I so desperately want to fall into his darkness.

Warm hands frame my waist before sliding down to rest on my ass, cupping me boldly. He gives me a playful little pinch and I squeak in surprise. Heat, awareness, and anticipation course through me causing a cascade of deeply inappropriate thoughts.

When the music from the ballroom changes to a Latin beat and a sensual rhythm, his eyes darken further. The movements of his body are fluid but raw at the same time. I am embarrassed by my inability to keep up with his steps, but he doesn't let me go, he just dips and sways, his body leading us further into the shadows. By the time my back hits the cold, hard brick of the building my heart is pounding erratically and my senses are muddled. All I can see, all I can think about, is him.

He waits three more beats as the music builds up to a crescendo. His hands move behind my neck and when the music pulses, he lowers his lips to mine. He tastes like a heady mix of champagne, cigarettes, and rebellion. I feel unsteady on my feet and he picks me up, his strong arms pinning me between him and the wall. My legs instinctively lock around his waist, pressing my core against the bulging evidence of his arousal. When he draws my bottom lip in between his teeth and bites down, I groan and rock my hips into his.

His lips trail down my neck, the stubble of his beard brushing against my pulse point in the most delicious way.

If this is a dream, I never ever want to wake up.

Instinctively, I arch my body into his further and he groans, looking up at me with wild eyes.

This isn't a dream. It's very, very real.

My body is on fire and I need more of him. I'll beg if I have to.

His eyes ask the question and I am breathless to answer.

"Please... don't stop," I manage before his lips crash back onto mine.

His kisses steal my breath and send me spiraling into this strange sense of ecstasy.

He's in total control and I am at his mercy.

The gentleness is gone. When he cradles my head with his hand anchoring me to him, his other slides between us, pushing my dress up my thighs and running his fingers along the edge of my panties. When he pushes aside the soaked lace and strokes me with his fingers, sensations explode around me and I moan into his mouth. His thumb slides over my clit, rubbing me in quick circles as he dips one finger in and then two. He's teasing me and I growl into his mouth, rocking my hips back to ride his hand.

There are approximately 7,000 reasons why getting fingerbanged by a stranger outside a political fundraiser for my father is a bad idea.

But for the first time in my life, I don't care about the optics or the consequences.

If I'm being truly honest, the idea of getting caught excites me.

My dark stranger might be my downfall.

But I am powerless to resist him.

His fingers move in me faster, answering my need with wicked skill.

He brings me closer and closer until I am writhing against him.

Overwhelming need blots out everything else—I am left only with heart-stopping desire.

When he bites my lip again, I shatter. My entire body vibrates in response as pleasure shoots through me and I come all over his hand.

He strokes me through my aftershocks, trailing kisses down my neck that cause me to shiver and shake. A persistent ringing breaks the silence and it takes me a moment to realize it's his phone. When he withdraws his hand, I feel an intense sense of loss. My legs unclench from around his waist and he helps me slide back down, holding me steady as I wobble and pressing a sweet kiss to my forehead.

Assured that I am not going to fall over, he steps back and looks at his phone before swearing viciously. He taps out a text and then shoves it into his back pocket, his face unreadable.

I don't know what to do.

There's no playbook for the awkward post-orgasm phase of an alleyway hookup.

Biting my lip, I tentatively step towards him, closing the distance between us. He watches me, his dark eyes still flashing with lust. But when I reach for his belt buckle, eager and willing to return the pleasure, his hand stops me.

"I have to go," he says gruffly, turning away.

I pull my hand back and look down, suddenly embarrassed. I busy myself with fixing my dress, suddenly wishing for a mirror to assess the damage before my mother sees me.

"Yeah, I should go too, I'll be missed before too long," my voice trails off and insecurity threatens to make me cry. My emotions are a bigger mess than my hair.

He's a stranger.

No promises were made.

We owe each other nothing.

"Sabine," he calls out softly before walking away, "I will find you again."

To hear my name on his lips gives me a stupid amount of joy. I don't question how he knows it, I just watch as he disappears down the alleyway and back into the shadows.

It's not until he's gone completely that I realize I never caught his name.

I stand out there for several more moments letting my heart rate go back to normal, hoping against hope that maybe he'll come back and steal me away.

But he doesn't.

I can hear emcee begin the opening remarks for the fundraiser and I know my freedom is up.

I turn back, smoothing my hair as best I can. It's time to face the sharks again.

My mother pounces on me the second she sees me.

"Where have you been? What happened to your hair? You are such a disappointment, Sabine. We ask so little of you and you can't even manage it." Under normal circumstances, her whispered vitriol would be like little stabbing pin pricks in my soul, but not tonight. My mind, body, and soul are consumed with someone else.

She grabs my arm and steers me towards the table where my father and Frederick are seated and forces me into a chair next to the older man. I know better than to allow myself to hope that I will get a second reprieve.

I try to relax into my chair, listening to the conversations around me quietly. While I am sipping my water and nibbling at the appetizers, I let my mind wander and the replay of my adventure in the alley plays over and over again. I scan the room, hoping to see him again, but my heart of hearts knows I won't. It's like he's disappeared. My dark angel has flown away.

* * *

Dominic

"You WENT OFFLINE. What the fuck, Dom? Where have you been? I almost called for backup!" Davis gets up in my face as soon as he sees me, almost falling out of the surveillance van in his haste.

I haven't seen him this pissed in a long time. I don't blame him. While my first instinct is always to punch first and ask questions later, Davis is the exception to the rule.

He's my most trusted lieutenant, and he's been like a brother to me. The only one I have since Luca died.

Everything I do is his business.

"We had a complication."

"A complication? What kind of fucking *complication*?" He follows me into the confined space and watches me shrewdly as I stagger to the chair in our mini command post and groan.

441

My impulsive actions have given me an impressive set of blue balls to add to my ever present rage. I can smell her on my fingers and it makes me ache even more. I shouldn't have touched her. I had no right to touch her. She's the job. Her future has been set and it's a tragedy, not a happily ever after.

I lift my fingers up to my face and inhale the scent of her again. They way she came all over my hand, her mesmerizing green eyes wide with surprise and need... it's like a drug. The only drug I want.

"Find out how long Confi plans to be in the building and how many of his men are here," I order, the rage building in my core as I think of what that miserable motherfucker will do to that woman. *Mine. She's mine.*

The idea of letting Confi have her makes me so livid that I want to stalk back out onto that dance floor and execute the sorry piece of shit and save us both the trouble.

She should be nothing to me. Collateral damage. The price of doing business.

But those pale green eyes are burned into my brain now. The touch of her and the taste are ingrained into my psyche. I can have any woman I want, but none of them appeal to me the way this one has.

I can't let her go. I won't.

Jesus Fucking Christ.

Sabine Christophe. America's Perfect Daughter.

Underneath that disguise of wholesome goodness is a spitfire who tastes like honey and sunshine and kisses like a goddess. She is like the first taste of spring after a long, cold winter. The promise of sunshine and brightness on a dreary day and the warmth of a bonfire. *Fuck.*

"He can't have her," I snarl, watching the monitors again.

Davis freezes and stares at me for a long moment. To disobey my father is to court death. We both know it's a gamble. If I fuck with the plans my father has put into play, there's a very real possibility of paying for any rebellion with our lives, and then the girl will go to Confi anyway.

There's a pause and I can hear a muffled conversation as Davis relays the information to the men at his station.

"Confi is present and we think he only has 4 men with him, boss."

A slow smile spreads across my face and I check my watch. That changes things. If Confi was cocky enough to only bring 4 men, and I have 7 of my crew... the odds are strongly in my favor.

"Change of plans, boys. I think we should join this party, don't you?"

According to the plan, I am to extract the *merchandise* at half past 10. That leaves me a little less than three hours to plan and execute a new objective.

"The parents. Get to them and see how much they owe. Then we see what Confi wants more than her."

Davis starts tapping out a text on his phone, setting plays into motion. "You've got it boss."

I turn back to the surveillance feed and scan for our target, my eyes dropping frequently to the blonde-haired beauty seated at the head table. She's scanning the room frequently and I know she's looking for me. I grip the edge of the desk to prevent myself from going back for her and stealing her away.

She's right. I am not the Big Man yet but I meant what I said. She wants a life outside of the arena and strangely, I want her to have it. What she said about duty? I get that. There will never be another life for me. I am a De Marchi. My family is my life. But her? She could have so much more. She could taste freedom.

I will rule over this empire one day and when I do, she will be mine. That kiss has sealed her fate. I can accept nothing less.

I'll be back for you, little spitfire. One day, you'll see. You're destined to be mine.

Chapter 3
Watched Over

Sabine
Present

Turns out Hot Yoga is actually really fucking hot.

And not the kind of hot where you lay out and soak up the rays, letting the sunshine warm you into a happy blob of languid contentment. Or the kind of hot when you collapse on a bed, exhausted by pleasure from a talented lover.

No.

This is something else.

It's the kind of hot where sweat pools on every surface of your skin, weird smells permeate the room, and the floor feels like lava.

You slide and move around the room like some sort of swamp monster, contorting your body into strange positions while a blonde-haired goddess in $300 worth of athleisure wear tells you she's your spiritual guide for the next hour. She makes it feel like she is doing you a service to charge you $90 for the privilege of sharing 'energy' with a bunch of strangers who may or may not believe that deodorant is a state of mind.

I stagger out of the class and wish for the thirtieth time that my therapist had recommended something more reasonable and less....wet to deal with my stress. There has to be a happy medium between sweating with strangers and their natural aromatherapy and living with the constant anxiety that is my life. She tells me that my previous coping mechanisms of wine and avoidance aren't working but maybe I need a second opinion.

Outside the studio, the breeze is like a welcome balm and does more for lifting my mood than any amount of patchouli and cucumber-crystal infused water ever could.

Unlocking my car, I throw my bags into the back and turn on my A/C. My Bluetooth kicks on and a piercing alert sounds as the automated voice reads my phone.

444

"You have eight missed calls and six voicemails."

Dread fills me. I ask my automated assistant to read the missed call list with a ball of nerves in my gut.

"You have eight missed calls from Mother, The and six voicemails from Mother, The. Do you wish to dial this number?"

Fuck.

There is no amount of yoga, hot or otherwise, that will save me from this. Few things can ruin my day faster than eight missed calls from my mother.

No matter how far away I move from her or try to establish my own life, she still tries to control everything. My therapist said I should stop letting her do it, but it would probably be easier to stop the ocean from having waves.

I wait until I am pulling my tiny Honda out of the parking lot and turning onto the main road before hitting 'call'.

She answers immediately and I have the presence of mind to turn the volume down on my headset quickly.

"Where were you? Why didn't you answer your phone? Eight missed calls, Sabine. *Eight.* What if there had been an emergency? What if I were lying dead in a hospital somewhere? What then?"

Her rapid fire questions are shrill, and I wince at the sharpness of the tone. The key to handling my mother is to... not handle her. Just let her rant. I don't care what my therapist says -- avoidance is a valid coping mechanism.

I slowly release the breath I have been holding and count to three before answering.

"Hello, Mother. I apologize, I had an appointment and turned my phone off. I called you back as soon as I saw the missed calls." I try to exude a sense of calm into my voice but talking to my mother is probably the least calming thing in the world.

"An appointment? There is nothing on your calendar regarding an appointment? I had Belinda check. What were you doing that was so important that you felt compelled to ignore your mother? Don't you dare lie to me, young lady."

I am a fucking adult, you crazy, meddling old bat! I don't have to tell you where I am all the time! I'm 28 years old!

I take another calming breath while my brain flounders for an acceptable lie. There's nothing wrong with what I was just doing, I just don't want to tell her. I hate giving her any information about my life that could be accurate. It gives her power.

Pedicure? No way. My home pedi will definitely not meet muster. Wax? She would probably want to see it to verify. Therapist? She'd set her assistant Belinda to the task of figuring out why I was in therapy.

"I was meeting with a consultant. A—a confidence consultant. You know. To improve my speaking. For Dad's campaign. She does... hypnotherapy. It's a very cutting edge therapy."

For three whole seconds my mother is silent on the other line and I almost congratulate myself on achieving something few people have ever achieved: getting my mother to shut up.

"Oh please, Sabine. The campaign doesn't need you to formally speak. We need you to show up and look pretty in the pictures. Surely you can manage a few simple sentences to the press from time to time and make small talk to the donors without a *confidence coach*."

The scathing reply shouldn't surprise me. My mother is known among her inner circle as a mercurial and biting woman, but I feel tears prick against my lashes anyway.

"You'll get the opportunity to show off what you learned tomorrow night. You have a date. Lawrence St. Martin—you will be charming, you will laugh at his jokes, and you will smile pretty for all the pictures. Do you understand me?"

My mother's voice comes through my Bluetooth loudly and I swallow a curse. The *or else* part of her statement didn't need to be verbalized. I know what's at stake as well as she does. The price of my freedom is my cooperation. It's been this way for ten long years. It doesn't matter that I am 28 years old and living on my own. Once a Christophe, always a Christophe. My father is on track to be nominated for Vice President this year and if my mother has her way, he'll follow that term up with a White House run for President. The agreement is clear: toe the line, help out with the campaign in whatever way possible, and don't cause a scandal. Noncompliance is met swiftly and my mother's reach is very, very long.

I know my role in my family's empire. I have been trained for it my entire life. If the price of my freedom is to occasionally serve as arm candy, God knows I will do it. I've appeared in public with a wide variety of men hand-picked by my mother to advance our agenda. From sports stars to minor royalty to business moguls old enough to be my father—I've done my duty and laughed on their arm, smiling pretty for the pictures.

But those men knew it was a means to an end.

There was no pretense of a relationship.

We each served a purpose to the other.

Lawrence St. Martin serves no such purpose and is bound by no such rules.

He's the sleaziest asshole I have ever met, and I grew up in the political arena. It doesn't help that he's the heir to a bank vault full of old money and in possession of even older family connections.

I have spent the better part of 15 years enduring his constant presence at political events, and the idea of being alone with him is not only distasteful but alarming. The more I rebuff him, the more he views it as a challenge. An involuntary shudder runs through me at the thought of going on a date with him.

"If you want me to do this, I have to have rules Mom," I finally continue, my heart beating rapidly as I try to assert my boundaries, "One: he doesn't touch me more than is absolutely necessary, two: I don't go home with him or have any media spin that implies that we are more than just family friends out for dinner, and three: if he gets handsy, I am allowed to leave."

The line is silent for so long that I think perhaps we got disconnected. Finally, my mother speaks and I can hear the tightness of anger in her voice.

"How *dare* you insinuate such things about Lawrence! His family is one of our closest allies. He is charming and has had a crush on you for ages. You will doll yourself up and you will attend to him in *any* way he asks, and you will do it with a smile. He is an upstanding member of society from a good family. He is not some sort of predatory monster."

My heart drops and I can hear ringing in my ears. I can read between the lines as well as the next woman and my mother basically wrote it out in sharpie for me. *Attend to him in any way he asks? Fuck. No. I may smile*

447

pretty for the cameras but I refuse to be pimped out for votes, business deals or anything else.

I choose my words carefully, my hand reaching for the small pearl pendant I wear around my neck. The smooth orb is comforting and gives me the strength to continue on.

"I am not accusing Lawrence of anything, Mom," I start, lowering my voice to placate her, "It's only that the media being what they are, the optics could be really negative for dad if it looks like his daughter is in an...untoward... relationship of some kind with one of his donors. I'm thinking of the campaign. Of course."

The lie comes so easily and I hold my breath, hoping that it will be enough to get my mother to back off the intensity.

"Your concern is noted, but unnecessary. It's a *date* Sabine, it's not a marriage. I had Belinda drop by your condo with a dress for you. The car will arrive promptly at 7 to pick you up. And Sabine? Do *not* disappoint me again."

The line went dead and I let my forehead fall onto my steering wheel in defeat. No amount of happy thoughts of a life without the press, hidden away up in the mountains with just my art, would stop the tears that leaked from my eyes.

I've lived my entire life in a gilded cage and all I've ever wanted is to be free.

CHAPTER 4

Sabine

S ixteen times.

That's how many times I have removed Lawrence's greasy paws from my knee during this clusterfuck of a date.

The next time he does it, I might stab him with my fork. It's clearly the only way he'll learn any manners. At this point, I don't even care if I end up getting injured in the process. The idea of driving a fork through his hand is so deeply satisfying I am minorly concerned that it might become a new kink of mine. *Memo to self: discuss with therapist.*

Draining my glass of wine, I try to ease my phone out of my wristlet to check the time. I chose this restaurant specifically because they close at 9 p.m. and I am alarmed to see that it's 9:15 and the staff are still serving. I know it's because they know who I am.

The only silver lining is that Lawrence doesn't require a conversation partner in order to fill uncomfortable silence. He is more than able to carry an entire conversation on his own. The more he drinks, the more verbose he gets. Thankfully, he has required my response on exactly none of these topics and seems quite content to just talk at me. *Charming.*

I motion for the server and ask for the check and that shuts him up. He rubs his hands together and licks his lips, much to my disgust.

"Ready for part two of this date, baby?" He asks, his voice slurring from the many drinks he has consumed. "Your place or mine?"

I quickly hand a wad of cash to the server and thank him before turning to my date. Lawrence is standing with his hand outstretched to take mine before I can even get my phone out to text my driver..

"Yours," I force my lips into a semblance of a smile to prevent any further outbursts. I decide to wait until the last minute to clarify that he will be going to his place and I will be going to mine.

No sense in making a scene.

Scenes end up in the tabloids.

Tabloids means more quality time with my mother and her battleax of an assistant Belinda doing damage control.

No, thank you.

Lawrence pulls me to my feet and I cringe as he wraps his arms around me, leaning in as if to kiss me. I turn my head at the last minute and his lips land in my hair. His hot breath in my ear makes my skin crawl.

"Ever the minx, Sabine! Don't worry. As soon as I get you home, I'll show you the proper way to thank me for this date."

He slaps my ass and I yelp in surprise, startling the staff that hover around us.

"Baby girl likes it rough," Lawrence's words are slurring even more now. I hate him with the burning passion of a thousand flaming suns but I just grit out a pained half-smile and count to ten in my head. As much as I might like to stab him with a bread knife, that would look really, really bad.

"Should we wait for the car here?" I ask, trying to extricate myself from his sweaty embrace with some semblance of grace, avoiding the eyes of the staff. I can feel the pity in their stares when they look at me. Belinda will have already ensured they all signed an NDA before we even arrived. They won't intervene. No one ever does. *At least not since Him.*

A memory flashes in my mind of dark chestnut hair and even darker eyes. *My dark angel.* He had intervened once. What started as a rescue off the dance floor turned into stolen moments in the shadows filled with wandering hands, soft lips and pleasure that had singed my soul. But then it was over. He disappeared, leaving me with an aching need that has never been fully satisfied. I looked for him and asked around but no one would tell me his name. He wasn't on the guest list. He never came back for me.

"I wanna smoke," Lawrence interrupts my memory and pushes me towards the door. The brick wall of reality crashes down on me and I check my phone. Lawrence is a handful when he's sober but he's impossible when he's drunk.

There's no dark angel waiting in the shadows to save me from this.

Outside Lawrence is struggling with his lighter and throws it to the ground in frustration.

"Goddamn it!" he screams out, kicking it across the street like a child having a tantrum.

I edge a little further away from him and contemplate calling a ride-share service or a taxi. At this point, I'm not even opposed to hitchhiking. I just want to get away.

The street is empty and the staff of the restaurant has already turned out the lights. An eerie feeling pricks the back of my neck and I feel like I'm being watched again.

Lawrence stalks over to me, still muttering under his breath about lighters and wanting a smoke. He grabs me from behind, holding my body up against his. I try to shrug him off but he's so much bigger than me and he doesn't budge.

His hands roam freely across my body, cupping my breasts while his hot breath blows into my ear. I want to vomit.

"Give me some sugar, baby. Show Lawrence how much you appreciate him, hmm?"

His breath smells foul and his stubble scratches against my cheek as I squirm.

"MMmm, no. No, thank you. Please don't." I claw at his arm but he just tightens his grip, pulling me off balance.

"Playing hard to get, baby? I like a challenge. You're *America's Perfect Daughter*. Maybe you don't know how to please a real man? Is that it? You too shy to tell me, baby? Why don't I show you how it goes?"

By the time he has finished his vicious little monologue, he has wound his fist in my hair. The aggression he showed earlier is more pronounced and when he yanks on my head, the pain is white-hot. My control snaps.

Flailing, I try to drive my elbow into his gut and stomp on his foot but he is able to dodge me. When I throw my head back in an effort to smash his face, he jerks my head away and brings his hand up to my throat. His large palm presses against my windpipe and his fingers wrap around my neck, tightening just enough to make me desperate.

I gasp for air.

"You're going to come with me, Sabine. You aren't going to make a fucking sound because if you do, you'll be on the cover of every newspaper in the nation tomorrow. Is that what you want? To go from *America's Perfect Daughter* to *America's Perfect Slut*? That's what they'll say when they see you on your knees in front of me."

My blood runs cold and tears drip down my cheeks.

"Lawrence, please. Please let me go," The pressure on my throat makes it hard to speak and we stumble as he drags me towards the dark alley.

"Bitch, you have led me on for years. You owe me this," he snarls, shoving me in front of him towards the wall of the alley.

My hands are shaking. I know I have pepper spray in my bag but fear and adrenaline make it hard to think.

"You scared, baby? I like that. I can feel it. It makes it so much better for me," His voice has dropped to a husky whisper and I am fighting the bile in my throat. I kick out in desperation and my foot hits his knee but it's not enough to drop him.

"Cunt, you'll pay for that!" he roars, backhanding me across the face before slamming the back of my head into the wall with such a loud bang that light flashes behind my eyes and I crumple. As I slowly slide to the ground, stunned, there's a flurry of movement in the corner of my eye.

People. Other people.

"Help me," I whisper hoarsely, trying to move my hand out to reach for them.

There's shouting and a muffled grunt before a gasp of pain. Something heavy falls against me, trapping me against the wall.

An overwhelming metallic and sickly sweet smell permeates my senses and I struggle to place it before it becomes clear. *Blood. The smell is blood.*

My head feels like it's been split in two and my vision is blurry but I am able to turn my head enough to see to look at what fell on me.

It's Lawrence. He's slumped over and blood is pouring out of a wide cut on his neck. His eyes are wide and lifeless.

I want to scream and throw his body off me.

My internal self-preservation is urging me to do whatever I can to get away, but I can't.

I'm frozen.

Everything around me feels like it's happening in slow motion and out of focus.

Low voices are talking quickly in a foreign language. I can't place it. I think it might be Italian or Spanish. Someone touches my shoulder and I strike out, my fist landing on a very firm chest.

"Easy, *gattina*. You're safe now."

The voice is deep and soothing as strong arms pick me up and nestle me close. I instinctively curl into the broad chest of whomever is carrying me. My vision is so blurry that it makes me nauseated so I keep my eyes closed. The person carrying me stops suddenly and there is a furious conversation over my head before I am carefully transferred to another set of arms. I am so dizzy that I feel like I might pass out.

I feel something wet wipe over my face before someone cups my cheek and shines a bright light into each of my eyes.

"You're going to feel a quick pinch and then it will be ok, *cara mia*."

My mouth is cottony and I can't answer. I feel the pinch and then the world falls blissfully into black.

Chapter 5
Guest

Sabine

My dreams are hazy, shapeless shadows moving in and out. Occasionally they speak to me but I can't seem to speak back. I am tumbling through a wave and everytime I get close to breaking the surface, I am sucked back down into the darkness.

I don't know how long I flounder, lost to the abyss, but when my eyes finally flutter open, squinting in the bright light, I know something terrible has happened.

Everything feels wrong.

I am in an unfamiliar room. The furnishings are sleek and modern with dark wooden paneling and brilliant chrome accents.

I am lying in the center of an enormous bed and there's an IV line taped neatly to my hand but it's not connected to anything.

A hint of sunshine is shining through an oblong window set unusually high on the wall.

A flat-screen panel is mounted on the wall directly across from the bed but it's blank, the reflective surface showing me only a shadow of myself.

My head aches and my throat is raw. I sit up and immediately regret it. A wave of nausea and dizziness hits me and I slump over.

Straining my ears, I can hear nothing.

I reach over to the bedside table and carefully switch on the lamp, wincing as the bright light hits my eyes.

Looking down, I see that I am dressed in an unfamiliar tank top and shorts. Inch by inch, I run my hands over my body, searching for injuries.

I am sore and there are fresh bandages on my legs and bruises on my arms.

My long hair is braided and I feel a neat row of stitches along my temple.

Wincing, I try to remember what happened but my mind feels hazy like my dreams.

454

Moving slowly, I ease myself out of bed and pad over the soft, lush carpet to the door. Turning the handle, I try to open it but it's locked. I look around the room for anything that might help but there is nothing, not even a phone.

Returning to the door, I try again, pounding and calling for help but no one answers.

A slow slide of tears make their way down my face as I sit back on the bed, hugging my knees to my chest.

I don't know where I am.

I don't know what happened to me.

Someone brought me here... and they aren't letting me go.

* * *

Dominic

"SHE'S AWAKE, Boss. We're ready for Phase 2 when you say the word."

Davis smirks at me as he pops his head into my makeshift office without knocking. He's lucky that we're so close. He knows the rules. When it's just us, he's my brother and he can speak freely. When we're in front of the men, he's my lethal lieutenant ready to shoot first and ask questions later at my behest. We're a team and he's the only one in this crazy, fucked up world that I truly trust.

The reason for his smirk is splayed out in front of me. Hundreds of glossy photographs from a well-worn file have filled every inch of the conference table. All of them have the same smiling face with pale green eyes and straw blond hair. *Sabine.*

Davis is the only one who knows the full extent of my obsession. He was there when it started and he's been there every step of the way as I set my plans in motion and built my empire from the ground up.

No one intended for me to take control of the De Marchi organization at such a young age. When my father got caught in the crossfire, everyone assumed control would pass back to one of my uncles.

They thought wrong.

For those that underestimated me it was a deadly mistake.

Davis and I fought side by side, leaving behind a river of chaos and blood, and we emerged on the other side.

When I rebuilt this family, Davis was there to enforce the new way of doing things.

Together we have expanded and grown past the wildest dreams of my father's generation.

Sabine was always in my plan. For ten years I've waited for her, watching in the shadows as she went about her life. She was always supposed to join me. Our destinies are intertwined and she is mine.

Just not like this.

Not because of Frederick *fucking* Confi.

I should have killed him when I had the chance all those years ago. He will never leave her alone. I know that now.

I twirl the knife on the table, wishing I could slam it deep into that slimy motherfucker's face again and again.

My blood is boiling and I need to hurt something. I slam my fists on the table with a roar. Seeing her covered in blood last night—the sunshine missing from her eyes, my temper is razor thin and I will snap. It's only a matter of time. No one puts their hands on my property and lives.

Pulling a second file over to me, I look it over. Lawrence St. Martin. He dared to touch what is mine. He injured her. I slit his throat and watched his lifeblood drain onto the street like the garbage he is but it doesn't seem like enough. It will never be enough.

Taking her off the street was impulsive but I couldn't leave her there. Not after what he did.

When a De Marchi vows vengeance, it is done.

To my men, she is merely an opportunity that fell in our lap. A chance to make money while sending a giant fuck you to our enemies.

Only Davis knows the truth.

Sabine isn't an accidental paycheck. She's the sun that we all orbit around. She just doesn't know it yet. And now, after 10 long years, I finally have her in my possession.

"What have we learned about the date?"

OBSESSION

I can't take my eyes off the photos while Davis gives his report, rattling off her health stats since she's arrived in our care.

The more he tells me, the more I want to destroy everyone who has ever even looked at her wrong. I would rip the world apart piece by piece for her.

"Have Giorgio meet her, befriend her and make her feel comfortable. Let him be the one to let her explore. She doesn't need to know about me yet."

Davis pauses clearly confused, but he understands I never do anything without a plan. He nods and exits to carry out my orders, leaving me alone with my thoughts.

Sabine's smiling face looks back at me from the stack of photos. I flip through them, easily finding my favorites.

There was her vacation in Jamaica a few years ago with the teal bikini that cupped her ass like a lover and her blonde hair streaming out behind her in a wave of woven gold. Two men were rude to her in a nightclub during that vacation and I ensured they were properly punished.

I flip the photos and land on the photo of her clad head to toe in white silk. She had attended a charity event that night and looked like an angel. It was the first event that featured one of the art pieces that launched her career. It sold for well over the expected asking price to an anonymous collector. It sits in a place of pride in my cabin in Aspen.

Flipping again, I land on my absolute favorite photo. She's in the bath and her hair pulled up in a messy bun on top of her head. She is half submerged in the bubbles and she's holding a glass of red wine, only the tips of her feet are visible. Her eyes are closed, as if she is relaxing after a long hard day. Her public mask is stripped away and all I can see is her delicate vulnerability.

It is intoxicating to me. My cock hardens with desire as I look at her and I shift uncomfortably in my chair. My beautiful spitfire. I have waited so long to have her. To taste her again and claim her as mine.

I pick up my phone and click to the surveillance camera I had installed in the detention suite. There's activity in the bathroom. Steam clouds my view but I can see the outline of her glorious ass as she bends over and wraps a towel around her hair. My cock throbs again, aching for release. The pounding need I have to be inside her grows stronger with every moment.

Sabine Christophe is mine.

She was mine the second she told me she would be the Queen to my King.

When our lips touched that fateful night, she sealed our destinies together.

The sooner my plan is complete, the sooner I can finally slake the ten years of desire I have had for her.

Sabine

I'VE SHOWERED. I've gone through every drawer and every cabinet. I've pounded on the door, crying hoarsely for help.

No one came.

My fear is quickly turning to anger and my anxiety is spiraling to new depths.

When the door finally creaks open and a tall, handsome older man dressed entirely in white appears—I want to throw something at him.

"Who are you? Why am I here? What happened?" I demand, looking frantically around the room for some sort of weapon. I reach for the lamp, curling my hand around the stem but he just laughs and produces a plate of food.

"You are here because you are meant to be here, Miss Christophe. You were injured and we rendered aid. We do not mean you harm. My name is Giorgio. I am here to assist you during your stay with us."

Blinking, I put the lamp back down and step back. I am at war with my senses. I both want to defend myself and scarf down as much of whatever is on that plate as humanly possible.

The man seems to understand that and he carefully places the plate of BBQ on the table and offers me a full set of silverware -- including a steak knife before stepping back and allowing me space to circle my food like some sort of feral hyena.

It really does smell divine, and once I'm confident that he's not going to attack me, I dig in.

He says nothing, just watches me eat with an amused smile on his face.

"I'm Sabine. But I guess you already know that." I say around a mouthful of potato. My mother would be horrified by everything in this scene. That thought actually makes me enjoy it even more. *Mommy issues? Check.*

"You said I was injured, I don't really remember what happened. Can you help me remember?" I finally ask, feeling sheepish for my outburst.

I take another bite, savoring the fresh vegetables and ponder my predicament.

"You were attacked several days ago. My men saw you and came to your aid. You were injured so we brought you here."

"I was attacked? Who attacked me? Oh..."A sick feeling started crawling over my skin as I remember Lawrence and the aftermath of our so-called date.

A flood of images crash into my brain. Lawrence forcing himself on me. The shine of his lifeless eyes as blood poured out of the wound on his throat. My stomach rolls.

"Oh my god, oh my god, I'm going to be sick."

I stagger over to the bench at the end of the bed and sit down heavily. Bringing my knees up to my chest, I wrap my arms around my body hugging myself close. The tears that threatened to fall earlier are falling freely now.

Giorgio grabs a glass of juice and comes over to me, staying just out of reach as he hands it to me.

"Miss Christophe, you are safe here. The man who attempted to harm you will never harm you again. Our men got to you in time and they alerted us immediately. Here, drink this. You've suffered quite a shock."

I take a sip of the juice and notice he's right, it does help a little bit.

"Your men? They saved me? You saved me?" I try to blink back the tears but they are still falling freely.

"We got there in time to stop the worst, *bella*, I am only sorry we were not there sooner to stop the entire ordeal." He steps closer and reaches out tentatively and places his warm hand on my forearm and it comforts me.

"I remember hitting my head and then there was so much blood.

Lawrence is dead, isn't he? Do I need to make a statement to the police? Have my parents been notified? What about the press?" The flood of questions tumble out of my mouth, one after another.

"The man who attacked you will no longer be a problem," he said smoothly, "As for the rest of it? We prefer to keep our privacy intact and we assumed that you would be the same. The police have not been involved and our private doctor is on the premises on standby to attend to your injuries. We have elected to allow you to make your own notifications as to who needs to know you are here."

Gratitude swells in me at his discretion. To know I don't have to deal with my parents, Belinda, OR the press right away is a gigantic relief.

Looking around the room again, I note the quiet opulence of the furnishings. Whoever this guy was, he definitely had a hefty bankroll.

Dragging my eyes up to meet his, I manage a wobbly smile. "I guess, I owe you my life. Thank you for saving me. Do I get to know who you work for?"

He doesn't answer right away, instead he offers me his hand to help me up and leads me over to the chair where the rest of my lunch is waiting. The first touch of his hand on mine gives me a little shock and I am suddenly aware that he is fully dressed and I am in a glorified set of underwear.

"I work for the De Marchi Family."

The name rings another bell but my head is so achy that I don't spend much time dwelling on it.

"My God, this is so good," I say around a mouthful of BBQ ribs. My mother would be utterly incandescent with rage if she saw my table manners, but something about Giorgio puts me at ease.

"I will give your compliments to my Chef," he stands to leave and then reaches under the table to hand me a shopping bag.

"I sent someone out for clothing since yours was... no longer usable."

I blush and look down at the clothes I am currently wearing, suddenly unsure of the timeline of events of the night before.

"Um, did you....?" My voice trails off as I realize *someone* must have undressed me and cleaned me up while I was unconscious.

"My housekeeper Anabel cleaned you up when you were brought here.

She thought you would sleep more comfortably if you were in different clothing," he answers my unasked question and I feel another pang of gratefulness for his discretion.

"Thank you. Seriously."

"I will leave you now, Miss Christophe. You are welcome to stay as long as you need."

The second he disappears back through the door, I relax against my chair and take another bite of lunch, my mind much more at ease now.

Chapter 6
On a Fucking Boat

Sabine

I feel like I'm being watched. Again. It's a constant feeling I have had for years. But it's especially strong today. My intuition is usually quite attuned to this, but when I look around the room, I see no one. A cursory examination of the light fixtures doesn't reveal any blinking lights or spy cameras.

I feel like a bit of an idiot for even looking.

Giorgio has been nothing but kind to me and here I am searching the gorgeous suite he has put me up in for cameras.

He doesn't even give me the creeper vibe. Powerful? Yes. Absurdly wealthy? Absolutely. But a creeper? Not so much.

Certainly not the kind that would wire a bedroom with cameras. If anything, I feel freer here than I do when I'm at home. If anyone in my life is going to create a loop of surveillance footage of me just existing, it would be my parents... not a complete stranger.

I write the feeling off as an overreaction and continue getting dressed.

The long jersey knit dress that the housekeeper, Anabel, acquired for me is marvelous and I hope I get to meet her before I leave so I can give her a hug of gratitude. Being clean and having something to change into goes a long way in helping me cope with the horror of the night before.

The purple, finger-tip shaped bruises on my arm ache and my mind flies back to the exact words Giorgio had used when she had asked about Lawrence.

"He won't be a problem anymore."

With considerable effort I am able to push the memories of his body falling on me away. *There was so much blood.*

For the five-hundredth time I wonder about the De Marchi family that Giorgio claims to work for. They could be anyone. Ultra-wealthy eccentrics. Organized crime. Hell, they could be a cartel for all I knew.

OBSESSION

My parents have ties to all sorts of criminal organizations. They're equal-opportunity when it comes to funding. Mother shields my dad from most of it, but I'm not blind. I've seen the scary Russian dudes who come for closed-door meetings after-hours. The suspicious circumstances by which political rivals have dropped out of key races. The whispered conversations at fundraisers and the men who travel with an entourage that barely conceals the outlines of their guns under their expensive suit jackets.

If it meant accomplishing their goals, my mother would make a deal with the Devil himself.

But that doesn't necessarily mean everyone else would.

I wonder if Giorgio will tell me the truth if I ask him outright. He's been extremely forthcoming thus far, and I have no reason to believe he is lying.

To my disappointment, it's not Giorgio who comes to my door next, but rather a tall behemoth of a man in a dark grey suit that he is bursting out of. He is carrying a small shopping bag.

He steps into the room and acknowledges me with a very regal nod. I feel like I am in some sort of movie.

"Miss Christophe, my name is Davis. I assist the De Marchi family with the management of their affairs. If you are done with your lunch, I would be happy to escort you on a tour of your accommodations."

I'm staring.

It's so rude, but I can't stop.

The disconnect between the Hulk Smash body and the Prince William accent is breaking my already bruised brain.

This man is the butler? Seriously? More like an enforcer.

I finally pull my shit together and look away, giving him a faint smile.

"Thank you, Davis. I prefer to be addressed by my first name. Sabine is fine. I would love a tour but, alas, I seem to have misplaced my shoes."

Like some sort of magic wish-granting genie, he hands me the shopping bag without speaking and I peek inside. A pair of stylish sandals are inside and I know without trying them on that they will be a perfect fit.

Sliding them on my feet, I beam up at Davis and together we walk through the corridor. The hallway is narrow and short, leading to a strange rounded door. As I step through it, I turn to Davis in confusion, "What kind of hotel puts boat doors in the hallway? That's so... Unnecessary?"

Davis' eyes twinkle and he gestures for me to walk up the spiral staircase.

I get halfway up and I see the sunlight. At the top I see a horizon of brilliant blue. *Oh. Oh no. No. No. No.*

"We're on a BOAT?!"

My screech is high-pitched and panicked. I can tell it startles the shit out of Davis and another man who is lounging on a couch to the side of the stairs springs up in a defensive position.

It doesn't matter.

I don't care if I scare them enough to piss themselves.

I'm on a boat.

A boat in the middle of the ocean.

I hate boats.

Fuuuck.

When I was a kid, my parents made me go to a summer camp for one summer that prided itself on being 'rigorous and physically strenuous' as a way to build character.

I rowed that summer. I rowed the whole damn summer long. And when we weren't rowing well enough, the counselor would tip the boat and we would have to swim. I have never been a strong swimmer and thus lived in fear of anything relating to the lake.

That was years ago, obviously, but even today I have a healthy respect for lakes and a genuine fear of the ocean.

My hands are clenched around the railing and I feel dizzy.

Everything outside is blue. A deep, sparkly, ocean-y blue. *I do not want to die in the ocean.*

"Miss? You're safe here. I promise," Davis' voice is placating as he pries my fingers off the railing with some difficulty and reattaches my hand to his arm. I clutch him tightly and together we slowly walk through the salon to a set of club chairs that are bolted to the floor.

As far as doomed water-vessels go, this one is a nice one. Everything is very tasteful and elegant. It screams money.

The second my ass hits the chair, my head is on my knees and I try to regulate my breathing.

"Why *the fuck* am I on a boat?" I whine.

'Technically, it's a yacht." A new voice sounds from behind me and I look up to glare at them.

"Excuse me?" I ask frostily.

"You keep calling this a boat. It's not a boat. It's a yacht. There's a difference. This isn't Uncle Joe's fishing charter. It's a fucking YACHT."

The arrogance in his voice makes me lose my fear for a hot minute and I turn around completely to face him with fire in my eyes.

He is an absolute mountain of a man. He reminds me of a Viking and his arms are barely contained by the strangely preppy business casual attire he is wearing. I can see the outline of extensive tattoos curling up his bicep through the thin white shirt. I follow the line of ink as it peeks out around his neck and then raise my eyes to his scruffy dark stubble and finally a pair of cool, hazel eyes that are looking at me with something akin to a challenge blazing in their depths.

He exudes a sense of danger from his pores and it does something to me. My body is in limbo, living somewhere between anger, fear and... arousal? I scoff, shaking my head as if to clear it before glaring back up at him. If *mountain man wants to play, I'll play.*

I try to remember my cool. The press may call me America's Perfect Daughter but I've had to build some survival skills in order to live in my parents world. Skills that enable me to *handle* any kind of Alpha asshole that comes my way.

I stand and will myself not to shake. This is a power move and there can be no shaking in power moves.

Taking two steps towards him, I raise my chin in defiance and look him up and down, slowly.

"Sorry, I don't know that it's big enough to be a yacht...so until otherwise, I'll call it a *boat* if I want to. Maybe even a *dinghy.* Who knows? I could go as far as to call it a *raft.*"

Davis chokes behind me but I don't look back. It's a cheap shot and probably an inaccurate one but it's easy pickings and I am mad. The guy in front of me puffs out his chest, his dark eyes flashing at me again. His teeth are bared in a snarl and he takes a step towards me in anger.

"Listen, bitch.."

I *hate* being called a bitch.

Hate it.

Add in the fact it's a strange man who calls me that?

I'm ready for war.

All the fear I should have had, all the apprehension from being on the water, and all the unknowns should have made me cower in the corner but I find myself walking towards the behemoth with murder in my eyes.

"Who are you calling *bitch*, you steroid-sucking bastard? *No. You* don't get to call me that. You don't get to call *any* woman that. You back *the fuck up*, do you understand me? I have had a supremely shitty day. I don't know who you are, or why I'm on a goddamn BOAT in the middle of the OCEAN, and I do not need your commentary. Get out of my face."

He looks like he might hit me. Davis steps around me deftly and comes between us. He looks murderous.

"Henri," Davis is in the large man's face and his voice is like molten steel. "Miss Christophe is our guest and is to be afforded *all of our hospitality as such*. I would hate to have to report to *her host* that she has been mistreated after such an express directive."

Henri pales a little bit but he still looks at me furiously. The code that Davis is clearly speaking in intrigues me and I jump on it.

"Davis, *who* is my host? Who is in charge here? If it's not you and it's obviously not Fuckface Mountain over here. Who is it? Who do you work for? I want to talk to the person in charge!"

Henri growls at me and takes another step forward, causing Davis to pull a very large gun from a holster at the small of his back. I gasp but Davis doesn't look at me. He calmly levels the weapon at Henri's head and his voice is flat and matter-of-fact when he speaks.

"Henri, last chance. Leave."

With a snarl like an angry bear, Henri stalks off towards the deck. I not-so-secretly wish for him a wave to crash over the boat and sweep his sorry ass out to sea.

466

I am still glowering after him when Davis turns to me, the expression he has had on his face is gone and so is the gun. But his patient calm has also disappeared and he seems harder somehow.

"Miss Christophe, I apologize for the disruption. I brought you up here in hopes it may ease your anxiety about the situation in which you now find yourself. You may avail yourself to our hospitality and the amenities of the yacht, or you may return to your room and stay there under guard. These are your only options. I have no patience for childish behavior. Are you going to behave yourself or shall I have you taken away?"

I swallow the angry retort the moment I see the seriousness on his face. He means it. As much as being out in the salon gives me anxiety, I really don't want to go back to the room I woke up in. My head nods in momentary submission to the rules.

"Who are you really? If I am on a fucking boat in the middle of the ocean, this isn't just a good samaritan rescue is it? Is it ransom? Whatever it is, my parents will pay it, I'm sure of it." I plead quietly, suddenly fighting off the urge to break down and cry.

Davis steps closer to me and places his hands on my cheeks.

"I can't tell you that. But all will be explained in short order. I promise."

It's not the answer I want.

It's not the answer I need.

Ignoring his warning about childlike behavior, I lash out. When I am under extreme stress, I tend to go back to the basics. As a petite person, my basics have to be fine-tuned to meet the rest of the world. Taking advantage of how close he is to me, I drive my knee up and land a direct hit on his balls. I follow it up quickly with a sharp elbow to the back of his neck. I score the element of surprise as he hunches over, holding onto the chair for support.

Knowing I only have seconds before he recovers enough to catch me, I dart through the hallway leading away from the salon, running through doors and slamming them shut behind me. I hear shouts as I run and my heart sinks.

Running is futile.

A part of me knows that.

I am on a boat, and an unfamiliar one at that.

Boats, even the super-rich-person-yacht that this appears to be, have a finite amount of space.

An alarm goes off and little white lights start flashing in the hallway. *Shit*. With a gulp, I spy a door to my immediate left and run inside it, bolting it shut and leaning against the door.

It's completely dark.

The sounds of large footsteps and shouts echo in the hallway and I watch anxiously through the peephole but no one makes a move to look in this room or even stop to investigate it.

I breathe a sigh of relief, resting my head against the wooden door for a moment.

Suddenly, an eerie sense of awareness falls over me. It's the feeling I get sometimes when I am by myself in public. Like I am being watched.

I'm not alone.

Very slowly I turn around, squinting in the darkness.

A large hand claps over my mouth, drawing me up against a hard, broad chest. Their arms are like steel bands, holding me tight. The cold metal of a gun is pressed against my forehead.

"Well, well, well. What have we here?"

"Oh my god, please don't hurt me. I'm sorry. I'll go back to my room quietly. I promise." I squirm and wiggle against the man who is holding me, trying to free myself. He growls menacingly in my ear.

"I'd stop wiggling if I were you, sweetheart. Unless you came into my room for a different purpose. In which case, by all means, wiggle away." His voice is velvety smooth but the underlying threat makes me freeze immediately.

He laughs in my ear and his hand comes away from my mouth. "Oh, you can follow orders, can you? That's excellent news, *principesa*. I am relieved to hear that."

Anger rises in me and I wish I could see him and give him a piece of my mind. Since I can't, I do the second best thing: bluff and name-drop.

"I am a guest of th-the De Marchi family. You can't hurt me. I would advise you to let me go immediately."

There is a long pause and the grip on my arms loosens and the gun moves away from my forehead. Finally he speaks again. "You are correct, Miss Christophe. You are a guest of the De Marchi family. No harm will come to you while you are under the Family's protection."

I relax slightly, reasonably assured that he is likely not going to harm me.

"Do you know where we are?" I ask my question softly, hoping the appearance of being meek might be more successful.

"Yes." *Thanks a lot, asshole. Super helpful.*

I take a calming breath and try again, "Can you please tell me where we are?"

"We're in my room, *principesa.*"

The man must be painfully stupid or deliberately obtuse. There can be no other explanation.

"OK," I drag the word out trying—and failing—to mask my irritation, "Where in the ocean are we? By we, I of course mean this boat—also called a yacht—where I am currently being held as a *guest.*"

"The Caribbean."

I want to scream. I want to stomp my foot, kick this guy in the nuts and scream until someone, hopefully the U.S. Coast Guard or the Navy SEALs or even a fishing boat hears me and comes and rescues me.

"Thank you. Can you please tell me what day it is?" A faint blue light flashes and I can see the dial of his watch light up. "It's Thursday."

"What. Is. The. Date. Today." I grit it out, my patience thin as ice in July.

He doesn't answer so I try to think back to the last thing I remember. I had spoken to my mother about a date. The details of the date are rather fuzzy but I think I remember it being on Wednesday because there was a special Happy Hour that Lawrence had taken full advantage of. The prick.

I suppose it's not inconceivable that I could go from New York to somewhere in the Caribbean in one day but it doesn't sit right with me. I've either been gone a day or a week. It will drive me crazy not to know.

I hear him mutter something into the radio in rapid-fire Italian. Shortly after, a knock sounds on the door before it swings open revealing Giorgio and Davis.

Giorgio's eyes are twinkling while he takes me in but Davis looks pissed.

"Question and Answer time is over for this afternoon, Miss Christophe. If you have more questions, you may ask them at dinner. Giorgio will escort you."

Before I can say another word, he shoves me in their direction and the door slams shut.

I am dismissed. Giorgio and Davis don't risk anything and then frog-march me to my room, locking me in without saying a word to me.

Chapter 7

Yacht After Dark

Dominic

I don't know whether to shake her for her stupidity in pissing off two of the most ruthless killers on this boat, spank her for trying to escape, or move her into my room so I can alternate between kissing the shit out of her and fucking her until she can't think of anything else. Having her break into my room and fall into my arms for however brief a moment is torturous.

The fact that she got the drop on Davis is impressive and something I will remind him of, at length, for the next 10 years. Henri will have to be dealt harshly for his disrespect.

Having her body pressed against me awakened a lust that is ten years overdue and my dick is still rock hard. Before I can strip and take care of the pressing need, Davis opens my door.

"Your girl is a fucking handful," Davis starts but something in me snaps at his humor and I stop suddenly, shoving him against the wall and holding my knife to his throat.

"You will remember your place in all of this, *old friend*," I grit out. He raises his hands in acceptance but his eyes narrow as he reads my face and I let him up.

"Sure thing, *Boss.*"

"Double check all the files. I want this airtight," I bark out "Make sure those documents are real. I want transfers and copies of trusts. She has to believe the threat came from inside her family. We begin at dinner tonight."

It's not like me to go to this much effort for anyone. I am a De Marchi. We are known throughout the world for taking what we want, often in the most brutal and lethal fashion possible. But Sabine is the exception to every rule I've ever made.

When Davis raises his eyebrows in surprise, I grant him an explanation.

"I want every avenue explored to encourage her to participate willingly."

He nods and turns to carry out my orders, pausing at the door, "And if she doesn't want to?"

The question is a loaded one and I hit him with a fierce look.

"She will lose the ability to choose."

He accepts this and closes the door behind him quietly.

* * *

Sabine

DESPITE MY HATRED OF BOATS, I can admit that a sunset on a yacht in the Caribbean is no shabby view.

Giorgio escorts me through the salon and up to the main deck. He is patient with me when I hug the wall as much as I can to avoid being near the railing. When we finally make it to the afterdeck, I see a table set for two. Uniformed stewards with trays of champagne are waiting and a man is leaning against the railing, watching me.

The closer I get, the more I am intrigued. He's wearing a crisp button down white shirt but the first two buttons are undone. I can see a gold chain around his neck and his muscular arms are tightly constrained by his shirt. He's wearing aviator sunglasses and the slight sea breeze tousles his hair. He looks like the love-child of a criminal mastermind, a Disney prince and an underwear model. Despite everything that's happened, I'm pretty sure I'm drooling.

If this is what a rescuing prince looks like, I would have thrown myself in front of a bus years ago in hopes of having him swoop in and save me.

Giorgio leads me by the elbow towards the table and the mystery man makes his way over to me. The man is built and he moves with a raw sensuality that sends a jolt of awareness to *every* part of my body.

Holy. Fucking. Hell. Hello Evil Yachty Prince.

"Miss Christophe, allow me to formally introduce your host," Giorgio began, gesturing to the man, "Mr. Dominic De Marchi."

The man takes off his sunglasses and I am at a loss for words. He greets me with a brilliant smile and a very European kiss on the cheek.

"It's a pleasure, Miss Christophe, to have you here and under the protection of the De Marchi Family."

Oh. Oh no. Oh no, no no. I know that voice.

"I believe we met this afternoon," I answer him tightly.

He nods his head in acknowledgement and smirks at me, gesturing for the steward to bring me champagne. I take it gratefully.

"You took out one of my best men with your little stunt, Miss Christophe." He is watching me over his glass and for some reason it annoys the fuck out of me.

"If I can get the drop on him, perhaps you need better men?" I take a sip of the champagne and try my hardest to look nonchalant.

"He saved your life, you might want to show him more respect." The seriousness of his expression shuts me up and I take another sip of my champagne.

"Does that mean I finally get to know what happened and how I came to be your....*guest?*"

He motions to another waiting steward who brings him a stack of manila folders.

"Do you want the long version or the short version?" The smile is gone and he is studying a folder in front of him. I blink and the fantasy I am having about climbing Dominic like a tree and riding him off into the sunset disappears in a heartbeat.

"Short version," I say finally. He looks up and studies me.

"We intercepted you. Consider it an impromptu rescue. You were on your way to be sold to a certain associate of ours and we declined to let him have you."

I blink. I'm not sure what I expected him to say but it wasn't that.

"Sold? Bullshit. The last thing I remember I was on a date with an appalling excuse for a man but he wasn't some sort of sex trafficker!"

"You are correct. Lawrence St. Martin was a lot of things, but trafficking was not his foray. He was just the mule this time. You were destined to be given to the Confi organization. A nasty bit of work. You're welcome, by the way."

The blood drains from my face and I study my plate for a long minute. I may not know the name De Marchi but I know the name Confi. I hope against hope that perhaps it's a coincidence.

"Confi. Any relation to Frederick Confi?" My voice is small and thin and I have to remind myself to breathe.

"They are one and the same."

I exhale shakily and try to make sense of it but to no avail.

"So, you nabbed me, and now I'm on a boat in the Caribbean and I can't exactly leave. How do I know you aren't just rival traffickers? I've never heard of the De Marchi family. How do I know you're legit and good people?"

"Miss Christophe, keep in mind that when we 'nabbed you' as you so eloquently put it, we also killed the man who was going to rape and abuse you before delivering you to his boss to be sold into a life of unimaginable horror."

Shame floods my face. When he puts it that way, he's absolutely right. Whoever he is or whatever his ulterior motives, he did save me. "So, you're one of the good guys?" I finally ask. I have to ask it but I already know the answer.

"No, Miss Christophe, we aren't the good guys. Our business lines are similar to Confi but we don't deal in flesh."

"But why?" I burst out, trying to fit the pieces of the puzzle together in my mind. "Frederick Confi was a friend of my family for years and so were the St. Martin's. What would they gain from... Selling me to some sort of organization?"

Dominic and Davis exchange another long look and my blood pressure rises.

"Frederick Confi is what we call an... opportunist. He has connections to the Russians. They are very helpful when someone needs to disappear. Particularly women. Your parents owe Confi millions of dollars. The St. Martin's family has had connections to Confi for years, and Lawrence also owed him a significant amount of money. We believe Lawrence was only meant to deliver you."

I stare at him, horror written in my eyes.

I can see where he's going with this, but my heart can't take it.

"Mr. De Marchi, are you insinuating that my parents—one of whom is a U.S. Senator, arranged to have me assaulted by a family friend before being delivered to a trafficker in order to pay off their debt? How would you even know that? That's preposterous! They have their faults, sure, but they are *my parents!*"

He stands, hiding his face behind his sunglasses again. He drops the folder next to my plate. "Read it for yourself, Sabine." His hand is warm on my shoulder for a brief moment before he walks off to the other side of the deck to stand with Davis and Giorgio.

I turn the pages with a sinking sense of doom and begin to read.

Page after page, I review the damning evidence of betrayal. It's all there in black and white. I have to give it to Dominic, he has good people working for him. This level of thorough rivals Belinda's packets on political rivals. No stone has been left unturned.

Familiar names pop out at me from all sides. Police reports for Lawrence Willhem St. Martin show six incidents of violence towards female partners in the US alone. Several other instances were reported through Interpol. No convictions. It would seem all the victims and witnesses either disappeared or no longer wanted to testify shortly after they reported

Marko, my parents private attorney, is listed as the attorney on record for each of Lawrence's police reports. There is no way they didn't know what he was accused of. I feel sick.

It's the last page that does me in. It's a copy of a bank statement and I know that number by heart. It's the business bank account for our household expenses in my parents household.

A single electronic payment is highlighted and next to it is a post-it note with an account number and banking login information.

I reach for the iPad that Dominic had left on the table and enter the information in with shaking hands. I mess up the username twice before I can get it to run correctly.

A single tear falls down my cheek as the most damning evidence of all stares me in the face.

The account belongs to an L.W. St. Martin.

The day before our date, a payment of $750,000 was received via wire transfer from my parents business account.

The same day my mother called me and voluntold me to go out with Lawrence.

It could be for anything but the coincidence is hard to ignore.

I am so confused and heartbroken. My mind is racing.

My parents betrayed me. Lawrence St. Martin attacked me. Frederick Confi tried to buy me. Dominic De Marchi saved me.

Thousands of questions pepper my mind and I rest my head on the table for a long moment. The sound of gentle waves lapping against the hull makes me anxious. When I look up, Dominic is sitting across from me, studying me with a great deal of intensity.

"You saved me." My voice is hollow. It's not a question. It's a statement of fact.

Dominic leans forward and grabs one of my hands. I feel a small shock when his fingers touch mine and almost pull away.

"No one will hurt you again. You are under the protection of the De Marchi family and everything I have at my disposal. You're safe here, *cara mia*."

His Italian accent is even more pronounced, as is the insinuation of being under the protection of The Family, but I don't doubt the sincerity and deadly seriousness of his promise.

I want to believe him.

That I will be safe and all will be well. That this is all a twisted fairy tale —a modern day Hades and Persephone story.

But I know better.

Mobsters don't just rescue people because they can.

There's always a catch.

And once again my freedom is on the line.

I want to scream and rage at the outrageousness and betrayal. I want to cry and then drink myself into oblivion and then plot out revenge. Anything that will make the pain stop.

But I'm terrified to ask the one question that burns in my soul.

Giorgio brings me a very large tumbler filled to the brim with whiskey and one ice cube. I don't question how he could possibly know my favorite drink, I just take it gratefully and gulp it down, the smokey burn a welcome distraction from everything.

The stewards bring out plates of food but I push them away.

It's not every day you find out your parents are ambivalent about whether you live or die so long as you serve as currency for their debt. That kind of news tends to not pair well with sea bass, no matter how well it's prepared.

Dominic studies me for a long while. The longer I spend in his presence, the more nervous he makes me. There's something about him that bothers me.

When I have almost drained my glass of whiskey, he finally speaks again.

"Ask me, Sabine. Ask me what you are burning to know."

I swallow heavily and drain the rest of the glass before looking him straight in the eye. "Why me? Why did you intervene and rescue me? What do you get out of this?"

He sighs and drains his own glass.

"I'm no longer the prince, *principesa*, but perhaps tonight you'll accept the King?"

I freeze. "What did you say?" I whisper incredulously, my eyes glued on the man in front of me. My entire body tenses and he gives me a wry little smile and moves to stand.

"Shall I have them killed for you? A terrible accident perhaps?"

The words are spoken so softly I almost miss them. But they are out there and suddenly it all makes sense. The reason why Dominic seems so familiar. The way my pulse accelerates each time I am near him. I slowly lift my head and meet his gaze head on.

It can't be. The probability borders on insanity yet I see it. Standing in front of me in all his brutal beauty is the nameless man of my fantasies for the last ten years. He finally has a name: Dominic De Marchi.

I swallow hard, unsure of what to do. I see the heat in his eyes and the recognition when he realizes I put two and two together.

"*Cara mia*," his voice interrupts my inner monologue. He proffers his hand and I stare at it, "Do you know who I am?"

I can't manage to speak, I just nod. "You're New York."

The realization that he is real and here is too much. He moves as if to embrace me so I do the only thing that makes sense.

I run.

CHAPTER 8
THAT FAMILIAR FEELING

Sabine

Once again, I knew that there's only so far you can run on a boat. No one stops me as I run down the deck and back down the stairs, darting through the salon with my chest heaving.

It's all too much. I find a corner between two leather couches and I squeeze myself into it. The act of crouching to the ground and hiding may be childish, but right now it's comforting to me. My world suddenly shrinks. I am no longer on a boat in the middle of the ocean—I am in a corner. Like a cat in a box, my world is only that which I can see and immediately touch.

Drawing my knees up to my chest, I bury my face in my hands and collapse onto myself. My stomach is coiled in painful knots and the tears slide down my cheeks. I've never felt more vulnerable and alone. I miss the simplicity of life when all I had to worry about was hot yoga and how to avoid Belinda and her spies.

The thought of my parents makes my heart clench in a particularly painful way. *Betrayal.*

Then there's Dominic. Twice he's saved me from Frederick Confi. He remains the only one who has ever intervened on my behalf. It's gone far beyond a rescue off a dance floor now. He *killed* someone for me.

That fact alone should scare the shit out of me. I am trapped on a boat with criminals and killers.

But that's not what scares me. If what he says is true, I was raised with criminals and killers.

It's *him.*

It's the way my body responds to him.

Even now, ten years later, I'm like an addict who has been craving my drug of choice for years.

The drug is here and all it would take is a single step and I could have that hit I've craved for so long.

A part of me wishes it were that simple. That I could mend this rending of my soul with mind-blowing sex and passion. I've never craved anything the way I've craved him. We could reignite those embers we stoked a decade ago into a full blown inferno that consumes us both and screams a giant fuck you to the rest of the world.

He's the only man to have truly set my blood on fire.

I would be lying to myself if I said he didn't still have that effect on me.

I want him.

I have wanted him for a decade.

My dark angel came back for me. Ten years ago I would have followed him to the ends of the earth no matter how nonsensical it was.....I just don't know if it's too late.

I lose track of all time as I sit, huddled in my corner. I can hear movement and the low buzz of conversation as staff and men pass my hiding place but no one acknowledges me or checks on me. I am not so stupid to believe that they don't know where I am. I think it's Dominic's way of giving me space. It's a kindness that is unexpected given what I now know about him.

I only wish my traitorous body would listen. Space is the absolute last thing I want to give him.

* * *

Dominic

SHE RAN AWAY from me and, to my great surprise, I let her. With a wave of my hand, I just let her go. It's a simple decision in the long run. An easy short-term victory for her. I'm not playing for the short-term, I have the long game in mind.

I instruct Davis to monitor the surveillance cameras and find where she squirrels herself away and intervene only if it looks like she might harm herself or go out on one of the tenders or jet skis. Sitting at my table, I finish the meal and study the folders I presented to her.

The information is damning. I knew when I first discovered the connection that showing her might make her world implode. It was a calculated risk. It wouldn't take much for me to press her. The fire flows through her veins as much as it does mine. Yet something stops me. If I were to share the rest of the information, the full depths of depravity that had been planned for her by the people she trusted the most...she would shut down emotionally and I might never get her back.

Pushing the folders aside, I call Davis on the radio.

When he arrives a short term later with Henri, I carefully remove my rings and roll up my sleeves.

There are some needs that have to wait to be satiated. Dealing with Henri is not one of them. If I can't have Sabine yet, I will have some blood instead.

Flexing my fists, I motion for Henri to step forward.

Disrespect to our guest is disrespect to me.

I don't tolerate that.

* * *

Sabine

HUNGER IS what ultimately drives me out of my hiding spot. At some point I must have fallen asleep. When I startle awake, I see that it's dark outside. The faint glow of a lamp is the only light in the room, and someone has dropped a blanket over me. Standing, my muscles scream at me for being forced into such a cramped position for so long. I stumble, making my way into the main living area to look around.

I never really gave Giorgio the opportunity to show me the full layout of the boat and I'm not sure where I would find the kitchen or galley or whatever they call it.

I wander the passageways of the boat, my mind too fucked up to worry about my fear of the vessel itself. When I find the galley, everything is pristine and locked down. It's a chef's kitchen and I feel nervous about messing it up, but the gnawing pain in my stomach wins out over my resilience to snoop and help myself.

I am so engrossed in my ingredients that I don't hear him approach.

When a hand lands on my shoulder, I whirl around, brandishing the knife I had been cutting apples with and narrowly missing my assailant.

Dominic's eyes narrow when he sees the knife and he quickly removes it from my grasp and places it back on the counter. His knuckles are a mess, split open and bleeding.

"You're hurt," I blurt out, shifting my weight from one foot to the other. My gaze alternates between studying his bleeding hands and wanting to get lost in his eyes. He makes me nervous.

Seemingly surprised by my declaration, he looks down and shrugs his shoulders at the state of his hands. "It's nothing you need to worry about."

I don't know whether it's his voice or the fact that he is standing so damn close to me but I can't stop staring at him.

"Too late," I whisper softly, reaching for his hand, "I'm already worried. You've done so much for me, allow me to do this one thing?"

Without waiting for an answer, I lead him to the kitchen island and take down the large first aid kit from its wall brackets. We don't speak as I painstakingly clean each of his cuts, bandaging each knuckle with steri-strips before wrapping his hands carefully in gauze and tape. My entire body is so aware of him that it's a miracle I don't shock him with the extra electricity running through my veins.

All too soon the bandaging is completed and the first aid box is put away. I no longer have a reason to touch him and it makes me feel sad. I turn away but he's faster than me and his hand latches on to my wrist, pulling me towards him.

"Dominic," I whisper softly, his name still unfamiliar on my tongue. He nods slowly and pulls me closer, his arms loosely embracing me. This time, when I step into his embrace, it's like coming home.

"Thank you, Sabine." His words roll over me like the caress of a lover and I close my eyes, resting my cheek against his broad chest.

"I don't want you to kill them. I want vengeance."

My voice is shaky but my resolve is strong.

He cracks a smile when he looks down at me, bending to press a kiss to my cheek.

"Then vengeance you shall have, *regina mia.*"

Perhaps, like my mother before me, I have made a deal with the Devil.

But unlike her, I have nothing left to lose.

I slide my hand slowly up his chest, reaching for his neck. Lifting my eyes up to meet his, I see my own desire reflected there.

So much of what has happened has not been my choice. It has been out of my control. I need to feel grounded again. I need to know that I can still have control over my own destiny.

I look at him, his beautiful face staring down at me with barely-controlled lust and I know what I want.

Tentatively, I go up on my tip-toes and press my lips to his. For one second he freezes and I wonder if perhaps I have read this situation wrong. I'm not sure my heart can handle rejection on top of everything else but before I could descend any further into my anxiety spiral, he responds. Gripping me to him, he takes charge of our kiss in a way that makes my body come alive. Gone is the gentleness from the last time I was in his arms. This kiss is aggressive and demanding and it doesn't allow me to think of anything other than him.

With his hands around my waist and my body flush against him, I can feel the power radiating from him and it's intoxicating.

He pulls back, the scruff of his beard scratching on my cheek as he looks down on me. "Tell me you want this, Sabine. Tell me you're mine tonight. If you don't want this, you need to leave now," he orders, his sharp eyes boring into mine.

I don't hesitate. Wiggling, I step out of his embrace and back up until my thighs hit the steel countertop. I perch myself on top of the counter and pull my dress off in one flourish. Tossing it on the floor, I beckon him with a crooked finger.

The tension between us is charged. He watches me, prowling closer with his heated gaze roaming up and down my body. Stopping just out of reach, he studies me.

"Say it, Sabine," he orders again, his tone leaving no room for argument.

"I want this," I whisper, forcing myself to meet his gaze headon, "I-I want you. Tonight I don't want to think of anything. I just want to be yours."

The tension between us is charged. He watches me, prowling closer with his heated gaze roaming up and down my body. Stopping just out of reach, he studies me.

"Your wish is my command. Lay back."

I shiver in anticipation as I comply, leaning back onto my elbows and propping myself up on the countertop. I am aching for him to touch me again but he makes no move to close the remaining foot of distance between us.

My breath catches in my throat when he picks up the knife I was using to cut my apples. He dances it around his fingers, toying with it while looking at me thoughtfully. The first feeling of apprehension floods through me but ten years of lust for this man drowns it out.

"Do you trust me, Sabine?" he asks suddenly, taking a slight step towards me, still casually holding the knife.

I pause and think for a second. I want him but *do* I trust him? Does it matter if I do or not? He's 100% a dangerous man and a criminal but my intuition tells me he doesn't want to hurt me.

"Um, enough to lie here and hope to God you are planning on fucking me soon?" I offer, trying to channel enough bravado to cover my anxiety.

Something flashes in his eyes but he accepts my answer.

"Hold still," he warns and I immediately freeze. He steps within arm's reach and runs the tips of his fingers up my legs, stroking me so lightly I can barely feel it.

I shiver and he pulls away abruptly, stopping just before reaching my soaking panties. Placing the knife back down on the counter, he reaches behind his back and pulls out a sinister looking handgun from a back holster. He checks the safety and places it on the table behind him.

Slowly he drags the flat of the blade up my inner thigh, the cold metal dances across my skin and I bite my lip in anticipation. While I believe he won't actually hurt me, the thrill and danger makes my nerves stand on edge. I am fighting against my natural instincts to get away from danger as he inches the blade up higher, caressing the steel against me, closer and closer to my sex.

He rotates his wrist quickly, pressing the flat against my underwear and dragging it slowly up and down my mound, the pressure rubbing deliciously against my clit. I gasp, biting my lip so hard I half-way fear I will draw blood. A small moan escapes when he drags the tip of the knife to the edge of my underwear, sliding it underneath the white lace.

My adrenaline is rushing and my pussy is throbbing, I want to buck against him and pull him close but I am at his mercy, the tip of his knife slowly moving further under the lace and towards the most intimate part of me.

"Exhale," Dominic orders suddenly and I comply immediately.

As my breath exits, he flicks his wrist again and slices through the lace with surgical precision.

"You follow orders so well, *bella*, perhaps you should be rewarded."

I've never had a sexual experience comparable to this before. His praise makes my whole body flush in pleasure and I ache for whatever reward he might dish out. I may have started this but there is no question in my mind that Dominic has complete control over me at this moment.

He puts the knife down and surveys his work. His hands are rough against my skin as he rips the rest of my underwear off, leaving me bare before him.

"Do you know how long I've wanted to taste you, *bella?*" He is staring at my glistening pink lips and before I can answer, his head is between my thighs and his breath hot against my inner thighs. At the first touch of his tongue, I moan and arch into him, my thighs clenching around his head.

I see stars. I can't tell if it's because Dominic is just that skilled or if it's the adrenaline from the buildup and situation or if it's because the object of a decade worth of fantasies has his head buried in my pussy and is pummeling my clit with his tongue with singular determination. Shifting my weight to one elbow, I bring my hand up to cup my breast, rolling my nipple between my fingers and pinching slightly. The combination of pain and pleasure is intoxicating and I can feel my climax building rapidly.

At my movement, Dominic flicks his eyes up to me and they narrow when they land on my hand. He pulls back and I whimper in protest.

"I told you to hold still, *bella*," He chides me, wiping his mouth with the back of his hand and straightening up to tower over me.

"Wh-what? I thought that was just for the knife thing! So I didn't get cut!" I protest, the electricity of my denied orgasm still pulsing irritatingly strongly through my veins.

"If I tell you not to move, you do not move." He continues, running his hands lightly over my thighs again.

I look down at the floor and try to make sense of the situation. I've never been this aroused in my life nor have I ever been left wanting like this. It's confusing and beyond infuriating given everything else. My temper up, I look back at him and sit up, scooting my ass closer to the edge of the counter. He's still standing between my legs so I take advantage of the situation and lock my legs around his waist.

He actually chuckles at my antics and presses a kiss to my lips. Still annoyed with his exquisite torture, I catch his lip in my bottom teeth and bite down hard. He growls, his hands gripping my arms tightly.

"Careful, *cara mia*. You don't want to play rough with me." The warning in his voice actually makes my skin goosebump. I have every reason in the world to heed it but I'm in the mood to let everything burn, so I don't.

"Or what?" I busy myself with unbuttoning his shirt, unveiling more of his toned chest to me. I have a strange desire to lick it. Scars and tattoos decorate the expanse of skin and I can't resist—I dip my head forward and press a kiss to the small round scar just below his collarbone.

He is gripping me so hard it actually hurts. His hands are over my existing bruises but I don't care. "What's the worst you are going to do to me, Dominic?" I ask, moving my lips down his chest to suck on his nipple and nibbling on it slightly.

"Are you going to beat me, threaten me with your gun or your knife?" I move my hands down his chest, hooking my fingers in the waistband of his pants, anchoring us together.

He hasn't said a word and his silence actually freaks me out more than his threats or his weapons. The only indication that I am getting to him at all is the grip he has on my arms and the rock hard bulge pressed against my aching pussy. Feeling devilish, I rock my hips again, rubbing up against him.

"I've got to say, Dominic. I don't think you will do any of those things," I move my mouth to the side of his neck, sucking hard on his pulse point. I am probably leaving a mark. It gives me no small amount of joy to think about marking this man and letting him do whatever the hell he does during the day with a hickey.

I wonder how much further I can push him before he snaps or tells me to get the fuck out of here. With a private grin, I move my hand down to cup him through his pants. The moment my hand grabs him, I bite down on his shoulder.

He growls into my ear, his fist suddenly bunched in my hair. He pulls my head back and forces me to look up at him.

"Don't say I didn't warn you, *cara mia*," He grits out between clenched teeth.

I debate whether or not I should push him further in my head. His eyes are wild and his one hand is fumbling with his belt buckle already. *In for a penny, in for a pound.*

"About fucking time," I shot back, shoving against him with my palms before reaching down to help him with his buckle. His pants fall to the floor and he steps out of them, kicking them to the side. His body is fucking beautiful. I reach out to touch him, but he captures my wrist before I can.

Reveling in this newfound defiance, I stare at him with a smirk and bring my other hand over to give him a languid caress up and down his shaft.

"You've only got two hands, choose wisely." It's like playing with fire. I know he could burn me beyond recognition but the potential reward of surviving is an addicting possibility.

He looks at me in a way that actually makes me pause. It's cold and calculating. He lets go of my hair and my wrist suddenly and bear hugs me, lifting me off the countertop and carrying me a few steps towards a passageway. Stepping through the door, he carries me with ease and we turn into a small elevator. Without letting go of me, he presses the button to call the lift.

"Where are you taking me?" I demand, leaning down to nibble on his shoulder again.

He slaps my ass hard and I yelp in outrage, biting down harder on his shoulder.

"If you want me to fuck you right here in full view of the security and crew, please, keep going, *cara*. Is that what you want? You want me to drop you to your knees in front of my men? Of course, then I'll have to kill them.

The only one who gets to look at you is me. What's your choice?" I freeze, looking around until I see the blinking red lights of cameras on all four corners of the room. I squeeze my body closer to his, hiding my nudity.

"Maybe someplace more private," I grumble, burying my face in his shoulder again, this time without teeth.

"A wise choice, *bella*." The elevator dings again and we step inside. He makes a sign to the camera and I notice the blinking light stops. I breathe a sigh of relief.

When we arrive at our destination, a warm breeze hits my naked skin and I look up immediately. We're on deck. *Oh fuck.*

"You have a fear of boats, don't you *bella*?" Dominic asks conversationally, as if we are just two friends catching up instead of two bare-ass naked people wound too tight.

I hesitate. My fear of boats is documented. He knows it. I know it. But this is a power game and I'll be damned if I let him win.

"I just don't like them," I respond curtly, trying to control my heartbeat as he moves closer and closer to the deck railing.

"Oh. Well, that's great news then," He sounds so sweet and considerate. Not at all like a criminal mastermind who is aiming to punish me for being a pain in his ass.

We walk leisurely towards the bow of the boat where a small cushioned seat is built in. *Fuck. Fuck. Fuck.*

The ocean is lit only by the stars and the deck lights on board. I peek over the edge and all I see is the inky blackness of the ocean. It's terrifying.

He drops his arms and I slide abruptly down his body. He doesn't give me any time to recover before he is roughly moving me back onto the cushioned bench. My back touches the cold railing and I feel panic rising.

"On your knees, Sabine. Your hands on the cushion and they don't move."

Slowly I draw myself up so I am kneeling. I am a potent mix of terrified and excited. He winds his fist in my hair again and tips my face up to face him.

My dark angel looks more like an avenging angel. The rational side of me says I should be scared. But I mostly want to see what he will do.

"You've been very mouthy tonight," he observes, stroking his cock leisurely, "I have a better use for your mouth."

Lining his blunt tip up with my lips, he presses forward and I open my mouth to taste him. He eases his girth in with a few shallow strokes before he brings my face forward, pushing his cock into the back of my throat. I gag and my eyes water, but I am determined to win whatever power struggle we are locked in. With his fingers knotted in my hair, he fucks my face in a punishing rhythm of shallow and deeper strokes until I am gasping and gagging, saliva dripping down my chin.

With a guttural roar, he suddenly pulls out completely, taking a few steps back from me. There's a white bag and a towel sitting on the bench and he digs through it, pulling out a condom.

"Turn around, *bella*," he snaps.

With shaking hands, I turn around and grip the sides of the railing in a death grip.

He reaches between us and rubs my clit, causing me to rock my hips back against him in wanton need.

"I want your tits over the bow. You may hold on to the railing as tight as you wish."

My heart almost stops as the fear rises in me. I start to shake my head, convinced I won't be able to do it, but he presses a small kiss to the side of my neck, nuzzling me.

"I won't let you fall, *regina mia*. Trust me."

With wobbly arms I get into position and lean my chest over the bow of the boat, my knees spread out and my ass presented to him. I am clenching the railing with white knuckles.

"Good girl," he murmurs, lining his cock up with my entrance. With a hand on the back of my neck to stabilize me and a hand on my waist, he sheaths himself in one thrust.

I cry out, his fullness is overwhelming and when he begins to move, the familiar aching in my core starts again with a vengeance.

"*Fuck,*" Dominic's prayerful epithet as he drives into me turns me on even further. I love that he is as affected by this as I am. Each thrust pushes me and rocks me forward, with my chest over the side of the boat it causes another thrill of fear and jolt of electricity to flow through me.

The sensations sizzle all the way through me and I know I won't last long. When he slaps my ass again, driving deep, I feel the rush of sensation starting. He pulls me back over the rail and sinks his teeth into the soft fleshy part of my shoulder. I cry out and tense before all my muscles spasm at once and I come on a white-hot wave.

He drives into me rapidly, his cock taking what he needs and soon his body tenses and he comes violently, his hands digging into my thighs as we ride out the aftershocks.

When he finally withdraws, I collapse in a heap, sliding backwards away from the rail. He sits on the cushions, his hands stroking my hair as I sit on the deck next to his feet and catch my breath.

"Are you ok, *bella?*" he finally asks, tipping my chin to look up at me. We're a mess. There's angry red scratches down his chest from my fingernails and I know my body will wear his marks for days.

I study his face. He looks genuinely concerned that he may have hurt me.

"I've waited ten years for that. I'm more than ok," I whisper back at him, leaning against his legs.

CHAPTER 9
Unraveling

Sabine

W hen I wake up, I notice two things immediately. One, it's morning. Two, I'm all alone. Once again, my body aches when I sit up but this ache is different. It's a deep, delicious throbbing from a night spent indulging my dark side. Looking around, I don't see Dominic anywhere. His side of the bed is cool to the touch and there isn't a clock anywhere to be found.

I'm in a different room than I was in before. This one is significantly larger. Where my room had chrome accents, this one has burnished bronze. It feels masculine and elegant, like an old world smoking club. There's a small sitting area/office space visible through an open door.

Curious, I wrap myself up in the sheet like a toga and prowl around the room looking for clues about Dominic and the De Marchi family.

Everything is orderly and clean. I have to resist my urge to casually knock things out of place on the shelves. Would he really notice if his pens were not lined up equally? Maybe. Would I enjoy being a brat and messing them up? Yes.

His office chair is a work of art. A sumptuous leather that I sink into as I twirl in a lazy circle, surveying the kingdom from behind the desk. It feels powerful and I don't hate it.

Finding nothing of immediate interest, I get up with the intention of stealing some clothing from a drawer and searching for some breakfast when I see the corner of a photo peeking out from a file in the corner of his desk.

Glancing around, I am aware that just because Dominic isn't here, doesn't mean people aren't watching. I can't see any tell-tale blinking red lights to indicate a camera but a shiver runs through me anyway. Careful not to disturb the rest of the files on the desk, I slowly ease the corner of the photo out a little bit at a time.

The corner is bent, as if it has been handled many times but slowly the image is revealed to me. I see a window and then a vanity. There's a head of hair and bubbles. It appears to be a black and white glossy taken of a woman in a bath.

A strange little tingle starts at the top of my scalp and trickles downward. Pulling hard, the photo comes out from the stack and I stare down at it with horror.

That's my bathroom and there, leaning back against the edge of the tub, my hair in a messy bun and a glass of wine in my head, is me.

Questions flood through my mind as I stare at the photo. My hands are shaking but my eyes travel to the folder and I grab it, uncaring about the mess I make.

The folder is labeled with my full name and birthdate and I have to steel myself before opening.

"Don't."

Dominic's voice from the doorway scares the shit out of me and I jump, dropping the folder like a hot potato. Another photo slides partially out and I can see the sand and teal bikini bottoms shining up at me.

"What is this?" I whisper furiously, unable to even look at Dominic for more than a few seconds.

I grab the swimsuit shot and hold it up, raising my chin in defiance.

"I asked you a question, Dominic De Marchi, what is this?"

He doesn't answer me. He just turns around and closes the door. The click of the lock makes me narrow my eyes. When he turns back to me, I instinctively back up, clutching my new-found evidence to my chest.

"I will only ask you once, Sabine. Put the photos down and come talk to me, " he warns, his hands out in a placating gesture while he takes small steps towards me.

I back away and more pictures cascade out of the folder, spilling out over the desk, the chair, and the floor.

I freeze, my eyes darting from picture to picture, a sinking feeling in my stomach.

When I look back up, Dominic is standing next to me and his face is stormy.

"I wish you hadn't done that, Sabine," he said with a dangerous calm to his voice, "that means we have to do this the hard way."

* * *

THIS IS the end of part 1 of "Obsession"

I know. I know. Cliffhangers. Dominic and Sabine's story can't be contained in the first 25k words so I had to do it. Good news though: *Obsession* releases in November 2020 as soon as Crimes of the Wicked is unpublished. After that the series continues with , *Blood Debt* in December 2020 and *Vengeance* in January 2021!

Follow along with the Dark Desires & Wicked Crimes series here:
https://beemurray.com/dark-desires-wicked-crimes/

* * *

SIGN up for my newsletter to get exclusive access to teasers, freebies, giveaways and more!
https://sendfox.com/beemurraybooks

About Bee Murray

Bee Murray is the pen name chosen by a quirky writer based out of the Pacific Northwest. A voracious reader turned writer, she dreams of everything from grand adventures with complex characters to pun-filled romantic comedy, weird paranormal situations, extra steamy romance, and anything else her heart comes up with! Come say hi on FB or IG: @BeeMurrayBooks or on Twitter: @HeyBeeMurray. Pronouns: She/Her.

Read more from Bee Murray
https://beemurray.com/

SAVING STONE

an Amaryllis Outcasts Romance

Mandy Melanson

Author Note

About Saving Stone: an Amaryllis Outcasts Romance

Stone Thompson lives the rockstar cliché lifestyle until one night his past catches up to him. He dodged a prison term by incriminating his girlfriend's sister. Now she's sitting in prison and he's living the rockstar dream. When the past catches up to him, he must decide between the life he loves or the woman who still has his heart after all these years.

CHAPTER 1

F uck.
My head is pounding. Where the hell are my pills? My hand lands on something soft and warm. Shit. I slowly open one eye and recognize the cherry blossom tattoo facing me. Why is she still in my bed? Tanya is a great fuck but she knows better than to pass out. Her ass should have been long gone by now. It's not about anything more than a good time with her, and she knows it. I nudge her in the shoulder.

"Uhh." she moans and rolls over draping one arm over my chest and here comes the leg...

Nope. We are not snuggling. Not tonight. Not ever. "Tanya, you fell asleep." My words are probably a little more harsh than totally necessary, but this is a complete violation of our deal. "I need you out of here."

Her eyes flutter open complete with mascara and eyeliner smeared from one side of her face to the other. We must have been wild, I just can't remember a damn thing about it.

"Tanya." I growl as I reach across the top of her to find my pill bottle. Her hands are exploring as my body drapes over the top of her. "Stop it. We've already done that. It's time for you to go." Finally. I grab the little bottle from the nightstand and pop one of those little fuckers in my mouth. At least the throbbing headache and feeling like I'm about to puke my guts out will stop within the next twenty minutes, even if she's slower than hell to leave.

"Sorry, Stone, baby." She flips the blankets back faster than I've ever seen her move before, and I've seen her do some crazy shit. "I didn't mean—"

I cut her off, waving my hand in the air. "I don't really care. Just can't happen again."

She nods and pulls her skirt over her hips. It shows just enough of her ass that it made me rock hard the instant I saw her in it. That doesn't really say much though. Some people say I have a sex addiction. Others say I'm just a dick. Either one might be true. Before Tanya showed up backstage, I had just fucked one of our groupies. I don't even know her name. She's been with us for over four months now. Oh well.

Bang. Bang.

The banging on the door makes Tanya jump and her tits jiggle underneath that thin white top of hers. I can see her nipples through the fabric. My dick instantly responds.

Fuck. Not now.

"Stone." *Bang.*

I recognize Nigel's voice immediately. He doesn't usually cause such a goddamn scene though. "I need you to go, now." I put my hand on the small of her back and guide her to the door as she fluffs her lavender colored hair in a weak attempt to take away from the freshly fucked look. "Not gonna work." I give her a wink and open the door, letting my hand push her past Nigel who is glaring at me over the rim of his wire framed glasses. "What the fuck do you want, Nigel? I need to get ready for the show."

"The show?" He snorts as he pushes past me and barges into my room. "The show happened about an hour ago. The band pulled it off, again— without you. Not that you'd actually give a shit."

"Ah." My fingers push through my hair. "So what you're saying is that I have the night off?" I laugh and grab a bottle of whiskey from the table.

He laughs, that annoying maniacal laugh that makes me want to punch him in the face every damn time I hear it. "No, Stone." He shakes his head back and forth and lets out a low whistle. "I'm saying you're on a one way track to having every night off. The way you're heading, you'll be kicked out of the band before we even get to the end of this tour."

I gulp down a swig from my bottle. "Bullshit." I drag my hand over my mouth capturing any stray drops of the alcohol. "They wouldn't dare. We've been together since... Since..." Nigel's laughter is condescending. Who the fuck is he? What the hell does he even know about me or the guys?

"Listen," he says handing me a napkin from the minibar stashed in the corner of my room. "I'm trying to help you, but you obviously don't want the help. You do what you need to do and Amaryllis—and The Machine—will do what we need to do."

My hand wraps around his pathetic excuse for a bicep and holds him in place. I can feel my grip tightening around his arm, but I can't stop myself. I shove him into the wall and hold him there. "Don't you fucking threaten me, Nigel." My finger is in his face and I can see the splatter of my spit on his glasses lenses. Rage boils just beneath my skin. Every single piece of my body is burning hot and all I need to release the pain of the searing heat is to pound his face into the wall.

"Stone!" Devon, the head of our security team, shoves me back and away from Nigel. "What the fuck are you doing?"

I lock my eyes onto Nigel and keep my finger pointing directly at him. "You don't know how lucky you are, Nigel."

"Oh, I think I do." His mouth curls up in a smirk as he straightens his tie. "I'm lucky enough that I don't have to put up your shit. Unfortunately, I'm not sure how much longer you'll be with us."

"Fuck you."

The door slams behind him as he runs away like the coward he is.

"What the fuck, man?" Devon's scowl grows by the second.

I shake my head and take another gulp from the bottle. "It's nothing."

"Like fuck it's nothing."

"What's that supposed to mean?"

Devon puts one hand on my shoulder, trying to soothe the demons swirling inside of me right now. "They're done with the games, man."

"I don't play games." I jerk my shoulder out of his grip. "Everyone else is busy playing games. I'm just living my goddamn life. Get out."

"I'm just trying to help you," he says as he reaches for the door. "You're on your way out. You need to pull your head out of your ass, Stone."

The bottle launches out of my hand just as Devon pulls the door shut behind him sending glass shards flying across the tiny living area.

Fuckers. All of them.

I grab my phone off the counter and swipe the screen.

Stone: I need something.

  Lexis: R U in Tulsa?

Stone: Wouldn't have messaged you if I wasn't.

  Lexis: Fine. Midnight. If UR not on time, I'm out.

I CHECK the time on my phone. Eleven-thirty? Fuck. I grab a pair of pants from underneath the bed and throw on a t-shirt from the floor. It smells. The whiskey must have landed all around the shirt because I'm feeling light headed just breathing it in. Nigel's words echo through my brain. I pound an open palm against my ear trying to beat his sniveling little voice out of my head.

The band pulled it off without me?

Yeah, right.

"Devon!" I yell down the hallway.

No answer.

The crowd's already thinned out and, from what I can tell, the crew's out too. I don't hear any sounds of the crew packing up, no random calls from one stage hand to the other, not even Carly yelling at Adair for being a dumb fuck.

I must've passed out hard tonight.

No guards.

No Nigel.

No drivers.

Guess I'll just have to do this myself. I flick the screen of my phone and tap to open the app ordering myself a driver.

They better be cool with this shit.

* * *

Lexis isn't here. The driver is tapping his thumbs on the steering wheel like that will somehow make her magically appear. I can't find my lighter and I need a god-damn cigarette. "Hey, man. You got a light?"

"No smoking in the car."

Right. Of fucking course. "Fine. I'll be right back." I let the door slam behind me as I head for the all night convenience store we've been parked in front of for the last ten minutes waiting on Lexis. She's a real piece of work. Telling me not to be late then not even showing up. If I was back home it wouldn't matter. I'd just call up the next dealer in my phone, but we're not at home and I don't have a backup in Tulsa fucking Oklahoma. "Welcome to the—"

"Fuck off." I growl to the overly chipper blonde attendant. She's hot though. If I wasn't in such a shit mood, I'd probably take her back to my bed. "Lighters?"

"Just down there," she points to an aisle behind me, "directly between fuck you and figure it out yourself." She flashes a customer service smile and I can't help but smirk. I like her style. No shit.

I find a lighter and toss a hundred on the counter. I don't wait for my change. She deserves the extra after putting up with my bullshit. I'm a piece of shit and I know it, but I also know that the people around me don't deserve half of what I give them. I just can't help myself though.

"Stone." Lexis's smoky voice cuts through my momentary soul searching. "I was about to give up on you."

"I've been here since ten till."

"Whatever." She wraps her arms around my waist in what looks like a hug to anyone watching, she drops the pills into the back pocket of my pants as she pulls back and looks up at me. Her dark red hair hangs in loose braids that drape directly over her perky tits and draw my eyes to her hard nipples poking through the bright white fabric of her tank top. She's still pressed close enough to me that I can feel the hard knobs against my chest and my

505

dick instantly responds. "Fuck, Stone." She grins and glances down at the growing bulge in my pants. "You really did miss me, didn't ya?"

Ugh. Not really. She's a headache and a half, but goddamn she's hot as hell. "You got new ink?" I say as my eyes follow the pattern of the snake slithering around her neck.

"I did." She winks and tugs her shirt down a little lower, exposing the dark pink circles around her nipples. "Do you like it?"

The tail drapes off her left shoulder, but the head... The head of the snake is nestled right between her beautiful full tits. "I like it." That's an understatement. It's teeth drip venom and fuck is it hot. I want to wrap my mouth around her full breasts and flick those sexy nipples with my tongue, just like that goddamned snake.

She reaches behind her back and pulls the fabric of her shirt covering everything right back up. "Too fucking bad." She shoves me in the chest forcing me to take a step back. "You still owe me for the last time."

"Oh, c'mon." She can't hold a grudge this long, can she?

"C'mon?" She snorts. "You got my sister ten years, Stone. You can go fuck yourself. The only reason I met you tonight is because I needed the money to go visit her tomorrow."

"Ten years?"

"Ten fucking years." She shakes her head and holds out her hand. "I don't really want to talk about it. Pay up and I'll be out of here."

I reach into my back pocket for my wallet, but it's not there. Fuck. "I... uh..."

"For fuck's sake." She laughs as she twirls one long red braid in her fingers and I can't help but think what her fingers wrapped around my cock would look like. "You're trying to get it for free, aren't you?"

"No." I check my other pocket. "I must've..." I remember pulling the hundred out and handing it to the cashier. "Fuck. I left the rest in my room. Let's go back and I'll make it worth your while." I wrap my arms around her pulling her in close, I make sure she can feel my excitement through my pants. She grinds her hips against me, which gets me more revved up as she nestles her nose against my neck.

I feel her breath on my skin as her lips part just slightly. "No," she whispers.

"Why not?" I say with a crack in my voice. I really need to fuck this girl.

"Because you're a piece of shit." She shoves me back and pulls out her phone.

Wait. "What're you doing?"

"Something that someone should've done to you a long time ago, Stone. Yes, I was just assaulted by Stone Thompson." She pauses.

"No, c'mon." She waves her hand in my face dismissing my protests. *Shit.* The driver is still sitting in the same spot waiting for me. "God dammit, Lexis."

She shrugs and goes back to the phone call with the fucking dispatcher. "Yes, Stone Thompson of Amaryllis. Sure. I'll wait for an officer."

Fucking great.

CHAPTER 2

The bus never felt so small. It's always been tight, but I usually just crash in my quarters and sleep until we get to the next stop on the tour. Tonight, the walls are closing in. I use my arm to wipe the sweat beading across my forehead. Lexis's words cut me to the core. The core I've tried to numb for years.

I'm a total fuckup.

Everything I touch rots and turns to garbage. Because I'm garbage.

Her smile flashes in my memory. The soft, sweet look I remember from high school when we were in love and the world seemed like it was at our fingertips.

Then I fucked it up.

The little brown bottle is perched over the head of the tiny bunk where I typically spend my time in here. I down two of the tiny pills and wait.

There it is.

The rush of ice floods my veins and numbs everything in its path. My body flops onto the bed. I swat at the light switch and cover my head with my pillow to block what little slivers of light are still streaming in through the windows from the neon signs outside.

Finally. I'm comfortable, in the frigid darkness, for the first time since I woke up after missing the show tonight.

Knock, knock.

Fuck. "Go away."

"Open the door, Stone." Carly's voice is soft but firm, like it always is with me.

Sigh. "Please just go away."

"Nope."

I groan and haul my heavy ass out of bed. It's hard to stand up with everything vibrating, so I grab the walls and try to hold myself up. It feels a little like what I imagine the little ball in a pinball machine feels like. Complete with the bells and alarms ringing in my head. Ugh. The headaches aren't fun, but it's worth it so I don't have to feel the weight of the memories.

"What do you want?" I growl as I open the door and see my sister standing there. Tears already welling up in her eyes and making me feel like a jackass before she even says a word. "Fuck. I'm sorry, Carly." I wrap one arm around her and try to pull her into a hug to comfort her, but instead I stumble and almost take us both down the steps leading down to the ground from the bus door.

She lets out a heavy sigh and pushes me back. "You have to get your shit together, Stone." She shakes her head and waves her hand toward the back of the bus. "Do you really think you can keep doing this? Keep sloughing off your responsibility to the band and they'll let you keep playing with them?"

"Don't tell me how to live my life, alright." I hold up one hand to signal her to back up the judgemental train and another to steady myself again. "The boys and I have an understanding. Always have."

"Really?" She folds her arms over her chest and glares at me with a force I haven't seen since I accidentally... maybe not so accidentally, ripped the heads off all her dolls when we were kids.

I was a mean little fuck. "Yes, really. Now get out and let me sleep." *Still am, I guess.*

"They're done, Stone."

"Why does everyone keep telling me that?"

"Who's everyone?"

Ha. "Devon and that weasel Nigel for starters."

"Maybe you should listen."

I shake my head as a chuckle escapes. "I think I'm good."

"Maybe that's the problem with you Stone." Her jaw clenches and I know that look. She's fighting back more tears. "I know you aren't the piece of shit you want everyone to think you are, but I can't keep fighting your battles for you."

"What do you mean fighting my battles for me?"

Her gaze drifts downward to the floor and her voice sounds softer now than ever. "If it wasn't for me, they would've kicked you out of the band before this tour even started. I helped you keep your job and you can't even pull your head out of your ass long enough to realize it."

"Bullshit."

"Okay," she swallows hard. "You know I love you, but I can't do this. It's not healthy for me, so I have to let you go. I hope you get help though." She reaches for the door but I grab her hand before she can.

"Where do you get off judging me? Your life isn't so perfect," I snort. "Jett's a real catch if you ask me."

"He's grieving. You're just a selfish prick," she says jerking her arm out of my grip. "There's a difference." The heartbreak in her eyes cuts me to the bone.

I want to take the words back, but it's too late for that.

Bang. Bang. The bus door rattles from the force of whoever's banging on it from the other side.

"Stone Thompson," a man's voice comes through loud and clear and my heart sinks further to the floor. I didn't think that was even possible.

Carly's eyes search mine for answers. She already knows who's out there and what they want. I see the disappointment drip out of her as she turns toward the door.

"Please don't open that," it comes out in almost a whisper.

Bang. Bang. "We have the bus surrounded. Come out now with your hands up and this can be nice and easy."

"What the hell did you do this time Stone?"

"It was Lexis."

"Why would you even see her when you know she's got it in for you over her sister?" She shakes her head. "And you tried to give me relationship advice," she scoffs. "I'm going out this door in exactly thirty seconds because I do not want to get shot for being caught here with my dickhead brother. Thirty... twenty-nine..."

The blood is pulsing through my veins with the exact force I tried to snuff out only a few minutes ago. *It's too much.* My fist lands in the television screen causing blood stained glass to shatter across the tiny living area. "Damn it," I growl, picking a shard out of my middle knuckle. "Go. Just go, now."

I don't have to tell her twice. She swings the bus door open and holds her hands up as one woman in uniform reaches out and helps her down the steps from the bus door and two more uniformed officers barrel through the door and wrap my arms behind me before I can even stutter out a protest. I don't give a shit anyway. Jail is exactly where a person like me belongs. The pain in Carly's eyes as they lead me toward the squad car is more than my heart can take. I thought I had numbed every part of me, but apparently I'm a dumbass and did a piss poor job of it. She looks away as the photographers finally break past the barricade security tried to offer. They tried... I see the face hiding behind the bright flash and shutter clicks coming from just a few feet away.

Shit. Fuck. Damn it. "Can you guys please get her out of here?"

"Don't worry. Where you're headed she won't be able to follow."

"Great. That's comforting." I duck my head into the car as another cop reads me my rights. I don't hear a damn thing he's saying. The only thing I can think about is how I can repay Lexis for this particular brand of bullshit.

* * *

I LEARNED my arresting officer's name is Maddox Wells and he just happens to be a retired marine. We had plenty of time to chat—*ugh*—on the long ass drive here. It probably wasn't as long as it seemed because of the endless swarm of paparazzi chasing the car and trying to get the money shot. They don't know it yet, but someone already got that shot and that someone just happens to be Adair's ex-wife. *My life is officially fucked.* Adair is our bassist, one night he got drunk and convinced himself it was a great idea to marry this random music blogger to get even with Carly for trying to move on with her life. Carly deserves a hell of a lot better than what Adair gives her. I don't know why the hell she still carries that damn torch for him.

Yes, I do. Because she's a fucking angel. And I'm a shitty brother because I've been caught up in my own shit instead of being there for her. *Fuck.*

"Inside, Thompson." Officer Wells ushers me inside through the open doors and the smell of piss and puke instantly assaults my nose. I fight back the bile rising in the back of my throat.

"I thought I smelled bad after a show," I snort through a cough-gag.

He shrugs and points to the blank white wall across from the camera. "Stand with your back against the wall and look directly into the camera."

Click. Flash. Click. Flash. Click.

"Not all that different from a normal night."

Wells cuts his eyes in my direction and slides some paperwork, no doubt the papers that will outline what a piece of shit I am and how I should be kept away from society, to the other officer. He's younger than Wells and looks like he would rather be doing just about anything other than booking me into a cell.

Me too, brother. Me too. "Do I get a phone call or something?"

The second officer, whose name I still don't know, points to a phone mounted to the wall. "You get one. Make it count." He unlocks the cuffs as the other two officers stand guard to make sure I don't try any shit.

"Right." I nod and rub the red marks on my wrist where the cuffs had been. "I'm in enough shit, I'm not going to try anything."

"That's what they all say."

Huh. He's probably right. I dial Devon's number and pump my fist lightly against the wall each time it rings. "Don't ignore my call right now, dude," I growl into the phone like he can actually hear me.

Beep. A robotic voice comes through the speaker, "We're sorry this voice mailbox is full. Please try again later."

Fuck.

My.

Life.

"Sounds like luck isn't on the table for you tonight," Wells says, nodding to the officers behind me to haul me out of the stark white holding pen and down the narrow hall lined with cells and drunks. The moans and bodily noises are enough to make me want to hurl.

"Welcome to your new home," they both laugh as they shove against my back causing me to lunge forward into the tiny cold space as the lock clicks into place behind me.

Fucking assholes.

The cell they shoved me into is no doubt the epicenter of the piss puke smell. Some dude is sprawled out on the only bunk in here. He reeks to hell and back. I'm not touching him. There's probably a pile of vomit underneath him. I'll just stand here in the corner and wait for my time to talk to the judge. It shouldn't be too long. They wouldn't keep a star locked up in here overnight. It'd be terrible press.

CHAPTER 3

The incessant ringing of an alarm forces my eyes open. I rub the back of my hand against my eyes trying to clear the fog. I instantly regret it. The smell hadn't just been a nightmare. Something in my back cracks as I attempt to unfold myself from the slumped over position I apparently passed out in last night. I wonder how long I was asleep for. Of course, I can't check because they took my phone and everything else I had on me before they threw me in here.

"Morning."

Shit. "Who the hell are you?" Obviously this is my cellmate but it's too goddamn early and my head hurts way too much to think about that right now.

He snorts out a laugh. "Liam."

"Ugh," I groan as I push myself up off the floor. I'm not completely out of shape. I mean, I probably could have laid off the booze and drugs a while ago and been pretty fit, but sleeping on the cold hard floor in a ball was a terrible idea. "I'm Stone."

"I know who the fuck you are." He nods toward the cell door. "Shouldn't your bandmates have sent someone to get you out of here by now?"

Great. A fan. "Uh…" I rub my hand across the back of my neck trying to pull the muscles loose. That was an awful idea. It hurts even more now. "I'm

514

not sure they'd even want me back. They're probably relieved I'm in here instead of on the bus."

"You think they left without you?"

I feel my fist balling up and I have to force the muscles to relax so I don't land a punch straight into the wall and get myself even more time in here... Or a few broken bones. "I wouldn't doubt it."

"Sounds like you're in a hell of a spot then." He wrings his fingers together and leans back on the pathetic excuse for a bed.

I shake my head and try to ignore the idea that I might actually be stuck here. "My sister will send someone... maybe."

"Sure." He closes his eyes and rests one arm over them to block what little light there is coming from the single row of fluorescent lights in the corridor ceiling. "I have a feeling I'll be out of here before you are."

"What makes you so sure of that?" I fight the urge to punch the wall since it's a concrete wall and I'm sure there are at least two cameras on us at all times.

He slowly opens one eye and sizes me up before deciding to answer my question. "I have a team. They'll take care of it."

"A team?" I snort. "Am I supposed to be impressed?" I wipe my forehead with the back of my hand. "And why the hell is it so damn hot in here?"

He shakes his head back and forth and throws his arm back over his eyes. "If your sister doesn't come through, let me know."

"I don't mean to sound like a skeptic or anything, but if you had a team then you wouldn't be laid out on a jail cell bed right next to me." I wrap my hands around the bars, tightening my grip until my hands are shaking. The door rattles as it knocks against the rest of the bars. "Fucking cage."

"Suit yourself." He lifts his arm and peeks out underneath it. "Looks to me like you're withdrawals are hitting you pretty hard there."

"What the fu—" I reach out to grab him by the collar and throw him against the wall, but remember where we are. "I'm fine. Thanks for your concern." The vomit I've kept barely under control since I got here threatens to come up again. I swallow hard and fight back the lump, choking on the metallic taste.

Liam shrugs and pushes himself up on the cot. "I can help you, you know?" He nods toward the edge of the bed and for the first time since I got here I think I have to sit down or I'm going to fall right over.

"I don't need any help," I say, taking the seat he offered.

"Sure. Whatever you say," he says through a thinly veiled laugh. "But in my line of work I see your type everyday."

"What exactly is my type?" I regret asking the second the words come out of my mouth but this headache has my filter at an all time low.

"I'm a coach. I know withdrawal when I see it."

"A fucking coach... What the hell is a coach doing in here?"

He flicks his fingers against the wall making just enough noise that I'd like to break his hand and shove his fingers down his throat. "Sorry, that noise is probably bothering you isn't it? I'm a coach. I got caught making some bets on my team. Big deal, right? You look like you know how to handle yourself. If you ever need to make some extra cash—"

"Right." I snort and hold up one hand as my head flops against the wall. The room won't stop spinning with me trying to hold the contents of my stomach in place. It's like a goddamn amusement park ride. "Listen, I know you think you're a badass since you got caught betting on your little league game or whatever, but if you don't mind, I'm going to take a nap."

Fucking little league coach.

* * *

"THOMPSON." The guard flings the cell door open causing my brain to seize from the pain of the noise.

"What the hell?" My heart's still pounding as he grabs my wrist and pulls me toward the door. "I'm going to need you to take me on a date first, playboy."

"Shut up." He pushes me forward with his baton. "You have a visitor."

Visitor? Thank you, Carly. I should probably apologize for being a dick the last time I saw her. The look she gave me as they pulled me out of the bus played on repeat as I slept. I feel sick.

"Have a seat." He nods toward the empty seat perched in front of a tiny metal table, and recedes back against the wall. The person sitting on the other side isn't Carly. He's at least six inches taller than me and looks like he just jumped out of Sons of Anarchy. He could probably squash my head between his thumb and forefinger, and I'm not tiny by any means. I'm six-foot-two and look like I've spent a fair amount of my time at the gym.

"Who are you?" The metal chair's legs scratch against the concrete floor, causing me to cringe. It's worse than that scene from the shark movie where the dude drags his nails down the chalkboard. *Shit.* I just made myself shudder again from thinking about it.

Charlie Hunnam part deux snorts and slides a paper across the table. "I'm your new best friend." I scan the paper and notice the raised seal at the bottom of the page.

"What's this?"

"It's your ticket out of here. You're welcome."

I shake my head and try to recall the last twelve hours. No one returned my call. No one knows I'm here except maybe Lexis and Carly. "Did Carly send you?"

"I don't know any Carly."

"I don't understand..."

He leans across the table so I can hear him even though he lowers his voice glancing back at the guard. "Liam."

"How did he—" I think back to when the guard jolted me out of my sleep. "Isn't he?" I turn and glance at the door and am quickly reminded that the guard is still standing there fully ready to knock my ass over the head with that club if I do anything he doesn't like.

He leans back in his chair, crossing his arms over his chest causing every vein in his arms to pop right through his skin. This dude is fucking ripped. I might need to hit the gym a little more when I get out of here. "Liam sent me. That's all you need to know." His jaw clenches, as he stares me down like I'm some whipped pup he found in the back alley.

It's starting to really piss me off. "I don't need Liam's help."

"Actually, you don't have a choice."

"I'm fine on my own."

"The bond is already posted, now you need to make good on it." He nods toward the paper. "Flip it over."

"And how am I supposed to do that?" My stomach instantly feels like I'm on one of those looping roller coasters as I scan the paper that had been hidden at the bottom of the stack. "My royalties?"

"Your royalties." He hands me a pen. "Sign it, or Liam will be forced to contact your family for payment."

Damn.

It.

"I'm not signing that." I shake my head and grit my teeth as a string of obscenities play on repeat in my brain.

"Oh, I think you are. You wouldn't want us to find Carly, now would you?" He nods toward the guard who steps forward and taps me on the shoulder with the club.

"Do we have a problem here?" he asks, making sure to push the butt of the club into my shoulder blade.

I grab the pen and sign the bond forms. "Nope. No problems." *Fuck.*

He grabs the forms and jumps up causing the table to rock from the impact of his fists pushing himself up. "Two things. Don't leave the state."

"What's the second thing?" I ask, rubbing my temples.

"You won't need to know if you don't leave the state."

Perfect.

Shit.

To be continued...

* * *

Enjoyed this story? Be sure to leave a review! You can also preorder the full story here: books2read.com/savingstone

About Mandy Melanson

International bestselling romance author Mandy Melanson creates stories to make people laugh out loud and ugly cry.

Want to hang out with the author, win book prizes, see the cool covers first, and support Mandy's books on social media? Join Mandy's street team here: https://bit.ly/mandymelansonsignup

Join Mandy on Socials
Facebook
Twitter
Instagram

CAPTURED BY THE CAPTURI MAFIA

A DARK MAFIA ROMANCE

Lashe Lacroix

Chapter 1

Asha Vivenzio

I had been waiting all my life for this day. Twirling in the mirror, I looked at the off-the-shoulder canary yellow dress that clung to my body. It fit my thick curves like a glove. I had gone on a liquid diet for the last two weeks to ensure I would be able to wear this dress. It was the only one in my size that was fifty percent off, which still took four months of savings to buy. Out the corner of my eye, I saw Telica turning up her nose at me. My baby sister was very stubborn, opinionated, and unapologetically harsh.

Just this one time, I need her to shove her pessimistic views up where the sun does not shine. I need her to be here for me. Is it too much to ask for her to be happy for me?

"Can we leave now?" Telica rolled her eyes and stood to her feet. The chair she was sitting in came crashing to the floor and the ladies that were in the dress shop all turned toward us. She opened the curtain and walked out the dressing room folding her arms over her chest.

My face felt hot as I rushed to pick up the chair. "What is your problem Teli?"

"I don't have a problem. If you want to marry a man that will be cheating on you as soon as you turn your back, that's your choice."

Narrowing my eyes, I glanced behind her, cringing as a small group of ladies formed a circle pointing and whispering about us. I hated when people looked down on us, and I did not like to look like a fool.

"Don't be jealous of Craig and my happiness. You could find someone who loved you too if you stopped being so judgmental." Unzipping my dress, I stopped midway and walked over and snatched the curtain closed.

Inhaling, I tried to focus on the day. In the four years I had been dating Craig Hastings, he had never taken me to dinner. In fact, because he was a Deputy District Attorney (DDA), he worked all the time. He was frugal to a fault stating that he needed to conserve his funds for rainy days. He planned things which was one of the many reasons I was attracted to him. I never meant to date him, but he wore me down until I finally agreed to a first date and the rest was history.

Sighing, I hung the dress on the hanger and jumped into my skinny-legged jeans. Reaching for my blouse, I heard my phone ring and glanced at my purse.

Telica yanked the curtain open. "Just remember when he breaks your heart don't bother running to me. I told you Craig Hastings doesn't love you because he was too busy loving himself." Tossing her hair over her shoulder she lifted her eyebrow.

Ignoring her I pulled my blouse over my head and rummaged through my purse trying to get to my phone. On the sixth ring, I found the phone but Telica snatched it out my hand and tossed it on the ground.

"Remind me again, what man asked you to marry him? What makes you the expert on relationships when you've never had a boyfriend. You don't even sleep with the same man twice. I would be stupid to take advice from you." Walking to the corner of the dressing room, I picked up my phone and inspected the screen.

Thank God the screens not scratched. I did not have insurance on the phone and could not afford to buy another one.

She snorted. Rolling her eyes, she shook her head. "I felt sorry for you, but not anymore. For your sake, I hope he does propose to you tonight. It took him over four years to take you out in public. What a shame."

Ignoring her, I looked at the call log. Nico had called twice. Our brother did not make good decisions and I worried about him constantly.

"That was Nico. When was the last time you talked to him Teli?"

Hearing from our older brother was bittersweet. I love him but I didn't love the trouble that followed him like a shadow. He only called when he wanted something. There was never a call to see if we needed anything because it was always about him.

"Like you care. You only care about Craig, so go be with him." She stomped out of the shop.

Frowning, I didn't recognize the number, so I hit redial. Slinging my purse over my shoulder, I grabbed the dress and walked to stand in the line to pay the final payment.

"Asha, where are you?" asked Nico.

"I was not far from the house. Whose number are you calling me on?"

"I got a new phone. I need you to come by the house."

"Why?" I looked around the store and there was no sign of Telica. We were far from the house which meant she probably hitch-hiked home. The District of Columbia was the nation's capital but that didn't mean anything. The streets were dangerous, and so were the people.

I should've just let her keep her attitude. When doesn't she have a stank attitude? Now, I will be worried about her all night wondering if she was dead in some alley.

"Just come now. I'll tell you when you get here."

"Shaking my head, my shoulders slumped as I moved closer to the checkout counter.

"Fine. I need to stop and get Telica."

"No, I don't want her to know. Come alone."

This was bad. My stomach rocked back and forth, and I covered my mouth with my hand. The last time Nico wanted to speak to me alone without Telica, was when our parents died, and we were being sent to foster care.

"I'm on my way." Hanging up the phone, I slipped it inside my purse and zipped it up. I took one last look at the dress. Something deep inside told me tonight would change my life forever and it had nothing to do with this dress. I stepped out of line and walked back toward the clearance rack.

"Ma'am, I can take you over here." The clerk waved me up to the counter. Smiling, I handed her the dress. No matter what happened tonight, this dress would serve as a beacon of hope. There would be many nights for Craig to take me to dinner.

The cashier swiped the barcode and took the machine and pulled out the ink antitheft device.

"The balance was sixty dollars."

Frowning, I looked at the total on the register. "The dress was two hundred dollars and I had already paid one-eighty while it was on layaway."

"Yes, but the store has a new policy that if the layaway wasn't paid in a week the item went back on the rack to be sold and you lose any monies paid while we reserved it for you. We held this item for two months. I was supposed to put it back on the rack to be bought but I knew you were coming to pay it off today."

He cleared his throat. Someone standing behind me said, "If you can't pay, put the item back so she can ring us up. I have somewhere I need to be."

Turning around, I looked at the rude jerk. He held a pale pink bra and panties set in his hand. "I bet you do. The clerk will wait on you after my transaction is completed."

Pulling out my wallet I handed her the last of the cash I had on me. "Here you go."

She bagged the dress and handed me a receipt. I put the receipt deep inside my purse and rushed out the door, the bag dangling in my hand.

I felt guilty for spending all that money on the dress. It was my money but Telica didn't work and was dependent on Nico and me. Normally, I spent money on both but for once, I wanted something for myself. Popping the trunk, I placed the dress inside and slammed it shut. I didn't want Nico to know that I had spent so much money on a dress. Nico had a job, but he always found ways to spend his money and mine too. This time I spent my own money.

Traffic sucked as usual, but I managed to get to Nico's apartment in forty minutes. Swinging into a parking space, I jumped out and ran up three flights of stairs to his apartment. When I reached the apartment door I was out of breath. Knocking on the door, I bent down trying to catch my breath. This was one of those times that reminded me that I was slightly out of shape. You couldn't tell it by my weight because I was thick in all the right places, but I needed to work on my cardio ASAP.

Nico opened the door and pulled me inside. He quickly locked the door. "What took you so long?"

Frowning, I stood up heaving deep breaths. "Traffic was hectic. What do you want to talk to me about?"

He took a deep breath then held it in. "I need some money."

Narrowing my eyes, I looked at him. Nico was always in a crisp suit and button-up shirt with cuff links. Ever since he got the job, the way he dressed was very upscale and professional. Today was different, and I was not liking that at all.

His clothing which was stonewashed jeans, were wrinkled and not starched. His white shirt looked more like cream with stains and black sweat marks. He didn't look so good. He looked high and that wasn't a good sign.

"What the hell Nico. You've started using again? You promised you would stop."

"I'm not on drugs."

"You're high. I know when you're high." I turned to walk to the door. He could've told me this crap over the phone. I was about to put my dress back and for what? So, he can buy more cocaine and be somewhere hiding out until he had come down from his high.

"You're not listening to me. I need money." He grabbed my arm his nails digging into my flesh.

"I don't have any money." I lifted my hands toward the ceiling in my frustrations. When he just stared at me blankly, I jingled my purse that was on my arm.

Frowning he looked at me. "You got paid today."

"I did and I owed a bill. I have got obligations. You can't always spend your money then come and demand mine." Snatching away from him I walked to the door.

"The one time I depend on you, and you let me down."

"You got paid too. Where was your money? Why were you always broke, and you make more money than I do?"

Nico was a master at playing the victim. I was tired of being everyone's punching bag. His debts were his not ours. I refused to feel guilty for spending some money on myself. Looking at my watch, I headed for the door. I still had time to get home and change in time to make my dinner date with Craig. After this crap with Nico, I would need all the alcohol that Craig was going to offer me. Tonight, I was going to accept. I've had it. You can't save people that don't want to be saved.

I opened the door. Nico slammed it shut before I could walk out.

"If I don't get the money, I'm going to be dead by morning."

"What are you talking about?" My mouth went dry. Walking past him, I went to the kitchen and opened the refrigerator. Nico had no food in there except beer and ten bottles of Dom Perignon champagne.

What the heck is he doing with this expensive crap in his refrigerator? How did he buy this and why?

Nico was always a beer and tequila kind of guy. He didn't drink champagne.

"I owe some really bad people some money. If I don't pay up, they'll kill me."

I wasn't completely in the dark on how the streets worked but when your life was being threatened, I knew it was time to call the cops. What was the alternative?

Whatever Nico had done must be big. He leaned against the counter and stared into space.

"Go to the police."

"The police can't help me. He owned them too, just like he owns me and you."

"How much do you need? I can talk to my boss and see if she would pay me earlier and say was a family emergency."

He laughed. "You work for scraps. I need two hundred thousand dollars or I'm a dead man."

"You can start by selling those bottles of wine in the refrigerator or getting your money back."

"Asha, I need your help."

"What do you want me to do?" Rubbing my temples, I tried to ignore the headache pounding at my temples.

"Nothing. I need you to work on your relationship with Telica. You guys will only have each other now."

"So, you're just giving up. Give the man the money back. You couldn't have spent all of it."

"I don't have it. I owed some people from when I was strung out. I was not using drugs like I used to, so he called in the debt. When the debt was called in you had twenty-four hours to pay it."

"So, you take money from someone else to pay off this debt and you still end up getting hurt or killed. Why didn't you just run and leave town? We could've all relocated and started over fresh."

"He wasn't just going to kill me. He was going to kill you and Telica. I never had a choice."

There was only one thing left to do. I needed to ask Craig for the money. It was a lot of money, but I would pay him back and I've never asked him for anything. There was no way around it. Nico had put himself and us in danger.

We are family and family take care of its own.

I RUSHED out Nico's apartment like the hounds of hades were on my heels. I drove straight to Craig's house. I wouldn't bother calling him in advance. He was supposed to pick me up for our date in a half-hour so he should have been home by now.

Punching his gate code in at the box, I tapped my fingers on the steering wheel, while the gate slowly opened. I didn't know what I was going to say to Craig to get him to give me the money, but it wouldn't be that Nico had taken money from someone. Craig was an attorney and he cared about his job more than he should. I would never tell him something that he could use to get a conviction on my family.

Driving through the complex I parked in front of building five and got out the car. I spotted Craig's Mercedes Benz in his assigned covered parking space. Punching the button for the elevator, I attempted to call Teli again. As usual, when she was mad, I got her voicemail. The elevator doors opened, and I left her a brief message before disconnecting the call.

I rushed down the hall. Knocking on his door, I waited for him to answer. Nibbling on my lip, I pulled out my key ring and used the key he gave me. I sighed in relief when the door opened, without resistance. Before today I had never used the spare key. Locking the door behind me, I flipped on the lights. There were strange sounds coming from the back. I looked at the kitchen and saw a bottle of champagne with two glasses set out, and a black velvet ring box.

Oh my god. I knew it. I knew he was going to pop the question. Should I peek inside?

My hands trembled as I picked up the little black box and opened it. It was empty. The ring box was empty. A high-pitched scream made me drop the empty ring box on the floor. Walking down the hall, I stopped in front of his bedroom door. Like always, it was open, he liked to have sex with the door open.

Craig was fucking some tall, lanky, blonde-haired woman. Squinting, I noticed the word "hoe" stamped on her right butt cheek. My eyes widened. It was Karen.

Karen Adams was supposed to be my best friend. She was the first friend I met when we moved to Washington, DC. I see now that she was not my friend at all.

"You are going to break it off with her? The poor girl thought you were going to marry her?" Karen lifted her finger as she leaned back taking Craig deeper as she stroked him slow. She had a sparkling ten-carat princess cut diamond on her hand.

Teli was right. Craig never cared about anyone but himself. They deserve each other. Four years, I wasted being true to him and he was screwing Karen my best friend.

"I was just using her, to get close to her brother Nico. We have obtained enough evidence to put him away. I don't have to pretend to like her anymore.

Craig was using me the whole time to tear my family apart and I let him do it. Biting my tongue, my mouth flooded with blood and allowed me to blink back the tears. *"Love don't love nobody."*

Turning on heels, I walked out the door without being noticed. There was no way I could help Nico now. We must leave town. There was a chance these people would get tired of looking for us and move on with their lives. I made it to the car before I collapsed on the seat in a ball of tears. I would've followed my first mind and stayed away from Craig, but I let him wear me down.

It was an hour later before I pulled back up to Nico's place. I had left twenty emergency messages on Telica's phone and I was tired of begging her to pick up. I had deeper problems than her hurt feelings. My only hope was that Nico's problems hadn't found her.

Running up the stair, I rushed down to his apartment. The door was wide open. Staring inside his couch and love seat were turned over. There was glass all over the kitchen floor. I pulled out my phone and dialed the police.

Forget this street stuff.

"Hello, what's your emergency?"

We need help. Now.

I crept down the hall holding my phone to my ear. "I'm at my brother's home. Someone has broken inside. There was glass everywhere. Send someone quick."

"Are you and your brother alright?"

"I don't know." My heart thundered in my chest. Swallowing hard past the lump in my throat, I reached his bedroom door and opened it.

Nico was down on his knees with a gun in his mouth. He turned to me, his face was bloodied and swollen. He mouthed something but I was frozen in place. Too late, I realized he mouthed, run.

"Now." My voice was calm considering I was sure that the horrible scene in front of me would be the last thing I ever saw. My twenty-two years of life flashed before my eyes as I watched resignation fall over Nico's face as he bowed his head and closed his eyes. A high-pitched scream tore from my throat.

Just then pain shot through my skull, and I dropped to the floor. Stars appeared in front of my eyes, as I spotted a pair of black boots in front of my face. The boots walked over to my phone and crushed it. Blood traveled down the back of my head, as I stumbled up and tried to run down the hall.

"Sorry love. You were in the wrong place at the wrong time." He picked me up from behind and something sharp stuck me in the neck. I felt my brainpower down like a computer and I slumped in his arms, as darkness engulfed me in his tight embrace.

Chapter 2

Cornelio Capturi

I should be down there busting someone's balls, but I can't seem to push
myself away from my desk and head down to the basement. The video
footage that I was staring at had me riveted to my seat. The star of the show
was that worthless piece of shit Nico Vivenzio a bookie of mine. Most people
were too afraid to steal from me, and yet this recovering junkie stole two
hundred thousand dollars. It was not a chunk of change for me, but that does
not matter. He took something that belonged to me.

The real question was who the hell was the blonde bombshell bleeding
all over my basement floor. A beautiful woman like that should never be
harmed. I usually don't harm woman, except on rare occasions, but she was
not a rare occasion.

What the hell was she doing there anyway? She looked worse off than
Nico, and he was the one who stole from me.

My office door opened, and Lucas waltzed inside. He popped a zanac
and sank down in the chair in front of my desk.

"John screwed up again. He brought Nico, but he also brought some
broad that was with him."

Lucas Puricello was my right-hand man. He was like family; we grew up
in Sicily together. He often knew what I was thinking, and I didn't need to
tell him what to do. We knew each other just that well.

"Who is she?"

"Her name is Asha Vivenzio, his older sister. They have a baby sister,
but she wasn't at Nico's house. I questioned John and he said she walked in
on them when they were about to finish him, and she was on the phone with
the cops." He handed me her driver's license.

Looking at it, I felt my cock grow hard. She would look stunning even in
a mug shot. There was something about her that drew me near. It puzzled
me that someone so beautiful was related to Nico. My lips curved. It was a

shame that her first time in Vegas had introduced her to the basement. I would've rather thrown a hundred stacks on the blackjack and watched her eyes light up as I won.

I always win. When it comes to getting what I want I never stop until I have it.

Handing him her license, I cracked my knuckles. "Fuck. I gave them a simple job, and he screws that up. I'm running out of ways for him to prove himself useful to me."

Forcing myself to stand slowly, I finished my shot of tequila and headed to the basement. If I wanted it done right, I had better do it myself.

Walking down the hall, I stepped in the elevator that took me down to the basement. There were several elevators in the house but this one went down to the basement. Reaching the basement, I nodded to my men and walked over to the captives. They were blindfolded so they couldn't see me. Walking over to Nico I picked up his head by his hair.

"You thought I wouldn't find out you stole from me. You must be the stupidest man on the planet."

Digging my fingers deeper in his hair, I brought my face closer to his. His eyes were dilated. My men had roughed him up, and it pleased me that his face was severely distorted. It didn't matter too much because he was going to die anyway.

"I had no choice but to take the money. I was going to pay you back. I just needed time."

I punched him dead center of his square jaw. I fucking hated liars, and he was lying straight to my face. Blood flew everywhere as his jaw cracked, and he slumped to the ground.

Taking out my handkerchief, I wiped the blood from my knuckles. "Yeah, that was why you snorted up two hundred thousand dollars. You would've done all of us a favor and overdosed."

"He didn't snort it up." Her voice quivered as she spoke up. Her husky voice was seductive, and I was impressed that she stood to her feet with her hands tied behind her back.

A slow smile spread across my face. I tried to ignore her enticing scent of hibiscus and ylang ylang oil, but it seemed she was determined to be involved, so why deny her.

"Baby doll, this doesn't concern you. If you keep your mouth shut, I just might let you go." Walking over to her, I circled her like a shark does its prey.

She turned her head left and right. "I'm involved. He stole to protect me and my baby sister."

What kind of heroic bullshit had Nico sold her? She was making him sound like a sacrificial lamb.

"Nico, have you told her some lies? You must come clean before you die, or must I expose you? I could show her the tape."

"Wow. He told her that he stole for her, and she believed it. I thought she was smarter than that. You graduated for Stanford College valedictorian despite being homeless, so why are you falling for this shit?" asked Lucas.

"Don't curse in front of the lady." I looked at John who was snickering in the corner and balled my fist up. I wasn't happy with him at all. If he were not careful, he would end up following Nico to the afterlife.

Nico shook his head, but he didn't speak. I didn't expect words, but I did want to hear him mumbling. His voice had always irritated me like salt festering in an open wound.

Snapping my fingers at John, I turned back to her. "Bring me the iPad. I guess she needs to find out the truth on her brother before he dies.

"I know that he snorts cocaine, but that wasn't why he stole the money. He owed some bad people, and they were going to hurt us before killing him." She licked her lips.

"Baby doll, you're in the presence of bad people."

Lucas snorted. "I bet she doesn't know what Nico does for a living? They lived in DC, so she was probably clueless."

John put the iPad in my hands and the video was already pulled up on it. I stepped closer to her and pulled down her blindfold. She tipped her head back and started to look at me. When she reached the tattoo of the phoenix rising from fiery ashes on my neck she stopped.

I waited. It felt good that I had her eyes on me. When her eyes reached mine her breath caught, and her mouth dropped open. She liked what she saw, and that pleased me. She attempted to school her features, but I had seen heat flare in her blue eyes. In her driver's license photo, her eyes were hazel.

"Your eyes change color." Inhaling her scent was driving me crazy. Standing here bleeding and confused she was the most alluring woman I had ever seen. It wasn't just her beauty, even though she was breathtakingly beautiful. There was something haunting behind her eyes.

She nodded. "Sometimes."

Pushing play on the video, I handed her the iPad. "It's time you learned who your brother really is?"

Nico got to his feet. My men punched him in the stomach, and he dropped back down on the hard concrete.

She looked at Nico then back at the screen. When she saw him snorting the cocaine, she turned her face away.

"Don't turn your eyes away from the screen. You already know he does drugs. Cocaine, heroin, molly, Percocet's, anything he can get his hands on."

She stared at me. As much as I loved her gaze on me, I pushed the iPad toward her face. "Look for yourself."

On the video, Nico followed Hyong Mun Hee back to the back room. I took my eyes off the screen and looked at her. I didn't need to see Nico sleeping with Hyong again. Homosexuals had been around since the ancient days, so that didn't bother me. I wasn't the type to want to watch other people fucking.

Her breath caught and she dropped the iPad. "Nico, were you sleeping with men? You said you didn't ..."

Raising my eyebrow at her, I waited for her to continue. She was surprised but not because he was homosexual. There was more here that I had missed. It seemed she had known him better than I thought she did.

"Were you forced to have sex with him in order to protect us?"

Nico was gay. He switched up men like he changed his briefs. He was a damn junkie nothing more or less.

"Just who do you think was after Nico? The man on the screen is Hyong Mun Hee, and he's part of the Korean Triad, but he was Nico's boyfriend if you can call him that.

"So, he forced himself on Nico by flaunting his power over him."

No. Nico chased after Hyong until he relented and started dating him. Nico's the type of man that liked the chase not the conquest, so once he's had you the thrill's gone."

You sound like you know a lot about that."

"I'm glad you're interested because you're going to find out the truth."

Chapter 3

Asha

I took a shaky breath. There was no way he heard me mumbling under my breath. It pissed me off that he knew Nico's personal business. Nobody but Nico and I knew that he gravitated toward men and why. What was Nico thinking sleeping with someone from the Korean mafia?

Why can't I keep my big mouth shut? He looked like caramel wrapped in sin.

Shaking my head, I stepped back putting some distance between us. "I'm not interested."

This man was drop-dead gorgeous. He looked like he should be on the cover of a modeling magazine. His body looked like it was chiseled from granite. The tattoo of the phoenix only made him look more rugged and dangerous. The thick, dark, wavy locks that were waved to the back of his head were molded to perfection. The thick curly beard that hung three inches down made me want to throw him against a tree, hook my legs around his waist and ride him until my orgasm could be heard from miles away.

I wasn't interested in him, however. When I'm interested in a man, that implies he and I might have had a future together. I was vulnerable right now, after realizing my best friend stole my man and had the ten-carat ring on her finger that should have been mine.

This man, whoever he was, wasn't dating material. He was dangerous and no matter how my lower lips quivered at his voice, I wasn't going there.

I'm not desperate and I'm not crazy. At least not certifiable yet.

"I hate liars. I usually cut out their tongues but since you and I hadn't met, I'll give you a chance to tell me the truth." He raised his head and crossed his arms.

"I am not interested in you. I want to discuss what my brother and I can do to make this right. You can't mean to kill him like those people". I pointed to the iPad on the floor.

"Do you know who I am?"

His voice was low as if he asked for some sugar for his coffee. He was not the least bit rattled about anything that was going on. He said he was going to kill Nico and he didn't even look upset. He looked bored. Nope, exchanging names wasn't necessary. The quicker Nico and I got out of here, we wouldn't see him again. Turning my head, I tried to see out the window. It was night and I could not see much from here.

"I prefer we don't exchange names. After we come to an agreement, we wouldn't see each other again."

His lips curved. "I'm Cornelio Capturi."

Glancing at Nico, who was lying prone on the floor, I looked around. Was I supposed to know him? I didn't and I didn't want to. He wanted to kill my brother, and he was probably going to shoot us in the head and go drink champagne. What was with all the pleasantries?

"I had a job. I had excellent credit, but no bank would lend me two hundred thousand dollars. I would make payments. I would pay off his debt. I would get you your money."

"You think it's about the money? I don't care about the money."

Searching his eyes, I didn't see anything. His expression wasn't giving me any clues to how he felt. This whole thing doesn't make sense. "I don't understand. If this isn't about the money..."

My eyes lit up. "He betrayed you. You thought you were the only one but then you found out about Hyong Munn-Hee."

The man standing at the door with his hand inside his coat pocket started laughing. "Well damn. This was a first."

"Shut up Lucas."

Cornelio shook his head. "I'm not gay baby doll. No one betrays the Capturi mafia and lives. Have you heard of anyone betraying the mafia and living?"

"HBO shows those kinds of movies all the time boss," said John.

"This wasn't the movies."

"Did he say mafia." My stomach dropped and my knees felt weak. He had taken my blindfold off. He's going to kill us. Telica will never find out what happened to us, and she was impulsive enough to look for us.

"Your wrong. You and I will get to know each other very well."

"Please," said Nico. He crawled lifting his hand to him.

"Don't hurt her. She was innocent." Nico wiped the blood from his swollen eyes.

"You put her in this, not me. You knew what would happen if you ever screwed me over. You knew when you started working for me, that I own you and everything you own."

"Please don't," said Nico. He tried to get to his feet but the man uppercut him and put the gun in his mouth.

"Don't. Please don't do this." I tried to run toward Nico, but he grabbed me from behind.

"He owns nothing of value. We are only common people working for a living. He owns nothing to his name."

Cornelio turned me around in his arms and let my feet touch the floor. However, his grip was not released on my arms. My chest heaved and because we were so close my breast brushed against his chest with each inhalation.

Closing my eyes, I tried to ignore the shock of heat from his arms on mine. His scent reminded me of a saltwater sea. Saliva pooled in my mouth.

"Wrong baby doll. Have you of no value?"

"Nico is my brother, but he doesn't own me, nor I him. People don't own people. That would be slavery."

He dug his hand in my hair and tilted my head. "Yes. I own you. You will serve me in every way."

His grip on my hair was rough. I expected to see a bald spot when he let me go. His hand traveled from my hair down to my neck and I swallowed. "You've lost your mind. I won't be your slave. Go pay a prostitute."

"Why when we both know that your pussy is as wet as the Yangtze River. Is it as beautiful?" He bent and placed a soft kiss on my neck.

I couldn't keep my legs from buckling. His rough handling, I could endure but his gentleness was destroying my soul. In that moment I hated my body for being weak. Most importantly, I hated Craig for not making me as hot and wet as the asshole who held me in his arms.

"Let me go." I dug my nails into his arms, but he just laughed.

"Oh, I don't think so. Lucas, take her upstairs while I finish Nico. Take her to the penthouse," He tossed me aside and strolled over to Nico.

The bastard was about to kill my brother. This can't be happening. Someone please do something.

"No, don't do this. I'll do whatever you want. Please don't hurt him."

"Yes, you will, but not for this piece of shit. You'll do it because those pretty pink lips, ache so bad that the thought of me was enough to make you orgasm on the spot."

"Never."

The burly man standing close to the door, caught my hand just as I swung it at Cornelio. The bastard didn't even turn around.

I fought with everything I had, but the man was too strong. He dragged me out of there just as Cornelio pulled a Glock from his jacket and attached a silence to it. Kicking and bucking, I tried to free myself. Nico looked at me and shook his head.

Damn him. He was asking me to accept that this was it. This was the end of my big brother who had always been in my life. I couldn't accept it. I refused. Jabbing my elbow in the man's gut, I jumped on Cornelio's back pounding my fist.

I was pulled off him, and he turned and looked at me.

"You'll do well. I like my women with spunk."

I opened my mouth and spit in his face. He raised his hand and wiped the spittle from his face. His face was dark with rage and I saw his hands trembling.

"Do your worse. I'm not afraid of you. I will never submit."

"I'll make you clean my face later." He smiled.

"You are failing miserably. You issued several challenges tonight and I accept every one of them. You bring me joy."

What the fuck? This man was a psycho.

"You want a rag boss?"

"No, she'll clean it with her tongue later."

I was lifted from behind and carried out of the basement over his shoulder. I watched as he pointed the gun at Nico. My heart slammed in my chest as the door slammed shut, and I heard two muffled gunshots.

Nico!

I fainted.

I came to on the softest mattress I had ever laid on. The penthouse was the lap of luxury. Under different circumstances, I would have enjoyed it. A flashback of Nico on his knees and the gunshots played in my mind. I fell on the bed, sobbing.

Why? Everything came down to money, it was the root of evil.

Chapter 4

Cornelio

A iming my gun, I fired two shots at Nico. Even with the door closed, I heard her muffled scream. She was magnificent in her rage. Asha had more balls than most mafia men. Nico should take lessons from her. He was a weakling. I looked at him and wrinkled my nose.

"Did you really just shit on yourself. Nico, you're really a piece of shit."

"I thought you were going to shoot him," said John.

I smiled but it didn't reach my eyes. John wanted me to shoot Nico. In fact, he had been counting on it.

"There was still a question that plagued me about Nico. How did he meet Hyong Mun-Hee? It was not like they traveled in the same circles or shared mutual friends." I pointed the gun at John.

"I don't know boss. Fetish Nights maybe."

"Nico was in the closet so why would he be at a gay club?"

I had already checked and knew that Nico wasn't openly gay. He hadn't had many male lovers despite my implication to Asha that he had. Nico slept around but he did so with women. He never discriminated. He liked woman big, small and anything in between. That was his way of coping with his situation. He used sex to stay off the drugs until he met Hyong Mun-Hee.

"You know how it is. One of his gay lovers must have introduced him to Hyong Mun-Hee."

Pow. I shot John in the kneecap. His lies were boring me, and he had a date with death. "You were mad that he turned you down, so you introduced him to Hyong Mun-Hee."

John rolled on the floor making high-pitched sounds like a hyena. He was pathetic and stupid if he thought I hadn't known that he had been working with the Hoon Mafia. Nae Seung Hoon, the Korean Triad don, was a greedy bastard, who had his eye on my infrastructure for some time now. John was his flunky.

"He led me on then laughed at me. How could he think he was better than me? Him and his whole family grew up in foster care. He's gay because he was raped. How sad is that? He takes drugs to numb his pain."

"He wasn't attracted to you John. Your stomach is so huge I wondered if you had seen your dick in ten years."

"I just introduced them. I didn't make him steal money from you." He sat up holding his hands up as he pleads his innocence to me.

"You were around the Koreans so long; you forgot what I do to liars. Let me remind you." I shot him in the other kneecap.

"Since you love taking dick you should lose yours." When he fell back on the floor, I shot him in the dick.

His incoherent screams were like Mozart to my ears. I nodded for them to hold this maggot still. Taking my Benchmade Hidden Hunter Cannon knife out, I waltzed toward him. "Hold his tongue out boys."

After two minutes of him squirming, I cut off his tongue and shoved it back in his mouth. "There was no need to tell me what you told the Hoon Mafia. Their faith would be worse than yours. At least you won't have to abstain long since I'll be sending them to hell to join you."

Pointing the gun at his head, I pulled the trigger. He slumped to the floor.

"Take this piece of shit out and leave his body on Korean territory. They can bury his ass."

Wiping the blood off my hands, I bent down and grabbed Nico's head. "You had better be elated that you didn't screw him. He was infected with the sauce, and he wanted to take as many people down with him as possible."

"Why?" His jaw was hanging at an awkward angle.

I shrugged. "Hell, if I know. My guess is he didn't like to use condoms, and he trusted the wrong man."

Nico shook his head. "Why didn't you shoot me."

"You have got information I want."

"Hyong and I didn't do much talking."

"Yeah, I know. You fucked like rabbits, but I don't want information on him." I walked to the door. I was done with Nico for now. I had better things to be doing like breaking Asha. I couldn't wait for her to shatter in my arms.

Opening the door, I turned to look at Nico. He looked confused.

"Asha, I want to know everything about her."

Nico shook his head. He jumped to his feet charging toward me. I lifted the gun and shot him in the thigh, making sure not to hit any major arteries. "You don't have a choice. She's belonged to me now."

"Leave her alone."

"No." I walked out the door. Two of my guards were posted at the door and Nico wasn't in any condition to move let alone escape.

Whistling, I took the stairs up. On the fourth floor, I opened the door and spotted, Sue Yong-Jin, the infamous Korean hitman. Sliding back through the doors, I ran back down the stairs.

"Lucas, get the men and Asha out of here. Sue Yong-Jin is here."

"Damn."

My stomach felt like hard pebbles pressed against my gut. "What. Spit it out Lucas."

"Asha got away from me. I'll get her back, just get out of here."

"Fuck that." I hung up on him.

I stopped on the first floor. "Parties over. Everyone out, Now." I snapped my fingers and my men jumped into action clearing everyone out.

Zetico Vertucci walked over to me with a Cuban cigar hanging from his lips. "What happened boss? Anything you need me to do?"

"Sue Yong-Jin paid us a visit. I don't want these people harmed. Get Nico from the basement and you and the guys meet me at the safe house."

"Got it." He lifted his AK47 and darted through the door. Zetico was fast. He was one of the tallest men in the Familia, and he used his height to his advantage.

Alcino and Siriano ran over to me. "What happened boss?"

"Sue Yong-Jin came here. We'll respond but not now when there are others that could get hurt. We'll meet up at the safe house."

"I want to stay with you," said Alcino.

"Come Alcino you can kill a lot of them cockroaches later. Let's go."

Alcino Santagata frowned. "I'm leaving when you leave."

Ever since I had saved his life, he was obsessed with paying back the favor. I appreciated it but he was driving me insane. "You can have my back later."

Running through the crowd, I darted through the doors. I slipped inside the small hidden door. Turning around, I swung my knife, at the man's throat.

"It's me," said Quintillo.

"One of these days, I'm going to kill you by accident."

Quintillo Tartalione was like a ghost.

"I've got your back, so tell me what we're doing?"

"Lucas lost Asha and Sue Yong-Jin is here." Turning I rushed through the door leading down the hidden narrow passage. It was a passage, only Luca, Eleuterio and I know about.

Quintillo glanced at his watch. "The bastard had probably rigged this place to blow up. He was known to set the five-minute bombs. How long has he been here?"

"I don't know, probably ten minutes." Pocketing my knife, I moved quickly to the library. Touching a hidden panel on the wall, it opened after it recognized my bio signature. I grabbed two AK 47s, slung the straps over my shoulder and pocketed several grenades as well as ammunitions. Strapping myself into the Kevlar vest, I tossed him one. "Put this on."

He caught it and put it on. "We need to evacuate now."

"Go I'll meet you at the safe house." I touched a button and the panel closed. Moving to the door, I lifted the gun.

"Hell no. Blood in and blood out."

I peeked around the doorframe. Rushing down the hall, I spotted Sue Yong-Jin, and I fired. He ducked behind the wall and fired off a couple of shots. Ducking, I waited until he stopped firing at me.

Quintillo tossed a smoke bomb down the hall. He slid next to me and pulled me toward the exit. He had to drag me out of there. I was like a rabid pit-bull feigning for blood.

What the hell is he doing?

"He plans to blow this place up. Lucas text me that he got Asha out. Let's go."

I bucked and fought, but he ran through the secret passage, instead of

545

hanging a left, he turned right leading us toward the road. He didn't put me down until we were standing on the backstreet hearing the parting sounds of the Vegas strip.

"I had him. What the fuck did you do?" My hands trembled. Shaking my head, I stomped back toward the passage before he could stop me.

Boom. Boom. Boom.

The blast shook everything, and the passage collapsed. I flew back several feet, knocking my head on a street pole.

"I told you, he was blowing up the place. He doesn't fight, he just blows shit up."

"You should've let me shoot him when I had the chance." I rubbed the back of my head, as I felt a lump forming at the base on my skull.

"We'll get him next time."

Tires screeched. I looked around him and saw Lucas jump out the car.

"I thought you were still inside."

"I was. Quintillo dragged my ass out." I ran to the front and leapt on the passenger side. I liked riding shotgun, but I didn't like to drive. Lifting my gun, I slipped inside the seat and slammed the door shut. After looking around and not seeing any threats, I turned to the backseat.

Oh no.

Lucas and Quintillo jumped inside.

"Where was she?" I narrowed my gaze on Quintillo.

"I told you she got away when you called." Lucas pulled off the side of the road and sped down the street.

"Quintillo, told me you had Asha."

His face turned red. "I lied. If I told you Lucas let her escape, you wouldn't have left the casino. You'd also be dead right now, and she needs you to save her from Nae Seung Hoon."

My fist balls up at my side. If he touched one hair on her head his whole bloodline would be wiped from the earth. He was already a dead man. "Drive Lucas."

Chapter 5

Asha

I lifted myself off the bed and wiped my face. He had killed Nico. I was going to kill him or die trying. What else would I have to live for? Telica was smart and had street sense. I did not, so she would be fine on her own. She wouldn't have a choice. I searched the drawers and the nightstands in the room. There were condoms, anal plugs, cock rings, dildos, and penis sleeves but no weapons. Unless he had a heart attack after the strongest orgasm of his life, I had nothing. The room was elegant. There were black and cream Dior crush velvet drapes that hung over the windows. From the balcony, there was a stunning view of Las Vegas. I could see that I was on the Las Vegas strip. Unlike, the parties down below, I was being held hostage and unable to go and comes as I please. My treacherous pussy clenched on the word come.

Rushing to the phone, I dialed Telica's number. My legs almost buckled when the phone started ringing.

Pick up. Pick up. Come on Telica.

"Hello. Hello."

"Telica. Are you safe? Me and Nico..." My voice trailed off as I recognized the voicemail. I had asked her to change this crap but like usual she didn't do it.

"Fool you. I'm not in. You know what to do next." Beep.

"Nico and I are in trouble. We ... never mind where we are. Get your stuff and leave the state ASAP. I do not want what happened to us to happen to you. These men were bad men they don't play around. I love you and don't try looking for us. You wanted to spread your wings, and I should've let you do it sooner. I love you butterfly." Placing my hand over my mouth I slammed the phone down and cried.

How do you tell someone goodbye that you never wanted to leave?

Walking to the bathroom, I flipped the light switch on. Splashing cold water on my face, I tried to think of my next steps. Looking around the bath-

547

room, I didn't see anything I could use as a weapon. Taking the towel holder, I flung it at the glass and ducked. Glass shattered everywhere, and some pieces cut my hands as I shielded my face from the shards.

Standing I grabbed a big piece of the glass shard and hid it underneath my shirt sleeve. Rushing into the bedroom, I heard heavy boots running toward the room. Tossing my hair over my shoulder I waited. The door opened and the burly man named Lucas stepped inside.

"What was that noise?"

"I don't know."

He walked past me, and I swung the knife at the back of his head. He ducked and reached for me, I swiped left and right backing up.

"Damn." He held his hand up and I tore his shirt.

I had cut him deep. Sprinting to the door, I ran down the hall. I hopped over the banister, lost my balance, and rolled down the rest of the steps. Jumping to my feet, I flung the front door open and ran out.

"Come back here." Shouted Lucas.

Dogs barking loudly weren't helping me. Coming to a chain fence, I kicked off my shoes and scaled it. Running behind the next-door neighbors shed, I placed my hands over my mouth. Someone was out here with me, and it wasn't Lucas. He had been too far behind me to catch up so quick. Whoever was out here wasn't a friend of Cornelio's, which made me a target. I was in deeper trouble than I had imagined. The shed door opened, and I had to cross my legs to keep from urinating all over myself.

A few minutes later, the shed door closed. I ceased breathing. Closing my eyes, I strained to hear how many men were out here with me. I couldn't hear anything past the dogs barking.

I could not wait behind the shed forever. This was my chance at freedom, and I was going to take it. I still intended to kill Cornelio but that meant I had to live through the night. Leaning over to the right, I peeked behind the shed. It was dark and impossible to see anything. There could be a Pitbull waiting to bite my face off and I wouldn't know it.

Taking a deep breath, I sprinted toward the right going around the house. Hopping the fence, I maintained my speed ducking behind trees and staying away from any light source. Tree branches crunched behind me, and

I crept behind another house. This house did not have shed. I balled myself up as small as I could and hid behind the trashcan.

"Are you sure she went this way? What woman runs from Cornelio? She had to crave a death wish to do that dumb shit."

Hey, if he can't keep his whore on a leash that's even better for us. When we send him her head, he'll know we mean business and that he can't mess with the Gorducci Mafia."

Who was the Gorducci Mafia and why do they want me? They need to take up their issue with Cornelio.

"Vincent I normally feel bad about killing woman, but I think I'm going to enjoy killing her. I might even make her do me before I slit her throat."

"Fernado, that is just sick. You are one sick fuck."

He wanted to rape me then slit my throat. I should've stayed in Cornelio's penthouse. At least I had a chance to kill him when he lets his guard down. I'm out here alone and there are two of them.

I wish I had a gun; Nico had always warned me that the city was dangerous and that I needed to start carrying a concealed weapon, but I didn't want to. If I had listened maybe I wouldn't be without it now. Cornelio's men didn't search me unless they did it when I was unconscious.

"Vincent you take the left and I'll take the right. She couldn't have gone far."

"I'll meet you back at this spot."

"Be careful Fernando. You tend to daydream when you smoke. Do yourself a favor and light up later."

I heard one of them take off. It sounded like he went left. That meant I was stuck with Fernando maybe. Those were better odds than trying to fight them both.

He struck a match and the light shined right on me where I was bunched up behind the trashcan. Dang, I have crappy luck.

"Well, well, look what I found. Don't worry. I'm not going to hurt you yet."

I stood up and swung the trashcan at his face. It hit him in the face, and I took off running. I heard him breathing behind me. I jumped over the fence and ran into a muscular chest. I fought hard.

"I'm going to kill you for that," said Fernando. He skidded to a halt as he saw the man holding me with a gun pointed at him.

Bam. Bam. Bam. He fired two shots to the heart and one to the head. The man holding me was wearing black leather gloves and smelled like old spice.

"Let me go."

"Why? You're obviously important if the Gorducci Mafia wants you."

"They don't even know me." I stopped struggling when he put the hot barrel of the gun to my cheek. I couldn't see it, but I felt it and my heart ached.

"Doesn't matter. You were at Cornelio's house and anyone that's around him is my enemy."

"He's my enemy too. I was running from him. Do I look like I was a guest?"

"You look like you're going to do what I tell you or I'm going to blow your head off."

Placing my hands up, I stopped struggling and walked in front of him. Something told me that this man was more dangerous than the Gorducci Mafia.

He led me around the corner away from Cornelio's house, and into an all-black sedan with tinted window. He pressed a button and the doors lifted like bird wings and shoved me into the back seat. I was grateful for some space between him and his gun. There was something about him that told me he was lethal. He pulled the trigger and shot Fernando in the face without hesitation. What had I gotten myself into?

I was wrong. My situation has officially gotten worse.

He slammed the door and slid into the driver's seat. He drove the car without putting a seatbelt on. He parked in the alley down the street from Cornelio's place. I had to admit if I had a choice, I'd choose Cornelio.

This man looked like a tall and lanky Jet Li. His suit was not tight on him, and he moved like the wind. He was stealthy and graceful. It was almost like his body was one with nature. I hadn't seen him do anything but shoot, but I was convinced that he knew martial arts. It wasn't because he was Asian, but there was something about his movements that suggested he studied martial arts.

"Who are you?"

"I'm Hyong Mun-Hee but most people call me the bogie man."

I'm not sure why I asked. I didn't know him, and I was sure I didn't want to get to know him.

"I'll be back." I leaned down and stuck something underneath the seat.

What the heck did he stick under there? Frowning I sat up and watched him as he got out the car. He stopped in front of my door and opened it.

"Don't go anywhere. I placed a bomb under the seat. If you move, leave the car, tamper with it, or if the car gets shot it will detonate. You can only disarm it is with my biosignature." He left my side car door open and moved several feet away from the car.

"If you don't believe me, try to get out." He stepped back several more spaces and leaned up against the tree.

I was right. He is worse than all of them. He wants to watch me blow up. He might blow me up anyway. Why should I trust him?

After several agonizing minutes, I realized that he was gone, and the door was wide open. Wiping my sweaty hands on my legs, I bent and looked at the bomb under the driver's seat. There were flashing red lights on it and the timer showed four minutes and sixty seconds.

Why doesn't anyone in the mafia make idle threats? Wiping the sweat from my brow I scooted down in the seat so nobody would see me.

This was an impossible situation. I was dead if I moved and dead if I didn't. The question was how I want to die. Do I want to be tortured or blown up?

Chapter 6

Cornelio

N ae Seung Hoon had made a fatal mistake. He came for me on my
own turf. He took what belonged to me, and now he will pay. Later I
will address Quintillo lying to me. It doesn't matter that he did it to save my
life. I refuse to tolerate liars on any level. If you deal with me, you deal
straight up or not at all. The gall to think he sent one man in, to kill my
whole infrastructure. Big mistake. Every man had a weakness and I won't
rest until I have found his.

Pulling out my phone, I scanned our surroundings. We weren't being
followed, but that was more disturbing than surprising.

"Alcino tell me you've got some information for me."

"Sure, do boss. I found two lacks from the Gorducci Mafia a few blocks
from your spot. It looked like Hyong Mun-Hee had gotten to them before we
could. I think they were following your girl and ran into him."

Gritting my teeth, I adjusted myself in my seat. "I can't talk to the dead.
Give me something I can work with." Rubbing my temples, I ignored the
sharp pain shooting through my temples. I didn't get to take my high blood
pressure medicine, so my head felt like an axe was buried in it.

"I have a meeting with one of their made men on the inside. I'll get something tonight. I don't trust him."

"He would do well not to trust me. When are you meeting with him and
what is his name?"

"His name is Po Hei- Ran and I'm meeting with him at The Venetian at
nine thirty tonight."

"Don't let him know we're coming. I want him to think you're alone."

"Got it."

Lucas pulled around the corner and drove down the street. He passed
the safe house. We never drive any cars into the safe house. We swung
around and went through a construction site, that was a secret entrance
underneath the underpass. There were always benefits to custom building

your house and owning all businesses around it. Hoping out the car, I walked deeper into the tunnel and touched a hidden spot on the wall. Once my biometrical signature was logged the door opened, and I walked inside.

There was a woman sitting handcuff to the table near Alcino. I looked at Eleuterio and Zetico, but they glanced at Alcino.

She bared a slight resemblance to Asha. Asha was stunning in an exotic way and this woman was pretty but forgettable. Alcino hadn't mentioned her

"Who is she?"

"I didn't want Nae Seung Hoon to get to her first, so I went and got her," said Alcino.

There was more to this story. If my suspicions were correct this was Asha's baby sister. That meant she was off-limits to Alcino. Knowing him he had already fucked her seven ways to Sunday. Alcino was the pretty boy.

He always gets what he wants, and women don't make him work for it, so he becomes bored. He's also a kinky fuck if what the women say is true, and I don't want him breaking this little girl's heart.

Alcino always breaks their hearts.

"My office." Tuning out Lucas', and Quintillo's snickering, I ignored Alcino handing Siriano a stack of hundreds. Those two were damn near inseparable. Siriano was the reasonable one and Alcino was the reckless one. Siriano was Alcino's light when the darkness became too much. Walking into my office, I grabbed the bottle of Armand de Brignac Champagne. I needed something smooth and nice, and this would do the trick. I did not drink it often, just on special occasions, and I wanted to introduce Asha to it. I doubt she had ever sipped something so extravagant.

Pouring us a glass, I sat down in my chair. Alcino came inside and shut the door. He had walked slowly which meant he was nervous about my reaction, and he should be.

I pushed the glass over to him. "Take a sip and tell me what you think."

He took a sip and put the cup down. "Tastes like a champagne I would spend on a girl that I was trying to screw that night. It's quality and smooth. It doesn't hurt that the bottle was pretty."

"Tell the truth. Who was the girl?"

"That was Telica Vivenzio, Asha's baby sister." He looked at me and stopped talking.

Great. He liked her. This was a freaking mess. I forbid it. He would just have to find another woman to screw. This situation leads to many broken hearts around the world and this was one girl I could save.

"Must I pistol whip you? The whole story. Don't make me ask you again."

"Telica and I know each other. We've been talking for five months and I fly down to the District of Columbia to see her. This weekend was the first time she agreed to come to Vegas so when everything popped off, I went and picked her up."

"You were screwing Thalia five months ago until she broke up with you."

Alcino shrugged. "I broke it off with her. She wanted more than I could give her."

"Bullshit. You broke it off with her because you were focused on this girl, but I forbid it. You can't have her."

Alcino leaned away from me. When my voice raised, he turned and looked at the door. "You don't understand; I have already had her. We are in a relationship."

WTF? Did he just say the r word? Alcino has never done relationships.

"If I call her in here now, she'll tell me you to are in a relationship?"

"No, she doesn't do relationships. If you asked her if we were monogamous in our relationship, she would still say no."

My mouth fell open. Alcino had shared women with some of the guys but I didn't think he let the woman be as free. "You allow her sex with other men?"

"No. Any man touches her is dead."

"Are you going to kill her too? It seems pointless to kill a man over a woman free with her favors."

"She's not, but she would say she was. She has commitment issues. She was not engaged like Asha, but she was a whore."

I spit the champagne out that was in my mouth. "Who was he?"

"I have a whole file on him. Let me go get it. I wasn't just going to

District of Columbia to check up on her. I was working." He jumped up and rushed out the room.

Asha hadn't mentioned a fiancée. Well, he was an ex-fiancée. There was no way he was marrying Asha now. She was mine the moment she woke up on my basement floor. Our sexual attraction sealed her faith. Why marry a man that can't please you like a woman should be?

Alcino came back in with a suitcase. He opened it up and pulled out a lockbox. He produced a skeleton key and opened it. Inside he had what looked like several years of files.

This doesn't make sense. Why so much research if you just met this girl five months ago?

"This looks like more than five months of research." I raised my brow as he took out another lockbox and opened it.

"These are all the recent files for this year." He handed me the green tin box and the key.

I looked at him then down at the box.

"Five months ago, was not when I met her. It was when she thinks we met. She was dealing with a bad guy. He's involved in human trafficking, mostly woman and kids. The ones he like he keeps and when he gets bored, he cuts them up and puts them in a deep freezer. At the perfect time, he thaws the pieces out and scatters them across the world."

Pushing my glass away from me, I lean back in my seat. I had lost my thirst for the champagne. "What was his name?"

"Daniel Pennington."

Why does that name sound familiar? I drummed my fingers on the table.

Oh, I know.

"I remember reading something on him, being found murdered with his dick cut off and his lips removed. There was something about two hundred kids being recovered."

Alcino was the one that tortured and killed him for the Familia. He had been killing people since he was five. He was the last man you would think would be involved with stalking a serial killer that alluded the government for seventy years.

Alicino's nickname was Black Shadow. He was seen only when he wanted to be.

"You saved her but why keep in touch. She doesn't have a clue that you've fallen for her, does she?"

"I haven't fallen. From time to time, I check on her."

"That guy that was found five years ago. How old was she then sixteen?"

"She was fourteen. I don't want her finding out. I just got out of the doghouse, and she was finally speaking to me again."

"What does she think you do?"

"She knows I'm a debt collector. I told her that I gamble on the side to make real cash."

I couldn't process everything Alcino had said and more important what he didn't say. He had been protecting this girl since she was fourteen, and he wasn't ever going to let her go.

He was right to bring her here with us. God help the fool who tries to mess with Telica. Alcino was one donut shy of a full box, from losing all sanity and most days we questioned what little he had. Fucking with this girl would send him over the edge and not even I would venture into the darkness to bring him to the light.

Sighing I pulled out the first folder. We had a few hours before we had to meet Po Hei- Ran, and I needed to know who Asha's ex-fiancée was.

"Her ex fiancée was Craig Hastings the Deputy District Attorney."

"Yes, and he was looking for her since she didn't end the relationship with him."

Frowning I looked down at his picture with the mayor of DC. He had a smug look of entitlement on his face. I couldn't picture them too as an item let alone her husband.

"He's not her type." Craig looked self-centered, and he did not look like he knew what to do with a passionate woman like Asha. He looked like the I got mine now you get yours kind of a guy.

"He never intended to marry her. He proposed to her best friend Karen, who he's been seeing their entire relationship."

"Does she know?"

Alcino tilted his head. "Maybe. He said it was not like her not to return his calls. If she does, she never confronted him with it."

Shaking my head, I rubbed my jaw. "How much does he know about Nico. Are we compromised?"

He was making a huge name for himself in the streets.

"I can't be too sure. Telica hates his guts and didn't approve of him so there was a lot of friction between her and Asha."

"Asha would just have to find out. For this to work you will need to do this. I'm thinking Siriano should do it."

"Do what?" Alcino frowned. His fist balled up and his body went rigid.

"Take Telica away for a while. When I tell Asha her sister's in danger and for me to save her, she needs to talk to Craig, she'll do it."

He smiled. "I can take her away for a while."

"I meant what I said. You need to break free from your infatuation with her if you really want to protect her. You can't have her. Your lifestyle would not be conducive to a healthy relationship."

Alcino clenched his jaw. "Siriano shouldn't go. Women fall all over him all the time. I don't want him to go."

"Your mine needs to be here and not wondering whether he's screwing her."

"I won't have to wonder." He cracked his knuckles.

Rolling my eyes, I stood up. "What was it going to take to get her out of your system?"

"I don't know. I had been trying. There was something about her that beckoned me near. We understood each other on a deeper level."

Chapter 7

Asha

This was the last moments of my life. My bladder made the life and death decision for me. I refused to sit here and piss on myself. I might not be able to determine how I was going to die, but I'd decided it wouldn't be with a pool of urine languishing down my legs. Scooting to the end of the car, I felt the cool breeze on my heated skin. Funny how during your last moments of life, you appreciate everything that you had taken for granted daily, wind, air, water, food, and tissue.

Closing my eyes, I bent my head and confessed my sins, not all of them but the biggest ones. I was going to see the creator soon enough, and my judgement was on the horizon, but I was still determined not to urinate on myself. Shaking my leg distracted me enough to finish the last of my prayer, pledges, and pleadings. I don't want to die, but I was at the crossroads. Grabbing the seat, I got in a crouching position and jumped out the car.

Landing in the street, my ankle buckled, and I fell hard on my knees scraping the flesh and fabric from my pants. Ignoring the sharp throbbing pain in my knees and ankle, I rolled until I was several feet away from the car. I took off running toward the house putting distance between the car and me.

Reaching the back door, I turned around. My adrenaline spiked in my veins and my temple throbbed from my jaw to my hair.

That rat-faced bastard had lied. He was bluffing. Well the joke is on him. I didn't stay in the car.

I opened the door. Boom. The force of the explosion threw me through the door and into the wall. My head hit the cement wall and slid to the ground. Blood trailed down my head. Stars appeared in my eyes as I blinked back tears.

I had to get up. Staggering to my feet, rapidly blinking, I stumbled a few feet into another door that was open. It was an office. Leaning against the large built-in bookshelves, I moved toward a doorway. The smell of leather and crisp paper reminded me of a real estate office, except cleaner.

I looked around for the restroom. Spotting the toilet, I didn't waste any time. Lining the toilet with four layers of tissue, I sat down.

He cleared his throat. "Don't bother rushing. I like what I see."

My stomach clenched and I let out a series of large farts. Closing my eyes, I tried to force the rest of the flow to hurry just in case he tossed me off the toilet.

What was wrong with these people? Opening one eye, I stared at the stranger. He was not the nut job that tried to blow me up, but he was not safe either.

"Who are you?" Tearing off some tissue, I tried to wipe as quickly as possible and get my torn pants up over butt.

"My name is Jered. I'm a friend of Cornelio."

Readjusting my clothes, I washed my hands.

"Nice to meet you."

"What's your name. Is it a game that you're not telling me?"

"Sara." Wiping my hands on the towel I waited for him to back up, so I could get out, but he did not move. He seemed content just standing there.

Jared looked like a dirty old man. He had a beard that hung down several inches past his chin, like Cornelio's but it wasn't well maintained. His clothes were loose-fitting like he had lost a bunch of weight recently and his face was hard with high cheekbones.

"He told me not to be long, so I had better get back." I pushed past him and felt his clammy hands on both butt cheeks. I ran to the door and down the hall.

An arm wound around my waist and lifted me off the floor. "Cornelio had to wait. You're here with Jared. I am not scared of him and I'm sure he would not mind sharing.

Twisting and kicking in his arms I tried to break free. "Let me go you pervert."

"You're not afraid of Cornelio. Wow. You must be stupider than you look."

Craning my neck, I looked past Jared and sagged in his arms as I saw Lucas. His lips tilted upward at my relief.

Lucas didn't seem like the smiling type. If he were about to shoot Jared, I hoped he planned that I would be standing beside him before doing it. Bullets had no names on them and would not discriminate.

"Sweetheart. You should have told me you were being shared with Cornelio. You can do us both. I don't mind sharing. My friends and I share woman all the time."

That is probably why you look like a skeleton serenading death. Whatever money you have can't cover up for your vile ways and disturbing sickly appearance.

Jared twisted so that he was facing Lucas head-on and one hand had slipped into his jacket. "Lucas do yourself a favor and mind your own business. When are you tired of being his dog, fetching and doing his business? Do you ever have an original thought, or does he have to hold your balls too?"

"Let her go." Lucas swung his right hand and Jared's body landed on the floor.

"Bastard." Jared made a high-pitched scream and dropped me as he fumbled to get his gun. I kicked him in the backside and ran down the hallway.

"Asha you're making a mistake." Lucas wiped his blade on his handkerchief and tossed it to the ground.

"Thanks, but I'll just be on my way now." Before I burst through the door I stopped and saw Lucas slit Jared's throat. He stood and shook his head.

"No good deed." Lucas began running down the hall after me. I swung the door open and looked at him one last time.

"I hope I never see you again." I ran smack into a wall of muscles. Before, I could draw breath his hands were gripping my neck. My air was cut off. I knew any second, my windpipe would be crushed.

"Lucas before I kill you, commit this image to memory. You'll live today so you can tell him what I did to her. How she suffered and cried out to him, but he failed her."

The pain from the pressure on my throat was unbearable. The psycho looked disappointed that I didn't blow up in the car.

I hate him. Why would I cry out for him?

"Hyong Mun-Hee why don't you just die? The world would be such a better place without you in it." Lucas took out a gun and fired.

Bam. Bam. The loud firecracker sounds happened quickly. Bullets whizzed past my head, and I ducked and tried to run, but Hyong used me as a human shield ducking his head and chest behind my body.

Pain shot through my leg. It felt hot and my leg got wet. There was a slight buzzing in my ears and my mouth fell open. My eyes widened when I saw Lucas flush and shrug. Opening my mouth, I attempted to yell but Hyong's hand was still wrapped around my throat. Everything started to become fuzzy, and I looked down and saw how much blood I was losing. There was so much of it, and everything was red.

Wham. The sting of a firm backhand across my face made me jerk awake in my bonds. I wasn't at Cornelio's place anymore. I tried to focus on my surroundings, but my blood was dripping in my eyes and my body was swinging left and right as I dangled upside down from being attached to a reinforced steel beam in the ceiling.

If I didn't bleed to death, I risked dying from head injury at this height.

"Hyong tells me that your Cornelio's prized possession."

Pinching my lips together, I tried to focus on the man sitting in the corner. It was dark in here and the only thing I could see, and smell was a shake and sushi.

"I've never seen you. What makes you so different from the other woman Cornelio fucks and leaves? You aren't beautiful and you should consider a diet."

Oh hell no. This prick is telling me I'm fat.

"Your man took the wrong girl. Cornelio's men picked me up because I was at the wrong place at the wrong time. My dumb ass brother stole from Cornelio, and I was visiting him when they were about to kill him."

"You think you can lie to me." The chair toppled over and a thin man, who moved like air was gripping my cheeks and pointing his blade close to my eye."

"I can prove it. Why would I lie? You're going to kill me anyway, so why lie. That Dipshit over there has already tried to blow me up in a car. It's not like I don't know you're going to kill me."

"You should be crying." He pulled back his knife and started to flick it near my face. There was no reason to flinch because I was a sitting duck suspended in the air. A man in the back must be controlling the levers because I was going up and down like a rollercoaster and my stomach rocked violently. Hot bile rose in my throat and I lunged upward latching on to my thighs as I vomited on myself.

Yup. Death by choking on my own vomit was rated up there with dying with urine on myself. I've always been a fighter and I can't stop now. I would fight until the end. Death wouldn't claim me so easily.

"I've never been shot before. Look, my leg feels like I was beaten with a baseball bat and it aches like a root canal. Just kill me and end this torture."

"Americans were spoiled and stupid. You don't know about torture, but you might find out." He smiled and pointed behind him.

My attempt to be brave let him know I didn't fear death had failed. He didn't care if whether I feared it or not. He must be twisted in the head.

"Hyong likes to kill and be done with it but I like to savor it and often resuscitate my enemies prolonging their death months on end, or until I get bored."

He bent down to my face. "Can you guess how many times I have gotten bored?"

"No guesses. If you don't want to play this game. I can always think of other games to play." He flicked his blade and pointed it toward my eye again.

"Fine. You've gotten bored five times, and it was three Americans and two Italians."

Retracking his blade he smiled. "Good guess, but no. I've killed over one million people man, woman, child and animals. That's the thing, I have never gotten bored."

Despite the controlled temperature in the room, I shivered.

"Do you have any information for me before I send you to hell?" He walked back and grabbed his tequila.

"No, I don't know Cornelio. Heck, I evidently didn't even know my own brother before that bastard murdered him in front of me. I was engaged to a district attorney planning a wedding before this. Check my social media. I am one of those stupid Americans that put everything on social media and hoped I would connect with others and feel close."

"You are pathetic." He snapped his fingers.

Blinking, I sighed when he moved away from me and sat back down at the table.

"Bring me the laptop." He rubbed his chin. He picked up something off the table and a flash of light lit up before he extinguished it.

A light. The bastard had a lighter for his cigars. I needed to get my hands on it. My hands were bound behind my back, but my mouth wasn't gagged. I just needed to get the light in my mouth then figure how to use it.

"If what you said was true, you might be useful to me after all."

How does my truth help me out of this situation? What was Nico thinking when he stole from the mafia?

I watched Nae Seung Hoon type on his computer. Frowning, I waited for him to ask me some questions, but he didn't. His fingers danced around the keyboard. He had my driver's license lying on the corner of the computer. Once again, my whole life hinged on Craig. Knowing him, that slime ball had taken every photo of us down and was probably parading Karen around the internet like a miniature Yorkie.

That backstabbing hussy should be the one strung up from the ceiling for perpetrating a fraud and stealing my man. If he belonged to me, he would still be mine.

"Yes, you were telling the truth, but unfortunately it looks like Craig, your fiancé, wasn't torn up over losing you."

No shit Sherlock. That was the understatement of the decade. He is a self-centered, entitled brat who did not care who he used to get what he wanted.

I shrugged. "Are you going to let me go?"

Karen has his lying ass now. I'm just disappointed that it took me all this time to see it.

"If you want to live, you're going to rekindle your relationship, like you don't know he's screwing every woman in the city and get some information."

The hair on the nape of my neck stood up. I didn't want to pretend I cared for him. I wasn't sure I could look at him without punching him in the face.

"I need to know the location of Gyeon Mi Young and everything that happened in her life from birth until now."

If he can't find her, what makes him think I can? If the mafia wanted to find you, they found you. Who was this woman anyway?

"If I find where she is then you'll let me go?" I licked my lips and squinted, trying to read his facial expression. He didn't give anything away.

Something deep inside me said he would never let me go. When he no longer needed information, I would be disposable. I was a pawn in this messed up game. I needed to be smart and find a way out.

"You had a direct connection to the DA's Office. I think after you are married, I could still use you. Especially if you told me ahead of time who they are investigating and warned me before they interfered into my business."

Did this man say marry Craig? There was no way. Pretending to be Craig's fool was a faith worse than death.

Swallowing past the lump in my throat, I closed my eyes. "Cut me down and I'll get the information you seek."

Hyong Mun- Hee laughed. His deep chuckles made me grind my teeth.

"She's so eager. Cornelio should've recruited her instead of her brother, then he might still be alive," said Hyong.

Turning my face, I closed my eyes and dug my nails deeper into my palm trying to banish the tears.

I might be defective, but I had my pride. I was done being a pawn in this game. It's a man's world but I refuse to be a victim.

The psycho came towards me holding something small, square and black in the palm of his hand.

"I hope you didn't think I would just cut you down and send you on your way, did you?"

Girl can hope.

"I was hoping you'd recover my purse and buy the plane ticket."

He bent and carved a square chuck out of my flesh near my ankle. "This is a present. Your location will be known at all times and if I need to, I will push a button and you will be blown up."

Squeezing my eyes shut, I ignored the pressure as he pushed the device inside my ankle. "What is it with you and bombs?"

"There effective, efficient and quick. It's not heartless the victims don't feel anything."

How does he know? Has he ever died before?

"You could've just had a man watch me."

Chapter 8

Cornelio

F our hours had passed, and I had already thought of one thousand five
hundred ways to die, and I wasn't trying hard. It was not a secret that
Nae Seung Hoon, the don, was a sick sadistic bastard. Hyong was addicted
to killing but his cruelty could not be compared to Nae's. There was something between Asha and me. Our chemistry was volatile, immediate, and
undeniable. I was excited for our next encounter. I wanted to see the
surprise in her eyes when I awaken her passion.

We arrived at The Venetian club two hours earlier at separate times. I
left Siriano and Quintillo at the safe house guarding Telica. She had looked
downright disappointed that Alcino was not staying with her. Her mouth
said she didn't care what he did, but her eyes showed her hunger. Their
chemistry was hotter than lava in an active volcano. I had never felt that kind
of animalistic sexual tension before today, before Asha, and I were like a
moth to a flame, I wanted more.

This was a damn mess.

It must be time for me to get laid. I liked sex like the next man but
running the mafia and controlling everything took time. Women come and
go, and I do not get attached, so I guess, I needed a submissive to visit
tonight, so I could fuck her hard.

Shaking my head, I walked through the double glass doors of the resort.
The floors were marbles and the entrance lightly scented with eucalyptus
and jasmine tea. The gold tones on the wall were soothing and reflected
nicely off the huge crystal chandelier. I needed the name of the interior
designer. It felt weird coming here.

I've been living in Vegas for over ten years, controlling everything, and
keeping the city I call home safe and running smoothly. In all my years, I had
never been to this resort. There was something about mingling with the fake
rich cowards that made saliva dry up in my mouth. They appealed to me like
having my dick cut off and blended in front of me.

Stepping inside the elevator, I saw a man at the bar in a dark navy-blue suit with a man weave. When Alcino and Zetico stepped inside the elevator, I pressed the button closing the door before other people could get inside.

Fuck. Just when I think this day can't get any worse, I spot a fed.

When the elevator started to move, I pulled out my phone and fired a code message to Lucas, who was in a separate room staying out of sight. When that text went through, I sent it to my men.

The vultures are here. Beware lest they pick the flesh from your bones.

This sentenced looked innocent enough and it was something we never physically spoke about, but we knew what it meant. It was one of my many code phrases for the Federal Bureau Investigation trying to close in on us. It's funny how they had no money to feed the poor or shelter the homelessness, but they squandered billions of dollars trying to investigate me and the other four families.

The doors opened and we split up. Alcino turned right and went inside his room and I went to my room. Zetico stayed on the elevator since his room was on another floor. My men were spread out in and out of the place. I had a sniper team on the roof hiding in the shadows. I was prepared for whatever I needed to do. Stopping in front of my hotel room, I heard soft sounds of Nat King Cole. Reaching in my jacket, I palmed my Glock 42 and slid the keycard in the door.

The door opened and I crouched as I entered. Lucas was sitting on the bed jamming out. I wasn't surprised. Nat King Cole was his favorite artist. He really had an old soul.

"Why aren't you in your room?" I slid my Glock in the holster and ran my hands through my hair.

"I got your text message."

This isn't our first rodeo with the feds so that didn't answer my question. Lucas was messing up. I still was pissed at him because he allowed Asha to be in the hands of our enemy.

Cracking my neck muscles, I snapped. "Spill it or and then get the hell out."

"You know I didn't lose her on purpose. It's hard trying to keep her from being raped and harmed when she's running from me straight into trouble."

"Refresh my memory again. Was that before or after you accidentally shot her?"

Taking my jacket off, I tossed it over the back of the chair. Walking to the bed, I opened my suitcase. I had two change of clothes, three stacks of money, and a pen that I could detonate to get out of a tight situation. I was a planner. I planned for the world to collapse around me and hoped I lived through it all.

He scrubbed his hand over his face. "Eleuterio will be here soon."

Three light taps on the door, and I turned and looked at the door. I had my gun out and was leaning against the desk with a clear shot to it. Lucas walked over to the door and peeped out. He opened the door and Eleuterio waltzed in.

"How are things at the spot?" I slid my Glock back in the holster and walked over and grabbed a cold bottle of water out the ice bucket. I tossed Eleuterio one since he looked like he was sweating bullets.

Eleuterio smiled, "Interesting. His girlfriend was pouting and giving Siri a hard time. It was funny to watch because you know he doesn't have the patience." He nodded, twisted off the bottle cap and drank almost all the water before speaking again.

Lucas snorted. "It was not like he could handle the situation like he normally does."

My lips curved upward. Siriano didn't have patience by nature. He had patience for what and who he wanted but that was very few people on a short selective list. Telica wasn't one of them. He would normally kill the person and move on, but he could not kill Telica, so he was forced to endure. I almost wished I had witnessed her driving Siri bat shit crazy.

Lucas pointed to ten of audio jammers located throughout the room. I never violated the no talking rule outside of my safe space. The feds were already here, and I wasn't opening myself up for their inquisition.

Eleuterio smiled. Yanking a piece of paper off the notepad on the desk he swiftly jotted something down. After a few minutes, he handed me the paper.

They are looking for her. There is a ten-million-dollar bounty on her head.

Gritting my teeth, I handed the paper to Lucas. He read it then gave it back to Eleuterio who pulled out a lighter and set the paper to flame.

Eleuterio pocketed the ashes in a zip lock bag.

Lucas' face flushed, and he jumped up and stormed out the room.

Nae Seung Hoon had put a contract on Telica. He wanted her alive. This was good news and bad news. On one hand, it meant that Asha was still alive. The bad news was that he knew she was engaged to the District Attorney, and he intended to let her go. He would always have his hooks in her until she proved no longer useful.

I was elated. I shouldn't be but that meant she was alive, and I still had time to get her back. Telica was safe in my camp. Well safe enough. It looks like I'll be heading to DC.

"You gave him a hard time. It wasn't his fault that he lost her. You should forgive him before he goes and get himself whacked trying to fix it."

* * *

Po Hei-Ran wasn't what I expected. He was fashionable and he moved like a ninja. There was something about him that was eerie. He wasn't the least bit nervous meeting Alcino and I. It was like he would have been there even if he had been surrounded by two hundred men. Whatever he wanted; he must want it bad.

"Nae Seung had taken her back to District of Columbia. She was now his eyes and ears for the District Attorney." He picked up his shot of scotch and drained the glass.

Po Hei-Ran is wasting my time. There is no way that the information he told me was all he knew. If he didn't talk fast with something I can use, he was going to eat my bullets.

Alcino crossed his arms over his chest. "Her ex-fiancée was hardly a wealth of knowledge. He was a Deputy District Attorney, which doesn't mean she could get the information he needed."

My jaw was set. I stood abruptly and my chair toppled to the floor. "This wasn't news. Nae always finds an angle that he could exploit."

I reached inside my coat. I watched Nae and I knew that he was aware that something was coming. What surprised me was that he didn't give a damn.

"You could shoot me and stumble in the dark or hear my demands and save her. You make a choice."

"Po you've been helpful in the past and I don't want to see you dead. What else have you got for me?"

"No, Alcino, this time I'll make the demands. You have failed me. You told me that you had the address for me, but all you had were excuses."

Chapter 9

Asha

I woke up strapped in a seat on a small jet. Jerking in the seat I unstrapped the seatbelt and pitched forward as the plane hit a rough patch of turbulence. Gripping the seat in front of me, I held on until I felt the turbulence even out. Me and heights didn't get along.

"Where do you think you're going?" Hyong was reclining back in his seat watching a movie on the screen in front of him.

"I need to use the bathroom."

The psycho looked elated that I was awake. He no doubt had more ways to torture me. My ankle was sore, and the pain was excruciating. I had a bomb inside me, and there was nothing I could do about it. My body was a slow ticking time bomb.

"Do you think you're on a commercial flight?"

Grinding my teeth, I took a breath. "Whatever." I walked past him and found a small bathroom. I slipped inside and locked the door.

Splashing cold water on my face, I weighed my options. There was nothing I could do until we landed. There was no weapon on the plane and any weapon Hyong had was not going to be easily taken. If he falls asleep, I can steal a weapon, and kill him.

My stomach ached. A generalized weakness flowed through me and I knew my body needed substance. Flushing the toilet, I walked back to my seat. We were the only passengers besides a pilot and maybe a co-pilot. Strapping myself in the seat again, I leaned back. Hyong would lower his guard if he thought I was sleep. Closing my eyes, I fantasized about the ways I might be able to kill him.

Something wet flowed down my cheek. Opening my eyes, I realized I had fallen asleep and drooled all over my cheek. Hyong's eyes were closed, and his breathing was steady. He wasn't snoring but maybe he didn't snore.

Everything looked how it did before I fell asleep. Looking out the window, all I saw was the night sky. I unbuckled my seatbelt. Digging my hand between the seat, I found a seat belt extender. Balling it in my hand, I stood and headed toward the bathroom. It was now or never.

Once I passed him, I kept walking toward the bathroom. I went inside and used the toilet. I tried to prepare for what I needed to do. I was not sure people are ever prepared to take a life. Splashing water on my face, I prayed. I didn't flush the toilet, so he wouldn't wake up. Hiding the seatbelt extended in my hand, I opened the door and walked toward him. When I got close enough, I wrapped the belt around his neck and started choking him.

I never saw it coming. He cut the seatbelt, and he was on top of me with the blade pressed to my throat. There was a sharp prick at the base of my neck, and I felt blood running down it. His arms were like titanium bands as he held me pressed to the floor

"I was impressed. You found the present I left for you."

"What?" I struggled against him, but he pressed the blade deeper into my neck and I stopped moving.

"I had to see for myself if you would try and kill me. Ever since you jumped out the car, I had to see if you really had courage."

"You didn't give me a choice." I glared at him hoping he saw my hatred for him burning bright in my eyes.

He bent and sniffed my hair. "It's a shame you and I didn't meet under other circumstances."

What is he doing? He tries to kill me and now he's trying to touch me. Heck no.

"Get off me." I shifted trying to move him off me. His weight was heavy on my limbs and my body was pressed against the floor.

"In case you hadn't noticed, I was not the one with the blade to your neck. Any strong turbulence and my hand could slip." He took the knife and moved it lower.

I moved and the blade cut me an inch below my collar bone. I didn't breathe. He laughed and cut the buttons off my shirt. There weren't many buttons to this shirt and soon I would be exposed from the waist up.

Something vibrated against my thigh and I sighed in relief when he pulled the phone from his pocket.

"Don't look so relieved. There was no guarantee that I would answer it."

572

Everything was a game to him, and I didn't have the rule book. Turning my face away from him, I looked at the pieced of the seatbelt extender.

He played me. He wanted me to try to kill him. What kind of man gives you a weapon to kill him with? I used to think death was the worst thing that could happen to you, but I was wrong. Rape was worse than death.

"No boss. I didn't kill her."

"You want to me put her on the phone."

Sighing deeply, he activated the flashlight on his phone and shined it in my face.

"I see he had some fun with you."

"Hyong, I didn't say you could violate her. Rape was worse than death and I could tell she wasn't willing."

"She will be."

"No. She needs to be able to fuck her way back in the relationship. She's off-limits for now."

"As you wish." He got off me and I scrambled to my feet and scurried to my seat. After I strapped myself in, I tried to repair my blouse but there was no use. He had cut off all my buttons but one. My breast was too large to only have one button holding everything closed. I had bigger things to worry about than when my large triple D cup breast was going to pop out of my blouse. Wiping my neck, the blood continued to run down it. I pressed my hand to the wound, but pressure wasn't enough.

"Here sew yourself up." He tossed me a small kit with some needles and thread. The package was unopened, so I opened it and walked to the bathroom.

* * *

FOUR HOURS later I was back at home. It was raining in the city, but I had never been so happy to see the streets blocked off by the secret service and the black tinted limousines driving down the street. It felt as if a lightyear had passed since I was home. Hyong had left my house with a promise that he'd be seeing me soon, and that made me cringe.

Locking the door after him, I ran to Telica's room. Everything looked like it did when I left. Nothing was out of place. Her bed wasn't made up, and she had ten outfits on hangers thrown across it. Her princess cup, which was her favorite was on her nightstand empty.

Nae Seung Hoon would kidnap Telica to make sure I did whatever he wants, but he never had her, or he would've shown her to me while threatening my life. I've always gotten on her about how secretive she tried to be with her personal life and her business. At the time I needed her the most, I would not have a clue where she was and who she was with.

Where is she? If I don't know then Nae and Hyong don't know either and maybe that is the best thing I've got going for me right now.

Limping to the refrigerator I fixed a glass of cold water and heated up the left-over beef stew I had saved for Telica. Lately, she had been staying out all night and being tight-lipped about who she spent her time with. I looked at the family portrait on the wall and doubled over.

Nico. I couldn't imagine a world without him. He and I were closer than Telica and I.

He had demons like all of us, but he didn't conquer his, and they came and dragged him to hell.

Walking to the bedroom, I stopped as the doorbell rang. Racing to the kitchen, I yanked a butcher knife from the rack. The door swung open and Craig walked in.

"Baby what were you doing?" He looked at the butcher knife then back at me.

My heart was racing. Memories of him and Karen flooded my mind and I closed my eyes and licked my lips. "I was going to see if I had any watermelon left."

Frowning, he closed the door and locked it behind him. "I was calling you like crazy and I left several back-to-back messages and you haven't returned any of my calls."

Why should I make an excuse? You are a lying, cheating, dirty dog.

"I lost my phone and I haven't had time to get another." I opened the refrigerator and sliced a small piece of watermelon.

"I appreciate that you stopped by, but it's been a long night and I'm beat."

He opened his mouth then shut it. "I never took you to dinner and I knew that you really wanted to go. I thought we'd go to that Thai Heaven Hut on Constitution Avenue and grab a bite to eat."

Oh, he remembers. I only mention that Thai restaurant over eight months ago.

"I went there with friends, so we don't have to go. Besides its eleven thirty at night, I've already eaten dinner."

"You're upset with me. I feel brushed off." He ran his fingers through his hair, walked over to the couch and adjusted himself before he sat down.

"Why would I be mad at you? You were busy and I understand that." He looked more like he was scratching an itch or maybe there was more going on down there. *You lie with dogs and you catch flees. Karen must be on her period because he's here to get laid, but he won't be touching me. Karen was always at the gynecologist with one issue or another. They could burn together for all I care.*

A knock on the door startled me.

"Who would be coming to the house this late?" Craig jumped up from the couch and headed toward the door.

"I don't know, maybe it's the neighbor." I sat the watermelon down but stayed near the knife rack.

Oh Lord, please don't be Hyong.

I was hoping it would be Telica and that maybe she was too drunk to use her key or something, Craig avoided confrontations with Telica at all cost and today I welcomed her interference.

"Man, who are you?" Craig's voice seemed to get deeper suddenly.

"Is Asha home?"

Placing my hand over my mouth, I stayed near the knife rack. Hopefully, Craig would say no and shut the door.

"We're coworkers."

I knew that voice. Cornelio was at my door. How the heck did he know that I was home? When Craig gets rid of him, I would get rid of Craig.

"She's not here." Craig snapped then tried to shut the door, but the door bounced back, and Lucas busted inside the house.

"Bullshit." He pushed Craig and he fell backwards. Cornelio walked past him and over to me.

"You bastard get out of here before I call the cops. You can't just barge in here."

Cornelio took a step toward him. "You don't live here."

Craig's face turned red. "How do you know?"

"Craig, I work with him, and I did say we would meet tonight, I guess it slipped my mind. I'll call you later."

"How are you going to call me when you have no phone? I don't feel comfortable leaving you with a stranger without a phone."

"I don't have a cell phone, but I have got a landline and besides he's not a stranger." I walked around Cornelio, but he reached out and grabbed me. He lifted the pants leg up and saw the bandage.

"I'm fine." I pushed his hands away and pushed my pant leg back down.

"You're limping, because you're doing fine." Cornelio lifted his brow and I rolled my eyes at him.

"What happened to your leg. You didn't mention anything about being hurt."

"I was on the phone and walking into a crosswalk and tripped over a homeless man's cart."

He shook his head. "I told you, that I had two left feet."

"I'll be careful next time."

Cornelio narrowed his eyes at Craig. "You have two minutes. I'm not a patient man."

"Craig, let me walk you to the door." I moved around Cornelio and walked to the front door. Craig hadn't moved and his face had turned red.

"I told you, I didn't feel comfortable. You don't know him."

Crossing my arms over my chest, I rolled my eyes. "You don't tell me anything Craig, this place belongs to me, you don't have a say in who comes and goes, just as I don't have a say who strolls in and out of your apartment."

"Asha don't be unreasonable. I am only thinking about your safety." He glared at Cornelio who was leaning up against the counter smiling.

"No, you're acting jealous and that is your problem not mine." I opened the door and waited.

He has the nerve to get jealous when he has been cheating on me this entire time.

He raked his hand through his hair and took a step toward the door. "You can't be serious. If I leave now, we're done."

"We're done then." I let the door close and grabbed my keys. I removed his spare key from my ring and handed it to him.

I snorted. "Do you want me to call Karen now and let her know or do you want to do it?"

He bucked his eyes. "What are you talking about?"

"The fact that you've been screwing my best friend the entire relationship and are now engaged to her must have slipped your mind."

Cornelio shook his head. The smile he had on his face fell, and he lifted his hand looking at his watch. *"He wasn't man enough for you anyway. Another man's trash is another man's treasure. Trust me Craig, I intend to treasure her."*

"Whoever told you that was lying. Did Karen tell you that?"

"Your time is up." Cornelio stalked toward Craig, but I slid between them and pushed Craig to the door.

"Karen is a liar. I never slept with her. You must believe me. Don't throw away what we had with this stranger he just wants to sleep with you."

"I saw you screwing her the other day. Information on my brother was all you wanted, and then you moved on to my best friend." Pushing him out the door, I slammed it and locked it. Unlike him, I never gave him a key to my apartment. I was working myself up to get to that point, but I never made it past the fear.

Leaning against the door, the realization of what I just did. I couldn't get information for Nae Seung Hoon. Craig now knew that I saw him cheating on me and I wasn't sorry. Something things were worse than death and allowing him to lie to my face after what he did was unforgiveable.

"Don't be sad. He didn't deserve you."

Clenching my jaw tight, I looked at Cornelio. "You have nerve. You can get the hell out just like him. You are worse than him."

One minute he was leaning on the counter and the next he had me pinned to the wall. "Don't say things you'll regret." He grabbed my face and leaned down. His minty breath tickling my upper lip.

"He could never hurt me like you did."

"No, he can't. I haven't hurt you yet, but when I do you won't know the difference from pain and pleasure." He captured my lips in a bruising kiss. He ravished my mouth like a wilderbeast.

Chapter 10

Cornelio

P o Hei- Ran was ready to die. I could see it in his eyes. He wasn't hiding anything from me. Despite my better judgement I was intrigued. What the hell was so important to him? I was a good judge of character and I liked him. I wouldn't hesitate to kill him if need be, but his honesty was honorable. I understood it and respected it.

What did he want so bad that he was willing to die?

"You aren't dealing with Alcino now. You're dealing with me. What do you want?"

"Yi So-Ran."

Narrowing my eyes, I searched his face. "Who was she?"

Po brow furrowed as he looked at Alcino. "You never had him check into it. I knew you had the connections needed to find her. I was not sure anyone could help me."

Po was determined. This wouldn't be easy. I have connections. My connections got connections, but something tells me, I'll need outside help on this one. I'm not certain he worth the trouble either.

Glancing at Alcino, I shook my head. "Tell me everything you know."

Po raked his hands through his jet-black hair. "She's my baby sister."

"Tell me or don't but you need my help. I haven't decided to help you. The information you gave me was weak. You haven't told me anything I didn't already know."

"I didn't always work for Nae Seung Hoon. I hated him. Our parents worked for him. My mother was a forger and my father one of his best hitmen. When my father was murdered ambushed coming outside the cancer center where mom was dying."

"How do you work for a man you claim to hate," asked Alcino.

"Nae and his men hand-delivered the photos of my father's mangled body. He had been shot twenty times and his ears cut off and his trigger fingers severed."

Alcino frowned. "He was the best?"

I glared at Alcino.

Alcino was a rude bastard. He didn't have any filter. I might have to stab him just get through Po story without his interruption.

"He killed sixty men before bleeding out. After texting me an emergency code, which meant get out quick, he severed his carotid arteries."

He lived by the sword and died by the sword. It was destiny that awaited all of us as made men.

"He used your mother and the cost for her treatment to get you to work for him."

"No, Nae shot her in the face when I refused to work for him. That was the worse day of my life, and I thought things couldn't get worse, but I was wrong."

"He took your sister," said Alcino. He leaned back and shook his head.

Po Hei Ran was twenty-eight-years-old even though he looked young. He had probably seen more in his lifetime than his parents ever wanted for him. Nae Seung Hoon was a ruthless prick, and he didn't take the word no. You did what he wanted, or he killed you.

"Nae kidnapped her and sold her into sexual slavery. He told me to work for him, and he would get her back. He told me five years ago, that she died."

I glanced at my watch. Po situation was fucked for sure. I would need to get outside help on this, but I hadn't decided I'd help. The bastard hadn't given me anything worth my help.

What do I look like? I'm the don. I don't help everyone that needs help. I help who I want to and right now I don't give a shit. He hasn't helped me.

"I understand your plight. Family was important but for your sake, I hope you get the answers you seek." I turned away.

"You could help me."

Turning, I walked back to him. "I can. I won't promise that she's alive or that I can even find her. Women in that kind of situation end up down two paths. There's no need to speak on the third path."

Po's face was shaking. His eyes clouded and his voice broke. "Find her." His movements were jerky as he looked at me then at Alcino.

Alcino reached inside his jacket and pulled out a cigar. Most thought he was a smug bastard, but he smoked cigars when he wanted to kill someone bad but couldn't or when he was unsettled like he was now.

Damn. I was beyond unsettled. I was repulsed and I wanted to kill Nae Seun- Hoon slow, but that didn't change shit now. Where is the information on my girl? Po came here with a problem fitted for the CIA/FBI and all I needed to know is where my doll is?

Running my hands through my hair, I stared into his eyes. "You don't have any information of value, do you?"

"Wrong. Hyong Mun-Hee implanted Asha with a bomb. It's in her ankle."

Grabbing him by the lapels, I flung him on the side of the wall. "You're just now mentioning that."

"Everyone knows that Hyong is the only one that can disarm his bombs," said Alcino.

"Wrong. I developed them. Who do you think taught him?"

"You're lying." My pulse leaped in my wrist. My adrenaline was making me high and I lusted for his blood. I was controlled but I felt it slipping.

"Nope. He thrusted his chin up and his lips curved.

My hand moved to his throat. His face turned several shades of red before I eased my hand away and allowed him to breathe again.

Po straightened his clothes. "Yi was taken from our home in Gwangji. Here are two names of the biggest traffickers in Korea. Bring me their addresses and the file on them, and the bomb will be replaced with a dud." He held up a piece of paper in front of me. I wanted to end his life right where he stood but I couldn't, not yet anyway. If he wasn't lying, then he and Hyong were the only two who could do about the bomb in Asha's ankle.

"If something happened to her, I'll deliver Yi in pieces to you before I send you both to join your parents." Snatching the paper, I left him before temptation grew too great for me to ignore.

I sipped my bourbon watching Greg Foster. He was eating his medium-rare porterhouse steak like he had never eaten in his life. His entire plate was blood and his chin dripped with blood. Each time I saw him, I dreamed of murdering him. He always did a number on my digestive system. Luck for him, his job saved his ass. I always needed the Central Intelligence Agency in my pocket. The information they had on everyone came in handy like now. I

"I need their entire file in one hour. If they took a shit an hour ago then I need to know."

Greg wiped his face and looked at the piece of paper. "These two assholes were on our radar. The girl's name doesn't look familiar, but I'll investigate it. I can't promise I'll have any information in an hour."

I shrugged. "An acquaintance has obtained the information. If I must deal with him to get it then I don't need you. If you do not have the information in the hour, our arrangement is done." I stood up and snapped my finger. Two of my men came and stood next to my table.

"He doesn't leave your sight. Where he goes you two go. If he does not have the information in an hour, he's all yours."

"I'll get it. I don't know about an hour though. I might have to go to Langley. I'll get you everything I've got in an hour and what I don't have, I'll get from work. I might not have the clearances and need to call in a favor so give me some time."

"I'll decide that after I see what you have for me in an hour."

Rain fell from the sky like God wept for humanity. Running up the stairs to my jet, I tossed my soaked jacket in one of the seats. I had several outfits on this jet, yet I couldn't summon the energy to go to my room and change. Greg had come through like I knew he would. I now knew more information on what had happened to Yi So -Ran, and I wish I did not.

The horrors that she must have faced at the tender age of fifteen made me sick. I had already vomited twice. Women were not meant to be treated like bloody tampons and tossed in the nearest dumpster. Taking out my phone, I dialed his number. His number was the only number that was not written anywhere. I was the only person that could reach him, so when I die so does the connection to him. That was my promise to him. Yi So Ran needed Willie Edward Carter. I gripped the phone as it rang twice.

The engines roared and the jet started to gain momentum. Looking out the windows, all I could see through the rain was dark storm clouds above. This was not the best time to fly but it was necessary.

"Why the hell are you calling here?" His gruff voice brisker.

"You owe me a favor. It's time for me to collect." I stood and walked down the aisle to my bedroom. This wasn't a conversation that my men would hear.

"I don't owe you shit. You promised, so keep your damn word or else."

In the background, I heard pots and pans. I knew the excessive noise was to camouflage what he was really doing. He was a smart bastard and one of the deadliest men alive. The government may have trained him, but he came to them with his own unique sets of skills.

I fell into the side of the sea at the back as the plane lifted off the ground and gravity took effect. I made my way into my room and closed the door. "Wrong. Who do you think keeps them off you? It cost three million a month to keep you there unbothered. You owe me."

"Why the call you and I both know you do what you want."

Closing my eyes, I held my stomach as the jet climbed higher in the sky. "Don't make me put a bullet in your head."

"How long?"

"Forty-eight hours tops." The turbulence shook the jet and I gritted my teeth.

Fucking airplanes. I take a bullet any day or falling out the sky. My pilots were the best, but they weren't god.

"Are you coming in hot?"

"I don't know yet." Rubbing my temples, I thought about Po Hei- Ran and Hyong Mun-Hee. Hyong might be on to Po and that meant I needed to be prepared for a double-cross when I arrived in Washington DC. It didn't matter, I would handle them before leaving the States.

"I'll be ready."

"Thanks."

Willie stayed ready. He took his guns apart blindfolded with a live bomb activated as timer. I wasn't concerned about him being prepared, he never relaxed. My surveillance on him showed he's killed a dozen men this month, so his killing skills aren't rusty either.

"Don't thank me. I'll probably slit your throat when you least expect it."

Hanging up the phone, I got up and walked to the closet. This was a good time to get cleaned up. All of my suits matched my Kevlar vest. There was my favorite bottle of Channel Blue cologne on board. Asha won't know what hit her. The flight back to Vegas will be enjoyable for the both of us. Eyeing my king size bed, I smiled.

* * *

WE TOOK FIVE SEPARATE CARS, and we were being followed. I was ecstatic. This was another way to vet the information Po gave me. It looked like three cars so far. I could keep at least one man alive, long enough to get some information.

"Pulling off the highway heading toward Silver Spring. Let's ambush these fuckers and get on with it." I checked my guns and slipped several ammo clips in my jacket. Lucas grunted in response and turned right down the street and gunned the car several miles until we came to an abandoned parking garage. Hopping out I grabbed the duffle bag, and Alcino had the other. We went to setup while Lucas hid the truck. All of us had our face mask covered our faces and gloves on, so the agency would only speculate. There was nothing linking us to this place, and the cameras were down for the next twelve hours, thanks to Greg. The all-seeing eyes would not see this.

Sammie and the rest of the men drove up and hopped out. Everyone set up. Ten of us were stationed in the parking garage, and the half of the men were in position on top of the three buildings near us. The other half were surrounding the outer perimeter.

Zetico checked the ammo in his AK-47. "Let's kill them quick."

I studied Alcino. He had been quiet ever since we found out the Hoon's men had been scouring the city looking for Telica.

"They are dead, but we need to know what they know first," said Alcino.

"Lucas kill the light now." I looked up and the lights went out. I went to stand behind the stone pillar. The silencers on or weapons would make this easier.

Tires screeched. Four doors slammed shut. The men came sneaking into the garage. So far, I spotted twenty men. They're holding machine guns and semi-automatic weapons.

"There were ten men were outside positioning themselves by the garage," said Leon.

"Five of them were in my blast zone. Just say the word," said Keith.

Keith Lee was obsessed with blowing stuff up. That was fine most of the time but now when we were so close to the nation's capital.

"We can't afford to draw attention to ourselves." I narrowed my eyes as I spotted five more men coming in from the right.

"Don't worry. It'll sound like fireworks and there won't be any evidence."

"Do it." I lifted my assault rifle and fired. The bullet went through the man's skull, and he dropped. Several shots went off as his finger was on the trigger. My men followed suit and fired.

I shot the three men toward the back. The two men dropped to the ground deeper into the shadows. Flipping on the heat signature, I saw two men sneaking up on Alcino. I saw one in the head and the other in the neck. A tin can toppled behind me, and I ducked and rolled to the next pillar. Lifting the gun, I saw the two men. One was far from me and the other was running right at me. I fired several shots at the man with the gun. Two bullets hit in the head and one in the heart. I grabbed my knife and threw it at the man running at me. It hit him in the gut, and he fell. Lifting my gun, I shot him twice in the head.

Gun fire erupted all around. There were multiple shots fired outside. All around me the garage smelled of blood and gunfire. Our shots were silenced but theirs were not, so the police would be here soon.

"The outside clear?

"Clear boss," said Lucas.

The cleanup crew had cleaned," said Keith.

"Police have been dispatched we must go. We have five minutes tops," said Zetico.

"Got it." Getting up, I navigated back to the spot near my men. There were dead bodies everywhere. The air was thick was blood. I barely managed to sidestep the puddles of blood.

"I kept the last one for you, boss," said Alcino. Blood covered the man's shirt and most of his face.

I walked over to Alcino who had his knife to the man's throat. The man was shot twice in the stomach and five of his fingers were lying on the floor.

"Why were you here?"

"We're here for Telica. The boss demanded that she be brought to him. She knew that she belonged to him, and there was nothing you could do about it."

"She belongs to me," said Alcino. His face turned red. He pressed the blade deeper into the man's neck.

"Have you heard enough? Can I," asked Alcino.

"Yes. Make it quick." I turned and walked away. I didn't hear the bullet, but that was because Alcino did not shoot him. He slit the man's throat. My men had cleaned up the shells and all of our weapons were on us. We jumped into the cars and hit the highway.

I smelled of gun smoke and blood. Hoon's men were crawling around the city. I didn't need that goon to confirm it. I needed to get Asha and get out of here. I was glad Telica was under my protection. Stealing a peak at Alcino, I shook my head. He hadn't cleaned a spot of blood off his neck. I knew that was deliberate. He liked wearing the blood of his enemies that had wronged them.

Damn psycho. I didn't need him losing his shit now.

"Telica needs you so get your shit together. We'll be back there soon enough, and I need you to focus."

"Here with you boss." He turned away from me and stared out the window.

It was two hours before; I reached her apartment. It wouldn't be long before we would have to be at the air strip. Taking the steps, I slowed down as I neared her apartment. There was a man in there, and he was not Korean. That didn't mean it wasn't a hitman, but it wasn't Hyong. Hyong probably wasn't far away and would be back soon. Removing my Glock from its holster, I slipped it in my pocket. With my right hand on the butt of the Glock, I knocked on the door. The door opened, and I came face to face with him. He was short for a man, standing five foot eight, with dirty blonde hair and blue eyes. He looked like a damn Ken doll. This must be Craig. His unblemished porcelain skin and cheap designer clothes.

"Man, who are you?" He frowned and held the door cracked open.

"Is Asha home?" My fingers caressed the end of my Glock. The feel of it between my fingertips calmed my temper a bit.

I DON'T NORMALLY KILL on emotion, but I want to kill Craig Hastings. His job makes him expendable, but his treatment of Asha made him an excellent target. Woman are meant to be cherished not used and abused. It was assholes like him that made it hard for the nice guys. I wasn't a nice guy, but I was honest with woman and I didn't fuck them up and leave them damaged for the next man. Women bring life and carry with the future in their wombs which demands a certain level of respect and patience.

It took everything I had in me, not to kill him where he stood. Craig didn't know how close he had come to death just now. I was expecting a fight with Asha when I arrived and had been looking forward to her spunk. I wasn't prepared for Craig to be here this late. The fact that he felt he could refuse to leave was hilarious. He had sealed his fate tonight. There was nothing he could do about it. He was on borrowed time. Asha won't even remember his name.

She belongs to me. It doesn't matter that she thinks she hates my guts. Asha will learn that the mind and the body are often at times opposite of the emotional spectrum and coming together, marring the emotions are what make life worth living.

When she slammed the door shut, I smiled. Craig deserved worse than that since he had disrespected her so, but she was too much of a lady to treatment like scum.

"He could never hurt me like you did." She narrowed her eyes at me.

"No, he can't. When I do you won't know the difference between pain and pleasure." I hadn't had time to ravish her like I wanted. Our first sexual experience wouldn't be a quickie. I hope she doesn't want those come quick type of men, because I planned to be knee-deep inside her all night long.

Her body muscles went soft in my arms. I felt a tremor run up her spine before her nails raked over my scalp. The soft scent of coco butter filled my nostrils. My cock grew hard, and I forced myself to step back and break the kiss.

"You want me, and I want you. You want to hate me, but your body doesn't give a shit. I can smell your pussy. You're leaking for me."

Tossing her hair over her shoulder she walked to me and backhanded me across the face. "It doesn't matter. Hell will freeze over before I sleep with you."

My cheek throbbed. The pain only heightens my pleasure for her. I was a kinky fucker and I liked rough. I was the nasty man she'd ever meet. "Get your stuff. We're leaving."

She swallowed twice then shook her head. "I'm not going anywhere with you."

Telling her the truth won't work. We don't have much time. Lying this once won't hurt. Besides how will she ever know I'm lying anyway. If we're both dead, it doesn't matter.

"So, you prefer to die Hyong's men come. They are ten minutes out right now, or maybe you're hoping he'll just detonate that bomb in your ankle."

"He just dropped me off. He's not coming to kill me."

"How do you think I know about the bomb in your ankle. Make your choice but you're running out of time." I shrugged and walked past her and out the door. I didn't expect her to follow me, and I needed the cool air on my skin. If I had to die, I sure as hell didn't want to die with blue balls. The door slammed behind me and I cause her scent on the breeze. I turned and looked at her.

"I don't have much choice and I blame you for that too."

Clearing my throat, I took the steps two at a time. "It rained today do you want to blame me for that too."

"Everything messed up that has happened in my life, is your fault. When I can, I'm going to kill you."

Turning around, I lifted from the last step and pushed her against the wall. "Next time you want to kill someone. Don't announce it, just do it." My gaze dropped to her lips that her teeth were gnawing on and pushed myself away from her. The flight to Vegas would give me time enough to put her in her place.

Forty minutes later we were in the air. I hated flying because I didn't like heights. I was surprised to see Asha doesn't like to fly either, or she did her best to hide that. Her emotions play across her face like a documentary. She can't hide nothing from me, and I find it refreshing. I hadn't thought about my men flying with us, my thoughts had been focused on her. I didn't want to share her with them. No one would hear her screams, pleadings or her orgasms. All of her belonged to me and me alone. Fuck, I don't share shit.

Can she tell how bad I want her? She owes me for my restraint.

This broad was getting under my skin. Once I got a taste of her, then this tension would leave me, and I could forget all about her. I didn't have time to be walking around with my cock swollen. She like to talk so much; I wonder how our conversation would go with her tonsils stroking my ball sack?

Chapter 11

Asha

I wasn't sure what I expected stepping on his private jet. This was not the first time that I have flown. I had flown a few times, but I had done very little traveling. The way my financials looked; I probably wouldn't be traveling much in the future either. It seemed like being in the mafia paid if you could get past the small fact that you would likely be murdered young.

The seats were cream leather. They were comfy beautiful chairs. There were about fifty seats on here, and each seat had its own television in addition to one overhead. The cabin smelled like a salty breezy day in Hawaii. An aroma of coconut and pink prosecco circulated through the recycled air. The table at the front of the jet was large enough to accommodate four people eating and it was made out of mahogany wood. The accent color was platinum. It was so nice on the inside, I almost forgot I was in a death trap.

I didn't wait for Cornelio to choose a seat. I rushed and sat down next to a caramel-skinned Adonis. I didn't choose the seat next to him because he was beautiful, but to piss Cornelio off. He couldn't assume I would sit next to him. The plane was full and there were twenty men in the back waiting for Cornelio to choose his seat. The man was far too conceited for my taste.

Why did I have to be attracted to Cornelio? My pride was torn to pieces when he said I was wet. That had been an understatement. I was wetter than I have ever been. Craig never sent my body into overdrive, not even after his flimsy attempt at oral.

I had to change my panties. When Cornelio had walked out my place, I had locked the door and ran and changed my panties. I took a spit bath and orgasmed right in my bathroom, with my leg up over the sink and the washcloth between my lower lips. If I hadn't thought I was in danger of dying, I'd still be there rubbing my lips until I had rug burn or carpel tunnel. It would take both conditions to stop me.

There was something about him that sent every nerve in my body alive. Breathing deep, I adjusted myself in the seat and slumped down in my chair. I'm not sure why I was the only female on the jet. Studying the man sitting next to me, he frowned at me. He rapidly spoke another language.

"Hi. My name is Asha." I held out my hand to him.

He looked down at my hand and shook his head. He turned and spoke with another man standing at the back of toward the restroom. When he burst into laughter, I decided then that all men suck.

"You don't speak English huh? Good. Your manners suck asshole. You don't want to sit next to me then free yourself." Crossing my arms over my chest, I closed my eyes.

"Jose doesn't want to die," said Cornelio. He looked down at Jose who had already unbuckled his seatbelt, and he stood and rushed to the back to of the jet.

"How would he die sitting next to me. It's not like I was contagious or something."

Cornelio buckled his seatbelt. "Oh, you're contagious, and we have infected each other."

"Great. You make me sound like an infectious disease. That's what every woman wants to be compared to."

"Your men are rude." I turned up my lips and looked out the window. I had been so distracted with Cornelio and his goons that I didn't realize we had climbed higher in the sky and seemed to be well on our way. I was ecstatic since I didn't like heights. I shouldn't have taken the window seat. I didn't want to look out the window.

"No, they don't want to die for a woman they will never touch."

How does he know who I slept with? It's not he had access to my body count, not that there was a count. I lost my virginity to Craig and I hadn't slept with another man.

I had always thought sleeping with Craig was safe. I practiced safe sex with him, and I thought we were monogamous.

There is no telling who Craig slept with.

"What makes you so sure, out of every man here there wasn't one that had touched me?"

"If he had he's a dead man." There was a tick that appeared in Cornelio's face. His smile was more reptilian than human, and his eyes had turned a smoldering amber.

I sighed deeply. "You don't own me. You kissed me but that doesn't mean you're my man or have some kind of claim on me. There was only one man that had that right and his name was Craig."

The wind became stronger, shaking the jet. I heard something shift as I felt the jet climb higher. Higher altitude made my ears pop and I had no chewing gum. The winds were still fierce, and we were bouncing up and down every second. His men ignored us, and someone pulled out a deck of cards. I loved to play spades. Telica sucked at playing cards, so I didn't get to play much.

Did I goad Cornelio too far? His arrogance was astounding, and I wanted to take him down several notches. I shouldn't goad him, but I wasn't the sharpest tool in the shed. I fought him with my tongue the only battle I could win again a man like him.

"So, you want Jose. Fine. You can have him."

"Jose do you want Asha?" Cornelio snapped my fingers at him. Jose looked like he'd rather eat a grenade than talk to me. I wasn't a vain person but damn, I had pride.

"No sir. I no want her. I love Gabriella."

"I won't get mad if you want her."

I had just met Cornelio and didn't believe that mess. He was very territorial and jealous. He acted like he owned me. I was trying not to panic about that. Didn't mafia men act like that toward all the woman they slept with?

He shook his head and leaned away from Cornelio. "She would cut off my pau and stick it in my mouth."

Something told me pau meant dick. I had to admit his crash language sounded better in his native tongue than in English.

"Who is Gabriella?" I swallowed and looked at Jose. Why the stupid man stared at Cornelio when I was talking to him, I'll never know. It bothered me more than it should.

Jose looked at me and I smiled. I hadn't given any of the men permission to speak with her. The only man that dared was Alcino. I let that past since he was probably trying to get on her good side, so he'd have an ally in his corner when dealing with Telica. His ass wasn't slick either. I had time to deal with him.

"She's his wife."

"You wanted him to cheat on his wife. Unbelievable. So, you cheat on your wife. I hope you allow her to cheat on you."

I rolled my eyes. "I'm not married. If you wanted to know if I was married all you had to do was ask."

"I don't care if you're married."

The plane had climbed high in the sky. At her back, I could see the night sky as we climbed higher. We hit a patch of turbulence and I bit my lip to keep from screaming. The smooth flight had turned into a rollercoaster.

My breathing was heavy, and I tried to calm myself. Unclenching my hands from the armrest I forced myself to lean back. The men sitting in the front of the plane didn't seem bothered by the rough ride. Most of them had turned out the lights above them and were recycling and sleeping.

How could anyone sleep on an airplane?

I didn't trust people and the thought that I was not in control over my life the pilot had irritated me. I wasn't a control freak, but I had to be in control of the situations I was involved in. I was comfortable that way.

Cornelio had leaned back and closed his eyes. I doubted he was sleep. Closing my eyes, I vowed to rest them and try to relax before figuring out my plan. I was heading right back to Vegas with the Capturi Mafia, who were the sworn enemies of the Hoon Mafia. My life had turned into a horrible b rated action movie where the girl was too stupid to live.

My body was exhausted, and my brain was too. I knew no one would bother me while Cornelio was around, and I couldn't be assured that he would stick around once we landed in Vegas.

I jerked awake when my head fell forward jerking my neck. Rubbing my neck, I tried to get comfortable, but I couldn't. Ever since I was a little girl, I was a terrible sleeper. It didn't take much to make me fall asleep, a warm place and a full stomach did it every time.

Cornelio was gone. The next to me was empty. It shouldn't bother me, but it did. I shouldn't feel anything but as tired as I was, I couldn't go back to sleep. Looking around, I noticed the men were sleeping and the one's awake were playing games. Jose sawing me looking and shook his head.

"He talks with the pilot. He'll be back."

The jerk speaks English. Why is he talking to the pilot? Is there a problem?

Biting my lip, I looked out the window. I couldn't see anything. It was dark out, and we weren't anywhere near the ground. Wringing my hand, I closed my eyes. My heart was pounding, and I needed to calm down.

"Don't worry no problem." Jose turned around and pulled a card from his hand and laid it on the table. He was playing a card game with his friend.

"Why else would he talk with the pilot. There must be a problem."

A man walked toward me and flopped down in Cornelio's seat. "We should arrive in a half-hour, but the pilot said we would be delayed by fifteen to twenty minutes, because of the windstorm."

"That makes sense, but what good does it do to talk with the pilot about that. He can't control the storm."

"Nope, God's work will be done. However, the pilot can land the plane safely in a location until the storm passes."

"I hope he takes us to his island again. I love that place," he said.

Josiah, you love that place because you love the clear blue water and white sandy beaches."

Wow. Having the island described like that, makes me want to see this place for myself. Who wouldn't want to take a beautiful sandy beach over a choppy flight through a storm?

"You were nice to me, so I must warn you. I don't think you should sit here in his seat. He seems to like that seat."

"My name is Alcino. He does not like this seat; I'd be willing to bet a million dollars he hates this seat. It's you that he likes." He smiled and extended his hand.

I shook his hand. "I don't like him."

"Why?" Tilting his head to the side, he studied my face.

"He killed my brother."

He rubbed his chin. "Can't you get over it?"

Chapter 12

Cornelio

As much as I liked our verbal sparring, I needed some shut eye. The trip to visit Willie would not be so smooth. He was a cantankerous man and he wore me out. Leaning back, I closed my eyes. After, twenty minutes, I opened my eyes and studied her. Her breathing was steady, and she was snoring softly.

Justin my pilot was texting me. He only texted when there was a problem. Things were going smoothly but it seemed that the time for smooth sailing and over. Asha was sleeping and I hoped she stayed that way. She was terrified with flying. Her nails had dug into the armrest and her claws had marked my leather seat.

Instead of being pissed about my Italian leather seats. I was jealous that her talon's dug into the leather instead of in my flesh. If she knew what I had in store for her she might beg Hyong to blow her ass up. She didn't trust people, and she had bet her pretty tight little ass that she was going to trust me. The walls she had built would keep her safe from everyone except me. I would be behind her fortress before she realized I was there.

I stood and walked down the aisle toward the cockpit. Stopping at Alcino's seat, I elbowed his ass. "Get up. I need to speak with the pilot. Keep your eyes peeled."

"I packed six parachutes."

Fuck the parachutes. Jumping my ass out an airplane was the last thing I wanted to do.

"I need you to watch her."

"No one will touch her." Alcino released his seatbelt and reached under his seat. Placing the little black box on his lap he opened it with an odd-shaped key.

Alcino started putting together the small Glock. I watched him as he put it together in record time. It was nice that he had it, but he was unable to shoot on the plane.

"She might touch them." The image of her sitting next to Jose was imprinted in my mind. He had a wife and was not interested in her, but I didn't want him tempted.

"Bullshit. She's pissed with you. She doesn't have eyes for anyone on this plane but you."

I walked over to the door of the cockpit and tapped lightly on it. Joanne, the co-pilot opened the door. "Cornelio."

She locked the door behind me. "We have spotted an unidentified aircraft heading toward us."

Justin snorted. "Baby, it doesn't mean it's a hostile. You always think it's a hostile."

Frowning, I turned to Joanne. "Did you try to hail it?"

She tossed her long hair over her shoulder. "Of course, and it didn't answer. It also tried to cloak itself but with our technology, thanks to Langley, I was able to see it cloak itself and hail another plane."

Hyong had left her alone because she was bait. If that ankle bracelet was powerful enough to blow more than just her up, it would have been done it already.

Fuck. I hate planes. We should have a shootout, but I wouldn't be the one holding the gun. It would be Joan and Justin. A gun fight at fifty-five feet above the ground wasn't optimal.

"Are we still fifty-five feet above ground?"

"We're higher and no I won't text you our altitude. Relax and worry about how you're going to deal with that female. She was more than a notion and you have your work cut out for you."

"We're about to be blown out the sky and you want me to focus on her?"

"We are starting our descent now. They won't get close enough to lock on us. They should've lost our signal fifteen minutes ago."

"You didn't tell me about that feature."

She squeezed my cheeks. "You didn't ask. Besides, you were terrified of flying. Why would I have you thinking that falling out the sky was an option?"

"You know Joanne. The government taught her well. She forgets they no longer own her."

"Can we make it to Vegas?"

"No. They can't see us and it's possible they could run into us. We must land and take care of them."

Parting my lips to speak, I raked my hand over my face. "Where were we landing?"

She smiled. "At your hideaway spot. If you must murder someone do it in paradise. Even a dying man appreciates beauty."

We are landing in Cabos San Lucas.

"I'll prepare the men."

Closing the cockpit door, I walked down the aisle. The men stopped playing games and the other men woke up. Asha was talking with Alcino. She was frowning at him. I wondered what he did to piss her off.

"We'll be landing soon and waiting out the storm."

Asha looked at Alcino. "Where are we exactly?"

"Cabos San Lucas. Buckle your seat belts and get prepared to land." I walked past her and Alcino and closed the door to my bedroom. There wasn't a need to lock the door since nobody would dare come in here without my permission. Asha might but I secretly wanted her to see this place. She'd be laying in this king-size bed soon enough.

Striding to the closet, I touched a secret panel and placed my hand on the biometric scanner. The flap opened and I bent down, opening my eyes, so it could scan my retina. A few minutes later, the door opened. I took out five hundred thousand dollars in cash and tossed the crisp stacks into the leather bag.

I had four outfits folded military-style in the bag already. It was the usual, two business suits, one all-black outfit for combat, and one casual outfit to blend in. Grabbing the grey bag out of the compartment I packed the entire bag in there. It had food rations, compass, GPS, Glocks, pistols, grenades, ammunition, assault rifles, machine guns, communication devices, satellite phones, and explosives. It was my on the go emergency survival pack. Zipping the bag, I closed the compartment and it retracted inside the wall.

My men knew what this bag symbolized. I wouldn't need to say a word, and everyone would be aware and on guard for our enemies.

I hadn't expected to have company but there was enough here for Asha and me to survive on in a pinch.

The plane made a right turn and started descending toward the private air strip. Closing my bedroom door, I marched toward my seat, putting my bag on the left-hand side of it in the lower storage.

I sat down and clicked my seatbelt. "Have you ever been to Mexico?"

She shook her head. "No. I hadn't done much traveling, but I planned to go to Amsterdam this year."

You aren't going to Amsterdam. It was probably Telica's ideal anyway. I could tell Telica was reckless and carefree and Asha was reserved, conservative, and innocent.

"I recommend visiting the Van Gogh Museum."

Jumping into the back of the Humvee Asha and I were the last to leave the landing strip. She was discovering just how beautiful Mexico was. Her expression after seeing a Mexican palm tree was priceless. I loved her appreciation for nature and the beauty that surrounded her. Mexican palm trees were one of my favorite trees. The huge fan like leaves grow tall and stretch wide. Their pointed leaves spread as if reaching for the heavens. It was also the reason why I had fifty of them surrounding my villa.

She pressed her face to tinted glass of the automobile as we got on the highway. "The sky in Mexico is so blue. It looks like God painted the sky with vivid baby blue, pink, and apricot colors."

I studied her face. "Lovely."

The moonlight over Cabo San Lucas was beautiful. I couldn't wait to see her reaction to the villa. The water was gorgeous and at night the sight was breathtakingly stunning. Turning to me she caught me staring. Adjusting my collar, I attempted to ignore the leap of temperature in the car.

She cleared her throat. "Why did you bring the bag if we were getting back on the plane?"

"We'll fly out in the morning."

"Of all the places to land, this was more of a vacation spot. I hope you weren't planning on seducing me."

"This was the last place I'd take you to seduce you."

Besides, we don't need to go anywhere to get our passions to rise. It seems we are always hot for each other. I can have her in the trunk of a car, and she will let me.

We arrived at the villa without any issues. Asha had not realized it, but my men were surrounding us on all sides forming a moving barricade. I had hoped to deal with the bastards before we reached the villa. Killing someone where I laid my head was always unsettling to me, yet it was where most hitmen thought you'd be laxed. Opening the door, I helped her out the truck. Heaving the bag over my shoulder, I opened the door. I had checked the surveillance and my men had check the house before we arrived, but the surveillance had gone down for ten minutes. Handing the bag to Levi, I turned to Asha. "Wait here."

Disappearing around the corner, I slipped out a back door. Walking through the thick garden, I took the hidden path around the side of the house to the detached in-law suite. After searching the suite, I went into the bedroom and stepped inside the walk-in closet. Touching a panel, I scanned my retinal and four cameras came out of the wall. I re-played the security footage. My backup security wasn't on the same servers so if the main security was hacked the hacker would have to know about the backup and hack it as well.

Replaying the footage from when the main security went down, I saw two Asian men enter the villa with black backpacks. The tall one had a man bun and the short one had an asymmetrical bob cut with his bangs dyed bright blue. Once the door shut, they removed AR 47s from the backpacks and searched the house. The bastards walked on my white carpet with their shoes on. The tall man stuck a microdevice on the laptop that sat on my bedroom nightstand. The bastards were going to blow my ass up the moment I went to stream my favorite television show.

I watched the footage until the main security came back online. The shorter man left. Checking the entire surveillance from the outer perimeter to the inside, there was no sign that the tall man had left.

Where are you? Duck, Duck, Goose.

Rewinding the surveillance, I examined everything looking for clues. Damn, I didn't see anything. taking out my phone I texted my men. Gunfire erupted on the screen, and I saw that my men that were outside on the veranda smoking Cuban cigars take a dozen shots to the heart and chest. Four men wearing all black with a green mask entered the house.

Fuck. The Mexican Mafia would pick this time to strike.

Snatching the hand-held portable security camera, I touched the secret panel, and everything retraced back into the wall. Reaching behind the dresser, I grabbed the Glock strapped to the wall. Two of the men headed toward the front door of the in-law suite. Bending low as soon as the door opened, I fired two shots and ducked inside the door as one man started to enter. The body fell to the ground and the second man opened fire from outside the front door. Watching the hand-held screen, I walked over to the window, aimed and shot him twice in the head. Picking up the first man's assault rifle, I ran down the hall past the kitchen to the powder room. Stepping inside, I pressed a hidden panel and the wall parted and I slipped inside.

Crawling through the hidden tunnel, I came out in the twelfth bedroom. Alcino and Lucas had killed the other two Mexican mafia assholes. Checking the upper level, I searched from room to room. The bastard was still hidden in here somewhere. Checking the security footage again, I stopped in my tracks and my heart leapt in my throat.

His Bermuda shirt was ripped open and his chest was strapped with several explosives taped to his bare chest. He had his gun pressed to Asha's temple. "You shoot me, and I shoot her. We're leaving, or we both die right here and now."

I flipped the cameras to the outside. There was no car waiting outside, which meant he hadn't planned to leave the villa alive.

I crept down the stairs. The floorboards creaked and he looked at me.

"Cornelio don't look so pissed. It could be worse."

His accent was thick. He was not with the Mexican mafia. He was either part of the Triad or he was an independent looking to make a name for himself.

Keeping my gun trained on him, I descended the steps and my men parted, so I could walk up to him.

"Don't come any closer." He pressed the gun deeper into her skull, and she winced. Scooting back, he fumbled with the door until it opened.

"Who are you?" This wasn't Nae Seung Hoon's style.

"Nobody you know. I got your number here, we'll be in touch." He walked out with Asha.

Watching them on camera, I saw the short-haired Asian man ride up on a motorcycle. He forced her on the back and the short-haired man rode off with her. A purple BMW drove up and the tall man jumped inside, and they rode off.

I screenshot the two Asian men and texted it to Greg Foster's phone, then I dialed him.

"I need to know who these two men are." I didn't give a damn that it was three o'clock in the morning there. He needed to get his fat ass up anyway.

"When are you going to call your men off?"

"When I feel you're trustworthy." I always had a small army following him. He was my flunky not the other way around. When he outlived his usefulness, he would be found floating in the Baltimore Harbor.

Hanging up the phone, I Grabbed the vase off the shelf and tossed it to the ground.

My phone rang. The number was blocked.

"Talk."

"Hyong will detonate the bomb in forty-eight hours," said Po.

Epilogue

If you want to find out what happens to Asha and whether Cornelio will save her and claim his prize, their battle continues in the novel *Claimed by Cornelio*.

https://books2read.com/u/mY7y0Y

ACKNOWLEDGMENTS

Thank you to my father, who died on active duty so that I live my life with the freedoms I have today. I am humbled and thankful for my mother, who encouraged me to pursue my dreams of becoming a published author.

Thank you to my fellow editors who read my early drafts and helped me believe in myself and this book. A special thanks to my editor Amanda Williams for doing an amazing job with this novel.

Enormous and overwhelming gratitude to my romance author friends, who encouraged me to tell Asha and Cornelio's story.

About Lashe Lacroix

Lashe Lacroix has always enjoyed reading all genres of romance. Her love for romance books started when she was given ***Captive Bride*** by Johanna Lindsey, and she has not looked back. Lashes' love for creating vivid characters and developing make-believe worlds began when she was four years old.

When she is not reading, writing, or traveling, you can find her on the ocean somewhere, sailing the high tides.
Sign up for the mailing list and find out about her latest releases, giveaways, and more.

Sign up here. **https://thomask24783-2336.gr8.com/**

If you enjoyed this book, you could help others enjoy it as well by recommending it to friends and family or by mentioning it in reading and discussion groups and online forums. You can also leave a review with the retailer you bought the book from. Thank you so much for taking the time to read my book!

TALLY

Lords of Exile

J.N. Pack

Author Note

Tally is an M/F new adult dark romance that deals with intense violence, excessive use of the word fuck and sexual content. I would advise skipping this story if you can't handle a badass chick who don't mind putting people in their places and surviving at all cost.

*Please note that the following story is only the part one of book one of my new standalone series, **Lords of Exile**. Each story will have a HEA but with this being only part one of **Tally** please be prepared for a cliffhanger. The rest of the story will be released once the boxset is unpublished.*

CHAPTER 1

The last place Korbyn expected to find herself was on a plane leaving Galway, Ireland to Stockton, California. Her brothers have done everything in their power to keep her in Ireland with their Aunt Keira. Unfortunately for them, she decided the day after Korbyn's eighteenth birthday, to ship her to the states. After the ten-and-a-half-hour flight from Galway to Portersville, CA, Korbyn is irritated and not ready to deal with anyone's crap. The uber ride from Portersville to Stockton was hell. The uber driver kept trying to make conversation with her just to hear her accent.

When he drops her in front of the Lords of Exile clubhouse and bar, Korbyn lets him have it, "Look you piece o' shet, nahbody wants to ride in yooehr car fahr three 'ooehrs and 'ave you say stupid shet joehst to 'ear dem talk. Get a clue mahron!" The angrier she gets the stronger her Irish accent becomes.

The man looks at her through the window and rolls his eyes. "You were prettier when you kept your mouth closed." Korbyn starts to grab him through the window, but he slams his foot on the gas and speeds away sending loose gravel flying everywhere. She turns looking at the bar and takes a deep breath before making her way to the front door, when she shoves through the front door every eye in the place turned her way. There were men of varying ages scattered throughout the bar. Some sat on bar stools nursing drinks, while some stood around pool tables. There were a few tables spread around the building, that had a few men sitting around them. The women in this building were outnumbered four to one. As she makes her way to the bar a younger guy with a prospect vest on yells, "We got another House Mouse!" If looks could kill he'd be dead and buried. Korbyn turns her attention back to the bar and climbs on one of the seats.

The bar tender walks over, "I think you're in the wrong place little lady."

Korbyn's eye begins to twitch and she literally growls, "I'm lookin fahr Cahnnor ahr Sean O'Clery."

The bar tender smirks, "You aren't from around here, are you?"

"What foehckin' gave it away?" she says rolling her eyes.

He cocks an eyebrow, "You'd get a lot further with sugar than vinegar little girl."

Irritated to the point of no return Korbyn climbs to her feet on the stool, "O'Clery, where de foehck you at?" she yells looking around the bar. All eyes were on her and the bartender was making his way around the bar to physically remove her from the stool.

A commotion is making its way from one of the backrooms and draws her attention. When a group of men walk from the back to find out what the commotion was about, Korbyn searches the group for any sign of her brothers.

"Not another crazy house mouse." One of the guys groans.

Korbyn cocks her eyebrow, "Get foehcked pretty bahy"

Someone shoves from the back of the group and when his eyes land on her, he pales, "Korbyn Leigh, is that you?"

She jumps to the ground and stalks towards him, "Mess me brahther"

He throws his arms wide and Korbyn jumps into them. "What are you doing here?" he says finally releasing her.

"Aoehnt Keira sent me, said she wasn't dealin' wit me anymahre." Korbyn says with her strong accent.

"Connor's going to kill you little sister." Her brother says throwing his arm across her shoulders and leading her down a hallway to the back. She rolls her eyes.

After passing three doors they turn into the fourth door on the right and come to a stop in the doorway.

"Connor? Um we have a problem." Her brother says drawing the attention of Connor from the desk. He slowly lifts his head until his eyes land on Korbyn. He shoots to his feet, "No, no, no. What the fuck are you doing here Korbyn Leigh?"

She sneers, "At least Sean 'ugged me befahre bein a deck."

Connor leans forward putting his fist on the desk and growls, "What did you do?"

Korbyn looks anywhere, but at Connor. She even makes a point to avoid looking at Sean.

At that very moment the phone rings and Connor grins seeing the name on his caller ID. "Don't bother coming up with a lie little sister, it's Aunt Keira." He snatches the phone from the desk and hits the talk button immediately putting it on speaker phone. "What the fuck is she doing here?" he growls.

"She's been causin' too many prahblems. She can't stay 'ere anymahre. If she's naht fightin, she's stealin. She was arrested ahn 'er birthday fahr fightin an ahfficer." Her Aunt Keira says.

Both Connor and Sean's eyes shoot daggers through her. "I'm sorry Aunt Keira, but I'm sure Korbyn Leigh will be on her best behavior when she gets back." Connor growls into the phone.

"She's naht combing back Cahnnor. I'm sahrry she's yooehr prahblem now." Aunt Keira says ending the call as soon as the statement leaves her.

Connor growls and throws his phone against a wall shattering it in a million tiny pieces. Nobody says a word. Korbyn's eyes are wide and she is the first to break the silence, "Foehck you Cahnnor. I'm nahbodies foehckin' prahblem. I can take care o' myself." She turns and shoves through the men standing behind her.

"Not so fast little sister." Sean says quickly gripping her arms and keeping her from making the escape she had planned.

Korbyn's wanted to be back with her brothers ever since she could remember, but this is far from what she expected to find when she got here. She knew he'd be angry, but he was treating her like he didn't want her here. Korbyn slams the invisible wall in place and growls at Sean, "Get yooehr 'ands ahff me. It's clear neither o' you want me 'ere, so let me foehckin' go. I do naht need you." Anger was coming off her wave after wave. She shrugs Sean's hand from her and starts for the door again.

"Ollie! Don't let her through." Connor growls and a tall guy with dark brown eyes steps in front of her.

Korbyn is ridged with irritation. She shoves into the guy's chest and growls, "Mahve jackass!"

He looks from her to Connor and then back again with his eyebrow cocked, "Is she for real?"

Sean smirks, "And she bites too."

Korbyn glares at Sean. Then turns her attention back to Connor, "I'm goin to foehckin' crepple yooehr friend if 'e doesn't mahve."

Ollie crosses his arms over his chest and watches her curiously. Connor half laughs at her and it sets her off. She turns rears back and swings with all of her might. Her five-foot four body had quite a bit of oomph behind it. When she lands the punch, Ollie hunches over and she shoves past him.

As they all clear a path for Connor, Ollie straightens and stalks behind her. Connor behind him and Sean behind Connor. The rest follow behind.

"When did she get so fuckin' mean?" Sean mumbles.

Korbyn storms out of the front door to the building and starts strutting down the sidewalk.

Ollie stops just outside the club watching her. Her green eyes had turned an olive green and her long red hair was braided over her right shoulder. Anger radiated off her in waves.

Sean walks just pass where Connor and Ollie stopped and yells, "Where the fuck are you going Korbyn?"

She throws her middle finger up over her shoulder and keeps walking.

CHAPTER 2

Tired and exhausted with nowhere to go, Korbyn walked the streets. She hadn't been in Stockton since she was twelve and her parents died. Korbyn was sent to live with her Aunt Keira in Galway. Her brother was given custody of her and Sean, but when her Aunt offered to take her in, he quickly put her on a plane and shipped her off to Ireland. She turns on Cherry Lane, where she used to live with her parents and her brothers, or at least Sean anyways. Connor had moved into the club as soon as he turned eighteen. She walks by the house and stares in the window from the street to see if anyone lived there now, if her brother had sold the place. He was left everything after their parents died. Not that Korbyn wanted anything, but what she didn't want was to be thrown away. She had expected her brothers to be angry, but she hadn't expected Connor to treat her like some kind of disease, he couldn't get rid of fast enough.

"Hey beautiful." Someone says from across the street.

Korbyn glances over her shoulder at him and cocks her eyebrow. Even in the dark his green eyes could compete with hers. He wore a red cap turned backwards on his head and a red tee-shirt. His jeans were slightly baggy, and he wore white sneakers. His head was cocked sideways assessing her.

"Beautiful night." He says glancing up at the stars.

Now that Korbyn has had a chance to cool off her accent isn't as strong, "If you say so." She crosses the street and walks into the park across the street from her old house. She drops down into a swing and digs the toe of her shoe in the sand. He walks over with his hands in his pockets and leans against the jungle gym.

"Who are you? Who sent you to fahllow me?" she asks.

He looks at the ground and then back up at her smiling, "Who do you think?"

"Tell Cahnnor to kess my ass." She growls, some irritation coming back to the surface.

He smiles and just shakes his head. "Yea I'm not going to be the one to do that. You'll have to pass that message along when we get you back to the clubhouse."

"Who are you? If Cahnnor wants me back there, he shooehld 'ave came 'imself." Korbyn says running her shoes through the sand and watching as the sand slid back down into the hole she was digging with her shoe.

"Roman. Connor didn't send me. He's still fuming. Looks like you and him have matching tempers. Sean sent me. He said you'd be here." The guy says.

Her face drops and Roman says, "Come on, you've got to be tired. I'm assuming it's a long flight from Ireland to here. I'll play peacekeeper until in the morning and you can sleep."

She does not argue, she has no fight left in her at the moment. She stands and walks in the direction of his bike. He follows behind her without another word. When they reach the bike, he pulls his helmet from the back and pulls it over her head and snaps the hook. He throws his leg across and makes himself comfortable. Roman reaches for her hand, "Come on little devil." And smiles.

Korbyn smiles as she takes his hand and climbs on the bike.

The ride back to the club house was short, but also peaceful. Korbyn enjoyed the sound of the engine and the wind blowing across her face and hair. She'd missed this in Galway. Her Dad used to take her on rides all the time. When he wasn't taking her on rides, he was teaching her about motorcycles and their engines. Connor took that from her. He sent her as far away as he could. He never once came to see her. Not in six years did he once come to see her. Sean came after he turned eighteen once, but even he didn't care enough to see her. Sean called her once a month. Connor hasn't seen or heard from her since the day their parents were buried.

Her Aunt Keira was nice somewhat, but she wasn't Connor and Sean. She wasn't the family that Korbyn had grown up with. She wasn't the family Korbyn wanted or needed. Things weren't that horrible in Galway, but they got bad at times. She wasn't happy and she didn't make it easy for anyone. She thought getting sent back here, back to her brothers would make things better for her, but turns out, they don't want her here.

When they pull back up at the club Roman backs his bike against the building and climbs from the bike offering Korbyn his hand to help her climb down. When she is standing, he unbuckles the helmet and takes her hand leading her into the club. As they walk in, he leads her to the hall at the back of the club. Seeing her walking down the hall with him Connor shoots to his feet at the bar. They continue down the hall. He opens the second door on the left, "You can sleep in my bed. I'll sleep on the couch in Ollie's room."

"Thanks." She says quietly, her mind a million miles away.

"Lock the door and don't open it for anyone. Things get pretty crazy around here." Roman says through the door.

She nods closing the door when he backs out the door.

Roman is shoved against the wall, "You're not fuckin' sleeping with my sister."

The door is swung open and as tired as she is, she growls, "Who the foehck do you think you are? If I want to foehck 'im, I will and dere is nahthin you can do abooeht it. You've made it abundantly clear, you dahn't want me 'ere. I get it, I'll leave as soon as me mahney clears de bank frahm Ireland. I do naht need you. Never needed you. All those years you wanted nahthin to do wit me, I made it. Without you. So foehck ahff." And she slams the door and slams the latch in place, but not before seeing the concern on Connor and Sean's face.

"She's tired, I was just giving her somewhere she can sleep. It's a ten hour or more flight from Ireland. She's angry, give her tonight and then you can tear each other to pieces if that's what you want, but tonight, well I'm pretty sure Emma has other plans for you." Roman says, playing the peacekeeper.

CHAPTER 1

The next morning when Korbyn wakes up, she calls and uber. Her plans are simple. Buy her old house back from the bank and fix it up. That had always been the plan. Korbyn pulls on some black tights and biker boots. She then puts on a white shirt that shows the bottom half of her stomach and fits tight in all the right places. She leaves her hair down where is hung to the middle of her back. Glancing at her phone she hurries out the door trying to beat her brothers up, so she could leave before they saw her. Walking through the club she smirks at the bodies lying all around passed out. She slips out the front door and makes her way down the street towards the bank.

Walking into the bank, she held her head high because she finally felt like she was doing what was right. People stared at her from every corner in the room. She approaches the counter, "I'd like to purchase a house on Cherry Lane."

The clerk looks at her as if she's grown an extra head. "I'll get my manager." She pushes a button and a few seconds later a man with hardly any hairs approaches the counter. "How may I help you?"

"I 'ad me money transferred to dis bank from Ireland a few days ago and I'd like to finesh setting up my accooehnt as well as poehrchase the old 'ouse for sale on Cherry lane." Korbyn says, getting irritated with having to repeat herself.

An hour later, Korbyn walks out of the bank with the deed and title to her old home. She's distracted when she walks out and doesn't realize she's not alone until Connor growls, "Where'd you get that much fuckin' money Korbyn?"

Startled she jumps. "You scared me." Looking up she realizes that he's not alone. Connor, Sean, Ollie and Roman stand beside their bikes.

"Where'd the money come from Little sister?" Sean asks.

She refuses to look at them. "It doesn't matter where it came frahm, it's mine. You dedn't want me around you." She holds up the deed and waves it at them. "Prahblem sahlved. You dahn't ever 'ave to wahrry yooehr lettle 'ead abooeht me again." Her eyes glisten for a second before she locks down all of her emotions.

Connor growls, "You're going back to Ireland Korbyn. You are not staying here."

Her cheeks flush and the tips of her ears flame red. Her eyes darken to an olive green and she rears back smacking the ever-loving shit out of Connor. His face flames red and Sean and Roman grab him to hold him back while Ollie steps between the two and tries to keep them from killing each other.

"Guess what beg brahther? I'm eighteen. I'm naht goin anywhere and dere is nahthin you can do to make me. Combing back 'ere I was supposed to get my family back. De family you took frahm me. Guess I was wrahng, because you're dead to me. I foehckin' 'ate you Cahnnor." As a tear slips down her cheek and she turns darting down the street.

The fight leaves Connor and his face looks completely crushed.

"What the fuck Connor?" Sean says running his hand through his hair. "I knew you were pushing too hard. Now what the fuck do we do?"

Connor drops his head, "I don't fuckin' know." He throws his leg across his bike and leaves the other three standing there.

Ollie says, "I'll go check on him."

Sean growls, "Fuck him right now! Find my fuckin' sister."

Roman says, "I'll go find her. He can go look for Connor. She's not very fond of Ollie after yesterday."

Ollie shrugs climbing on his bike and pulling away from the curb.

Roman pats Sean's shoulder, "I'll call when I find her."

Sean nods looking devastated. He runs his hands through his hair and waves Roman off.

CHAPTER 4

Korbyn allowed herself to cry for ten minutes, then she did what she always did, sucked it up. No purpose in crying over something you can't change. Her brothers have been her end goal for the past six years and now she was letting them go. Her heart was crushed. After going to the electric company and water company she stops at a diner and orders a burger, fries, and strawberry milkshake. She sits on the deck outside nibbling on her food, but not really tasting it.

The sound of someone hopping the fence draws her attention. She looks up just as Roman flops down in the chair across from her. He's got a huge smile on his face as he does something on his phone and then snatches one of Korbyn's fries. "You know these are better like this?" He pulls the lid off her shake and dips the fry in her shake then shoves it in his mouth.

Not in the mood for company she grumbles, "Have it. I'm done."

The smile fades a little from his face, "I'm not going to defend him for being a royal ass, but maybe... Maybe you should ask him why he doesn't want you here."

"Thank's Dr. Phel, boeht I've waited six lahng years for me brahther to show me 'e wants me in 'is life and 'e's done nahthin. I meant what I said, they're dead to me." Korbyn says through gritted teeth.

Roman just watches her for a minute before saying, "So what's the plan?"

"I'm goin to me 'ouse. I'm goin to clean it. I'm goin to fex it up and once I'm done, I'm goin to live in it. Other than that, I 'ave no plan. I grew up in dat 'ouse. It's me 'ahme."

He smiles up at her, "Wanna get drunk with me?" His smile is contagious. "I'll even help you clean."

She is smiling and needed to feel like someone wants her around she agrees. "Meet me at my house in about two hours."

He smiles and pushes her food back to her, "Eat." Then he jumps the fence and he's gone. Leaving her smiling like an idiot.

Korbyn grabs a few things she needs and takes an uber back to her house. It wasn't what she remembered, but it has been six years. There is still some old furniture in it from back then, but it's in bad shape. Kind of looked like someone had been sleeping in the house. She planned on putting Roman to work putting new locks on the doors as soon as he got there, until then she was going to start cleaning the main areas of the house. She starts with the kitchen, throwing everything away and washing the sink out and wiping down the counter tops. Then she used a broom she bought to sweep the cobwebs from the ceilings and then sweeping the floor up.

She then moves to the rest room where she scrubbed the toilet first because she had been holding it for hours now and figured it was time. She then moved to the shower, where she scrubbed it until her knuckles nearly bled. Swept the floor and mopped the floor. Then she started to put things she'd bought away. A couple of towels, rags, shampoo, soap, the basics. She'd get more later, but for now she had what she needed.

Back in the living room she finds a vacuum in the corner and plugs it in. Lucky for her, it worked. So, she picked up anything it couldn't vacuum up and vacuumed the rest up. She also vacuumed the dust from the couches and chairs. When she's done, she leans back on the couch remembering how her mom used to dance from the kitchen to the living room singing to her and her brothers. Her mom could be so mad at her Dad, but the second he walked in from one of his trips, she was throwing herself in his arms. They'd dance around the kitchen until the early morning hours with the music blasting. Korbyn missed those days more than she missed anything. Missed having a real family. Someone she knew loved her beyond the shadow of a doubt. She hadn't had that in a long time, and she missed it.

Korbyn climbs to her feet and grabs the bottle of fireball she bought earlier and pops the top. She turns it up gulping down about two shots of the liquid. The burn heats her from the inside out. Roman should be there in a bit, so she goes to take a shower before he gets there. She has a towel wrapped around her hair and a long sleeve tee-shirt with a pair of black booty shorts with socks that came up to her knees. Sitting on the kitchen counter, she opens Spotify on her phone. She grabs the bottle of fireball and takes another gulp. Then lays back on the piece of crap couch listening to music and remembering when life didn't suck so much.

Roman is thirty minutes late and she's starting to get a little irritated when someone knocks at the door. Expecting Roman she answers the excited to have someone to hang out with. Only it's not Roman, it's Ollie.

He smirks when I open the door, "You expecting someone?"

"Where's Roman?" she asks feeling slightly disappointed.

His smirk turns into a full-on grin, "He got a better offer, he won't be coming to hang out."

Her heart drops to her feet and she smiles trying to put on a show like she doesn't care, "Ahh ahkay. What can I 'elp you wit?"

He shoves past her and throws a bag on the couch, "I'm under orders to babysit you, so how about you be a dear and don't give me shit."

The smile slowly begins fades from her face and she turns up the bottle again. When she pulls it back down and swallows the liquid she says, "I don't need a babysetter."

"No?" he asks with an eyebrow popped.

"No, I dahn't. I'm eighteen and I've been takin care o' myself fahr de past sex years. I dahn't need you, or them fahr dat matter."

He drops his ass on the couch making himself comfortable.

Feeling slightly defeated in that moment she walks past him knocking his foot from the coffee table and dropping into an old recliner that sat by the window, "Don't expect me to offer you a blanket or anything."

He smirks and rolls his eyes as he pulls a hoodie from his bag and pulls it over his head. "Wouldn't think of it, Princess."

Curling the bottle of fireball into her side, she laughs, "I'm no Princess, I'm a foehckin' Queen."

She fell asleep to dreams of anything, but sugar and fairies. The ultimate betrayal. Her brothers were standing over her body with blood dripping from their hands and smiles across their beautiful faces. Even though she couldn't see herself in her dream, she knew her body was lifeless. An empty feeling took over and she shivered in her sleep. The dream was so lifelike when she wakes drenched in sweat, she has to look around to make her there was no one around. Only she's not alone. Ollie is sitting on the couch watching her closely. She looks at her body expecting there to be blood, but there is nothing.

He stands and walks to the kitchen, when he returns, he has a glass of ice water. He leans over taking the bottle of fireball from her and handing her the glass of water. Reluctantly, she takes it and then he digs in his bag and comes back with two white pills.

She cocks her eyebrow, bringing a smirk to his face, "Tylenol."

She takes the pills and he sat back on the couch. Stretching back on the couch, she checks her phone. Only the message their makes her blood freeze in her veins.

M: *One, Two, Three Micah's coming for you! You can't hide from me Korbyn!*

She knew it was going to happen, but she never expected it to happen this soon. Micah was a prick and she had fucked him over. He was going to get her for that, and she'd pay a price. A huge price.

"Who was that?"

Korbyn's head snaps up and she sneers.

"Whoever it was scared you. You do know whatever it is you are hiding; Connor and Sean will find out. Secrets don't stay secrets for long, they always find their way to the light." He says.

She winces knowing it's true, but she never came here with the intentions of keeping secrets from anyone. She was who she was, and she didn't intend to hide that from anyone. Especially not her brothers. That was until they decided that they didn't want her in their lives. They'd rather ship me to Ireland so they can go on pretending I don't exist.

"It's none o' your business. It's not even their business. They didn't care the six years I was gone, I come back and all dey want is to shep me back to Ireland. foehck dem, foehck dem both." Anger boiling her insides.

He shrugs and leans his head back on the couch, not willing to make excuses for her brothers. Assuming he had let it go, she hoped he had let it go. She should have known better. The next morning when she wakes up her brothers, Ollie and even Roman are seated around the rickety table in her kitchen. She quickly glances around for her phone and freezes realizing it's in the kitchen on the center of the kitchen table between the four of them. Her eyes roam to each of their faces and stops when it reaches Roman. He is sporting a black eye and busted lip.

"You assholes do that to 'im?" she asks from her seat on the recliner.

Four sets of eyes shoot her way. Not one of them responding to her question. "Password?" Connor growls.

She smirks, "I'll never tell Beg Brahther."

He jumps to his feet and stalks over to her, "I will find out Korbyn."

Sean stands, but doesn't make a move to approach her. "You know we'll find out, save yourself the heartache and give us the password."

She climbs to her feet and adjusts her shirt before shoving past Connor and making her way to the table, ignoring Sean altogether. She stops by Roman on the way to the sink and touches his cheek, while glancing back at Ollie, "Better offer, hmm?"

He smirks and Roman is tense knowing her brothers are going to try to beat the shit out of him for this. She drops her hand and snatches the phone from the table quickly shoving it in her bra and continuing to the sink. She fixes herself a glass of water and turns to them all, "You can see yourselves the foehck out."

Roman and Ollie fall in line with her brothers when they come to stand in front of her. "Nothing happens in Stockton that we don't know about. If we don't give the okay, it doesn't fuckin' happen. I don't know what you got into the past six years but bet your ass we will be digging, and we will know every little detail from the past six years. I'll know everything you do in this town before you fuckin' do it." Connor growls.

"Good luck with that brahther." She says laughing. "I'm a foehckin' O'Clery, "If I dahn't want you to know what I'm up to you'll never know. Now get de foehck ooeht, lettle sester 'as plans."

Ollie smirks as he passes her walking out, Connor growls in anger following behind Ollie. Sean just drops his head as he passes. Roman is last, but he is certainly not least, he smiles and winks at her as he pulls the door shut behind him.

Soon as they are gone Korbyn leans against the door sliding down until her butt hits the floor. She runs her hands through her hair pulling it back from her face and right at that moment she wished she was a normal person. She wished she could go back six years and fight to stay but would it have mattered. The past six years she's fought to get where she is. This was always the end goal. Coming home was always her end game.

CHAPTER 5

K orbyn wasn't afraid of what was headed her way, but she didn't want her brothers to know everything that went down when she was in Ireland. She did what she did, and she was okay with that. Korbyn took a few days to herself, only leaving the house to get paint and food. She'd had to purchase a new fridge because the one that was in the house was crap. Two days in and her milk was lumpy, bad.

She'd slowly started making purchases to make it her home. After two days of boredom, she decides to paint them entire house inside. She paints all the walls gray and then paints the trim a bright white.

She's in the middle of painting when there is a knock at the door. Walking to the door slowly, she peaks through the curtains to see a smiling Roman on the other side.

She cracks the door, "What?"

He smirks, "You got a little something," he says rubbing her forehead with his thumb.

Korbyn shrugs him off. She then steps to the side allowing him to walk in. She pulls her black bandanna back around her hair to keep it out of her face and paint from her hair. Roman looks around smiling, "Can I help?"

She sneers at him.

"For real, I like to paint." He says grinning.

Korbyn hands him a paint brush and they start painting. The only noise in the room was the sound of music coming from her phone. She didn't make any attempt to talk. She was lost in thought when he sneaks up behind her with paint on his fingers and runs them across her cheek.

Her mouth drops open as she slowly turns towards him, "You've got to be kidding me?"

His smile only enrages her more. She goes after him with the roller soaked with paint. His eyes widen as he dodges her catching the paint roller across his backside. He freezes glancing back at the paint running down his back.

Korbyn stands admiring her work and his ass all at the same time. When her eyes meet his and she notices the paint brush in his hand, it's all-out war. He slings paint and she tossed the roller at him. In the end they are both covered in paint from head to toe. They end up grappling with her straddling him trying her best to finger paint his beautiful face. He grips her hips drawing attention to the serious hard on he was sporting. She glances down and then back up to his face. His face is sober and clear of all emotions. He's trying to gauge her reaction when she leans in connecting her lips to his. There was no denying the attraction between the two of them in that moment. Roman deepens the kiss if that's even possible.

Korbyn tenses under his hands and pulls back. He can see the minute regret seeps into her eyes. She pulls away from him and climbs to her feet. Roman climbs to his feet watching her. When she goes to the window and instantly starts chewing at her fingernails he says, "Don't do that."

She turns to him with a questioning look, "Don't do what?"

"Don't over think this. It is what it is. You stopped it before it went too far. Nothing for you to *regret.*" He's says as he makes his way to the front door. He looked angry. Not angry at Korbyn, but angry with himself.

"Ro.." He shuts the door before she can get his name all the way out. She watches him cross the street and throw his leg across his bike. He sits there for a minute staring at the sky. He runs his fingers through his hair and then starts the bike and drives away.

Korbyn felt like complete shit for that. She liked Roman and he was the only person who's been kind to her since she got here. She honestly didn't regret it. He was an awesome kisser, made her toes curl. Genuinely, fun to be around. He made her forget all the crap in her life right now. Including her two brothers who like to pretend she doesn't exist. A weight settles on her chest.

Korbyn's phone buzzes alerting her to a new text message. Her shoulders sag a little as she leaves the window to check the message.

M: *Guess I'm coming to California to collect what's mine. The money too.*

That was fast. Korbyn didn't know how he connected the dots so quickly, but he had, and it was only a matter of time before he's knocking on her door. Time to get back to what she does best.

Korbyn joins a gym that very day and spends most of the rest of the day working out and training. She knew it was a matter of time before she found what she was looking for, so she'd train until that time came.

CHAPTER 6

Roman avoided coming around for a few days after what happened that night, but the attraction was too strong, and it wouldn't last. It couldn't. Her brothers had sent Ollie over every single night and he stayed on the couch in silence. He was always quiet and never made much noise, so it was easy for Korbyn to pretend he wasn't there at all.

Korbyn made a few friends at the gym. She met Max her sparring partner. He's a pretty boy, but too smooth around the edges. Nice to hang with, but definitely not someone she would crawl in the sack with. Then there is Benny. Benny owns the gym. He's a pretty decent guy. Older, set in his ways. Doesn't believe girls have any place in a gym. Korbyn is okay making men eat their words. Then of course theirs Zina. Zina is a one of a kind hooker. Literally a hooker. She is as out there and outspoken as they come.

Today she is sporting orange pleather pants and a neon pink pleather sports bra. You could quite literally see her from a hundred miles away. With the outfit she is wearing, you could probably see her from Mars.

Today Ollie followed Korbyn to the gym. Unfortunate for him, Zina is working. Walking in the gym, Korbyn stops just on the other side to peer through the glass and watch.

Zina approaches Ollie while he removes his helmet. She leans into him and takes a deep breath. "YUUMMMMY!" she moans into his ear.

He groans, "No Zina."

She whines, "Come on Ollie. I need to make some money."

He steps off the bike, "That would be a no! Not fuckin' happening."

She leans into him and you can see a shiver wrack his body from where Korbyn stood watching. Dying not to laugh.

"I'll make it really good for you." She says rubbing her hand down his chest.

A laugh escapes Korbyn and he glares at her. She quickly turns trying to escape his wrath.

She's not quite fast enough. He grips her arm before she enters the gym and shoves her against the wall. "Think you're funny, do ya?"

A laugh slips from her mouth and startles them both. "Do not encourage her!"

Korbyn smiles, "Sure thing Boss man."

He smirks, "I'm starting to agree with Roman's assessment of you."

"And what is that?" she says irritated.

"You're one hundred percent devil." He releases his hold on her.

Korbyn full on grins, "You have no fuckin' idea." She shoves past him.

He follows behind her plopping down on a seat close to the ring.

Korbyn stretches before she starts grappling with Max. Ollie is watching entirely too close for her comfort. She freezes when her phone rings loudly giving Max the advantage. Ollie dives for her stuff and grabs the phone. Korbyn shoves Max away and tries to snatch the phone from Ollie. He answers, "Hello."

"Who the fuck is this?" Micah says on the other end of the line.

Ollie smirks, "Wouldn't you like to know."

Micah growls, "I will foehckin' bury you bahy. Put Korbyn on the phahne!"

Ollie laughs, "I don't think I will."

Micah says, "Tell 'er I'll be seein 'er." and hangs up.

Korbyn swings hitting him square in the jaw. He grabs her by the throat slamming her against the wall. There's absolutely no fear in her eyes, just anger. She tries to swing again. He stops her and leans in whispering in her ear, "I told you secrets don't stay secrets for long." He then releases her.

She growls, "You're goin to wesh you dedn't know." Snatching her phone from his hand, she leaves the gym heading straight for the Lords of Exile Club.

She shoves through the doors and stalks down the hall to her brother's office, slamming through the door only to find a big tit blonde bouncing on Connor's dick. She clears her throat and growls, "You foehckin' dahne 'ere?"

Connor freezes peaking around the blonde bimbo and growls, "If I say no will you leave?"

Korbyn grabs a shirt from the floor and tosses it to the blonde, "Not foehckin' likely. Get off my brahther's cahck and make yooehrself scarce."

Tally

The blonde climbs from his dick and walks out stark fuckin' naked rolling her eyes at Korbyn as she passes.

"Nice Cahnnor. Real Foehckin' nice." Korbyn says shaking her head.

Connor actually smiles, "She gets the job done."

Sean walks in laughing, "I would have warned you if I thought it would stop you."

She rolls her eyes at him and growls, "Call ahff your foehckin' dog. I dahn't need a foehckin' babysetter."

Ollie chooses that moment to walk in. He laughs behind her. She turns to see that Ollie wasn't the only one to come in. Roman has entered quietly and was sitting in a chair behind her watching.

Sean laughs, "Ollie my boy, you keep popping up with bruises on that pretty face of yours I'm going to think you're fighting again."

Ollie actually grins at her like he was fixing to let the cat out of the bag, "Nah, I'm not fighting anymore, but someone has been."

Korbyn's eyes widen slightly. She trains her face as Sean says, "Better not fuckin' be."

Connor just watches Korbyn. He knows. The pieces are falling together for him. "Sean, Ollie's been fighting his entire life aside from the past year, he can recognize a fighter from a mile away."

Korbyn refuses to look at him.

Sean is looking at her like she's a stranger. "Korb?"

She swings her head his direction, "What? You dink because you talked to me wance a mahnth, you know me? You dahn't know de first foehckin' ding about me."

She tries to make her escape, but Ollie steps in front of her blocking her escape.

He looks over her to Connor, "She got a call from the guy who was texting her and I answered it. She has him saved as M. He's Irish and he said to tell her he'd be seeing her. He wasn't very happy that I answered." He says smirking.

All eyes in the room turn to Korbyn and she swings at Ollie again, only this time it's Roman who stops her. He maneuvers her around Ollie and towards the door. She glares at him, but bolts for the door. Shooting glares at anyone who looks in her direction.

"What the fuck Roman?" Sean growls after Korbyn's gone.

Roman never lifts his head, "I can get in her phone."

Connor sits straighter, "How?"

"I watched her put the code in the other night." He says. When they were painting, she was relaxed and didn't think he was paying attention to her.

Connor's chin drops because he knows that currently Roman is the only person his sister has any trust in right now and if he does what he's going to do, she won't trust him right along with the rest of them.

Sean steps forward, "Get the phone Roman."

Roman drops his head as he walks out of the room.

Connor looks at Sean, "You know she'll consider this the ultimate betrayal from him."

Sean grins, "If it will keep him out of her pants, so fuckin' be it."

Connor grimaces.

Ollie looks between the two of them and then at Connor, "She already hates me. I'll steal her phone. We can tell her our tech geek broke into it or that I saw her put in the code."

Sean smirks, "What fuckin' tech guy?"

Ollie grins, "The one she doesn't know we don't have."

Connor nods, "Do it. I'd rather her not feel completely alone. Roman is a good kid."

Chapter 7

Korbyn is fuming when she makes it home. She is pacing her living room chewing her fingernails. Every sound is making her more and more irritated. When someone knocks on the door, she stops pacing and walks slowly towards the door. God help her if Micah has made it here already. She peaks through the curtain to find Ollie standing on her porch.

He has a fuckin' death wish!

She swings the door wide and leaps at him. He sidesteps her and walks into the house uninvited.

"What de foehck are you doin 'ere? Get Ooeht!" she growls.

He smirks dropping down on the couch. She reaches behind the door and comes out with a Louisville slugger. He freezes gulping down a deep breath before darting from the couch and away from her. "You crazy?"

She smiles like a crazy person and starts towards him. She swings and he dodges it. Swinging again, she smashes the coffee table between them. The next swing connects with his midsection. He sucks in air as he bends over to catch his breath, "Crazy bitch."

When she swings again, he catches it. He snatches her into his chest using the bat and then tosses it aside still holding her there. When she tilts her head up, he smashes his mouth to hers. She relaxes into his kiss and he deepens it. When he releases her and walks out the door, she is left stunned and silent. Her heart beating out of her chest.

It took twenty minutes for her to realize she hadn't just misplaced her phone and a matter of seconds to realize Ollie had snatched it when she was trying to hit him with the bat. Grabbing her bat, she storms out of her and leaves a path of destruction the entire way to The Lords of Exile Clubhouse.

Storming through the front door wielding her bat, everyone freezes staring at her with their mouths gapping open.

Breathe by SKitz Kraven starts playing on the stereo system and every person in the room turns their attention to the stereo. Roman leans back against the stereo watching the show. When Korbyn swings the bat shattering the glass case holding a remodeled bike and a few trophies everyone

635

jumps from their seats and a few even made a b line for the front door. When she doesn't get the audience she wants, Korbyn climbs on the counter dragging her Louisville slugger behind her along the top of the counter leaving the bartender scurrying away from the bar. She swings again knocking multiple bottles of alcohol to the floor shattering them.

Finally, Connor, Sean and Ollie come rushing down the hall.

"What the fuck Korbyn?" Sean yells.

She whirls their direction spinning the bat in her hands.

Ollie growls, "Fuck!"

Connor keeps his mouth shut assessing the situation and trying to develop a plan that doesn't include putting a bullet in his sisters' ass.

She picks up a full bottle of liquor off the counter and turns it up gulping down at least four ounces of it. She then slings the bottle at the stereo Roman was leaned against. He sidesteps the bottle and it smashes into the front of the stereo instantly cutting the music. She turns her attention back to her brothers, "You really want to know yooehr little sester? Let me enlighten you." She swings the bat again smashing a bottle that was on the counter.

"You've dahne your research and by now I know you're a little froehstrated because you keep combing up empty. Yooehr boys in Ireland can't tell you shet, right?"

Connor tilts his chin up knowing he's not going to like what his sister is about to tell them. Ollie watches curiously and Sean looks confused. He's never seen this side of Korbyn and it worries him. Roman has no emotion on his face, he just watches her closely.

"You'll never comb up wit anythin if you keep lookin under Korbyn O'Clery. Let me 'elp you out!" She lifts the bottom of her shirt exposing a tattoo on her hip bone of six tally marks. They didn't look professional and they could have been done by Korbyn herself.

Sean takes a step forward but stops when she points the bat at him and continues. "Dey call me Tally. De stories you'll 'ear, they're all true. Remember I warned you, you want like what you fend." She drags the bat one last time along the counter before smashing several more liquor bottles and then hope from the counter to a stool and then to the floor. She steps

636

over the carnage and heads for the door, stopping long enough to look back, "I want me phone back by de end o' de day." Slamming the door behind her.

"Tally? What the fuck is that? Why didn't we know what the fuck she's been doing?" Connor growls.

Sean shakes his head looking at his brother, "Let's find out."

He follows Connor and Ollie down the hall with Roman trailing close behind them.

Connor calls his first Ireland contact and puts his phone on speaker. It rings three times before he answers, "'ello."

"Tell me you've got something O'Malley?" Connor growls.

"De girls a ghahst. No one 'as ever 'eard o' 'er." He says nervously.

Connor runs his hands through his hair in frustration. "Tell me about Tally."

The guys on the other end of the line nervously says, "Dahn't say dat name. She's dangerous. I can't tell you anything abooeht 'er and even if I could, I wouldn't. Ploehs she screwed over Micah befahre disappearin. You dahn't want to get ahn Micah's bad side if you know what I mean."

Sean mumbles a few cusses under his breath.

"No, I don't know what you mean O'Malley, enlighten me." Connor growls.

"Well, people tend to fend demselves dead when dey mess wit Micah." He takes a sort breath before saying, "Tally and Micah were dick as dieves. It blew everyone's mend when she screwed 'im over and disappeared."

Connor glances around the room before finally saying, "Thanks O'Malley, we owe you one."

He laughs through the line, "Nah, de Lord's 'ave 'elped me more times dan I can cooehnt. Just keep me name away frahm Tally if you comb acrahss 'er."

Connor smirks, "Done."

Chapter 8

Korbyn walks into her house dragging the bat behind her. She looks around and the realization that what she wanted when she came home was probably never going to happen sends her into a rage. She slams the bat into the sheet rock in the living room send pieces flying around the house. Turning she slams the bat into the kitchen counter and the corner or the wall. A ragged scream leaves her, and she balls her fist up need to feel some kind of pain, she slams her hand into the wall. She winces as she pulls her hand back to her chest. She grabs a bottle of fireball from her refrigerator and opens the bottle turning it up, then slamming the bat through a window. Lost in anger, she doesn't hear anyone come in. Not until she's being slam against the wall and the bottle snatched from her hand tossing it to the floor behind him. Roman grips her face and makes her look up at him. She does and he says, "Feel better?"

He can see every feeling she has in that very moment. Then she crashes her lips to his. His hands slide from her cheeks to the sides of her throat. His thumbs at the base of her neck making small circles causing her body to instantly going lax. She drops the bat from her hand and her hand goes to his hip while the other lies on his chest. Her hand trembles against his chest. He slides one hand down to hold the trembling hand. When he pulls his lips away and leans his forehead against hers, he can see the wheels turning and her fight or flight kicking in. He whispers, "Don't over think it. You're into this as much as I am. Don't deny that."

She wraps her legs around his waist and presses her lips down on his again as he grips her thighs holding her as close as possible. When she pulls back flinging his hat across the room and gripping the hair at the base of his neck, she whispers, "I 'ave no intention o' denyin what I want."

He carries her down the hall kissing her every step of the way. After kicking the door to her room open, he drops her on the bed. Standing at the foot of her bed, he starts slowly stripping his clothes. First his shirt, leaving his magnificent abs and upper body exposed. He kicks his shoes off and sits on the edge of the bed beside her where he rubbed his hands up and down her bare legs. He removes his socks, then grabs her shorts wiggling then down her hips, tossing them across the room. Korbyn watches him as he unsnaps the button of his jeans. "Tell me you want me Korbyn." He says quietly.

She moans, "Like a foehckin' rainstorm in a drought."

He smiles shoving his jeans away from his hips and kicking them to the side with his feet. Korbyn wiggles impatiently, coming to her knees in front of him. He drops his lips to her gripping the back of her hair as they kiss. She pulls away taking his impressive shaft in her hand and runs her tongue along the length of it, looking up to see his reaction. He smirks, but it fades the moment to takes the length of him into her mouth. Her eyes drift closed, and his head softly sits on the back of her neck as she takes him as deep into her mouth as she can. A moan slips from his lips and Korbyn's eyes slip open to watch him as his head rolls back so that he's staring at the ceiling. Honestly, his eyes could be closed, but from her view, who knows. When his head comes forward and he's looking at her he smirks gripping the back of her neck and thrusting into her mouth deeper and deeper. She moans around his dick and her hands grip the outside of his thighs as he thrust one last time emptying himself into her mouth.

When he pulls back, she uses her finger to wipe her lips and then very slowly runs her tongue along the tip of him.

He pushes her back on the bed and crawls up between her legs, spreading them apart. Running his one hand up her torso he runs a finger along her core. She moans and lips her hips up needing more. When his other hand reaches her neck he grips, not enough to cause pain, but enough to heighten what she's feeling right now. When his finger slips between her folds, she nearly comes unglued. Thrusting towards his hand. "Are you wet for me Little Devil?"

Ignoring his comment, she grinds against his hand. He grips he hips and dips his head lightly blowing on her core. Shivering she growls, "Stop foehckin' teasin me."

He begins by kissing the very top and then he very leisurely began his torturous journey of bring her to the best orgasm she's ever had. Gripping his shoulders with her legs, she shivers through it with one hand gripping his hair.

When he finally comes up for air, the cocky asshole smiles as if he knows how good it was. He crawls up her body until he is laying comfortably between her legs and kisses each one of her breasts. Leaning his head to the side, "I can do this all night long and never get enough of you."

Korbyn smirks, "Care to test yooehr deory?"

He smirks, "Your accent is adorable."

She glares at him as if he kicked her dog, "Is naht. I"s... It's... Whatever."

He burst out laughing. When she gets enough, she tries to push him away and get up, but he grips her hips, taking her nipple into his mouth. Her body instantly responds. She moans and pulls his mouth up to hers. He adjusts himself so she can feel how much he still wants her right now. She reaches down taking his dick in her hand and moving her hand up and down it until it is standing at full mass, which didn't take much. He was already pretty much there. When he leans back on his knees and positions himself in front of her, she bites into her bottom lip. As he slides inside of her, she throws her head back grip the sheets on both sides of her. He leans in kissing her as he thrusts into her sending her body over the edge.

CHAPTER 9

R oman had left the room ten minutes before to get a bottle of water and hadn't returned. Korbyn climbs from the bed and puts her shorts back on, then smirks as she grabs his black tee shirt from the floor and pulls it on. When she walks out of the bedroom and down the hall, her feet falter when she sees her brothers sitting on the couch and Ollie standing by the door. He sneers and shakes his head looking back out the window on the door.

When Korbyn's eyes land on Roman and he's got a freshly busted lip and his eyebrow busted, she steps in his direction. Connor steps between them. "Hope you got your fill."

"Roman?" she calls over Connor's shoulder.

He shakes his head and turns towards the door, storming out.

Sean tries to take her hand and she snatches it away as the first tear drops down her cheek. She steps to the door and calls out to him again. He stops just beside his bike running his hand through his hair and staring at the sky. Something Korbyn realizes he does in frustration. He throws his leg across the bike and glances at her one time before pulling away from the curb.

Sean reaches for her again and she reels on him. "Foehck you! Dahn't you foehckin' tooehch me!" She shoves him ready to fight. She pulls her fists up and when he steps towards her again, she swings. He luckily dodges it.

"What you want to hit me now?" Sean growls his own anger growing.

She swings again connecting with his gut. When Ollie steps forward, she spins around kicking him in the jaw. Sean comes at her, trying to grab her again. She jumps up, but arms circle around her midsection holding her tightly, but her feet still connect, knocking Sean back to the floor on his ass.

Through tears she yells, "What? You dahn't lahve me so no one else can either." She cries struggling against Connor. His grip loosens for a second when the words leave her mouth. "You want me gahne?" Connor releases her and she drops to her knees, "Fine! Whatever makes you 'appy. I'll disaapear again. I'm naht goin back to Ireland, but I'll foehckin' leave. I'll be gone by mornin'." Like a broken little girl, she climbs to her feet and uses her arm to wipe the tears running down her face. Ollie uses this as a moment to walk out deciding this was something family needs to handle. Connor steps forward and scoops her up. She struggles, but he asks calmly, "Is that really how you think we feel Kor?"

Korbyn uses the back of her hand to wipe her face again and shrugs giving up the fight to escape.

Connor sits on the couch with her in his lap. "Hell no, Korbyn. None of that is true. Every decision I've made in the past six years has been to protect you because I fuckin' love you."

She sniffles and he continues. "I guess its time we all clear the air."

He sits her on the couch beside him and she snuggles into a pillow, throwing a piece of sheet rock from earlier to the floor. Sean walks over, "If I sit down are you gonna hit me again?"

She smirks and shrugs. He drops to the couch beside her.

Connor leans back and says, "I may as well start at the beginning. When Mom and Dad died, I was terrified. I didn't know how I was going to protect you. Then Aunt Keira offered to take you, it was perfect. You'd be away from all of this. So, I jumped at it." He runs his hands through his hair. "Then come time to say goodbye and I couldn't so I disappeared. Sean told me you cried and fought all the way to the plane, and it broke my heart. I sat on my car and watched the plane take off, but I couldn't bring myself to say goodbye. Not to you."

"Why ded I 'ave to leave?" she whimpers. "Why couldn't I stay?"

Sean takes over when he sees the tears clouding Connor's eyes. "The people who killed mom and dad are out for blood and you, you were the intended victim. Not mom and dad. We had to protect you with any means necessary. I didn't understand to begin with, but then Connor explained, and I understood."

"I dahn't understand, why me?" Korbyn asks.

Connor shrugs, "That we still haven't figured out yet."

"Why dedn't you comb see me? Or even call me Connor? Sean came at least wance and called wance a month, boeht you, you never called nor did you ever comb see me."

Connor drops his head. "I made it to the plane a hundred times and turned around. I knew that if I saw you, I'd have to say goodbye and it'd break your heart all over again. We protected you by sending you to Aunt Keira. I couldn't be selfish and make you go through all that again."

Korbyn's eyes widen slightly as if he was missing something and Connor asks, "What Korbyn?"

She just shakes her head. Sean leans back on the couch, "Now we need to know your secrets Korbyn. We can't protect you if we don't know what we are protecting you from. Or what has followed you from Ireland."

Korbyn takes a deep breath. "Well, you see, de only din I ever wanted was to comb back 'ahme. I ded everythin in me power to make Aunt Keira send me back." She wipes away some remaining tears and looks up at Sean. "I met a boy two weeks after I gaht to Ireland. "He was a little older dan Sean, but younger dan you, Connor. Micah." She takes a breath and stands walking to the door looking out the glass at Ollie, wishing Roman was still here. "I was getting poehshed around because I was small and 'e stood up fahr me. I was alone and I was scared and 'e offered to be me friend and we were de best o' friends." She turns back to them, "Or at least in de begennin. Kater I saw 'im as me way 'ahme and I took advantage when de time was right. At least 'e dinks I ded anyways. 'e taught me to fight, to defend myself. I was good, better dan good, I was de best." She paces the wall behind the couch kicking sheetrock and wood splinters out of her path. "Den I started de deat matches. I gave up 'ope o' ever combing 'ahme, so I dedn't care if I was livin or breathin."

Connor and Sean both sat forward ready to pounce, "Death matches?"

Korbyn shoves her hair from her face, "Yea." She pulls her shirt up exposing her tally's, "One fahr every life I took."

"Jesus." "Fuck!" her brothers say in unison.

"De call me Tally, because I keep track o' de lives I've taken by carvin' tally marks into me sken." Korbyn's broken out into a nervous sweat as she wrings her hands together and continues to pace. "Micah made me stahp. 'e said 'e wouldn't let me kell myself. 'e took me ooeht o'f de deat matches and threatened de lives o' everyone who 'osted dem." She stops pacing and looks out the window again and Ollie is watching her. She rolls her eyes in irritation. "Dat was sex months ago. Den I was approached by an Irishman. 'e wanted me to throw a fight. It wasn't a deat match, boeht 'e 'ad a lath o' money ridin on it. De match was a week before me eighteenth birthday."

"You through a fight to get back home?" Sean asks.

Connor shakes his head knowing what was coming, "No she didn't, but the money was wired anyways and made her look guilty when she lost."

She points at Connor and grimaces, "Micah dinks I screwed 'im and all de proof 'e needed was de million dollars settin in me account and o' course me disappearin'. Now Micah is on 'is way 'ere and dats not a conversation I want to be present for."

Connor runs his hands through his hair again and says, "He'll have to come through the Lords of Exile before anything happens to you."

Sean stands, "Can you at least come back to the clubhouse tonight? We can get your windows fixed and that door you busted up in a temper tantrum."

She cocks her eyebrow, "The only way I'm going back to that clubhouse is if I can sleep in Roman's bed."

Connor drops his head shaking it and laughing.

Sean growls, "Fuck that."

This time Connor looks at Sean laughing, "She's eighteen, we can't stop her. If he is willing to risk what you threatened him with earlier, he's good for her in my book."

Korbyn's eyes round and she spins in Sean's direction, "What? What did you do? What'd you say to him?"

Sean quickly makes his way towards the door. "What? What um, happened to your accent?"

She growls.

Connor puts his arms around her, "Grab some stuff. I'll talk to the both of them when we get to the clubhouse."

Korbyn looks up at him, "It doesn't bother you? I mean Roman and me?"

Connor shrugs, "Not as much as it does Sean. I know Roman's not a bad kid and he's loyal, you could do a lot worse."

Korbyn smirks as she disappears down the hall to grab some of her things.

CHAPTER 10

When I walk in the clubhouse behind Connor and Sean all eyes turn our direction. The older men who were present for my temper tantrum earlier hover close to the door in case they need to leave in a hurry and the bartender grimaces.

Connor smirks, "It's okay Jameson, I made sure she left the bat at home."

Korbyn smiles wickedly at the bartender and winks as she walks by. When they get to the hallway, Korbyn is determined to prove to Sean that he's not going to push her around. She stops outside of Roman's door. Sean drops his head, "Please Kor?

Connor laughs, "Let it go Sean. She's proven she can take care of herself."

Sean drops his head as Korbyn rolls her eyes before walking into Roman's room. She drops her bag in the corner and glances around. Not much has changed since she was in here last. It's mostly clean, besides a couple half empty bottle of water on the bedside table and clothes that got dropped on the floor beside the hamper instead of in it. The bed is partially made but looked mostly clean. Korbyn goes into his bathroom and splashes water on her face to erase the day. It started out as hell and hopefully things can even out from here. She's been on such a high lately she sometimes doesn't know if she's coming or going. She's just in survive mode. That's what she does, she survives. She stares at herself in the mirror for a few minutes noticing the dark circles forming around her eyes and the worry lines creasing her forehead. Smoothing her hand across her forehead, she smirks at herself before shutting the light off and walking back into the bedroom. She's not delusional, she knows that whatever is happening with Roman is probably not something that's going to last, but nobody has the right to have a say in what they do or don't do together.

Korbyn drops her shorts to the floor beside his bed and climbs in with his tee shirt wrapped tightly around her. She switches the nightstand light off and curls into his pillow where she falls hard and fast asleep.

Korbyn has been asleep for hours when Roman stumbles in the door.

She blinks her eyes open at the intrusion of light from the hall. She quietly watches as he stumbles to the bathroom and she smirks as he leaves the door open as he relieves himself. One hand resting on the wall to keep himself on his feet. The other holding his dick. He moans and rolls his head back on his shoulders before shaking and shoving it back in his pants. Without buttoning his pants, he shuts the light off and walks over to the bed. It's dark and she can hear him drop his pants to the floor and then the distinct sound of his shirt being pulled over his head. The bed dips and he falls back on the pillow closest to the outside of the bed. When he turns on his side and adjusts himself. Korbyn eases up behind him and wraps her arms around him.

In a split second he is jumping from the bed and knocking things off the nightstand trying to turn the light on, when he finally flicks it on, Korbyn laughs.

He grabs his chest, "What the fuck Korbyn?"

She bends over in a fit of giggles.

"What the fuck are you doing in here?" he growls finally get his breathing back to a somewhat normal pace.

"Well... See.... What had happened was..." she starts being a complete smart ass.

"Stop bullshitting me, I can't fuck with you no more. Your brother made it perfectly fuckin' clear." He groans.

Humiliation replaces the giggles and anger bubbles in her gut. "So, dis is 'ow it is, huh?"

He drops his head and then rolls it around on his shoulder, tension clear in his shoulders. He rolls his head to the side, "You know there's no right answer for me in this."

Korbyn shifts her feet uncomfortably standing in nothing, but his tee shirt. Hurt clear on her face.

He roles his head back staring at the ceiling, he growls, "I don't want to hurt you, but this club is all I've got. I've got no fuckin' family. The only friends I have are in the Lords of Exile. What do you want me to do here, because either way I'm fucked."

Korbyn quietly grabs her shorts and pull them up her legs as he stares at her quietly. When she turns for the door, he growls frustrated and in three steps he's behind her pushing the door shut and wrapping his hand around her waist. "Wait please?"

Her hand grips the doorknob and she whispers, "Let me go."

He kisses the side of her head behind her ear, "Please understand."

She squeezes her eyes closed as he backs away, turns the knob opening the door, "Lesson Learned." She slips out of the door and he steps to the door and watches her disappear down the hall.

Roman lays in bed for at least two hours unable to fall asleep. He reaches for his phone on the bedside table and checks the time. It's only one am and he knows the bar is still pretty packed right now, so he gets dressed and steps into the hall. He follows the noise coming from the bar and when he walks in his eyes widen, "Fuckin' hell."

Korbyn is barefoot on the bar dancing. She has a bottle of fireball in one hand and the other one is spread wide as she wiggles her little body to the beat of the music. Roman looks around for Connor and Sean, hell even Ollie. Connor and Ollie sit at a table with a bottle between the two. Connor's pretty gone, but Ollie watched Korbyn closely. He finds Sean in the corner with some blonde that's been hanging around the bar the past few weeks. He stalks over to Sean, "You just gonna let her do that shit?"

Sean glances at the bar and laughs, "Who's gonna fuck with her with Zina up there with her?"

Roman glances back at the bar and notices Zina bent over rubbing a feather boa between her legs. Sean turns his attention back to the blonde and Roman glances around the room at all the men with their eyes trained on Korbyn like she's a piece of meat, all praying she's going to lose the shirt. Korbyn was pretty drunk and stumbling around slightly on the bar. The bartender shook his head as he did his job. When Zina stumbles and trips, Jameson makes a disgusted face, but he catches her and eases her to her feet on the floor. Roman glances back at Connor and Ollie. Connor is watching the show amused. When he notices Roman, he cocks his eyebrow at him. *What you gonna do now?* Ollie watches in amusement. Roman turns his attention back to the bar just as another song comes on. When Korbyn grips the bottom of the shirt like she is going to pull it over her head, Roman is at the bar in three steps. He reaches for Korbyn, "That's enough. Come on."

Korbyn snatches her hand away and ignores him. With a guttural growl, Roman grabs her and tosses her over his shoulder. She's kicking and hitting him in the back as he marches across the room. Connor and Ollie are both bent over laughing. Sean just shakes his head as he walks by headed for the hallway.

"Put me de foehck down Roman!" Korbyn growls while wiggling trying to get free from him. He kicks the door open to his bedroom and kicks it shut behind him. He drops her on the bed. She climbs to her feet ready to fuckin' fight, only Roman beats her to it. "What the fuck is wrong with you?"

She stumbles, but catches herself more than a little drunk, "Foehck you deckhead. Lesson learned, remember?"

He starts pacing around the room stuffing his shit in bags, not even looking in her direction anymore.

"What the foehck are you doin?" she asks.

He doesn't look at her nor does she stop what he is doing, "Hope you want a fuckin' roommate?"

She shoves hair away from her face, "What are you talkin abooet?"

He stops and looks at her, hurt eating away at his insides, "I'm out! Done! I fuckin' went against them because of you and I'm fuckin' out. I have nowhere else to go, so yes, I hope you don't mind company for a while."

CHAPTER 11

K orbyn bends at the hip laughing. Roman drops the bag with his stuff in it and growls, "What's so fuckin' funny?"

Korbyn tries to fight the laugh as she walks towards him, "Roman, you're fine. Connor loves you like a little brahther. 'e's not goin to keck you out."

Roman rolls his head to the ceiling, while she puts her hands on his chest, "You don't understand how any of this works, you don't know them like I do."

Korbyn drops her head to his chest, "Don't I? I may 'ave been gone for sex years, but before dat I saw every move dis club made. My Dad trained me just as much as 'e did my brahthers."

Roman looks to the side and Korbyn grabs his chin turning him to face her, "Just anybody doesn't get in. Connor and Sean both saw something in you, dey aren't goin to just keck you out. You should know it's not dat fochckin' casy."

Roman leans his forehead against her.

"Especially, not because o' me. Dey may rag you, dey may even beat de shit out o' you, but dey're too attached to do anything as drastic as keck you out."

Korbyn sways in front of Roman and he smirks down at her, "You're to wasted to be angry with me."

She grins putting her fingers an inch from the other, "Maybe just a lettle."

He picks her up in his arms and drops her to the bed. She leans up on her elbows as he tosses his shit in the corner and turns the lights out one by one. He then sinks to the bed beside her and curls her into his side. Korbyn snuggles her face into the curve of his neck and throws her arm across his hip.

When Roman starts laughing quietly, Korbyn leans back, "What de foehck are you laughing at?"

He smiles to himself, "The look on Jameson's face when Zina fell off the bar."

Korbyn leans her head back into his chest and giggles, "Please tell me you're not one of the regulars she has told me about?"

He leans back in disgust, "Hell no! Do I look like I have to pay to get laid?"

Korbyn smirks, "Maybe, maybe naht, I dunno."

He straddles her taking her hands in his above her head, leaning down he smiles, "I can assure you I do not have to pay to fuck anyone." He leans down kissing her nose, "Goodnight little devil." Then he falls to the side and pulls her back against his side.

Korbyn wiggles deeper into his side with her head on his shoulder. He kisses the back of her head.

The next morning Korbyn wakes up with hers and Roman's legs tangled together. She runs her finger lightly over his chest and then an idea pops into her head. Climbing under the covers, she starts easing his boxers down his legs. She a little distracted so she doesn't notice when he lifts the blanket to look at her under the cover.

"What are you doing?" he asks with a grin on his face.

Korbyn smiles glancing up at him, "Having breakfast." And she takes him in her mouth. She strokes him with her tongue. His head is propped up on the pillow watching her. Korbyn moans deep in her throat as she takes him deeper in her mouth. She can feel him at the back of her throat, but she wants to feel all of him. She begins to stroke him faster and she can feel him tightening up just before he explodes into her mouth with a moan, "Fuck."

Korbyn climbs out from under the blanket just as someone knocks on the door. Roman calls out, "Yeah?"

Sean of all people asks, "You hungry?"

Korbyn giggles and puts her finger over her lips looking at Roman, "Thanks, but I just ate." She calls through the door.

Roman's eyes bug out and Sean yells, "Fuck Korbyn, keep that shit to yourself." Sean shuffles on the other side of the door. "Remind me to black your eye Roman for that image."

Roman's stare flies to the door and he yells, "Fuck, that's all her. I haven't opened my mouth."

More shuffling and Connor says, "You guys get the fuck up, we got shit

Tally

to do today." Then there is the sound of Connor shoving Sean down the hall and then what can be assumed is Ollie following behind them chuckling.

Roman glares at Korbyn who is pulling on a pair of ripped jeans and a tank top, "You're going to get me killed asshole."

She smirks, "Not today! You heard 'im, get the foehck up! We got shet to do today."

Chapter 12

Korbyn steps into the bar with Roman close behind her sending a groan from Sean. She smirks as she takes a seat at the bar with Connor. Roman drops to a stool across from Ollie who grins and then shakes his head at him.

Connor glances around the room and then starts giving orders. Sending several groups in different directions.

Korbyn's phone buzzes loudly drawing the attention of everyone in the room. She quickly sends it to voicemail knowing exactly who it is. Connor cocks an eyebrow at her before returning to passing out orders. Korbyn's phone beats signaling an incoming message. She quickly flips her phone to silent, catching the last of Connor's orders.

"Since my dear sweet sister has destroyed her new home, we now have to make time today to get it back in order for her." He says grinning in Korbyn's direction.

She makes a face at him and sticks her tongue out pulling a laugh from him and Sean. This is the side of her they remember. The side that's not ruined by death, blood, anger, and self-destruction. The side they want to remember.

After he turns his attention away, she glances at the messages that came through on her phone.

M: *You can run, but you'll never be able to hide Sweet Tally.*

Micah never calls her Tally. It just goes to show how angry he is with Korbyn.

M: *I'm coming and you're going to regret everything!*

Korbyn pales even though she knows she'll walk away with her life.

Ollie drops to the stool beside her and whispers, "No secrets."

She glances up at him and cocks her eyebrow.

His face sobers, "I'm not the enemy here Korbyn. I'm really not, but you see those two guys over there." He points in the direction of Connor and Sean and Korbyn turns her attention in their direction. Ollie continues, "They have done everything in the past six years to keep you safe. They aren't your enemy, so if you wanna hate me, go for it. But those two... give them a break."

She glances back at Ollie and then her brothers. Roman drops to her other side but is quiet. He's watching Connor and Sean, but she is sure he was paying close attention to her and Ollie. She looks back down at her phone and then at Ollie and Roman. She's not worried about herself, but she wants to protect her brothers and the rest of these idiots from Micah. He may not have a biker gang behind him, but he is not someone to be messed with, and Korbyn did just that. Or at least he thinks she did. Believes she did. He'll break her and if he has to go through these guys to get to her, he will. That's the thoughts running through her head when she takes a deep breath and finally unlocks her phone and hands it off to Ollie, who quickly looks over the messages, grimaces and then stands carrying the phone to Connor.

Connor looks over the messages, looks up at Korbyn and shows Sean. They both look worried. Connor walks over taking the seat that Ollie vacated slinging his arm around her shoulders, giving her a quick squeeze. "Let him come. We'll leave blood from one end of Stockton to the other."

She smirks up at him,even though her stomach was churning on the inside.

A loud noise sounds down the hall and horrid singing follows behind it. Everyone's head jerks in that direction. Roman even took an inconspicuous step between the hall and Korbyn, until the sound of Zina's heels clunking down the hall draws a groan from everyone. When she steps into the bar, Jameson disappears from behind the bar quietly disappearing into the back. She stops in the doorway and yells, "Ollie, where the hell you at?"

Ollie blanches and I swear if he would fit, he'd climb under the table. Nobody moves. She calls out again, "I need me some Ollie time. Where are you hiding?"

When she see's Korbyn she grins, "Hey girl!" and waves above everyone else. Korbyn grins and waves back. "You seen Ollie? That boy is as fine homemade wine."

Korbyn starts giggling and the other men in the bar laugh. Ollie is slowly making his way towards the door when she catches sight of him. "There he is! Damn baby hate to see you leave, but damn if I don't love to watch you walk away."

The room fills with laughter as Ollie hightails it out of there.

Zina squeezes between Roman and Korbyn. Roman quickly moves away to take a seat at the table with Sean.

Connor smirks over Korbyn's shoulder, "You ever gonna give my boy a break?"

Zina giggles, "O hell no! One day he's going to give in and I'm going to rock his world. Or even better, he's going to rock mine."

Connor snorts as he takes a drink of Bourbon.

Korbyn gives a little laugh and Zina pins her with a cocky grin, "So you and pretty boy, huh?"

Connor quickly stands and says, "That's my que to leave."

Korbyn glances at Roman and then back at Zina, "Dunno, but I'm sure as fuck not gonna miss the chance to find out."

Zina grins from ear to ear, "That's what I'm talkin' about! Well, I got to get to work." She adjusts her boobs and then makes a beeline for the door. "These bad boys didn't pay for themselves." She winks over her shoulder and grins, "Or did they?"

Korbyn laughs as she makes her way out the door. Sean sits on the stool beside her, "We are getting ready to head over to the house and start making a list of everything that needs to be fixed so we can send the prospects to get what we need. You wanna ride with me?"

Korbyn looks between him and Connor and then to Roman who smiles and winks at her as he walks out the door. She grins to herself and then looks over at Sean, "My ride just walked out."

Sean smirks, "You're never going to let me get a moments' peace, are you?"

Shaking her head, "No chance in hell." She says as she walks towards the door Roman just left.

CHAPTER 13

When she walks out the bar and over to Roman, he smirks down at her. "You know you're torturing him, right?"

She smiles brightly, "I've got sex years to make up fahr."

Roman grins and leans down pressing his lips to hers before quickly handing her the helmet he usually wears. As she pulls the helmet on, she notices a black charger sitting across the road. Korbyn's stomach knots as the car pulls away from the curb squealing tires. Roman watches as the car pulls away and then turns back to Korbyn. "Friend of yours?"

Korbyn nods slowly as tears fill her eyes, "Something like that."

He sits on the back and holds her hand as she climbs behind him.

The ride to her house was stressful. Not that the ride was bad, she was with Roman. He'd become the one person that eases her mind, but he also now has a target on his back. Micah had to see them kiss. He'd for sure try to end Roman. She had to talk to Connor and Sean. She had no other choice, but how could she do that with Roman and Ollie always around.

Her phone vibrates in her pocket and she already knew exactly who messaged her. A tear slips from her eye as regret seeps into her heart. Her heart shattered because she knows the monster Micah is becoming because he believes she could betray him. In a sense she did. She didn't tell him that someone had come to her and made an offer like they did. Hell, she betrayed him by even considering the offer to begin with. She was just so desperate to get home. To get to her brothers. To get home.

When they pull up at her house, she's somewhat gotten her emotions under control, but they leave her in a pissy mood. As soon as she climbs from the bike she stalks toward the house, locking herself in the bathroom. She pulls her phone from her back pocket and reads the message.

M: LOL Bullet to the head and he's dead, that what you want Tally? Pretty boys blood will be on your hands.

Korbyn tries desperately to control her raging emotions. After not replying for weeks, she finally messages him.

KL: Please Micah!

It takes him a split second to reply.

M: Begging is beneath you.

Korbyn knows now her only option is to go to Connor and Sean and pray they can protect Roman. When she steps out of the bathroom, all four of them are leaning against the hall, waiting.

She looks up at Roman but speaks to Connor and Sean, "I need to talk to you guys. Just you and Sean." She turns looking at Connor, who drops his head and nods. HE looks to Roman and Ollie, "You guys can go ahead and start tearing out what needs to be torn out."

Ollie turns doing what he was asked and Roman quietly follows behind him.

She starts down the hall to her bedroom and drops to the edge of the bed as Connor and Sean shut the door behind them. She unlocks her phone and she handed it to Sean. After reading the text he growls. "Fuck!" then hands it off to Connor, whose eyebrow shoots up.

He looks at her smirking, "Never gonna fuckin' happen. I need to know what the fuck we're dealing with and who."

Sean says, "We need to know all there is to know about him. His full name, what he's into? Everything."

The corner of Korbyn's mouth lifts in a smile, "It wasn't always like this with Micah and me. When we first met, he was like you guys. Protective." Sadness was crushing her. She was drowning in it. "We were best friends. We were always together. He saved me more times than he probably should have. When I was in the ring, he was always ringside and when the match was over, he was the first one at my side. He was you guys when you guys weren't around."

Korbyn forced down a sick feeling before continuing, "Not just me, but all of Galway." Korbyn lost in thought begins to chew on her fingernails as Connor's eyes round and he asks, "Who? Who is he?"

She drops her hands looking up at him, "Micah Daniels."

Connor and Sean's eyes bug out of their head. "What the fuck Kor?"

"I saw home in him. He reminded me of you guys." She says quietly looking down at her hands that are fidgeting in her lap.

Connor growls, "He's a fuckin mercenary for the Lords Korbyn."

Tally

If possible, her chin drops further, "I know."

Sean grabs her chin making her look at them, "Please fuckin' tell me you were not involved in any of that? Please tell me?"

Korbyn cringes before looking up pointedly, "I can't do dat. I wesh I could tell you dat I'm stell de lettle girl I was when you sent me to Galway, but I'm naht a liar Sean. I ded what I did."

Connor looks down, "Fuck. Roman needs to know so he can be more careful until we get this figured the fuck out."

Korbyn stands, "I'll tell 'im."

They all stand and start down the hall. When they walk in the living room, he's not there.

Turning to Ollie, who is snatching a piece of broken sheet rock from the wall, Connor asks, "Where the fuck is Roman?"

Ollie looks over his shoulder and when he sees the worried looks on their faces, he turns his complete attention to them, "He ran to the store around the corner to grab a few drinks."

Connor races for the door before anyone could say anything. Sean grabs his hair and growls. "Fuck!"

Chapter 14

F ear paralyzed Korbyn making her legs go weak. She sinks to the floor and pulls her legs to her chest, shoving me head down on her knees. Sean squats beside her and whispers, "Shhhh... Connor will get to him. Watch."

Her voice trembles as she says, "His bloods on my hands."

Ollie growls, "What the fuck is going on?"

Sean doesn't take his eyes off of Korbyn, "Micah is Micah Daniels and he's going after Roman."

All the color fades from Ollie's face as he races for the door, shortly after there's the distinct sound of his bike roaring to life.

Korbyn starts scratching at her hands, "No matter 'ow much I scrub dem. Dere's too much blood."

Sean slides to the floor beside her pulling her into his chest trying to give her comfort as she breaks.

It's ten minutes before Connor calls, and Sean answers. Korbyn's too fucked up right now to follow the conversation. When Sean hangs up, he urges Korbyn to get to her feet. Concern is written all over his face. "Come on Kor, we need to go." He leads her out to his bike and very carefully pulls his helmet on her head. He grabs the sides of the helmet making her look up at him, "I need you awake. I need you to hold on to me. Keep yourself up on my bike."

She nods, but she's zoned out, so he shakes her quickly. When he finally gets her on the bike and is sure she is holding onto him. He speeds away from the curb. Korbyn is mid breakdown so she really isn't focusing on the route they are taking, but the minute they pull up to the hospital, she sprints for the double doors of the emergency room. Her blood is boiling under the surface of her skin. She slams into a hard chest and her hand slams into it over and over again. "Calm down Kor." Connor whispers in her ear. Her head flies back looking up at her brother, tears clouding her eyes. "He's alive. He was sitting on the sidewalk when I got there. He was confused and disoriented, but he's going to be fine. Someone rammed his bike, he wasn't going fast so he wasn't hurt too much, but his head hit the pavement and he has some road rash. The only reason he's here at all is because there's a possibility he has a concussion."

He leads her to a chair, and she sinks down into it, pulling her legs up into the chair with her and leaning her head against the window and staring out. Ollie paces the wall closest to the hallway the doctor will come. Every few minutes he sticks his head out checking to see if anyone is coming down the hall.

Connor and Sean sit close to Korbyn without crowding her. Her tears have dried, anger and hurt root deep within her heart.

Ollie peaks into the hall and then rushes down the hall. Sean and Connor rush to the hall just as Ollie comes in helping Roman. Korbyn doesn't move, but she checks him over from head to toe, making note of every single scratch, bruise, or knot on his body.

Roman quickly whispers, "Get me the fuck out of here."

Ollie laughs as Connor and Sean both grin.

Korbyn had turned back to the window. Putting distance between her and Roman. Distance that Roman's not going to put up with. He takes a step towards her and Sean puts a hand on his chest and drops his head as he shakes it.

Roman calls her name, but Connor urges him towards the door and whispers, "We need to talk. We'll talk when we get back to the club I promise."

Roman looks from Korbyn up to Connor. Connor looks sad and just nods his head and Ollie leads Roman to the exit. Connor squats in front of Korbyn and grips her chin, "Look at me little sister."

Korbyn turns her eyes from the window to Connor.

"Climb back out of that head. This isn't your fault."

She pulls her chin back out of Connor's hand standing. "Boeht vengeance'll be mine." She stands and steps away from his hands. When she walks off down the hall, Sean whispers, "We just got her back Connor, I watched her break! I watched her as every ugly thing she's done in the past six years crawled to the surface."

Connor looks to the hall she just walked down and shakes his head walking the same path she just took, when he gets to the front of the hospital Ollie is loading Roman into Jameson's old pickup truck.

"You see where Korbyn went?" he asks when he gets to Ollie. Ollie shakes his head, "Nah I was trying to get Roman to get in the truck. He's being an ass."

Connor turns shaking his head and to himself he says, "They're prefect for each other." Pulling a laugh from Ollie. Sean is sitting on his bike waiting for Connor.

Connor climbs on his bike bringing it to life and then he says, "We need to get Roman back to the club where he can be protected, I'll send the boys out to watch her. We'll find out. Ollie's going to follow Jameson back to the club."

Sean nods and they drive off in different directions.

K orbyn walks in her house in search of her bat. When she finds it she grabs it stuffing it under her arm, a bottle of whiskey and a kitchen chair. She slides it to her front porch and sits in the chair watching and waiting. She twirls the bat in her hand and leans back propping her legs on the porch rails. When the car she's been looking for pulls to a stop out front she stands at the top of her steps with her shoulders firm. When he stands from the car crossing his hands in front of him, anger raging behind his eyes, she shivers.

Anger pulses through her and she yells, "You'll be foehckin' sahrry Micah! You foehcked up. You'll regret every fuckin' ding dat's 'appened since I left Galway."

He laughs bitterly, taking a step in her direction, "I regret nothing. I'm a fuckin' mercenary. I have no fuckin' conscious, but you sweet Tally, you can't control that little heart of yours. Always chasing what never wanted you."

She twirls the bat in her hand again and drags it behind her as she steps to the first step. Rage poisoning her veins.

He stops, but not in fear, more so in amusement. "Your little toy doesn't scare me. Remember I get off on the pain. I taught you to use that, don't forget that."

She takes the next step, "You may 'ave taught me, but remember, I perfected it. Remember de deat fights, because I do." She simmers with anger.

Fear flashes across his face quickly, but he is fast to hide it away. "Things are different now."

She scrunches up her nose nodding, "You're right! Everythin is different." She fights to control the anger bottled up in her.

He shoves his hands in his hoodie and presses his lips in a firm line. He takes a step back nodding his head, "Decisions, decisions. We both know you'll pay for your sins..." he snorts in disgust, "and theirs." He turns climbing back into the car shutting the door behind him. He pulls from the curb.

When he pulls away it's not even two minutes later and a bike pulls to the curb out front. Korbyn drops to the chair propping her legs back up on the railing. Expecting Connor or Sean, she's surprised when Ollie hops up on the railing. He smirks as he pulls the bottle of whiskey from her hand and turning it up.

"Where are dey? You send dat message I know you can't wait to send?" she growls under her breath.

He laughs, "We knew you were here the minute you walked through the front gate. You think it's a coincidence I pulled up when I did?"

She shrugs not caring, "Do I look like I give a foehck?"

Ollie's wide set mahogany eyes blink unaffected by her attitude. "I'm not the one."

She stands swinging the bat in a complete circle, annoyance written deep within her face. "You could very easily be de one."

He shoves the bottle back in her empty hands, "Save it."

She takes the bottle and drinks several more swallows before sitting it on the porch beside her. Ollie stays sitting with her. When her eyes begin to get heavy and she drifts off to sleep in the chair, he lifts her carrying her to her bed. He quickly throws a blanket over her and props her bat in the corner before leaving the room.

The next morning when Korbyn wakes up, she finds a bottle of Tylenol and a bottle of water. She runs her hand through her hair and groans. After taking two Tylenol and chugging half the bottle of water, she climbs in the shower hoping to wash away some of the hopelessness she woke up feeling. When she climbs from the shower, she walks down the hall, hoping the asshole who slept on her couch didn't eat all of her fruity pebbles. When she gets in the living room and there's a whole crew in her living room, she pauses looking from person to person, freezing when her eyes land on Roman, who should in no way be in here working after the day before. Roman glances back at her, disappointment sagged through him. Her own grief drowning her, she tears her eyes away. They freeze on her brothers who are at her kitchen table each with a bowl of cereal in front of them. Korbyn

Tally

marches over snatching Sean's bowl and leaning into Connor's ear whispering, "De last foehckin' place 'e needs to be is workin."

Connor snorts, "You tell him that." She drops in the chair across from Sean and beside Connor. Sean rolls his eyes and climbs to his feet fixing another bowl of cereal.

Sean looks at her from his place at the counter, "So what's your plan? This shit with Daniels won't just go away."

Korbyn swallows a mouth full of cereal and looks up at Sean, "Whatever the foehck it takes!"

Sean stares at her until she looks back down to her bowl. Then his attention turns to Roman, "And what about him?"

She glances at him and he's doing his best to avoid looking at her. She shrugs, "What about 'im?"

As Sean walks by he leans down to her ear, "You didn't pitch that big of a fit, just to walk away. You may not think we know you, but deep down you're the same little girl you've always been. You've never been able to let go of something you fought for."

She rolls her eyes, shoves from the table and walks to her porch dropping down on the steps. She glances at Ollie in the living room. He watches Roman like a hawk. Korbyn wonders what the deal is with Ollie and Roman.

Chapter 16

Tired of sitting around waiting for something to happen, Korbyn makes her way to the gym. Zina is on her normal corner outside of Benny's. When she spots Korbyn approaching the gym she starts waving and quickly walks over to meet Korbyn. Korbyn smiles, "What's good Z?"

Zina glances around and then quickly looks behind Korbyn, "No pretty boys following you today?"

Korbyn grins, "Don't worry dey'll be along wance dey realize I've disappeared."

Zina smiles and leans in close, "Don't worry, there is a newbie and he's not bad to look at either."

Korbyn shrugs, "As lahng as 'e stays out o' my way, I'm good."

A car pulls to the curb and whistles at Zina. She looks back and then a huge smile stretches across her face, "Gotta go girl, Mama gotta go catch this big payday."

Shaking her head Korbyn enters the gym. Benny stops her at the door, desperate, "Korbyn, we got a heavy hitter here today training, we need you."

Korbyn nods to the locker room, "Let me get changed and I'll meet you guys out frahnt."

Benny rushes back to the front and Korbyn disappears in the locker room. After quickly changing into her gym clothes, she does some basic stretches and then makes her way to the front.

She freezes when she hears him talking to Benny and Max. Recognition causing her stomach to knot as anxiety swirls around her. It's quickly followed by anger. Korbyn walks around the outside of people standing close by watching, not making a sound, just watching. After realizing it looks like he's alone, she cuts through the crowd. Her jaw set, her eyes flaming with fury.

His desire for her flickers to life, drawing a grin from him.

Korbyn stops at the side of the ring, "What de foehck you doin 'ere Micah?"

Tally

He leans on the top rope of the rings with his chin on his arms, "Hello my sweet Tally."

"Stop foehkin' callin me dat. I'm naht leavin Stockton, take what you want. Kell me but get it de foehck over wit and leave me family alone." Anger pulsates through her in waves.

His face falls, "I am your fuckin' family, Korbyn. I didn't toss you away. I didn't send you to live with a fuckin' child molester either. You will pay for betraying me, but it won't be with your fuckin' life. Get in the fuckin' ring." He leans on the ropes pulling the middle rope down and pushing the top rope up.

Korbyn climbs through the ropes, Max takes her hand trying to stop her, "We didn't know you knew him. You don't have to do this, Korbyn. Nobody would care."

Korbyn looks up at Micah and then back to Max, "I either do dis, or 'e makes everyone I care about pay." She pulls free from his hand and climbs the rest of the way through the ropes. Once she's inside, she doesn't try to move far away from him, there's no purpose. She throws her shoulders back, "I'll never run, you foehckin' wit de wrong one."

He spins out kicking her legs from under her, knocking her to her ass. He leans down in her face, "The last thing I want is for you to run, *TALLY!*" Backing away, he pulls his long sleeve tee shirt over his head and tossing it to the floor by the ring. She climbs to her feet and with his head held high and shoulders back she stands tall. When he swings out, she sidesteps him and jumps up ramming her knee in his chin. Micah stumbles back, grabbing his chin and rubbing, he grins. Before shaking his head and coming at her again. This time he trips her again and when she lands on her knees, he slams his fist in her jaw. Drawing blood from her nose and splitting her lip. She knows he's punishing her, and she refuses to defend herself. He should have known the truth. Anger flares to life in her again and she goes at him hard. She spins tripping him and spins around kicking him in his jaw. She spins the opposite direction kicking him in his ribs, causing him to hunch over. He laughs holding his stomach, "Is that your price *Tally?* A million dollars? Is that what it costs for you to turn your back on your family?"

Korbyn turns her back prepared to walk away, only he wasn't done. He

665

pulls a gun from his waistband and growls, "Do not walk away from me Korbyn Leigh!" She glances over her shoulder seeing the gun trained on her forehead. She slowly turns with her shoulders back and her chin held high. "Knees, now!" he growls. She drops to her knees, but keeps her mouth sealed in a firm line.

Max and Benny step towards the ring and Korbyn's eyes fly to them, "DON'T!" They stop in their tracks.

She turns her attention back to Micah. He tucks the gun back in his waistband and walks over to her gripping her hair and pulling her head back, looking down at her, "You should have never taken that money, K?" He slams his fist down in her face. She sways and falls catching herself with her hands and letting the blood dribble from her nose before pushing herself back up to her knees and pulling her head back up. Blood runs down both sides of her mouth from her nose. A nasty bruise developing at the corner of her eye. Korbyn forces her mind to stay in the present knowing that it'll end soon. A Fist slams into her chin and she falls forward again and again she pushes herself back up. His foot slams into her left side and she doubles over grabbing her ribs. When she's able to breathe, she pushes herself up again, taking another kick to the ribs on the opposite side. Her body crumples to the side and she curls in fetal position on the floor. He leans down and grips her hair, "You don't have to leave Stockton, K. You'll fight every fuckin' fight I set up and you'll win. You'll earn my trust back or I swear I will make you pay by permanently taking away that pretty boy your so fond of and those brothers you so desperately wanted to get back to."

Before his fist slams into her face one final time, she pleads, "Nooo Micah." She groans fighting consciousness. When his fist slams into her face again, she crumbles to the floor unconscious.

CHAPTER 17

Korbyn groans as arms lift her from the floor. Her eyes flicker open to see Connor's concern, then quickly drift closed again. Connor loads her into Jameson's truck and quickly circles around to the driver's side. The drive back to the clubhouse was a tense one. Connor checks her pulse every few seconds and yells at traffic for being in his way. When he pulls into the parking lot at the clubhouse and lifts her from the truck she groans, "foehck." She grips his shirt tightly, only to pass out again.

When Connor walks into the bar with her in his arms, Ollie and Sean both jump to their feet.

Connor growls, "Keep Roman in his room until I can get her in my room."

"On it." Ollie shoots down the hall and slips into Roman's room quickly shutting the door behind him.

Sean follows behind Connor, "What the fuck happened?"

Connor growls, "Micah Daniels happened!"

Sean grabs Connor's door quickly opening it and Connor slips in laying Korbyn on his bed. He grabs his phone and shoots Ollie a text. Not two minutes later Ollie slips into Connor's room locking the door behind him, getting his first real glance at Korbyn. He sucks in a breath, "Fuck!"

Connor's heart is pounding as his eyes fly to Ollie, "Help her."

Ollie's eyes widen, "I dunno Connor. She needs a hospital."

Sean growls, "Fuck!"

"Do what the fuck you can Ollie." Connor growls.

Ollie gets a washcloth from the bathroom and runs hot water over it. He sits in a chair beside the bed and slowly dabs the blood from her face. Connor sits a bottle of vodka beside him and he soaks the tip of a rag in it cleaning the cuts on her face with it. She moans in pain and Ollie freezes. Connor nudges him, "Just finish it."

Ollie looks up at Connor, "I can clean it up and stitch this one, but I can't help her if she has a concussion."

"Just do what you can, Ollie." Sean grumbles worried about his sister.

Ollie grabs some thread and a needle he burns the tip of the needle and then dips it in the vodka. He then proceeds to stitch the gash on Korbyn's eyebrow. When she wakes in a panic, Connor and Sean hold her down while he finishes stitching her eyebrow. Anger pulsates through them all. The room is thick with rage.

Connor growls, "This shit is over!"

Both Ollie and Sean nod in agreement. Connor lounges back in a chair close to the bedside, "I'll watch her."

Sean drops his head, "Any ideas about keeping this from Roman?"

Ollie turns back from the door, "He'll find out enough when he sees her. No need saying anything."

Connor nods as they walk out the room. Connor turns the lights down low and watches Korbyn's every breath.

At some point Connor dozes off. When Korbyn wakes up she groans fighting the nausea. She pushes up on her hands in pain. She slides one leg off the edge of the bed and whimpers as her ribs scream in agony. When she is completely sitting on the edge of the bed, she nudges the chair Connor is in with her foot. His eyes drift open and she shoots up into a sitting position, "You need to lay down."

Korbyn snorts, "Says foehckin' who? I need to get out o' dis foehckin bed."

Connor raises his eyebrow, "You're a stubborn ass, you know that?"

She tries to grin, but it hurts so she settles for a smart-ass comment, "I learned form the best."

He smirks, helping her climb to her feet.

"I need a hoodie." Korbyn grumbles.

Connor leaves her long enough to go to his closest and grab a black hoodie form his closet. He pulls it over her head, and she pushes her arms up into it humming through the pain in her ribs. When the hoodie rubs across her face, she winces. Her face is riddled with cuts and bruises. When the hoodie is on and the hood pulled over her head to hide away some of the bruises she looks up at Connor, "How do I look?"

Connor grins, "Like you went to hell and back with the devil and came out on top."

She tries to smile again, but it doesn't meet her eyes, "I need alcohol."

He opens the door and she follows him down the hall slowly, when Connor walks into the bar Sean shoots to his feet. Connor holds his hand up and Korbyn slowly walks into the bar holding her right side drawing Roman's attention. Roman stands quickly watching as she walks slowly to the bar. He starts for her and only stops when Connor puts his hand in his chest and slowly shakes his head. "She feels like shit, don't make it any worse."

Roman looks from Connor's hand on his chest to his face, "I've got all the fuckin' respect in the world for you but get your fuckin' hands off me. She looks like she's been run over by a goddamn elephant."

Connor growls, "At least let her get some alcohol in her before you start in on her." Roman watches as Jameson hands her a full bottle of Fireball without looking at her face. He looks up at Connor, "How bad is it?"

When Connor grimaces and presses his lips in a firm line, he turns to Sean, "How fuckin' bad is it?"

Sean lowers his head watching his feet.

He looks to Ollie and he just shakes his head, "It's not fuckin' good."

When she starts to a table and the light hits her face, Roman sucks in a breath. He jerks his head in Connor's direction, anger radiating off of him, "Who the fuck did that to her?"

Sean doesn't lift his head, "A dead mother fucker."

Roman growls hitting the table, "Who?"

Connor looks over at his sister who is huddle in the corner with her bottle of fireball and her head lying on the wall beside her, fidgeting with a coaster, "Micah. Micah Daniels did that to her."

Chapter 18

After an hour of watching her slug fireball and play with the coaster on the table, Roman's had enough. He slams his beer bottle on the table and walks over to her. He stops beside the table and she refuses to look up at him. "Look at me Little Devil."

Korbyn shakes her head and fidgets with the label of her bottle of fireball. He puts his finger under her chin and pushes up. When her eyes want meet his and a tear leaks from the corner, he squats beside her. "Please look at me Korbyn." She has her head propped on her hand and turns to look at him. He grimaces, "Even the most beautiful angels are marred with scars and splattered with blood." Tears begin rushing down her cheeks as she throws her arms around his neck and wrapping her legs around his waist, abandoning the bottle of fireball on the table. He buries his face in her hair and lifts her in his arms. Without another word to anyone he carries her down the hall to his room.

Roman eases her to the bed and climbs in beside her. She turns into his chest wincing as she eases her face into his chest. She crawls as close to him as she can get needing his closeness. He runs his hand across her head trying to give her some form of comfort. When she breaks in his arms, it solidifies to what needs to be done.

"Sshhh... I got you and I'm never letting you go." He runs his hand though her hair. He holds her close and lets her cry until her tears turn to whimpers and her whimpers turn to sniffles. When the sniffles turn to soft breathing, he allows himself to drift off to sleep.

Korbyn is startled awake to the sound of people yelling and then the sound of feet tearing up and down the hall. She winces as she climbs from Roman's bed. A bed he was missing from. She eases Connor's hoodie over her head and pulls on a pair of jean shorts she had in her bag from before. After putting on a pair of worn Vans she makes her way out into the hall, making sure no one accidentally rams into her as they make their way to the front the building. When she makes it to the bar, she follows the men as they make their way out to the front of the building. Korbyn shoves through the crowd stopping a few feet to the left of Connor. Her eyes go from Connor to what had gained his attention.

Micah is leaning back against his car with his legs crossed at the ankles. When he notices her, a grin spread across his face.

Connor growls, "You have a fuckin' death wish."

Micah looks back to Connor, "Nah, there's no threat here. She'll never let you kill me."

Korbyn speaks up, "What makes you so sure?"

Micah laughs, "Because family remember."

Korbyn glances around her and her eyes land on Connor and Sean. She looks around the crowd, realizing Roman is missing. "Family?"

He looks directly at her, "Yeah fuckin' family, K."

Korbyn's hand goes to her right side, "*Family,*" she says the word like it's diseased. "Doesn't take de word o' an enemy. Dey chase the foehckin' facts. I shouldn't 'ave to defend myself to you."

His face drops, "Family doesn't just disappear leaving family no other choice, but to find answers through the enemy. I spread their blood from one end of Galway to the other."

Korbyn shakes her head, "You were always quick to expect de worst o' me."

"Tell me different." He growls.

"NO!" Korbyn growls. "I don't 'ave to defend myself to anyone. Especially not you." She takes a few steps in his direction. "So, if you wanna comb beat it out o' me, 'ave at it. If you wanna aim dat shiny lettle pistol at my head again, 'ave at it." She takes another step towards him, "But, I prahmise you, if you don't pull de tregger, you'll be lookin over your shoulder for de rest o' your life. I'll foehckin' end you."

Micah takes two steps in her direction and stops, "Who the fuck is going to make me pay, *Tally?*"

Connor smirks, but doesn't say anything.

Korbyn glances around the crowd again. She tilts her head to the side, "I can think o' a few, but you don't 'ave to wahrry about dem. You know me Micah. I always 'it my target."

Micah steps forward, "You may always hit your target, but it's never been me Korbyn."

Korbyn notices Roman behind Micah's car and her eyes widen. His green eyes are shadowed as he steps around the car soundlessly and sticks the barrel of a nine-millimeter to the back of Micah's head, "Hey motherfucker!"

The end!

* * *

THIS IS the end of part one of, **Tally**, the rest of the story will be available after ***Crimes of the Wicked*** is unpublished.

About J.N. Pack

J. N. Pack is an author of New Adult romance books. She is a junk food and red wine junkie. Born and raised in South Carolina, she enjoys the simplicities of life. She is a married mother of three crazy kids who keep her on her toes, and she wouldn't have it any other way.

Read more from J.N. Pack
https://www.facebook.com/groups/1228119297520248

BLOODY UNION

Made Seies
Part 1 of Book 1

Brooke Summers

Bloody Union

Marriages are meant to be sacred but when an arranged marriage turns bloody a war is started.

Mackenna Gallagher's life is anything but ordinary. After experiencing something traumatic her life changes and not for the better. When she meets the man that she is expected to marry she knows that keeping her secrets is only going to get harder.

When Dante Bianchi sees his wife-to-be, he's surprised. She doesn't look anything like the sweet and innocent fourteen year old who he had agreed to marry five years ago. He looks forward to making her his.

When their wedding ends in a gunfight, he's surprised to see his wife handling a gun with ease and when he watches her kill a man he doesn't know whether to be angry or turned on.

Every family has secrets, but Mackenna is drowning in hers. Will she sink or swim when hers turn deadly?

Author Note

Please note the following story is only the first part of book 1 of my new Mafia series, **Made***. Each story will have a HEA but as this is only part 1 of* **Bloody Union** *please be prepared for a cliffhanger. The rest of the story will be released once this boxset is unpublished.*

* **Bloody Union** *is an M/F (one male, one female) darkish contemporary Mafia romance that deals with intense violence and illicit themes. I would advise skipping this story if you don't like curse words; guys that use ANY means to get what they want; or have a problem with badass chicks that don't bow down to anyone and who have no problems in taking people out.*

PROLOGUE

Makenna

There's a slight tremble to my hands but I try to hide it. The Famiglia are in my father's office. Matteo, is the Capo sits in front of my father, Matteo's son Dante – the underboss sits beside him, while his brothers stand behind them, all of them tense and ready to start killing if need be.

The darkening of Dante's eyes tells me that he's seen my hands tremble. My breath hitches as I take in his gorgeous green eyes, to the sadistic grin and the dark stubble that surrounds it. "Makenna." My name slides off his tongue like silk, making my body break out in goose bumps. I swallow harshly and raise my eyes to his.

"Makenna..." my father growls and I turn my gaze to him. His tone is harsher than it usually is with me and I know that it's because of the men that are sitting in his office. My father is head of the Ceannaire ar chách. The Irish mafia, he has been since my grandfather had taken a bullet to the heart by the Bratva. "Matteo Bianchi..."

My body tenses, I hate the Capo. Have since I was twelve years old.

Nobody knows about my hatred of Matteo and no one ever will. I know the consequences of what will happen if anyone finds out the truth about that night.

My father carries on talking, "And I have agreed that our families being bonded is the only way to guarantee peace." I hide my scoff. This is absolute bullshit, there's no way that anything can be guaranteed; it'll be put on hold for a while, but something is bound to piss one of them off at some stage. And then all hell will break loose. "You and Dante will marry."

I grit my teeth, I knew one day I'd have an arranged marriage; it's the way our world works. A woman in the mafia doesn't have the life like a normal woman. We're to be seen and not heard; we're to be at the beck and call of our father and then our husband. I've been lucky, my father isn't a monster to his family, unlike some of his men and from what I've heard most of the made men. They beat their women and children to submit to their wishes. Break the woman so they won't disobey them.

I take a deep breath. "Yes, father." My gaze moves to my brothers who are standing in the corner of the office; they are looking at me with a weird expression. Did they think I'd object? I've not got a death wish. I'm not stupid, and I'd never disrespect my father; not in front of his men and definitely not in front of men that are our enemies.

My father nods his head. "You are fourteen, Makenna, and the wedding will take place when you are of age." His tone is darker once again, this isn't for my benefit, this is for the Famiglia.

"Of course," Dante says harshly.

Matteo shakes his head, "As soon as you're of age, we'll have the wedding." He turns his gaze to me. "You can go."

My brothers tense, their hands on their guns, all of them eager to be the one to shoot him.

"Makenna, go to your mother," my father demands and I hold back the protest. I give my brothers a smile as I leave the office.

My mother is waiting for me in the living room. Her hands by her side and a smile on her face. She rushes over to me. "You're finally getting married," she says and to anyone else it would be as though she's congratulating me. To me, I know better, she's been waiting for this day for a long time. Waiting for me to leave the house where she knows that the secret I carry will no longer have the possibility of being spilled.

CHAPTER 1

Dante

Five years later

The looks I get as I walk into the bar are nothing unusual. The women's eyes are full of arousal, want, and fear; the men's are either full of fear and respect, or fear and hatred. It's always been like this, since I was twelve when I had my first kill. The fucker had it coming, he had his knife to my mother's neck, by the time my bullet had entered the asshole's head he'd slit my mother's throat. The next day, I became a made man.

"Dante," Alessio, my youngest brother, growls, and I smirk when I see three of the Irish mafia men sitting at the bar. "Fucking hate those Irish bastards."

"We're at peace now," I tell him, even though I'd love nothing more than to put a fucking bullet in their brains.

He scoffs. "Please don't tell me you believe that shit."

Of course I fucking don't. "Do I look like I'm stupid?"

He laughs. "No, but then again, you're marrying the Gallagher girl."

The mention of her name has my gut tightening. I've not seen her in the past five years. Seamus Gallagher, is the Ceannaire ar chách, the head of the Irish mafia here in New York. Fucker thinks he's leader of all; hell he's not even the leader of New York. That would be us. He's managed to keep his daughter out of all rags and newspapers. Not a fucking picture of her online at all.

"I am."

In a few I'll see her again, and in a week, we'll be married. Fuck.

One of the Irish men lifts their cell to their ear, not once have they taken their eyes off of me. I smirk, I don't give a fuck if they're on edge that we're here. When he puts his cell in his pocket I raise my brow, "What's the matter boys?" I grin as their bodies tense. "We're going to be family soon." I'm taunting them and they fall into the trap, their fingers edging closer to their guns. "Reach for them and I'll rip your fucking heads off," I grit out as I walk toward them. Their eyes narrowing but they're not quick enough to hide the fear that seeps into them. "We're here for a drink, not to kill you." The threat of it hangs in the air and Seamus walks up behind me.

"You'll not be harmed while you're in my establishment." His Irish brogue thick as he walks over to his three men. "Why aren't you at the airport?"

They straighten their backs, the respect shining in their eyes. "Boss, she told us that she wasn't arriving until morning."

Seamus narrows his eyes. "Finish your drinks, we're leaving."

They're instantly on edge, something is going down.

"Need any help?" I ask quietly and Seamus grins. "I take that as a no. But if you change your mind, you've got my number."

He nods. "I'll see you in a few days, Dante." Just as I thought, he wouldn't ever accept my help. It would be seen as weak. "Enjoy your evening." There's a reproach in his voice, is he warning me to behave. I grin darkly at him, I'll do whatever the fuck I want, *whenever* the fuck I want.

Romero slides over beside me. His face deadpan but I know him, he's boiling with rage as we watch the Irish leave.

"Not now," I warn him.

"It'll be a bloody wedding yet." He grins.

There's not been a bloody wedding in the Famiglia for over a decade. "They won't start a war, not at a wedding."

He raises a brow. "You sure about that?"

I glare at him, of course I'm not fucking sure. But they'd be dead by the end of it. "Fuck, I need a drink."

"You need to get your dick wet."

I grit my teeth, trying not to kill my brother.

"You never know when to shut the fuck up do you, Romero?" Alessio grins.

Romero shrugs. "I'm going to die somehow."

I ignore their stupidity and turn my eyes to the women that are around the bar, some have their heads down, others giving me the *'fuck me'* eyes. None of them hold my attention for very long.

Romero lets out a low whistle. "Fucking finally," he mutters and my gaze follows his where two women have just walked into the bar. There's a busty brunette who's wearing a tight pink dress and matching heels, but it's her friend that I'll be fucking by the end of the night. Black leather pants that look as though they've been painted onto her, black boots that reach her knees, and a red fucking top that clings to every curve of her body. Her blonde hair curls down her back. Both walk in as though they own the place, heads held high as they saunter toward the bar. The Barman's eyes widen but he serves them.

They find a corner in the bar and stay there, not caring about the appreciative looks that they're getting. Not once have they glanced around the bar to see who's here. Fucking stupid.

"How the hell are they not surrounded by now?" Alessio muses and I agree. Not that I'd admit it. They've been left alone even though their beauty by far outshines any other women.

The night wares on and the women haven't so much as looked at anyone in the bar. It's pissing Romero off that they haven't glanced at him, he wants the brunette.

My hand reaches for my gun when I hear a man growl, "Bitch!" Three fucking Russians stalk toward the women. I'm slightly impressed that both women stand and glare at the Bratva bastards. Fucking hell, they have a death wish.

One of the Russians backhand the brunette viciously making her fall backward to the floor. The blonde woman steps forward and raises her brow. Jesus Christ. The hum of bikes is in the far distance. I watch as she tells the Russian that he's a dead man. Right before one of the other Russians punches her in the ribs, knocking the breath from her lungs, she doesn't back down, she stands tall and glares at the Russians.

Alessio, Romero, and I get to our feet. I notice the barman is tense, his eyes on the girls. The rumble of bikes grow closer; they're outside. Within seconds, eight fucking bikers walk in. The women sigh and turn to the door where the bikers have their eyes on them, the blonde steps back, whereas the brunette takes a step toward them.

"Which one?" the biker asks and the brunette smirks as she slides her eyes to the guy that backhanded her. "Time for you to go home," he tells her and she nods. The blonde steps toward her and they walk past us. One of the bikers grabs a hold of the blonde's arm and pulls her toward him. "You good?" he asks, his eyes taking her in and for some reason I want to rip his fucking hand off her.

She steps out of his hold. "No worries, Ace, I'm grand." Her Irish accent thick and velvety.

"You sure?"

She nods. "Positive."

The biker regards her closely. "Time for you to go on home." I can't make out the blonde's reaction to his demand but I see the smirk on his face. "Before your brothers catch you here."

Her bell like laughter rings out and I feel it in my gut. What the fuck is going on? "Come on, Kinsley," the blonde laughs, "before your brother starts to lecture us."

The biker grins as the girls leave the bar. His eyes narrow in on me, a warning in his eyes. He nods to his brothers and they pick up the asshole that backhanded his sister and the other two fuckers that are with him.

"What the fuck was that about?" Romero asks as he makes his way out of the bar behind the bikers.

I have no fucking idea.

* * *

"Are you ready for this?" Romeo asks causing me to glare at him.

"Of course he's ready," my father says. I shift my glare to him, unlike my brother he doesn't back down. "War between the families has been going on for decades, this wedding is finally a way to bring peace." It's a warning. He's telling me not to fuck up.

"I know my duty, Father," I say through clenched teeth.

"The wedding is in three days, Dante. One mistake and we'll pay dearly."

I don't answer him, instead I keep my gaze firmly in front of me. Seamus, Finn, Patrick, and Cian Gallagher stand at their door, all of their eyes on us. Seamus glares at my father, whereas the Gallagher brother's death glares are aimed at me.

"Do they really think they can out shoot us?" Alessio comments as he takes in the guards that surround the monstrosity that is the Gallagher mansion. The fucking Irish don't do things small by any means. They're flashy assholes.

Our father gives Alessio a harsh look, we've seen that look a thousand times. It doesn't work on any of us. Not anymore. "Enough of your shit," he demands.

We walk toward the Gallagher's, none of us are happy about this but right now, we've got to deal with it. "Gentleman," Seamus calls out, just the way he says it grates on my nerves. I'm going to get a headache from gritting my teeth.

"Where is she?" my father asks and there's a bite to his tone.

Christ.

"She'll be here soon. Right now, we've some things to iron out." Seamus' eyes are hard as he glares at my father.

As Capo my father leads. I, as his underboss, follow. Although, if I have anything to say about it, Romeo will be my underboss when I become the Capo. My father's time as capo has come to an end and it's only a matter of time before he meets his death. My father is a monster; we all are, it's who we are. But unlike my father, I'm not a fucking monster to those closest to me. I protect those that are and retaliate against those that hurt them.

My father nods; that's his signal that we're to follow the Gallagher's into the lion's den. My father first, followed closely behind me and then my brother's, our men hidden around the perimeter of the Gallagher mansion. Seamus and his sons lead us toward his office. I haven't been here since we agreed that I'd marry his only daughter, Makenna. She was fourteen when I last saw her over five years ago, she was small and scrawny, pretty in an inno- cent way but I didn't pay too much attention. I'm not into kids and Makenna certainly was a child. I'm curious to see how she's changed.

Seamus opens the door to his office and I notice that he hasn't redecorated since I'd been here last. The huge mahogany desk takes up half the fucking office. Yet again, it makes me wonder why they have to try and be so flashy, are they trying to make up for something?

My father takes a seat and I sit in the one beside him, both my brothers and the Gallagher brothers stand.

"This is a waste of our time," my father grits out. We had come under the impression that we'd be seeing Makenna today, instead, we're sitting in this fucking office doing stupid chitchat.

"My daughter's well-being—" Seamus begins. "Is not a waste of time," he growls and this is the first time that I've seen this side to him. Usually he's calm and composed. Sitting across from me now isn't the Ceannaire ar chách, instead he's a dangerous man who's determined to make sure that I look after his daughter.

This should be fun.

"Are you trying to insinuate that my son won't be a gentleman?"

I glance to my side where Romeo is standing, a smile tugging on his lips. My name and the word gentleman don't belong in the same sentence. I'm anything but, and if Seamus thinks telling his daughter that will help, he's sorely fucking mistaken.

"Like Dante knows what being a gentleman consists of," Finn growls.

These men are playing a dangerous game, they've shown us their ultimate weakness and by doing so, they've shown us where to target them if need be.

"You have something to say?" I ask with a raised brow.

Seamus regards my father first and that pisses me the fuck off. I'm a grown ass man, one that has killed hundreds of men. My name is feared by everyone and yet I'm ignored because my father's the capo. My father nods, and Seamus turns his gaze to me.

"My daughter is..." He pauses if to find the right word. "Unique," he says with a glare at me.

"Difficult," Cian says and I see the loving smile on his face.

"A pain in the ass." Patrick grins.

"A fucking princess," Finn replies darkly and that right there is a threat.

"I can handle a woman."

The look the Gallaghers give me would make a grown man quiver, but not me, I stare them down.

"Fuck, you're as stubborn as she is," Seamus says, and the grin on his face makes me brace for what he's about to say next. "You two are going to be a match made in fucking hell."

"Is that all?" my father asks. "I'd like to see the girl now."

I grit my teeth, that fucking look in his eye is enough to tell me why he wants to see Makenna. Asshole.

Seamus narrows his eyes at my father, but stands. I hear a door opening and Seamus grins. "She's here." He walks out of his office and we all follow. "Makenna," he calls out just as I hear the sound of heels clicking against the floor.

As we enter the sitting room, my gaze follows the Gallaghers'.

"Shit," Romero curses.

"Holy shit," Alessio mutters.

Standing in front of us is, Makenna, the blonde from the bar. She's wearing a tight tank top and even tighter fucking jeans. She's fucking gorgeous, but if the narrowing of her eyes is anything to go by, she's going to be defiant.

My anger begins to rise as I remember the punch she took a few nights ago. She has her arms crossed over her chest and stares at her father. Yet again she's not looking at me or my family, just as she did in the bar.

"I'd like to have a talk with my *Fiancée*, alone." I growl, just barely able to contain my bubbling anger from the glares of her family but I just stare them down.

Seamus glares at me but nods, indicating to his son's to leave. My father and brothers following behind. I turn my attention to Makenna once the door is closed behind them. "Show me," I growl, needing to see the damage. She raises her brow at me, the defiance clear in her eyes. I take a step closer to her, she holds her head high. She's changed a lot from the fourteen year old who trembled when she was in a room full of made men. Now, she stares me in the eye. She's good, she doesn't show any fear. "Lift your top and let me see," I growl.

"And why should I do that?"

My mouth goes to her ear. "I watched you take a punch, Makenna. I want to see the damage."

She steps back and lifts her shirt, a black bruise marks her creamy skin. "Happy now?"

I grit my teeth. "Ecstatic."

"It's nice to know that my husband-to-be watches as a man hits me." She takes another step backward. "Guess what they say is true, hmm? The Famiglia really know how to treat a woman."

I reach for her and pull her toward me. "I will not raise a hand to you. Ever."

She looks at me in disbelief, but doesn't answer. My fingers caress her bruise and she winces before closing her eyes. When she opens them again, they're clear, unreadable. Damn, the Gallagher's have taught her well. I'm going to find the man that hit her and gut him like the fucking animal he is. She pulls down her top and looks at me, curiosity in her eyes.

I take a step closer to her and watch as she gulps, fear creeping into her eyes. "Make no mistake, Makenna, I am underboss of the Famiglia and you'll give me the respect that I have earned," I spit out through clenched teeth. That fucking fear has no place between us, but at the same time, she needs to realize who I am.

I reach into my pocket, and pull out the ring that has been in there since yesterday. I place it on her finger, loving the way her eyes widen as I touch her hand. "A week and then your mine." I step back before I do something stupid like fucking kiss her. Once I do that, I'm going to fuck her until she passes out.

Makenna's eyes flash with heat and indignation. Before she's able to say anything the door opens, she turns to see who's there and that's when I spot the white raised scar at the base of her throat.

I know what that scar means. What the fuck happened to her and who the fuck did it to her?

Chapter 2

Dante

S eamus walks in and glances between me and his daughter, his eyes like a fucking hawk as he spots the diamond ring on her finger. He gives me a nod and I understand. I give Makenna one more glance before I leave and pull the door behind me. I don't close it fully as he intended, instead, I leave it open slightly so that I can hear what's being said. "Makenna?" His voice is fucking soft. This is why he didn't want me in the room with them

She gives him a smile and that fucking smile hits me in the gut. What the hell is wrong with me? She's a woman, I've had countless over the years and yet this one makes me fucking lose my head. "Yeah, Da?" Just as her father's was, her voice is soft and gentle. It's clear to see that they have a lot of love for each other.

"Behave tonight." He warns her as he takes a seat in the chair, and I watch as she bites her lip trying to stifle her laughter. "Makenna..." he glances at the door but I stay hidden. "Matteo is..."

Her eyes flash with pure hatred for my father, something I hadn't thought I'd see from anyone but me and my brothers. "I know, Da, don't worry."

Seamus shakes his head. "You'll be the death of me, Kenna. I swear to God, you'll put me in an early grave."

She cocks her brow. "Early would have been twenty years ago, Da."

I tamper down the smile. Fuck, she's a smartass.

"Thank fuck you're out of my hair soon." There's no heat in his words but I see the hurt flash through Makenna's eyes. "Does your mom know you're here?"

The pure hatred that flashed through her features at the mention of my father's name is nothing in comparison to what she has at the mention of her mom, she looks as though she wants to kill her. "Nope, but I guess you'll tell her."

Seamus sighs, as he gets to his feet then pulls her into his arms. The softness he has for her is definitely his weakness, if he shows this to anyone they'd use it against him; they'd hurt Makenna just to hurt him.

She pulls out of her father's arms. "I'll go find *mother*." The way she spits out the word makes me wonder what the hell happened between her and her mom, she walks toward a different door and leaves, slamming it shut behind her.

"I should kill you for listening in on the conversation," Seamus says to me even though he can't see me yet. I walk into the room again, where he's glaring at me. "Did you get what you wanted?"

I glare at him. "Seamus—" I say, my tone serious. "What happened to her?"

He sighs. "Fuck knows." He mutters, "Was attending to some fucking animal, and got a call from Finn. He'd just returned home to find Kenna on the floor beaten and bleeding out." His voice breaks, he's unable to talk. I leave him be for a moment, let him get his composure. My blood is boiling, my hands balled into fists. "Someone slit her throat, luckily we found her in time. Haven't found out who did it yet, but when I do, I'm going to carve them like a fucking pumpkin."

I nod. "I'll be there when you do it." Seamus looks at me in shock. Fuck, this woman is getting to me and I have no idea why. "She's going to be my wife."

He looks at me with respect. "Okay."

"How old was she?"

He shakes his head again, his eyes dark and I can see the storm raging in them. "She was twelve."

Fucking hell.

"When she was released from hospital, I sent her to stay with my brother," he informs me. He wanted her safe, so he sent her away. I'd have done the same thing. It also explains why her accent is thicker than her brother's; she sounds like her father. "She came home every Christmas and some weekends."

He's silent for a moment and when he talks his tone full of barely concealed rage. "Your father is an asshole, Dante." I glare at him, he's treading a fucking thin line right now. "It's true, we both know it. The only reason I agreed to this fucking shit was because of you."

I raise my brow in confusion.

"You think I haven't looked into you, into your family?" He snarls at me, "I have, I know exactly who your father is. I know what he does to girls like my daughter. Do you honestly think I'd have let her marry you if you were just like him?"

I laugh, it's bitter and cold. "You have no idea what I'm like. I'm worse than my father."

He nods. "That maybe so, boyo, but you're not a fucking asshole to women like your father is."

I tense at him calling me boyo. What the fuck am I, five?

"She's my daughter, Dante. I want peace between us. But I will go to war with you if my daughter gets hurt."

"She's going to be my wife."

He stares at me in disgust. "You're forgetting something, Dante," he snaps taking a step toward me, his voice low and bristling with anger. "I watched your mother wither away under the beatings she took from your father. I won't sit back and let that happen to my daughter."

I step up to him so we're face to face. My body tight with my unleashed anger. He's lucky, I haven't broken his jaw. No one speaks to me like Seamus has and gets away with it. "I am not my father. I will not lay a hand on my wife in anger," I say through gritted teeth. "Let me make myself extremely clear, Makenna is going to be my wife, she's mine."

He takes a step back, a slow smile sneaking across his lips. "Okay then." He turns and walks out of the room, leaving me wondering what the fuck is wrong with the man?

It doesn't take me long to catch up to him and we walk into the dining room where everyone is already sitting, waiting for us. Makenna's sitting beside Finn, an empty seat beside her and another empty seat at the top of the table. I walk over and sit beside Makenna, she's glaring at her mom who's looking down at her hands. My father has his sadistic grin on his face, loving the way things are tense.

Mrs Gallagher clicks her fingers and the maids come in carrying the food.

"That's a nasty scar you have." My father grins as he leers at Makenna.

I watch as she grips her knife, her eyes full of hate. She looks as though she's dying to kill the bastard. Her mother gasps and covers her mouth with a shaky hand. I turn my gaze to my brothers, they both have no expression on their faces, almost as if they haven't noticed but I know they have. There will be questions later and I'll get my fucking answers.

"Is Killian coming to the wedding?" Finn asks and I notice that Makenna sits up taller. The hand that was gripped around the knife loosens; she's relaxed. Her mother on the other hand looks as though she's about to faint.

Seamus grins. "He should be arriving in the next couple of days."

"Killian?" I ask. Knowing damn well who they're talking about, I turn to Makenna in time to see that she's giving me a warm smile.

"He's my brother," Seamus says, but the way the Gallagher brothers are glancing at one another, there's a hell of a lot more than him being Seamus' brother. I need Orion to look into this shit; one fucking thing I hate is being in a situation where I'm going in blind.

Makenna's attention is on her cell phone, I glance down and see the message from Kinsley. From the intel I gathered, Kinsley is her best friend and has been since she was a child.

Party tonight?

I grit my teeth remembering what happened the last time she went out. I see her reply saying that she can't, but will ring her later. Kinsley Anderson is the only daughter of Julian 'Jaws' Montry, the president of the Fury Vipers motorcycle club. They're fucking animals who party hard and kill harder. They're ruthless, and have no loyalty to anyone but the Fury Vipers brothers. They'll do whatever the hell they want and don't care about the consequences. Much like la Famiglia, they're feared by most. Whereas we keep a low profile and have businesses as fronts and are fucking gentleman in the presence of the public, those animals couldn't give a fuck. I know that when Makenna and I are married, I'll be putting a stop to her going to that damn club house.

The dinner is quiet, Mrs Gallagher keeps glancing at Makenna as though she's waiting for her to lose her damn mind. Something about this family doesn't sit right. The hatred that my brothers and I have for my father isn't publicized. We don't want the fucking world knowing that when my father goes down, it could be, and probably will be at our hands. The Famiglia won't allow me to become Capo if I've killed the previous Capo. Hell, it's against our oath to kill another made man. But fuck, I've broken that oath before and I'd happily do it again if the fucker needs to be put down. Traitors are different, as soon as they become rats, their made man status dies and they'll soon follow after we torture the fuck out of them. But we extract as much information as we can before their death. Whereas Makenna's open hatred for her mom is something I can't understand. I've witnessed the way she is with her father, they have a great relationship. It's obvious she has a lot of love for him along with her brothers, her eyes soften whenever they talk to her. Whenever her mom speaks to her, her features harden and she glares at her.

"Mrs Gallagher," my father says once the dinner is finished, and I watch as she bows her head, "thank you for a wonderful dinner."

The woman gets to her feet, "It was a pleasure to have you." She practically curtsies as she walks backward to exit the room.

"Seamus, I ensure that everything will be ready for the wedding in three days." The harshness to my father's tone has the Gallagher men's hands twitching for their guns.

"Matteo—" Seamus glares at him, "what do you take me for?"

"And her..." my father continues, not knowing when to shut his fucking mouth. "She's pure?"

Makenna smirks, not what I'd expect from her. Most woman in our life are untouched. Therefore when men talk about sex, they blush and bow their heads with embarrassment. Not Makenna, she smirks and her eyes twinkle. "I'm catholic," is her response, her accent is thick and full of sarcasm.

"That means nothing," my father says in outrage.

Makenna shrugs, the hatred she has for him is making her disrespectful. She needs to be careful. I reach over and grip her arm. Her gaze snaps to me, eyes narrowed, but she raises a perfectly sculpted eyebrow.

"Watch your mouth," I say through clenched teeth. "Respect."

She glares at me for a moment before smiling and I know that whatever is going to come out of her mouth isn't going to be good. "I'm sorry," she snarls. "Don't worry, Dante here will be the only one to defile me." My grip on her arm tightens. Does she really believe that I'd defile her?

My father nods, pleased with her answer. "And I see that she's drinking." His tone reproachful.

Makenna reaches for the glass of wine that's in front of her and downs it in one swallow. Romero's eyes flash with humor, but his face is void of emotion. Alessio on the other hand, is unable to stop his lips twitching with amusement.

"I'm Irish," Makenna drawls with a smile and her brothers laugh.

"We can handle our drink, Matteo." Seamus grins. "Have no fear, Makenna can and will drink you and your Italian boys under the table anytime she likes."

Why do I think there's a double meaning to this?

Father gets to his feet and my brothers and I do the same. "Seamus," he says as a way of saying goodbye.

I lean down so that my mouth is level with Makenna's ear. "Soon, Makenna," I whisper and enjoy the tiny shudder she has. "Three days and then you're mine."

She gets to her feet, her expression blank. "Oh, Dante," she whispers, "You're in for a surprise."

"No, darling," I return. "You are. You've lived sheltered for so long. When we go home, you're going to find out what it's like to be in our world. Not to mention what it's like to have my cock inside of you."

The sharp intake of breath is all I needed. I walk away from her, I'm tempted to push her against the wall and kiss her, but knowing that the first time we kiss will be when she's mine. Right after we say 'I do.'

Once we're outside, my father turns to me. "When you wed her, make sure you teach her manners." He sneers and I glare at the fucking bastard. "Damn bitch," he mutters. "I've got a meeting. Pietro is with me," he says talking about his consigliere. "The sooner this wedding is over, the fucking better."

I don't rise to his bait, he's trying to get a rise out of me. Wondering if Makenna has gotten to me. My father believes that a woman is a man's downfall. That all they're good for is fucking and baring children. While my father is a monster to his women, I on the other hand won't hurt my wife. Although, I do agree that love is for fools.

"Good," he says, whatever he saw on my face must have satisfied him. "You've three days, Dante. Three days before you take that fucking bitch to become your wife." He turns and goes to his car. I stay where I am and watch him leave.

"Bro..." Romero says, "I'll fucking take him out."

"Anytime, anywhere," Alessio agrees.

I shake my head. "Not now." But our time will come.

"What the hell is with him and Makenna?" Alessio asks. "I've never seen someone affect him as she does. He wants to rip her head off." I shake my head but it's what I've been wondering too.

"I don't know, I saw the way they acted. Something's up and I'm going to find out what." I make my way to our car, needing to get the hell away from the Gallaghers. Makenna is making me lose my damn, fucking mind and I'm not even married to her yet.

"What I want to know is what the hell her mom did to her? I've never seen a woman look at their mom with such hatred." Romero chuckles, "That woman should sleep with one eye open from now on."

I frown. "If Makenna was going to kill her mom, I think she'd have done it by now." I slide into the driver's seat and wait for Romero and Alessio to climb in. As soon as they do, I drive, needing some distance between me and Makenna.

That just makes Romero chuckle louder. "Oh, dear brother," he tuts, "I wasn't talking about Makenna, I doubt she can hurt anyone. I'm talking about you. When you find out what happened, you're going on a rampage."

I glare at the asshole. Why does he have to be so astute? "Fuck you."

Both he and Alessio laugh. "Who'd have thought that Dante 'Ice' Bianchi is being led by a woman. One that he's not yet fucked."

My hands tighten around the steering wheel.

"I wonder what it'll be like to fuck her. Will she fight? Or lay there and take it like a good girl?" Romero laughs.

I slant him a look, one that has him shutting the fuck up. My knuckles turn white from the grip I have on the wheel. "One more word about my Fiancée and I'll gut you where you sit."

"Fuck," Alessio whispers.

Yeah, I'm deadly serious about gutting my brother, we've all made threats before but never meant it. Until now.

"Makenna is mine."

Romero grins but keeps his damn mouth shut. Both he and Alessio have fucking knowing smiles on their faces and if they continue, I'm going to wipe them off their faces.

"We've got your back, bro," Alessio says after a couple of minutes. "We won't let dad get to her."

Damn fucking straight we won't. I know what that asshole is capable of.

"Where are we going?" Romero asks.

I grin. "I've a Russian to find." My mind is filled with the images of the bruise on Makenna's creamy skin. Some bastard laid a hand to her and for that he's going to pay.

Chapter 3

Makenna

"Makenna..." The gentleness of my mother's voice has the hair on the back of my neck standing up. She's being nice, that can only mean she wants something.

"What, Ma?" I'm tired of this bullshit, the sooner I'm away from her the more I'll be able to relax. I glance in the mirror and look back at myself. The scar on my neck shining like a beacon against my tanned skin and white robe, it's a reminder that I'm nothing more than a victim in this world of monsters.

"You won't..." She stops and I turn to face her, she's sitting on the sofa. "You won't tell anyone, will you?"

I let out a bitter laugh. "Don't worry, Ma, your secret is safe with me. I'm not stupid. If I tell them what happened, what do you think is going to happen?"

She glances down at her hands, wringing them together.

"It'll mean war. Something I don't want, nor does Da, hence why this farce of a marriage is happening."

She sighs, her body slumping forward with relief, but she frowns. "You don't like your fiancé?"

I shrug. "I don't know him well enough to make that assessment."

She lets out a little laugh and it grates on me. "You're so cynical. You've been around your uncle too long."

I take a step toward her, her eyes flash with fear before she masks it. "Why do you think that is, Ma? Hmm? If the truth comes out, what do you think is going to happen to you?"

She folds her arms over her chest and leans back against the sofa. "I'm married to your father, Makenna, you know just as well as I do that the Irish Mafia don't harm women."

I roll my eyes; she's fucking naïve. "You really believe that if da finds out what happened, he'll let you live? That if Killian finds out he will?"

She gasps. "Makenna, you can't tell them."

A knock at the door gives her the reprieve she needs. "Get out, Ma, and leave me the hell alone. Today I'm getting married and then I don't ever want to fucking see you again."

"Watch your language, Makenna. I'm still your mother."

I shake my head, she's a fucking bitch. "Get out. I have to get ready."

She huffs but does as she's told. When she opens the door it's to find Kinsley standing on the other side glaring at her, her silver purple bridesmaid dress hugging her curves in all the right places. She looks gorgeous. Once mom's gone, Kinsley closes the door and locks it. "What the hell did she want?"

I sit down and grab the champagne glass that's on the table. "She wanted to make sure I'd keep my mouth shut."

Kinsley's eyes flash, she's the only person that knows the truth and I trust her more than I trust anyone in this world. Kinsley will take my secret to the grave, just as I will hers. "She's a bitch, Kenna, I wish you'd change your mind and tell your dad what happened."

I raise my brow. "Take your own advice and tell Ace."

She shakes her head, her long brown hair cascades down her back. "I can't, you know that."

I nod. "I do, and you know I can't tell my da. It'll cause a fucking war."

When she looks at me, I see the sorrow deep in her eyes. It's the worst thing about her knowing what happened, the look in her eyes whenever she thinks about it. I feel like I'm twelve and lying in a pool of my own blood.

"Shall we get you dressed?" Her voice is soft but full of support. I take another sip of champagne and get to my feet. My hair and makeup are done, all that's left is to put on my dress. "Your dress is beautiful, Kenna, you're going to look stunning."

I give her a small smile. Beautiful isn't something I consider myself, not with the scar that I have. Growing up, boys would always say I was pretty, shame about the scar. Girls would make fun of it, laugh and point. I got thick skin fast, but the shit they said, it stuck. The words Makenna and beauty don't belong in the same sentence.

She helps me get into my dress, it's tight fitting but as soon as I tried it

Bloody Union

on, I knew it was the one for me. It's got lace covering my neck so it hides my scar, but it's backless and sleeveless. It hugs my hips and flows down to the ground. Beauty isn't me, but this is as close to beauty as I'll ever get. I don't think I've felt as sexy as I do wearing this dress.

Kinsley lets out a low whistle. "Damn, Kenna, Dante is going to lose his damn mind when he sees you."

At the mention of Dante my heart beats faster, there's something about that man that makes my knees go weak. I've never been one to swoon over a guy, until Dante. Whenever he touches me, my body trembles in ways that it shouldn't. I should be afraid of him, I've heard the stories about the Famiglia made men and the way they treat their wives and daughters. Yet whenever I look into Dante's eyes, I find a sense of peace I haven't had in a long time. To me, that's the ultimate danger. I learned that trust isn't something I should give, with the exception of Kinsley. I don't even trust my brothers. To them, the family comes first and I'll always be second. I understand that, I've known that my entire life. It's our way of life and that's the reason I can't trust them. I know if they ever knew that, they'd be hurt.

"Kenna?" Kinsley says softly, pulling me from my thoughts. "Are you okay?"

"I'll be okay," I reply, not sure what else I can say. I'm marrying a man I know very little about, his father is someone I hate, and I'm leaving my family behind to live with said husband.

She pulls me into her arms and I go willingly. "Promise me that you'll still come visit. That we'll still be the same. Promise me." She chokes on her words.

"Oh, Kins, of course I will. Me and you, we're not changing." If Dante thinks he can forbid me from seeing her, he's sorely mistaken.

She gasps for air and I lead her to the sofa. I should have realized she was worried. Kinsley and I, we're practically sisters. Even when I went to live with Killian, Kinsley was there, always at my side. Hell she even came to Ireland to stay with me during the summers. If Dante doesn't allow Kinsley and I to be friends, I'll run away. For Kinsley, it would be her worst nightmare, for me, it would be the ultimate heartbreak.

"It's going to be okay, Kinsley."

She shakes her head unable to breathe. Shit.

There's a knock at the door and I quickly open it needing to help Kins, I see Finn standing there with a huge smile on his face. "Finn," I whisper and his smile drops, he peers past me to see Kinsley in the midst of a panic attack. "I need your help."

He looks at me, his eyes soft, "What do you need?"

I take a deep breath, "I need you to get Dante to come here." He opens his mouth to protest but I stop him. "Please, Finn."

He nods once and turns, I close the door again and go back to Kinsley. Her face is red and her eyes glassy as she tries to suck in air but she's panicking too much.

I kneel down beside her, pulling her head to mine so that our foreheads are touching. "Kins, please," I say softly, hoping that she'll hear me. I need to try and get through to her. "You're supposed to be the strong one. You're the one that keeps us together remember?" I bite my lip hoping to stop the onslaught of tears that's threatening to spill over. "Kinsley, you are the strongest woman I know. You are my sister."

"I'm..." she sucks in a deep breath, "scared."

I nod, my thumbs caressing her cheeks. "I know, but don't be."

"I—can't—lose—you."

I close my eyes, the pain I feel right now is unlike anything I've ever experienced. "Kins, you're not going to lose me."

"I—almost—did—once. Can't—do—it—again."

My hands on her face tighten. "You won't."

"You—almost—died. They—nearly—killed—you." Her breathing is hard, every breath she takes sounds painful.

"Kinsley, I survived that shit. We're here. Together, we've overcome so fucking much. We're fine."

"You—don't—know—that.   He—may—forbid—us.   Seeing—each —other."

I let out a small laugh, "You make us sound like lovers."

"You're—my—sister, Kenna. My—protector. I—need—you. Please—don't —go. Please—don't—let—him—break—us." She's crying now, it's adding to the panic.

I suck in a sharp breath, what am I supposed to say to that? She's right, if we're not allowed to be there for each other, it will break us.

"I won't." A deep voice breaks through mine and Kinsley's moment. I turn and see Dante, Romero, Alessio, and Finn standing in the room. All of their eyes on us, Dante's on me, his expression hard. Romero and Alessio's gazes bounce between Kinsley and me, whereas Finn is having a hard time keeping his emotions in check.

"You won't?" I ask in disbelief as I stand and position myself in front of Kinsley.

He stalks toward me, "I won't keep you and Kinsley away from each other. When you're at the clubhouse, you'll have three guards."

I hear Kinsley slowly start to regain her composure, her breathing doesn't sound as painful as it had.

I step closer to Dante, we're almost touching. "Just like that?"

His eyes scan my face, almost as if he's searching for something. "Not just like that. Today we marry, then tomorrow, you and I are talking."

I bite my lip, I should have known that he'd have stipulations.

He lowers his head, our lips almost touching. "You're going to tell me what's happened, Makenna. I can't help you if you don't." His voice gentler than I've heard before but it still has a bite to it.

"No one can help me." I confess and watch as his eyes darken. "Thank you," I say and his features soften.

Kinsley gasps and I turn to face her, Dante's hand goes to my waist and goose bumps break out over my body. "You're not supposed to see her in her dress before the wedding."

I laugh, "Kins."

She shakes her head. "Kenna," she returns. "It's bad luck."

I roll my eyes. "That's our middle name."

She laughs and to my utter surprise, walks over to Dante and hugs him. It's awkward as he's got his arm on my waist but that doesn't bother Kinsley. "Take care of her." I hear her whisper and Dante's hand on my waist tightens.

Finn clears his throat, "Hate to break this up, but everyone's waiting on us."

703

Kinsley pulls away from us and gives me a smile. "You ready for this?"

I shrug. "Sure, as long as there's vodka, I'm good."

She laughs and I'm glad, it's better than hearing her cry. "Why is it that Irish people drink as much as they want and it's normal?"

I smirk as I move out of Dante's hold. "You mean, when you do it, you're labelled an alcoholic?" She narrows her eyes. "It's because we can handle our liquor, you... Well, Kins, you get on top of a bar and start stripping."

I hear Finn's chuckle and I turn to see him, his emotions are in check and he's smiling. "That was once!" She gasps in mock outrage. "Better than stealing a cop car and spending the night in jail."

It's my turn to laugh. "You spent the night in jail with me, or did you forget?"

Pain slashes through her face and I feel like an ass. She quickly recovers and snorts, "Hardly. Besides, it was a good night." She slaps my ass and I narrow my eyes at her. "Your tramp stamp is something I'll never forget."

Tramp stamp. "It's not a tramp stamp when it's on my ass, Kins."

"Who the fuck tattooed your ass?"

"What the fuck?"

Dante and Finn say in unison.

Kinsley laughs and I glare at her. "Fuck, will you both calm the hell down?"

"No, I want to know what fucking asshole put his hands on you and tattooed your ass," Finn demands causing Kinsley's eyes to widen. He's not normally as aggressive around Kinsley as he is now.

"Why?"

"Because I'm going to kill him," Dante snarls.

I can't contain the burst of laughter that escapes me.

"Makenna this isn't funny," Finn growls.

"What's not funny?" Da asks as he strolls into the room, Patrick and Cian hot on his heels.

"Makenna let some asshole tattoo her ass."

"What the fuck?" Patrick snaps and I resist the urge to roll my eyes.

"Shit," Kinsley whispers.

"You all need to calm the hell down." I tell them, glaring at them all. Da however is standing in the doorway with a smile on his face.

"Tell us, Kenna," Cian pleads with me.

"Makenna's right, you all need to calm down. What the hell did I raise? A pack of wild animals?"

Finn turns his gaze to our father, his features cool and calm but I can see him internally battling with his anger.

"Christ. It was Kinsley," Da tells them. "You know what those two are fucking like when they've been on the tear. They do stupid shit, hell getting a tattoo wasn't even the worst shit they did that night. They thought it would be funny to get a tattoo and I told them both that they weren't allowed to have anyone tattoo them. They decided it would be funnier if they tattooed each other. So they each tattooed the other. Now do you want to calm the fuck down and relax? Today is supposed to be a joyous occasion, we finally managed to get someone to marry your sister."

"Hey!" I cry out. "I'm a fucking catch!" Da grins and my brothers laugh. "It's these fucking idiots you have to worry about. None of them know how to keep their cocks in their pants. No woman is going to want to marry their crotch-infested asses."

"Leave me the hell out of this. I did nothing wrong!" Cian says holding up his hands.

"Oh, I'm sorry," I say sarcastically. "I forgot who it was that I walked in on while they were fucking two whores."

"You should have knocked," he growls.

"It was in the fucking pool at seven in the damn morning!"

Da smacks him around the head. "What did I tell you about those fucking whores?"

"Okay, it's time for you all to leave. Makenna needs to finish getting ready and Dante needs to be at the altar waiting for her," Kinsley proclaims while sharply clapping her hands.

Everyone except Dante leaves. When I turn to him, butterflies swarm in my stomach as I wait for him to say what he wants. He turns to Kinsley, "Will you give us a minute?"

She bites her lip and gives him a tight nod, before turning to leave.

"Are you okay?" he asks closing the distance between us.

I look at him in shock. He's showing concern for me; that's something I didn't think he'd do, ever. "I'm okay." I tell him gently and I'm rewarded as he gives me a stunning soft smile.

He's so close, I could reach out and touch him. Actually, I'm itching to do it. His eyes soften as he looks at me. "That was fucking intense, Makenna."

I do what I've been itching to do and place my hand on his chest, his heart beat is slow and steady and it settles me. "Kenna, my family call me Kenna."

He searches my face and nods. "Kenna." It rolls on his tongue and I let it wash over me. Loving how he says it. "It was intense, she's your girl. Are you okay?"

I bite my lip to stop my tears from falling, I feel his strong heart beat and let it settle me again. "I'm okay. She's not had a panic attack in quite a while and seeing her like that hurts, but I'm okay. *And* thanks to you, she's going to be."

He's quiet for a moment. "I meant what I said, tomorrow, we talk."

I nod. "I understand and I think I knew this day would come. Not tonight though, Dante. Let's just enjoy today and then tomorrow, we'll deal with the ugly stuff."

His head lowers so that our lips are barely touching. "You're ugly stuff is going to be mine. The sooner you realize that I'm going to protect you from anything and everything that poses any harm to you, the better we'll both be."

"I know you want to help, but it's going to take a while to trust you." His eyes narrow at my words and for some reason I want to ease his worries. "I don't trust many people, including my brothers, so please don't be offended."

I've shocked him, but he quickly recovers. In doing so, he lowers his mouth to mine giving me a quick, hard kiss.

"Fuck," I mutter when he leans back.

"I'll see you at the altar," he says as he walks to the door. My heart is pounding and yet he seems completely unfazed. "And, Kenna..." He calls out as he opens the door, "You look beautiful."

My heart melts at his words.

This isn't good. This marriage was supposed to be an arrangement; I wasn't supposed to get attached, to catch feelings. The stories of the Famiglia men and how they treat their wives made me believe that my life as a married woman would be full of hurt. But Dante, he's given me hope and that's one thing that could break me.

CHAPTER 4

Makenna

"You really do look beautiful, Makenna," Kinsley tells me as she dabs her eyes.

My stomach is full of butterflies. My nerves have kicked in but for some reason I'm not scared. When I was told that I'd be marrying Dante, every scenario went through my mind. I always pictured being scared, being so distraught that I'd be a shivering mess. Instead, I'm calm and ready. Everything I've come to know about Dante is that he's a monster, but not to me. The soft look he gives me makes my body react in ways I can't explain. Thinking about this day, I thought I'd be in hell, where I'm actually looking forward to our future. Although, I'm not sure how it will go, but I'm hopeful and that's a good thing.

"What do you think of Dante?" I ask her, smoothing down my dress.

Her eyes widen, "Um..."

I laugh, "Kins, you're my best friend, but you know how to read people. You've been doing it since you were a child. What do you think of him?"

She sighs and takes a seat on the sofa, "Makenna, that man doesn't know how to love..." Hearing her say those words is like a punch in the gut. "From the little I've seen you interact, he's not a maniac around you, the two of you could have a reasonable marriage but that's about it."

I close my eyes and sit beside her. "Do you think he'll push me to tell him what happened?"

She nods. "Definitely. He's possessive of you already. The hand to the waist, the smouldering looks. He's going to want to know everything about you, including what happened that night you were hurt."

"I can't tell him everything," I whisper. There's no way I can.

She reaches for my hand and gives me a reassuring squeeze. "You need to set the boundaries, Kenna. Make him be truthful, that way, there's no surprises. But if that happens, it means you have to be completely honest too."

708

"Grr," I cry. "Why do you have to be so wise?"

She laughs before sobering. "You need to decide what you want. You can keep him in the dark, but I know you. I know that if that happened, you'll be miserable. If you're honest, then make him be too."

"Let's see how tonight goes and then I'll decide." I still don't think it'll be wise telling him everything.

"Okay, but think about how it will impact your marriage if you don't be honest with him." She gives my hand one more squeeze before getting to her feet.

"Kins, he'll want to know about you too."

She nods. "Yeah, I know, I'm okay with that."

I get to my feet. "You are?" Since fucking when? "You've made me keep this shit quiet for years, Kins. Years! I could have had Da sort this out, hell I would have done it."

"It would have caused a war!" she whisper-yells.

"And you don't think telling Dante what's going on will cause one?"

"You won't let it."

I laugh, I can't help it. She's got an awful lot of faith in me. "I don't see how that will happen. Anyone who finds out what's happening isn't going to sit back and let it happen any longer." I hate that it's gone on for this long already. If I had a choice, I'd have made sure it ended from the get go.

She shrugs. "When my father dies, then I'll be free."

I shake my head. "Your dad is a piece of shit, Kins. He's letting you get hurt and doesn't give a shit."

"I think that Stuart has something on him, that's why he's letting him do it."

My anger is bubbling beneath the surface, we've spoken at length about this in the past and this is the first time that she's telling me this. "It doesn't matter if he has something on him. You don't let your daughter be abused! You just don't fucking do it."

"I think my father killed my grandfather."

I suck in a sharp breath, Kinsley and I aren't supposed to have secrets, but we do. We've both hidden things from one another in the past, this is one of them. "What makes you think that?"

709

She glances down at her hands and then back to me. "He was a bastard, Kenna. He really was, he was worse than dad. He lashed out on Ace more than anyone, but then Ace got bigger and then he turned his attention on me."

I know what happened. Ace came to me, hoping that I'd help him by asking my father for a favor. Ace believes that my da will call him when he needs a marker.

"What happened to him?" I never want anyone to know that I was the one that poisoned the bastards coke stash. If it comes out, then there will be war. The secrets I carry are there to stop the people I love from getting hurt.

She shrugs. "The cocaine he had was shit." She shakes her head, a small smile playing on her lips. "He wasn't found until morning."

"Why are we even talking about this? The man's been dead for almost six years, why bring it up?"

She bites her lip, she's thinking carefully about what she wants to say. Everyone looks at her and sees this gorgeous brunette who is *only* the princess of the Vipers Fury motorcycle club, but she's manipulative when she needs to be and that's most of the damn time. "Don't." I warn her, she's never like this with me and I'm pissed that she's starting now. "Kins, whatever the hell you have to say, say it."

"Fine." She huffs. "We're talking about this because I need to know what happened, Kenna. I need to know why the hell my father is letting that animal hurt me whenever he likes."

"I don't know, Kins. I really wish I knew why this was happening. I've tried so hard to take you away from them but you never would leave. You kept going back." I would have kept her with me at all times. Every time she went back made me lose a part of myself. How can I protect my best friend if she willingly went back into that hell? Instead, each time it happened, she'd call. I'd be the one to get her. Bring her home with me, stitch up her wounds, clean up her cuts, and hold her until she cried herself to sleep.

"I had to go back. If I didn't, they'd have come for me. You and I both know that. We're the same, Kenna. We both do whatever the hell we have to, ensuring the ones we love are safe. So I go home, take what that asshole does, and then I call the only person in this world that I can rely on. The girl that's been my best friend since as long as I can remember, the one who's had my back from the very first moment we met, and the woman who's been my backbone."

I will the tears not to fall. "Don't make me cry!" I warn her. "You've been here for me just as much as I've been there for you. You also cleaned up all the cuts and bruises I've had."

She nods. "Let's hope I'm right about your soon to be husband. I don't want to clean up any more cuts."

I reach for her and pull her into my arms. "I don't want to clean anymore of yours, but until your father dies, I'm going to have to." I release her and take a step back, once again, smoothing down my dress. "It's time."

She reaches for the bouquet and hands it to me. "Try not to kill my father as you walk past him."

I grin. "Your dad's here? Who the hell invited him?"

She shakes her head, gone is all the seriousness and in its place is happiness, just the way it should be today. "Let's get you married."

I exit the door and am greeted by my father. "Have you two been behaving?"

"Don't we always?"

His brows practically hit his forehead. "Now, the day you two start acting like ladies, is the day, I begin to worry."

"You really love us, Mr Gallagher." Kinsley grins.

Dad shakes his head. "Kinsley, how many times have I told you to call me Seamus?"

She ignores him and turns to me "I'll leave you both alone for a few moments."

Dad waits until she's out of sight before turning to me. "Baby girl."

I shake my head. "Don't, Da..." It's been a long time since I was this emotional. Today, my life is changing and I'm not sure if it's for better or worse.

"No, I've failed you."

"You haven't," I implore, needing him to realize he did what he needed to do.

"Kenna, will you be quiet for a minute so I can talk?" I nod. "Thank you, as I was saying. I've failed you. I couldn't keep you safe even though that was my job. You're my baby, Kenna, and I've fucked up in more ways than one. I'm sorry."

"Da, you've done what you thought was right. This is our way of life; this marriage is what we do. It's going to bring peace between the Italians and the Irish. Besides, I could marry worse than Dante."

Da scoffs, "Yeah, if you say so. The boy's a fucking psycho. He's not what you think, Kenna, he's everyone's worst nightmare."

I laugh. "And, I'm the one that gets to marry him."

"Remember, you're a Gallagher, Kenna, through and through. Even after you take the Italian bastard's name, you're still ours, and we'll always protect you." There's a promise in his words, he's letting me know that no matter what, he's going to be there for me.

"I'll be fine." I promise him.

He kisses my cheek. "I know you will be. I'm proud of you."

My heart swells at his words. "Da, you've got to stop, otherwise I'm going to cry."

He shakes his head. "My Kenna doesn't cry."

"You don't know me, Da, not anymore." His eyes flash with guilt and I feel bad. "Sorry, I didn't mean it like that."

"You did," he says simply. "I sent you away hoping to protect you."

I know he did, if only he knew the life he had sent me away to.

"You hate me for it, don't you?"

"Da, I don't hate you..." Not anymore. "You did what you thought was right. That's all that I can ever ask of you." I place a kiss on his cheek, "I don't hate you, Da, I don't. So, we're going to put a smile on our faces and I'm going to get married. Besides, I'll be back on Sunday."

He smiles. "Yeah, you will. You're not allowed to miss Sunday dinner unless you're dying. That includes that husband of yours."

I lift my brows. "Dante doesn't seem to go anywhere without his brothers."

Dad's eyes narrow. "Fuck, do I really have to sit around a table with those Italian bastards?"

"Da!" I gasp, "You've got to stop calling them bastards."

He laughs and I can't help but smile. "Let's get you married, huh?"

He holds out his arm for me to take and I do. "I love you, Da," I whisper as the bridal march song starts.

"And I love you, Makenna."

The door opens and my breath is taken from me when I see Dante standing at the front of the altar, his eyes on me.

Kinsley walks ahead, I notice that Romero's eyes follow her every move, her body tenses ever so slightly as she passes her father and brother on her way to the altar.

My arm tightens on dad's as we move toward Dante and the priest. My mother has outdone herself today, the church is full to the brim, the who's who of the mafia world are here and then some. The men of the East Street Kings are here, Landon, Scantor, Miller, and Prior. In front of them is Hudson Brady, his wife, Mia, and his right hand man, Jagger, plus Jagger's wife, Sarah. Dante's family take up a huge portion of the church, each and every single one of them are armed to the teeth.

I finally make it to Dante and once again, my breath is taken from me. His gaze is piercing me as he stares at me. He shakes Dad's hand and the priest begins to talk; I'm unable to concentrate on what he's saying. Dante has a hard grasp on my hand, his thumb rubbing circles against my palm. I'm in a daze, I can't help but glance up at him throughout the ceremony, whenever I do, he always seems to catch me.

When the priest says, "You may now kiss the bride." My heart speeds up as I glance at Dante once more. His eyes are filled with lust and need, but when he lowers his lips down on mine, it's gentle and yet promising. It's a promise of what's yet to come. I cling onto him as though he's my lifeline and I'm wondering when the hell I became this woman? The woman that wants someone in their life, to be a part of it, in ways that no one else has?

"Dante..." I whisper and his gaze hits my lips.

"Kenna..." he replies and I practically whimper.

The sound of glass shattering, breaks through our moment. I cry out as something hits my arm; I'd have fallen to the ground if Dante hadn't held onto me. His eyes narrow in on my arm and I'm too scared to see what's wrong. What's made that dark look come onto his face?

Then all hell breaks loose as the doors burst open, showing the Bratva holding guns. Dante pushes me behind him as he pulls out his own gun.

Shit, this is going to be a bloody wedding.

CHAPTER 5

Dante

My heart pounds against my chest as I watch Makenna walk down the aisle, there's something about this woman that fucking gets to me and I don't even know her. When my father told me that I'd be marrying, I had assumed that the relationship I'd have with my wife would be cold and sterile. I know the way things work in our world, woman are to be seen and not heard. They're to make a home and look after the children, but as I watch Makenna walk toward me I know there's no way things will be cold or sterile. The woman makes my blood run hot, she's brought out a protective instinct I never knew I had. When Finn told me that Makenna wanted me, I didn't know what to expect but walking into the room and watching her kneel in front of a panicked Kinsley wasn't it. Hearing them talk made me realize that I've underestimated my soon to be wife. Her words hit me like a fucking sledgehammer, *"I survived that shit. We're here. Together, we've overcome so fucking much. We're fine."*

She's far from fucking fine, seeing the two woman huddled together, heads touching, made me see that there's things Makenna hasn't let anyone see. I'm determined to find out what the hell she's been through and I'm not going to stop until I find out all of her secrets. I'm unable to take my eyes off her, she has a bright smile on her face. You'd think we've known each other for years the way her smile lights the room, whereas the truth is so much worse, she's been handed to me in a fucking deal, and yet she's not showing an ounce of fear. She's strong and vulnerable. She's a walking, talking contradiction and yet I crave her.

I shake Seamus' hand then instantly reach out for Makenna's. My thumb moves in circles over her skin, needing this contact, goose bumps break out over her skin and I bite back a smirk; she's affected by me. When my lips touch hers, it takes all my restraint not to take it further. Instead I pull back, my hands on her hips, holding her tight. Her eyes are heavy with lust, she's fucking gorgeous, she's holding onto me as though she needs the strength to keep her upright.

"Dante..." she whispers and my cock stirs, my gaze goes to her lips, plump and kissable.

"Kenna...." I reply gruffly, pissed that we're in a church and not near a bed.

Glass shatters and she jerks in my arms just as a cry escapes her lips, I reach for my gun as the doors to the church burst open.

The fucking Bratva.

The blood on Kenna's arm has my blood pumping; murder running through my veins. They fucking shot her. They're going to pay for it. Tightening my grip on her waist and I twist her so that she's behind me, my gun in hand and I start shooting.

"Shit," Romero says and I glance at him, his eyes on Alessio, who's on the floor bleeding.

Kenna pulls out of my hold and I hear material ripping, more shots are being fired and I focus on the bastards shooting at my wife and brothers. As far as I can tell there's thirty if not more Russian bastards here. They picked the wrong fucking wedding to hit. Every man here is firing back at them, we're taking them down but they just keep coming.

"We need to get him out of here." Kenna's voice pulls me through the blood lust I have. "Dante, if we don't he's going to die."

Fuck.

"Finn!" she yells and instantly her brothers are by our side. "I need you to cover us, we need to get Alessio out of here."

He instantly nods, crooking his finger, his men surround us.

"We need to go out the back, there's a car waiting."

I turn back to my wife and I'm fucking shocked, she's torn off the bottom half of her wedding dress. Blood covers her torso, and I'm not sure if it's hers or my brother's seeing as the bottom half of her dress is on Alessio's body, where Kinsley is applying pressure. But what shocks me the most is her calm like appearance, her mind clear as she barks orders at people.

"Romero, I need you to carry Alessio out. Kins, Ace is waiting for you."

"Keep a tight perimeter. Shoot anyone who gets close." Finn tells his men and they instantly nod. "Let's go."

"Dante," Kenna whispers. "If you have to stay, I understand."

Fuck, this woman. She understands. I don't even have to say a word and she knows what I need. For the second time today, her hand lays over my heart and she takes a deep breath. "Be safe," she whispers and places a kiss against my lips before she releases me and they leave.

I turn back to the foray and see that most of the attendance have left, leaving my men, the Irish and a few others left, there's still some Bratva left but nowhere as near as there was. I walk toward my men, "I want at least one alive." I want to find out just why they started shooting up my wedding.

"How's Makenna?" Seamus asks and it's in that moment that I realize, I didn't even check. I knew she'd been shot, but I don't know how bad. Fuck. He shakes his head.

"Finn's with her, they're making their escape."

He nods. "Let's get rid of the rest of these bastards and then you can go and check, yeah?" There's a fucking threat in there somewhere; there always seems to be with Seamus. He can't just come out and say whatever the fuck he wants, instead the asshole has to say some cryptic shit.

"Boss," I hear one of my men call and I turn to face Stefan. He's got a cut to his eyebrow, a bruise forming on his cheek and he's grinning like a crazy asshole.

"What?"

"Boss, the Russian's have retreated, there was four Escalades coming to the entrance and then they left. We've got three in the back of the car, we're bringing them to the warehouse."

My gut tightens at his words. "I need to find my wife. Fuckers are probably following her."

Stefan's grin fades, "Boss, what do you need?"

"Get them to the warehouse. Make sure you're not followed and that they have no weapons. Once I make sure my wife is safe, I'll be there." He nods once and turns.

"Want me to help locate her?" Seamus asks.

"No, it won't take me long." I turn, not wanting to deal with this shit any longer. She's my wife now, he has to come to terms with that. I make my way out the back just in time to see my wife shooting a fucking Russian bastard. Why the hell has she got a gun in her hands? My rage starts to surface again, she's already been hurt and now she's just killed a man. Fuck.

"Kenna," her name is a growl from my lips.

Her back stiffens and she turns to glare at me, "You here to help?" Her Irish accent thicker than I've heard it before.

My cock starts to stir again, her defiance shouldn't be a turn on, but it is. "Sure," I drawl and see her lips turn up before she quells her features.

"There's six out front," she tells me. "Fucking Finn told me to stay here while he took the men with him. Asshole." She shakes her head. "Fuck knows where they've gone. Thankfully, Romero isn't stupid and had a gun."

"Where did you get that one?" I ask her and I'm surprised I'm able to keep my tone even.

She raises her brow and shakes her head. "When Romero put a bullet into asshole number one—" She points to the dead body on the floor beside her. "I picked his gun up and used it on asshole number two and three. Now, I've answered your question and as you can see I'm not going to have a melt down because I killed someone; wasn't the first time and certainly won't be the last. How about we cut the chit chat and get to the car before your brother bleeds to death?"

I bite back my chuckle, whereas Romero and Alessio don't. Fuck, I should hate that she's not the quiet, shy woman I had expected but I'm not, I'm glad. I don't want a docile wife, I want someone who's full of life. And looking at Kenna that's what I've got. "Let's go."

"Atta boy," Kenna laughs and I shake my head, fuck, how can I want to laugh during a moment like this? "The black Rolls, that's where we're heading. Try not to get shot," she tells me.

"Don't worry, Princess, I'll be fine."

She smirks at me. "Good, you have your husband duties to take care of tonight."

Jesus! My cock twitches at the thought of being inside of her. "Oh, Princess, nothing, and I mean nothing will stop me from fucking you tonight."

Her pupils dilate, she shakes her head, turns and runs out of the back door, firing her gun as she does.

"I'm going to kill her," I grunt as I follow behind her.

She's standing in the middle of the parking lot shooting at the bastards. I snap out of my shock and start shooting too. There's only a couple more of the fuckers left and within seconds there's more gunfire. The Irish are coming out of the front and taking them down. "Kenna, into the car now," I shout at her and thankfully she has more sense than to argue with me, she runs to the car, fucking runs in her six inch heels like she's been doing it every day of her life. She pulls the back door open and jumps into the driver's side.

Romero's right behind me, pulling Alessio along with him. I reach for Alessio and Romero runs around the other side of the car. Looking down at my youngest brother, I see the pale skin and the sheen of sweat on his head, he's not doing good. FUCK! Romero slides in and helps me get Alessio onto the back seat. Within seconds I'm around the car and sliding into the passenger's side. Makenna doesn't wait for me to put my seatbelt on, she puts the car into drive and pulls out of the parking lot like a bat out of hell.

When we put some distance between us and the church, my pulse starts to slow down but the anger I have is still palpable. The fuckers shot my brother and wife; I'm going to kill every single one of them as soon as we get this car load safe.

"Phone, please?" Kenna asks not looking at me and I frown but hand it to her. "Thanks," she whispers and gives me a small smile as she punches in some numbers.

Ringing filters through the silent car and I realize she must have put it onto loud speaker. "Hello?" A man answers.

"Doc, it's Makenna."

"Ah, my dear, congratulations are in order so I hear."

"Thanks, Doc. We ran into a bit of trouble," she tells him, not once has she taken her eyes off the road, glancing at the dashboard, I see she's doing 120 and not even breaking a sweat.

"Say no more. Same place?" he asks and my body tightens.

"Yep, I'll be there before you." Her face is blank, not a single emotion is running through her head.

"Okay, dear, I'll be there shortly."

She ends the call and I'm surprised to see her once again punching in numbers, the car's filled with the sound of ringing. "Hello?" This time it's a woman that answers.

"Angela, I'll be there in fifteen minutes. Get the guest room set up, the doc's on his way. I'm going to need the usual shit."

"Of course, Ms Gallagher."

"Bianchi," she replies instantly and I smile. Damn, she surprises me at every turn.

"Of course, I'm sorry. I'll get right on it, Mrs Bianchi. And congratulations, darling." She once again ends the call and this time she passes the cell back to me.

"Where are we going?" Romero asks.

"My place. This is off the grid, nobody, other than Angela and the doc knows where it is. Keep the pressure on his wound," she instructs him.

"Why?" I ask, why would she need a house off the grid?

"Why what?" she says with a frown.

"Why does nobody know where it is?"

She shrugs. "Because I didn't want them to know. I prefer having somewhere I know is clean and that if I need to I can go."

"So many secrets, Makenna." My voice is low but there's a bite to it.

She laughs. "Oh, Dante, you have no idea who the hell you've married. I've so many fucking secrets I'm drowning in them."

Everyone's silent as we weave through the city, heading toward the suburbs. I'm wondering where the hell she's leading us, when we reach the suburbs she comes to a stop at an iron gate; trees surround it so you can't see anything. From outside it looks as though it's an abandoned lot, but when Makenna drives through the gates, I realize it's a fucking mansion. The garage door opens and she drives into it, before anyone can react, she's turning off the car and sliding out. I'm a nanosecond behind her, rushing to her side and opening the door to get Alessio out. "Let's go, we need to get the bullet out and stop the bleeding."

She leads us to an elevator, where she punches in a code, the doors slide open and she waves for us to go ahead. The doors close and she hits the button, the elevator purrs as it starts to ascend. "Holy shit, this is like some James Bond type shit." Romero breathes and I want to rip his fucking head off for the look he's giving my wife.

"Angela?" Makenna yells as soon as we're out of the elevator.

"Mrs Bianchi..." a woman in her late fifties appears, wiping her hands on a cloth that's attached to her apron. "I have the room set up, please let me know if you need anything."

The two women start walking and I'm getting fucking annoyed, I hate being in the dark. Finally we reach a door and Makenna opens it. "Put him on the bed," she instructs gently as her eyes survey the room and the instruments at the side of the bed. "Angela, the doc will be arriving soon, please let him in when he gets here."

"Of course, Mrs Bianchi."

"Shit." Makenna groans as she rubs her head, "Angela this is my husband, Dante, and his brothers Romero and Alessio."

"Mr Bianchi." She grins at me and shakes my hand, taking my attention away from my wife and to the woman shaking my hand as though she's just met the damn pope. "It's a pleasure to meet you. Can I get you anything? Coffee, beer, whiskey?"

"Whiskey, neat please, ma'am."

She nods. "Certainly, sir." She turns on her heel and leaves the room.

"Dante, take your belt off please?" Makenna asks and I see her looking over Alessio, she's taken off his jacket and ripped open his shirt, the blood pooling from his wound, he's lost a lot of blood; too much blood.

I frown but do as she asks. As soon as I hand it to her, she folds it in half and turns her attention back to Alessio. "I'm really sorry, but this is going to hurt, I'm going to need you to bite down on this." As soon as he does, she goes silent, putting on a pair of disposable gloves and picks up tweezers. "He's going to end up passing out. There's no other way, I don't have anything to give him for the pain." She looks at me and I see the depth of despair in her eyes, she's worried about hurting him, does she think that I'll hurt her for doing so? I nod, unable to say anything.

721

I watch in sick fascination as she gets to work, pulling the bullet out of him. Alessio grunts around the belt, his eyes full of pain. Romero slides up beside me, he too hasn't been able to take his eyes off the scene in front of him. "Angela?" Makenna yells and instantly the lady is rushing into the room, two glasses of Whiskey in her hands and passes them to Romero and I.

"Yes, Mrs Bianchi?"

"Jesus, Angela, how long have you known me?" Her tone isn't impatient, instead full of love.

"Since you were six."

Makenna nods, "And yet you still won't call me Makenna."

Angela shakes her head, "Oh no, I can't do that."

Makenna grimaces before sighing. "Fine. Will you please call the doc and see what's taking him so damn long." She glances at me, "What blood type is Alessio?"

I stare at her in confusion, how the fuck am I supposed to know that shit?

"Angela find out his blood type and inform the doc, he's going to need a transfusion."

"Of course, I'll do that right away. Do you need anything else?"

"No, thank you. I'm okay. I'm almost done here, I just need doc and the blood."

She nods and runs out of the room. "I just have to stitch him up, thankfully it didn't hit anything major, he's lost a lot of blood but he'll be fine as long as it doesn't get infected. Once the doctor gets here, he'll give him the antibiotics and transfusion."

"Jesus, how the hell do you know how to do this shit?" Romero asks as she begins to put stitches in Alessio.

"Practice, years and years of practice," she murmurs, her attention fully on what she's doing.

I'm wondering even more what secrets she holds, this woman is a mystery, one I intend on solving.

CHAPTER 6

Makenna

I stare down at my hands, Alessio's blood coats them, even with the disposable gloves on. Alessio is asleep, he passed out once I took the bullet out. For the first time in my life, I was worried. Usually, it's only Kinsley or myself I have to stitch up, but today I had to do it to Alessio, knowing that there was two people watching as I did, two men that wouldn't hesitate in putting a bullet in my head if I messed up. I was worried that if I did mess up, what would happen? I hate this unnerving feeling I have. It's not me. I don't care what people think, I never have. Growing up with older brothers helps shape you, they take you under their wing and help you. Show you how to be strong and resilient, show you what it's like to not be afraid and I wasn't. Until that day. The day when the facade fell and I came face to face with the devil incarnate. Then the young girl that was fun and outgoing became the woman I am today. Since then I've learned a lot of things about myself, about the world, and I've used every single thing to my advantage.

"Kenna?" His warm tone makes me look up from my hands.

"Mrs Bianchi..." Angela calls out just as Dante's hand grips hold of my hip. Having him so close makes me shiver. "The doc's here."

I nod. "Thank you, Angela, you may go home now."

She glances between me and Dante. "Thank you, I have dinner for you all, and the guest rooms are made up."

I give her a soft smile, one that she returns. "Send the doc up and have a good evening."

Within seconds, the doc walks into the room, takes a sweeping glance of us before moving to Alessio. "Nice work, Makenna, not that I should be surprised. You're an old hand at this now. Must be quite a change from stitching yourself up."

The hand on my hip tightens as the air in the room changes, this is more dangerous.

I ignore everyone and focus on what the doc's doing. Hanging the antibiotics, before giving him the blood transfusion. It takes a while, nobody says anything, we're all watching the doc intently, or Romero and I are. Dante however, has his gaze firmly on me. I glance up on him and I'm shocked by the intense gaze he has on me. My hand reaches for his and I hold on tight. Up until today, I haven't had someone to lean on, but now, I have Dante. I'm not sure how long it will last but I'll take however long I'm given.

"Do you want me to have a look at your arm?" Doc asks and I shake my head. Up until that moment, I had forgotten that I had been shot, it's just a graze, but the shock has worn off and the pain has registered now. "I'll leave the gauze and things for you. You know the drill. I'll be by tomorrow to check on Mr Bianchi here." He packs up his bag walks to the door.

"Thanks doc, I'll see you tomorrow." He nods before he leaves the room.

"Romero, would you like me to show you to your room?" At my words, Romero's gaze leaves Alessio and moves to me; the softness in his eyes is unlike I've ever seen. He gives me a sharp nod. "Follow me." I take my hand away from Dante and realize I've left blood on him. "Sorry," I whisper as I rip the gloves off me and throw them into the bin beside the bed.

He doesn't take his hand from my hip, instead his other hand goes to the other side. We're all still in our wedding attire and I'm dying to strip off and put on something more comfortable, but first, I need a goddamn shower.

We walk out of the room, Dante's still holding onto me and I leave the door ajar, needing to hear in case Alessio needs any help. We walk down the hall, "Romero, your room is on your right. There's food in the kitchen, help yourself to anything you need."

He gives me a nod as he walks toward the bedroom door, until his hand touches the handle. "Thank you for saving him," he says softly.

"Good night, Romero," I reply, not wanting to answer any questions. I know they all have them but there's only one person who's going to demand them and right now, I don't have it in me to answer them. Not now.

Dante and I are silent as we make our way to my room. I've not been here in a couple of weeks. This house has been my safe haven. It will always be and yet, today, I let three men walk into it. That's something that has never happened before and I'm still trying to figure out why I did this.

Once we reach my room, I close the door behind us. The floor length mirror in front of me shows me just how fucked up I look. When Alessio went down in the church and I saw the blood pouring out of him, I did the only thing I could. I reached for the skirt of my dress and I pulled as hard as I could, ignoring the ripping sound as I tore it from my body. I couldn't think about what I was doing, I just did what I had to. But staring at myself, all I see is what I am. A bloody bride. Blood covers my dress, my legs, my arms, and my face. I look like a fucking corpse. My gaze goes to the man behind me, his focus is on me. His eyes dark and hard, as he too takes in my appearance.

"I guess I know what everyone's going to call me now," I say with a laugh, although it's forced, it's all I can do to stop the tears.

"And what's that?" His voice is a rumble.

"Bloody bride."

"Anyone calls you that, I'll kill them." It's a promise.

I shrug. "It's what I am. Our wedding turned into a bloody union, Dante."

He spins me around and I crash against his body. "I don't give a fuck." He growls, "You're not a bloody bride. Why wouldn't you let the doctor see your arm?"

I shake my head. "I don't like anyone touching me."

I watch as his features darken. "You let me."

I'm speechless, I have no idea what to say without making me sound like a complete bitch. "I haven't let anyone near me with a sharp object since someone slit my throat." He goes to say something but it's too much. I pull away from him and walk into the bathroom, I need to see what my arm is like. I managed to tie a piece of fabric from my dress around it after Kinsley helped me in the church with Alessio. Untying the fabric I see the bleeding has stopped, it's not as bad as I had feared, I won't need stitches but it'll leave a mark. What's one more to add to the mix? I clean the wound and leave it be, I need a shower and putting a bandage on it will be pointless at this stage.

"Kenna..." It's a gruff whisper, I shouldn't turn around and face him, but he has a pull over me, one that I can't ignore. "Fuck." He grabs hold of my waist and spins me around so that I'm facing him. "You're supposed to be this docile woman who knows her place."

I scoff. "Whoever gave you that impression needs to be shot."

His lips twitch. "How did you know how to fix Alessio? How do you drive like you're born to do it? Drive at full speed, without breaking a sweat? How the fuck do you know how to shoot a gun and hit the target every time?"

"Dante..." I whisper, we weren't supposed to be doing this tonight. "Tomorrow." Even then I doubt I'll be able to do it.

"You drive me fucking crazy. What the hell am I going to do with you?"

I laugh. "You're my husband, Dante, I'm sure you can come up with something creative..."

His hands tighten on my hips and he lifts me up, instinctively my legs wrap around his waist, my arms going around his neck, his lips are on mine. It's hot, hard, demanding. I sink into his embrace, his hands sliding from my hips to my ass, pulling my body against his thickening cock. I moan, grinding against it. There's something about Dante that makes me lose myself. Whenever I'm around him, I feel the heat between us. His tongue sweeps into my mouth, stealing my breath, I push back with my own. My hands fisting into his hair, pulling his head closer to mine.

It's only when my back hits the bed and he's leaning over me do I realize that he walked us from the bathroom to the bedroom. I'm in such a lust filled haze that I had no idea what's going on. "This dress needs to come off," he growls, the sound reverberating in his chest.

I lick my lips. "You don't like it?" I'm breathless.

His eyes are dark with lust, "I didn't say that. It's fucking tight, it clings to you. It shows me what's underneath and right now, I need it off, so I can see all of my bride."

I squirm beneath him. God, why do I find that a turn on. I hear the unmistakable snap, my body freezes as I see his switchblade in his hands. Is he for real? I don't fight, instead I stay still. I learned from a very young age not to show fear.

"Kenna..." His voice sounds hoarse but I ignore it. "I'm not going to hurt you." Now where have I heard that before? Oh yeah, right before my throat got slit. I don't trust anyone, I can't afford too, look where trust got me. "Baby, I promise." He sounds as though he's hurting, but I'm not focusing on him, my eyes are glued on the knife in his hands.

"Do it." I demand, whatever the fuck he's doing, just do it and get it over with.

With the flick of his hand, the knife slices through my dress, the ripping sound loud through our silence, as soon as he's finished cutting my dress, he folds the knife away and puts it back in his pocket. The dress falls away from my body, leaving me completely naked except for the tiny white lacy G-string.

"Come back to me—Kenna—come back." His lips are on my neck, kissing and sucking. "Baby, come back." My hands go to his hair and my back arches as his lips capture my nipple, his teeth grazing them and I gasp. "That's it."

My hands tighten in his hair and I pull, he raises a brow at me, the stupid asshole has a smirk on his face. "Next time you hold a knife against me, I'll kill you."

That smirk of his widens but his eyes flash with something dark. "Yet another question. Tell me something, Makenna, why do I get the feeling that killing me would come easy to you?"

I ignore the stupid question, my hand reaching between our bodies for his zipper. I pull it down and his cock springs free. "Are you going to stare at me, or are you going to fuck me?" I breathe, needing him. He only has to touch me and my body is alight, it's as though my blood is on fire as it runs through my veins.

He sucks in a sharp breath. "I know what you're doing," he murmurs as he lifts off me, I watch as he strips down. His shirt comes off first and his muscles are tight, just as he probably is. Dante is a closed book, or so they say. He doesn't show any emotion. Yet looking at my husband, I say they're wrong. Dante's lust is an emotion and I'm wondering what other emotions I can invoke.

My legs wrap around his waist as soon as he's on top of me. The heels of my feet against his ass and I'd love nothing more than to reach down and touch it, in fact, there isn't any part of him that I don't want to touch. His mouth crashes down on mine, his tongue sweeping in and I'm lost. That's all it takes from him, a kiss and I'm putty in his hands. I arch back when his finger enters me, his mouth still on mine, his other hand, he's trailing his fingers along my body. His touch searing against my skin. It's too much, he's everywhere and yet, I don't want him to move. My body starts to grind against his finger and I feel his smile against my lips, thankfully he doesn't say anything.

My pleasure climbs and I'm grinding harder and harder against his hand. He tears his mouth away from me and I whimper, instantly missing the soul splitting kiss. "Give it to me, Kenna. Come for me." I shatter at his words, my breathing coming out in pants as I try and come down from the intense orgasm.

"I'm sorry, baby, but this is going to hurt," he murmurs. I should have prepared, but I was otherwise occupied. He slams his cock into me and pain tears me apart. I cry out and Dante stills inside of me. "I'm so fucking sorry." He holds me until I get accustomed to having him inside of me. I wiggle beneath him, testing to see if it still hurts. He lets out a sharp hiss. "Fuck, Kenna, I'm barely hanging on, don't do that again."

Instead of wiggling, I grind down against him, my pussy contracting around his thick cock. "Are you going to stay there all day?" I drawl, my legs tighten around his waist, "or are you going to fuck me."

"Christ," he growls but starts to move.

I've never known pleasure like it. Having Dante inside of me, filling me up, I feel something I never thought I'd feel. I feel like I'm home and that scares me. I push that thought out of my mind and focus on what's happening between us. "More... Harder," I beg, my fingers digging into his shoulders as I hold on.

"Makenna, I can't, I'm barely holding on..."

"Dante, do you think I give a shit if you lose control?" My fingernails dig into his shoulders as he thrusts into me harder than before. "God. Oh, please, Dante. I need more."

His mouth smashes against mine, and I know that he has finally released those reins he held in check. The kiss is hectic, hard, furious, and bruising. He thrusts into me and it's painful but the pleasure I'm feeling far outweighs the pain and I'm clawing at him as I try to reach that peak once again. It doesn't take long before that pleasure once again washes over me and I let go, screaming his name as my pussy spasms around his cock.

He thrusts, once – twice – three more times before he releases inside of me. "Fuck," he bites out, his breathing labored. He pulls out of me and lifts me into his arms. "Shower time."

"I can wash myself," I tell him although there's no heat in my words. "What the hell are you doing to me?" I ask once he sets me down on the counter in the bathroom.

He shakes his head. "Fuck, you're driving me crazy. You've gotten to me and I'm not sure I even want you there."

I laugh, at least I'm not the only one that's feeling this way. "You're stuck with me, so deal with it."

His eyes darken as his gaze sweeps across my naked body. "Oh, baby, you have no idea what you've gotten yourself into."

I smile, because I know exactly who Dante Bianchi is, the problem is, Dante has no clue as to who I am and that could be the biggest problem I've ever faced. "Shower time." I tell him as he turns it on.

* * *

I HEAR movement in the kitchen and smile, Angela's back and I'm starving. "You're awake," I say as I walk into Alessio's room, I'm not sure where Romero is, I'd assume he'd have spent the evening in here with him. I've checked on Alessio every few hours and Romero wasn't in here any of those times.

He's frowning as he croaks. "I am. What the hell happened?"

I sigh as I walk over to him. "How much do you remember?" I lift up the blanket and check the bandage, there's no blood, which is fucking great. It means the stitches haven't busted.

His tongue darts out and he glances at me and then to the doorway, I know Dante's just walked in. "You got married, then all hell broke loose, I got shot—" his eyes move to my arm, "you got shot." I nod, even though there's no need, he obviously knows what happened. "Then we came here and you were—" he glances down at my hand on his stomach, "and here I am."

I smile. "You passed out, either from the pain or the blood loss, I'm not sure which. You're fine, the bullet was taken out and it didn't hit anything major. You're all stitched up. The doc gave you antibiotics and a blood transfusion. You really shouldn't move for a couple of days and even then, it shouldn't be anything too strenuous."

A hand clamps on my waist. "What she means is, no fucking around. Once the doc has cleared you, then you can get back to work." Dante's voice is hard.

Alessio groans but nods. "Do you need anything? Angela's here, so if you're hungry, just let her know. For as long as we're here, she's going to be here." I turn, wanting to set some space between Dante and I. I know what's coming and I'm not ready for it.

"Thank you," he says and I nod.

I make my way toward my room and I smile when I see bags by the door. I arranged for Finn to get our things from the hotel and bring them to Angela. At least this way, the men have some of their own things. I pick up the bag and walk into the bedroom, I instantly hear the door close behind me. Shit. Dante followed me.

"Okay, Makenna, I've had enough. It's time for us to talk."

I turn and face him, he's staring at me intently. He really does want me to bear all to him; unload all of my secrets. The problem with that is, it's giving him power, power that I've never let anyone have before.

"Kenna, start talking."

"What do you want me to say?"

He takes a step closer to me. "I want to know exactly who I fucking married. I've done a lot of research on you and yet, staring at you now, I know that I don't have half the fucking info. So, who the hell are you?"

I sigh, there's no way out of this. I open my mouth and decide to take a chance on a man that's made me feel things I shouldn't feel. If he betrays me, I'll kill him. I'm not the twelve year old girl who watched as her mom slit her throat, I'm stronger than that.

Bloody Union

* * *

The End

* * *

This is the end of Bloody Union, the rest of the story will be available after
Crimes of the Wicked is unpublished.
https://brookesummersautho.wixsite.com/website/the-made-series

* * *

Newsletter
http://tiny.cc/BrookesNL

About N.K. Stackhouse

I'm Brooke, I'm a Londoner born and raised. I live with my fiancée and our daughter.
I'm a foul mouthed, dirty minded weirdo. I'm an introvert who would rather spend the night in front of the fire reading than go out.

Read More from Brooke Summers
https://brookesummersautho.wixsite.com/website

JAMESON'S DEBT

Forever Midnight MC Novella

Victoria Gale

Jameson's Debt

Not all families are made from blood.

Carina never took an interest in her family's business until it took an interest in her.
Now, it threatens her freedom, her family, and her life.
Only Jameson can save her.
He has a debt to pay, but how far is he willing to go to repay that debt?

Author Note

*Please note the following story is a short standalone story in the **Forever Midnight MC** series. Each story can standalone and have a HEA.*

__Jameson's Debt__ is a M/F contemporary romance, crossing over between the Forever Midnight MC world and Jameson's previous Mafia life. The series contains scenes of drug use, violence, and frequent 'F-bombs'.

CHAPTER 1

Carina

T he second his eyes hit mine, I knew I was in trouble. There was
something possessive in his gaze, something dangerous. A rush of fear
struck deep in my chest, my vision blurred, and the club whirled around me,
a maelstrom of noise and color. I was used to meeting those some might call
bad men. Men who stole and killed and used people to keep themselves in
the life they were accustomed to. Hell, my own family had exploited those
weaker than themselves for generations. They were no saints, but still, they
maintained a certain level of humanity and compassion. They took, but they
also gave. The man talking to Gabriel, my brother, had no such traits. I'd
never been more certain of anything in my life.

My first instinct was to turn and run, but years of living up to the Rizzo
name and upholding the reputation of my family stalled my steps.

I couldn't hear what he was saying, but it was obvious my brother had
realized something was wrong when he froze and followed his companion's
gaze. A troubled look flashed over his face when he found it resting on me,
but he didn't hesitate in stepping in front of the man and blocking his view.

With his gaze no longer burning into me, I took a gasp of air while
Gabriel motioned a couple of women, one blonde and the other brunette, to
welcome his guest. A pang of guilt formed a lump in my throat at the
thought of what those women might be getting themselves into, but I pushed
it away. My brother never made any woman do something she wasn't willing
to, and they were as free to leave as I was.

With that thought in my mind, and with the strobe lights and the
thumping base now making my head ache, I decided it best to call it a night.

"Let's get outta here," I said to Rahat as she edged through the crowd
toward me and suggested we grab another drink from the bar.

"But we've only been here an hour," she said and flicked her lustrous
black hair over one shoulder. She looked stunning in her black, strappy
catsuit. The sheer mesh bodice left no doubt that Rahat liked to keep in

shape, in much the same way the molded bra cups left no doubt that her ample bosom was the result of implants. I looked down at my own natural E cups and wondered why anyone would willingly make their chest the same size as mine. To say they had been the bane of my existence since I turned fourteen would be an understatement. Although, you wouldn't know it with the metallic mini dress I wore that delved into a deep V at both the front and back, highlighting all my assets.

"Please, let's just go." I reached for her hand. I couldn't leave my friend in the club, not with a man who made my every nerve ending scream to run away or cower in fear.

Rahat brushed my hand away. "Jeez, Carina. What the hell's gotten into you?"

"It's nothing. I just…" I shrugged and glanced around the club, trying to spot the man with Gabriel again, but at the same time, hoping I wouldn't find him. When I saw him in the VIP section deep in conversation with the blonde, I quickly pulled my eyes away and took Rahat's hand again. "I've got a really bad feeling about tonight. We need to leave. I'll explain at my place. We can watch a movie or something."

She stared at my face, her own burning with questions. After a moment, she huffed out a breath and nodded. "Fine. You win. But can we please grab a bottle or three of Prosecco from the bar to take with us?"

"That we can do."

Rahat flashed me a beaming smile. "You get the bottles and I'll grab our jackets. We can meet at the front door."

"Thanks, Rahat. But make sure you're there in five," I said, knowing full well that the only reason she'd volunteer to grab the coats was to say goodbye to Don, who was working tonight in the back office where we'd stashed them.

She winked. "See you in five," she said and disappeared back into the crowd.

I sighed, resisted the urge to glance at the VIP section again, and headed to the bar. A path cleared. Not every customer knew who I was, or that my family owned the place, but the regulars had an idea that I received special treatment at the club. Plus, I normally gave off a vibe showing that I wasn't to be messed with. When a hand snaked around my waist and pulled me backward into a hot and clammy body, I guessed today, with my insides rattled, that vibe was absent.

"Get the fuck off me," I said, trying to break free.

"Come on, love. Just one dance." In his free hand, he held what smelled like a glass of whiskey, only just discernible beneath his stench of BO and booze that stood out amongst the other drinking bodies in the club.

I stifled the roil in my stomach, stomped on his foot, and elbowed him, forcing him to break his hold and drop his glass.

He cursed and reached to grab me again. A mask of anger flashed over his face. "Fucking stuck-up bitch," he almost spat. "You think you're too good for me."

I was about to come back with an appropriate response when someone beat me to it.

"The lady *is* too good for you," someone said in a voice cold enough to freeze the whiskey puddling on the floor.

Two men grabbed my assailant and dragged him from the club. I could almost feel sorry for what would happen to him, but my mind was focused on the man who'd spoken. Gabriel's companion.

Although my legs were weak and my stomach felt like lead, I lifted my gaze to meet his face. To some, he would appear handsome: tall, dark, with full lips, and a strong, defined face that matched perfectly his sun-kissed Italian skin. But, up close, the look he gave me was even more terrifying than it had been from across the room. It was hard to explain what I saw, but it wasn't beauty. It was more a disconcerting mix of hatred, lust, and a need to control.

"Thank you," I said, and moved to turn.

"Thank you, Xander."

"Sorry." I halted my steps.

"My name. Xander Caruso."

I took a deep breath and plastered a smile on my face. "Well, thank you, Xander Caruso. If you'll excuse me." This time, I shut my ears to any potential response, turned and walked to the far side of the bar, as far away from Xander Caruso as I could get. "Nicki," I called to the bartender as soon as I arrived. "I'll take three bottles of Prosecco to go." Anxious to be gone quickly, I added, "I'm in a hurry."

Nicki nodded, stopped what she was doing, and grabbed the bottles. She was placing them in a carrier for me when Xander appeared at my side.

"Perhaps I could buy you a drink?" he asked, his commanding voice easily heard above the music.

"I'm actually leaving," I said and resisted a shudder. I hated the way he made me feel weak and powerless when I'd always been confident and self-assured.

"One drink as a way of thanking me properly."

I bristled at this and found some of my usual self rising to the surface. "I have already thanked you twice. Aside from the fact that I never once asked for your help or needed it, I think that is more than adequate for any service you believe you served. Now, if you'll excuse me."

Nicki gave us both a weary look and placed the bottles on the bar in front of me. I reached up to grab the handle of the carrier, but Xander snatched my hand and held it tight in his own.

"Let go of me," I said, although my mouth was dry and the words hard to come by.

He leaned in close to my ear. "Do I make you nervous?" he asked.

"Nothing makes me nervous," I lied.

He smiled. "Perhaps you are correct and a thank you is not required. However, it is customary and polite to offer someone your name when they give you theirs."

"Fine! My name is Carina Rizzo." The second the words were out of my mouth, I regretted them. The dryness in my throat became unbearable when his smile shifted, and I knew that my name had granted him some extra power over me.

"Rizzo," he said as if to confirm my thoughts. "Of course, I should have seen the family resemblance. Your beauty is very much like your mothers."

"My mother passed away fourteen years ago."

I tried to pull my hand away, but he held it tighter, pulled it to his lips, and brushed a soft kiss that made my skin crawl on the inside of my wrist.

"Which is why it took me a while to register the familial resemblance," he said, peering at me between his lashes. "Your father passed away soon after if I remember correctly. Not that his death was unexpected. He often crossed the wrong people and the stress must have taken a toll on his heart. A problem I hope your brother has enough sense to avoid."

My blood boiled. Who the fuck did this man think he was?

"Carina," Nicki called from across the bar. "Do you need me to get the bouncers or your brother?" she asked.

Xander patted my hand and released it. "No need. I'm just leaving. In fact, I'm due to meet with Gabriel shortly myself." He nodded to the carrier holding my bottles of Prosecco. "Have a good evening," he said to me. "I trust we will speak again soon."

"Carina!" What happened to five minutes?" Rahat's voice sounded shrill in my ears as she shouted over the music and emerged from the crowd carrying our jackets. She eyed Xander next to me and a smile played at the edge of her lips. "Oh, I see. If you've changed your mind and would like to stay, that's fine by me."

"No, we couldn't possibly cancel our other engagement," I said, grabbed her arm, and spun her around. I didn't look back as I dragged Rahat to the exit.

As soon as we were out the door and down the steps, she pulled me to a stop. "Carina. What the hell is going on? You are not acting like yourself at all."

I glanced back up at the club entrance. Three doormen covered the door and ushered in the line queuing outside a group at a time. Xander was nowhere to be seen. He hadn't followed me. Not that he needed to with whatever connection he had to my family.

"Carina," Rahat said again. "Speak to me. Is everything alright?"

"That man at the bar--"

"The hot Italian who looked like he wanted to eat you right up?"

I winced at her words. "Yeah, that man."

Rahat handed me my jacket and slipped hers on over her catsuit. "So, what's the problem? You suddenly developed an aversion to drop-dead gorgeous men who clearly have money and want to devour you?"

"Only this one." I thought about her words for a moment and the way

Xander sent cold tendrils of fear snaking up my spine. "The problem is," I said, "I can't shake the feeling that this particular man wants to chop me into little pieces with an ax before devouring me, if that makes sense."

"If you're getting a creepy serial killer vibe from him maybe you should talk to Gabriel." She motioned for me to go back inside, but I shook my head.

"Let's just go back to my place for now and open these bottles. Maybe I'm overreacting and all this will seem silly in the morning," I said, knowing full well it wouldn't. Besides, for the first time in my life, I had a feeling Gabriel wouldn't be able to protect me.

We spent the next five minutes flagging down a taxi.

"Frognal, please," I said, climbing in when one finally stopped for us.

We shut the doors, slipped on our seat belts, and pulled away. Rahat pulled one of the bottles from the carrier.

"Do you mind," she asked the driver.

"Not if you're willing to pay for any damages and lost fares for the night if you soil or break anything."

"Deal," Rahat said and popped the cork on the Prosecco.

She took a sip and handed me the bottle. *Why the hell not?* I thought and took an extra-large sip myself. By the time we reached my flat in Hampstead, we'd finished the first bottle and were ready to open a second.

"What have you got to eat?" Rahat asked as we pushed inside, hung our coats on the rack, and took our shoes off so as not to damage the parquet floor.

"Not a lot. Let's finish the second bottle, then order Chinese."

"Sounds like a plan," she said and linked her arm in mine. "Although, let's drink the next bottle out of glasses."

"That might be an idea."

My mind was a million miles away from events in the club when my phone rang.

"I'll pour us a drink," Rahat said and released my arm and toddled toward the kitchen.

"Hello," I said, answering the call.

"Carina, thank fuck you're home. I need you to pack a bag. I've booked you on a flight from Heathrow to New York in four hours. I'll arrange for someone to meet you when you arrive. They'll get you some-where safe."

I sobered instantly at his words and leaned against the wall, allowing my head to fall back against it. "It's because of Xander Caruso, isn't it?"

Gabriel huffed a breath down the line. "Ah, fuck. I just... I just wish you weren't at the club tonight. Then he would never have seen you."

Not liking the tone that implied somehow this was all my fault, I straightened and said. "I'm at the club every fucking Friday night."

"I know, I know. I'm not blaming you. If I'd had the slightest inclination he was coming, I would have told you to stay home."

Rahat entered the room brandishing two glasses. As soon as she saw my face, she put them on the side table and gave me a questioning look. I pulled the phone away from my mouth and told her what Gabriel had said.

"Serial killer guy?" she asked.

I nodded and returned to the call. "Who the hell is this Xander Caruso?" I asked.

"Let's just say he's a bad man who will stop at nothing to get what he wants. And tonight, he's decided that what he wants is you."

"Well tell him he can't fucking have me."

"Don't you think that's exactly what I've already done," Gabriel said in a strained voice.

"Then why do I have to run away?"

"Like I said, he's a man who gets what he wants."

"There is no way in hell you are going to New York without me," Rahat said. "I am not leaving your side until this serial killer Xander guy is dealt with."

I pulled the phone away from my mouth. "It's not going to be a fun shop-ping trip," I said. "I can't ask you to drop everything and hole up in some room for God knows how long."

My friend crossed her arms and gave me her stubborn pose, complete with tapping foot.

"Carina... Carina..." Gabriel's voice came muffled over the line.

"What now?" I said, returning to the phone.

"Did Xander meet Rahat at the club?"

747

"They didn't exactly meet, but he saw her talking to me, and he knows we left together."

"Then she's going with you whether she wants to or not."

"You can't tell her what to do."

"What did he say?" Rahat asked, picking up her glass and taking a swig.

"He said, you have to come with me whether you want to or not."

"I already said I was bloody coming, Jeez."

I rubbed my head. This three-way conversation was impossible. "If Xander finds me in New York and Rahat is with me, that places her in danger."

"If you disappear and Rahat is left behind for questioning, that places her in even greater danger. As she knows where you are going, her torture and subsequent death at Xander's hands set him straight on your trail." He said the words in a deadpan voice, and I knew he was serious.

I glanced at my friend. I always worried that her association with me would be her downfall. Now, there could be no doubt.

"What's he saying?" she asked.

I sighed. "We're going to New York," I answered. "Gabriel?"

"Yeah?"

"What about you? Are you going to be alright?"

"I can take care of myself," he answered and fell silent for a few seconds. After a moment, he added. "I'll book Rahat on the same flight as you and email you the details. Get packed and get a taxi to Heathrow as soon as you can. I'll speak to you in a few days when you're safe and settled. Oh, and leave your mobiles. They'll only be good for tracing you now. I'll find another way to contact you."

"Okay. Stay safe," I said.

"You too."

Jameson

"Me hold the baby," Charlie giggled as soon as Cane entered Caleb's office with Thea, who carried their two-month-old daughter in her arms. She jumped up on the spare chair next to Rex and patted her lap.

Amber came around from behind the desk and held her hand out. "Charlie-baby, How about me, you, Aunt Thea and Toni-baby go downstairs and leave the men to their boring conversation?" she said. "I'm sure Aunt Thea will let you hold Toni there."

"Okay," Charlie said and jumped up from the seat before reaching ahold of Thea's hand and moving to drag her from the room.

Cane gave Thea a quick peck on the cheek and took the seat Charlie had just vacated. From the corner of my eye, I couldn't help but note the love that shone in Caleb's eyes as they all left.

Lucky passed them as they were on their way out. The last of our group to arrive. He patted Charlie's head in passing and cooed at the baby before perching on the edge of the side-unit. I sat on the windowsill and stared outside. The sun stood high in the sky and a warm breeze blasted in my face through the open window.

Lucky cracked a joke about the clubhouse turning into a nursery. Everyone laughed when Cane responded with a quip implying Lucky was the biggest kid of them all. I smiled. It was weird how close I'd become to each of these men. How much I'd invested in their lives and happiness. I would die for any one of them, and I never doubted they would do the same for me.

Cane and Caleb were blood brothers, but we were all brothers of Forever Midnight MC. Our motorcycle club, our family. I never thought I'd find another after saying goodbye to mine, after turning my back on the family business all those years ago.

Caleb had called the five of us together. The one brother missing, who

749

was usually in attendance at meetings, was Bono, but he was taking a much-needed break to reconnect with his fiancé, Hope.

The laughter died down and Cane asked, "What's up?" kick-starting the meeting.

"The dispensary up in Fort Collins has been seeing a lot of trouble of late. Nothing major. Vandalism, broken windows, graffiti. That sort of fucking thing. It started a month or so back, and Bono was going to take a trip up there and find out what was going on. But we all know that trip got derailed."

"You want me to head up there?" Cane asked.

Caleb shook his head. "I've more sense than trying to drag you away from Thea and the baby. The trip could take anything from a day to more than a couple of weeks. I need you three to go," he said, addressing the last part to me, Lucky, and Rex.

"Not a problem," Rex said. "When do you want us to leave?"

"Yesterday," Caleb said and smiled.

Lucky nodded and stood to leave, Rex followed suit. I shifted on the windowsill.

"What do you expect we'll find?" I asked, curious as to what we weren't being told. We often made trips to check on the brother's various business interests, but these were normally scheduled in advance. Small things like vandalism would be left to the local chapter to deal with.

Caleb leaned back in his chair and huffed out a breath. "Fuck if I know," he said. "It could be some petty beef or it could be the first move by a rival group to take over the town. But it seems to be escalating. I'm hoping you'll be able to figure out what the fuck is going on when you get there."

I was about to answer when my phone rang. I pulled it from my jacket pocket. "I gotta take this," I said, recognizing the number as belonging to Jordan.

Caleb nodded, knowing I wouldn't interrupt the meeting unless it was something serious, and I left the room.

Jordan was my blood-brother, though none of my new brothers knew that. I wasn't someone who liked to talk about myself or my past. It was something better left buried. My club-brothers had a running joke about the time I turned up at the bar, Midnight Anchor in a slick suit, looking close to breaking point. Although, the truth was, I was beyond breaking point. The brothers took me in and made me a better person than I ever was before. They gave me a simpler life where things were often black or white and not fifty different shades of grey. They gave me a family I could respect.

I'd avoided anything to do with my birth family for over six years, but need had driven me to contact them, and my brother hadn't hesitated in helping out when we needed to protect Amber and Hope. Although, that help came with a price tag, a debt owed.

I closed the door behind me, huffed out a deep sigh, and answered the phone. No doubt, Jordan was calling to collect on that debt.

"What do you want me to do?" I said, deciding to dispense with any formalities.

"It's good to hear your voice, too," Jordan said, unable to keep the bitter tone from his own voice.

"I didn't take this for a social call."

He fell silent for a few seconds and a vice clamped around my chest. "You remember Xander Caruso?" he asked, and the vice started squeezing ever tighter.

"How could I forget?"

Jordan scoffed, and I knew he was biting back a comment on how I'd forgotten my own family. "Gabriel Rizzo called from London. His sister's in trouble. Caruso wants her big time," he said instead. The vice became too tight, so I sat on the floor, and leaned my head against the wall. "She and a friend are due to arrive at J.F.K in eleven hours. Being as you're in the market of protecting women, I need you to keep them safe. Gabriel's sister especially."

I remembered Gabriel's sister from her father's funeral, and her mother's before that. Carina, I think her name was. She was a skinny little kid, drowning in loss and the sea of corruption that surrounded both our families. But she'd stood tall and shook my hand when I'd offered it in condolence for her loss. It rankled me that Caruso had set his sights on her, especially considering his father had been instrumental in her mother's death.

"Send me the details and a recent photo and I'll be there," I said before adding that I'd text back to confirm if I was able to make my own flight arrangements from Denver, and hung up.

I glanced at the door to Caleb's office and shook my head before dragging myself to my feet and going back inside. "My contact in New York is calling in my debt," I said as soon as I entered. All eyes flashed to me. "There's a couple of girls due to arrive in New York. I need to get a flight from Denver within the next few hours."

Caleb stood. "I'll get Amber on it," he said, as she worked at the airport and was often able to book us on a flight at short notice. "Rex is going with you," he added. I was about to object when he raised his hand to still my voice. "This is our fucking debt, not just yours, he's going."

My phone buzzed with a text from Jordan confirming the flight details.

"We need to move fast," I said.

Caleb edged around his desk and moved to leave; we all followed suit. "Lucky," he paused for a moment at the door, "you okay to grab a couple of brothers and head on up to Fort Collins?" he asked, remembering the original reason for our meeting.

"Not a problem," he said, echoing Rex's earlier words.

CHAPTER 1

Carina

I was exhausted by the time we arrived in New York. Rahat had been all abuzz for the first hour or so of our flight, and then promptly fell asleep for the remainder of the journey. She had woken refreshed with just enough time to head to the toilet and replenish her makeup before the pilot announced our imminent arrival. I hadn't managed a minute's sleep, and not for want of trying. My mind kept drifting back to Xander Caruso and what he would do if he found me. Hell, I didn't even know the man. I wished I'd asked Gabriel more questions. Hell, any questions. I kept imagining that the name Caruso was somehow familiar, but that wouldn't be a surprise. I tried to keep out of the day-to-day logistics of the family business, but I knew most of the key players, and other names were often bandied about. No doubt, Caruso was one of them.

It was a little after 5 a.m when we collected our bags and headed outside. My nerves were rising, and I was beginning to worry who Gabriel would have sent to meet us. There were a few mafia families he worked with in New York. He had contacts everywhere, families allied to our own. I could think of at least two of them who my brother might turn to for help in the city.

I scanned the thin cluster of people waiting to greet the arrivals and take them onto their next destination. A man a few years older than me, at maybe twenty-eight, pushed between me and Rahat, shouting a belated, 'Excuse me,' after he did so. I mentally forgave him as soon as he ran up to a brunette who was holding a sleepy child and encompassed them both in his arms.

"I don't think anyone's here for us," Rahat said. "Maybe we should get a taxi and check into a hotel in Times Square. We could call your brother from there. And who knows, maybe we could get in a little shopping after all?"

I sighed, not sure what to do. Rahat's plan was as good as any of our other options. Which mostly consisted of standing around and looking confused.

I was about to agree when a firm voice sounded behind me. "Carina Rizzo."

I froze for a second, before taking a deep breath and turning. *Fuck me!*

To say I was surprised to find the sexiest man alive standing before me would be an understatement. He was all muscle and power and screamed sex. My panties flooded just looking at him. He was accompanied by another man, and they were both dressed in jeans and leather biker jackets. I shifted under his gaze. He didn't seem like the type of person my brother would know.

"Carina Rizzo," Mr sex-on-two-legs said again. I looked him up and down. He was handsome and intense. His deep midnight eyes burned into me. "Rahat Jones," he added while glancing in her direction before turning his gaze back to me. She eyed him cautiously. Neither of us confirmed our identity. "Our flight leaves in forty minutes," he said. "We should go."

My insides clenched and I tried to imagine what he looked like without his clothes on. In the movies, men like this were covered in tattoos. I licked my lips and resisted reaching out to run my hand over a chest that seemed made for ink.

His eyes flickered with something for a moment before he turned to leave, while his companion reached out and offered to push the trolley holding our bags.

Unconsciously, I moved to step in line behind him. Rahat grabbed my arm and gave me a pointed look, making me come to my senses.

"We're not going anywhere with you," I said. *What the bloody hell was I thinking?* I didn't know who this guy was from Adam, but if he had the slightest idea that I was going anywhere with someone who looked like they just stepped out of the TV series, *Sons of Anarchy*, he had another thing coming. Even if he had a body that oozed sensuality and power, and intense eyes that made me wet just thinking of them roving over my naked form.

I glanced down and tried to push aside the reactions my body had to his presence, but this only served in highlighting them more when I spotted my nipples poking through my T-shirt, demanding to be squeezed.

I suddenly felt very conscious that Rahat looked like she'd just stepped from the cover of a magazine while I looked like... well, I looked like a sex-starved nymphomaniac who hadn't slept in more than twenty-four hours and was being plagued by the hangover from hell after imbibing far more Prosecco than was good for me.

I cleared my throat, drew my eyes away from the black T-shirt that did nothing but highlight the firm muscle of his chest, and stared into those magnificent eyes. Doing my best to ignore the trickle of wetness between my legs and my aching core, I stood as tall as humanly possible for someone only five foot, four inches in height, and said, "Who the hell are you and who bloody sent you?" I kept my face blank but inside I felt a little satisfaction that my voice hadn't wavered.

A slight smile flickered at the edge of his lips. I could almost believe I imagined it with how quickly it disappeared.

"This is Rex." The other man tipped his head and gave us a warm smile. "You probably don't remember me. My name is Jameson. We last met at your father's funeral."

It was then I realized that I did recognize this man, from the funerals of both my parents. Most of the men in attendance never so much as looked at me, let alone spoke to me, even though I stood next to my brother both times. All their words of comfort had been for Gabriel, but this man had offered me his condolences and shook my hand. He looked different then, younger, most certainly, and his mode of dress had also been remarkably more refined. And as a grieving child, I'd certainly never reacted to him the way my body did now.

"I remember," I said. "Did my brother ask you to come?"

"He spoke with my brother, Jordan Swash. Jordan asked me to come," he said, and I couldn't help but notice the slight shift in his eyes to his companion when he said this. The Swash family were one of the two I thought my brother would turn to, so instead of asking more questions, I nodded and consented to leave with them.

"You said we were getting on another flight," Rahat said. "Where are we headed if we're not staying in New York?"

Rex looked at her with a big beaming smile on his face. "None other than the great Centennial State," he said.

"Where?" Rahat's confusion matched my own.

"Colorado."

"Colorado!" Rahat and I both said at the same time.

Rahat froze in her tracks and folded her arms across her chest. "I'm not being funny," she said. "But are there many people like me in Colorado? You know, of Indian heritage? Like my grandparents came from *India* heritage."

Rex laughed. "It's not the back of beyond."

"It's not as if you'll be leaving the house when we get there," Jameson added, dampening Rahat's spirits further.

My stomach roiled as I followed Jameson. Rahat and Rex were chatting like they were old friends. Rahat liked to play dumb but as soon as someone mentioned a computer, she would turn into a complete tech-nerd. From the slivers I caught of their conversation, she might have found a soul mate in Rex.

As we boarded the plane to Denver. I tried to stop thinking about Jameson crawling between my legs and nipping my clit with those perfect teeth, and strove instead to think of what I knew about our destination. I'd been to New York hundreds of times, L.A, and Los Vegas too, but Colorado was a new one for me.

I'd heard it was filled with canyons and high desert plateaus, as well as forested mountains. I remembered, years ago, a friend from university mentioned they were headed there on a skiing trip. But that was the extent of my knowledge.

Jameson's clothes had me thinking too. Not that I minded in the slightest the way his jeans hugged his tight ass. Fuck, everything about him was so tight and perfect. It's just... his clothes were a long way away from the Armani business suits Gabriel's associates normally wore, and the one Jameson used to wear if memory served. Although, maybe he always dressed like this and put on his Sunday best for the funerals. The leather jacket was a little weird with a skull sprouting wings and a full moon behind. The words, 'Forever Midnight' were written underneath. Rex had the same emblem on his jacket.

I shook my head trying to dislodge the notion that they might be involved in a weird cult or something. That shifted my thoughts to hoping it was a sex cult where Jameson would tie me up and tease me 24-7. *What the hell is wrong with me?* More likely the clothing was part of a planned disguise to keep us safe. I looked down at my Dior jeans and T-shirt, and decided that Rahat and I might be overdressed.

I racked my brain trying to remember all I knew about the Swash family. I'd seen Jordan a time or ten when he'd visited my brother over the last ten years, but Jameson never accompanied him, which made him something of a mystery, especially as I believed Jameson was the older of the two brothers. He had the same strong and angular jawline as his brother, and they were both tall, but physically that was where the similarity between them ended. Jameson was the larger of the two, bulked with muscles instead of the sleek lines his brother possessed. Although his waist looked just about perfect for wrapping my legs around.

I let my gaze travel his body and decided I needed to know everything there was to know about him, and to see every inch.

"Rahat," I said as soon as we boarded the plane to Denver. "Will you be okay next to Rex for a while? I need to talk to Jameson."

Rahat glanced at Rex, who once again beamed at her. She laughed and confirmed she'd be just fine.

I took a deep breath and glanced around the cabin. The flight was only half full and our group was not seated close to any others.

"I'll take the aisle," Jameson ushered me to take the window seat. "You have questions," he said as soon as we were comfortable. It at least gave the outward appearance of being that way.

My mouth suddenly became very dry and I licked my lips. Jameson shifted his gaze as though refusing to look at me, and stared at the monitor on the back of the chair in front of him. I swallowed quickly, feeling for some reason like I'd been caught doing something wrong.

Jameson no doubt thought me a fool, all but demanding to sit with him, and then being lost for words. I huffed out a breath and shook my head again.

What the fuck was I doing and why the hell should I care what he thinks of me? No matter that his slightest glance sent bolts of need straight to my core. Maybe it was for the best he stared straight ahead. I'd be wise to do the same.

"I want to know what you know about Xander Caruso," I said, more of a statement than a question. "And why my brother needed to send me away." They might not be my intended words, but the questions were ones I needed answers to.

Jameson didn't respond at first and I wasn't sure if I should rephrase my statements as questions or if he was simply mulling over his response. After a moment, he said, "Have you ever met Xander Caruso?"

"Yes."

"Then you have your answer."

I stared at him dumbfounded for a minute. *What the hell was that supposed to mean?* "No, I don't," I said, a note of incredulity in my voice.

Jameson leaned his head back against the chair and gusted a deep breath out of his nostrils. "When you met Caruso, did you get the impression he was a nice man?"

"You sure like to answer a question with another question, don't you?" I asked. Jameson looked at me and I saw that quick flash of a smile at the corner of his lips again. He brushed his hand under his chin, and I imagined it brushing under mine, lifting my head higher for him to kiss me. I turned my gaze away again, and said, "No. He was most definitely not a nice man. But I could have handled him," I added, even though I knew that wasn't true.

"Do you think I'm a nice man?"

The unexpected question caught me off guard.

My stomach flip-flopped. What I thought was that he was a man I wanted to do dirty things with. "My brother wouldn't have trusted you to keep me safe, if you weren't," I said, pushing away thoughts of him spanking my bottom.

He reached across the chair and dragged the tip of his finger across my lips, dragging my bottom one down. My heart pounded and my insides clenched as thoughts of his cock pounding in and out of my mouth flooded my mind.

"You've the body of a woman now, but you're still a naive little girl at heart."

He pulled away and my heart sank to the pit of my stomach. I bristled at his comments, grabbed the headphones provided by the airline before slapping them on my head to block out any further attempt at conversation with music. Turning to look out the window, I ignored the new flood of wetness in my panties, and resolved I'd damn well show him just how much of a woman I'd become.

Chapter 1

Jameson

A s I'd intended, Carina turned away from me in a huff.

It had been a shock to see the little girl I met all grown up in the photograph Jordan sent me, and an even bigger shock to see her in person. Any thoughts of her still being a little girl fled in an instant. She was full of delicious, natural curves. And the way she looked at me... fuck... those eyes flashed with a myriad of emotions all at once. And those lips, all pouty and kissable. She had me imagining just what it would feel like to explore those curves with my tongue.

The rest of the flight seemed to take an age. I couldn't get the image of Carina tied spread-eagled to my bed with my tongue exploring every inch of her pussy out of my head. The journey from the airport to the safehouse seemed to take even longer. She was still pretending to be pissed at me. But the look in her eyes said otherwise, and made my cock twitch to life in my pants. I shifted in my seat, and Rex gave me a knowing smirk from the passenger seat. Fucking juvenile. Like he hadn't had a stiffy the entire time he'd been talking to Rahat.

I growled under my breath and shook my head. I may want nothing more than to thrust my engorged cock in and out of her tight pussy, but I was here to keep her safe, nothing more, nothing less. Besides, I'd said goodbye to my family because of the backstabbing and drama, because of too many games being played. Carina Rizzo was nothing but a big fucking time bomb full of exploding drama. I just wish my fucking cock would realize it.

A little after mid-day, we pulled up outside the safe house as it was fast becoming known. A colonial-style farmhouse set amongst a few acres of land. It was one of a number of properties in the portfolio my brother and I inherited, and had been my original destination when I'd decided to settle in Colorado for a while. That had been more than seven years ago. I'd never made it to the house then. Meeting the brothers of Forever Midnight saw me settling in Castle Rock instead. We'd originally used the house to keep

Amber hidden away from the leader of a rival motorcycle club, an act that reconnected me with my brother and led me to the debt I was repaying today.

Carina and Rahat jumped out of the car as soon as it came to a halt. Rex and I grabbed their bags and directed them inside. Carina glanced back at me, biting her bottom lip and smiling.

"Nice place," she said, having obviously given up on the idea of pretending to be pissed.

I growled and tried not to look at the sway of her hips as they wagged back and forth.

Excusing myself as soon as we entered the house, I checked in with both Caleb and Jordan while the ladies freshened up before Rex gave them a tour.

"Xander's still in London," Jordan confirmed.

"Did Gabriel tell you what he intends to do?" I asked while staring out the window. Rex was pointing to the electrified fence that we'd had installed around the grounds after we last used the property.

"He's trying to broker a deal that he hopes Xander will find more attractive than his sister."

"It won't work," I said. Xander Caruso was a lethal combination of powerful, dangerous, and obsessive. When he set his sights on something, he wouldn't stop until he got it. "How's his father these days?"

Jordan huffed down the phone. Caruso's father, Manuel was the underboss of our connected families, second in command to the big boss himself, and the root of all Caruso's power. "There's talk that he doesn't have much time left--" that was nothing new, but given he had to be in his mid-to-late nineties by now, maybe there was some stock in the talk these days "--I suspect that's why Xander was in London."

"Shoring up support to take over his father's role." Maybe, if he needed Gabriel's support, Carina's brother would be able to broker a deal after all.

"Yeah, his *father's* role," Jordan said, unable to keep the scorn from his voice.

"Keep me updated," I said, choosing to ignore it, and ended the call.

Not willing to dwell on the drama, I searched the cupboards and fridge to see if we had any food, but Rex and I had only decided to come to the safe house on the flight to New York and hadn't arranged for any supplies to be provided. I debated calling Caleb again and asking if he could arrange for one of the brothers to make a run to the store for us, but Rex volunteered as soon as he came back inside.

"Oh, me too," Rahat said and collapsed onto his arm.

Rex couldn't keep the grin from his face, and I knew neither of them planned on spending the night alone.

"Xander's still in London," I said. "You'll be safe for a quick trip, but don't call home and don't draw any attention to yourselves."

"Do you want to come?" Rahat asked Carina, but Carina only shook her head and said she was staying right here, with me. The look she gave me couldn't have been any clearer.

As soon as the others left, she asked me for a glass of water. I reached into the cupboard and removed a glass before pouring her a drink from the tap.

I handed her the glass but instead of taking it, she clasped her hand around mine and stepped in close, eyeballing me suggestively.

I lifted her chin, so our eyes met. "I don't play games and won't be teased," I said.

"Who's teasing," she answered before she placed the glass on the counter and planted her lips on mine, never breaking our gaze.

CHAPTER 1

Carina

J ameson kissed me back, setting molten fire flooding deep to my core. I
knew he would. His attraction to me was as evident as my own to him.
We kissed deep and fast. His tongue explored my mouth and my heart
raced. A desperate need to feel his cock overwhelmed me.

I slipped my hands to his jeans, opened them and delved inside. I gasped
when I felt the size of him against my fingers. He grew even thicker and
engorged as I touched him.

"You don't know what you're starting," he whispered and pushed me
away a little.

I licked my lips. "I know what I want."

I squeezed tighter and he growled. Before I knew it, his hand snaked
around my head and into my hair. His fist closed tight at my scalp and he
wrenched my head back sharply. I gasped and let go of his cock. My panties
became wetter.

The edge of his lip curled, and this time, there was no missing the smile
at their edge or the glint in his eyes. "Take your clothes off," he said and
released his grip on my hair before taking a step back.

"What?" My voice trembled with need.

"I want to see you naked."

Before common sense could take over me, I reached for the hem of my
top and lifted it over my head. His eyes dipped to my breasts and my flesh
tingled. I kicked off my shoes and unfasted my jeans before wriggling my
hips and pushing them down. I stepped out of them, kicked them away and
stood in front of Jameson in nothing but my underwear: a lilac sheer satin
bra and panty set.

"Take everything off," was all he said, and so help me, I obliged.

I stood stark naked before him in the kitchen, while he remained fully
clothed. He did nothing but look at me. I'd never felt more exposed, but my
core clenched with growing need, and I was getting wetter by the second.

"A body that beautiful should never be covered," he said after a moment and I felt my cheeks flush. He stepped forward and dropped to the ground before me. I shivered and moaned as he planted a soft kiss on my stomach. His hands touched the back of my calves. He trailed them up my legs, cupped my bottom, and squeezed tight. My legs faltered and I tried not to stagger forward into him.

While one hand continued its journey and came to a rest on the small of my back, the other snaked around the front to my neck before trailing a strong path all the way down the front of my body. His fingers slid over my mound. I shivered and cried out in need as he pressed them inside me. My core clenched around them, wishing them deeper, and my hands fell to brace myself on his shoulders.

Jameson made a low growling sound, he looked up at me and his lips twitched. He removed his fingers and lifted them up to show me. Like I didn't already know how fucking wet I was.

"Lick them clean," he demanded.

Fuck, help me, I wanted to. I wanted to taste just how wet he'd made me by barely doing a damn thing. I pulled his fingers into my mouth and swirled my tongue around them.

"I need you to fuck me," I said and shuddered under the weight of my own need.

Instead of answering, he moved his head to my breast and gently kissed my nipple, making both harden into stiff peaks. The palm of his hand cupped my breast, and he sucked hard, sending ripples of pleasure shooting down my spine. He released my nipple from his mouth with a popping sound. The bereft feeling that flooded my chest was short-lived when he grabbed my nipple again between his fingers, plucking and twisting until I cried out in pain. Bolts of pleasure rushed straight to my core and my clit ached as much as the tight bud of my nipple.

"Fuck!" Jameson said. Suddenly, he stood, lifting me with him.

The firmness with which he pushed me down on the center island in the middle of the kitchen, turned me on even more.

I sucked in a breath when he spread my legs, and his fingers explored the wetness between my thighs, rubbing at my opening agonizingly slowly. My wetness poured out and he pushed inside. My breath hitched as they delved deep, scissoring, and thrusting. His thumb circled my clit and I thrust into his magical hand.

He trailed his tongue up my body and finger fucked me harder. He nipped my nipple, and then sucked it into his mouth. Through heavy eyelashes, his eyes bored into mine with heat and lust. A low grumble built in his chest and he bit my nipple.

My head fell back. I ran my hand over his short, dark hair and pushed him tighter to my breast while rocking into his fingers.

"You like that?" he asked and bit me again. My nipple tightened further, pleading for more erotic pain.

"Yes," I gasped. "B-but I want... I need you to fuck me, Jameson."

He stopped what he was doing and straightened. "Do you think you're ready for me?" he said, which caused me to lift my head and look at his crotch.

His member popped completely erect, and pressed tight against his belly by the remaining bounds of his jeans. I gasped, worried that it was bigger than my arm. I didn't think I'd ever be ready. But I also thought I'd die if I didn't feel him inside me.

"Yes," I said. "Fuck me. Now."

He raised an eyebrow and lifted my legs to rest on his shoulders. There was no teasing, not testing to see if he'd fit. He pushed himself in. I cried out. The pressure built and I felt fit to burst, but still, he pushed in deeper, and deeper... and deeper, widening me with his girth.

"Oh, fuck me!" I screamed, not sure I could take it.

"Halfway there," he said, and I realized my earlier assessment had been way off. This was him taking things easy.

My heart raced. "It won't fit," I said.

"You can take it. And when you do, I'm gonna fuck you hard." He grabbed hold of my ass, and pulled me closer, filling me even more. "Now relax and accept me."

Easy for you to fucking say!

I bit my lip. I'd never been more aware of my body and it felt electric. I wanted to be able to take all of him. I needed him to fill me. He thrust deeper. I tossed my head back and stifled another scream.

"One more push," he said as a pang of nervousness flushed my body.

I closed my eyes and gasped, not knowing whether it was pleasure I felt or pain. He slid deeper inside.

"Oh, God!"

He pulled back, slowly, before pushing inside again. The same slow measured movements over and over, allowing my body to accept him.

"Fuck! That's an incredible fucking pussy," he groaned.

His hands gripped my hips. He held me tight, stretched me, filled me. He pulled back and then slammed forward. I screamed, unable to stop myself. His cock claimed every depth of my core as he fucked me hard. Need, pleasure, and pain shook my whole body. My core clenched greedily around his cock, wanting everything it gave me. He plunged into me, again and again, taking me hard and fast. I bucked into him, willing him deeper still, fighting to take everything he offered me.

His fingers pressed into my clit. He tweaked and teased mercilessly. My body was on fire, everything throbbed and pleaded for release. I'd never felt anything like it.

My eyes rolled in my head, my body tensed, and I exploded. Hard. My orgasm crashed over me with an intensity I'd never known. Still, he didn't stop. If anything, he fucked me harder, just when I thought my orgasm would end another followed in its wake. Only then did Jameson still, holding himself still hard deep within me. I lay there panting, trembling with the intensity of my climax. Jameson lay soft kisses on my chest and allowed my breaths to calm before slowly withdrawing. As he pulled out, I realized just how big he'd been.

He stepped back, fully clothed where I was completely naked. I sat up and pushed myself from the counter, licking my lips.

"I want to lick you clean," I said, and Jameson smiled.

CHAPTER 1

Jameson

Although I'd wanted to, I hadn't planned on fucking her. I thought she was being a little tease, messing around and trying to fuck with my mind when she grabbed the glass of water. She knew exactly what she was doing to my cock and enjoyed watching me squirm. I wanted to show her I was nowhere even close to being a nice man.

I thought she'd be intimidated and shy when I told her to take her clothes off. I should have known better, she was anything but. I knelt and probed her pussy, being exposed made her slick and wet. I trailed my hand down the full length of her body, looking for any trace of fear or doubt. There was none.

Desire twisted like a knife in my gut, and I just had to feel that tight pussy wrapped around my cock. She had no clue what she was asking for. I'd had women up and leave at the size of my cock, but seeing how wet she got, I knew she could take it.

I want to lick you clean, she'd said. Fuck! She was heaven. I couldn't help the smile that spread across my face. She was also insatiable.

I clasped my hand around her neck and claimed her lips while walking her backward. Her legs hit the chair near the back door, and I pushed her down into it. I stood in front of her with my cock almost level with her face.

She didn't hesitate. She looked up into my eyes as though challenging me, opened her mouth and licked at the fucking tip of my head like it was a fucking lollipop. I shuddered and moaned. She did it again.

Her eyes fluttered closed as though she was the one being pleasured. She took her time, licking every fucking inch of my rigid flesh. I wanted to pound into her mouth, and find release, but I wanted to watch her suck me even more.

She wrapped her hand around my cock and pumped slowly before finally drawing me into her mouth, slurping at my shaft with eager wet lips.

My thighs trembled and I growled in appreciation. She groaned and shifted in the chair a little and I knew she was getting wet all over again. I stared at her perfect breasts and tight pink nipples. I wanted to squirt all over them. She was so fucking perfect, so round, soft.

"Fuck! That feels... just... just like that."

Carina moaned and with agonizing slowness, she took me further into her mouth. She used her hands, her mouth, her tongue. She fondled my balls. Her every focus was on pleasuring me, and fuck was she! I felt as hard as a rock and fit to explode. She opened her mouth further. This time, I couldn't help but push inside, but I kept my movement gentle. She could work her way up to taking me fully. Even though I almost fucking came when she hummed against my cock.

She must have noticed as she hummed some more and sucked me in as deep as she could. I couldn't hold back any longer and tried to pull away, but she pulled me back, sucking on my rod with animalistic fervor.

"Oh fuck," I said and shuddered, spilling everything I had into her perfect mouth.

She lapped up my cum greedily, and when she pulled back and wiped the bottom of her lip suggestively with her finger, I knew she wasn't done with me yet. My cock knew too and instantly started to harden. I lifted her head and studied her face, flushed and needy. There were so many games I knew she'd be interested in playing.

The phone rang, making us both jump. I quickly tucked my cock back in my jeans and answered the call.

"Rex," I said, having seen his name displayed on the screen.

"If it's okay to take a few more hours. Rahat and I are gonna grab some dinner out."

"Not a problem," I said and ended the call, eager to drag Carina upstairs and see just how far she would go.

Carina stood from the chair still completely naked, still completely confident in showing everything she had. "Is everything okay?" she asked.

"Rahat and Rex are gonna be longer than they first thought."

A slow smile spread across her face. "How long do we have?" she asked.

"Enough time for me to explore every last part of you," I answered. Carina may be all soft and gentle curves, but there was a need in her that demanded to take everything.

CHAPTER 1

Carina

I shuddered at his words. God help me, I wanted him to explore every last part of me. Jameson reached his hand out to me and I took it. Without saying a word, he led me upstairs and into a bedroom. I should have felt embarrassed that I was still ass-naked, and he was fully clothed, but all I felt was a thrill that made my core clench at the thought of being at his mercy.

As soon as he shut the door, he said, "I want to look at you."

"Aren't you already?" I couldn't get enough of his eyes on me. I loved the way he stared into my eyes, the way his gaze roved around my body with utmost concentration as though he was etching every last detail into his brain, but always came back to my eyes as though he was looking deep into my soul.

He growled and motioned to the bed. "I want to see your pussy."

I laughed. No-one had ever spoken to me like that before. Jameson kicked off his boots and stripped his T-shirt off. He was fucking perfect. His shoulders, chest, abs, thighs. He even had that perfect V on his hips pointing down to his cock. And just as I'd wondered, tattoos adorned his chest and arms. I reached out and relished the hard muscles of his chest. My mouth suddenly dry, I licked my lips.

Jameson wrapped his arm around my waist and turned me away from him. His hard chest pressed against my back and his hands explored my body. One massaged my breast, teasing my already-taut nipple, while the other wound into my hair. He yanked my head back and grazed my neck with his teeth before he trailed feather-light kisses along my shoulder and all the way to behind my ear. My eyes fluttered closed and my head fell back against his shoulder. He pinched my nipple and I groaned in response. Who knew a little pain could lead to ultimate bliss?

"Keep your eyes closed," he said.

His hands left me for a moment, and he stepped away, but I kept my eyes closed as he'd asked. A few seconds later, a soft blindfold wrapped around my eyes. I shuddered and my body burned with excitement. Jameson was a man who knew what he wanted and wasn't afraid to demand it.

He walked me to the bed. "I want to see your pussy," he said again. "Climb on your hands and knees, and then drop down on your elbows."

Excitement fluttered through my body all the way down to my needy core. I climbed slowly on the bed and did as he asked. My ass stuck in the air and my breath hitched. I couldn't see his actions behind me and that made everything all the more exciting, but I heard the ruffle of denim as his jeans came off.

I felt him edge closer. "Getting a good look?" I asked.

He laughed. A low masculine sound that reverberated through my entire body. "Tell me if I go too far and I'll stop," he said as soon as he sobered.

I didn't know what he meant, but I felt both nervous and excited. "What are you going to do?" I asked, my voice a moan of anticipation.

He didn't answer. Instead, his large warm hand stroked my bottom, and his fingers slid over my folds, making me shudder. He rubbed over my clit, and pleasure sparked. He pulled away and I pushed my bottom higher.

"Such a perfect ass," he said.

The slap that came down was hard and unexpected. I cried out and he did it again.

My breath hitched waiting for another slap. Instead, he entered me with his fingers. I was soaking wet. He withdrew and I moaned as he circled and pinched my clit. My core clenched, needing his fingers back inside me. Still, he teased, his touch too light. Then, he lightly slapped my pussy. The shock of the sudden sharp pain hitched my breath. Wetness dribbled down my leg.

I'd never been treated like this before and wasn't sure how to respond. He told me he'd stop if he went too far, but so help me, I wanted to see... to feel what he would do.

The next spank made me whimper. My body simmered with need. I wanted to feel his cock between my legs. I spread my thighs wider, hoping he would take the hint.

I felt his weight shift on the edge of the bed and held my breath, he grabbed my cheeks with both hands, pulled them apart and buried his face in my pussy. His tongue licked a hard sweep from my clit up to my ass and back. It delved into my core.

My legs almost buckled. "Oh, fuck!" My body burned as though I'd been set on fire.

He interspersed blow after blow on my ass, my pussy, with the most delicious teasing with his tongue and fingers, Sweat trickled down my forehead. I wanted to come, needed to come, but each time I came close, his hand fell down with a responding crack. Tears of frustration pooled in my eyes.

"Please, Jameson," I said.

"Do you want me to stop?" he asked as if he couldn't see how wet he made me.

I laughed and wriggled. That was the last thing I wanted. "No."

His tongue teased my clit and he made a satisfied groan in the back of his throat. "You taste unbelievably good," he said. He sucked and licked, driving me so mad, I thought I'd die if I didn't come soon. He swiped his tongue along my pussy and sucked hard on my clit. My body shook and my orgasm built as the tingling sensation in my throbbing nub spread, electrifying my senses. I couldn't catch my breath. My heart beat so fast. When my orgasm hit it was like a tsunami, wave after wave crashed against me. I trembled and quivered, losing myself in the powerful sensations.

Jameson withdrew his mouth and plunged his fingers inside. I gasped, still sensitive from my climax. My core clamped around him. He scooped out my wetness and drew it up my folds and circled it over my bottom hole.

I quivered, not quite sure whether I should feel shame or embarrassment. No-one had ever touched me there.

"Remember," Jameson said. "I'll stop if you want me to."

"No. Don't stop." The words came out breathless and needy.

"Good girl," he answered in response.

I quivered in excitement, a sensitive, aching bundle of nerves. He pushed his fingers inside my pussy again, used them to spread the wetness over my bottom, and then slipped inside. I cried out at the sensation, the pressure somewhere on the cusp of pleasure and pain. I felt dirty. But my clit throbbed, and my nipples hardened like solid marbles against the bed coverings. I was unbelievably aroused. It felt dirty, but it felt good.

He pushed deeper, working his finger further inside my ass. Then he started to pump, and so help me, I was ready to come all over again. It felt too good, crazy good. Pleasure swept through my body.

"Does it hurt?" he asked.

"Yes... No," I gasped. "It... it feels great."

Jameson ran his other hand over the round of my ass. I desperately wanted to see his face, to know what he was thinking. His weight shifted again and it felt like he was fumbling with something. He removed his finger from my ass, and it sounded like he was unscrewing a cap. I wanted to shift and look, but was worried removing the blindfold might stop him.

"This might be cold at first," he said.

A sudden chill hit me, and I flinched. Jameson held me steady and something pressed against my ass. I let out a surprised gasp when it pushed inside. At first it burned, and seemed only small, but Jameson pushed it deeper and deeper with agonizing slowness, and I realized it had to be getting wider.

"Oh fuck," I cried out. "Fuck. What is that?"

"A butt plug." *What the fuck!* "Talk to me," Jameson continued. "Can you take more?"

My pussy throbbed and my back arched. "Y-yes. Don't stop."

Jameson pushed the plug deeper still. It filled my ass. He only stopped when a flat end hit the outside of my bottom. He left it and teased my folds, dipping his fingers into my wetness, and massaging my clit.

I trembled and pushed against his fingers. He hit the base of the plug. I moaned at the sensation. Pain but not as I'd ever known it. Something that hurt but also felt too fucking good. A sweet, delicious pain. The touch of Jameson's fingers as they plunged into my core only amplified the ecstasy building inside me. A voice deep inside told me I shouldn't like such things, that I didn't even know Jameson, so why the fuck was I allowing him to do this to me, but an even deeper one begged him to never stop.

"You're so fucking wet," Jameson said, not needing to tell me I was drenched in my own juices. "I'm going to fuck you now."

I swallowed and tried not to scream out in relief. *At fucking last!*

Still, he took his time. His strong hand crept under me, and cupped my breast, pinching and tweaking my nipple, and sending waves of pleasure straight to my core.

The tip of his cock nudged at my entrance. The heat of it was a stark contrast to the initial cold of the plug. I groaned and pushed back, but shuddered when it made the butt plug twitch. My whole body shook.

He teased me with just a couple of inches, allowing my body to adjust.

"Oh, my God," I moaned, my breaths ragged.

The plug already felt as though it filled me completely, and I felt fit to burst. I closed my eyes behind the blindfold and told myself to relax.

His hand left my breast and he grabbed a hold of my hips. Seconds later he cranked it up a notch, slammed forward and plunged his entire cock into me, letting out a deep moan of pleasure. A jolt of pure ecstasy swept through my entire body all the way to the tips of my toes and fingers.

With the plug, he felt even bigger than he had in the kitchen. I moaned loudly. My body struggled to take everything it held. He pulled out slowly, and then used my hips as leverage to pound into me again. This time, his pelvis smacked against the edge of the plug, reflaming the delicious ache in my bottom hole.

I screamed and almost blacked out. I was blind and deaf, my every cell felt as if they were being ripped apart. It felt too fucking good. A beautiful aching fullness. I shouldn't like this. It shouldn't make wetness trickle from my core. It was too much, too good, too unbelievable. I was so damn full, so engulfed in a deluge of pure sensation, and I'd never experienced anything better.

My core clenched greedily around him, even as my bottom clenched around the plug. Jameson knew exactly what he was doing. He took me roughly. The angle and the intensity of his pounding made the plug feel so much more. Agonizing ecstasy shot up my back, heralding the onslaught of my orgasm. It brewed stronger and stronger. Jameson didn't stop. He pushed deeper, harder. A scream ripped free from my lips. The rush of pleasure was so intense, my skin felt like fire.

Jameson shuddered and moaned his release. He held me close. His hand snaked around my waist, and his head rested on the small of my back. I wanted to fall forward on the bed, but I worried what the movement might bring, and Jameson's hand kept me in place.

We stayed like that for a few minutes. I savored the touch of his body against mine, the hot air of his breaths and the beating of his heart.

After a moment, Jameson planted kisses on my shoulder and down my back. He slipped free from me and brushed his hand over the plug. My breath caught when he grabbed the end and gave it a slight tug. I pulled my ass away and he released his grip. He slapped his hand down on the end and it thrust back inside me. I gasped.

"Hold still," he said. Grabbing a hold of it again, he eased it from my ass. "Are you okay?" he asked and rolled me onto my back before removing the blindfold. He looked at me with such earnest concern it made me smile.

I brushed my hand against his cheeks and pulled him over me, claiming his lips. "I've never felt better," I said after I caught my breath.

He pulled back and looked at me again. "You can't be real."

I lifted my head and nipped at his bottom lip. "Did that feel real?" I asked.

A devilish grin played at the edge of his lips and his hand delved between my legs. He latched onto my clit. I gasped.

"Does that?" He clamped me tight as he claimed my mouth with his own, stealing my breath completely.

Chapter 1

Jameson

Insatiable didn't even come close to describing Carina. We'd briefly acknowledged the arrival of Rex and Rahat and then holed up in my bedroom for the rest of the night. After we finally managed to get some rest, my cell phone awoke us. The light seeping around the corner of the curtains told me it was morning.

"What have you learned?" I perched on the edge of the bed and answered the phone to Jordan.

"Manuel's dead and Xander's on his way to New York to gain the final support he needs before staking his claim to his father's role."

I scoffed. Normal children would want to be with their father during his final days. They wouldn't be traveling around the globe in an attempt to take over his job. "Will he get it?" I asked.

Jordan huffed down the line. "Gabriel has already been on the phone," he said instead of answering my question. "He doesn't see how he can withhold Carina from Xander any longer. He wants her to call him so they can talk through her options."

"Are there any?"

"If Xander takes over as second in command, no."

"I won't let him take Carina."

"Then you'll have every soldier under every caporegime after you. You're talking about thousands of men. It won't be like last time when Dolmilo was on his own," he said referring to the mob killer who had come after Caleb's wife after she put him behind bars for ten years.

I rubbed at my head and glanced back at Carina, lying in the bed and staring at me with a worried look on her face. She'd only heard my side of the conversation, but it was enough to know that things were not going well.

"You do have one option," Jordan said, and I knew exactly what he meant.

"That's not an option," I closed my eyes and answered.

Pressure built and I felt the entire weight of my family responsibilities fall on my shoulders. Manuel Caruso had taken on the role of second in command when our father had died. At twenty-two, I'd been too young to be considered a candidate for underboss, leaving the position free for Manuel to assume. But both our families knew, the second I turned thirty, I'd have had a claim to the mantle and could have challenged him for it. Instead, a year before that happened, I'd turned my back on my life, and I'd never looked back, never even thought about it. Until now.

"Jameson," Jordan said along the line.

"We'll see what Gabriel has to say to Carina before making any decisions," I said and hung up.

Carina lifted herself on the bed and shuffled beside me. She used the bed sheet to cover her nakedness and looked at me wide-eyed. It was the first time she'd looked vulnerable and afraid.

"You can't protect me, can you?" she said.

"Xander's father, Manuel Caruso is dead," I answered, ignoring the question. "Do you know who that is?"

She shook her head, but froze when realization struck. "I've heard the name Manuel, he works with Don Bianchi."

"That's him. He was Bianchi's second in command."

Carina rested against the headboard, closed her eyes, and pulled the sheet tighter around her. "Why did Gabriel even try to send me away? What was the point when he knew it was fruitless?"

I thought about her words for a moment before everything became clear. Gabriel and Jordan had known exactly what they were doing sending Carina to me. And Carina, she'd played me like a fucking fiddle. I stood and paced the room. My fists clenched and rage built like an inferno inside me. My heartbeat thumped in my ears, unable to stop myself, I walked over to the closet and punched the door. My hand throbbed, but I punched it again, satisfied this time that the wood cracked.

Carina drew her knees to her chest and hugged them tight.

"Did they tell you to act like a fucking whore?" I asked, my voice tight.

"Was that the plan? To seduce me and lure me back?" Tears formed in her eyes and a pang of guilt squeezed at my chest. I pushed it away and threw my phone to land on the bed beside her. "Call you brother," I said and pulled on my jeans before storming from the room.

Carina

I had no idea what had gotten into Jameson. When he punched the door, I couldn't help but flinch. He seemed like a man possessed. I didn't know what was going on, but it was clear that Jameson no longer wanted anything to do with me.

With shaking hands, I lifted the phone from the bed beside me and tried to remember my brother's mobile number. It took a few minutes, but eventually, I heard it ringing.

"Gabriel," I said as soon as he answered.

"Carina. You heard, I take it."

I couldn't stop the sob that bubbled from my throat. "I haven't heard anything," I said. "I have no idea what's going on. I just know that Jameson's mad at me, and I'm stuck in the middle of nowhere with Rahat --" if she was even still around "--I just... I don't know what went wrong."

"Xander saw you at the club, that's what went wrong," Gabriel said, missing my meaning.

"Why did you send me here?" I asked.

"To keep you safe."

"No, just... just tell me what you're not saying. For once, please let me in. I need to know what's going on. Who is Jameson? Why have I never heard of him or seen him in London when his brother comes all the time?"

Gabriel sighed and I heard his muffled voice telling everyone to leave. I wasn't sure what time it was in London, but he must have been in a meeting from all the scrapes of chairs that echoed along the line. After a minute, a door clicked shut and Gabriel returned to the phone.

"Jameson Swash is the rightful head of the Swash family. For generations, they have served as second in command to the Bianchi's."

"Jameson said that Manuel Caruso was second in command."

"He was, but mostly in a caretaker role until Jameson turned thirty."

779

"That must have been years ago." If I had to guess, I'd put Jameson at around thirty-five, at least. "What happened?"

"Jameson left. He turned his back on the life. Handed control of everything over to his younger brother. Hell, until two days ago, I thought he was dead."

I couldn't make sense of what I was hearing, and I wished I'd taken more of an interest in the family business over the years. But the year after mum had died, dad had been inconsolable. He'd ranted about how the family business had led to her death. How he hated the life and wished he'd never been born into it. It took both of them from me, so I'd tried to stay as uninvolved as possible. I guessed a small part of me understood why Jameson had turned his back too. But if what Gabriel was telling me was true, then it meant, apart from the dom's, no-one's family held more power than Jameson's. And he just walked away from it, and what... decided to live like some biker dude in Colorado? I rubbed at my eyes and leaned my head against the headboard. "Please. Just tell me what this means," I said.

"It means that if Jameson comes back, claims his rightful place, and forbids Xander Caruso from even looking at you, Xander obeys or he dies."

I understood everything then. Jameson wanted to be free and I'd been sent as some sort of trap to lure him back. No wonder he hated me.

"How did you know?" I asked.

"Know what?"

"How did you know he'd be attracted to me and we'd end up in bed together?"

"Fuck! Carina. Jordan mentioned that Jameson spoke well of you after our parents' funerals. He and his biker friends have been running some sort of protection racket for women in trouble. I never thought you'd bloody fuck him. After meeting Xander, I thought you'd just be fucking scared and he'd want to help you."

"Yeah. Well, all that's gone out the window now he thinks I'm some sort of fucking honey-trap." Or whore, I didn't bother adding. It didn't matter, he was right either way, even if Gabriel didn't think we'd end up sleeping together. Without waiting for a response, I hung up and sunk into the bed. Pulling the covers over my head, I allowed my tears to flow freely.

I couldn't tell how long I lay there before a soft knock came at the door. When I didn't answer, it opened, and I peeked my head over the edge of the sheet, hoping for all the world to see Jameson.

"Are you staying in bed all day?" Rahat asked before plopping herself down next to me.

"Have you seen Jameson?" I asked.

She sucked in her bottom lip and nodded. "He's been stomping around the garden for the last half an hour and looking like he'd murder the air if he could."

I dived under the covers again, but Rahat pulled them back. "What happened? From all the noises coming from this room last night, I thought the two of you had well and truly hit it off."

"Oh fuck," I said. "Everything is so bloody fucked up." After another bout of tears, I told her everything that happened.

"Ugh," she said and pulled a disgusted face. "On the kitchen counter. I've just eaten breakfast there."

"That will make up for the time you and what's-his-name did it in my car," I said, unable to stop the small smile from forming on my lips at the details she'd latched on to.

"Gavin. Ugh, don't remind me, that was a huge mistake."

"And what about Rex?"

"Rex is a cutie," she said. "But we're not talking about me, we're talking about you and Jameson."

"There is no me and Jameson."

"Honey," she said and stood before gathering me some clothes. "No man would get that worked up over a *'honey-trap'* if he didn't fall hard for the bait. Now get some clothes on and talk to him. Ninety-nine percent of all your problems, family or otherwise, come from the fact that no-one ever tells anyone else what the fuck is going on." She pushed the clothes into my arms and left the room. "It's time for that to change."

CHAPTER 1

Jameson

I should never have made any form of bargain with my brother. If I'd learned anything over the years, it was that family couldn't be trusted. I guessed my brothers at Forever Midnight had made me start to forget that one simple fact. I was the elder brother, Jordan deferred to me, but I hadn't wanted to wield that power, and instead I'd agreed to owe him one for all the help he gave in protecting Amber. I should have bypassed him and gone to the other families myself, but that would have put me exactly where I am now. The worse thing was, I'd fucking fallen for it, hook line and sinker.

Fuck!

Out of the corner of my eye, I saw Carina open the back door and slowly close it behind her. She glared at me before straightening her back, lifting her chin, and walking straight towards me. So help me, I fucking loved that about her. I was easily twice her size with steam practically coming out of my nostrils, but she approached without a shred of fear showing on her perfect face.

"I spoke to Gabriel," she said.

"And?"

If anything, she stood taller and stared into my eyes. "And, I'm sorry. I didn't know who you were or what Gabriel and Jordan planned."

"They just told you to do anything I asked," I said, the words making my anger bubble to the surface again. I thought I'd found the perfect woman: strong, sexy, with intelligent, thoughtful eyes. One whose sexual appetites might mirror my own. But she'd just portrayed the woman she thought I wanted her to be.

"They told me nothing, maybe if they had this whole thing could have been avoided." She grumbled under her breath and sucked in a gulp of air. "It's not as if you've told me any-fucking-thing either."

"What's that supposed to mean?"

She ran her hand over her dark hair and cleared her throat. "You turn up at the airport, looking like a fucking biker--"

"I am a *fucking* biker."

"That's bullshit. Gabriel just told me exactly who you are. You're coming across all high and mighty like I did something to you. You were the one who told me to take my fucking clothes off... Is that your life now? You come to the rescue and pretend to protect some poor helpless woman, act like her savior, and then fuck her?"

"You have no idea who I am."

"Then tell me. Tell me why you left New York and came to Colorado."

God damn it, Carina made me feel... I don't know what the fuck she made me feel besides confused. I let a deep breath out through my nostrils and tried to make sense of my thoughts. "I came to Colorado to escape exactly the life you lead," I said after a moment. "The manipulation and games. I came because it's a good place to find out what you're made of."

"Yeah, well I hope you're proud of who you found. I did what I did because I wanted you. I slept with you because you are the sexiest, most intense man I've ever met. Why the fuck did you sleep with me?" Before I had the chance to answer she raised her hand to stop me. "You know what, none of it matters. I don't care. It's not as if you know me any better than I know you. Neither of us owes the other anything. Rahat and I are leaving. I've booked us on a flight to New York later today. You don't have to worry, we'll be out of your life in no time." Without saying another word, she handed me my phone, turned, and left. So help me, I let her.

I debated going after her, of stopping her. But what would that mean? Was it a price I was willing to pay?

I watched her open the back door and enter the house, and a pang of guilt washed through me again. Carina would be handed over to Xander Caruso in New York. He would use her and spit her out, just as his father had wanted to do to her mother. The Rizzo family was a good one, but not a strong one amongst our hierarchy. When Lina, Carina's mother, had chosen to marry Petra Rizzo instead of Manuel, he had made sure her family paid for it. Petra could do little but stand by and watch. The stress had proved too much for Lina's weak heart, and losing Lina had proved too much for Petra.

I clenched my fists and huffed out a breath. "Fucking, damn it," I said, but still didn't follow after Carina. Instead, I lifted my phone and did something I promised myself I would never do.

"I need to speak with Dom Bianchi," I said as soon as someone answered.

"Who is this?" The voice on the other end of the line asked.

"Jameson Swash."

CHAPTER 1

Carina

After speaking to Jameson, I asked Rex if there was a phone I could use, and excused myself to go upstairs and call Gabriel again when he handed me his smartphone. I might have lied in the heat of the moment when I said that Rahat and I were booked on a flight back to New York, but I would make that lie a reality now.

Gabriel sounded resolved when I spoke to him. He confirmed he would get back to me with all the arrangements and that he would see if Jordan could meet us in New York. He'd also be getting a flight out from London, but would undoubtedly arrive later than us.

"Why me?" I asked before he had a chance to end the call.

"What do you mean?"

I stopped pacing the room and perched on the end of the bed. "Xander Caruso saw me for like 5 seconds and apparently decided I was his. I get that he's a nutjob, but it doesn't make any sense." Sure, I wasn't bad to look at, but it wasn't as though I had magical powers that made all the boys fall madly in love with me.

Gabriel took a deep breath and I pictured the twitch he got at the corner of his eye whenever I asked him something he didn't want to answer. After a moment, he said, "I think he saw our mum when he looked at you, even if he didn't realize it at first."

"And what, he had some creepy obsession with mum? She had to be twenty years older than him."

"I think it's more to do with the fact his dad had a creepy obsession with mum. Manuel was in competition with Dad for her hand. At the time, the power dynamic between our families was equal. The consigliere who mediated disputes decided Mum had the right to choose who she wanted to marry. She chose Dad. Manuel married someone else."

"But that wasn't the end of it," I said as a rock sank into the pit of my stomach.

"No. When Manuel became second in command, the power dynamic between our families shifted. Manuel left his wife and demanded Mum leave Dad. Of course, they were having none of it, but Manuel made both their lives hard as a result. Mum couldn't take the pressure, she wanted to stay, but worried that it would be better for the family if she left. She started drinking. You know where that led."

Tears flooded my eyes at his words. I'd been so young, I knew Mum had been drinking a lot, but she was always happy and smiling around me. I could never have imagined what was going on underneath. And after the accident... Dad had fallen into depression and died when his heart gave out. "Why didn't you ever tell me this before?" I asked, wiping away my tears.

"Mum's death was an accident. Dad died of a broken heart. You didn't need to know more than that."

I sniffed my tears back loudly at his words as anger flared. "I had a right to know," I said and stood before resuming my pacing of the room. "And now what, I'm supposed to be some plaything for the son of the man who destroyed our family?"

"No. Not a plaything. Xander has claimed you as his wife. A union between our families that was previously denied his father."

"His wife! This is fucking bullshit. I'm not going to marry this guy." I ran my hand over my head and continued pacing, my feet as fast as my muddled thoughts. "What about this mediator. This consigliere guy. Can't we appeal to him? If mum had the right to choose, shouldn't I be granted that same right?"

"Besides the fact that the role of consigliere has been vacant since Manuel took over from Jameson's dad. You're forgetting the power dynamic. Xander's going to be the underboss, he takes commands from no-one except Dom Bianchi himself."

"Then we appeal to Dom Bianchi," I said and sat on the edge of the bed again.

"To override Xander. The Dom would see us six feet under for even suggesting such a thing."

I shook my head. Jameson was right to want to be away from all this crap. What I wouldn't give right now to be free, to live a life away from all these games and manipulations, all these people who think they are entitled to tell others what to do. "Then there's no hope," I said.

"As the wife of the underboss, everyone will treat you with respect."

"Except Xander Caruso," I said and closed my eyes, wishing the world would just open up and swallow me into a black hole. "Send me the flight details as soon as you have them," I added before Gabriel had the chance to say anything else. "I'll see you when you get to New York."

With that, I ended the call and looked around the room. I decided to shower and change and then get a cab to the airport, even if that meant having to wait there for hours before our flight. Better to accept my fate and get on with it than sit around wallowing, wishing Jameson was the protector of women Gabriel thought him to be. Hoping with all my heart, he'd swoop in and save me.

I STEELED myself to go downstairs after the shower. Jameson had made up his mind about me and I couldn't blame him, but there was no way I would hide upstairs like some frightened doe. I took a deep breath and opened the door onto the landing. Voices greeted me as I stepped down the stairs, but none of them belonged to Jameson. That was no surprise. He didn't seem to say much around others.

When I pushed through the door to the kitchen, only Rahat and Rex were inside. Rex nodded his head at me and excused himself. My eyes darted outside, but Jameson was nowhere to be seen.

"He left about twenty minutes ago," Rahat said.

"Who?" I asked, pretending nonchalance.

It didn't work. Rahat knew me better than that. We'd been friends since we started nursery school together at 3-years-old. She walked over and put her hand around my shoulder, pulling me in for a hug.

"You okay?" she asked. Alone with Rahat, I broke down in tears and hugged her tight. "I'll take that as a no," she said and stroked my hair. "You up for sharing what happened when the two of you talked earlier?"

I pulled back and between sobs told her that as well as Jameson hating me, I had to go to New York and meet Xander, who was apparently now my fiancé.

"What?" Rahat almost screamed. "You are so not marrying that guy."

"What choice do I have?" I asked and started crying again.

Rahat pulled me in for another hug. "Let's not go to New York. I have some money saved, we could head to L.A or better yet, the Outer Hebrides. No-one will ever find us there."

I couldn't help but smile at the thought of Rahat on a small Scottish island. "And what would you do there?" I asked. "The population's probably less than thirty-thousand. That's nowhere near enough eyes fawning over you."

She smiled. "Maybe not, but you can be damn sure every set would be. Besides, I heard they have the best internet connection in the whole of the UK. I'll be just fine."

I huffed out a breath and wiped my tears. "It's a nice idea," I said. "But no, for Gabriel's sake, I have to marry Xander." As I said the words, I knew just how true they were. Xander's father had hounded our family until my mother drank herself into an early grave. I could understand the pressure she felt now. I couldn't do that. I could see Gabriel hurt or punished for my rebellion.

"Gabriel will understand," she said. "He can be a bit of a twat at times, but he loves you."

"I know. And that's why I have to do it."

Before we had the chance to say anything more, Rex's phone beeped in my pocket. I pulled it out and found a text with all our flight details. I held it up and showed Rahat. "We'd better call a taxi and get to the airport," I said.

"Rex will take us," she answered, and I felt a pang of guilt at separating them.

CHAPTER 1

Carina

R ahat was relieved when Jordan met us and took us directly to a hotel. No doubt she thought no harm could befall us in a public establishment. I knew better.

"I'm not leaving Carina," Rahat said when Jordan showed her to her room.

"Gabriel has asked me to keep you safe," he said. "Unfortunately, for now, that also means keeping you separated."

"Like hell it does."

I rested my hand on her shoulder and told her I'd be fine. It was obvious I was being taken to meet Xander Caruso and the last thing I wanted was Rahat saying something inappropriate and paying with her life. "Please," I said and squeezed her hand tight. "Stay here and stay safe. I'll come back as soon as I can. I'll be fine," I added, trying to reassure myself as much as Rahat.

She pulled me in for a quick hug while scowling at Jordan.

The sound of our footsteps as we continued on to wherever Jordan was taking me, pounded a rhythmic beat that echoed the thumping of my heart. Dread weighed heavy in my stomach and I wished for all the world that Jameson was with me and not his brother.

When we reached another room. Jordan stopped and nodded at his men to fall back. I gulped in a breath and stared at the door, knowing I was about to meet a very dangerous and very powerful man. The man I was set to spend the rest of my life with, however short that may be.

Jordan was about to say something, but I raised my hand to stop him and straightened my back. There was nothing he could say that could help.

"Just open the door," I said, glancing at the keycard in his hand.

"Jameson said you had guts," he said and smiled, while I wondered when he'd had a chance to talk to him about me.

The door swung open and without a backward glance, I stepped inside.

My stomach churned, but I kept my face passive, even when Jordan pulled the door shut behind me. I glanced around the suite looking for Xander. Only the empty room with a small breakfast table with two chairs and two ornate couches facing off against each other either side of a round coffee table greeted me. I took a few steps further into the room and noted the closed double doors to both my left and right. Xander could be behind either one of them.

I realized then that I wasn't ready for this, that I'd never be ready for this. If only I could have spoken to Gabriel first and reaffirmed my lack of options.

I almost jumped when the jarring sound of a handle turning came from the doors to the left. I wanted to run, but the sight that greeted me stalled my steps.

"Jameson," I said as his intense gaze bored into me. "What are you doing here?"

"Family business," he answered.

"H-how...?"

"I chartered a flight and arrived a few hours ago." Without saying another word, he lifted his T-shirt over his head and threw it on the floor. I itched to reach out and touch his sculpted flesh but instead averted my eyes.

"I thought you were sick of games," I said, unable to keep the note of desire from my voice.

"I'm going to undress you," he said, ignoring my remarks.

My feet remained rooted to the spot. He moved towards me slowly, his eyes never leaving my face. When he reached me and slid my jacket off, his eyes dragged down my body and rested on my chest. I shivered and told myself to push him away, but the needy part of my mind told me that I wasn't married to Xander yet and if I could have one more time with Jameson then I should.

He flicked at my buttons with practiced ease, undoing each and every one at a slow and steady pace. His fingers traced over my shoulders and down my arms as he slid me free of my shirt. My shoes, jeans, and underwear followed suit.

Goosebumps stood out on my flesh as, once again, I stood before him completely naked.

He brushed the hair from my shoulder. My breath seized in my lungs and need pulsed straight to my core. My fingers itched to reach out and touch him, but I kept them firmly by my side.

"What do you want?" I asked.

"I was about to ask you the same thing?" He reached to the top of his jeans and unbuttoned them, setting free his thick, rigid cock. I imagined it pounding into me, filling me completely. Just the thought of what he could do to me had me gasping as my core clenched against nothing. Willing him inside, I licked my lips and instantly berated myself.

What the hell was I doing? No man had ever made me feel the way Jameson did, but strangely no man had ever hurt me the way he did either. I didn't want to process what that meant about my growing feelings towards him. Not when this was all there could ever be.

He reached to the waist of his jeans and unthreaded his belt. I took a shuddering breath and relished knowing just how wet he was making me. The pulsing need between my legs intensified and Jameson gripped my hand and brushed his thumb over the pulse point on my wrist. A small smile played at the edge of his lips as though he was pleased to find my heart racing for him. Without a word, he pulled me into his body with my arms pressed behind me.

I felt small encompassed in the warmth of his arms, but also safe. My whole body felt alive. I lifted my head to look into his eyes. He stared back and his lips lowered to mine. Capturing me, he thrust his tongue inside. My legs threatened to buckle, but he held me tight. There was nothing soft or gentle in his actions. Only possessive. His kiss claimed me as his hands worked to fasten my arms behind my back.

"Do you want me?" he asked, his breath like fire against my ear.

"Yes," I almost gasped. The memory of how good it felt for him to claim every part of me circled forefront in my mind. I wanted that again. Needed it.

He lightly brushed his hands down my chest and stomach, creating a trail of goosebumps wherever they touched. Heat soared through my body. I could barely breathe when they trailed over my mound. I shuddered in anticipation.

He flipped me around, guided me to the couch, and pushed me bent over the arm. My face pressed into the coarse material of the cushions. I wanted to use my hands to push me up, but they were wrapped tight in the belt behind my back with Jameson holding onto them with one hand. The other ran a trail over my folds.

CHAPTER 1

Jameson

Ever since speaking to Carina in the garden, I'd planned exactly what I wanted to do, and had set things in motion to ensure they were done. And right now, that plan involved stripping Carina naked... again.

She'd stood, strong and determined in the hotel suite and my cock had responded by becoming hard in an instant. I'd have fun reassuring myself that she was worth the sacrifices I'd decided to make. As if there could be any doubt.

Her bottom pointed in the air over the arm of the couch, giving me a perfect view of everything she had. She was so incredibly wet and begging for me to touch her. I obliged.

"How many men have you been in this position with?" I asked.

"Only you."

She gasped and bit her bottom lip as I ran ruthless circles around her clit, pinching and teasing without mercy. She liked it rough and I liked giving her what she wanted. But on my terms. I softened my touch, knowing it would make her beg for more. With the gentlest of movement, I stroked her clit and teased her entrance with my fingers.

Carina squirmed and tried to push back onto them, but I lifted her bound arms and forced her deep into the couch, forbidding her to move.

"Please," she said after a moment.

Before she could utter another word, I delivered a sharp slap to her pussy. She cried out and I delved my fingers inside, plunging them in and out and working her wetness around her throbbing clit.

"What did you know about me before you met me at the airport?" I asked and delivered another slap.

She screamed. This time I licked up and down her folds and sucked her clit roughly into my mouth. She tried to squirm, but I wouldn't release the pressure on her arms.

"Answer the question," I said and teased her swollen bud before pushing inside with my tongue. Fuck! She tasted so sweet like Halloween candy. Dangerous and delicious.

"N-nothing. I didn't... I didn't know who was coming?"

I heard the truth in her words. They made my heart sing. She hadn't been sent to trap me, to drag me back to the life I'd left. And because of that, I'd return to it. For her.

Without another word, I released her arm and grabbed onto her hair, pulling her head back to make her look at me.

"You're mine." I claimed her lips with a brutal kiss and speared her with my cock. Pushing my way fully inside without waiting to see if she could take me. I already knew she could.

CHAPTER 1

Carina

Fuck! I couldn't hold back the scream that ripped from my throat. Jameson plunged into me again and again, fucking me hard. Each thrust went deeper and deeper, making me undone.

"Oh, fuck," I screamed, as I exploded with pleasure, almost blacking out. My core clenching around him. He pulled out and pinched my clit, delving inside with his fingers, while his other hand worked to untie my arms. Another orgasm rocked me.

"You're incredible," he said and slapped my ass cheek, hard. "Your ass is made for fucking." He ran his hand over the curve of my bottom, and pumped his finger in and out of my pussy. "Has anyone ever fucked your ass?" he asked.

I closed my eyes and willed him to do it, even though I was afraid. "Never," I answered.

"I'll stop if you want me to." His hands spread my cheeks, and he twirled my wetness around the entrance.

I closed my eyes and enjoyed the sensations.

I gasped as a cold sensation hit me and I realized it must be lube. Slowly, he pushed his finger inside. With my hands free, I dug them into the cushion on either side of my head.

"Relax," he said. "Remember, I'll stop if you want me to."

I calm my breathing and try to relax. "Fuck!" I scream as his finger pushed all the way inside me while his thumb circled my clit.

He hooked his finger slowly and worked it in and out. "Touch yourself," he said and grabbed my hand, pushing it beneath me and between my legs. I circled my sensitive nub and probed between my folds, all while Jameson worked his finger inside my ass.

My eyes rolled in my head and my breaths came in desperate pants. Still, I worked my pussy while Jameson finger fucked my ass, soon we were working in unison, pumping inside me in time with each other.

"I-I can't," I said. "D-don't stop. I'm going to come." Just as I said the words, Jameson pushed in a second finger. My senses flipped into overdrive, and my whole body flared and pulsed with delight. I screamed as my orgasm struck, sending me over a chasm as shudders racked my whole body.

Jameson withdrew and grabbed onto my hips. He let out a deep groan and pushed his cock inside my pussy, pounding me through my release. "Do you think you can take more?" he asked and my fingers dug deep into the couch.

A strangled noise escaped my lips. I didn't know if I could, but I did know, I never wanted him to stop.

He slowed, but continued moving inside me as his hands worked a trail up my back. He rubbed the back of my neck before working them back down. I moaned as he moved his finger over my back entrance. He pushed his finger inside again while his cock filled my pussy. A second finger joined the first, but this time his movements were different. I felt like a powder keg set to explode, but sensed that Jameson was keeping me on the cusp of pleasure and making sure I was relaxed and loose enough to take what he wanted to give me.

My thoughts and emotions were all a muddle. Everything inside me wanted to stay here forever, but knowing that couldn't happen, I wanted... no, needed to have Jameson claim every part of me. I focused on every sensation I felt, etched them into my memory.

After a moment, Jameson removed himself from me completely. I felt the tip of his cock touch my ass. He spread my cheeks wider and pushed inside. The pressure was blinding.

I jerked away but he clasped onto my hips and drew me closer to him. "Don't stop. Please," I screamed though I felt fit to burst. "Don't stop."

Jameson pulled me up, so my body was flush against him, and pressed all the way inside me. He moved in and out slowly at first, but faster as my body became accustomed to this delightful yet strange intrusion. He kissed and nipped at my neck. His one hand reached around and pinched my nipples, driving me delirious with pleasurable pain. The other pinched at my swollen clit. His fingers pressed inside my pussy and circled my bud.

"I'm gonna fucking come inside your ass," he said as he pushed me closer and closer towards oblivion.

Lost in sensation, my head dropped back to rest on his shoulder. My eyes closed tight.

The orgasm that struck was unlike any other I'd ever experienced. Like a raging storm, it ripped through my being, unstoppable and relentless. Wave after wave crashed through me and a scream ripped from my throat. Every nerve ending in my body burned. I needed Jameson to stop, to set me free, but I couldn't stand the idea of him leaving me. I was paralyzed as pleasure tore through my body with Jameson's relentless actions.

He kissed me madly and muttered my name as he jerked, and his hot seed filled me.

CHAPTER 1

Jameson

A call from Jordan pulled me from the bed the next morning. Carina lay sound asleep, so I quickly answered and left the room to stop her being disturbed. A smile edged onto my mouth at the thought of all we'd done. She'd earned her rest. For now. And I'd claimed every last inch of her, leaving no doubt that she was now mine.

"It's time," Jordan said.

"I'll be out in five," I answered, knowing it was time to claim something else.

I showered and pulled an Armani suit from the closet. I finished by straightening a tie for the first time in more than seven years, gave a quick look in on Carina, who was still sleeping, and stepped out into the hallway where Jordan was waiting.

"You sure about this?" he asked.

"Are you?" I answered.

He laughed and shook his head. We both knew there was a chance neither one of us would come out of this alive. Despite the situation. I couldn't help but smile in response. We'd been close, once upon a time, maybe we could be again. If we lived.

A limo took us to a nondescript office on the lower east side. Jordan left me in a side office to wait until it was time for him to collect me. I spent the time wondering if Carina was awake and hoping I'd get the chance to see her again.

Voices sounded on the other side of the door. Dom Bianchi's louder than all, even though I knew he wasn't in the room, but rather displayed on a monitor on the wall via an online chat. I could tell when he'd made his announcement as the room erupted in a cacophony of voices. My cue to enter.

All heads turned to me as I stepped through the door. Xander Caruso stood from his chair and glared.

798

Jameson's Debt

"Sit down," Bianchi told him, his face larger than life on the screen. Small squares depicting the caporegimes who couldn't be in New York in person lined the screen beneath him. Everyone present for the vote. Everyone, the head of their respective families.

It was plain Xander wanted to object, but nobody disobeyed the dom, and he wasn't someone who liked to repeat himself. Xander sat, but the glare he shot my way couldn't be clearer. It matched the glare that some of the other family heads shot me. Half of them had assumed me dead, the other half wished it was so. That was their way. Always wrangling for power and position.

"Jameson," Bianchi said. "Sit." I nodded to the dom and did as instructed. "Now," he continued. "We are all here to vote on a replacement for the dearly departed, Manuel Caruso. My trusted friend for many years. May he rest in peace."

"May he rest in peace," everyone echoed.

"Two families have a valid claim, Caruso," Bianchi said, "and Swash."

Xander stood again, but Bianchi made him sit with a glance. "Forgive me, Dom Bianchi. Jameson Swash surrendered any claim he had to the position of underboss more than seven years ago. He has no claim."

Bianchi's eyes flashed to me through the screen. He sat back in his chair and opened the large wooden box on his desk, pulled a cigar from it, and chewed on the end. Xander gulped. That was never a good sign.

To save the dom repeating himself Espsotio, the man to Xander's right growled. "If Dom Bianchi states that both Swash and Caruso have a claim to the position of underboss then Swash and Caruso have a mother-fucking claim to the position of underboss. You understand? Now shut the fuck up."

Xander eyeballed him but wasn't capable of keeping quiet. "I understand. My apologies again, Dom Bianchi. I spoke out of turn." His gaze flashed to both me and Jordan sat beside me and a triumphant glint appeared in his eyes. "As only the caporegime of a family can be present under such circumstances as these, I had been momentarily confused. As you have stated, Jameson Swash has every right to stake a claim to the position of underboss. His brother, Jordan, however, is unwelcome at these proceedings and as such is in forfeit of his life."

Murmurs of agreement echoed around the table and through the chat link, but the dom only continued to chew on the end of his cigar.

I kept my face straight, but inside, I smiled. I'd spoken to Dom Bianchi at length regarding Xander's suitability for the role. He was far too full of his own self-importance to stay within the bounds of his role, and I had no doubt he would eventually try to usurp the dom's power. With my presence in the vote and Xander's overriding need to have his own way, he had already shown a lack of respect.

"If I may, Dom Bianchi," I said and continued when he nodded. "You are correct Xander, I do have every right to claim my father's position as underboss. A claim which supersedes your own." When he opened his mouth to object, I raised my hand to silence him. "However, you are also correct in stating I surrendered that claim more than seven years ago when I handed my family over to my brother."

"Then the matter is fucking settled," Xander said.

"It is not," Bianchi said, and all eyes returned to the screen. "I have spoken to Jameson at length and the time he has spent away affords him a unique perspective. I have therefore decided his talents are best suited in the role of consigliere. From now on, he will be my most trusted adviser, and any disputes you have will be mediated through Jameson."

A few shocked gasps and curses sounded around the room. Manuel had ended the position when he became underboss and undertook the role as a second duty for himself. No doubt, Xander had thought to do the same. Underboss may be second in command and consigliere third, but the consigliere's loyalty was only to the dom and had his ear in all matters. From the way he stared at the desk, Xander was running through the implications of this in his mind.

"Enough," Xander said after a moment, slamming his hand down on the desk. "Fine, Jameson is fucking consigliere. We are here to vote on the position of underboss."

The dom told us when to speak, when not to speak, and who to fucking kill. We certainly spoke to him the way Xander just had. Everyone listening knew his days were numbered. They were just waiting for Xander to realize it himself. Manuel was no saint, but he knew his place. It was clear for all to see, he hadn't passed that knowledge onto his son.

Dom Bianchi spat the end of his cigar out and waved the remains at Xander. "For someone who likes to tell others about procedure, you are forgetting one very important one yourself." The dom motioned for me to continue.

"Thank you, Dom Bianchi," I said. "As is custom, to ensure a fair process, any disputes against the Caruso family must be ruled on before the vote. Does anyone have an issue with Xander Caruso they would like to raise?"

On cue, Gabriel smiled, thanked the dom for his wisdom in appointing me, and gave Xander a pointed look. "Xander Caruso has demanded the hand of my sister in marriage. Given our family's history, I feel the demand is outrageous."

"How does your sister feel?" I asked, knowing the answer.

"She is very much against the union."

"Then much as your mother was free to make her own decision in this matter, so too is your sister."

Xander took deep steadying breaths, but a wry smile played at the edge of his lips. No one in the room doubted he intended to make the Rizzo family pay for any decision not in his favor, in much the same way as his father had. "Then the matter is settled," he said, still not picking up on the dom's mood towards him. Xander was used to getting his own way. Manuel should have taught him better. "As no-one else has raised an issue, we are free to vote. We have wasted far too much of the dom's time already."

"Making the right decision is never a waste of time," Bianchi said.

"Does anyone have an issue with Jordan Swash," I said and took great delight in watching the change come over Xander's face. "The head of the Swash family."

"No fucking way," he screamed and stood, slamming his fists on the table. "Jordan has no fucking claim to the position."

"On the contrary, Dom Bianchi has already stated that both the Swash and Caruso family have a claim. Are you fucking correcting the dom again?" Espsotio asked, his voice like ice.

Xander's face reddened and he looked fit to explode. He stood, his fists clenched against the table. He tried and failed to get a hold of his emotions. "You're not going to get away with this," he snarled. "I'll make each and every one of you fucking pay."

"Sit down," Bianchi said.

"You," Xander said, pointing at the screen and then at me. "The two of you. You did this. You had no fucking right."

Espsotio stood along with the others at the table. The dom quietened their threats with one word, *silence*. Only Xander continued his tirade.

"It seems we have another dispute for you to mediate," Dom Bianchi said to me and raised his eyebrow as a signal to what he wanted me to do.

I nodded, pulled the gun hidden beneath my jacket, and shot Xander Caruso in the head.

EPILOGUE

Jameson

If anyone had told me a few days ago that I would be back in New York and working for the family again, I likely would have shot them in the head. But all things considered, we had the best possible outcome. My brother was quickly voted in as second in command. A role I had no doubt he would excel at. Gabriel didn't have to worry about Xander and neither did Carina.

I'd always been one of the dom's favorite nephews -- it's the only reason I was allowed to walk away from my life and not killed all those years ago -- so to say Bianchi might have been biased towards today's outcome was an understatement. Still, he wasn't pleased with my decision to turn my back on the family, and the outcome could have gone in Xander's favor. Too bad, he was too much of a narcissist to keep his own superiority in check for half an hour. And me, I had the luxury of being able to live in both my worlds. To maintain my impartiality, I was free to live in Colorado and stay out of the day to day running of the business. Dom Bianchi and I would chat online every week and I would offer what little advice I could and deal with any disputes that arose. I could live with that. Maybe the families would be quick to realize that I hated playing games and had no intention of standing for their petty squabbles and manipulations.

The dom had disconnected after the vote and most of the others left, but Jordan and Gabriel stayed to discuss business. Not wanting to be involved, I'd grabbed the limo back to the hotel. The sky was overcast with gray clouds and rain pounded on the windows. If I was lucky, I could be on the next flight out of this God-forsaken place.

I spotted Carina standing in the lobby, staring out into the street before the car came to a stop. The second it did, she ran forward, ignoring the rain that plastered her dark hair to the side of her face and seeped into her flimsy top.

"Gabriel told me what happened," she said as soon as I stepped out of

803

the car. "W-why? Why did you do that? I know how much it meant for you to stay away from the life."

"It was the only way to keep you safe."

She ran her hand over her wet head, and I did the same. "Because that's what you do, you protect women. Is... is that why?"

I smiled. For the first time, Carina actually looked a little afraid. I touched the side of her cheek with my hand. "That's not why," I said and brushed the rain from her lips. "You look so beautiful right now. You always look beautiful. I did it because I never want to take my eyes off you. Come back to Colorado with me and see if you feel the same way about me."

A slow smile spread across her face. "I'll go anywhere with you. But I don't need to go to Colorado to know that I never want to spend another minute without you. I already know it to be true."

With that, and with rain drenching every part of us, she stood on tiptoes and sealed her lips against mine.

* * *

The End

* * *

This is the end of *Jameson's Debt*. Check out the compete Forever Midnight MC series and subscribe to Victoria's newsletter to learn more about the upcoming Bianchi Mafia Chronicles.
https://magicbookdeals.com/author-spotlight/victoria-gale/

* * *

Newsletter
(https://www.subscribepage.com/victoriagale)

About Victoria Gale

Victoria Gale writes short romance stories. Whether steamy or full of suspense, they'll keep you on the edge of your seat.

Delve into a romance with determined, resourceful women and strong, fearless men.

https://magicbookdeals.com/author-spotlight/victoria-gale/

Made in the USA
Columbia, SC
14 September 2020